VENGEANCE AND VAMPIRES

THE COMPLETE SERIES

ALICIA RADES

Published by Crystallite Publishing LLC.
Edited by Megan Linski.
Cover design by KnesArt.

aliciarades.com

VENGEANCE AND VAMPIRES

Ravenite
Resilience
Resolute
Retribute

ALSO BY ALICIA RADES

HIDDEN LEGENDS: ACADEMY OF MAGICAL CREATURES

The Fire Prophecy

The Water Legacy

The Earth Legend

The Air Omen

The Elemental War

The Soul Sacrifice

HIDDEN LEGENDS: COLLEGE OF WITCHCRAFT

The Coven's Secret

The Reaper's Shadow

The Cauldron's Curse

The Demon's Spell

The Warlock's Trial

The Witch's Fate

HIDDEN LEGENDS: PRISON FOR SUPERNATURAL OFFENDERS

The Villain Institute

The Criminal Lair

The Infernal Underground

The Assassin's Destiny

The Devil's City

The Elven Gate

The Phoenix Dawning

SEA OF MERMAID SECRETS

Deep Waters

Rising Tides

Crashing Waves

For the ones still searching for themselves.

RAVENITE

BOOK ONE

1

Vampires are easier to kill after you've pecked their eyes out. This vamp was dangerously close to finding out exactly what that felt like.

I grabbed a fistful of his shirt and shoved the vampire up against the side of a brick building. He was at least four inches taller than me, but I easily matched his strength.

The darkness of night blanketed the damp, narrow alleyway. Humidity hung in the air from the recent rain, carrying the scent of putrid garbage over to us from the dumpsters nearby. Brick buildings rose on either side of us. Each was two stories high, with restaurants, bars, and the occasional boutique shop on the lower levels and apartments on the upper. I never ventured into this part of town during the day, but this street crawled with vampires at night. I was a sucker for vampires looking for a stake through the heart. They usually found it.

"Tell me where the Soulless are hiding!" I demanded.

The vamp's canines elongated until fangs protruded from his mouth. "Look, lady," he said, showing them off. "I'm not scared of you."

Lady? Who the hell does he think I am?

"If you knew who I was, you'd be scared," I snarled.

"I'm a Soulless. I have no reason to be scared of you." He raised his left hand and pulled back his sleeve to prove a point. The mark of the Soulless was carved into his wrist—the same mark I'd noticed from my perch atop the bar's roof. The scar was shaped like a *V*, with two dots in the middle, one atop the other— fang marks.

"You should be the one who's scared," he threatened.

Okay, maybe he had a point. The Soulless scared me shitless, but Fangs here seemed harmless enough—for a vampire.

"I don't play games." My fingers tightened around his throat. "I could snap your neck right here, right now."

Fangs scoffed. "That ain't gonna kill me, honey."

"It'd give me plenty of time to get the job done," I countered. "Now tell me where to find your friends."

"What do you want with them?" he asked, narrowing his silver eyes at me.

"It doesn't matter," I said. "All that matters is that you're dead if you don't tell me."

Laughter bubbled up from his throat, and I nearly gagged at the scent of copper and vodka on his breath. Vampires didn't have to breathe, but it must've been habit. "You'll only consider killing me once I tell you."

Poor guy. He won't know what hit him.

"You obviously don't know who I am." I had a reputation to uphold, which meant if he didn't talk, he most certainly would die.

"*Should* I know you?" Fangs said with a suggestive smile.

Pig.

I slammed my fist into the side of his face for that one. He fell from my grasp and stumbled sideways but stood straight up again in less than a second. His lip was split where my knuckles connected with it, but like all vampires, he didn't bleed. The wound would heal within the hour, though.

"All I know, lady, is that you're in trouble," Fangs sneered.

Before I had a chance to respond, he lunged forward. A sudden sharp pain shot across my thigh. It felt like I'd just been impaled by a freaking sword. Was it forged in the fires of Hell or something? My leg felt like the flesh was burning off it.

I cried out and fell onto one knee. When I glanced down at my leg, I saw it was only a pocket knife.

Only a pocket knife. And it was sticking three inches into my flesh.

Lovely. I'd paid a high witch three months' worth of wages to enchant this outfit to shift with me, and now I'd forever have this hole in my jeans. My favorite pair of jeans, too. My ass looked perfect in them.

A moment of lust crossed Fangs's eyes as he stared down at the blood rushing out of my wound.

Yeah, that's right. I'm a shifter, I wanted to yell. *I bet I taste fan-freaking-tastic, you jackhole!*

I ripped the knife from my skin and pressed my free hand to my leg to slow the bleeding. Either Fangs had enough to drink earlier or he saw the fury etched into my face and thought better of sticking around, because after only a moment of hesitation, he turned and hightailed it down the alley.

A string of curse words trailed after him. It took me a moment to realize I was the one shouting them. I pulled my arm back and hurled the knife at his back, but it flew past his right hand, missing him entirely.

I was *not* done with this vamp. I rushed to my feet, ignoring the pain shooting up and down my leg and the blood soaking into my jeans. I was two steps from tackling him when a figure sprang out from the shadows. He slammed into Fangs's side and knocked him to the ground. I stopped in my tracks. The newcomer scurried to his feet and smashed a foot into the vamp's gut before he had a chance to move.

Oh, good. He's on my side.

I took a moment to steady myself against the side of the building and pressed my hand back over the wound. It burned more than it should, which could only mean one thing. The knife had been laced in vampire venom. Which meant I didn't have long before the blaze hit full force and I was down for the count.

"Cowen, you bastard!" the new guy shouted. His fist connected with Fangs's face.

Good shot, I thought. Except…

"Hey," I snapped. "I'm not some damsel in distress. I've got this."

The new guy was tall—at least six foot—with short black hair the same color as his skin. With those broad shoulders and all that muscle, he was the living embodiment of the phrase *tall, dark, and handsome*. I might've gone weak in the knees at the sight of him if I wasn't already feeling unsteady from the wound.

Handsome was too preoccupied with hauling Fangs to his feet that he didn't look at me when he replied. "No offense, but I need a moment with this vamp."

Wait. What?

"Uh, no," I objected. "He's mine."

Fangs grunted as Handsome shoved him up against the building in the same position I just had him in. Handsome landed another punch to his jaw with a loud *thud*.

"Hey!" I shouted. "Go easy on him. I need him to talk."

Handsome's striking brown eyes met mine, and they widened in shock. His gaze flickered down to my bleeding leg, and his face immediately fell. He hesitated for a moment, but it was one moment too long. Fangs swung his knee upward to connect with Handsome's groin. Handsome grunted and sank to the ground, while Fangs took off running.

I didn't waste a second. I sprinted after him. My leg burned like the sun, but I managed to put one foot in front of the other.

But Fangs was fast—faster than any human alive. It was one of the perks of being a vampire. Sure, vampirism had its drawbacks, like sensitivity to sunlight, bloodlust, and the fact that they couldn't breed the traditional way, but it also came with flawless beauty, quick healing, supernatural strength, and super speed at least five times faster than a normal human. Not to mention immortality—or at least a killer anti-aging enchantment. There were very few things that could kill a vampire. Luckily for me, I was pretty good at it.

I stumbled forward, and my hands slapped on the sidewalk. I caught myself and hurried back to my feet. The throbbing had spread down to my ankle and up my hip. I couldn't feel my knee anymore.

Chasing him on foot was useless.

I paused on the deserted sidewalk, only long enough to shift. Within seconds, my body shrank to the size and shape of a raven. Shifting didn't help the searing pain burning through my body. In fact, it only made it worse. But in my raven form, I didn't have to put weight on my leg. I shot into the air and flew down the street at top speed. My eyes caught the vamp turning down another alleyway up ahead.

I pumped my wings harder, but I'd lost my visual on him. I flew so fast around the turn into the alley that I nearly missed it. I quickly corrected my flight, but by the time my eyes focused, the alley was empty. The burning pain reached my wings, and I struggled to continue flapping them. I shot out of the alleyway onto a busy street bustling with nightlife. My eyes flickered from face to face, but Fangs was nowhere to be seen.

Frick!

The pain was more unbearable than ever. My vision blurred, and my head grew fuzzy. I wasn't ready to give up yet, but I didn't have the strength to keep going.

Just my luck.

I turned down a quiet street away from the bars and restaurants and shifted back into my human form. I sank to the ground and rested my head against the closest building. A string of curse words escaped my mouth. This was the closest I'd come to a Soulless in two years, and I'd let him slip through my grasp.

The distinct scent of dog hit my nose, and a low growl met my ears. My eyes shot open, only to be met by a pair of dark brown eyes just inches from my own. A black coat of fur covered the creature's body.

My heart hammered. Vampires weren't the only ones with supernatural perks. As a shifter, I was as strong as a vampire, a heck of a lot stronger than I looked. Plus, the vamps' heightened sense of smell and hearing didn't work on shifters for whatever reason, which made it hella easy to sneak up on them. But none of those perks would help me now. With the venom pulsing through my veins, I didn't have the strength to fight off another shifter.

"Please. I—" I started.

My voice cut off when the black wolf rose to its hind legs. His body lengthened, and his snout shortened as he shifted back into human form, his fur shrinking into his skin. Handsome stood fully-clothed in front of me.

"You're hurt," he said breathlessly, kneeling to my level to inspect my injury.

I resisted his touch and kept my hand pressed over the wound. Sweat dripped down my face.

"We have to get you to a hospital." He reached for me.

"No," I groaned, my head lolling to the side.

"Yes, we do," Handsome argued, like I didn't have a choice. His arms folded around me.

"No," I said more clearly, pushing him away. "A hospital won't help. The knife was laced in vampire venom."

Handsome's jaw tightened, and he cursed under his breath.

"It's not enough to change me," I told him through labored breaths. "Just enough to hurt like hell." I didn't mention the part about its anticoagulant properties, which meant if I didn't get this wound taken care of soon, I was going to bleed out. A wound infected with vampire venom didn't just heal on its own. It required a vampire's saliva or a healing spell. Luckily, I had one of those. I just had to get to it.

"Let me help you," he offered.

"I can do it myself," I protested. I pushed myself to my feet to prove a point, but I didn't have the strength to stay upright. I stumbled forward.

Handsome caught me before I smashed my face into the concrete below me. He smelled familiar, like cinnamon. It was the scent of my mom's kitchen on Thanksgiving morning… God, I missed her.

"You need help." He wasn't informing me; he was demanding.

There was no denying the truth, but…

"I don't know you," I said, harsher than I intended.

"I'm Venn," Handsome introduced. "And you?"

Yeah… I wasn't giving him my name.

"You're the Ravenite, aren't you?" Venn's voice was soft in my ear.

"Don't call me that." I drew away from him but only stumbled again. I had to do something *fast* if I didn't want to pass out.

"You are, aren't you?" he pressed.

Nausea twisted in my gut. I thought I might vomit from the pain. I only nodded as I sank to the ground and pressed my face into my bloody hands.

What's that healing spell again? I need to start memorizing these things.

"I have to call you something," Venn said. "If you don't want me calling you Ravenite, how about Rae for short?"

Close enough.

I nodded.

Venn knelt beside me. "Now that we know each other, will you let me help you?"

The sidewalk swayed in front of me. Unless I wanted to spend the night bleeding out here, I had no choice but to accept his offer.

"Okay," I agreed, though I was barely able to spit the word out. "No hospital, though. My apartment."

"No—" Venn began to protest.

"My apartment," I repeated, cutting him off.

Venn must've noticed the urgency in my tone, because he quickly scooped me into his arms. I gave him my address. Within moments, he was racing down the street, cradling me.

It wasn't like me to lead strangers back to my apartment, but I couldn't walk or fly, nor could I stay out on the street all night. I'd get home, heal myself, and figure the rest out later.

All I knew was that once I was back on my feet, I was going after that Cowen bastard.

It was my only choice if I ever wanted to see my sister again.

2

Venn burst through the door of my studio apartment and rushed across the room to the bed. I groaned in agony as he set me down. The feeling of the blanket on my skin was torture, as if I'd just been tossed onto a bed of needles. This was *so* not how I pictured things going the first time I brought a guy back to my place.

"Where's your med kit?" Venn demanded.

I tried to spit the words out through clenched teeth, but they wouldn't come. Instead, I pointed to my spell book on the table across the room.

"You don't have a first-aid kit?" Venn asked in disbelief.

I shook my head and pointed again.

His brow furrowed. "You want the book?"

I nodded, biting back a cry as the pain pulsed up my abdomen. "Now!"

We were running out of time. As Venn raced across the room for the notebook, I struggled to unzip my pants. There was no time for modesty.

"Help?" I asked desperately as soon as he returned.

Venn dropped the book next to me and began stripping my boots off. His fingers fumbled with the button on my jeans before he pulled them down my legs, careful not to touch my wound. Not that it mattered. Even the smallest touch sent a trail of fire across my skin. When he peeled my jeans back, it felt as if my skin was being ripped off with them.

"The book." I tried to point, but I could hardly lift my limbs.

Venn hurried to my side and flipped my spell book open.

"Page..." *Where was the spell again?* "In the middle somewhere."

"Tracking... Truth... Protection..." Venn read off the words I'd written in the headers of the pages.

"Keep going," I croaked out.

"Healing… Healing!" Venn stopped and scanned the page, then flipped to the next one. "Which one? There are a ton of them."

I struggled to sit up and somehow managed to prop myself up on my elbow. Venn turned the book toward me. The words swam in front of my eyes, and though I had perfect twenty-twenty vision, I squinted to see them more clearly.

"Next page," I told him.

Venn turned the page so quickly that he tore it a half inch. I cringed.

"There!" I cried.

I scanned the incantation. *Fantastic.* This was going to be one of the toughest spells I'd ever performed. I let out a shaky breath. Let's hope nothing went wrong. I began muttering the words under my breath.

Go away, pain! I thought to myself. Whoever said becoming a vampire was comparable to labor was insane. I was experiencing a mere taste of what vampire venom could do. If labor was even a fraction this bad, I was never having kids. And let's hope to *God* no vampire ever tried to change me.

I reached the end of the incantation, but the pain only burned more intensely. Had I made it *worse*? This spell was supposed to counteract supernatural injuries.

Where'd I get this crappy spell from anyway? I glanced at my notes in the header of the page. It came from one of my boss's clients, Mrs. Carlyle. She was the sweetest old lady you'd ever meet, but this wouldn't be the first time she sold us a shoddy spell.

What a bitch. Devin *had* to stop offering her money.

"Go back," I instructed though clenched teeth.

Venn flipped to the previous page.

This was a basic healing spell. I'd used it the last time a vamp tore a muscle in my shoulder, so I knew it worked, but it wouldn't do anything about the venom. That, I was going to have to ride out.

If I don't die first, I thought to myself. *Okay, here it goes.*

I pressed my hands to my wound. I could hardly open my mouth, but I pushed past the pain and whispered the incantation under my breath.

I can't die. I need to find the Soulless. I need to save my sister.

I couldn't explain how I knew Jenna was still alive after all this time, but I couldn't bring myself to believe she was dead. I'd felt a piece of myself die with my parents, but I hadn't felt that with Jenna yet. She was still out there somewhere.

I couldn't tell if the incantation took, so I recited it again. A sharp, stabbing pain shot down my leg and up my hip. The fire in my body filled my lungs, and I gasped for air.

This was it. I was going to die. My body was ripping into a million pieces, and there was no spell in the world that could piece me back together.

An earth-shattering scream filled the air around me, and then… nothing.

⁂

My mind swam through a fog as thick as syrup. I was vaguely aware I was still alive, but I couldn't seem to hold on to the memory of what had happened to me.

Where am I? I repeated to myself each time my mind cleared enough that I could manage a coherent thought. *Why does everything hurt so much?*

My mind slipped back into oblivion.

What felt like hours later—or days—I finally became aware of my body again. The light weight of a blanket settled over my legs, and the heavy, humid air left my skin slightly damp. A dull ache spread across my thigh.

"Ugh," a voice filled my ears. It took me a moment to realize the groan had come from me.

"Rae?" a second voice said softly.

Rae? That's a strange thing to call me. Only a moment later did I realize I'd told Venn to call me that.

My eyes shot open. I knew I was lying in my bed because of the ache in my back that I woke to every morning. The familiar water stain on the ceiling stared back at me.

"You're awake." Venn sat at the edge of my bed in my dining room chair. It was the only place to sit in my entire apartment.

The dull glow of morning light filtered in through the dusty window next to my bed. I struggled to push myself to a sitting position. The fire in my body had subsided, but my muscles hurt when I moved them, like I'd just finished running a marathon—and I wasn't a runner. My stomach twisted in hunger.

When my eyes landed on Venn's face, my hunger didn't seem to matter anymore. My stomach shifted for entirely different reasons. I'd invited this guy to take my pants off last night. *How embarrassing!* I mean, it was to save my life, but still...

I couldn't take my eyes off Venn, off his smooth skin and strong jaw. I wanted to throw my arms around his neck and drag him into bed with me.

It's the adrenaline from last night talking, I told myself. *You're acting weird because he helped you.*

"What?" Venn asked innocently. He'd *totally* caught me staring.

Of course he did! You're barely two feet from his face.

I didn't know what to say. "Have we met before?"

Venn shook his head. "Not that I remember, anyway."

"What are you still doing here?" I asked in barely a whisper. We were strangers, after all, and he'd been watching me sleep all night like a creep.

"I wanted to make sure you were all right," he replied.

Okay, so maybe he wasn't a creep. Maybe he was a gentleman. He'd draped a blanket over my exposed legs while I slept, so there was that.

"You're feeling better, aren't you?" Venn asked.

I lifted the covers to inspect my injury and was surprised to find a washcloth taped over the wound. The dry, crusted blood I expected to find wasn't there.

"I couldn't find a first-aid kit, so I had to improvise a bandage," he admitted.

The tension in my chest softened. "You cleaned it for me?"

"I did what I could."

My face heated at the thought of him tending to me while I slept. He could probably see the blush on my pale cheeks. I avoided his gaze and carefully peeled back the tape on my thigh. The washcloth dropped away to reveal that the wound had mostly healed, but a large, tender bruise remained. I pulled the covers back over my legs.

"Since you're okay now, I think I'll go." Venn lifted the chair and returned it to its spot at the table.

"Wait," I croaked out.

He paused and looked back at me. His eyes drooped, as if he hadn't slept all night.

I cleared my throat. "You're not going to turn me in, are you?"

His eyebrows drew together. "Turn you in?"

"Yeah, well…" I glanced around the tiny apartment, not really looking at anything—not that there was much to look at. I just couldn't manage to meet his gaze. "You know what I am. You know what I've done."

Venn inched his way across the room and shoved his hands into his jean pockets. "You mean that I know you're the Ravenite?"

I internally flinched at the word. I didn't deserve the respect that came along with the name. I was Rachel Collins, low witch and raven shifter in hiding. I was just a cashier at a spell shop who happened to kill vampires on her off-hours. But I wasn't special. I was barely an adult. I could hardly remember to do my own laundry, for heaven's sake! I wasn't the fierce, confident vigilante everyone thought the Ravenite was.

But I *was* the girl the police wanted.

"I've killed enough vampires to earn me a life sentence," I said.

As far as I was concerned, I was doing the police a favor by taking out vile vamps. *They* weren't going to kill them, not without a trial, at least. Some people still saw them as human. They called them *diseased*, but I'd seen enough to convince me otherwise. Vampires lost their humanity the moment they changed.

It wasn't like I had a grudge against vampires or anything. Okay, maybe I did. But I didn't kill just anyone. I only killed the ones who deserved it.

"Relax," Venn said. "I'm not going to tell anyone. The vampires are better off dead."

Exactly! Except Venn didn't say it with vengeance in his tone. He said it more like it was fact.

And let's face it, Venn was still a stranger to me. I couldn't just *trust* that he wouldn't out me. I was going to have to ditch Nocton and move to another city, preferably somewhere far away from Illinois where no one had ever heard the name *Ravenite*. It didn't matter where I went as long as there were vamps to slay.

Great. Bloodstone was the only place I'd ever manage to find a job that taught me anything about magic. Not to mention I was never going to find another place this cheap. I mean, it was a total dump, but at least I could afford it. I'd have to find a roommate.

Oh, God. Not a roommate.

Not to mention there was this Soulless guy running around now. I couldn't just walk away from that, not if I could use him to find Jenna.

Venn eyed me.

"What?" I asked innocently.

"I'm curious... how've you gone this long without getting caught?"

I shrugged.

Venn continued to stare at me, waiting for me to answer.

I wasn't interested in opening up to a stranger, but I had questions of my own to ask him, and it wasn't like he couldn't figure this one out on his own.

I sat up straight in bed and pulled the blanket around me. "I'm not registered as a shifter."

Venn raised an eyebrow. "Just a witch, then?"

I nodded.

"That was a pretty decent spell you cast last night," Venn pointed out. "You must be at least a mid-witch."

I shrugged again. "Somewhere between a low witch and a mid-witch. I'm still learning how to control my magic."

Venn bit his lip, like he wanted to say more but wasn't sure he should. I stared back at him with a questioning gaze.

"What were you doing with that vamp last night?" he asked.

Wait. Did he think I was just going to spill all my secrets because he helped me home?

"You already asked a question," I pointed out. "It's my turn."

Venn hesitated but eventually sank into the chair behind him, like he was settling in for a long conversation. "Fair enough."

My mind raced through fifty different questions at once. If we were going to play twenty questions, I had to make mine count.

"I want to know more about that vamp," I settled with. "You seem to know him."

"Not exactly," Venn said. "He stole something from me, and I tracked him down to get it back. What were *you* doing with him? You know he's a Soulless, right?"

"Yeah." *That was kind of the idea.*

Venn leaned forward in his seat and rested his elbows on his knees. "You know who the Soulless are, don't you?"

I scowled. "Of course I do. I'm not an idiot."

The Soulless were an elite group of vampires—*the* elite group. They were the ones created by Valkas, the original vampire. He showed up eight years ago at the same time magic appeared in our world. The Soulless were the worst of the vampires, the ones in Valkas's immediate circle. He left his mark on them when he changed them so that everyone would know to be afraid. Their mark was a warning. And there wasn't a soul in the world who wasn't afraid of them.

Except for me, of course.

I'm a terrible liar.

"If you knew he was a Soulless, what were you doing getting into a knife fight with him?" Venn asked.

Was Venn *mocking* me? He didn't deserve to know my whole life story. Then again, he'd found Cowen once already. Maybe he could help me find him again.

I swallowed hard. "He has something I need, too."

"What's that?" Venn's gaze bore into mine, challenging me to reveal more.

My teeth ground together. I *really* didn't like all these questions.

Venn leaned back in his chair when I didn't answer. "I don't know yet if you're friend or foe. What if we're after the same thing?"

Good point.

"You can relax," I said. "All I need from him is information."

Venn's expression hardened, and I thought I detected a hint of concern in his tone. "You really don't want to mess with a Soulless."

I scoffed. "Says the guy who punched one in the face last night."

Venn crossed his arms. "Yeah, well, I had my reasons."

"So do I," I replied flatly. "Can you hand me my pants?"

"These bloody ones?" Venn rose from his chair and bent to the floor beside my bed.

"Yeah. They're my best pair," I said, reaching for them.

Venn averted his gaze as I pulled them on. I could only guess it was out of respect, but I kept the blanket draped over my legs, so it's not like he'd see anything even if he wanted to. After I was dressed, I pushed back the covers and hung my legs off the side of the bed.

"So," I said, running my fingers through my tangled black hair. "Now that we've established that we're friends, what's the plan?"

Venn furrowed his brow. "Plan?"

"Yeah." I rose to my feet.

My thigh protested since the spell was still working to heal it, but I'd endured worse. I crossed the room and grabbed the bag of bread next to the fridge. Venn's eyes followed me the whole time.

"Are we going after this guy or what?" I asked as I shoved a bland piece of bread in my mouth. I would've toasted it, but I was too hungry and impatient.

An expression of disbelief washed over Venn's face as he stepped into the small kitchen beside me. "*Go after*? As in, together?"

I nodded. If he didn't help me, I may have to wait years before I found another Soulless with answers.

"You know I'm good with vampires," I pointed out. "I'm a shifter. I'm strong —and fast."

"So am I," Venn said in a clipped tone.

I took a step back, holding up my bread up in surrender. "Right, I know. But don't we both stand a better chance together?"

"No," Venn said with conviction.

What? He didn't think I'd slow him down, did he?

"I can't let you get involved with someone like this," Venn said.

I let out a breath of disbelief. "I'm already involved!"

Venn pursed his lips. "Well, maybe you should get *un-involved*."

I swallowed my final bite of bread and leaned against the counter. "I told you last night, I'm not some damsel in distress."

Venn opened his mouth to say something but only exhaled. After a moment of holding my challenging gaze, he finally spoke. "You're hurt. I don't want you to get hurt again."

He didn't even know me; he couldn't mean that.

"I can handle getting hurt," I said with my head held high. What I *couldn't* handle was letting this opportunity pass me by. "I'm going after him with or without you. You wouldn't want me to find him first, would you?"

Venn's teeth clenched. "You're going to be a problem no matter what I do, aren't you?"

I put on my best innocent face. "My friends don't call me *stubborn* for nothing."

I internally laughed at the mention of friends. I didn't have any friends—not anymore—but Venn didn't need to know that.

"How do I know I can trust you?" Venn asked.

A hundred versions of the answer flew through my head, so I was surprised by the words that actually left my mouth. "You don't."

I didn't exactly know if I could trust him, either. We were just going to have to take a chance on each other.

Venn stepped forward and narrowed his eyes at me. My backside was already pressed against the countertop, so I had nowhere else to go. My skin heated, and my mouth went dry. He was testing me, waiting for me to back down.

I won't.

"All you want from this guy is information?" Venn asked, his hot breath brushing across the top of my head.

"Yes," I stated without blinking, despite my racing heart.

How did this guy's challenging gaze send my heart hammering harder than it did when I stood up to a freaking *Soulless*?

"What kind of information?" Venn pressed.

"That's personal," I replied, refusing to answer. He was already objected to me getting involved with *one* Soulless. What would he think if I told him I intended to crash their hideout?

"Tell me again why I should help you," Venn insisted.

He was only inches from me now. Had this guy ever heard of a personal bubble? Not that my apartment left much room for personal space.

"Be—because," I stuttered.

Stupid mouth.

I cleared my throat. "Because I need your help."

No! That's not what I meant to say!

It wasn't like I could shove the words back down my throat.

Venn's expression softened, and he took a step back.

"I can help you, too," I said in a rush, standing up straighter. "I'm a witch, after all. I can perform spells, and—"

"Fine," Venn said with a heavy sign.

Wait. What?

"Really?" I asked, not quite sure I believed him.

"Against my better judgement, yes, I'll help you."

I jumped in excitement, startling Venn and sending a fresh wave of pain through my thigh. I quickly composed myself. "Cool. When do we start?"

"Whenever you're ready," Venn said.

I ran my fingers through the knots in my hair. "I'm ready. So... where do we find this guy?"

Venn shook his head. "It's not that simple. I think we should head back to my place first. We'll talk to the family and come up with a game plan."

I passed Venn and headed to my dresser to gather my purse and the few belongings I carried when I wasn't out getting myself into supernatural trouble.

"*The family?*" I asked without looking back. "You spend *one* night at my place, and suddenly I'm meeting your parents?" I turned from my dresser and slung my purse over my shoulder. "Sorry, Venn, but we may want to slow this relationship down a little."

Venn leaned his shoulder against the refrigerator and smirked at me from across the room. "To be fair, *you're* the one who invited me back to your place and had me take your pants off."

"Oh, God," I groaned, shoving my face into my hands. "That's how you're going to introduce me to your parents, isn't it? I'll never live it down."

"Relax," Venn said with a laugh. "You don't have to meet my parents. They're dead."

My entire body tensed at the words. It was official. I was the worst person on the planet. My hands slowly dropped from my face, and my mouth hung open. All I wanted to do was tell him that I knew how he felt, but my lips refused to move.

"Come on." Venn straightened and crossed the room toward the door. He acted so casual, like my comment hadn't bothered him in the slightest. "We should get going. Ryland's going to be mad enough at me as it is. The sooner he's done yelling at me, the sooner we can go after Cowen."

I grabbed my spell book off the table then followed behind Venn into the hall, flipping off the light and locking the door behind me. I bent and peeled back the loose baseboard in the hall next to my front door and placed my key inside the crack. It was easier to leave it there than coming up with the money to enchant it to shift with me.

"Who's Ryland, and why would he be mad at you?" I asked when I stood.

"You'll meet him soon, but be careful," Venn warned. "He'll be mad at me for bringing home a stray."

A stray? I almost asked before realization hit. *Me. He means me.*

This Ryland guy was going to be mad at *me*. Too bad he had no idea I was a fighter. And when I fought back, I fought back *hard*.

3

"Is there anything I should know before I meet your family?" I asked Venn once we reached his car. It was a black four-door sports car with a sleek, modern design. Though it looked at least a few years old, its paint shined as if it'd been recently cleaned. The car was parked a few blocks away next to the bar we'd both confronted Cowen outside of. The street was quiet, in stark contrast to the bustling nightlife of last night. "Anything that will help me make a good first impression?"

Not that I care.

Venn turned the air conditioner on full-blast before it had a chance to cool. Hot air burst from the vents and blew in my face. The air today was thick and far too hot for a summer morning.

Venn pressed on the gas, and the car sped forward with a quick jolt. This thing clearly had its fair share of horsepower. "You could've started with a better pair of pants."

"I told you these were my best pair," I defended. "You of all people should know how valuable clothes that shift with you are. Yours are obviously enchanted."

Venn glanced at my pants then back to the road. "They're that valuable?"

My brow furrowed. Was he toying with me, or did he really not know? Either he was made of a crap ton of money, or he was sleeping with a high witch. His car was nice, but it wasn't *that* nice. I had to guess it was the latter.

"Do you have a cleaning spell in that book of yours?" Venn asked, gesturing to the bag on my lap. "Something that will get rid of the blood?"

I scoffed. "Sure I do, but if I could actually perform the spell, don't you think I would've done something about that water stain on my ceiling?"

"I thought you said you were a mid-witch," Venn said.

"No," I corrected. "I said I was somewhere between a low witch and a mid-witch. There are some spells I can't get right, okay?"

"Whoa." Venn held up a hand in surrender. "I didn't mean to hit a nerve."

Had I been that harsh about it? *Woops.*

"It's okay," I told him in a softer tone.

I looked out the window as we turned down a residential street. The houses here were small and cramped together, but they looked well taken care of, which was in total contrast to the dump neighborhood I lived in. Here, the houses actually had a homey charm to them.

Venn pulled into the driveway of a white two-story home. A bright flowery wreath hung on the front door. My thoughts immediately went to Jenna. Every spring, we'd pull out craft supplies and make a wreath for Mom for Mother's Day. It would hang all year until we made her a new one. My heart ached at the reminder of my family.

"What's wrong?" Venn asked as he shifted into park. He sounded genuinely concerned.

My face must've gone pale—paler than normal. I shook my head, as if trying to rid the memory from my mind. "Nothing. It's just a lovely home."

Venn opened the door and stepped out of the vehicle. "Yeah, we got lucky."

I slung my purse over my body and followed behind him up the sidewalk. Nerves twisted in my gut. Sure, I had no problem confronting a Soulless in a dark alley, but something about voluntarily meeting new people was terrifying.

Venn led me inside. I warily stepped over the threshold into a narrow hallway. The first thing I noticed was the faint smell of cinnamon. It was the same scent I'd noticed on Venn, the smell of comfort, of home. Hardwood floor spanned in front of us, reaching back into the house where it met an open doorway that led to a bathroom. A flight of stairs rose to our right. Framed drawings hung on the wall and climbed upward with the steps. Two other doorways opened from the entryway, one leading to the living room on our left and the other to a dining room on our right. I noticed six chairs set around the table, so I figured Venn's family couldn't be *that* big. I hadn't had a chance yet to ask more about who lived here with him. If his parents weren't around, who did he live with?

"Venn Jason Michaels!" a deep voice boomed from upstairs.

A shudder traveled through my body. We were in trouble. Well, Venn was, and I'd walked straight into it. Part of me wanted to stay just to see the fight while another part of me felt like ducking out of the house the first chance I got. I kind of had a love-hate relationship with drama.

"I'm back!" Venn shouted before lowering his voice and gesturing to the living room. "You can set your stuff down in here."

I followed behind him and sank onto the couch, but I didn't accept his invitation to set my bag down. Instead, I held the strap close to my chest.

My eyes swept across the room. This room alone had more decor in it than my entire apartment, though it wasn't like my apartment was much bigger. A

TV hung on the wall across from me, and a coffee table sat in the center of the room with a vase of flowers placed on it. A brick fireplace was built into the far wall, and a painting of a landscape hung above it. On either side of that stood two bookcases filled with old books and picture frames. I noticed a skinny redheaded teen girl in several of the photos and wondered who she was. Her pale skin was in stark contrast to Venn's dark complexion, so I guessed they weren't related.

Just as I thought it, the same redheaded girl rushed into the room. She stopped abruptly in the doorway, and her wide eyes locked on Venn. He faced the doorway with his arms crossed, bracing himself for whatever came next.

"Ryland's pissed," Red warned.

"I know," Venn replied tensely as heavy footsteps pounded down the stairs.

"Venn," the deep voice came again.

Red stepped aside as the man the voice belonged to stomped into the room. His facial structure was similar to Red's, but he had chestnut brown hair. He didn't look much older than me, yet he towered at least a foot above Red. If I thought Venn was made of muscle, he was nothing compared to this guy. His biceps were as big as the trunk of the tree my dad built my childhood treehouse in. In other words, the guy was *massive*.

"What happened—?" Tree Trunks started to say, but his voice cut off when his eyes fell on me. His jaw tightened. "Who's this?"

Venn raked his fingers through his hair and sighed. "This is Rae. I mentioned her last night."

"She's the *situation?*" Tree Trunks boomed in disbelief. He cursed under his breath and clenched his fists tight. He spun around and took a few paces—which basically covered the whole room with his long legs—before turning back to Venn. "You let Cowen get away for *her?*"

"I—"

"What did you *do* to her?" Tree Trunks cut Venn off and stared down at my bloody jeans.

I was stunned by the accusation.

"Nothing," Venn defended.

Tree Trunks shot him a look of disbelief.

I stood abruptly. "This was Cowen's doing. Venn saved me."

Tree Trunks hesitated for a moment, but he didn't reply. He turned back to Venn. "Why'd you bring her here?"

Venn's gaze darted between mine and Tree Trunks's. "She's on our side."

"So what?" Tree Trunks objected. "She's a complete stranger. You can't just bring strangers into our home. This is supposed to be a safe place!"

"She needs our help," Venn replied, calmer than I expected him to.

"You should've at least asked first," Tree Trunks insisted.

"Asked who?" Venn's voice rose. "You? You're not in charge here. Sondra would've—"

"It doesn't matter what Sondra would've done," Tree Trunks argued. "While she's gone, I *am* in charge."

This was getting to be too much. I was a sucker for violence, but only when it involved kicking vampire ass. I didn't want to be the reason this home turned into a war zone.

"Hey," I said to get their attention. All eyes turned to me, including Red's in the doorway. "All I need is—"

Tree Trunks held up a hand to stop me. "Hold on. I'll get to you in a minute."

"Excuse me?" I snapped. This guy was a total asshole. I knew it was his house and everything, but I couldn't just stand around and let him treat everyone like dirt.

Tree Trunks blinked at me, like he couldn't believe I'd objected to his orders.

"You interrupt people an awful lot," I observed. And I hadn't even known the guy for two minutes. "As I was saying, all I need is help finding Cowen. Venn offered his expertise. As soon as we find him, I'm gone."

Tree Trunks's jaw tightened. "This isn't about you. This is between me and Venn."

"Fine," I agreed. "Have your little chat, but you can't stop Venn from helping me."

"Believe me," Venn said with amusement on the corner of his lips. "She'd castrate you if you tried."

I smiled proudly, glad he understood me. I adjusted the strap on my purse and stepped out into the hall while Venn and Tree Trunks continued yelling at each other. I took a seat on the bottom stair, intent on waiting out their fight where I could still eavesdrop. Though at their volume, I could probably easily hear them halfway across the street.

"Hey," Red said as she sat next to me. "I'm sorry about Ryland. He's never like this. He's actually really sweet, and I say that as a sister who can't stand him half the time."

He could've fooled me.

"He's only mad because he's been up all night worrying about Venn," Red explained, keeping her eyes fixed on a hangnail she was fidgeting with. "Venn called to let us know he was okay, but Ryland couldn't help but worry, you know?"

My shoulders relaxed. It sounded like the time I was fifteen and snuck out of the house to attend a party. Jenna wouldn't take me because I was only a freshman, but I went anyway. We both got an earful from Dad the next morning.

"I'm Fiona, by the way," Red introduced.

I cleared my throat. "Rach—Rae. I'm Rae."

"Cool, so why—?"

"Back off, Ryland!" Venn's voice boomed from the other room, cutting Fiona off.

She glanced to the living room, looking positively embarrassed by the guys she lived with.

"You don't have to worry," Venn continued. "I'll take care of her."

Take care of me? Who says I need taking care of?

"That's not the problem," Ryland responded. "How do we know we can trust her?"

I raised my eyebrows at Fiona. "They're just going to keep talking about me like I can't hear them?"

Fiona crinkled her nose and nodded. "Probably."

"We *can* trust her," Venn emphasized. "Because..."

I couldn't see Ryland from the hall, but I pictured him crossing his arms when he spoke.

"Because...?" Ryland prompted.

"Because..."

Every muscle in my body tensed. *Oh, God. He's going to out me as the Ravenite. I know he said he wouldn't turn me in, but what if one of his friends does?*

Venn let out a frustrated growl. "I just trust her, okay? Isn't that enough?"

I relaxed. He was keeping my secret.

Venn lowered his voice, but I could still make out his words clear as day. "There's just... something in her eyes."

Ryland paused for a beat. "That doesn't give you the right to act without consulting us first."

Fiona turned to me, ignoring the on-going argument. "So, how'd you meet Venn?"

I still didn't know this girl—or Venn for that matter. I didn't know any of them, so I was hesitant on how much to say. I avoided her gaze, looking anywhere but her eyes—at the front door, at my boots, up the stairs at the sketches on the wall. Even though her question was innocent enough, I purposely didn't answer.

"Those are nice," I said flatly, gesturing to the closest drawing. Venn's eyes stared back at me from the paper. Whoever had drawn him had managed to capture the soft beauty in his eyes perfectly.

"Yeah," Fiona agreed. "Sondra drew them all."

I twisted further to view the portraits. I noticed a drawing of Fiona beside Venn's, and Ryland next to hers.

"Who's Sondra?" I asked.

"She's mine and Ryland's cousin," Fiona answered.

"So, you're all related?" I asked. "Even Venn?"

Fiona shook her head. "Not by blood. We sort of adopted Venn and Teagan."

"Teagan?" I asked.

"She's probably in her room listening to music to drown out the guys' argument." Fiona gave a light giggle, as if it was a common occurrence.

"You all live here together?" I asked.

It felt like there should be an adult in the house, until I realized *I* was an adult. *When did that happen?*

Another voice in my head quickly responded. *The day Mom and Dad died.*

"Yep," Fiona answered.

I eyed her curiously. She definitely looked younger than me. "How old are all of you?"

"Venn's nineteen, and Ryland and Teagan are twenty. I'm seventeen."

I was eighteen and couldn't afford a place a quarter this nice. How did they do it?

"Sondra owns the house," Fiona explained, like she could read my mind. "She's a lot older than the rest of us. She inherited the house from her parents and then took me and Ryland in when ours died."

"Oh," I said softly. It sounded like Sondra was running some sort of orphanage. I'd fit in perfectly.

Great. Because that was just the kind of place you wanted to fit in at.

An uncomfortable silence hung between Fiona and me, but Venn's and Ryland's voices in the other room somehow made it less awkward.

"So, what do you need to find Cowen for?" Fiona asked. "You don't seem like the kind of girl to get involved with people like him."

I laughed a deep, full-belly laugh I couldn't control. "You'd be surprised."

If my job was any indication, I was *exactly* the kind of girl to get involved with people like Cowen. Bloodstone wasn't exactly legal, and neither were my... hobbies.

Eight years ago, Valkas showed up and started changing a bunch of people into vampires, presumably recruiting them for his Soulless army—until the Soulless fell off the radar two years ago, not long after they kidnapped my sister as a blood slave. Anyway, when I was a kid, the new vampires went on killing sprees all across the US. No one knew for sure if it was the product of bloodlust or if it was under Valkas's orders. Maybe he just wanted to spark fear in the masses. Which, by the way, totally worked.

At the same time, ordinary people began to discover they had magic. Shifters started shifting, and witches started casting spells. It began with adults, but kids my age followed a few years later as we grew older. Magic usually appeared at first during times of high emotions, but the more we used it, the more we could control it. Most people never changed, but you never knew if you'd end up supernatural or not. It was clear from the beginning that shifter magic ran in families, but witch magic was random. There wasn't a genetic component that anyone knew of.

But of course, witches and shifters were lumped into the same supernatural category as the heartless, murderous vampires. A civil rights movement fought to treat all supernaturals as equals to humans. In a compromise, the government ruled that supernatural creatures couldn't be charged for what they were, only for the crimes they had committed.

Magic was outlawed except in special government-approved cases, and supernaturals were required to be registered as such. Blood banks were set up for vampires who'd already been changed so that they could satisfy their cravings without killing or changing more people. It was a great solution but a crappy deal. The government didn't even pay people for their blood, but they sure liked to charge vamps for it. And people bought into the whole thing out of fear, because at least there were fewer vampire attacks.

Obviously, however, if there are laws in place, people are bound to break them. Vampires continued to feed without consent, shifters continued to shift, and people like me continued to deliver justice in a world with a broken justice system. Magical objects and spells were sold on the black market for a pretty penny, which meant that if Bloodstone were ever discovered, I'd already have a decade or two in the slammer just for working there. If all my crimes were laid out on the table, I'd be in for life. But seriously, who's counting?

"Yeah…" I said to Fiona, dragging out the word as all these thoughts rushed through my head. "We probably shouldn't get into that."

"Hey," Ryland's clipped tone came from behind us.

Fiona and I both turned. The anger had melted from his face, but I still sensed something in his expression that told me he wasn't entirely pleased.

"You can stay for now," Ryland told me.

From beside him, Venn shot me a reassuring smile. I wasn't sure what he'd said to Ryland to change his mind, but I was grateful that he fought for me.

Ryland's eyes flickered down to my thigh. "Find her a clean pair of pants, Fiona. Teagan should have some that'll fit her."

"I can try," Fiona said, "but you'll have to wish me luck getting anywhere *near* Teagan's closet."

"Good luck." Ryland didn't sound the least bit genuine. "Just be quick. We're leaving in ten minutes."

My brow furrowed. "Leaving where?"

Ryland's jaw tensed. "To get Cowen."

4

When Fiona said we'd have a hard time getting into Teagan's closet, I
pictured walking into a blonde bimbo's glittery pink bedroom. Imagine
my surprise when we entered her room just in time for a knife to whizz past my
head. The blade hit the wall beside me with a *thud*.

I jumped back from the door, my heart racing.

"Tea," Fiona scolded, ripping the knife from a board screwed into the wall.
Every inch of the board was filled with nick marks. "Are you *trying* to scare our
guest away?"

Teagan eyed me from across the room. She was strikingly beautiful, with tan
skin, high cheekbones, and full lips. Her dark hair was twisted into a braid
down her back. Teagan wore a skin-tight black tank top tucked into a pair of
brown cargo pants that hugged her curves. A pair of sheaths hung from her belt
on either hip. My guess was that she was some sort of badass shifter who could
rip a vampire's throat out with her teeth.

I think I'm going to like this girl.

Teagan stepped forward and snatched the knife from Fiona's outstretched
hand. She ignored Fiona's question but kept her eyes on me.

"So, you're the girl Venn brought home?" Teagan asked as she slid her knife
into its sheath.

I nodded. "The one and only."

"You heard all that?" Fiona asked, like it wasn't obvious. "Maybe you can do
something to calm Ryland down later?"

Fiona made it sound like Teagan had some sort of power over Ryland.
Maybe she wasn't a shifter but was a witch… or, like me, perhaps she was both.

My gaze traveled beyond Teagan. I took note of a queen-sized bed and two
dressers side-by-side. The decor was simple and accented with neutral browns.

That's when it clicked what kind of power she had over him, and it wasn't anything supernatural. Ryland was her boyfriend.

I need to get myself one of those.

The problem was, I had to actually leave the house if I wanted to meet anyone. I was never going to meet a guy while patrolling for vamps causing trouble.

"This is Rae, by the way," Fiona introduced. "She needs to borrow some clothes."

Teagan didn't say anything as Fiona crossed the room to her closet. Instead, she kept her attention on me. She stood so close that I could smell the scent of lavender on her clothes. She was two inches taller than me and stared down at me like I was supposed to be intimidated by her. I stared back with an equally intimidating glare.

"What are you?" Teagan asked curiously.

My brow furrowed. "Excuse me?"

Could she sense I was supernatural? She must've been a powerful witch.

"Venn wouldn't bring just anyone home," Teagan pointed out. "What kind of shifter are you?"

My eyes darted to Fiona across the room, but I only saw a glimpse of her backside in the walk-in closet. I didn't tell people I was a shifter. The only reason Venn knew was because he saw it. Even the witch who enchanted my clothes didn't know what I was. Luckily, she wasn't the kind of person who asked questions. She just took the money and did her thing.

I wasn't about to give up my secret to a girl I just met, no matter the fact that she could probably give me a run for my money in a fight.

I cleared my throat. "I'm a low witch. You?"

"Vampire slayer," Teagan said confidently, without missing a beat.

"Seriously?" I asked in disbelief.

Was she suggesting she was a supernatural "chosen one?" That didn't happen in real life, did it? Then again, eight years ago I would've said vampires, shifters, and witches didn't exist either.

"Don't let her fool you," Fiona said, emerging from the closet with an armful of clothes. "Teagan's entirely human."

"No way." The words slipped from my mouth before I could stop myself. Teagan seemed… tougher than that.

"What?" Teagan raised an eyebrow. "Humans aren't good enough for you?"

"No, I just—" I fumbled for the right words. *Crap.* "You really fight vampires?"

Teagan sucked her teeth. "On occasion."

"You *have* to have shifter blood in you," I insisted.

"Nope," Teagan said with certainty.

"How are you fast enough?" I asked.

"She doesn't need supernatural speed," Fiona said, like she was quoting

Teagan's own words. She dropped her pile of clothes on the bed before turning to me. "All she needs is a clear shot of their heart."

"Yep," Teagan agreed proudly. "Stab them in the heart with anything, and they die."

I knew the drill. Vampires only dropped dead from a wound to the heart or brain, decapitation, or fire. They healed quickly from other injuries.

"You just have to get to them before they get to you," Teagan continued.

"*Stab first, ask questions later,*" Fiona said. "That's Tea's motto."

Teagan smirked. I liked her motto.

"Ryland would never let a vamp hurt her," Fiona said. "Anyway, Tea, are these pants fine to lend Rae?"

Teagan glanced at the cargo pants Fiona held up. "Not those."

Teagan marched across the room and scooped up the clothes on the bed and returned them to her closet. Fiona shot an apologetic look at me while we waited for Teagan to return.

"So…" I dragged out the word, partially to fill the silence. "Venn's a shifter, and Teagan's human. What are you?"

Oh, gosh. I hope that didn't sound rude.

Fiona sat on the bed. "Fox shifter."

Which meant Ryland was a shifter too.

"Is Sondra a shifter?" God, I was nosy. If she was Fiona's cousin, she could be anything depending on which side of the family Fiona inherited her shifter magic from. "When do I get to meet her? I want to tell her how much I love her drawings."

Teagan exited the closet while I spoke. She froze in place and exchanged a wary glance with Fiona.

Fiona was the one to answer. "Sondra's… not here right now. But if everything goes well, you should be able to meet her soon."

I didn't have a chance to ask where Sondra was or when she'd return as Teagan shoved a pile of neatly folded clothes in my direction.

"Here," she said. "These should fit. You can change in the bathroom. It's the next door on the right down the hall."

I took the pile of clothes in my hands. "Thanks."

Teagan grabbed a jacket off her dresser and slipped it on. It fell to the top of her thighs and covered up the knives on her hips.

Fiona stood. "Let me know when you're done so we can throw your pants in the wash."

I shot back a smile. It was nice of her to offer. It'd save me a few quarters and a night at the laundromat.

I turned and stepped out into the hall just in time to see Venn climbing the stairs. A smile spread across his face when he spotted me. My breath stalled in my chest, and my knees went weak under his stare. What the frick? My insides were rock-solid. They shouldn't be turning to mush, especially not for a guy I just barely met.

Venn reached the top of the steps and stopped with one hand on the banister. "You almost ready?"

"Yeah, I…" I didn't know what to say. My eyes dropped to the clothes in my hands. "I just have to change. I'll be out in a minute."

"Try not to be too long," Venn suggested. "Ryland wants to get going soon."

I was about to turn to the bathroom but paused. "Hey, Venn."

"Yeah?" he asked softly, his eyes still fixed on me.

I wasn't sure why I stopped or what I was going to say. All I knew was that I didn't want to step out of the room without him.

Stop acting weird!

"Thank you," I finally said while fidgeting with a loose thread on the tank top I held. "I mean, Ryland was right. You don't have a reason to trust me. So I just wanted to say thanks for offering to help."

Venn stepped forward and reached out like he was about to touch me, but he pulled away at the last second. I had the unnatural urge to accept his invitation and close the distance between us.

"It's no problem," he said.

An awkward silence followed, and I contemplated saying more. Several seconds passed, but nothing came out of my mouth. It felt too late to break the silence now, so I turned to the bathroom without another word.

Inside the bathroom, I forced Venn from my mind, and my thoughts turned to Cowen. My heart pounded as I rushed to slip into Teagan's clothes. In a matter of minutes, I'd be back on my way to tracking down the Soulless.

Watch out, Fangs. Here I come.

***

When Ryland said we were going after Cowen, I thought we were headed to kick some vampire ass. As in, I thought Ryland knew where to find him. Turns out he didn't have a clue.

We pulled up in front of the bar I cornered Cowen outside of last night. The sign above the door read *Red Whiskey*. This was a hot hangout for vamps since they sold alcohol *and* blood—fresh from the blood banks, thank God—but we wouldn't find a vamp hanging out here in the middle of the day.

"I thought you knew how to track this guy down," I accused Venn when he parked the car.

Venn turned in his seat to explain. "This is as far as we tracked him. We got a tip that this is his favorite hangout spot, but now that he knows we can find him here, we're not sure he'll be back. We're here to figure out where to find him next."

"Unfortunately," Ryland cut in, "Venn acted on pure emotion last night without calling in the rest of us, so I'll be doing the talking this time."

"Or maybe *I* should," Teagan offered from next to me in the back seat.

"No," Ryland stated sternly.

"You scare people away," Teagan accused.

"If you don't want to scare people, send me in," Fiona argued. With her small frame and sweet smile, she didn't look like she was capable of hurting a fly. She was right that no one would be intimidated by her.

Before the group could come to an agreement, Venn opened his door and stepped out of the car. Ryland fumbled with his door handle and kicked the passenger-side door open. I draped my purse strap over my shoulder and scrambled out of the car behind them. Teagan and Fiona followed closely behind.

Ryland's long legs carried him ahead of Venn so that he was the first to reach the door. He gripped the handle so hard that I was surprised it didn't crush beneath his grip like a soda can.

The building had no windows, and the lights were dim when we entered. A long bar lined with stools ran the length of the building to our right, while other tables filled the rest of the space. The chairs were all empty, and the building was silent apart from the sound of an air conditioner whirring. The back of the bar housed a lounge and a pool table. The distinct smell of floor cleaner filled my nostrils, masking any other scents that may have permeated into the walls and furniture.

Before any of us had a chance to speak, a man emerged from a door behind the bar. He held a drying towel in his hands and had a bored expression fixed to his face. He was attractive and looked to be in his late twenties or early thirties. For a vamp-friendly bar, I expected to find vampires running the place, but this guy's eyes were blue—not a hint of silver present.

Probably a blood slave, I thought. I hated that I couldn't tell what he was. Someday, I was going to figure out how to identify the difference between witches, shifters, and humans.

Fiona's eyes traveled the length of his body. It took everything I had to hold in my laughter. He was at least a decade older than her, and she was totally checking him out.

"Sorry, folks," he said in a smooth voice. I noticed the name on his uniform read *Alex*. "We're closed."

"The door was unlocked," Ryland responded, as if that was an excuse for the guy to serve us a drink—not that any of us were even of legal age. A lot had changed in the past eight years, but the drinking age was still twenty-one.

"Our hours are posted out front," Alex informed us, like leaving the door unlocked during off-hours was a common occurrence. "If you want to avoid the vamp crowd, it's best to come early."

Ryland stepped forward until he was right next to the bar. "Thanks for the tip, but actually, we're not here for a drink. We're looking for someone who frequents this establishment."

'Frequents this establishment?' He sounds so formal when he wants to.

"Can you help us?" Ryland asked.

Alex tossed the towel over his shoulder and leaned against the counter behind the bar, looking amused. "Who are you looking for?"

"His name's Cowen," Ryland answered.

Alex pressed his lips together. "He's a vamp? Brown hair, scar on his wrist?"

So Alex knows Cowen's a Soulless. Am I the only one who didn't know there was a Soulless running around Nocton?

Ryland nodded.

"Yeah, he's a regular, but I don't know where to find him," Alex said.

Too bad. I was really looking forward to beating information out of someone. Except Alex didn't look like he deserved a beating, and I didn't pick a fight without a reason.

Alex cocked his head in the direction of the kitchen and raised his voice. "Hey, Kieren. Come here a minute."

A huge guy that took up the entire doorway stepped into the room. Ryland's arms were like twigs compared to this guy. It didn't matter that I didn't have the sense to spot supernatural beings; I was totally pegging this guy as a shifter.

"They're looking for Cowen," Alex explained.

Kieren crossed his massive arms, and his eyes traveled over the group; first to Fiona, then to me. I shifted uncomfortably, like I'd just been violated by a simple glance. Maybe *this* guy deserved a punch to the groin. His gaze skipped straight over Venn and landed on Teagan. She didn't even blink.

"I might know Cowen," Kieren said in a deep voice.

"Well enough to know where to find him?" Ryland asked.

"That depends..." Kieren dragged out.

"On?" Ryland pressed.

Kieren smirked. "On how valuable the information is to you."

I glanced to Venn to see his jaw was tense. His eyes met mine, but I couldn't read his expression.

Ryland sighed, like he was hoping it wouldn't come to this. "What's your price?"

Kieren still hadn't taken his eyes off Teagan. She held his gaze without a single sign of fear. It was like she was used to guys looking at her like that—like a piece of meat. I think I felt uncomfortable enough for the both of us.

"What are you willing to pay?" Kieren asked with a raised eyebrow.

Ryland dug into his back pocket for his wallet and slapped a pile of bills on the bar. "Look, we don't have a lot of money, but we really need to find this guy. Can you help us or not?"

Kieren glanced down at the money but didn't move to take it. Beside him, Alex looked like he was itching to snatch it up.

"I can help," Kieren stated flatly, "but I don't want your money."

"What *do* you want?" Ryland asked.

Kieren didn't even hesitate. He cocked his head toward Teagan. "I'll take the girl."

Disgust hit my stomach at the suggestion. Fiona gasped, and Venn's expression hardened. Teagan just rolled her eyes, as if it was all too predictable.

"No," Ryland declined immediately.

Kieren stepped forward and placed his palms flat on the bar. Though there was a countertop between them, Ryland took a step back to distance himself from Kieren. A tingle spread across my skin in preparation to shift.

Cool down, I told myself. Even though I had a rule about shifting in front of people, I *would* shift if it came to that.

"Maybe let the girl decide for herself," Kieren suggested.

Ooh, what a gentleman...

Teagan's expression remained static. Clearly, this guy didn't scare her. Finally, she turned to Ryland. "Let's go. We'll find Cowen another way."

Teagan started for the door, but Kieren's voice stopped her.

"Come on," he said. "I'm only asking for one night."

Teagan whirled around. "And I'm saying *no.*"

"Fine," Kieren said with a shrug, like it didn't really matter to him either way. "But I know where to find him. If you leave, you might never know."

"Stop pushing it!" Ryland snapped. He leaned over the bar until his nose was only inches from Kieren's. "She said no."

I held my breath as the two stared each other down. I half expected one of them to spontaneously combust under the other's narrowed gaze.

Teagan stepped to Ryland's side, breaking the staring contest between the two guys. "Name us another price."

Kieren straightened. "I gave you my price. Take it or leave it."

Teagan gritted her teeth. "We'll leave it. Have a nice day."

Teagan's hand slapped to the counter to grab the wad of cash Ryland had placed there. In a flash, Kieren's arm shot out to grab Teagan's wrist.

And that's when Ryland lost it.

5

Chaos broke out all within a single second.

One moment, Ryland was looking up at Kieren with a narrowed, challenging gaze, and the next, his legs lengthened so that he towered above Kieren. Ryland's arms thickened, and brown fur sprouted all across his body.

Kieren dropped Teagan's hand and jumped back. His body shortened and morphed into a black creature not much bigger than I was.

At the same time, Venn whirled around and spread his arms out, catching me and Fiona at the same time. I stumbled backward into the table behind us, and the edge of it slammed into my backbone. Fiona fell over one of the chairs and crashed to the ground.

I suffered only a moment of disorientation, but when my attention turned back to the rest of the room, Ryland and Kieren had already fully shifted. Teagan had her knives out in under a second, looking determined to use them if she had to.

A terrifying roar filled the room, sending a surge of adrenaline through my veins. Ryland had grown to three times his normal size, so big that four stools and a table had been knocked out of the way in his transformation. He bared his large, pointed canines as a deep roar erupted from his chest.

A bear. Ryland's a freaking bear shifter.

That explained the tree trunk arms he had.

In front of him, a large cat with a black coat stood atop the bar, its lips curled back over its teeth. The t-shirt Kieren had been wearing hung from the jaguar's body.

That tingle of shifter magic returned and traveled all the way up my spine. I was a split second away from shifting, ready to peck some eyes out if necessary. I stood farthest from the bar in human form, bracing myself. Venn and Fiona

32

stepped forward, Venn in his wolf form and Fiona in her fox form. Alex raced through the door to the kitchen, running away from the fight.

Another beat passed as Ryland and Kieren bared their equally terrifying teeth at each other. Then, without warning, Kieren lunged.

It all happened in a blur. One second, Kieren was standing atop the bar in his jaguar form eye-to-eye with Ryland's bear. The next, he was on top of him, clawing into the flesh on his neck. Teagan lunged forward, swiping one of her knives at Kieren. She just barely caught him in the back leg.

Ryland spun around. His head jerked from side to side as he tried to throw Kieren off of him. His body slammed into Teagan, knocking her off balance and sending her crashing into a nearby table. Ryland didn't even notice.

I rushed across the room to Teagan and helped her to her feet. She shrugged me off but followed me in haste around the bar. Venn's howls filled the air, as if he was trying to talk some sense into Ryland in his shifted form.

Ryland went wild trying to buck Kieren off of him, but Kieren's claws dug into Ryland's back. Table and chairs screeched across the floor as Ryland slammed into them. Beside me, Teagan popped her head up over the bar and pulled an arm back, a knife ready between her fingers.

I caught her wrist before she could throw it. "Don't," I hissed. "You could hit Ryland."

Teagan didn't have a moment to respond. A split second later, Kieren's teeth sunk into the back of Ryland's neck, and Ryland shot to his hind legs. If I hadn't stopped Teagan, there was a good chance Ryland would have a knife sticking out of his back right now.

Ryland fell sideways. The nearest table crumbled beneath his weight, and the two shifters crashed to the ground. Ryland twisted his massive head, and his powerful jaws snapped at Kieren, who still hadn't loosened his grip.

This was *way* out of hand.

I didn't think. I just *acted*. In a mere second, my five-foot-four-frame shrank. The clothes I'd been wearing dropped around me in a heap. I flapped my wings and shot across the room until I was in Kieren's face, clawing at any flesh I could find and blocking his vision with my wings.

While I had him momentarily distracted, Venn jumped forward. His weight slammed into Kieren, knocking him several feet away from Ryland. A high-pitched whimper filled the air. Ryland regained his footing, but Kieren collapsed under his front paw when he tried to right himself. Venn stood between the two, growling at Kieren.

Finally, Kieren dropped his gaze in surrender, and Venn's growl died down. Ryland shifted back into human form and wiped the blood from the puncture wounds left by Kieren's teeth.

I landed behind the bar and shifted. Teagan's eyes went wide. Fiona rushed around the side of the bar while I was pulling my shirt back on. Luckily, I'd kept my enchanted underwear on from earlier, so I didn't have to flash anyone. Good thing, too, because Teagan's wide eyes were still on me. I would've felt a hundred times more uncomfortable if my tits were hanging out.

"Are you two okay?" Fiona asked in a rush, kneeling down beside us.

Teagan ignored her. "Why didn't you tell us you were a shifter?"

I stood to pull my pants back on. "I didn't realize I was obligated to."

"A *raven?*" Teagan hissed.

I ignored her. I snatched up my bag and hopped over the top of the bar. By now, Venn and Kieren were back in human form, but Kieren was still on the ground. He wore nothing but his ripped t-shirt, leaving all his goods hanging out in the open. He didn't even seem to notice as he clutched his left hand with his right.

"You broke my hand!" Kieren roared at Venn before proceeding to call him a slew of horrible names.

"Yeah, well, you deserved it!" Venn snapped back.

Kieren sucked in deep breaths as he got to his knees. "Leave! All of you!"

Ryland didn't waste a second. He took Teagan's hand and started for the door.

"Alex!" Kieren called on his way to the kitchen. "Lock the doors and get the car. We're going to the hospital."

Ha! The hospital. Too bad he didn't know a good witch. Though, healing spells could be just as costly as hospital bills, but at least he wouldn't have to suffer through the pain. Which, judging by this guy's use of colorful words, could really brighten his day.

"Wait!" I blurted before I could stop myself.

Everyone froze to look at me.

Oh, crap. I couldn't go through with what I was just about to say. Sure, I could heal myself from time to time, but I'd never healed someone else before. He could end up with boils across his skin or something gross like that. There was a reason I didn't conjure magic for profit.

But... the chance to find Cowen—to find my sister—was *far* more valuable than any monetary payment. Could it really hurt to *try?*

Yes, I told myself. Everyone was eyeing me, waiting for me to explain my sudden outburst.

I can't believe I'm doing this, I thought, my hands shaking.

I cleared my throat. "I'll help you."

"Help me?" Kieren asked skeptically. He was behind the bar now, struggling to pull on his pants with one hand—thank God, because I didn't think I'd be able to look him in the eye otherwise.

"I'm a witch," I explained. "I'll heal your hand. It will save you a trip to the hospital, emergency room bills, and weeks of recovery."

Kieren hesitated. "You'll do all that *if* I tell you where to find Cowen?"

"Yes," I replied.

Kieren scoffed. "Screw you."

"Seriously?" I snapped as he turned away. "The information is *that* valuable to you?"

"No," Kieren barked, spinning back toward me. "But pissing you people off is pretty damn satisfying. Now get out of my bar."

"Come on," Venn said to me in a low voice, encouraging me to follow him. "You don't have to do this."

Kieren cursed under his breath.

"I can make the pain go away," I stated confidently. The truth was, I had no idea if my healing spell would work on someone else. But it wasn't like I was above conning a guy who clearly had worse morals than I did.

Kieren grimaced, like he was fighting an internal battle on whether or not to save his hand or save his pride.

"All you have to do is tell us where to find Cowen," I pressed.

Kieren's jaw remained tense. "So you break my hand to use it as a trade for information? You should be fixing it without asking anything in return."

"Hey," I said like it didn't matter to me one way or the other. I was totally bluffing; I really wanted the information. "I'm not the one who broke your hand. If you don't want to take my offer, you're free to go to the hospital on your own."

A long pause passed through the bar. My shoulders tensed with each passing second.

Finally, Kieren spoke. "Fine."

Yes!

"First you give us what we want," I demanded.

"No way," Kieren protested. "You'll just walk out of here without helping me."

"I won't," I swore. But I needed him to fulfill his side of the bargain first in case my spell didn't work.

"How do I know you're not lying to me?" Kieren asked.

Good question.

I held my head high. "I guess we're just going to have to trust each other."

Kieren didn't look like he trusted me one bit, but he *did* look desperate.

"Okay," he reluctantly agreed. "Cowen lives with a group of vampires on the corner of Cramer and Valander. It's the big white house with red shutters. Now will you fix my effing hand?"

A sense of victory washed over me. *One step closer.*

My excitement didn't last long. If this spell didn't go well, I'd better be ready to run.

"Sit," I instructed Kieren, pulling out one of the stools next to the bar.

Kieren glared at the group of shifters—and one human—behind me, but he rounded the bar and sat anyway. I took one glance at Venn and his family to see they all had a look of intrigue in their eyes. They were probably just as curious as I was to see how this was going to pan out.

I ignored their stares and pulled a second stool up beside Kieren. I grabbed my spell book from my bag and flipped it open to the spell I'd used last night. My eyes scanned the incantation. I should've had it memorized by now, but I had a terrible memory when it came to spells. That was probably one of the reasons I was such a bad spellcaster.

"Are we gonna do this or what?" Kieren asked through clenched teeth. "Because this hurts like a mother—"

"Yes," I replied quickly. "Give me your hand."

Kieren's bruised hand hung limp as he extended his arm toward me. Gently, I took his wounded hand in mine. He didn't show any emotion, like he was too tough for that.

Seconds ticked by, but I couldn't bring myself to mutter the incantation.

"Let's get this over already," Kieren mumbled.

Right. Okay, Rachel, just say the incantation, then you can get out of here.

I began reading the spell from my book, focusing only on the words and Kieren's hand in mine. I neared the end of the incantation, but Kieren's face remained expressionless. I couldn't tell if he was still in pain or not.

Here come the boils.

Just as I thought it, a sharp, stabbing pain shot through my left hand. It hurt so bad that I sprang up from my chair and let out a high-pitched squeal. Kieren's face lit up with alarm, but by the time he spoke, the pain in my hand was already gone.

"What happened?" he demanded.

I didn't have an answer. I'd never experienced something like that before. Had my spell backfired? Could it do that?

"It didn't work!" Kieren roared.

"It—it didn't?" God, I sounded like I had no idea what I was doing. Which, to be fair, I didn't. Not really.

"No, it didn't!" Kieren cried, shooting up from his stool. He looked like he was two seconds away from going all maniac-jaguar on us again. "I gave you the information you asked for. You owe me a good hand!"

Venn rushed forward before Kieren got mad enough to punch me out with his good hand. "Let her try again. Sometimes it takes a few tries."

Kieren paused, but he didn't look convinced.

"I saw her perform a healing spell last night," Venn said in an attempt to calm Kieren down.

Just tell the whole world, why don't you, Venn? Everyone's going to want me to heal them. The joke's on them, since I can't cast a decent spell to save my life.

"She can do it," Venn said. "Let her give it another shot."

Okay, maybe I could cast a spell to save *my* life, but I wasn't sure I could cast a spell to save someone else's.

Kieren slumped back into his stool. "Fine, but if this doesn't work..."

I was incredibly grateful that he didn't finish that sentence.

Venn stood behind me and squeezed my shoulders. Warm tingles spread down my arms, calming me. It was almost as if he had magic of his own, though

I figured he would've told me by now if he was a witch. My shoulders relaxed beneath the weight of his comforting hands.

"You can do this," Venn whispered in my ear. "You cast the same spell last night, and it worked. You can do it again. I know you have it in you. You just have to believe in yourself."

I took a deep breath. *He's right. I can do this.*

Taking Kieren's hand in mine again, I reread the incantation. This *had* to work.

"It's not working," Kieren said, disgruntled.

Or not...

"Remember why you're doing this," Venn whispered from beside me.

I'm doing this to find Cowen, I told myself. *Because without him, I'll never find Jenna. I'm doing this for my sister.*

I read through the incantation a third time. All my thoughts turned to Jenna. I pictured her soft blue eyes and long brown hair. In my mind, she hadn't aged a day since I last saw her. She was still eighteen and drop-dead gorgeous, with long lashes and a dimple on the right side of her face. I imagined the smile that would spread across her face when I found her. I pictured her pulling me into a tight hug. She'd squeeze me until I couldn't breathe, like she used to do when we were kids.

I missed you so much, rugrat! Jenna would say.

I would cry, even though I'd try not to. *I missed you, too, Jenna-Bean.*

Before I realized it, I'd already reached the end of the incantation. Kieren continued to stare at me in skepticism.

"Better?" I asked. I couldn't read him.

"Better," Kieren said bitterly, "but not fixed."

I could hardly believe my ears.

"Then it worked," I told him, standing and scooping up my spell book. "The pain will start to go away slowly, and it should be completely healed within a couple of days."

Kieren didn't look happy, but he couldn't deny that I'd held up my end of the bargain. Which I still couldn't believe.

"Thank you for your cooperation," I said before turning to leave.

Kieren scoffed, like he didn't think of it as cooperation in the slightest.

Venn, Ryland, Teagan, and Fiona all headed to the door with me, no doubt as eager as I was to escape this place as quickly as possible.

"I don't want to see any of you back here!" Kieren called before we stepped outside. "You hear me?"

Obviously, I was never going back there. He'd probably demand we pay for the broken tables, and I certainly didn't have that kind of cash lying around.

Outside, Fiona rammed into me, pulling me into a tight hug.

"*Ohf.*" A breath of air escaped my lungs.

"Thank you *so* much!" Fiona continued to squeeze me.

"For what?" I asked on our way to the car. "All I did was heal the guy's hand."

And I probably didn't do a very good job of it, I told myself.

"You did more than that, though," Venn insisted, pulling out his keys. "You got him to tell us where to find Cowen."

"Yeah," Fiona agreed. "Teagan wasn't any help."

Teagan slugged Fiona as she ducked into the car.

"Ow!" Fiona complained, holding on to her shoulder.

"You seriously expected me to sleep with that guy?" Teagan asked in disbelief.

"No," Ryland said firmly as he slid into the passenger seat. "None of us would've let you do something like that."

Teagan's expression softened, but it only lasted a second before she turned to me with a raised eyebrow. "I thought you said you were a low witch."

I shrugged. "Mostly. I guess I just have a gift for healing."

"And a bit of shifter magic," Fiona pointed out, gazing at me in admiration. "You're the Ravenite, aren't you?"

I sighed. There was no point in denying it. There weren't exactly hundreds of raven shifters running around Nocton.

"I do what's necessary," I said, adding a hint of warning to my tone. "So… are we gonna go get this vamp or what?"

Venn pulled out onto the street.

"Believe me," Ryland said. "I wanna go after him as soon as possible, too, but you heard what Kieren said. Cowen lives with a bunch of other vamps. We have to be careful. There's a good chance they outnumber us."

"So, what do we do?" Fiona asked, hopeless.

Ryland paused a beat and glanced to the sky. The sun was hidden behind a thick layer of clouds, so it wasn't going to help us much today. Sure, it would slow the vampires down and maybe give them a few blisters, but it wasn't enough to make them retreat like it would if the sun were out.

"We wait until nightfall," he decided. "It'll give us enough time to scope out the place. Plus, most of the vamps will leave by then, so we can crash the nest while there are fewer to deal with. Maybe Cowen will make an appearance himself."

"I say we bust down the place right now," Teagan voted. "We don't have the time to waste."

"Yeah, well, I'm not gonna walk straight into a full vampire nest and lose any one of you," Ryland replied with a harsh tone. He had a point.

"In that case," Teagan agreed, "I'm going to need more knives."

6

Night fell, and darkness enveloped the city, but the minutes on Venn's dashboard continued to tick by, and still no sign of Cowen. We'd been sitting in the car a few doors down from the white house on the corner for hours, and we had yet to see a single person come or go.

"Maybe Kieren lied," Fiona theorized, pausing momentarily from blowing air across the back of Teagan's neck. She'd been doing it for the last several minutes to try to get a reaction out of her. Either Teagan hadn't noticed or she was purposely ignoring Fiona. I'd been trying to hold in a laugh because it seemed like something my sister would do when she was bored.

Venn shook his head. "I don't think he lied. I mean, the house is here like he said."

There was no arguing that, considering it was probably the only white house with red shutters in town. The house was old, with various peaks in the roof, two chimneys, and peeling paint siding. Crooked wooden stairs led up to a front porch that looked like it creaked with every step. The house rose two stories high and looked big enough to have at least five bedrooms on the top floor. It certainly *looked* like something a vamp would live in, with the whole haunted-house vibe it had going on.

"If he didn't lie, then where's Cowen?" Ryland asked with a tense jaw, as if Venn was supposed to know the answer.

"Calm down, love," Teagan said in a soothing voice.

She reached forward from the back seat to run her hand across Ryland's shoulder. He breathed a sigh and laced his fingers through hers, pulling her hand to his lips and brushing a kiss across it.

Damn, they were so cute together. I needed to get myself someone like Teagan, a partner who could calm me with a single touch.

Teagan jumped in her seat and swatted at Fiona. "Would you stop it?!" she snapped.

Or, you know, I could just get myself the type of person who would bite my hand off just for kicks.

"Are you being annoying again, Fiona?" Ryland scolded.

Fiona rolled her eyes. "*Again?* You mean *still?*"

Ryland didn't even justify her answer with a response. Fiona frowned and folded her hands in her lap. Clearly, sitting still was getting to her.

"Maybe we missed the vamps," I suggested. "They could be leaving through the back door."

Ryland let out a groan, like he couldn't believe he hadn't thought of it before.

Yeah, we were officially idiots.

Ryland kicked his door open before anyone could get in another word. "You wanna come stake it out with me, Tea?"

A wide smile spread across her face, like she was hoping they'd run into trouble at the back of the house.

"I'm coming, too!" Fiona volunteered, rushing out of the car behind Teagan.

An uncomfortable silence filled the air when the doors shut behind them, leaving Venn and me alone in the car. The only sound came from Venn reaching into the glove compartment followed by the rustle of a plastic bag. Judging by the scent that hit me from the back seat, I guessed he was snacking on cheesy snack mix. My favorite, too, and the greedy bastard didn't even offer to share.

A full minute must've passed without either of us saying a word, but it felt more like an hour. I wanted to say something, but I couldn't come up with anything that wouldn't make me sound like an idiot.

"You can come sit up here," Venn offered.

"Oh, thank God," I blurted, grateful that someone finally broke the silence. I wanted to shove the words back in my mouth as soon as I said them.

"God has nothing to do with it," Venn joked as I climbed over the middle console and settled into the front seat.

"He doesn't?" I teased back.

Good thing, too, since I didn't believe in God. Somehow, I didn't think vampires and shifters fit into the God story, though some people claimed that vampires were just demons who'd escaped from Hell and had come to possess their loved ones. It might've been believable except for the fact that crucifixes and holy water didn't work on them. If I had a nickel for every time I rolled my eyes at the demon theory, I'd be able to afford a *far* better apartment.

"So, you don't think vampires are spawns of Satan?" I asked, mostly to keep the silence from once again entering the car.

Venn smirked and let out a light laugh. "No, I don't."

I leaned toward him with curiosity in my eyes. The scent of the snack mix in his lap filled my nose. My pulse quickened with each inch I came closer to him, but I ignored it. "Then where'd they come from?"

"Well, I won't claim to know *everything*," he admitted, holding out his bag toward me.

Score!

"But what I do know makes a lot of sense," he said.

"Oh?" I raised my eyebrows and plunged my hand into the bag. "What is it that you know?"

Venn smirked, looking positively proud of himself. "For starters, I know how magic works."

I scoffed and tossed a handful of cheesy crackers into my mouth. "No, you don't."

Even Devin, my boss, didn't truly know how magic worked, though that shouldn't have surprised me. It was clear he was only in the business for the money.

Venn returned the bag to his lap. "You've never hung out with a high witch before, have you?"

"I paid a high witch to enchant my clothes, if that counts," I told him.

Venn shook his head. "Doesn't count. Not unless she told you how she did it."

"She didn't," I said with a full mouth.

I must look like such a lady.

Venn popped another handful of snack mix into his mouth then wiped his hand on his jeans. "Ever heard of Synchrony?"

I furrowed my brow, not sure what he meant. "I've heard the word before."

"But do you know what it means?" he asked.

"Um... are you asking me to recite the definition from the dictionary?" I replied, insulted.

Venn laughed. "No. I'm talking in a philosophical sense. Synchrony is the force that creates and sustains life. It's responsible for the balance within the universe."

"Okay..." I dragged out the word. "I'm intrigued."

Though it's probably just nonsense.

"Essentially, Synchrony is God but without conscious thought," Venn explained. "It's more closely related to nature. It's just something that *is*, like electricity."

"Really?" I asked skeptically. He expected me to believe this? I didn't know what to believe these days, but I wasn't buying that.

"I can't explain it like Sondra can," Venn said, "but basically, she says that Synchrony is the life-sustaining force that's been around since the Big Bang."

"You're saying magic has been around forever?" I asked. Some theories claimed magic was always there. Others said it came here from another world when Valkas showed up—and that he was from that other world, too. I still didn't know which theory to go with.

"Yes," Venn answered. "Magic has always existed in our world. It just wasn't made public until eight years ago. Before that, the secrets of Synchrony were kept within the supernatural community. It was the only way people escaped persecution."

"So in your story, magic and Synchrony are the same thing?" I asked.

"Not exactly," Venn said. "That's like asking if light and electricity are the same thing. Magic is what happens when you access Synchrony, but Synchrony itself is bigger than that. It's what creates life—creates souls—and what drives fate."

"Fate?" I laughed. Venn was officially a nutcase... A nutcase who made butterflies dance around in my stomach. I mentally squashed the suckers.

"Yes," Venn stated flatly.

My laughter instantly died. Woops. I was being a total ass.

My voice softened. "I'm sorry. I'm listening. Tell me more."

Venn eyed me, like he couldn't tell if he should keep going or not. I really did feel bad about laughing at him.

Finally, he continued. "I believe there are no coincidences in life; only balance. We have an equal give and take relationship with Synchrony. If you bring positivity into the world, Synchrony will deliver more positive things into your life. Accessing the Synchrony force—or doing magic—has consequences because it all balances out."

"Okay," I said, trying to keep an open mind. "But not all magic *does* have consequences."

"Not all consequences are negative," Venn said. "But Synchrony always reacts. *How* it reacts depends on your intentions when you cast a spell. If you cast the spell with positive intentions, you will get positive results. The bigger the spell, the more consequences, like how trying to bring someone back to life could trap their soul in their body. Well-intentioned spells won't have bad consequences. That's probably why you're so good at heal-ing. On the other hand, dark magic almost always results in negative outcomes because there are very few dark spells that can be cast with pure intentions."

"Why would anyone practice dark magic, then?" I asked.

Ha! Plot hole!

Venn frowned. "Because they honestly believe they're in the right."

I narrowed my eyes in thought, trying to absorb everything he was saying.

"Synchrony reflects your intentions back on you," Venn continued. "You can never cast a perfect spell if you're doing it for selfish reasons or if you're trying to hurt someone else."

"That doesn't make any sense," I argued. I don't know why I didn't want to believe Venn. Maybe I didn't want to believe there were people out there with the answer and I'd gone so long without knowing it. "I tried to heal Kieren earlier, and the spell backfired on me. I wasn't being selfish or trying to hurt him."

"Maybe not," Venn agreed with a shrug, "but you were still projecting nega-tive energy."

"No, I wasn't," I insisted. He couldn't even *do* magic, but he was going to sit here and tell me all about how I'd been doing it wrong?

Jerk.

Venn didn't seem to notice my furrowed brow. "The thing about Synchrony is that it doesn't recognize good versus evil. Instead, it recognizes positive energy versus negative energy. Your beliefs and intentions affect how Synchrony responds."

"How so?" I asked. He wasn't suggesting I was carrying around negative energy like some sort of evil witch, was he?

"You have to believe in your ability and the reasons for why you're casting the spell." Venn looked at me with a pointed expression, like he was accusing me of something. I just wasn't sure what he was accusing me of. "A witch who doubts herself is much more susceptible to consequences."

"I do not doubt myself!" I defended.

"Yes, you do," Venn said, like it was fact.

Any lingering butterflies in my stomach were now officially dead.

"You don't know anything about me," I replied in disgust.

Venn shrugged. "You're right, I don't. But I know how Synchrony works, and I know you're a lot more powerful than you give yourself credit for."

Ugh, here comes the flattery, like he wasn't just insulting me a moment ago.

"I know what I'm capable of," I stated.

Venn peeled his gaze off me and looked back toward the house. "Do you? Because you said you've never worked with a high witch before. You might learn a lot by having a mentor."

"Yes," I agreed sarcastically, "because high witches willing to mentor me on my budget drop out of the sky every day. How do you know all this anyway?"

Venn blinked several times before answering. "Because Sondra's a high witch. She told me."

My blood stopped in my veins. Mind. Officially. Blown.

These people were living with a high witch, and this just happened to be the first time anyone mentioned it to me? High witches were rare, and most of them were living in luxury, not still hanging around in a city like Nocton.

"Seriously?" My tone came out softer this time, all the offense removed from my voice. "Could she teach me?"

For free, obviously, because Devin barely pays me minimum wage.

"I can't speak for her," Venn said, "but I'm sure she'd be happy to teach you a thing or two once we get her back."

I nearly choked on the handful of snack mix I'd just shoved in my mouth. "Get her back? Where is she?"

Venn swallowed hard, like he was contemplating whether or not to trust me with the truth. "She was... taken."

"Oh, my God!" I cried. "Like, kidnapped?"

Venn nodded somberly. "Yes. She's being held for ransom. That's why we're after Cowen. He stole the thing we need to get her back."

I was just about to ask what it was he needed when Venn's entire body stiffened, halting my words in their tracks. I followed his gaze to see a male figure emerging from the house we'd been watching.

This jackhole is officially going down.

Before I could suggest calling Ryland and telling him we spotted movement, Venn's car door slammed behind him. Outside the car, Venn lunged forward, shifting into wolf form mid-air.

He raced after Cowen.

7

I kicked my door open and sprinted behind Venn. In his shifted form, Venn was *fast*. The black wolf slammed into the vampire and knocked him to the sidewalk before I was even halfway across the street. Venn's head snapped to the side as the vampire's fist connected with his jaw. It didn't even seem to faze Venn.

Venn's jaw snapped at the vamp in warning, and his paws pressed down on his chest. The vamp stopped struggling to hiss in Venn's face just as I reached them. Every muscle in Venn's body froze—like time altogether had stopped.

The light from the nearest street lamp caught the vampire's face. I, too, stopped in my tracks. The man stared back at Venn with hauntingly silver eyes. Fangs protruded from his mouth, but the shape of his jaw was unfamiliar. His hair was slicked back, like he was trying to channel an old-school Dracula vibe. Though he had similar hair color and an almost identical build to Cowen, we had the wrong guy.

Dracula's head swung forward in a flash, knocking into Venn's snout with a sickening *thud*. Venn reeled backward on instinct. Dracula rolled in the grass, freeing himself from Venn's grasp. He dodged around Venn's outstretched paws and made a run for it, but he must've not seen me there, because he headed straight in my direction.

I didn't have time to think about what to do next. All I knew was that I wasn't ready to let this guy go without asking him some questions. I sprang from the pavement and leapt forward, catching the vampire around the middle and tackling him to the ground.

He quickly freed himself and scurried to his feet. Before he could make it far, Venn was on the other side of him, blocking his path. Dracula whirled around, but I skirted in front of him, ready to kick him in the royal jewels if it came to that. He hesitated, his nostrils flaring. His eyes dropped to my neck with a hungry look in then.

Oh, hell no. He looked like he had every intention of ripping out my jugular and using it as a straw.

"We're not here to hurt you," I said in a rush, hoping we could work this out civilly.

Dracula held his hands up in surrender, but I suspected he only stopped because I'd piqued his interest. My eyes darted to his wrists, just in case, but the skin on his arms was smooth.

"Then why'd your boyfriend try to knock me out?" he asked begrudgingly.

Boyfriend?

Venn stood on his hind legs, and the fur disappeared from his body as he shifted. He wiped the blood from his lip but barely stole a glance at it, like it didn't really matter.

"We thought you were someone else," Venn said without regret. "If he'd seen me first, he would've run."

Strike first. Ask questions later. I like Venn's style.

"Obviously, you have the wrong guy," Dracula snapped, glancing between the two of us.

"Is Cowen around?" I asked—or rather, demanded.

The vamp narrowed his gaze, but his eyes continued to flicker down to my throat. "Cowen? He hasn't lived here in years."

Venn cursed under his breath, and I was sure the blood had drained from my face.

"Years?" The word passed by my lips breathlessly.

"You deaf?" Dracula mocked. He inched away from us like we wouldn't notice.

"No," I answered, "but I'm a shifter who's strong as hell, so I suggest you refrain from the insults."

The vamp stopped retreating. "What do you want?"

"We want to know where to find Cowen," Venn answered. "That's all."

"I don't know where to find him." Dracula sounded like he was telling the truth. But then again, he *was* a vampire, and I had yet to meet a vamp who wasn't completely heartless.

"Are you sure?" I asked, using my most threatening voice.

I liked to think I sounded terrifying, but I must've not looked the part, because he didn't seem particularly scared of me. When his eyes darted to Venn, though, he sure looked wary.

"I hardly knew the guy," Dracula admitted, still looking at me like he'd enjoy me for his next meal. "He was just a roommate. He left a few months after I moved in."

"Were any of your other roommates close to him?" Venn asked.

The vamp rolled his eyes and turned to the car beside us on the curb to climb inside. "I'm not some messenger boy. If you want to know more about him—"

I grabbed his door before he could slam it. He sat in the driver's seat, trying to wrench it out of my grasp, but I had a firm hold on it. The vamp looked up at me in shock, like he thought I'd been bluffing when I said I was strong.

"My *boyfriend* asked you a question," I stated in my most intimidating voice. "I suggest you answer."

Dracula hesitated. "I don't know anything about Cowen, and I doubt my roommates do, either. The most I know about him is what's in the box he left behind."

Every word sounded genuine, but I wasn't ready to accept we'd hit a dead end. If only he'd given me a reason to beat the answer out of him...

I think I enjoyed confronting vampires a little too much. If I treated humans half as bad as I treated vamps, I'd already have my ticket to Hell in hand. I was about to give up and let the vamp go, ready to call this mission officially a bust, when Venn quickly stepped in.

"Do you still have the box?" he asked in a rush.

Dracula's jaw tensed. He was totally over this interrogation. "I might know where it is."

"We'll buy it from you," Venn offered.

The vamp's eyes lit up in intrigue.

"How much do you want for it?" Venn asked.

"I don't want money," Dracula declined, his silver eyes staring greedily at me.

Seriously? Another lonely bastard looking for a good time? He'd be sorely disappointed.

"What *do* you want?" Venn asked.

Either he was dumb or blind. It was obvious by the way the guy eyed me like a piece of meat. *I* was his price.

Screw him. Wait, no. Not what I meant.

"I just want a taste," Dracula said, like it wasn't a big deal.

He can shove his offer—wait... a taste? As in, my blood? Okay, not as bad as I thought, but still...

"No," I answered automatically, my voice filled with disgust.

"Then I think we're done here." Dracula reached for his door handle.

"Wait!" Venn insisted, catching the door again before he could close it.

Dracula looked up with a sardonic smile. "You seem to really want that box."

Venn hesitated.

What was Venn hiding? He *did* really want that box, but I wasn't sure why. He didn't think the thing Cowen stole from him was in there, did he? I mean, this vamp said Cowen had left here years ago. Unless he thought there might be something in there that could help us track Cowen down.

Tracking...

Of course! A tracking spell required an object belonging to the person you were trying to locate. We could use anything in the box to track Cowen, as long as no one else had claimed ownership of the objects inside since he'd abandoned them.

"I lied," I said quickly. "I'll do it."

The vamp smirked the same time Venn spoke.

"No, Rae," he objected. "You don't have to."

"I do," I countered. "We need that box."

Venn whirled toward Dracula. "Feed on me instead."

The vamp stood in the grass beside the curb and shut his car door behind him. He shook his head. "No. I named my price, and I asked for the girl."

His nostrils flared, inhaling my scent—not that he could smell me well considering I was a shifter. He must've *really* had a thing for female shifter blood. That wasn't surprising, though, since shifter blood tasted best, or so I'd been told. Vampires could feed on animals, but I'd heard it compared to the taste of dirt and the energy boost of an ice cube when you're craving a double bacon cheeseburger. Human blood did the job, but it was like eating salad when shifter blood was a triple-layer chocolate cake with ice cream on top. Vampires didn't get many chances to drink shifter blood since most of us weren't up for donating it. Not to mention that shifter blood slaves were rare. Vamps only took the ones who couldn't fight them off.

I took a step back to distance myself from him. Dracula looked two seconds away from pouncing on me and sucking me dry. He almost had me second-guessing the deal, but then I reminded myself what would happen if I refused. We really would hit our dead end, and I'd be no closer to finding Jenna than I was the night the Soulless took her.

"I'll do it," I said, "but you only get five seconds—"

"A minute," the vamp countered.

"You'd have me drained dry! Five seconds," I replied firmly.

"That's barely a sip!" he complained, like I was being totally unfair.

Frankly, I thought I was being awfully generous for a box of junk that didn't even belong to him.

"Thirty seconds," the vamp negotiated.

I crossed my arms. "Ten, and that's my final offer."

His eyes locked on my jugular as if he could hear my blood pulsing through my veins. I knew he couldn't, not like he could with humans.

Finally, he scoffed. "Forget it. I can buy blood for less than that box of crap is worth."

"You and I both know that my blood fresh from the source is a heck of a lot more valuable than what it sells for at a blood bank," I countered.

Blood from the blood banks was like eating that chocolate cake after it'd sat on the counter for three days—dry and stale. He knew my offer was well worth it.

"Rae," Venn said sternly, trying to talk some sense into me, but I'd already made up my mind. We needed something of Cowen's to track him down.

Dracula's lips tightened. "Fine," he caved. "Ten seconds." He stepped forward and reached out for me.

I quickly dodged out of the way. "Whoa. We get the box first."

Dracula glanced to Venn, as if to ask, *Is this girl for real?*

"And if you try anything," I warned, "you're dead. If you release venom, take longer than your ten seconds, *anything…* my friend here will make sure it's the last drink you ever take."

Dracula gritted his teeth. "Yeah, I get it. No tricks."

"Rae, come on," Venn protested, his voice growing harsher with each passing second. "We'll find another way."

I ignored him. We might find Cowen eventually through other means, but this was our quickest option. "Let's do this," I said to Dracula, sealing our deal.

"No," Venn demanded like I didn't have a choice. He grabbed me by the arm and pulled me away from Dracula.

On instinct, I ripped my arm out of his grasp and swung my fist at his nose. He stumbled backward from the impact, his hands immediately covering his face.

"Damn, Rae," he said with a mixture of anger and amusement in his tone. "You have one helluva swing."

Dracula laughed, but I ignored him. I wasn't amused in the slightest.

"Let's make something explicitly clear," I said, my eyes trained on Venn's. "Just because I asked for your help does *not* mean you own me. I'm doing this on my own, so you can either stay and help or leave without answers."

Silence settled over the lawn.

A muscle fluttered in Venn's jaw as he considered my words. Finally, his shoulders relaxed. "I'll stay."

Dracula smiled triumphantly. "The box is in the garage."

He gestured for us to follow him, but my feet remained firmly planted in the grass. Venn didn't move, either. Dracula glanced back and frowned, like he didn't have all night.

"I said no tricks," I told him.

"This isn't a trick." The vamp sounded annoyed. "I'm upholding my end of our deal."

Maybe he was telling the truth, but how could I trust that there wouldn't be twenty vampires hanging out in the garage waiting for us?

"Bring the box out here to us," I demanded.

Dracula shook his head, like I was being completely ridiculous.

"Do you want my blood or not?" I asked. The truth was I'd follow him into that garage if I had to, but I hoped it didn't come to that.

"Fine," the vamp sighed. "Wait here."

He hurried off toward the side of the garage, leaving Venn and me alone on the dark sidewalk.

I turned to Venn, who stared after Dracula with a hard expression. "He's not coming back, is he?"

"That, or he's bringing a bunch of vamps back with him," Venn said. "We should leave before he comes back. This is a bad deal."

"No," I insisted. "We need that box to track Cowen. Don't you want to save Sondra?"

Venn hesitated. Before he had a chance to answer, Dracula had already emerged from the garage. He carried a white cardboard box not much bigger than a paper grocery bag.

Maybe there are vampires out there worth their word.

Dracula dropped the box beside Venn's feet. It landed with a *smack* on the sidewalk.

That was... too easy. We could've just walked in there ourselves and taken it. A minor breaking and entering charge was nothing, and I wouldn't have to give up my blood for it.

I stared into the silver eyes of this Dracula-Cowen look-alike, praying to God—or Synchrony or whatever—that he'd keel over and die right there so I wouldn't have to go through with this. But I knew praying wouldn't do me any good.

"I'll take my payment now," Dracula said, licking his lips.

My skin crawled, and every fiber of my being told me to take the box and run, but I found myself stepping toward him anyway. I wasn't the type of person to go back on my word. I know... shocker. Rachel Collins actually had morals.

But when Dracula took my wrist in his cold hand, I wasn't sure I could go through with it. Suddenly, I wanted to hurl.

I hope my blood tastes like horse shit.

"Wait!" Venn couldn't take it. He threw himself between us, forcing Dracula's hand off mine. "Don't, Rae. You don't want to become a blood slave, believe me."

"Hey!" Dracula rose his voice and shoved Venn aside with his elbow. "No one said anything about blood slaves. We had a deal. You're not trying to double-cross me, are you?"

Venn held Dracula's gaze, his lips tight and nostrils flaring, but he couldn't come up with a rebuttal.

"Are we going to do this or not?" Dracula's teeth gritted. He looked at me in a way that told me that one way or another, he *would* receive his payment.

"Venn, I told you this was my deal," I said.

"Watch out," Dracula warned. "You don't want to get punched by a girl again, do you?"

I almost struck Dracula for the insult. I wasn't just some tiny, weak-ass girl, though he had to know that by now.

I placed a gentle hand on Venn's arm. "Ten seconds. That's it. Ten seconds, and it will all be over."

I stepped toward Dracula before Venn could respond. My hands shook. I knew it wouldn't be anything compared to the pain I felt when Cowen stabbed me with vampire venom, but I still wasn't looking forward to vampire fangs sinking into my neck.

Ten seconds. Then we're out of here.

I ignored Venn and nodded toward Dracula.

"Rae—" Venn started, but I didn't hear the rest of what he said.

Dracula wrapped his arms around me possessively, and a sharp pain shot across my neck. My breath hitched, and my entire body tensed.

Ten... nine...

I started counting down in my head, but two seconds in, I'd already lost track of the numbers. It only took a moment for the initial shock to fade and the pain to go away. Instead, a light tingly feeling danced across my skin, melting away all the tension in my muscles. I forgot about Venn's protests, about the fangs in my neck, about the box near my feet that could hold the key to finding Cowen... all that mattered was the feeling of euphoria filling my body.

Had I really only offered this guy ten seconds? If this was what being fed on felt like, he could take me for ten goddamn years. The pleasure only built within my body each passing second. I yearned for more, but I never got a chance to learn what that might feel like.

My mind was instantly pulled back to the present, to the reality that a *vampire was sucking my blood,* when the deafening roar of a massive beast cut through the night.

8

A moment of disorientation overcame me as the fangs in my neck drew away.

"Step away from the girl," a threatening female voice met my ears.

The pressure around my middle disappeared. I hadn't even realized there'd *been* pressure on my body until it was gone. My legs felt like noodles. Without the strength to hold me up, they crumbled beneath me. A pair of strong hands caught me before I slammed to the ground. It took only a split second for my head to clear, as if I'd just broken the surface of a very deep lake and taken my first life-saving breath.

The first thing I noticed was that Dracula had dropped me. He stared with wide eyes at something beyond me and backed away slowly. The faint scent of cinnamon filled my nose, and I realized it was Venn who had caught me.

A second chilling roar filled the air just feet away from me. I steadied my feet and turned to see Ryland in bear form, glaring at Dracula and poised for attack. Fiona had shifted into a fox, and Teagan was ready with her knives out.

This was *bad*. Ryland had to know this wasn't at all what it looked like.

"Wait!" I cried.

I rushed out of Venn's arms and threw myself between Ryland and Dracula. But Ryland was quicker than me. He'd already leapt into the air, his sharp teeth bared toward Dracula's throat. Ryland's massive paws slammed into my chest. I fell to the ground, feeling as if I'd just been hit by a truck. Ryland quickly righted himself and shot me a glare as if to ask if I was insane.

Possibly.

I sucked in a heavy breath and tried to force out an explanation, but the words didn't come before Dracula had already ducked into his car. Ryland rushed forward, and his heavy shoulder connected with the driver's side door. It crumpled like a soda can. Dracula quickly shifted into drive, flipped us the finger, and sped off down the road.

"Ryland, stop!" Venn yelled to get his attention.

Ryland was already racing after the car, but he didn't get far before realizing he'd never be able to keep up with Dracula's increasing speed.

Teagan rushed over to me to help me to my feet. My chest heaved as I struggled to inhale steady breaths, and my head swam in a lightheaded daze. A warm sensation rushed across the skin on my throat. My hand slapped to my neck and came away sticky with blood.

Great.

I pressed hard over the vampire bite to stop the bleeding. My eyes remained fixed on Ryland as he abandoned the car chase and raced back to the lawn. Even in his bear form, he looked *pissed.*

"Ryland," Venn and I said in unison, in a matching tone that said we had a lot to explain.

But we never got a chance. Fiona's scream of terror ripped across the lawn, startling all of us. Venn, Teagan, and I whirled around, only to be met by half a dozen pairs of silver eyes. Six vampires flooded out of the house. The first vamp already had Fiona by her hair. He was tall, with skin as dark as Venn's and arms as big as Ryland's.

Ryland showed no signs of slowing down.

"Ryland, stop!" I shouted.

He was already flying through the air.

I was so over this *act first, ask questions later* thing.

Alpha Vamp dropped Fiona and ducked out of the way before Ryland's claws could catch him. Ryland's massive bear form flew over the top of him and slammed into the petite female vamp behind him.

"Stop!" I screamed again, but no one listened.

The female vamp was already back on her feet. She drew her arm back and smashed it into Ryland's nose. Ryland swiped his paw out at her, but she ducked. Her clothes fell to the ground as her body shrank to the size of a medium dog. There was a distinct pattern to her brown fur. *A wolverine.*

Whoa. I was totally not expecting that. Vampire-shifter hybrids were rare, especially since shifters weren't common in the general population to begin with. Unlike witch magic, vampires kept their shifter magic when they changed.

Venn shifted and sprang forward to defend Ryland. Teagan grabbed a fistful of Ryland's fur and hoisted herself onto his back. In the blink of an eye, one of her knives flew from her hand and landed square in the center of the female shifter-vamp's chest.

Terror entered the woman's eyes, but it was gone a moment later as the magic keeping her alive left her body and reduced it to a pile of ash.

Me? I was still holding on to my neck, trying not to bleed out the open wounds Dracula had left. I needed to perform a healing spell—and fast.

What's the incantation? Come on, Rachel, you can do this.

I racked my brain, thinking back to the words I'd uttered only earlier today.

The incantation is only four lines. It shouldn't be this hard to remember. Just start somewhere.

I began muttering the first words I could remember. No, that wasn't right. That was the second half of the spell. How did the beginning go?

Three of the remaining vampires had Ryland and Teagan surrounded. Another had chased Fiona up onto the porch, and though the vamp was fast, Fiona was agile enough to avoid getting caught. The vamp was probably a total newbie still getting used to his supernatural speed. Nearby, Venn's wolf claws sank into a vampire's arm. The vampire bared its sharp fangs and hissed.

They need help. I need to get in there.

Suddenly, the incantation clicked. I whispered the four lines from memory under my breath. The moment I finished, Alpha Vamp leapt on top of Ryland and sank his teeth into the back of Teagan's neck. An invisible force slammed into my gut.

"No!" I shrieked.

I didn't have time to check if the spell had taken. I instantly shifted. My clothes dropped away behind me, and I shot into the air, my wings flapping hard. I landed on Alpha Vamp's shoulder and pecked my beak at the first piece of flesh I could find. *His ear.*

Alpha Vamp cried out. His hand shot toward me, but I was already out of reach before his large hands could wrap around my small throat. I flew to the other side of him, and he twisted to follow me. He swatted at me in the air, intent on knocking me out of it. My talons caught him and sliced across the back of his hand. I'd distracted him long enough that when Ryland spun around, Alpha Vamp didn't have time to grab on to any fur. He flew through the air off Ryland's back and landed so hard on the front lawn that his elbow skidded through the grass and left behind a divot.

A quick motion closer to the house caught my eye. I looked just in time to see the vampire chasing Fiona grab ahold of her tail. She shifted back into human form, and her tail disappeared from his grasp. She tried to dodge out of the way, but he was too fast for her. The vampire jumped forward and tackled her to the ground. Her foot flew out and slammed into his nose, but he held her down and climbed on top of her, like he didn't even feel it. The light from the nearby street lamp reflected off his pearly white fangs as they elongated past his upper lip.

Hell no.

I dove toward him, passing through the narrow space between his face and Fiona's neck. He pulled back, startled. I flew in an arc and aimed my body at his face again. He leapt backward, completely disoriented as I flapped my wings in his face over and over again. It was a handy trick. He stumbled back so far that he ran straight into Ryland's backside. Ryland was still trying to fight off two other vampires, and so he didn't even notice when one of his huge back paws stepped on the vamp's foot.

I took the brief opportunity we had to escape. I shifted back into human form and grabbed Fiona's arms to help her to her feet. She followed behind me as I raced across the lawn—in nothing but my enchanted underwear and boots. I scooped up my clothes on the ground and tossed them on top of Cowen's box.

"Come on," I said in a breathless rush as I grabbed the box.

I raced out across the street, and Fiona sprinted behind me. My heart hammered at a million beats per minute once we reached Venn's car. I flung the driver's side door open and tossed the box on the passenger seat. Inside, my hands found the keys Venn had left in the ignition. I twisted, and the car roared to life. I hadn't driven a car in years and didn't have my license, but I remembered enough from my driver's ed class.

I shifted into drive and pressed down on the pedal before Fiona even had the back door shut. Tires squealed when I slammed on the brakes in front of the vampires' house a few doors down from where we'd been parked.

"What—?" Fiona started, but I laid on the horn before she could finish, drowning out her question.

Everyone's heads jerked in our direction.

"Open the door!" I instructed in a rush.

Fiona quickly opened her door and franticly gestured for everyone else to make a run for it. Ryland whirled his head to the side, slamming it against the nearest vampire, who was trying to get on top of him. He broke free of the vamp and barreled his way between two others. Teagan grabbed a handful of fur and leaned over, nearly touching the ground but still holding herself up on his back. While Ryland ran, Teagan scooped her knife up from where it stuck in the ground. Ryland shifted not a moment too soon, and he and Teagan stumbled into the back seat.

"Venn!" Teagan cried in a high-pitched shriek I never would've guessed she was capable of.

Venn raced toward us, but two vampires leapt on top of him at the same time. He clawed at them and managed to slice one of them across the cheek.

I was a split second away from streaking across the lawn in nothing but my undies and kicking some vampire ass when a loud *bang* filled the vehicle. The entire car shook, and my heart jumped into my throat. My head snapped in the direction of movement to find Alpha Vamp perched atop the hood of the car. His silver eyes bore straight through the vehicle to the back seat. He glared at Teagan with a look of vengeance in his eyes.

Not today, buddy.

"GO!" Venn's voice filled my ears from mere feet behind me.

Relief flooded through me when I heard his voice. He was all right—for now, anyway.

Without a second thought, I floored the pedal. Alpha Vamp steadied himself on the hood of the car. In my rearview mirror, I saw four vampires rush out onto the street, following much closer behind us than I would've imagined they could. I swerved to the left, then to the right, almost hitting into a vehicle parked at the curb. I must've missed it by inches.

"The brakes!" Venn shouted.

I immediately applied the brakes, and Alpha Vamp went flying. I was half surprised he didn't splat onto the pavement like a bug against a windshield. A *thud* sounded behind us as the four remaining vamps ran into the back of the vehicle, stunned by the abrupt halt.

"Hang on!" I warned as I wrenched the shifter into reverse.

I whirled around to look out the back window and stomped on the gas. The car jolted as the tires passed over at least two separate bodies. It wouldn't kill the vamps, but it would sure slow them down. Shifting back into drive, I put the pedal to the metal and hightailed it out of there. Alpha Vamp leapt from the middle of the road out of my path. Our speed increased rapidly, and I swerved around a slow-moving vehicle ahead of us on the street.

I didn't pay attention to the vamps behind us. I let Fiona—who was screaming at me to step on it—worry about that. Instead, I focused on not crashing as I turned down another street in an attempt to lose the vamps at our tail. I never even saw the stop sign on the next block, but I sure saw the black sedan I almost t-boned. I pulled the wheel to the left as the driver in the other vehicle slammed on his brakes. I just barely missed him.

On the next block, we broke out from the residential area onto a street with more traffic. I made a sharp right turn, and by some miracle, I managed to slip right into traffic without hitting anyone.

Fiona breathed a sigh of relief. "They're gone."

I slowed to follow traffic, but my heart continued to slam against my rib cage. I glanced back briefly to see that Venn was still trying to get situated, but it was nearly impossible with Ryland taking up half of the back seat. Apparently, Venn decided he had enough of trying to fit four people in the back, because he ducked his head and climbed over the middle console. It took him a good ten seconds of struggling—since there wasn't exactly much room for a guy his size —before he was seated in the passenger seat with Cowen's box on his lap.

"What the hell happened back there?!" Ryland exploded.

I opened my mouth to explain, but before I could, Fiona's small voice cut through the brief silence in the car.

"Um, guys," she said with concern.

"What?" Ryland snapped, like he didn't have time for her.

I glanced to the back seat to see that Teagan's body was slumped against Fiona's, her eyes closed. Fiona slowly drew her hands away from Teagan and stared down at the blood on them in horror.

Fiona shook. "Teagan's not breathing."

9

I was pretty sure *I* stopped breathing when I heard Fiona mutter those words. I wrenched the wheel to the right and slowed to a stop in a gas station parking lot. I kicked my door open and rushed out of the vehicle, still half-naked and everything. I pulled Ryland's door open so fast that I was half surprised it didn't rip off its hinges.

Ryland didn't even notice me there. He leaned over Teagan and shook her, begging her to wake up. Because *that* was totally going to work.

I reached two hands around Ryland's bicep—and they didn't even reach all the way around—and pulled at him. "Move! Let me help her."

It took several tugs before Ryland acknowledged me. Then, as if he suddenly remembered I actually *could* help her, he dropped her shoulders and jumped out of the car.

I climbed into the back seat and knelt over Teagan. The first thing I did was check her chest while Fiona pressed her hands over her wounds. I was relieved to see that it was rising and falling, though slowly.

"She's still breathing. That's a good sign," I said. "Help me, Fiona."

Together, we propped Teagan up in the middle of the back seat.

"What happened to her?" Ryland demanded desperately from outside the car. "Is she going to be okay?"

On the other side of Teagan, Fiona was breathing heavy, shallow breaths, like she was doing everything she could to keep from freaking out.

"How can we help?" Venn asked from the front seat. His head was screwed on straighter than Ryland's, but his tone still sounded rushed and worried—for good reason.

"What's wrong with her?" Ryland's voice rose as he began pacing.

I didn't answer him right away. I reached for Teagan's dark braid and pushed it out of the way. Fiona lifted her hands, exposing the back of Teagan's neck. Two puncture wounds lay side by side on her skin, confirming what I'd seen earlier. My stomach churned at the sight of the raw, swollen skin and the blood soaking into her shirt.

"What?" Venn demanded.

I could hardly get the words out past the lump in my throat, but somehow, I managed. "She's been bit."

Ryland stopped pacing abruptly. "You can help her, can't you?"

I turned to him, hoping the fear I felt for Teagan didn't come across in my expression.

"Can't you?!" Ryland shouted.

I swallowed hard. "I can try."

The truth was, I knew there was nothing I could do. The only spell I had that I thought might help—the one to counteract supernatural injuries—was clearly a dud. But if we didn't do something about that venom, we could be waking up to a vampire in the morning.

"I need that shirt, Venn," I demanded.

Venn tossed me the shirt I'd been wearing earlier.

"How did this happen?" Ryland asked, to no one in particular. "She was with me the entire time."

"That big vampire bit her while she was on your back," I said, wiping the shirt across the blood. "I saw it."

"Is she going to—?" Ryland started, but I cut him off before he could finish.

"No," I told him. "We're going to fix this. But either way, she's going to have a rough night."

"*A rough night?*" Ryland repeated, like he couldn't believe my words. "So you're saying you can't do anything? I thought you could heal!"

"I'm going to do my best!" I shot back at him. "Stand back if you don't want blood all over your shoes."

Ryland's hands shook, like he was trying to physically hold himself back from ripping me out of the car just to hold Teagan in his arms, but he stepped aside anyway.

Peeling the soaked shirt off her back, I took a deep breath to ready myself. The longer I thought it through, the deeper the venom would penetrate into her body. So, ignoring my instinct to brainstorm further solutions, I lowered my lips to her skin and sucked her blood into my mouth.

A fire burned across my lips and raged through my mouth, scorching every millimeter of my body that her tainted blood touched. There was no taste to it; only fire. It was like eating the hottest ghost pepper in the world, if that pepper had been coated in red-hot molten lava.

I longed to cry out, but I resisted the urge. I didn't need everyone worrying about Teagan *and* me. My mouth filled with blood. I turned my head out the open door and spit. Blood sprayed across the pavement. I quickly returned my lips to her wound and repeated the procedure until the pain in my mouth stopped building and became a constant dull, but intense, pain.

"I got most of it," I slurred, my tongue barely able to move in my mouth. "Just need to stop the bleeding."

Before I had a chance, Teagan lifted her head slightly. A small groan escaped her lips.

"Tea?" Fiona asked in a rush.

Teagan only replied by gritting her teeth and letting out another sound of discomfort. I was surprised tears weren't rolling down her cheeks.

"We need to get her home," Venn insisted.

Just as I placed my hand over the bite marks on the back of Teagan's neck, the door beside me slammed closed, making me jump. A second later, Ryland was climbing into the driver's seat. I ignored Ryland's curses and Venn's instructions that he thought were helping. Instead, I focused on channeling my magic into Teagan's skin. On the other side of her, Fiona rubbed her back.

I muttered the incantation two more times just to make sure. Before I could start the incantation a fourth time, Teagan's head snapped upward, and a high-pitched shriek filled the vehicle. I nearly jumped out of my skin. As fast as the screech came, it was gone, and Teagan slumped back against Fiona.

Ryland whirled around in his seat, completely oblivious to the cars in front of him. "What'd you do to her?"

"It's the venom," I bit back. "Eyes on the road!"

Ryland twisted back around just in time to slam on the brakes. He barely missed hitting the car in front of us that had stopped at a red light. Venn braced himself against the dashboard.

"Calm. Down," Venn barked at Ryland. "You're not going to do Teagan any good by getting her killed before we make it home."

The sound of Ryland's heavy breaths filled the car, but he ignored Venn. The light turned green, and the car jerked forward. Ryland weaved between vehicles and sped through a yellow light, then took a sharp left turn.

I wiped the remaining blood away from my mouth and Teagan's back with the t-shirt. I was satisfied to see her swelling had gone down and the bleeding had almost stopped.

Several minutes later, we pulled into the driveway of their home. I jumped out of the car so that Ryland could scoop Teagan into his arms and carry her up to the house. Fiona rushed out of the car behind Ryland.

Finally, I took a moment to breathe. I stared after them. After everything that happened today, I needed a minute to absorb it all.

"Here." Venn's voice cut through the darkness.

I tore my gaze from the house to see him holding my pants and purse in one hand and balancing Cowen's box in the other. He avoided my gaze.

"Thanks," I said shyly as I took the pants from him. I *so* needed to get my own clothes back. Running around half-naked every time I shifted was not high on my bucket list. I held the pants close to my chest, covering up as much exposed skin as I could. I mean, I wasn't exactly showing off more than I ever did at the pool, but still… My off-white underwear didn't exactly scream *sexy*.

I stood there awkwardly, going beet red under Venn's gaze. I wasn't sure if I was supposed to get dressed right here in the middle of their driveway or what. And what was our plan going forward?

"We should get inside," Venn suggested.

The tension in my shoulders eased. At least I had a plan for the next five minutes. After that… I had no idea.

10

I followed Venn into the house. Teagan's cries of pain traveled down the stairs and to the front door.

Venn exchanged a glance with me. "You're sure there's nothing more you can do?"

Fiona's voice came from the top of the stairs before I could answer. "You probably shouldn't even try, unless you want Ryland to bite your head off."

I hated to think that he literally could do just that.

"That bad?" Venn asked.

Fiona descended the stairs and held out a clean shirt to me. "He says Teagan needs space. He's cleaning her up and trying to make her comfortable right now. I think this is harder on him than it is on her."

"She's tough," Venn said.

Fiona stared up at Venn with tears at the corner of her eyes. "She'll be fine, won't she?"

"Yes," I said, hoping to sound reassuring. "I don't know everything about vampire venom, but I know there's not enough in her system to cause long-term damage."

Fiona bit her lip, and her voice cracked. "You're sure?"

"Hey, Fiona," Venn said softly.

He set down the box in his hands and stepped forward to pull Fiona into a hug. She hugged him back, looking comfortable in his arms. It wasn't the type of hug that made me suspect there was something between them. It was more like the type of hug a brother and sister might share.

Still, it didn't feel right to be standing there watching their family moment. I slipped out of the hallway into the dining room, where I finally pulled on the

61

clothes in my hands. Though I wasn't thrilled to still be in Teagan's clothes, I felt a hundred times more comfortable now that everything was covered.

I sensed Venn in the doorway before I saw him. He entered the room looking like he had something he wanted to apologize for. Probably for dragging me into all this, even though I was the one who insisted on coming. He seemed like the kind of guy who would do that.

Fiona followed behind him.

"So..." Venn dragged out the word and glanced down to the box he carried. "Should we check it out?"

I nodded, because my mouth still burned. Apart from the pain, I was running out of strength anyway. How late was it? I was used to staying up late, but tonight, I was completely drained.

Venn sat and set the box in front of him on the table. I sank into the chair beside him. He pulled the top off the box, and together, we leaned forward to peek inside. My stomach fluttered at the close proximity.

I didn't know what I expected to find, but I thought it'd be more... vampire themed, though I had no idea what that would entail. Vials of blood or something? Instead, all we found was a pile of junk: pens, a phone charger, an old watch, a thin roll of duct tape. There was even a pack of mint gum, which seemed weird for a vampire, but I guess when you didn't need to eat regular food anymore, gum was a good way to add flavor to your diet.

I frowned, but inside, I was completely heartbroken. I let a vampire bite me for *this*? This probably wasn't even Cowen's stuff. Dracula could've just grabbed a random box of junk from the garage so that he could get consent for a taste of my blood.

Venn took a deep breath and stood. A curse slipped out under his breath.

"What's wrong?" Fiona asked. She stood behind the chair across from me and looked into the box. "What's with the box anyway?"

Venn raked his fingers through his hair. "It's Cowen's. We were hoping to use it to track him. What you saw... Rae agreed to it as a trade." He shot me a look like he still wasn't pleased about the whole thing.

"You should've called us," she said. "When we went to check out the back, we didn't see anything. Then we heard your voices at the front of the house, and we came to check it out. If we knew what was happening, Ryland never would've—"

"I know," Venn cut her off. "I just saw the vamp, and I didn't think we had time..."

Fiona shook her head like she'd never understand men. She stood on her toes and leaned over the box, shuffling through the random junk. "So, we can use any of this stuff to track Cowen?"

"Probably not," I said. "Tracking spells work best with sentimental objects, but even then they're tricky. We might've had a chance with something else, like a piece of clothing. But this stuff... I don't think it'll work."

"What about the watch?" Fiona asked, holding it up.

I reached for it. "It's worth a shot, but the real challenge is going to be coming up with the money for a tracking spell."

Fiona and Venn both stared at me blankly.

"What?" I asked. "Any witch with a business sense is going to charge us double for asking to track a guy with a watch he abandoned years ago."

"We… um… we don't need to pay a witch, do we?" Fiona asked with hesitation. "I mean, what about you?"

Venn raised his eyebrows, like he agreed Fiona had a point.

"Me?" I asked in disbelief.

"You have a tracking spell, don't you?" Venn pointed out.

"Well, yeah," I said. "I have the spell, but I'm only a low witch."

The corner of Venn's lips turned down. "You know that's not true. No low witch can heal like you do."

"Okay," I agreed, "so I'm on the low end of a mid-witch. I still don't have enough magic to perform this type of spell."

"I don't think you give yourself enough credit," Venn said.

Really? We were back to this again?

"I know what I'm capable of," I snapped. "Witches have *died* trying to access power beyond their capabilities."

"Yes," Venn agreed, "but you can also improve your powers by testing those limits, by practicing magic."

He thought I was being lazy? Like I hadn't *tried* testing my limits before? Because apparently my notebook full of spells wasn't proof that I at least had an *interest* in getting better at magic…

"Do you really think I'd be here right now if I could perform this kind of spell?" I asked. It wasn't like I hadn't tried. If I could do this, I would've found my sister ages ago.

"You can do it," Venn promised. "You just don't know you can."

"Fine," I said with determination in my voice. "I'll prove it to you what my limits are. Get ready to write a big check, because when you turn to another witch for this, it's not going to be cheap."

"Hold on," Venn protested, but I was already moving Cowen's box off the table.

I pulled my spell book from my bag and flipped open to the tracking spell I'd copied from a book at work.

"You need to—"

"Hey, Fiona," I interrupted without looking at Venn. "Can you get me some salt from the kitchen? Also, I'm going to need a few candles if you have them. Four, at least."

Fiona nodded and hurried into the kitchen.

Venn sighed, like I was being ridiculous. "Rae, this isn't going to work like this."

My eyebrows shot up. "Oh, so you're the spell expert now?"

"No," Venn replied, "but remember what I said about Synchrony? You can't do this just to prove me wrong."

I opened my mouth to counter, but I hesitated. Maybe he was right and I was totally going about this the wrong way. I would've loved to prove him wrong, to show him he had no right to be making assumptions about me, but the truth was that I didn't have time for this. None of us did.

Fiona returned and set a salt shaker in front of me on the table. She found four candles and a lighter in a nearby cabinet and returned to her seat with all of them in hand.

"Okay," I caved. "You seem to know how I *can* do this. What do I have to do to make it work?"

Venn finally relaxed and sank back into his chair. "The first thing is that you have to let go of all that negative energy you're holding."

Yes, because telling me to do that will make it all magically disappear.

"How do you suggest I do that?" I asked.

Venn shrugged.

Great. He doesn't even know.

"How do you normally relax?" he asked.

I kill criminal vampires.

"Ice cream," I said instead, because even though I had no problem killing vampires, I didn't want to come across sounding like an insane serial killer. Ice cream sounded like a safe bet, and I was hungry anyway. Plus, it might help cool the heat on my gums. "Do you have any?"

"I'll get it," Fiona offered.

I returned my attention to Venn. "Once I'm relaxed, then what?"

Venn leaned forward in his chair and laced his fingers together on the table-top. "We talked about this earlier. You have to perform the spell without doubt. If you're focusing all your attention on how the spell won't work, it will fail every time."

He said it like you could just switch your doubt off at the snap of a finger.

"Okay," I agreed. "I won't doubt myself."

Venn shook his head. "You can't just wish you won't doubt yourself. You have to truly believe it."

I gritted my teeth. He made it sound so easy when it wasn't.

"Clearly, you know I don't think this is going to work," I pointed out. "Why are we even bothering?"

"Because," Venn said, "I still think you can do it. I think, deep down inside, you have the power to become an amazing witch."

The corners of my lips twitched involuntarily. "Keep talking..."

Venn smirked. With enough compliments, I might just believe in what he was trying to tell me.

He leaned even closer until he was just inches away from me. I could smell the scent of cinnamon on his skin and feel the rush of his breath across my arm.

My breath hitched, and it took everything I had not to close the distance between us. All I wanted was to touch him.

"I think you've been on your own for too long," he said softly. "And I think that without someone there to believe in you, you forgot how to believe in yourself."

So much for the compliments.

"Wait." Venn grabbed my hand before I could pull away. My skin tingled at the touch, sending warm vibes up and down my arm. "The thing is, it will never matter how much I tell you how beautiful or strong or smart I think you are if you don't feel that way yourself. I can't give you faith. That can only come from inside you. But I will tell you this…" Venn's gaze dropped to my hand as he ran his thumbs over the back of it, sending my heart going haywire and making me forget all about the pain on my lips. "I absolutely believe that you can do this, that one day, you will embrace Synchrony and do amazing things with it."

I scoffed lightly. "You say that like you can predict the future." Which would've been strange, even in our effed-up world.

Venn shook his head. "I don't know the future, but I know you've done amazing things with magic before. Your soul is powerful, Rae, and once you come to realize that, nothing will be able to stop you."

I couldn't help but smile. He was trying a *little* too hard. It was quite amusing.

"What?" Venn asked innocently.

"You think I'm beautiful?" I teased.

Disappointment crossed Venn's face. "*That's* what you got out of that?"

"That, and you can't tell the future."

Venn sighed and dropped my hand. He leaned back in his chair. "All I'm saying is that I believe in you, and *maybe* that's enough magic to make you see it, too."

Oh, wow. He really meant it. He wasn't just telling me what he thought I wanted to hear.

I narrowed my eyes. "I thought you weren't a witch. You don't *have* magic."

He nodded in agreement. "Not like you do."

"Here you go." Fiona set a bowl of vanilla ice cream in front of me, then one in front of Venn.

"Thank you," I said before digging in.

Fiona sat across from me and dipped her spoon into her ice cream. "Is there anything else you need? I mean, for the spell?"

I glanced at the notebook beside me. "Nope, that's it. But according to Venn —" I shot him a glance "—I need to find a little confidence."

"What?" he asked with a mouthful. "It's true."

I rolled my eyes. *Okay, maybe he has a point. It's not like it'll hurt to be open-minded, about Synchrony, about everything. Just try it.*

I sat quietly, letting the ice cream melt in my mouth and focusing on the cooling sensation and sweet flavor. I forced my shoulders to relax and pictured the negative energy in my body melting away with the ice cream. Fiona exchanged a skeptical glance with Venn, but neither of them said anything. I finished my ice cream far too soon, but I thought it would be rude to ask for another serving.

"So, here's how the spell works." I pushed my bowl aside and stood. I placed Cowen's watch at the center of the table, then situated the four candles in a square around it. I popped the top off the salt shaker and emptied the entire contents in a thick circle around the candles. I took the lighter and lit each of the candles.

"Should I get the lights?" Fiona asked.

I shrugged. "It doesn't say anything about lighting, but if you want to, go ahead."

"Will it help you concentrate?" she asked.

I thought about it for a moment, then nodded.

Fiona rose from her chair and flipped off the light switch. In the darkness, it felt eerie to be sitting in a stranger's home performing a spell.

"Now what?" Fiona asked curiously.

I didn't have much to go off of, only my notes on the ingredients needed and the incantation I was supposed to mutter. Beyond that, I wasn't sure how the spell actually worked to track someone down. I just hoped this wasn't another one of Mrs. Carlyle's shoddy spells.

Venn set his bowl aside. "Remember, Rae, you can do this."

I nodded. I just needed to believe in myself, or so Venn said.

I shut my eyes and took a deep breath, letting out the remaining tension in my body on the exhale. *This is going to work*, I told myself. I did my best to shut out the second voice in my head telling me I was wrong. *Just believe. It can't be that easy, can it?*

Finally, I opened my eyes. I spoke the incantation in my notebook, but the words hardly sounded like my own. They sounded strong and confident, and I had no idea if I was doing this just for show or if I truly felt it in my heart.

By the time I reached the end of the short incantation, nothing had happened. Further down the page, my notes read that the incantation needed to be repeated several times.

No giving up, Rachel. You've got this.

A light breeze passed through the room, rolling from the kitchen to the dining room windows and rustling their curtains.

Maybe I'm actually doing something, I thought.

The breeze grew stronger the longer I repeated the words in my spell book. A prideful smile swept across Venn's face, and Fiona shifted in her chair in excitement.

Right in front of my eyes, granules of salt began to swirl together, rising up from the tabletop in a smooth, controlled manner, as if somehow my magic had created a tiny invisible twister on the table.

I held in my urge to cry out and rejoice, to gloat to Venn that I was actually doing it, but I couldn't stop the incantation now. I continued, and my chest filled with a sense of victory. We were going to find Cowen. The thieving bastard was going to get what was coming to him, and I was going to finally get the answer to the question that had been burning inside of me for years.

The remaining granules of salt rose from the table until they all come together to form an orb in the middle of the candle square about a foot above Cowen's watch.

Fiona leaned over to Venn and whispered, "Is that supposed to happen?"

Venn simply held and index finger to his lips, instructing her to stay quiet.

Then, in the blink of an eye, the salt orb exploded, blasting back into my eyes. I instinctively flinched and fell back into my chair, my heart racing.

It didn't work. I failed.

I forced my breathing to slow and the heat to leave my eyes before I opened them. A knot twisted in my chest, but I did my best to hide it.

"Was that it?" Fiona asked, rubbing her eye. "Do you know where Cowen is?"

I gritted my teeth. "Did it look like it worked?"

"I—I," Fiona stammered. "I've never seen this spell done before. I'm sorry."

"Don't be." Regret filled my voice. "It's not your fault. It's mine."

I couldn't keep my anger in any longer. I shot to my feet and raced out of the room.

11

———————

The front door slammed behind me. By the time I was outside, I realized I *really* didn't know what I was doing because I'd left my spell book, my purse, and my good pants behind. I couldn't just leave right now. Well, I could, but then I'd have to come back to retrieve my things later.

Instead, I sank down onto the steps and covered my face with my hands. *Where did I go wrong? I believed in myself like Venn said I should. Maybe he was wrong. Maybe I don't have enough power for this. I'm only a low witch. I'm never going to find Jenna.*

The door creaked open behind me. I *really* didn't want company right now. But apparently whoever had followed me outside couldn't read minds, because they sat on the step beside me. I thought it was Venn and was about to tell him to leave me alone, that I'd be back inside when I was ready, but then Fiona's voice reached my ears.

"Hey, Rae," she said softly. "It's okay. It really is."

I dropped my hands from my face and lifted my gaze to hers. It was dark out, but it was easy to make out her soft features with the light from a nearby street lamp.

"No," I stated flatly. "It's not okay. We need this to work. If I was a better witch, you'd be closer to rescuing Sondra, and I wouldn't still be wondering if my sister is dead or alive."

Fiona cocked her head. "Your sister? That's what you're doing this for?"

I nodded. I wasn't sure why I opened up to Fiona. Maybe it was my emotions running high and the inherent *need* to talk to someone, or maybe it was because I thought she and her family could help me. Whatever the reason, I found myself telling her things I'd never talked to anyone about before.

"Two years ago, vampires raided our house," I said. "They killed my parents and kidnapped my sister as a blood slave. I tried tracking spells on my own, but they never worked. I turned to a witch the first chance I got, after I saved up enough money, but she couldn't do the spell. She said I'd already claimed ownership of everything I had left of my sister's, so she couldn't use any of that to track her."

The sorrow on Fiona's face deepened the longer I talked.

I dropped my gaze to my hands. "I'd pretty much given up hope trying to find her until... until I met Cowen."

"You think he knows something about your sister?" Fiona asked.

I nodded, and a silent beat passed between us.

"The Soulless took her, didn't they?" Her voice was so soft, so full of sorrow. "That's why you need him?"

I closed my eyes and took a deep breath. "Yeah. I just wish I could do it on my own."

"You're the *Ravenite*," Fiona said in admiration. "You can do practically anything."

I rolled my eyes. "Don't fool yourself. I'm not what they make me out to be. I've never been good at magic. I work at this magic shop downtown because I thought it would help me get better at magic, but the whole thing is a joke."

Fiona scoffed. "Most of them are."

"My boss is an idiot," I complained. "For one, the shopfront is a bakery, but he'll just leave charms and shit lying around by the donuts. And he basically has no protocols for when people come in the back where I work. He's barely a low witch but sells charms he claims are enchanted with protection spells. He resells spells that barely work, at best. He's a total con artist. I only stayed because I need the money."

Fiona nodded like she understood. God, it felt good to finally talk to someone. And Fiona just sat there listening without judgement. For the first time in years, it felt like I could actually make a real friend. But I didn't let myself entertain the idea. Now was not the time to get distracted.

"Anyway," I said, changing the subject. "I'm really sorry that I can't help you."

"It's not your fault," Fiona replied. "Venn's being too hard on you."

"Thank you!"

Fiona giggled but quickly composed herself. "He can't just expect you to jump into a complicated spell like that. He needs to realize that it takes small steps and a lot of practice."

I frowned. "I have been practicing."

"Right," she said. "That's why you can heal, because you've already done the spell before and know you can. Next, you need to try something just a little bigger, until you know you can do it, rather than jumping straight into something so different."

Fiona made a lot more sense to me than Venn did. You don't just become powerful by *believing* in it. It took practice.

A slight smile spread across my lips. This sounded like the kind of pep talk Jenna would give me.

"So, you're not mad at me?" I asked. "For not being able to perform the spell, I mean?"

"Of course not!" Fiona said. "None of this is your fault."

"But Sondra's still missing," I pointed out.

"Again, not your fault," she said. "I'd blame a hundred different people before I'd blame you."

An uncomfortable silence hung in the air. I dared to break it.

"Whose fault is it?" I wanted to take back the question as soon as I asked it. It wasn't fair of me to ask something like that when I didn't even know Fiona.

She didn't even hesitate to answer. "Matias," she snarled in disgust.

Okay, now I *had* to know.

"Who's Matias?" I asked. "Wait. *Matias Vayne?* The richest vampire in the state? The one who owns like fifteen skyscrapers in Chicago?"

"The one and only," Fiona confirmed. "But you forgot *manipulative and controlling jackass.*"

I chuckled. "Doesn't that apply to all vampires?"

Fiona smirked. "It certainly does. But Matias is worse than most. He has hundreds of supernaturals working for him who basically bow down to him. He'll do anything to maintain his power."

Power was always a dangerous motivator.

After a beat, I spoke again. "So, what happened?"

Fiona turned to stare me straight in the eyes. "First, a little backstory. Sondra's a high witch—the low end of a high witch, but still a high witch. She runs a business collecting and selling magical artifacts—totally underground like your boss does. She does other things, too, like sells protection charms, performs spells, stuff like that…"

"Why haven't I ever heard of her?" I asked. I liked to know what was going on in the magical community. It was one of the other reasons I stayed at my job. There was always gossip running through that place.

"She likes to keep a low profile," Fiona answered. "She's pretty selective about her clientele. A few years back, she was involved with some bad business deals. She ran into a lot of debt with some other witches while she was trying to get her business off the ground, but the interest was so high that we've just been falling further and further behind." Fiona dropped her gaze and pursed her lips. "At this rate, we'll never be able to pay off the debt, even if we sold the house."

My heart broke for her family. It didn't sound like Sondra deserved that.

"Anyway, Matias offered us a job." Fiona spoke slowly, like the story was about to get really bad. I held my breath, bracing for it. "The money he offered us would've been enough to pay off the debt. We could've even moved out of the city. All any of us really want is to lead a quiet life, maybe use our magic to do some good in the world."

Fiona sighed. "We spent months looking for this artifact he wanted to pay us for. We even had to ask for more time, and Matias let us have it. But... then Cowen came along."

"Venn told me he stole something from you," I said solemnly.

Fiona nodded. "It was the Leora Locket. It's a magical artifact named for the witch who created it. As the story goes, the owner of the locket can use it to predict the future."

I narrowed my eyes. "Why are you telling me this? I mean, if I find Cowen, I could just take it and run."

"For one, I don't think you're like that," Fiona answered.

"You don't even know me," I pointed out.

"I know," she said, "but I just feel like I can trust you. Besides, the locket isn't as great as it sounds."

I cocked my head. "How so?"

"It can only *predict* the future, but the future can still be changed," Fiona explained. "The locket was created using a spell designed to connect the wearer with the spirit realm so they could communicate with loved ones—"

"Wait," I stopped her. "The spirit realm? We're talking about *ghosts* now?"

Though I was shocked by Fiona's mention of ghosts, it shouldn't be so hard to believe after everything else I'd seen in the last eight years.

"Not *ghosts*, exactly," Fiona said, "but yeah. Anyway, the locket became connected with Synchrony—you know what that is, right?"

I nodded. "Venn explained it."

"Right. So, Synchrony is connected to everyone, and so it can see other people's intentions. The locket detects that and shows you how the events would play out."

"That still sounds useful," I said.

"Oh, sure," Fiona agreed, "but intentions can change, and you have to know whose future you're looking into for the locket to work. But someone else's intentions might get in the way of that future. Matias wants power, and he thinks the Leora Locket will give him that, but it really can't. There are too many factors at play."

"So, you're conning him?" I asked, slightly amused.

"No," Fiona stated flatly. "We're doing the job he asked us to do."

"But you didn't tell him about the locket's limitations," I pointed out. "Why tell me?"

Fiona paused. "I don't know. There's just... something about you."

The way she looked at me, it was like I was supposed to know what she meant, but I was only confused.

"Anyway," Fiona continued. "Cowen knew some stuff about the locket, and we ended up turning to him for answers. Once he knew what we were after, he waited until we got our hands on it, and then he stole it. Needless to say, Matias was *not* happy. After already granting us more time, he wasn't exactly inclined to wait any longer."

"So he kidnapped Sondra," I guessed.

Fiona pursed her lips and nodded. "She went to have a meeting with him, and he wouldn't let her leave. He's using her as collateral to motivate the rest of us to deliver the locket."

My chest felt empty. I hadn't even met Sondra, and here I was feeling like I'd lost her, too.

"Do you think she's okay?" I asked in a whisper.

Fiona didn't answer right away, as if she wasn't quite sure what she thought. "She better be. Otherwise, Matias isn't getting anywhere near that locket."

I chewed the inside of my lip, hoping I'd find the right words for her, but nothing I thought of sounded right in the moment. Still, I found the words coming out of my mouth anyway. "We'll get that locket, Fiona. I don't care if we have to sell our kidneys and pay a high witch to track Cowen down." *Not sure why I haven't thought of that before...* "One way or another, we'll find him, and we'll both get back the people we lost."

The door creaked open behind us, and Fiona and I both turned to look. Venn had a frown fixed to his face.

"What is it?" Fiona asked.

Venn sighed, stalling his answer. "I talked to Ryland. We agreed it's time to call Genevieve."

I glanced between the two of them, hoping someone would explain who Genevieve was, but neither of them did.

Fiona stood and pursed her lips. "I was really hoping it wouldn't come to this. We don't have any other options?"

Venn shook his head. "It's too late. I've already called her."

Fiona stared at him in total disbelief, her mouth agape. "Uh... okay. When are we meeting her?"

"In the morning," Venn answered. "We all need to rest. If you want to stay, Rae, we can make up Sondra's bedroom for you."

My heart lifted in my chest, feeling a hundred pounds lighter for a second. "Are you sure?" I asked uncertainly, not wanting to intrude.

"It's totally fine," Fiona assured me. An inviting smile spread across her face.

"Thank you," I accepted, making sure they heard the gratitude in my tone. I didn't feel like going back home to my lonely apartment tonight. "I'm exhausted."

"It's the spell," Fiona said. When I shot her a questioning look, she explained. "Most of the spells you've cast probably haven't drained you because they were well within your abilities. But when you try to cast a spell beyond your abilities, the energy starts to draw from your body instead of Synchrony. Don't worry about it. The more you practice, the more you'll expand your abilities. You'll be able to draw from Synchrony more and more without feeling the drain on your body."

My jaw went slack. "You say that like it's not a big deal. Something like this could kill me!"

"Believe me," Venn said, "you're far from conducting spells that could kill you."

At least that was comforting, but he could've mentioned the whole energy-draining thing before I tried the spell.

"Come on." Fiona gestured for me to follow her. "I'll show you to your room."

12

"You can stay in here," Fiona said, opening the door to the room farthest from the top of the stairs.

She flipped a switch on the wall, and two lamps on either side of the queen bed lit up, bathing the room in a soft glow. The comforter was a dark purple to match the walls, like the color of royalty. Matching curtains with intricate gold patterns stitched into the fabric covered a pair of wide windows that looked out over the front lawn. In the corner sat a table with three plants and four unlit candles. A yoga mat was rolled up beneath it.

"Thank you," I said, inching my way into the room.

Fiona crossed the room to the closet. "I think Sondra might have something you can wear to bed. If you need a shower, there are clean towels in the cupboard in the bathroom."

I figured I'd have to take her up on that offer. I set my purse on the bed and ran my hand across the soft blanket. Part of me felt weird being in someone else's room without them knowing, but another part of me just wanted to crawl under the covers and sleep in a decent bed for once.

"Here you go," Fiona said, handing me a silky black robe. "Let me know if you need anything else."

"I will," I said with a smile.

Fiona left the room, and I heard her footsteps pad down the hall. The house was quiet, and I assumed Teagan had fallen asleep. Normally, the quiet made me uneasy, but in this house, it felt comfortable, peaceful even.

With the silky robe in my hands, I headed to the bathroom. The shower looked inviting. The water was actually warm, and the pipes didn't squeak when you twisted the faucet. The water hit my skin like a soft caress, washing away most of the tension in my shoulders. I stayed under the cascade of water far longer than I needed to.

By the time I stepped out of the shower, the mirror above the sink was completely fogged up. The soft towel I found in the cupboard felt good against my clean skin, but the silk robe felt even better. After drying my hair out, I ran a brush I found on the counter through it, then gathered my dirty clothes.

As I exited the bathroom in a cloud of steam, I caught Venn's eye just as he reached the top of the stairs. He looked surprised to see me, but the corners of his lips lifted into a slight smile. Butterflies danced in my stomach at the sight of him.

"Hey, Rae," he said softly, gazing at me from under dark lashes. "I'm sorry about earlier. Are you okay?"

I nodded. Even though I still felt bad about the unsuccessful spell, the shower had helped calm me down. I felt like I should say something to him but didn't know what.

"Can we do another load of laundry tonight?" I heard myself say. Apparently, that was the best I could come up with. "The other half of my wardrobe could really use cleaning."

"Yeah, no problem." He gestured for me to follow him.

I softly descended the steps behind him in silence. I tossed my clothes and a bit of laundry soap in the washer, and Venn started the machine.

"Is there anything else you need?" he asked kindly.

Several answers rushed through my mind, but nothing I dared to say aloud to him.

"No, thanks," I replied as we headed back down the hall. "It's so nice of you to let me stay here."

Venn shrugged like it was no big deal. "Don't worry about it. We had the extra bed tonight anyway."

My stomach dropped as I thought of Sondra. It didn't seem fair that I was showering in her house and sleeping in her bed while she was being held captive. But there wasn't exactly any more I could do to help tonight.

My gaze drifted to the drawings on the walls as I climbed the stairs. Each was a portrait of a different person. They looked incredibly realistic, down to their stray hairs. It almost looked as if they'd been photographed in black and white. Some portraits looked more modern, but others wore their hair and clothing as if they'd lived centuries ago.

"Are these Sondra's ancestors?" I asked, mostly because I wasn't ready to say goodnight to Venn.

"No," he said simply. "It's history."

"History?" Okay, now he had me intrigued. "History of what?"

"Of magic," he replied. He reached the top of the steps and turned to me with a smile. "Recent magic, anyway."

"What do you mean?"

Venn smirked. "You up for a history lesson?"

It sounded like a challenge. "I suppose I have time."

Venn's smile widened, and he pointed to the portrait on the end. "Here, we start with Elizabeth Martin. Ever heard of her?"

"I don't think so," I said, shaking my head. The name sounded vaguely familiar, but maybe it was just a common name.

I stepped closer to the portrait for a better look. Like the drawing of Venn at the bottom of the stairs, Elizabeth's eyes looked incredibly real, as if she was staring back at me through the photograph. An eerie shudder traveled down my spine. She wore a long-sleeved dress that covered her collarbone, and her hair was fashioned in an elegant updo.

"She was the witch who created Valkas," Venn said, like he knew it for a fact.

I furrowed my brow. "How do you know? I've heard stories and speculation, but no one can actually know for sure where vampires came from."

"Sondra does," Venn stated. "Valkas was the first vampire."

"I know *that*." But that was all I knew. That was all *anyone* knew.

"Well, Elizabeth was the one who created him," Venn said. "Not on purpose or anything. It was a revival spell gone wrong. Valkas came from a very powerful family. He recruited Elizabeth. She believed she was to perform a healing spell. He was very sick, but instead of allowing the illness to take him, he wanted to die and come back to life to show that he could conquer anything, even death. She refused to perform the spell, but he threatened her with her family's death if she didn't comply."

"So he knew about magic before everyone else did?" I asked.

Venn cocked his head, confused by my question. Suddenly, his face softened in realization. "Oh, you think Valkas was changed eight years ago? No. This was *centuries* ago. Magic has always been around. But the people who knew about it before kept it secret."

"Right," I said, remembering something he'd said earlier. "Persecution and all that."

"Yes," Venn agreed. "Valkas changed that when he returned eight years ago and everyone freaked out."

I pressed my lips together. "What happened after he threatened Elizabeth?"

"He gave his blood for the spell, but it went wrong," Venn explained. "He died, and she brought him back to life, but he wasn't quite human anymore. He was overcome with bloodlust and couldn't control his power. His family was scared of what he'd become, and he was hunted. He lost the power he once had. That's why all these years later he wants that power back."

"No one's heard from him in two years," I pointed out. "No one's heard from the Soulless at all. You think he's still out there?"

Not everyone believed he was still around, but no one was able to confirm his death, either. Somehow, I *knew* they were still out there, and I knew they had Jenna.

"I think it's possible." Venn shrugged, then pointed to the next picture on the wall. "That's him."

I hadn't noticed the drawing before because my attention had been so absorbed by Elizabeth. When I looked at him, my mouth went dry. I'd seen pictures of him on TV and online, but it was nothing compared to this picture. Fangs protruded from his open mouth, and he looked as if he was screaming. I could practically hear the fear-inducing howl through the portrait. His eyebrows twisted into an enraged expression, every muscle in his face tense. There was a hunger and a lust for power in his evil eyes that sent shivers down my spine. Seeing him like this, I could actually believe he was responsible for all of the terrible things he'd been accused of. Like all vampires, he was flawlessly beautiful, but I there was something in the drawing that told me to be very, *very* afraid.

"That's what he would've been like right after the spell changed him, back in seventeenth century Europe," Venn explained. "He started changing other people, and vampires spent the next one-hundred years spreading across Europe, then to the rest of the world."

How could Venn know all this? He told the story like it came straight from a history book. I'd never met someone before who didn't show skepticism in the vampire stories they'd heard. No one, as far as I knew, had the truth.

"For a long time, Valkas saw vampirism as a curse," Venn continued. "He couldn't go out in the sun, and so he couldn't show off his power. Years later, he came to terms with the bad things about vampirism and started focusing on how much power he did have, like extra strength and the ability to kill so easily. That's when he started thinking bigger. He's already conquered death. Time to conquer the whole world."

Venn frowned, like the very thought of Valkas disgusted him. "Anyway, for many years, humans and witches alike hunted vampires and tried to eradicate them before their population became too large. But about a hundred years in, vampires began to spread wider and faster. The witches were having a hard time finding the vampires. In the mid-seventeen-hundreds, a husband and wife team, Abigail and Charles Williams, set out to protect the world from vampires, who were killing humans and causing mass panic."

Venn gestured to the next set of portraits. A beautiful woman who looked to be in her thirties smiled back at me. Beside her in another frame, an attractive man smirked, like he knew something I didn't. The way Sondra drew his eyes looked strikingly similar to Venn's, though they otherwise looked nothing alike.

"How'd they do it?" I asked, completely engrossed in his version of the story. "Protect people, I mean."

"Abigail was a powerful witch, and Charles was human," Venn explained, like he was excited I took interest. "Using wolf's blood, she performed a spell that bound his and the wolf's bodies together."

"A wolf shifter like you," I said with a smile.

"Yes," Venn agreed with a light laugh. "Exactly like me. Charles became the first shifter, meant to combat the vampires. He was able to sniff out vampire lairs in his wolf form, helping them reduce the population. Better yet, the spell incorporated protective magic. That's why vampires can't smell us or hear our heart beats. With the help of their hunter friends, Abigail created several other shifters, each a different animal species with their different strengths. They reduced the vampire population to almost nothing and thought they'd eradicated them.

"Another hundred years passed of shifters hunting vampires, but they couldn't completely take them out. The shifter boom set the vampires back for a while, but then they stopped running around killing for survival and began taking blood slaves. They became more organized and grouped together, growing their numbers in secret. By then, the vampires were in the US. People started to go missing quietly, but no matter how many vampires they killed, the witches couldn't manage to kill them all. A team of witches came together just before Valkas was going to unleash his army of vampires."

Venn pointed to the next row of drawings. My eyes remained fixed on the portraits as I descended the stairs, inspecting each face.

"These were just some of the witches who came together to stop him." Venn stood on the stair above me to look at the sketches. He was so close that I could feel the heat radiating off his skin. I had the urge to lean into him, but I resisted and focused on the images instead. "With the help of the shifter population, the witches were able to take out most of the vampires. But they couldn't kill Valkas."

"So, he went into hiding?" I guessed.

"No," Venn answered. "In 1847, they locked him away in a supernatural prison. That way, he couldn't create any more vampires, the shifters could kill the rest of them, and the mass killings would stop."

I thought about his story. It made so much more sense than the other theories I'd heard—like how vampires and shifters had been created by mad scientists, which didn't explain our magic. I'd been mostly accepting the theory that magic came from an alternate universe, but trying to follow the parallel universe theory hurt my head. So far, I was really digging Venn's story.

"The thing is, something went wrong with the spell," he continued.

"Something that affected magic?" I asked. It only made sense.

He nodded.

"So, magic got trapped in the supernatural prison with him?" I guessed.

"Not exactly," Venn clarified. "Magic is all around us, all the time. Always has been. Somehow, the spell took away our ability to *access* magic. We're just not entirely sure why."

"Any theories?" I asked, sensing he might have one or two up his sleeve.

Venn shrugged. "The thing about a spell like that was that it required so much magic that the witches had to work together. There's strength in numbers, after all. But the more people you have trying to accomplish one goal, the trickier it is to carry out. My guess is that not everyone was working together as well as everyone hoped. Synchrony didn't know how to respond.

But to wipe out access to magic completely… that's huge. It never could've happened without so many witches participating in the spell."

"What happened while he was trapped?" I asked. "Everyone just forgot magic existed?"

"Basically," Venn said. "Many generations passed, and as technology advanced, most people wrote it off as legend, as make-believe. But the stories of magic were still around, just twisted in different ways. I mean, you knew what magic was before you ever saw it, right? And there's always been a small community of people who still believed magic existed. It's just that most people didn't want to listen until they saw it with their own eyes. Even then, people denied it. They still do."

Don't get me started on those whack-jobs.

"So when he escaped, our ability to access magic returned?" I asked. *Obviously.* "Shifters started shifting, witches started… witching."

Venn laughed. "Yeah."

"You seem to know a lot about this," I stated. "Any idea how he actually escaped?"

Venn shook his head regrettably. "No, unfortunately. That one's still a mystery."

A beat passed between us as I considered his words. I was all too familiar with the rest of the story. Once Valkas showed up, mass panic ensued. Not only was Valkas and his army of new vampires slaughtering, changing, and kidnapping thousands of people like they were trying to win a record on terrorism, but now a bunch of people were discovering they had powers. Everyone was afraid. Afraid of the vampires. Afraid of the shifters. Afraid of themselves. I understood the fear—and the equivalent thrill—because I'd lived through it. The civil rights movement, the blood banks, the new laws, and all of that followed shortly afterward until supernaturals were forced to either suppress their nature or unlawfully succumb to it.

"Is there a history book or something that explains all this?" I asked. "How did Sondra get so detailed with these portraits?"

Venn shook his head. "No history books. She remembers."

Hold up. She remembers? How's that possible?

"Anyway," he said with a yawn before I could ask. "It's getting really late, and we should get some sleep before we meet up with Genevieve in the morning."

"Who *is* Genevieve?" I asked. "How can she help us?"

Venn dropped his gaze, like there was something about Genevieve she didn't want to tell me. "She's a witch," he finally said. "But an… unconventional witch."

My jaw practically dropped. Venn didn't have to say anything more. Somehow, I knew by the look in his eyes that we were about to meet up with a witch who practiced dark magic.

<h1 style="text-align:center">13</h1>

Genevieve wasn't just into dark magic. She was into dark *everything*.

The next morning, Venn, Fiona, and I walked up the steps to a large house with dark stone and a black roof. Teagan was feeling better but still not back to normal. Ryland had insisted on staying back at the house with her, so it was just the three of us.

A tall, thin woman answered the door. She looked old enough to be my mother, but her skin was smoother than Fiona's. I was willing to bet she had an anti-aging spell up her sleeve. Her hair was jet-black, in stark contrast to her pale skin. It was short and stuck up at every angle, but in a way that looked like it belonged in a fashion magazine. Her brown eyes were outlined in a dark layer of makeup, and her black dress was made almost entirely of lace.

Genevieve, I presume.

"Come in," she offered in a cold tone. She turned on her heel and started down the hall, leaving the door open behind her.

I warily stepped through the door behind Venn. Inside, the lights were dim. The dark gray walls housed black and white images of random landscapes. At the end of the hall sat a Victorian-style chaise covered in black fabric. The only pop of color was a deep red throw pillow on top of it.

Genevieve led us into a room at the end of the hall. The room was dark, like the rest of the house, but was small and cluttered. Black curtains covered the window. They let in only enough light to make out the shadows in the room. A bookcase spanned one wall. Books without names on their spines lined the bottom shelves, looking old and tattered. On the upper shelves were hundreds of jars of all different sizes. Some held various colors of liquid, while others looked to house different types of herbs and spices. Against the other wall, unlit candles lined the top of a long dresser, surrounding an open book that looked centuries old. I figured it was just for show, but it intrigued me none-theless.

In the center of the room sat a round table with four chairs and a crystal ball in the center. That *had* to be for show, because as far as I knew, crystal balls didn't actually work. All the room needed was a skull and a cauldron for decoration and you'd be ready for Halloween—not that anyone celebrated Halloween anymore. It'd become far too real and horrifying.

Genevieve raised a thin, dark eyebrow at Venn. "I understand that you'd like me to perform a tracking spell."

"Yes," Venn said with a nod.

Genevieve pursed her lips. "You're well aware that I require payment up front."

The way she said that… it was like they had history together, like she'd given him chances before and wasn't about to put up with any more crap. Not that I could picture Venn giving *anyone* crap—unless for a good reason.

"Of course." Venn didn't look Genevieve in the eye. Then again, neither did me nor Fiona. The woman made my skin crawl.

Venn reached into his jacket pocket and placed a pile of cash and a vial of red liquid in front of Genevieve.

Blood. Venn's blood. Shifter blood.

Not only was it illegal to sell blood anywhere but a government-approved blood bank, but it was *definitely* illegal to sell shifter blood. Devin didn't even deal with shifter blood, and he dabbled in some questionable things. There weren't very many spells that used shifter blood for good, none that I knew of, anyway. But that wasn't saying much.

Genevieve swiped her payment from the table and turned to a small hutch behind her, where she slipped the money and blood into the top drawer.

"Please, take a seat," she said without turning to us.

We did as we were told without muttering a single word. I sat across from where Genevieve stood, while Fiona took the chair on my left and Venn sat to my right.

"How's Sondra doing?" Genevieve asked with her back to us as she reached into a cupboard. She didn't sound the least bit interested in Sondra's well-being. It almost sounded like she was mocking Venn and Fiona.

Fiona clenched her fists, like she'd really like to take a swing at Genevieve. On the other side of me, Venn's jaw tensed.

"You know we wouldn't be here alone if she was fine," Venn said with a hint of malice to his voice.

"Of course not." Genevieve turned around, an attempt at a smile fixed to her face. "Shall we get started?"

She snapped her fingers, and the crystal ball on the table rose into the air. It hovered across the room and landed softly on another table. Six candles floated over to take its place on the black tablecloth. They neatly arranged themselves into a circle.

"Ardeat ignis," Genevieve muttered. The candles lit on her command, licking tall flames into the air.

My palms grew clammy. Every fiber of my being told me to run, to get as far away from this place as possible, but I remained rooted in my chair. I didn't come here just to leave without answers.

Genevieve took a large glass jar of salt and poured it in a circle around the candles. She set the jar on the hutch and then gracefully slid into the chair across from me.

"You have the watch we discussed on the phone?" she asked Venn, holding out her palm toward him.

Venn quickly dug into his pocket and placed Cowen's watch in her outstretched hand. She dropped the watch into the center of the table, eyeing it like it was infected with germs. Fiona glanced to me as if I should know what was going on, but I had no reassurances to give her.

My mouth went dry. Part of me was excited to see how this spell would actually work, but another part of me feared that it wouldn't.

Genevieve began chanting under her breath. Her words were the same I spoke last night, but they were different, too. She pronounced them with an accent, making the spell sound more mysterious and… authentic.

I tried not to breathe as the salt rose above the table, afraid that just the smallest breeze might throw the granules out of the air. The candle flames licked higher, something that hadn't happened when I'd tried the same spell last night. The salt swirled above us, spinning faster and faster until it all came together to form a tightly compact ball the size of my fist.

And this is the part where it explodes, where we fail.

On cue, the salt ball burst, as if someone had shot a bullet through it. I flinched away, expecting the granules to assault me, but I never felt a thing. Slowly, I peeled my eyes open.

The salt had stopped a mere foot from my face. The granules had expanded outward to create a ball at least three feet in diameter. They moved in unison, twisting around an invisible axis like a globe. Colors flashed inside of the ball. It took me a second to realize the colors made up real images, as if there was a hidden projector somewhere in the room using the spinning salt granules as a screen. The images flickered by so fast that they were almost impossible to make out. I caught a glimpse of Cowen's face and then the bar we'd tracked him down to, Red Whiskey. Several more images passed by quickly, but they were too hard to see, like we were speeding down a road at an insane, inhuman speed.

The images slowed to settle on an old mansion. Perhaps *mansion* wasn't the right word. It was more like a castle. It was beautiful, with a huge fountain on the front lawn and three big towers reaching into the sky. A security wall ran the perimeter of the property. Beyond that lay a lush green forest.

The image disappeared almost as quickly as it came. In the blink of an eye, the salt stopped spinning and dropped out of the air. Salt littered the table, the floor, and my lap. I sat there speechless, unable to believe the level of magic I'd just witnessed.

Fiona had an expression of sheer terror fixed to her face. She stared across the table at Venn, barely even breathing. Venn cursed heavily under his breath, and his nostrils flared. He looked like he was about to go on a rampage. Somehow, he managed to keep his temper under control, but it was clear that something had *seriously* hit his enraged button.

Genevieve laughed lightly, but it sounded less like she was actually amused by something and more like she was taunting us. "I should've known. What kind of trouble have you gotten yourself into this time?"

Venn shot up from his chair and snatched the watch from the center of the table. "That's none of your business."

"I'm only trying to help, darling," Genevieve replied in a smooth voice, but it sounded fake.

"Yes," Venn agreed, "but we've already paid for all the help we can afford."

Genevieve rolled her eyes and sighed. "Fine. If that's all you wanted, you can help yourself out."

I had no clue what was going on here, but when Fiona stood, I followed behind her. Venn waited until we were both out of the room before turning from Genevieve, as if he wanted to make sure we were both okay before leaving. Nobody spoke as we made our way down the long hall. My stomach dropped further and further with each step I took. I *had* to know what those images meant. Something told me they were bad. *Very* bad.

But I didn't speak, not until we escaped Genevieve's house and could no longer hear her laughter echoing down the hall. I managed to keep my mouth shut until I climbed into the passenger seat of Venn's vehicle.

Finally, I burst. "What happened? What did those images mean? You know where to find him, don't you?"

Venn's jaw remained tense. He didn't meet my eyes as he turned the ignition and shifted into drive. "Yeah," he finally said. "We know where to find him."

"Where?" I asked desperately. "What aren't you guys telling me?"

"You didn't recognize the mansion?" Fiona asked in a small voice.

"No," I replied. "Should I?"

Fiona cleared her throat. "Ever heard of Maliya Valerik?"

I drew in a sharp breath. "Please don't tell me that's who I think it is."

I'd heard whispers. Devin had let the name slip once when he was talking with a client. But he never talked about vampire politics with me. He always shrugged me off when I asked him what he knew.

"If you think she's one of the most powerful vampires in all of Nocton, you'd be correct," Venn said, never taking his eyes off the road.

"That last image we saw... that was her mansion," Fiona explained. "Which means that's where we'll find Cowen. And wherever we find Cowen, we find the locket."

Venn growled in frustration, startling me. "I should've known he was one of them."

"One of who?" I demanded, glancing between Fiona and Venn. "Will someone *please* fill me in."

"Maliya runs her own vampire nest," Fiona explained. "She's recruited hundreds of vampires to do her bidding for her, and they're always the worst of the worst."

"What kind of bidding?" I asked, fearing the answer.

Fiona's skin paled. "Maliya's in the blood slave trade."

My heart stopped. Maliya was basically a pimp. A drug dealer and a pimp. She was likely guilty of the most inhumane things possible. Theft. Abduction. Rape. Murder. It made me nauseous just thinking about it. There was a reason I didn't agree that vampires deserved a trial. Vamps like Maliya didn't belong in this world.

"Why hasn't anyone done anything about it?" I demanded.

"Because she's smart." Disgust filled Venn's tone. "No matter how many times they investigate her, they never find enough evidence to try her."

"But there have to be witnesses!" I insisted.

"Of course there are," Venn agreed, his eyebrows tight. "But talking to the police is a death sentence for a blood slave. Do you really think any of them will talk?"

I didn't answer. Venn had a point.

"If Cowen's working for Maliya, do you think he stole the locket for her?" Fiona asked Venn.

Venn's fists tightened around the steering wheel. "He must've. The vamps who work for her worship her." He sounded hopeless.

"We'll get it back," I said in determination. "We'll crash the nest, find Cowen, and get your locket back."

I twisted in my seat to look at Fiona, but she bit her lip in uncertainty. I glanced to Venn, waiting for him to agree with me. He just stared straight ahead at the road, looking furious.

"What?" I demanded. "That's the next logical step, isn't it?"

"No," Venn said in a clipped tone, but he didn't care to elaborate his blatant disregard for the idea.

"If we're going to run straight into a vampire nest, we might as well forget about the locket," Fiona said. "We could just break into Matias's and rescue Sondra instead."

Except you're forgetting one thing...

I hated that that was where my mind went first, that *I* needed to get into Maliya's to face Cowen. Obviously if they had the choice between helping me and rescuing Sondra, I was clearly lower on their priority list. But still... I felt an incredibly selfish need to convince them to reconsider.

Venn and Fiona sounded hopeless, but I was still determined as ever. Come hell or high water, I was tracking down the Soulless. And that started with crashing Maliya's vampire nest.

14

"**I**'m leaving."

The words didn't sound right coming out of my mouth. They *should've* felt perfectly natural. I hardly knew Venn or Fiona, so what was this guilty sensation doing in the pit of my stomach?

"Leaving?" Venn's face paled.

We stood on his porch. Fiona had already gone inside, but I couldn't bring myself to join the family. We couldn't help each other anymore. I'd managed on my own for years, and one way or another, I'd manage this alone as well.

I shrugged. "Yeah, I mean, you have to go rescue Sondra. I have to find Cowen. This weekend has been fun…" *If you can call it that.* "…But I have work tomorrow, and—"

"Rae, we haven't made any decisions yet," Venn said, like I was crazy to consider leaving. "I told you I'd help you."

"I know," I replied, "but you've already helped. I can figure the rest out on my own."

"No," Venn said sternly.

I took a step back and crossed my arms. "You don't think I'm strong enough to handle myself?"

"That's not what I meant," he insisted. "I'm not going to go back on my word. I want to help you."

"I told you I'm not a damsel in distress," I reminded him. "I don't need a knight in shining armor."

Venn laughed so loud that it caught me off guard. "Believe me, I'm no knight."

No, of course he's not.

I didn't *want* to leave. For the first time in years, I'd met people I could actually get along with. But there were more important things in life than friends.

"Come inside," Venn suggested. "We'll get everything figured out."

"No," I protested with a sigh. We no longer shared a common goal. There was no solution. "I'll just slow you down. Besides, I have nothing to offer you. I can't even cast a decent spell, so I'm not sure why you want me around—"

"Is that what you really think of yourself?" Venn asked.

He stepped forward to close the distance between us. He stood only inches from me. My breath suspended in my chest, but my heart *pitter-pattered* against my rib cage. What *was* it with my body lately? It totally betrayed me every time Venn got within inches of me.

"You think we don't want you here?" he asked.

I couldn't look into his eyes—his gorgeous dark brown eyes. "Well, yeah. Why would you? We barely know each other."

Venn reached up to brush the hair out of my eyes. His touch was like a warm summer breeze across my skin. Calming. Inviting. Desirable. Damn it all if I didn't welcome the gesture. I caved and looked up at him. He gazed down at me with a soft expression, like he was looking into the eyes of someone he knew, someone he felt comfortable around.

My mouth grew dry the longer I stared up at him. I didn't know what it was about the way he looked at me, but it made my fingers quiver and my knees grow weak. Something in his eyes tugged at my heartstrings, making me feel at home—like this was where I was meant to be.

Was it Synchrony talking?

Don't be ridiculous, Rachel. It's called lust.

Venn glanced down at my fingers with a look in his eyes that said he wanted to take my hand in his. I suddenly felt myself itching to accept that offer, but he didn't make the move. Maybe he thought it was too soon for that type of physical contact. To be fair, it *was* too soon for… pretty much anything. But I still felt like I should be melting into his arms.

It'd been *way* too long since I had a boyfriend.

"Please don't leave yet," Venn begged. "At least stay for food."

Was this guy a mind reader or something? Because in my book, free food was always a good reason to stick around. Somehow, he knew exactly what to say to make me reconsider. But still, the stubborn part of me refused to accept. If I stayed, I wasn't sure I'd ever leave.

"Teagan's a great cook," Venn pressed. "You won't regret it."

Damn Venn with his temptation of a home-cooked meal. It totally beat another afternoon of peanut butter and jelly sandwiches.

"Okay," I caved. "I'll stay for lunch, but after that, I really do have to go home. I can't stay."

"I know," Venn said, but it didn't sound like he was actually agreeing with me. It was more like he was just telling me what I wanted to hear. Venn turned and opened the front door. He stepped aside so that I could enter first.

He might not be a knight in shining armor, but he sure is a gentleman.

The sound of voices in the kitchen caught my attention, and Venn gestured toward the back of the house. We crossed through the dining room and stopped in the doorway to the kitchen. The delicious smell of lasagna filled my nose.

"It's true?" Ryland asked Venn. He leaned against the counter with his arms crossed. "Cowen took our locket to Maliya?"

Venn nodded. "That's where Genevieve tracked him down to."

Teagan peeked into the oven door and then slammed it. I was glad to see she was doing better, but she still looked pale.

She pulled off her oven mitts and threw them on the counter. "I can't believe this!"

"I say we're better off launching a rescue mission into Matias's," Fiona said.

Ryland frowned at her. "And if we're caught without the locket, we're all dead."

"We're dead if we try to get the locket from Maliya, too," Fiona countered.

Teagan looked deep in thought. "Not necessarily."

Wait. They were still going after Cowen?

"What do you mean?" Venn asked.

The anger etched on Ryland's face melted away, like he was catching on to what Teagan was saying.

"Wouldn't they see us coming?" I blurted.

Everyone turned to look at me.

"I mean, because they have the locket," I explained. "It can predict the future, can't it?"

Venn shot me a questioning glance, as if to ask how I knew about it at all, but then he looked to Fiona in realization.

"They wouldn't see us coming," Ryland answered. "Not unless they were watching for us."

"Which they could be," Venn pointed out. "They know we want it back."

Fiona threw her hands up in the air and sighed, as if she was *so* done with everyone's crap. "And this is why we don't have a chance."

"Matias's security is twenty times stronger," Ryland said. "From the moment we step into the building, there will be eighty floors between us and Sondra. Not to mention the cameras on all floors, security guards, restricted areas... The list goes on." He turned to Venn. "You've said yourself Maliya's place is in serious need of a security update."

"Yeah," Venn agreed, "but who needs a security upgrade when no one's stupid enough to break in?"

"Not to mention that we already know our way around Maliya's mansion," Ryland continued, like he hadn't heard him.

I stood silently, wanting so badly to agree with Ryland but not sure if I had a place in the conversation. If we didn't make it to Maliya's, I would never get a chance to confront Cowen.

Venn's jaw tightened. "You can't be serious. We're not doing this."

"Oh, really?" Ryland challenged, straightening. "And I suppose you're going to stop us?"

Venn scoffed. "If you want to run straight into an active vampire nest, be my guest. But we both know you need me to navigate the mansion, and I'm not helping."

"Fine," Ryland said with a shrug. "We'll go without you. Of course, that makes our chances of survival very slim, but—"

"Stop it, Ryland," Venn demanded. "I know you're bluffing. I'm not an idiot."

"You're acting like an idiot!" Ryland boomed, making me jump.

"Calm down, love," Teagan said, reaching for him.

Ryland shrugged her off without even looking at her. His eyes were still trained on Venn beside me. "I mean it. What's your plan, Venn? Leave Sondra to rot in Matias's tower? You know he won't let her go without getting what he wants. And if we don't show up with it, he'll force her to work for him or kill her. Or are you planning to barge into one of his highly-secured skyscrapers and bust her out without anyone noticing? We can't handle Matias on our own, but we *can* handle Maliya. Besides, once we hand off the locket to Matias, it's not our problem anymore. Maliya will go after him, and Matias will let Sondra go free."

"You really think that?" Venn asked flatly. "You know Maliya doesn't play fair. It won't matter if we don't have the locket; she'd still kill us for stealing from her."

Ryland shrugged. "Then I guess we're just going to have to get in and out of there without getting caught."

Venn gritted his teeth, his nostrils flaring. His skin rippled as if he was fighting the urge to shift.

"Maybe…" Fiona said cautiously. "Maybe Ryland's right. Maybe this is our only option."

"See?" Ryland pressed. "Even Fiona agrees with me."

Teagan sighed and shot Venn a somber expression. "I agree, too."

I would've put my vote in, but it would've been a selfish vote. And I was pretty sure my vote wasn't needed anyway.

Venn fumed, pressing his hands to his face and then raking his fingers through his hair. He took a long inhale and then let it all out in a *whoosh*. "I can't believe we're doing this. Fine. I will help you. I just hope you know what you're getting yourselves into."

Hope surged through my chest.

We're back in business!

15

S neaking into a vampire nest in the dead of night should've scared the shit out of me. Instead, my heart pounded in exhilaration. This was way cooler than sitting on rooftops hoping to find trouble. This time, I was *causing* trouble. And I was pretty darn proud of it.

We waited until nightfall to crash the nest. Vampire nests were packed during the day since they were all sleeping to avoid the sunlight that burned their flesh. At night, vamps were either working or hanging out at bars or casinos, giving us the perfect opportunity to slip inside unnoticed.

According to Venn, most of Maliya's business took place inside the mansion, but the worst of her henchmen would be out "recruiting" blood slaves or making deals. The place wouldn't be completely empty, but there'd be significantly fewer vamps to risk running into. Plus, Venn guessed that we'd find the locket near the sleeping quarters, which would be virtually deserted by now.

How he knew so much about Maliya's mansion, I didn't know. By the look Fiona shot me when I started to ask about it, I was pretty sure it was a story for another day.

We were all dressed in black, making us almost invisible against the night. The moon was high above us, casting a dull glow across the forest, just enough to make out the shadows of the trees. Ryland, Fiona, Venn, and I wove through the trees, careful not to make any noise. Teagan hadn't wanted to stay behind, despite the fact that she still looked like she needed rest, but Ryland insisted on it. He finally convinced her when he pointed out that her human heartbeat was enough to break our cover.

The mansion was tucked in the forest a half-mile off the road just outside of Nocton. The trees stopped at a brick wall surrounding the property.

"You're up, Rae," Ryland hissed through the darkness.

I didn't think Ryland trusted me, not when I agreed to play my part only if Venn helped me navigate the mansion after we retrieved the locket. Ryland was adamantly against that, saying he wouldn't let Venn hang back for me, but Venn insisted it was his own choice. Ryland finally caved, since I was their only hope of avoiding security cameras and alarms.

I jumped and shifted mid-air, grateful to be back in my own enchanted clothing. I flapped my wings until I was high enough to perch on the edge of the wall, which stood at least ten feet high. I already knew what the mansion would look like from the image I saw in the salt at Genevieve's, but that quick glance wasn't enough to truly prepare me for the beauty of the property.

I faced the West corner of the mansion, where the windows were dark. A vast garden surrounded by a manicured lawn stretched out toward the back of the property. It met up with perfectly trimmed bushes lining the side of the building. The front exterior was lit up like there were tiny little stars embedded into the brick. A long driveway circled the fountain near the main doors and seemed to go on forever before it reached a big iron gate by the road. The mansion itself was styled with white brick, and several towers with balconies reached up three stories. The building was divided into at least five different sections, each one bigger than the last. It seemed to go on for miles.

The property was quiet. Almost too quiet.

This is going to be a piece of cake.

Once I had a chance to take in the grandeur of the mansion, I turned to focusing on the smaller details. I spotted two security cameras hanging from the wall, pointing at the lawn. Another was secured next to the balcony doors looking over the garden. I scanned the area again, just to make sure, but it looked like I only had three security cameras to deal with.

I launched myself into the air and landed on the wall beside the first camera. I shifted back into human form and balanced myself on the edge of the wall above the camera. My feet dangled on either side of it. I grabbed the camera and twisted slowly, making sure not to make any sudden movements. I didn't want to catch anyone's eye if they were watching the security footage. The camera pivoted on its mount with ease. I pointed it toward the opposite end of the lawn and then shifted back into my raven form and did the same with the other two security cameras.

I glided over the top of the wall and circled around my co-conspirators. As soon as I cocked my head at them, they sprang into action. Ryland laced his fingers together and helped boost Venn over the wall. He landed quietly in the grass on the other side. Next, Fiona stepped into Ryland's hands, and she pulled herself over the wall. Venn helped her down on the other side.

Ryland backed up and took a running start. He launched himself upward and just barely caught the top of the wall with the ends of his fingers. He pulled himself up easily. Frankly, I was impressed. This guy must've been a champion at chin-ups. He jumped down from the wall and rolled onto the grass to slow his momentum.

Nobody spoke. Instead, we communicated through small hand gestures. Venn pointed to a balcony on the second level, and Ryland shot him a thumbs up. Then Venn gestured to one of the five chimneys. I nodded before he, Ryland, and Fiona hurried away from me across the lawn.

The plan was simple. I'd fly down the chimney to get inside undetected. Meanwhile, Venn, Ryland, and Fiona would climb the balcony. Once I reached the target room, I'd unlock the door from the inside to avoid triggering any alarms.

I flapped my wings and rose high above the mansion, my eyes fixed on the chimney. My heart pounded, partially because I feared what might be at the bottom of it—perhaps a room filled with hungry vampires—and partially from the thrill.

Bring on the vampires.

Without hesitation, I dove into the deep darkness. The chimney was cramped. It certainly wasn't wide enough to spread my wings. Despite clawing at the bricks to slow my fall, I spiraled downward, slamming into the sides and picking up mounds of soot as I went. I landed at the bottom in a pile of ash with a hard *thud.* The wind knocked out of me, but I ignored the burn in my chest as I righted myself, prepared for whatever might be waiting for me.

I was relieved to see that the room was empty. I stepped out onto a brick base that surrounded the fireplace. The room was dark, but I could make out shadows of bookcases and a long desk in the corner. It appeared as if I'd entered a study, which was exactly where Venn had told me I'd end up.

I shifted back to human form, ignoring the soot in my hair, and hurried to the door. I opened it a crack and peered down the hall. It was deserted.

Slowly, I pulled the door open and scurried down the hallway to the door on the end. It was open, revealing a long flight of stairs leading to the basement. I descended the stairs, my footsteps far too loud in the empty stairwell. At the bottom, a long, dark hallway stretched in front of me. The only light seeped in from an open door toward the end of the hall.

My heart pounded, and I welcomed the adrenaline. It'd be nice to get in at least one vampire ass-whooping tonight. Except for the part where Venn told me to avoid a fight unless absolutely necessary. And even then, he didn't want me killing any vamps. He said it'd only earn me a target on my back. Not like that was anything new, but I'd do my best to follow his instructions.

I inched forward, making sure my footsteps were soft as I passed door after door. I counted each door as I went, knowing I needed to pass three on the right before I reached my destination. I only crept closer to the door with the light on.

Finally, I reached out for the door I needed. Just as I twisted the knob, the door at the end of the hall swung open wider.

"Hey!" a deep voice shouted.

Instinct told me to spring into action, but instead I froze. Plan B: If caught, just play the part. According to Venn, so many people milled around this place that most wouldn't give it a second thought, but they *would* come after you if you ran.

"What are you doing down here?" A huge guy emerged from the room and locked eyes with me. Even in the dim light, I could make out his pale skin and silver eyes.

I could totally take him. Maybe. Probably not. He was built like a bodybuilder.

"Laundry, sir," I lied, using my best submissive tone. I dropped my gaze to the guy's chest. Venn told me not to look the vamps straight in the eye.

Bodybuilder glared down at me disapprovingly. "Laundry runs during the day. You should know that."

"Sorry, sir," I said, improvising. "I'm new. I came in with the last group of blood slaves and was assigned to laundry duty. I just wanted to learn my way around."

"I thought they had a tour yesterday." Bodybuilder inhaled, as if searching for my scent. When he didn't find it, a smile crept across his face. He could tell I was a shifter, and he knew I'd make one heck of a meal.

"There were some reassignments," I lied. "I missed the first tour."

Bodybuilder stepped forward, gazing at me like he wanted to eat me. Which was probably true. "So, you haven't been assigned to anyone yet?"

I stepped back, still clinging on to my submissive act. "I thought you weren't supposed to feed off anyone but your own. Isn't Maliya strict about that?"

Bodybuilder scoffed. "She doesn't care unless you've already been assigned."

"I'm being assigned soon," I said. "I'll need my strength."

I loved how frightened I sounded. It was damn convincing.

"Assignments won't be for another week." Bodybuilder said, taking another step closer to me. "You'll regain your strength by then."

"Won't you lose your job?" I pulled at any strings I could. Not because I was scared, but because I didn't want this to get messy.

"I'll bring that up with Maliya myself," Bodybuilder snarled. "You should really learn to keep your mouth shut, shifter girl. You'll not want to *ever* forget your place here."

Bodybuilder lunged for me so fast that I didn't have time to react. His strong arm gripped my wrist, and his fangs elongated. I quickly calculated my options. On the one hand, I could play the part. On the other, this sure fell into the *absolutely necessary* category.

I'd already been bit once. And damn, it felt great. No one ever told me it would feel so good, like all the worries in the world didn't matter. If I'd let that vamp feed on me any longer, I might've never wanted him to stop. Maybe there was a reason blood slaves didn't run. It was like a drug. But I wasn't a druggie. No one got anywhere near my blood without my consent.

I swung my elbow upward. It connected with Bodybuilder's nose with a sickening *crunch*. His hands flew to his face. I didn't waste any time swinging my knee into his groin as hard as I could. He let out a grunt and sank to the ground, but not before reaching out and grabbing my arm, pulling me to the floor with inhuman strength. Pain shot across my shoulder as my body slammed into the ground. Bodybuilder jumped on top of me, his fangs heading straight for my neck.

I struggled against him, my breathing ragged. Maybe attacking was a bad move. A vamp of Cowen's size I could handle, but I didn't have the strength to combat this guy. He held my wrists against the ground and used his weight to keep my hips against the floor. It all happened so fast, and I mentally screamed at myself for letting him get me in this position. Rule one of fighting vampires: Don't ever let them get the upper hand. If you do, you're dead.

Shifter magic tingled through my body. My wrists shrank out of Bodybuilder's arms, and within a second, I was free. Bodybuilder nearly squashed me, but he caught himself. I managed to squeeze out from beneath his giant belly. I dove for him and slashed my talons across the top of his head. It was enough to make him pause, though he didn't cry out in pain as I expected him to. I was about to go for his eyes—always the eyes; those were the best part—when Bodybuilder's arm shot out and he scooped me out of the air.

For the first time all night, my heart pounded not from the excitement but from fear. Bodybuilder drew his arm back and whipped me against the wall. My small raven body slumped to the ground as I gasped for air, my back throbbing. Bodybuilder stood and stalked toward me, a triumphant smirk fixed to his face.

I didn't have time to catch my breath. If Bodybuilder got ahold of me, he was going to suck me two pints from dry. I was sure of it.

Not today, asshole!

He loomed over me and reached down. Before his hands could touch my feathers, I sprang out of his reach. Within a second, I was already shifting back into human form. Using all my strength, I jumped and kicked off the wall then spun mid-air, my leg aimed at his face. My heel cracked against the side of his head.

Bodybuilder's entire body flew sideways. His head slammed into the wall, and he slumped to the ground, unconscious.

I gazed down at him for only a second, trying to decide if I should leave him, kill him, or hide the body. I didn't know how long I had before someone else came down here, so I didn't want to leave him. Venn made it clear I wasn't to kill anyone, so that was out of the question. *If we kill one of them, they'll come after us with an army*, he'd said. If I left him here, I only had to worry about one vamp with a vengeance. Which meant I had to hide him and hope he didn't wake up anytime soon.

I hooked my arms under his. With all my strength, I dragged the huge dude down the hall and dropped him into a storage closet.

A moment later, the sound of footsteps reached my ears. My whole body tensed, alert. Without another thought, I raced into the room I'd intended to enter earlier. It was so dark that I couldn't see. Instinctively, I ducked into the first hiding place I could find with my hands. Fabric brushed by my face as I crouched in a narrow cubby space. Curtains, maybe?

"Dave?" I heard a deep voice outside the room. "Where'd you go? I brought you a soda."

My guess was soda was code word for "fresh blood."

Footsteps continued down the hall, and then I heard the sound of a door swinging open. Every inch of my body tensed as the footsteps neared the room I hid in. I held my breath, and my fingers curled into fists. Maybe this whole thing was a bad idea. We should've just forgotten about the locket.

Retrieve the locket, and Venn will help you get to Cowen, I reminded myself.

The door swung open. I squeezed my eyes shut, like that might make me invisible.

Don't be scared, Rachel. Vampires don't scare you.

True. They didn't scare me... when I had a chance at escape. But here, my only chance at escape was the door I'd come through, the door a vampire was standing in right now.

"Dave?" the vampire called loud and clear.

I pictured him glancing around the dark room, but I didn't open my eyes to check. I just held my breath, feeling like my lungs might explode. Thank God I wasn't human. He'd hear my heart pounding for sure.

The door clicked shut, and I finally let my breath out. It felt like the first breath I'd taken in the last five minutes. Slowly, I emerged from my hiding spot.

My eyes finally adjusted to the darkness. A small window set high in the wall let in a small amount of light. I noticed several large appliances lining the far wall. When I glanced back to where I'd been hiding, I realized I'd been behind a row of clothes hanging off a closet rod. I'd known I was headed for the laundry room, but I pictured a small room with one washer and dryer, not a huge room fit for a resort. Then again, I suppose they needed it when they had a house the size of a hotel.

I crossed the room and stopped when I reached the opposite wall. Just inches above my head, a square tube came down from the ceiling.

Bet they thought their laundry chute was safe. They should know better than that.

I shifted into raven form and flew up to the laundry chute, wedging myself in. Like the chimney, it wasn't large enough for me to spread my wings in, but I was able to wiggle my way up by digging my talons into the wood on one side and pressing my back against the other.

The chute was cramped and stuffy, and I swore I only moved an inch a minute, but eventually, I reached the top. I kicked at the door, and it popped open. It took a crazy ninja move to launch myself out of the chute without falling all the way back down. Somehow, I managed to rustle my way out, though a couple of my feathers were now crooked.

I shifted and glanced around the room bathed in darkness. It was vast, with doors heading off in all directions. I guessed one of them had to be the bathroom, and another a closet. The two double doors must've led out into the hall.

A king bed stood at the center of the room, with a plush chasse situated at the end of it, and a chandelier hung from the tall ceiling. A long line of windows lined one wall, all covered in dark black curtains that had been pulled aside to offer a view of the garden.

Voices in the hall reached my ears, sending another surge of adrenaline through my veins. Getting caught was *not* part of the plan. I wouldn't be able to talk my way out of what I was doing in Maliya's bedroom. I scurried under the bed and tried to control my breathing, but it was shallow and ragged. I covered my mouth to keep from making any kind of noise.

To my relief, the voices continued down the hall. I still waited at least another minute before I crawled out from under the bed and got to my feet. I rushed over to the glass doors leading onto the balcony and twisted the lock. Ryland, Fiona, and Venn hurried over from where they hid in the shadows when I opened the door.

Venn's hands were on the side of my face immediately, his eyes roaming mine for sign of injury. When he didn't spot any in the darkness, he pulled me into a hug, sending my heart pounding so quickly that I was sure he could feel it. His breath rushed across my face, and my chest pressed against his. My whole body warmed in his arms. He held on to me protectively, and for a moment, I truly felt safe in his arms—albeit at risk of a heart attack.

This was the perfect time to make some snarky comment about how he could at least take me on a date first, but I held my tongue. I rather preferred the comforting embrace.

"Thank God," Venn whispered. "We thought you'd been caught."

"What took you so long?" Ryland hissed.

"I fell in," I deadpanned.

"What?" He looked completely confused.

I shook my head as I drew away from Venn. "Never mind. Let's find that locket."

We all split off in different directions. I headed straight for the jewelry on the vanity across the room, Fiona silently opened drawers on a dresser nearby, and Ryland felt around on the bed.

Because she's totally keeping it under her sheets. It's not a freaking diary.

"Over here," Venn whispered. He cocked his finger for us to follow him.

Venn led us over to a door with a keypad above the knob. He took a deep breath.

"How can he know the combination?" I whispered to Fiona.

She just gave me a shrug, but something told me she knew exactly how. Venn knew *way* too much about this mansion, about Maliya. It wasn't hard to figure out why, but I didn't want to believe it. And that wasn't exactly the kind of thing you just brought up in casual conversation.

The keypad beeped twice. Victory surged through me, but the feeling didn't last long. Venn cursed under his breath. My face fell. Those weren't the beeps of a successful combination. It was an error message.

"I thought you knew the passcode," Ryland whispered.

"I did." Venn scowled at him. "But I also told you it could've changed. There was more than one reason I didn't want to go through with this plan."

"So we can't get in?" Ryland sounded less than pleased.

I was feeling pretty much the same way. This plan was never going to work in our favor. How could I have thought it would?

"I get three tries. Let me try something else." Venn placed his fingers at the corner of his eyes, like he was thinking really hard.

Seconds ticked by. The room was eerily silent apart from everyone's breathing. I was half considering jumping forward and entering a random combination myself—even though there were probably a million combinations.

Finally, Venn opened his eyes and input a four-digit code. To my surprise, the lock disengaged. Venn twisted the knob, and the door swung open. When Venn said we'd have to break in to Maliya's vault, I pictured a bank vault with safety deposit boxes or something. I didn't picture a freaking room full of treasure.

Soft lighting illuminated the room when we stepped inside. It was the size of a large walk-in closet, with display cases lining the walls. Expensive jewelry sparkled beneath the glass. When I said expensive, I meant *expensive*. Like, probably in the millions. There was even a tiara placed in the center of the display case on the left, embedded with hundreds of shining diamonds. It wasn't just jewelry, either. I spotted a knife and an old coin, too. I wasn't sure of the significance of it all, but everything either looked old or worth a fortune. It took my breath away.

"Be quick," Venn warned.

I stepped further into the room, searching for any sign of a locket. My heart leapt in my chest when the door beeped. I whirled around. We all exchanged a quick, alarmed expression, but it only lasted a split second. The door began swinging shut on its own.

"Run!" Ryland commanded the same time Fiona cursed under her breath.

Everyone sprang toward the moving door at the same time. Ryland made it out first, followed by Venn. I sprinted behind Fiona. Just before I made it to the door, my eyes caught sight of a golden locket in one of the display cases. I didn't think twice of my next move. I reached for the glass and flipped the top up. I snatched the locket out of the case.

Fiona cried out in pain. The door had caught her on her way out, pinning her shoulder to the frame. There was no way I was fitting through the opening behind her. I shifted in a flash and scooped up the locket in my beak. Fiona managed to wiggle herself free, no doubt thanks to someone on the other side tugging at her.

I didn't question my chances. I jumped for the crack in the door. The edge of the door brushed by my feathers. I thought for sure it would squash me and cut my head off or something, but by some miracle, I slipped out of the door with my head still intact.

Venn had stopped in the middle of the room and was ushering everyone toward the balcony. Fiona held on to her shoulder and sprinted behind Ryland. Venn's eyes met mine, and I spread my wings. Venn took it as a cue to whirl around and follow behind everyone else. He knew I was right behind him.

We did it!

I couldn't believe it.

Doors banged open behind me. I didn't have time to react before something wrapped tightly around my leg and dragged me out of the air.

I spoke too soon.

The blood drained from my face as my eyes connected with Venn's. Horror washed over his expression, but he'd already taken the leap over the balcony. His hands reached out, desperate to grab on to anything to come back for me, but his body betrayed him. Within a mere split second, he was gone.

Somebody grabbed me by the back of the neck so hard I couldn't move. I feared whoever had ahold of me might crush the vertebra in my neck if I did. Strong hands lifted my raven form until I dangled several feet off the ground. My vision began to blur due to lack of blood flow, but I saw enough to count at least five male vampires surrounding me. One of them rushed past me and leapt from the balcony, pursuing my friends.

And then a woman's voice reached my ears. A thin figure with wide hips that swayed with each step entered through the double doors. "What do we have here, boys?"

Maliya.

I swallowed deeply and locked my jaw tight. The necklace hung from my beak.

Never let a vampire get the upper hand, I repeated. *If you do, you're dead.*

I didn't know what would happen next, but one thing was for certain: No matter what, I was already dead.

16

I had a rule about death. If I ever faced it, I was fighting back until my last breath.

My eyes darted to the lamp on the bedside table mere feet from me. Within a split second, I shifted. My hand shot out and clamped around the lamp, and I swung it above my head with as much force as I could. It slammed into the vampire's head behind me and snapped at the base.

Big Bad Vamp released his hold on me just enough that I was able to duck and spin out of his grasp. I sprinted for the balcony doors, but a shadow leapt in front of me. All I saw was orange hair glistening in the moonlight before strong hands slammed into my chest, sending me flying backward across the room. I landed on the bed, bouncing across the mattress as all the wind left my chest.

Before I had a chance to process what had just happened, another vamp with dark hair and a square jaw was already on top of me, reaching out for the locket hanging from my mouth. One hand pressed down hard on my throat while the other pulled at the necklace. I bit down on the chain as my fingers reached for the other bedside table, blindly searching for another weapon. My left hand curled around something cool and hard. I swung it toward the vamp's head.

Before it could connect with his skull, the ginger guy leapt onto the bed. His hand shot out of the darkness and grabbed my wrist. He threw my arm sideways with such force that I couldn't control my own body's momentum. The object in my hand crashed into the edge of the table, and the sound of breaking glass met my ears. Cool water rushed over my hand, and I realized it was a vase.

Ginger plunged his fingers into my hair and wrenched the strands backward as he squeezed my lower jaw, trying to force my teeth apart. I refused, welcoming the fire across my skull and the intense pressure on my jaw more than I welcomed failure.

My fingers tightened around the broken vase. With all my strength, I thrust it upward. The sharp, ragged edges sank into Ginger's chest. In an instant, his hands in my hair and on my jaw disappeared. Ash rained down on me.

Square Jaw's eyes darted momentarily to where his friend had just been. It was enough of a distraction that I was able to swipe his hand off my throat. I thrust my hips upward, spinning our bodies until I had him pinned down on the bed.

A look of desire crossed his eyes, and he opened his mouth. But he didn't even get a chance to take a breath before the shards of glass in my hand entered his heart. I didn't stick around to enjoy his body disintegrating to ash. I leapt off the bed and shifted, aiming for the balcony doors. The locket still hung in my beak.

Without warning, my skull slammed into a solid, invisible barrier. My neck twisted, and pain jolted through it as the ligaments twisted. I fell to the ground in a daze. The room swam around me as a strong hand reached out and curled around the back of my neck. Big Bad Vamp squeezed tightly. I swore he was a second away from snapping my neck. It freaking *hurt*.

Maliya only laughed and stepped forward. Her long dark hair swayed around her. She snatched the locket out of my beak. Though I tried to hold on, it slipped through my grasp.

"Shift," she commanded in an unforgiving tone.

I hesitated. I didn't take well to those types of demands.

The hold on my neck tightened again. I did as I was told. My body lengthened, and my wings grew into arms. My nostrils flared. Almost immediately, Maliya's hand cracked across the side of my face. Pain pulsed across my skin, but I didn't make a sound.

Maliya leaned in close to me. She stood several inches higher, but I guessed she was wearing heels under her dark red dress. "How *dare* you," she hissed, sounding strangely reminiscent of a snake. "How dare you steal from me!"

My captor hurled me across the floor, his fingers leaving my neck as I flew through the air. I landed with a *thud* and skidded across the carpet past Maliya and straight between the double doors leading to the hall. I was already dizzy from the earlier impact, but my headache intensified at the sudden movement. I glanced toward the balcony and finally saw what I had missed a moment ago. The doors were shut, the glass blocking my only chance of escape.

A vampire by the doors—the one who'd shut them, I assumed—stepped forward. *Cowen.* He had a look of fury etched into his eyes. There was no doubt in my mind that he recognized me.

Maliya knelt to my level, fuming. "Who sent you? Who are the other people you were with, and how did you manage to get the passcode to my vault?"

I held my tongue. I may be going down, but I wasn't taking Venn and the rest of them with me. They'd been nothing but nice to me. It was almost a glimpse into the family I once had, before the vampires stole them from me.

Shock riveted through me when Maliya grabbed me by the shirt and hauled me to my feet. I stumbled backward, and she slammed me into the wall.

In the hallway light, I finally got a good look at her. She was flawlessly beautiful, with long dark lashes, high cheek bones, and manicured eyebrows. Her skin was pale, but not as pale as the other vampires, as if her skin had a darker hue during her time as a human. Her black hair fell in perfect waves around her shoulders. Her long-sleeved dress gave her breasts the perfect lift—to the point where I was a little jealous. She looked like she might be in her forties, and *my* breasts weren't even that perky. Everything about her screamed *cougar*, though there were the obvious silver eyes and elongated fangs that said *vampire*. Who knew, though? She could be a vampire cougar. Probably was.

Maliya's snarl turned into a sardonic smile. "Don't want to talk?" she taunted. "Fine with me. It's not going to save your sorry shifter ass anyway."

This bitch has no right to talk to me like that!

My head snapped forward, cracking into hers. Her head reeled backward, but it barely looked like she felt a thing. Meanwhile, my head and neck throbbed. Big Bad Vamp stepped forward, but she held up a hand to stop him before he could get to me. I was probably more shocked than anyone. I hadn't planned on head-butting her.

Maliya's silver eyes slowly roamed over me. "I've been looking for you for a long time, *raven shifter*. How fortunate that you just happened to find me on your own."

Looking for me? Great. Who'd I kill?

"You *are* the Ravenite, aren't you?" Maliya accused in a smooth, even tone.

Ugh. That name again.

I didn't even bother responding. I wouldn't play into her games.

"Will you kill her?" Cowen asked.

I'd kill all these jackasses first.

A smile spread across Maliya's face, but she didn't tear her gaze off mine. "No. That would be too easy. I want the Ravenite to *suffer*."

What had I gotten myself into?

Maliya dropped her grip on my shirt and whirled around. She unclasped the locket in her hand and secured it around her neck, placing it over several other necklaces that hung there. "Lock her up. Don't provide her any food or water. I'll be back to deal with her later."

Big Bad Vamp grabbed on to both of my arms as Maliya headed down the hall with Cowen at her heels. I kicked my legs into the air, trying to struggle out of his grasp, but he was too strong. He squeezed my arms together behind my back until I thought my shoulders might pop out of their sockets.

"What'd I do to you?" I blurted. I hadn't intended to speak, but for the life of me, I couldn't figure out what I'd done to get her attention. I mean, besides try to steal from her and head-butt her in the face. But she spoke of me—of the Ravenite—like she already had something against me long before tonight. "Did I kill one of your security guards or something?"

That was very possible. I'd killed a lot of vampires. I couldn't exactly keep track.

Maliya spun toward me and was back in front of me in an instant, her breath rushing across my face. "No," she snarled. "You killed my *husband*."

Every muscle in my body froze at her words. I really had gotten myself in too deep. Whatever torture she had in store for me, it wasn't going to be pretty.

And still, I couldn't seem to bite my tongue. The next words slipped out without my approval. "I'm sure he deserved it."

Big. Mistake.

A scream ripped out of my lungs and echoed down the hall when Maliya's fangs sank into my neck and a shock of vampire venom entered my veins.

17

Excruciating pain seared through my body. I could hardly focus on my limbs, let alone my own thoughts. Each time my consciousness broke through the pain, I racked my brain trying to decide if there was a stronger word than *bitch* to describe Maliya. I'd run into my fair share of bitches in my lifetime. I survived high school, after all. But *bitch* was such a petty little word. Maliya was pure evil.

She barely bit me for a second. It was hardly deep enough to bleed and wasn't long enough to change me—just enough to make me suffer. She knew exactly how much venom would keep me just on the edge of consciousness so that I could feel every nerve ending in my body ablaze. It started at my skin, the hot, widespread pain of being cast into the fires of Hell. Then it moved to my muscles, where the pain transformed into sharp, repetitive jabs. It was like being stabbed over and over again with long surgical needles on every inch of my body. And then it reached my bones, where it felt as if someone was cutting them open with a chainsaw and shoving metal rods through them.

I almost wished the pain meant something, like I'd come out on the other side of it with flawless beauty and immortality. But I'd rather die than join the ranks of the most hated and heartless species alive. Still, immortality beat this fiery pain burning through my veins.

It seemed like days that I'd been stuck inside my own head, trying to claw my way through agony. Eventually, the pain eased to a dull ache, and my mind cleared enough that I managed to force my eyes open.

The first thing I noticed was a charge like electricity buzzing through the air. I was in a small room no bigger than my bathroom, lying on a stone floor with identical walls on three sides of me. A layer of bars blocked me from a larger room that spanned beyond my cell.

I lifted my head, which was still foggy from the venom, and squinted into the darkness. There wasn't much of a room outside my cell. It was more like a hallway, with at least a dozen other cells identical to mine lining the walls on either side. A soft light cast shadows across the room. When my eyes finally focused, I saw that the light came from a single candle near a large metal door. A vampire sat in a wooden chair next to it.

A guard.

His eyes were closed, like he didn't take his job seriously. I couldn't help but think that the stone cells and candlelight were all there for show, just to give me the creeps. I mean, who had a freaking *dungeon* in their house?

I had to remind myself that Maliya literally had blood *slaves* living here. This was probably where they went to get punished.

I pushed myself to my elbows, but I could barely make my muscles comply to my demands. This was a thousand times worse than last time. It was less like I was recovering from a marathon and more like I was a cadaver waking from the morgue.

My tongue felt like sandpaper. I tried to lick my lips, but there was nothing left to wet them with. They were dry and cracked, like my throat. My stomach twisted in hunger. I didn't know how long I'd been here.

My thoughts flickered to Venn, the look in his eyes when he realized I'd been caught and that he couldn't save me. I wanted to believe he'd come for me, but it didn't matter how much he knew about this mansion. There was no way he was getting down in this dungeon—past Maliya, who now had the power to predict the future, past the security cameras, and past the guard at the end of the hall. I wouldn't be surprised if there was another guard posted outside the door.

Not to mention that I was pretty sure Ryland would talk anyone out of coming back for me. I mean, he wasn't a terrible person or anything, but he seemed like the kind of guy who wouldn't risk his family for a girl he just met. I wished I could believe Venn would defy Ryland's instructions and come after me like a true knight in shining armor, but I wasn't holding my breath.

Which meant I was on my own. I'd shift, slip through the bars, attack the guard, and figure out the rest as I went. It was a long shot considering my whole body trembled in weakness, but I held on to my slim chance of survival.

Shifter magic tingled across my skin. As quickly as it came, it disappeared. What the hell? I tried again, but it was like trying to run through a brick wall. My skin rippled, but the change never happened. Was it the vampire venom? No. That shouldn't affect shifter magic.

I tried again. The strange buzzing I sensed intensified as if pushing back against my magic. Terror consumed me when I realized the energy in the air was a strong enchantment keeping me from shifting. Strange. I'd never felt someone else's magic before. I'd heard it was possible, but I'd never been strong enough to recognize it.

Hopelessness consumed me, sinking like a rock in my gut. I curled my knees to my chest as every curse word I knew flew through my mind. I screwed up *big* time. I should've gone after Jenna sooner. I shouldn't have begged Venn for help. I should've let the vamps take the locket so I could escape. I should've fought harder. I should've done a lot of things… Then I wouldn't be in this mess.

Who was I kidding? This was where my search for Jenna was always going to end. I was actively pursuing the Soulless, which meant I was going to die at the hands of a vamp one way or another. It was kind of in the job description.

I pushed the unkind words I had for myself from my head. My mind drifted to a simpler time. I was seven, pumping my legs on the swings at the park near our house, trying to swing higher than Jenna.

I was eight, running through the sprinkler in our back yard on a hot summer day while Jenna chased me around with a pool noodle.

I was ten, sitting in front of the mirror in Jenna's room while she dusted blush on my face and nearly impaled me in the eye with a mascara brush.

I was twelve, sneaking out to the treehouse after bedtime to meet up with Jenna and "practice magic." Mom and Dad didn't approve of magic, so mine and my sister's curiosity had to go under the radar. We didn't know then that I was a witch.

My head snapped upward as it hit me. What was I *doing*? I was a witch. I could get out of this place on my own. I mean, I didn't know a spell to unlock jail cells or anything, but I was desperate. Maybe that was enough to save my life…

I tried not to make any sudden movements so that the guard wouldn't notice. First things first—get rid of the guard. I was too weak to take him one-on-one.

Slowly, I rose to my feet. My whole body tensed with nerves. There was nowhere in the cell to rest my shivering body, not even a cot to sit down on. So I stood there with my knees quivering and my hands curled into tight fists. I narrowed my eyes at the sleeping guard, focusing intently on aiming my magic at him like a laser beam. Maybe if I concentrated hard enough, he'd have a heart attack or burst into flame or something.

Several minutes passed, and… it was incredibly anticlimactic. The guard didn't move, and all my concentration did was give me a headache.

So maybe I couldn't make vampires spontaneously combust. Instead, I turned my attention to the lock on my cell. It was my only other option. I didn't know the incantation to unlock a door—I'd never needed it before—but it couldn't be that hard. I was sure any low witch was capable of it.

I stepped forward and reached out until my hands closed around the cold metal of the lock. I pictured the locking mechanism disengaging and the door swinging open, but when I pushed at the cell door, it remained firmly in place.

"Come on," I growled under my breath. *I can do this.*

The tension in my head intensified. Okay, so maybe it wouldn't work with all this negative energy pulsing through me. Freaking Synchrony. How was I supposed to channel positive energy in my situation?

Just try it.

I closed my eyes and took a deep breath, forcing out the tension in my head. But all it did was transfer that tension to my shoulders. I tried again.

This has to work.

I pushed at my cell door again. It didn't budge. My jaw tightened, and I resisted the urge to kick the metal bars.

This is dumb! I bet Synchrony isn't even real. It's the freaking enchantment working against me.

The sound of a lock slipping open echoed through the dungeon. It startled the guard awake and sent me stumbling backward into the far wall of my cell.

"This shouldn't take long, Cowen," I heard a female voice say on the other side of the door. "You'll have plenty of time to make your flight to Seattle. You can tell Ellwood all about the raven bitch once you get there."

Seconds later, the door at the end of the hall burst open. Maliya entered the dungeon, flanked by four male vampires. Through the darkness, I recognized Cowen, Bodybuilder, and Big Bad Vamp beside her. The other guy was new. Maliya's heels clicked against the stone in a quick staccato that matched the pace of my pounding heart.

I am not afraid, I told myself, despite every biological process assuring me I was. I ignored the warnings my own body was giving me and straightened in my cell. My eyes locked on Maliya's, and my face softened into a perfectly indifferent expression. The sound of her footsteps stopped once she was within arm's distance of my cell. I could've reached through the bars and clawed at her face.

"Let her out, Dave," Maliya commanded in a cold tone. She never broke eye contact with me.

Dave—a.k.a. Bodybuilder—stepped forward. He glared at me with a hard expression. No doubt it was more than a little embarrassing that a huge vampire like him lost a fight to a little girl. I expected him to whisper some sort of threat, but he didn't speak. He simply unlocked my cell and stepped aside.

"Get her," Maliya instructed before turning her back to me.

Dave reached into the cell. Though I ducked out of the way on instinct, he had me in his hands in under a second. His grip was so tight on my arms that I was sure he'd leave hand-shaped bruises behind. I stumbled out of my cell, a thousand curses thick on the end of my tongue. I didn't speak. I didn't need to add fuel to the fire, though I would very much enjoy seeing how that would go down.

"Bring it in, Vincent," Maliya called to the guard.

Dave hauled me down the long hallway, even though he didn't have to. I would've walked on my own if he let me, but the more I struggled to regain my footing, the more he fought against me.

The guard appeared in the doorway, dragging a chair behind him. It was the size of my dad's old plushy recliner, only it was made entirely of wood. Two of the legs screeched across the stone floor, and the other two connected with the ground with a loud *thud* when he dropped it into place at the end of the line of cells.

I spotted the shackles connected to the arms and legs of the chair, and that's when I freaked out. My legs thrashed, and my arms flailed. My elbow caught Dave in the nose. Two of the other vampires reached for me and held my legs. Maliya just stood there with a smirk on her face, watching her henchmen force me into the chair.

"Get off me!" I screamed.

Of course, they all ignored me. The cool metal of the shackles touched my skin, and I heard the sound of them locking. I continued to struggle, though it was clearly no use. An icy cold hand shot out and grabbed my face, squeezing my cheeks until my teeth hurt.

"Stop!" Maliya demanded of me.

Despite the urge to spit in her face, I did as I was told. If I complied, maybe she'd have a little mercy on me.

She's a vampire, I reminded myself. *They have no mercy.*

"This entire room is enchanted," she warned. "Don't even think about shifting. It won't help you get free."

Maliya dropped her hand from my face, but she leaned in so close that I could smell the copper on her breath. I noticed the locket hanging from her neck. The candlelight near the door cast dancing shadows across her face. I pressed my head against the back of the chair, trying to get as far away from her as possible.

"Ivan Valerik," she whispered, accenting each syllable.

Huh? Was that some sort of incantation?

"Say his name," she instructed.

I kept my mouth shut.

Her palm cracked across the side of my face. My cheek stung, but after the pain I'd endured with her vampire venom, I barely felt it.

"Say. His. Name!" she shouted. "Ivan. Valerik!"

"Go to hell." The words slipped out before I could stop myself. But damn, they felt good.

Maliya plunged her hand into my hair and yanked back until my face tilted upward to look into her eyes. Her hold was so tight that I thought she might pull my hair out.

"It's not that hard!" she roared. "Say his name. Ivan Valerik."

It wasn't hard, but it sure gave me pleasure watching her lips continue to tighten. I told myself I should just comply, but my mouth wouldn't move. My stubbornness could be a curse sometimes.

"You killed him!" she growled, pulling even harder on my hair.

"I don't remember an Ivan," I said in a completely calm and collected tone. Boy, did Maliya squirm. She didn't like it one bit that I wasn't crying out and begging for mercy. I sure loved toying with vampires. Might as well get one final game in.

"You're lying," Maliya accused.

She dropped my hair, though a dull ache continued to pulse where she'd been tugging at the strands. She stepped back a foot and held her hand out to Cowen. The bastard pulled a dagger from a sheath on his boot and handed it to her.

Maliya held the blade to my neck. It took everything I had not to blink, though my breathing was ragged. Instinct told me to fight back, to survive, but I didn't see a scenario where I made it out of here alive.

"I know you remember Ivan," Maliya insisted.

"I've killed a lot of vampires."

"Yes," Maliya agreed, "but you'd remember Ivan."

"Why's that?" I asked.

"Because," Maliya said, tightening her grip on the blade. "He was your first kill."

18

A sharp breath passed by my lips as the images of that night came flooding back. It was just over a year ago, a few months after I filed for emancipation, left my foster family, and moved to the city. I'd been plagued by insomnia and nightmares ever since my parents were killed. I'd stepped out onto my fire escape that night to get some fresh air since I couldn't sleep.

My chest tightened when I thought back to what I'd seen.

A woman's scream cut through the silence on the deserted street below me. My fingers tightened around the railing as I looked over the edge of the fire escape three stories down. Below, a man had cornered a woman in an alleyway across the street.

He's going to rape her, I thought immediately. I'd already lived through my parents' deaths and my sister's abduction. I couldn't take witnessing another act of violence.

"Please!" the woman begged, but the man continued to advance on her like a predator stalking his prey.

I couldn't let this happen. I shifted into raven form. It wasn't the first time I'd shifted, but I hadn't had many opportunities to fly—since I didn't want anyone knowing what I was. As I spread my wings and jumped off the fire escape, I found that flight came naturally to me.

I dove into the alleyway and tore a chunk of skin from the man's hand just moments before he touched the girl. He pulled away from her, holding on to his hand and cursing. I didn't see his silver eyes until I soared in a loop, preparing for my second attack.

My body should've been pulsing in terror, but my fear was pushed down by some-

thing else, by another internal instinct that told me to protect, to save. There wasn't time for fear.

Somehow, the silver eyes didn't intimidate me. He—Ivan—must've thought they should, because when I landed and shifted back into human form, he only laughed. Here I was, a seventeen-year-old girl who was half his size and butt naked, thinking I could take him on. He drastically underestimated me.

"Leave her alone," I demanded.

Ivan smirked, ignoring the girl he'd been stalking. Instead, he advanced on me. "A shifter?" he said suggestively. "You'll be worth quite a bit."

He lunged forward. I saw it coming and ducked out of the way, but he was too fast for me. He wrapped his arms around my chest. One hand assaulted my exposed breast while the other squeezed so tight I thought my ribs might crack. I cried out in pain, then dipped my head and bit down as hard as I could on his arm.

He growled and whipped my body around, flinging me across the alley. I skidded across the pavement. Tiny little pebbles and bits of dirt ripped through skin. Adrenaline shot through my body, and hot breath passed by my upper lip as he advanced. Bitch, I was only getting started.

I sprang to my feet. "Touch me again, and you'll regret it."

Ivan only smiled, as if he was amused by our little game. "Is that an invitation, shifter?"

"Hell no!" I jumped forward to attack, but he was already moving.

His fist connected with my gut, sending me reeling backward. My spine slammed into the nearby dumpster. I reached for the edge of it to catch myself, but my hand slipped inside. A jagged piece of metal at the top of the trash pile sliced across my palm. I inhaled a sharp breath and held my wounded hand in my good hand. Ivan's eyes darted to the blood dripping onto the pavement.

He licked his lips. "I always did like playing with my food."

"Too bad your mother never taught you manners."

Ivan leapt forward, his fangs bared for my bleeding hand. I didn't think; I only acted. I snatched up the scrap metal and aimed for his heart.

It cut into his chest like a knife through butter. A moment of shock crossed his face before his body disintegrated into a pile of ash. His clothes crumbled into a heap where he'd stood only a moment before.

For the first time in a year, I actually felt something more than misery. For a second, I wasn't suffering, because no matter how much anguish had come into my life recently, I could still do good in the world. I could still make a difference. I could save people from evil, keep them from suffering the way I had since the vampires stole something from me.

The woman I'd been protecting was already long gone, but I felt like she would've thanked me if she could.

I returned to my apartment that night never knowing I'd left a raven feather behind, not until the news reports came out the next day. As time went on, I got smarter about my attacks, but I always left a raven feather. That way, the vampires would know there was someone out there protecting Nocton.

That way, they knew to be afraid.

They named me the Raven of the Night, but a misprint from an online new source led to the shortened version—Ravenite. They'd called me that ever since. They hadn't really gotten my personality down, though, always calling me a vigilante and saying I was greater than I really was. One blog claimed I was as strong as ten male vampires put together, and one theorized that I must've been a vampire-shifter hybrid.

I'd managed to get away with it due to not being registered as a shifter and killing every vampire who saw me shift. I'd worried for months that the girl from that first night would turn me in, but she never did.

I didn't intend to become a vigilante. I just wanted to protect people...

Because I couldn't protect Jenna.

"Say. His. Name," Maliya repeated, pulling me back to the present.

I wouldn't. He didn't deserve to be acknowledged, not after what he would've done to that girl in the alley. I realized now he wasn't trying to rape her, but kidnapping her for the blood slave trade wasn't any better.

"All I want is for you to acknowledge that you killed him," Maliya said. "So, let's try this again."

Maliya slowly brought the blade between her lips and ran the dagger gently across her teeth. In a flash, she swung the dagger downward. The blade cut across my left forearm, sending vampire venom into my bloodstream. Fire ignited across my arm, burning down to my fingers and up my shoulder. Blood flowed out of the wound and crept down my arm. I shrieked like banshee, my scream echoing off the stone walls. The guard, Vincent, covered his hears with the heels of his hands and cursed.

"Say it!" Maliya demanded.

She sliced at my skin again, just above the last cut. It felt as if the blood in my arm had been replaced with hot lava. It compounded with the ache of venom that had saturated my body down to the bones last night. It was like Maliya's blade was skinning me alive, like the skin was ripping from the muscle and everything. It was unbearable. *Effing bitch.*

I just wanted the pain to stop.

"Ivan!" I cried before I consciously decided to give in. The name came out so high-pitched that it hardly sounded like a name at all.

"Again!" Maliya commanded as she slashed the blade across my skin a third time.

"Ivan!" I repeated. The words fell from my lips against my command as my self-preservation instinct kicked in. "Ivan Valerik."

Maliya paused with the blade at my skin, ready to make a fourth cut above the other three. I held my breath, forcing back the sobs bubbling up in my throat.

"There we go," she said happily. "Now, why couldn't you do that in the first place?"

My head hung in defeat, but I didn't respond. Beneath my waterfall of dark hair, my jaw clenched, and my nostrils flared.

Maliya held her head high. "I want you to admit what you did. You remember killing him, don't you?"

My hands shook, and though the shackles dug into my skin, I clenched my hands into fists. Every muscle in my body tightened, the tension most intense in my lips and eyebrows. Blood dripped from my arm and onto the floor.

Slowly, I lifted my head. "Yeah," I answered in a clipped tone. "I remember killing him. I remember everything."

My tone shifted, becoming light as air… almost dream-like. I knew it would piss Maliya off, and I loved to watch her squirm. "I remember the way the metal fragment cut through his chest. I'll never forget the look in his eyes when he realized me, a tiny little raven shifter, defeated him. I mean, he was *Ivan Valerik*, and mine was the last face he saw before he died. Before he was reduced to nothing more than a pile of ash at my feet—"

Maliya's hand shot out and clamped around my throat. She squeezed so tight I couldn't breathe. My eyes rolled back, and I gasped for breath that didn't come. I was pretty sure she was two seconds away from collapsing my trachea.

A *thud* sounded beside me, and then a grunt. Maliya's grip on my throat loosened momentarily. My eyes shot open just in time to see Dave's body crumble into a pile of ash beside Maliya. A knife clinkered to the ground atop his clothes.

As soon as that knife entered Dave's chest, hope entered mine. Teagan had made it, and she'd come with a message.

Today wasn't the day I'd die.

19

A low growl echoed down the hall and into the dungeon. *Venn.*

He'd come to save me. I could hardly believe it. And yet... I couldn't believe I ever doubted him.

"Get them!" Maliya shouted.

My back was to the door, and the chair I sat in was too big for me to peek around it, so I couldn't see what was going on. Three of Maliya's men disappeared from view to pursue my rescuers.

The growl behind me turned into a full-on howl. A breeze passed through my hair as a massive shadow leapt over my chair. In wolf form, Venn slammed into Maliya and knocked her flat on her back. I could hear the shuffling of bodies and the shouts that came from Maliya's men. Fiona's *yip* and Ryland's roar met my ears.

They were all here. For me. I was so happy I could cry.

Maliya held her hands over Venn's throat. His jaws snapped at her face, but she held him far enough away that he couldn't cause any damage. Maliya's fist swung upward and connected with the underside of his jaw. He let out a pained bark.

"Venn!" I cried in a shaky voice. I struggled against my restraints, but even my shifter strength wasn't enough to release me from the shackles.

Maliya lifted her knee and got her foot under him. She used all her leverage to hurl him off of her. He flew through the air faster than I could blink. His body crashed against one of the cage doors so violently that it made me wince. The door clanged loudly, masking his whimper of pain. My whole body ached for him.

"No!" I shrieked. It was horrifying to watch it happen without being able to help.

113

Venn slumped to the ground. He blinked rapidly, disoriented.

Maliya stood with a smirk on her face. "Venn," she said in mock disappointment. "I should've known it was you. Who else could've guessed the code to my vault?"

Venn finally got to his feet, but his chest heaved shallow breaths. He looked weak, like the blow to the bars had broken a rib or two. I wanted to rush over to him and heal him, but I couldn't move.

Maliya stalked forward. I expected her to kick Venn, but before she could, a small figure with red fur darted between her legs. Maliya tripped over Fiona in the most un-graceful way I'd ever seen. It was so satisfying to watch that I almost burst out laughing.

While Fiona had Maliya temporarily distracted, Venn shifted and rushed over to me.

"Are you okay?" he asked with worry in his eyes. He pushed my hair out of my face, and then his gaze fell to the gashes across my arm. I didn't have time to explain or to tell him how it felt like I'd reached my arm into the fires of hell.

"There!" I cocked my head toward the pile of clothes next to me.

Venn rifled through it and quickly found Dave's keys in the pants pocket. It took him a moment of shuffling through them to find one that resembled the right shape for the shackles. He shoved the key in the lock at my feet and twisted. I barely noticed the pressure on my ankles disappear; I couldn't feel much of anything outside of the sting shooting up and down my arm.

As soon as my hands were free, I jumped out of the chair and flung my arms around Venn's neck. I didn't even stop to think about what I was doing. I pressed my entire body to his and lifted my lips to meet his.

It was only meant to be a peck, a thank-you for rescuing me from Maliya's torture, but the moment our lips connected, time altogether seemed to stop. The grunts and screams around me faded, and it felt as if the floor fell away beneath our feet. Even the pain in my arm seemed to numb to nothing.

Venn wrapped his arms around me and squeezed me tight, like he wasn't at all surprised by the kiss, like he welcomed it, *craved* it even. My heart flipped in my chest. But it wasn't just a little flutter, like the tummy tickle you get when you drive over a hill too fast. This was wild and filled with adrenaline, like jumping out of a plane without a parachute. It was scary and exhilarating all at the same time. And I didn't want it to end.

But it did. One moment, we were in our own little world, our bodies colliding, and the next, the sounds of battle and the pain pulsing across my skin returned. I suddenly remembered where I was and what I was doing there.

A woman's high-pitched scream tore through the dungeon. My fingers tightened around Venn's arms. Both our heads snapped in the direction of the scream. It echoed in my ears over and over as sheer agony tore through my body.

Fiona was back in human form, and Maliya held her by the hair. Her dagger pressed into the skin on Fiona's neck.

"Stop!" Maliya shouted.

The entire room quieted. Everything was so still that all I could hear was the sound of Fiona's breathing. I glanced around me to see that two of Maliya's men remained. Cowen paused between Ryland and Teagan in the hall, his fangs bared. The other—the new vamp—was on top of Ryland, his massive biceps curled around Ryland's thick neck. Slowly, he loosened his hold on him and climbed off the bear. Ryland shifted back to human form but stood completely still. He stared at his sister with apology in his eyes.

"If you touch any more of my men, the girl dies," Maliya threatened.

A beat passed. If we moved, Fiona was dead.

If we don't do anything, we're all dead, I told myself.

"Cowen, Evan," Maliya instructed, "bring the other two in."

The new vamp, Evan, pushed Ryland down the hall. Cowen smirked as he grabbed ahold of Teagan's arm and shoved her through the door.

"Don't touch her!" Ryland roared.

"Shut up, or I'll hurt the girl," Maliya warned.

Ryland quieted and followed Evan into the room. His lips tightened, but there was a fire in his eyes that told me there was still a lot of fight left in him.

"Call Dreyfus," Maliya told Evan. "He needs to get his ass down here with all his men, and then he's fired."

Evan nodded and pulled a phone from his pocket.

"The rest of you..." Maliya snarled. She cocked her head toward the open cell I'd spent the night in. "Get inside."

Venn shot me a glance I couldn't read. We were out of time, and we all knew it. Our only options were to enter the cell or watch Fiona bleed out in front of us. I didn't care what they did to me after they locked me back up; I wouldn't be the reason she died.

Venn stepped forward before any of us had a chance to move. "Maliya..."

"Venn," Maliya said with a click of her tongue. "I was really hoping I didn't have to kill you."

Venn inched forward another step, testing her. Maliya's lips curled back over her teeth to reveal her fangs. Her dagger left Fiona's neck, and she pointed it at Venn.

"Take one more step," she dared him.

I suddenly realized what that look he'd shot me meant. He was buying us one more moment. It was now or never.

I didn't give it a second thought. I jumped forward and shifted mid-air. Before Maliya had a chance to react, my sharp beak clamped around her outstretched hand. She let out a scream, and the dagger fell to the ground with a *clink.*

The room exploded again. Venn shifted, and his powerful jaws sank into Maliya's ankle. My talons dug into her other hand. I squeezed harder and harder until she dropped Fiona's hair. And still I ripped at the flesh on her hand.

I didn't pay attention to what everyone else was doing. I could only guess

Ryland and Teagan were dealing with the other two vamps. All that mattered to me in that moment was causing Maliya pain.

My talons clawed at Maliya's skin as she shrieked. I found pleasure in the feeling of my claws tearing through her flesh. I ripped at her hands, her face, and her chest—anything I could get. My talons caught on one of her necklaces. I tugged harder until the tension in the chain tore away. The necklace snapped off her neck and flew through the air away from us.

The sound of Venn's wolf whimper reached my ears.

No.

I turned to see what was going on, but all I saw was a fist flying at my face. Pain shot out across my entire head as I flew backward across the room, unable to control my trajectory. I slammed against the stone between two cells. I gasped for air that didn't come. I shifted back to human form, hoping that might help me catch my breath. When my head cleared, I looked up to see that Teagan was on Ryland's back. They were still taking on Evan with Fiona's help. Venn struggled to his feet. It looked like someone had targeted his ribs again to knock him down.

Cowen was at Maliya's side, supporting her as they raced past cells toward the open one on the end. Dave's keys dangled from Cowen's hand.

Beside me, Maliya's dagger caught my eye. I snatched it up from the ground with my good hand. Fury ignited throughout my body. My teeth gritted, and my eyebrows tightened. A scream ripped out of my lungs as I drew my arm back and hurled the dagger at Maliya's back.

It flipped over and over in the air. Maliya and Cowen reached the open cell, and Cowen swung the door shut. The dagger connected with the bars with a loud *clank* that echoed throughout the dungeon.

I scurried forward, my sights on the dagger. Before I could reach it, a pair of arms wrapped around my middle. I struggled against them, but it wasn't much use when I could hardly use my left arm.

"We have to go," Venn's voice came in my ear.

I instantly stopped struggling.

"They're coming," Venn cried. "We have to leave. Now."

He tugged at me again. I told my legs to move, but I couldn't tear my gaze away from Cowen. He stood in the middle of the cell with a wide, taunting smile on his face. He knew he'd won this battle. I wasn't getting past those bars before the rest of the vamps showed up and killed us.

"Come on!" Teagan's urgent voice filled the dungeon.

I tore my gaze from Cowen's, and my feet finally complied to my demands. I hurried to my feet beside Venn, and we raced behind Ryland, Teagan, and Fiona. My gaze flickered across the floor as we ran. A fresh pile of ash told me they'd killed Evan. And then my eyes caught a glimpse of a small object reflecting the candlelight.

The locket.

"Wait!" I cried, pulling against Venn.

He was still headed toward the door but didn't let go of my hand. I swore I almost pulled my shoulder out of the socket. He paused just long enough for me to scoop up the locket. I glanced back to the cell at the other end of the room just in time to see confusion cross Maliya's injured face. Her hands shot to her chest, and her face contorted in fury when she realized she no longer had the locket. Cowen realized the same thing a split second later and immediately began fumbling with the keys.

Looks like you didn't win this battle after all.

Venn and I sprinted down the hall, and Cowen and Maliya disappeared from view. We followed Ryland in his bear form up a flight of steps and then down another long hall. It was like a freaking maze in this mansion.

Finally, we broke out of the dark hallways leading to the dungeon. My heart nearly stopped in my chest. When we reached one of the main halls, a swarm of vampires was headed our way, blocking our escape from the mansion.

Ryland didn't even hesitate. He bowed his head and barreled his way through the crowd. We sprinted closely behind him. Hands flung out toward me, but I dodged out of their way. Vampires screamed as we entered the main foyer. A marble floor stretched out in front of us, and the ceiling reached up three levels. The only piece of furniture was a small table at the center with a potted plant on top of it. The front doors looked miles away.

Suddenly, my legs seized, and I fell face-first into the ground as a vampire tackled me. As soon as I hit the floor, I regained control of my legs. I swung my foot out, and it connected with the vampire's nose.

Just as I managed to free myself from him, another set of hands grabbed me, a woman this time. She bared her fangs at me. I held the locket tight in my right fist and swung it up at her jaw. She stumbled back just enough that I managed to wiggle free. I rushed to my feet.

In front of me, Venn struggled against another vampire's hold. I sprinted forward and sank my teeth into the vampire's hand, clamping down as hard as I could. I didn't have sharp fangs, but it got the job done. The vampire leapt backward, freeing Venn. Pretty good for a girl whose left arm was out of commission.

Ahead of us, another vampire lunged forward and caught Fiona by the tail. She let out a yelp as the vampire dragged her backward across the floor. As we raced by the table at the center of the room, Venn grabbed the plant. He held it high over his head, then dropped it straight on the vamp's head.

Fiona scurried from his grasp. I scooped up Fiona's small body. We sprinted the remaining distance to the front doors and broke out into cool air behind Ryland and Teagan.

There was just a sliver of sunlight on the horizon, casting a dull glow over the landscape. I had no way of telling if it was dawn or twilight, because I didn't know how long I'd been writhing in pain on the floor of that cell.

My legs burned as we continued sprinting down the long driveway. I glanced behind me to see vampires flooding out of the front doors. Some quickly sank back into the safety of the house, while others sprinted into the sun rays, risking severe burns to pursue us. They advanced quickly.

Teagan aimed a knife at the closest one. It flipped through the air and sank into his chest. His body disintegrated into a pile of ash when he was only three feet from me.

"Good shot!" I called.

Teagan smiled in satisfaction then hurled another knife at an oncoming vamp. He too crumbled into a pile of ash behind us. Teagan reached for her hip, but despite the many sheaths that hung off her belt, her hands found nothing.

"I'm out!" she cried to Ryland just as we reached the perimeter wall. In one swift motion, she brought her knees up, pressed her heels into Ryland's back, and leapt off from him, scurrying over the wall.

Ryland turned and sprinted in the opposite direction, heading straight for the vampires behind us. His teeth bared, and his frightening roar sounded across the vast lawn. Venn jumped and caught the top of the wall and pulled himself up. He paused at the top and reached out his hand. I tossed Fiona up to him. Biting on to the locket chain, I shifted and flew over the wall. I stole one glance behind me to see Ryland swinging his massive head into three vampires at once, knocking them all off their feet.

Once he saw we were all over the wall, he turned and raced toward it. He reached up with his bear paws but pulled himself over in human form, landing with a *thud* in the grass on the other side.

"Come on!" Venn shouted.

Everyone sprinted behind Venn through the trees while I flew above them, dodging tree branches as I went. The adrenaline helped me push past the pain in my left wing. I didn't look behind me this time to see if we had any followers. A break in the trees loomed ahead, where I saw Venn's car parked along the edge of the road.

We all scurried inside. Venn, Fiona, and I were in the back, and Ryland was in the passenger seat. Teagan twisted the key in the ignition. Tires squealed as we made our escape.

I shifted back into human form and glanced behind us. Two vampires had made it through the scorching sun and were pursuing us, but they couldn't keep up with Teagan's increasing speed.

Finally, I had a chance to catch my breath, though my heart hammered. It only served to push the pain of the venom faster through my body.

"Everyone okay?" Ryland asked through heavy breaths.

"We're alive," Venn said, like that was all that mattered. He clutched on to his side.

I wanted nothing more than to help. I reached for him, but he just shook his head.

"Rae's bleeding," Fiona said with worry. I barely remembered the blood but saw that it was still oozing out of the wounds on my arm.

Ryland flung open the glove compartment and tossed us a stack of napkins. Fiona took half the stack and pressed it to my arm to slow the bleeding.

"What now?" Teagan asked. "What's our next move?"

I held out the locket in my hand. "Can we use this to decide what to do next?"

"You got it!" Fiona squeaked.

"Please tell me it's the locket you were looking for," I begged. I didn't want all that to be for nothing. I offered her the locket while I took over wound duty.

Fiona gently took it. "Yes, this is it."

"Sondra taught you how to use it, didn't she?" Teagan asked.

Fiona nodded in excitement.

"Then use it," Ryland instructed. "Figure out if we can go home."

Fiona went to put the locket around her neck but quickly realized the clasp was broken. Instead, she held the locket tight in her hand and closed her eyes.

"It works for anyone?" I asked Venn while Fiona concentrated. "Not just witches?"

Venn nodded, though the movement appeared strained. "That's why it's valuable to vampires, since they can't conduct magic of their own."

"They're coming after us," Fiona stated. "But it'll take them a while to find us. They have to go through some contacts to track us down. We have until dawn."

"Okay, here's what we'll do," Ryland said with a tone of authority. "We'll head home and pack up what we can. We'll leave before daylight and head straight for Matias's. We'll figure out our next move once we have Sondra. Sound good?"

Everyone nodded in unison.

"Okay, let's—" Ryland didn't get a chance to finish his sentence.

Beside me, Venn's face went pale, and his eyes rolled back in his head.

He was out cold.

20

"How are you feeling?" My voice was hoarse. An hour had passed since Venn had blacked out. I was just glad he was alive and healing.

He pushed himself up to a sitting position on his bed and glanced around. Venn's room was clean, but otherwise totally not what I expected. The navy-blue color scheme made sense, but then there was a bookcase along one wall filled with fiction books. An acoustic guitar was situated on a stand in the corner. I wouldn't have pegged him for a reader or a musician. Learning he was both… well, it was kind of hot.

I'd walked around the room while he was sleeping, after I'd performed the healing spell on his ribs. We weren't entirely sure why he passed out, but my guess was because it'd gotten hard to breathe.

While I explored his room, I found a picture of him in a frame on the dresser. He looked around twelve. He stood with his arm around another boy who looked several years younger than him but had the same dark skin tone and full lips.

Above the dresser, three hand drawings were taped to the wall. They looked a lot like the ones in the hall, so I guessed Sondra had drawn them. The pictures showed different poses of a couple hugging. The guy was tall, with dark skin, and the girl pale with long dark hair. I couldn't see their faces in any of the pictures, but I thought for sure the guy was Venn.

I didn't want to ask who the girl was. She could've been an old girlfriend or something.

It was interesting, to say the least, to be in Venn's bedroom. It was like I knew him better now.

Eventually, Venn's eyes fell on me seated in the big comfy chair by his closet.

A hint of a smile touched his lips. "I'm feeling better, actually. I guess I have you to thank for that."

My cheeks flushed, and I nodded. What the heck? I wasn't the blushing kind of girl.

I stood on shaky feet, ignoring the fire raging through my sore muscles. I crossed the room to the duffel bag in front of his dresser. "I was hoping you'd wake up soon so you could tell me what to pack for you."

Venn glanced to the empty duffel bag. "You don't have to do that."

"I do," I insisted. "You're still healing."

Venn pulled the covers aside, revealing his toned torso. Bruises splayed across his skin, but with the healing spell, they were already starting to look better. It would take a couple of days until he was back to normal, though. He stood, as if to prove a point.

I rushed over to him and pushed on his shoulders. "Venn, you—"

He grabbed my wrists gently. His touch was like an electric shock, and not just because my arm was still prickling with searing pain from the vampire venom.

"I'm fine, Rae," he whispered.

He stared down at me, his eyes flickering to my lips. Oh, how I would love to kiss him again, but I couldn't. I shouldn't have kissed him in the first place. It was a huge mistake, because now I felt... I felt things I shouldn't be feeling. I couldn't get attached. I mean, Venn didn't even know my real name.

"Rachel," I said breathlessly. The name slipped out before I could stop myself. I cleared my throat and repeated my name. At least if he knew it, we might be able to find each other again... someday. "Rachel Collins," I said. "That's my name."

A smile crept across his face, widening slowly. "I like it. It's a pretty name."

Heart. Officially. Melted. And not because he gave me a compliment. That smile was to die for.

Our eyes locked, and my gaze traveled down to his lips. Now that he knew my name, it couldn't hurt to—

No, I scolded myself. I barely knew him. For starters, there was clear history between Venn and Maliya. And it'd be insanely rude to ask about.

"What's the story with you and Maliya?"

Holy crap! Where had that come from? My mouth wasn't supposed to work without my consent!

Venn tensed for a moment, then dropped my hands. He stepped around me to his duffel bag and opened the top dresser drawer. He riffled through it and pulled out clothes to shove into his bag, all without looking me in the eye.

"I thought you would've figured it out by now," he said tensely.

I bit my lower lip and sank onto the bed. "I have a good guess. If it's what I think it is, I'm really sorry, Venn."

He tossed a pile of clothes into his bag. "Don't be. It's not your fault."

I wasn't going to push it. It wasn't fair of me to dig into his past like this. "I'm sorry. I didn't mean to bring it up."

He paused and then shrugged. "It's not a secret. It's pretty obvious. I was her blood slave."

Holy crap! I'd assumed he was a blood slave in her house, but the way he said it… *her* blood slave. He'd been her personal pet. The thought made me want to vomit. I forced down the lump in my throat.

"I know what you're thinking," he said solemnly.

"What am I thinking?" I asked curiously.

Venn took a deep breath. "You must think the worst of me. You must be wondering why I stayed."

"Of course I don't think any less of you," I assured him. "You were forced to stay."

"Yeah, but I wanted to," he admitted without meeting my eyes.

He *wanted* to?

Venn ran his fingers through his hair and returned to packing. "Most people are very judgmental. They don't get what it's like to be fed on."

"It's like a drug, isn't it? For both of you." I remembered what it felt like the moment Dracula sank his teeth into my neck. It was blissful. Addicting.

Venn nodded, slowly folding clothes into his bag. "It's… a hard habit to break."

"How'd you end up with her?"

I shouldn't have been asking these personal things. My mouth apparently had no filter.

Venn hesitated.

"Never mind," I said. "You don't have to tell me."

"I know." He finally turned to me, a look of sadness in his eyes. "But the crazy thing is that I want to tell you. I want you to know. It's just… hard to talk about."

"Then don't worry about it," I told him. "Really, Venn. I don't want—"

"My parents fell into a bad deal with a group of shifters when I was fourteen," he interrupted. "They died."

My heart sank. Of course. Because everyone here had lost their parents. It didn't seem right.

"My brother and I went to live with my grandfather," Venn continued. "It was… not the best situation. My grandfather was just as emotionally abusive to us as he was to my dad. But I had to stay… for my brother."

Venn zipped his bag and sighed. He crossed the room and sat on his bed beside me. "We lived there for about a year before my brother was attacked by a vampire and changed."

My hand shot over my mouth. I couldn't believe all these terrible things had happened to him. Why was he telling me all this?

"I left. Maliya found me not long after that. Believe it or not, she treated me well… at first. It was only after she had my trust that she started to show her true side. But it was still a warm bed to sleep in."

Tears welled in my eyes. I thought my past was horrible, but it was nothing compared to the story he just told me. I couldn't imagine.

"Luckily, Sondra came along as things started to get worse," Venn said.

"She saved you?" I asked in a small voice.

Venn nodded. "She was working a deal with Maliya, but Sondra refused monetary payment. She ended up trading me for payment instead."

I didn't know it was possible for my heart to break any further. It wasn't fair that Venn had gone through all that. He didn't deserve it. He deserved happiness and love.

I didn't know what I was doing when I reached out to touch him. My hands ran over his exposed shoulders. A tingle spread through my body upon contact. He gazed down at my arms, his eyes slowly drifting past the bandages until they landed on my hands. A hint of a smile touched his lips, like he welcomed my touch. I gently wrapped my arms around him, and he rested his head on mine. His body heat was strangely comforting. I didn't know how I could sit there with him feeling so comfortable, like this was where I was meant to be.

Now's not the time to get attached, I reminded myself. But I didn't pull away. I let myself enjoy the moment. I forgot how good it felt to hold someone, to be held.

Venn took a long breath. "Anyway, I've been with the family ever since. What about you? How'd you get here?"

I was shocked by the question, but for some reason, it felt perfectly natural opening up to Venn—like we'd had conversations like this a million times before.

"I grew up in a really close family," I said, surprised to hear the words tumbling out of my mouth with such ease. "It was just me, my sister, and my mom and dad. My life was basically perfect before the vampires came."

Memories of that night flickered through my mind. The screams. The blood. The mark of the Soulless.

I swallowed hard. "When I was sixteen, a group of vampires raided my house in the middle of the night. I heard my parents' screams downstairs. I remember shaking in fear. I'd never felt so scared in my life. That was the first time I shifted."

I took a deep breath as images flickered across the back of my closed lids. I remembered a vampire's voice from Jenna's room. *'No, she's mine,'* he said. The sound of her voice shrieking at me to run… A vampire barged into my room, but I was in raven form, crouched into the small space between my bookcase and the ceiling. The vampire flipped my mattress and pulled my closet door off its track. I remembered how he reached up to the bookshelf I was on. His hand getting so close to me, the mark of the Soulless coming closer and closer… I remembered how I thought he'd found me. He just knocked all the books off the top shelf instead. He never saw me.

But I didn't tell Venn any of that. I didn't want him to know I was after the Soulless. He'd want to protect me from them.

"I tried to follow them when they took Jenna, but they piled in this van and disappeared." A sob broke out in my chest, but I held the tears back. I shouldn't be crying. I was stronger than that.

"It's okay," Venn told me, readjusting so that he held me close to his chest.

I wanted to tell him it wasn't, but in his arms, I could almost believe it was okay. It felt as if a huge weight had lifted off my shoulders when I shared my story. It was different than when I'd told Fiona. Fiona got the vague, watered-down version, but with Venn, all the memories came rushing back as if I was reliving them.

I sniffled and wiped the tears from my eyes. "The police investigated my family's murder, but the vampires responsible were never caught. I had no other family, so I was put into foster care. I was only there a few months before I filed for emancipation and moved to the city. My landlord gave me a deal on my apartment."

Though, my landlord was a pig who raised my rent as soon as I turned eighteen. I was sure it was because I wouldn't indulge in his advances. I didn't mention that to Venn.

I shrugged. "One thing led to another, I started killing vampires on my off-hours, and here I am."

Venn pulled me even tighter and placed a warm kiss on my forehead.

Damn it. He was going to make it hard to leave. I wanted to be close to him. I wanted to get to know him better. I wanted to stay with this family because for the first time in years, I finally felt like I belonged.

And that scared the hell out of me.

"I'm so sorry," Venn whispered, the sound of his voice melodic, entrancing.

Before I knew what I was doing, my body leaned into him as if magnetized. My lips brushed against his. The kiss was like magic, melting away the pain in my veins and making me feel as if I was floating. Venn kissed me back, and desire ignited deep in my belly. I parted my lips, inviting him to deepen the kiss. His tongue grazed against my lower lip. For a moment, all was perfect in the world.

And then reality came crashing down on me.

"No!" I pushed him away and sprang to my feet.

He stared back at me with utter shock, as if to ask what he'd done wrong.

"I—I'm sorry." My voice shook. "I just can't do this."

"Rae," Venn whispered, reaching out for me.

I took another step back. "I'm sorry, Venn. I've already lost too many people I love."

Venn bit his lower lip. "You're saying you don't want to lose me, either?"

I wasn't sure what I was saying, but that was a pretty darn good way of putting it into words.

I nodded. "I can't go with you, Venn."

He didn't say anything for a long time. My chest started to hurt as I stared down at his wounded expression. *I'm sorry* didn't even begin to cover it.

He finally lifted his head. "What will you do without us?"

I considered his question for a moment. I was leaving the city. I knew that much. But I was leaving alone.

I sat back down beside him. "I'm going after my sister."

I didn't know how I was getting to Seattle, but assuming Cowen made his flight Maliya mentioned, that's where I'd find him. And he was my only lead on Jenna. One way or another, I'd get to him.

After a beat, Venn spoke softly. "I don't want you to go alone."

"But I have to," I countered. "You have Sondra, and I have my sister. I can take care of myself."

"I know. You told me that the night we met."

It already felt like a million years ago.

"Stay with us, Rae," Venn begged.

I shook my head. "I don't think I can."

"You can't go alone," he whispered. "Is there nothing I can say that'll make you come with us?"

He was already saying all the things that could make me stay, but I fought against them.

I shook my head. "I can handle myself, Venn. Don't worry about me."

"I'm going to worry," he promised.

Damn it. Why was this so hard?

"I have to go," I insisted. "Alone. I can't stay here, and you can't come with me."

I knew I was being unfair. His family just risked their necks for me, and I repaid them by hitting the road. But my only choices were to walk away from them or walk away from Jenna. Guilt twisted in my gut, wrenching at my insides so fiercely that it almost overshadowed the venom.

"Yes, I can," he insisted. "I can—"

"Venn," I cut him off. "This isn't up for discussion. I've been on my own for years. I'll be fine."

Venn sighed. "I just want to be with you, Rae… I want to keep you safe."

The guy was tempting as hell.

"Please don't treat me like I'm incapable of making my own decisions," I said, tears welling in my eyes.

Sorrow crossed Venn's eyes. He still didn't want me to go, but he knew he couldn't stop me. He had no choice but to give in.

"I hope you find what you're looking for," he whispered. "If you ever feel like your journey is over, you can always come find us."

I cracked a smile. "Thank you."

Venn stood and crossed over to his dresser. He grabbed a pen that lay there and returned to my side. He scribbled a number on the palm of my hand. "There's my phone number. And if you can't reach me there, take this."

He held an object so small in his hands that I couldn't see it. I held out my palm to accept his offer. He placed a piece of blue plastic the size of a quarter in my hand. A guitar pick.

"You don't get to keep it," Venn said.

Of course not. How could I find him if I claimed it as mine?

He reached out and curled my fingers around it. "I want it back. When you find me."

I pressed my lips together to keep the tears from falling. I nodded. Damn him. Why was he making it so hard to leave?

A light knock came at the door. I quickly dashed the tears away.

"Come in," Venn called.

Fiona stuck her head inside the room. "Oh, good. You're up. I was just wondering if you needed anything."

Venn shook his head. "I have a few more things to pack, and then I'm going to take Rae home."

Fiona's face fell. "You're leaving?"

I nodded because I couldn't bear to speak. I bet I could've been really good friends with Fiona.

"But we just…" Fiona stared at me like a deer in the headlights. After a beat, she crossed the room and pulled me into a hug. "We're going to miss you, Rae."

"Don't be silly." My voice cracked. "You just met me."

She drew away and wiped at her eyes. "Maybe in this life, but I feel like I've known you forever. We all do."

It was strange how I felt the same way about them.

Maybe I should stay, I thought.

I pictured myself with the family, leaving the city and leading that quiet life they talked about. In my mind, I rocked on a porch swing. Fiona sat curled up next to me in her fox form, and Sondra sat in a chair nearby sketching the landscape. The sun was high in the sky, spreading happiness across our property. The wind gently rustled through my hair. The wrap-around porch we sat on overlooked a wide-open lawn that stretched out to a line of trees that blocked our view of the quiet road. In the distance, Ryland and Teagan tended to our garden, and their future son pedaled his tricycle down the driveway. The strum of Venn's guitar and the melodic sound of his voice filled the air. He smiled at me from where he sat playing on the steps. Everything was perfect… except Jenna wasn't there.

I returned to the present. It was clear to me now why I was doing this. If Jenna was still out there, I'd never find her if I went with the family. And I'd never be happy with them without closure.

"Are you ready to go?" Venn asked.

As much as it broke my heart, it was time to leave.

21

I t was incredible how you could feel so strongly for someone you just met. I sat on my bed alone in my apartment, rolling Venn's guitar pick around in my fingers. I couldn't stop thinking about him, about leaving him.

The pain in my muscles had eased to a dull ache. There must've not been as much venom on Maliya's blade as I thought. My bag sat beside me, packed and ready to go. I didn't have many belongings, so it only took me five minutes or so to pack everything up.

All I needed to do was leave my key on the table and slip the note I'd written under my landlord's door explaining I was leaving and he could lease the room to someone else. Luckily, he was lazy with his record keeping, so he wouldn't have much luck tracking me down for unpaid rent on the contract. I'd take what cash I had and head to the bus station, where I'd hop on a bus to Chicago and take the first flight to Seattle. There, I'd find Cowen and get answers.

And yet, I couldn't bring myself to actually rise to my feet and leave. It wasn't like I was attached to this place. I mean, I just used it as somewhere to crash and keep my stuff. It barely fulfilled its purpose. At least I was able to get a shower one last time. I wasn't sure when I'd see a bed or a shower again. It could be weeks.

But it still felt like I was leaving something behind. I racked my brain, trying to think if I'd hidden anything in the cupboards or behind a baseboard, but I figured if something was valuable enough to hide, I would remember it. I wouldn't miss this creaky old bed, the pipes that made noises every time I turned on the faucet, or the water stain on the ceiling. I wouldn't miss my job, though Devin deserved a phone call to know I quit. About the only thing I'd miss was patrolling. It was the only time I ever felt something. Before I met Venn, of course.

That was what was holding me back.

I wasn't ready to take a break from slaying vampires... from being the Ravenite.

One more night, I told myself.

The last night I went patrolling, I ran into Cowen, and he got away. I wouldn't let that be my final fight in Nocton. This city may've sucked as bad as Hell's armpit, but for the last two years, it'd been my home. The people here deserved one last fight from the Ravenite.

I shot up from my bed. Fiona said I had until morning. I wouldn't let tonight be a night I'd forget. I was going to find the biggest, baddest vamp I could, and I was going to kick his ass. It would be my greatest fight yet.

I sat perched on the roof of Red Whiskey, knowing that if I was going to find a vampire worth killing, this was as good of place as any to hunt one down.

So far, the night was a total bust.

I was disappointed, and frankly a little bored, but my determination hadn't waned. A vampire *would* die by my hand tonight. I'd wait all night if I had to.

The sidewalk in front of the bar was quiet, apart from the heavy bass shaking the building and spilling out onto the street every time someone opened the door. It was a slow night, nothing compared to last Friday when the street was buzzing with nightlife.

A group of people—humans, it looked like from this distance—walked along on the other side of the street. Other than that, there wasn't much to see. If there was anything worth watching, it was all going on inside the bar.

Which was why I decided I should check it out. I never admitted to being the sharpest tool in the box, but this girl really needed to see some vampire action or she was going to lose it.

I swooped down into the alley and shifted. I peeked around the corner of the building, but there was no one close enough to see me slip out of the shadows.

The music pulsed through me like a bass drum when I stepped inside Red Whiskey. It was like the building had completely transformed since I was in here last. There were fewer tables than before—all thanks to Ryland, I'm sure— so most people stood and danced. Women wore short skirts and held their drinks in the air. Most of their glasses were filled with a thick red liquid, and they sure as hell weren't Bloody Marys.

I was about to sit at the bar, but then I spotted Kieren and immediately turned in the other direction. I'd probably get thrown out if he saw me. I threw myself into the crowd so I wouldn't be seen. Bodies pressed in on me. I swayed my hips to the music to blend in.

"Hey," a girl beside me called over the music. She had long blonde hair, pale skin, and silver eyes. She held a red drink in her hand and moved her hips expertly to the beat of the music. "You looking for someone?"

I hadn't realized I'd been that obvious scanning the crowd.

"My friends," I lied.

"You can dance with us until they come back," she offered. The hot vampire lady grabbed my wrist with her cold fingers and pulled me toward her group of friends.

What was I doing? They probably wanted to eat me alive.

The girl swayed her hips beside me, bumping into me every so often.

"Come on," she encouraged. "You're not scared of me, are you?"

Hell no! I just wasn't used to dancing like this. Heck, I hardly ever danced at all. This girl knew what she was doing with her hips, and I'd been wondering how to use mine since puberty hit.

Vampire Girl grabbed my hand and held it up above my head. I twirled for her, but my eyes remained on the crowd. So far, no one caught my eye.

She laughed when I completed my twirl and faced her. "You from around here?"

"What?" I shouted over the music.

My eyes locked on a group of three guys who'd all stopped dancing. They glanced down at a phone then back up, scanning the crowd like they were nervous.

"I said, are you from around here?" she repeated.

I barely processed what she'd said. "Huh? Oh, I'm sorry. I think I see my friends. It was good dancing with you."

She winked at me. "Feel free to come back if your friends aren't any fun. I'll show you a good time."

It wasn't until I pushed through the crowd and was halfway across the bar that I realized she'd been hitting on me. Weird.

The guys I had my eye on hurried off the dancefloor and down the hall that led to the bathrooms, where there was some relief from the music.

I followed behind them and dropped my head. My hair fell in front of my face as I pushed myself into the girl's bathroom. It was empty, so I didn't feel weird about opening the door a crack and peeking through it to spy on the three guys. Two had silver eyes, but the other guy's were dark brown. My guess was he was either a shifter gone bad or a blood slave. With his strong build and smug expression, he certainly seemed to fit into the vampire crowd. Maybe these three would be worth taking out tonight.

"What'd she say?" the short vampire asked.

"Maliya found them," the taller vampire said.

All the blood drained from my face. *Please don't let him mean what I think he means.* I thought the family had until tomorrow. I listened as closely as I could, ignoring the music.

"She wants everyone but Cowen to report to the location now," the tall vampire said.

"What's Cowen doing?" the guy with brown eyes asked.

"He's headed to round up some old friends on Valander," Tall Vamp replied.

I swear my heart stopped. That was where we'd gone before, where Kieren had led us and Teagan got bit. I could easily intercept him on his way and finally get the information I needed from him. But—

"I'll let the others know," Short Vamp said. "What's the address we're supposed to meet at?"

I held my breath, praying he wouldn't say the address running through my mind. Every muscle in my body froze when the words I'd been dreading left his lips. *112 Amore Drive.*

Venn.

They'd found the family, but it was too soon. Fiona said they had until morning. Then I remembered what she told me about the future. It wasn't written in stone, which meant something had changed.

"Anything else?" Short Vamp asked.

"Yeah," Tall Vamp said. "Leave no survivors."

I dropped the door handle and stumbled back several paces, knocking over the garbage can. My gut twisted, and I thought I might puke. I almost tripped over my own feet as I crossed the room and caught myself on the counter. I braced myself over the sink, and my arms shook. This couldn't be happening. I had to warn them.

I reached for my pocket before I realized I didn't have my phone on me. Of course not. It wouldn't shift with me. I never brought it on patrol.

Voices passed the door, snapping me back to attention. They were headed to round up Maliya's cronies. I needed to get out of here. I rushed across the room to the door, but before I could reach the handle, the door swung open. Vampire Girl from earlier nearly ran into me.

"Hey," she said with a smile. "You again. You ready to bring your friends over and dance?"

"I—I have to go." I pushed past her and into the hall. I raced to the end and blasted out the exit. I didn't check to see if anyone was watching as I shifted and flapped my wings, launching into the air.

It took me several seconds to realize which direction I was headed. I was flying in the direction of Valander, toward where Cowen was supposed to be. It was a closer flight, and I could be there in a matter of minutes. I couldn't stop thinking about Jenna, how if I got what I wanted from Cowen, I'd finally be able to find out what happened to my sister.

But then images of Venn invaded my mind. His soft, familiar eyes, his full lips and gorgeous smile, the warmth of his embrace...

It didn't make sense for me to want to save someone I'd just met over my own *sister*, but at the same time, it seemed like the only rational course of action. Jenna had been gone for two years. I wasn't even sure if she was still alive. If I didn't act *now*, I was certain that Venn and his family wouldn't make it.

I hesitated a moment longer.

Screw it. I have to warn Venn.

I just hoped I wasn't too late.

I was in such a hurry that I couldn't slow my momentum when I came in for the landing. My entire body slammed against the glass window at the front of the house. I dropped to the porch, heaving in deep breaths. I shifted back into human form where I lay. Every muscle in my body ached.

"Oh, my God! What are you doing out here, Rae?" Fiona's voice reached my ears as she rushed outside.

"I—I needed to—to warn you," I managed to spit out between heavy breaths.

Fiona helped pull me to my feet. "Warn us? Rae, what's going on?"

I finally steadied myself on two feet and caught my breath. "They're coming here. Now."

"But the locket showed me—"

"Something changed."

Fiona's entire body froze, and her eyes went wide. She whirled around and raced back into the house. I followed quickly behind her.

"It's time to go!" she shouted up the stairs.

Fiona hurried down the hall and flung open the cupboard beneath the stairs. My jaw dropped when I saw the pile of weapons hanging from the walls. Guns, daggers, axes... There was even a sword and a crossbow with a full quiver attached. It looked high-tech, like the kind that auto-cocked itself.

Fiona caught the look on my face while she grabbed for the weapons. "We don't get much chance to use them since we prefer fighting in our shifted form. And Teagan would rather use her knives."

Fiona shoved the handle of a dagger into my hands. It was completely silver, with intricate designs carved into the blade. She took a gun for herself, an old-style revolver that only held six bullets. She quickly checked the chamber to confirm it was full, then cocked the firing pin before grabbing the crossbow.

I glanced down at the dagger in my hand, my heart pounding. "You don't understand. You can't fight them. They're coming with all they've got. They're going to kill you. You have to leave now!"

Footsteps pounded down the stairs. Venn stopped at the bottom, and his eyes locked on me. A smile touched the corner of his lips, like he was glad to see me. Which totally would've melted my heart if he wasn't about to be ambushed.

Fiona glanced up at him. "You have twenty seconds to get the rest of the bags in the car. Rae says the vamps are on their way."

"What?" Venn gawked. "How do you—?"

"No time to explain," I said. "You all have to leave immediately."

"You wanna go bad-ass wolf shifter, or do you want to play slayer?" Fiona asked Venn.

"What's going on?" Ryland demanded as he descended the stairs with Teagan close behind him. "I thought we had another few hours."

Fiona tossed the crossbow up, and Teagan caught it.

"Something changed," I said in a rush. "You're out of time—"

As if on cue, the front door burst open, sending slivers of busted door frame flying across the front hall. Ryland and Venn shifted before I could blink. Fiona pulled the trigger on her gun, and a loud *pop* cracked through the air. Teagan brought the bow to her shoulder in an instant.

Ryland lunged forward, and the bodies of the closest vampires flew backward through the door. His huge bear form blocked any others from getting through. The sound of shattering glass and the pumped-up roar of invading vampires filled the living room.

"Run!" Teagan screamed.

I sprinted as fast as I could down the hall, never looking back as I hightailed it to the back door near the kitchen. My blood ran cold and I stopped in my tracks when a scream of terror erupted from Teagan's lungs. Fiona and I whirled around just in time to see a vampire with his arms wrapped around Teagan, his fangs headed for her throat. Three others were already racing down the hall toward me, while dozens more flooded in through the broken window in the living room.

I didn't hesitate a moment. I rushed forward and sank the dagger into the closest vampire's chest. I didn't wait around to watch him disintegrate into a pile of ash. My dagger was already speeding toward the chest of the next vampire.

Fiona got off five more shots. I saw several vamps turn to ash out of the corner of my eye, but I didn't count how many. Fiona dropped her gun once she was out of bullets. She grabbed a picture frame off the wall and swung it toward the closest vampire's head. The glass in the frame shattered. She swooped down and snatched up the sharpest fracture and stabbed it straight into the vampire's chest.

Ahead of us, Teagan had dropped her crossbow and was holding a knife in either hand. She swung her arm backward, slicing her knife through a nearby vampire's eye. He screamed and stumbled backward. Teagan whirled around and sank her other knife into his chest. I still couldn't believe this girl was only human.

Meanwhile, Ryland and Venn had pushed the vampires at the door outside. I couldn't see them, but their growls told me they were still alive. For how much longer, I didn't know. All I knew was that I couldn't let this family die. I had to help them make their escape.

Fiona reached back inside the cupboard under the stairs and grabbed the sword. She sliced it through the air, nicking a vamp's neck when he tried to grab her. I'd plunged a knife into two other vampires' chests by the time I made it to the front door.

Outside, dozens of vampires flooded the front lawn, and there were only more coming from down the street. When the vamps said Maliya wanted *everyone* to attack the house, they weren't kidding. She'd called in every favor she could.

There was no way we were making it out of here alive. It only made me want to fight harder. It didn't matter what Maliya did to me; she wasn't taking this family down, too.

Three vampires jumped Venn at the same time. His sharp teeth sank into one of the vampire's hands. The vamp screamed, and his face contorted in pain. I realized the moment I saw him that I recognized his large frame and dark hair. He was the Alpha Vamp who had bitten Teagan. The whole lot of them were back to get their revenge on us.

I sprinted across the porch and jumped the banister to reach Venn as fast as I could. One vampire had ahold of Venn, while the other swung a foot at his face to force his jaws off Alpha Vamp's hand. Venn let out a whimper.

The vampires never saw me coming. I jumped down off the porch and sank my dagger into the back of the nearest vampire, the one who held Venn down. The second vamp whirled toward me, just in time for my blade to enter his chest.

Venn rolled over in the grass, finally free of the vampires. Alpha Vamp completely forgot about him as his eyes, etched in fury, turned to me. Before I could get out of the way, he lunged. His strong fingers clamped around my throat, and my body crashed to the ground. A satisfied smirk spread across his face as I gasped for air. Pain filled my chest, and my vision clouded. I thought for sure this was the end.

Then a howl cut through the night, and a shadow flashed in front of my eyes. Alpha Vamp's weight lifted off of me, and air filled my lungs again.

I sat up, sputtering. "Venn!"

I tossed my dagger into the grass two feet away from him. It stuck into the earth right where I'd been aiming. Venn shifted back into human form and grabbed it. Alpha Vamp didn't have time to react before Venn shoved the blade into his chest. Alpha Vamp crumbled into a pile of ash.

Venn rushed over to me as I jumped to my feet. Most of the vampires had made it into the house now. I glanced to Ryland on the front lawn. Nausea slammed into my gut so hard that if Venn hadn't been there to steady me, I would've fallen right back down. Time seemed to slow as the scene played out in front of me.

Four vampires wrestled Ryland in his bear form. I spotted Cowen among them. He threw himself onto Ryland's back but made the mistake of getting within reach of Ryland's powerful jaws. Ryland's sharp teeth clamped around Cowen's leg, and he whipped his body around. Cowen landed with an audible *thud* in the grass. His scream echoed through the air, but it was silenced by the weight of Ryland's strong paws pressing down on his chest.

Ryland's teeth ripped at the flesh on Cowen's neck. Pieces of skin went flying, exposing the raw flesh and bones beneath it. It was horrifying to watch. Ryland took one final swipe at him, severing his head from his shoulders. Cowen crumbled into a pile of dust on the front lawn.

My body shook, and I thought I might vomit. But it wasn't just horrifying to watch the gruesome death unfold before my eyes. With it, I watched the mark of the Soulless on Cowen's wrist vanish. I watched my one chance at finding out what happened to my sister disappear like dust in the wind. Any sliver of hope I had for Jenna perished in that moment.

An unsteadiness consumed me. I fell to my knees in the grass. Venn's voice swam in and out of focus. I was sure his hands were on me, but I couldn't feel him anymore.

It was over.

Somewhere beyond the dizziness, I heard the sickening crunch of breaking bones and Ryland's roar of pain. Four vampires leapt on top of him, twisting and pulling his limbs in different directions.

My stomach bottomed out. We were done for.

23

"Don't kill him!"

Maliya's voice sounded like it was coming from under water. She emerged from the house in her velvet, long-sleeved dress. She walked with grace but wore a tight expression on her face. The wounds I'd slashed across her face with my talons were barely visible. Damn vampire healing abilities. The image of her descending the porch steps swam in and out of focus.

"Don't kill him... yet," Maliya repeated. "I want them all out here. Now."

Four vampires followed out of the house, each of them holding on to one of my friends' arms. Teagan struggled against the two vampires dragging her outside, while Fiona remained still, tears streaming down her face. Their weapons were nowhere to be seen.

The feeling of strong hands snatching me up from the ground sent a shot of adrenaline through my chest. Venn shouted curses from beside me. Suddenly, the world came back into focus.

At least two sets of hands clung on to me and forced me forward. I stumbled into the porch light illuminating the lawn. I tried to struggle out of their grasp, but I'd lost my strength. Even shifting wouldn't save me now, and if it did, I'd never be able to save the rest of them.

"Ah, Venn," Maliya said with a smile when she turned to see her henchmen dragging us toward her. "Nice of you to join us."

The vampires forced me and Venn to our knees beside Ryland. He lay in the grass in his human form, his left arm twisted in an unnatural direction. His face was pale, and his eyes were closed.

Please don't be dead, I thought.

Maliya's henchmen positioned Teagan and Fiona on the opposite side of

Ryland so that we all knelt in a line. I could see at least a dozen other vampires inside the house, moving by the windows as they raided the place.

They're going to kill us off one by one and make the rest of us watch, I thought. I wasn't sure I could stomach it.

One of the vamps ripped the dagger from Venn's grasp and threw it several yards away. Venn's lips curled, and his nostrils flared. He glared at Maliya with pure hostility.

Maliya paced in front of us. "You all know why we're here. You stole something from me."

"You stole it from us first," Teagan snapped.

Maliya glared at her, but the corners of her lips slowly turned up. "Yes, I suppose I did. And I want it back."

Teagan turned her face away when Maliya leaned down to run a manicured finger across her cheek. The touch was harmless, but I knew she was doing it to scare Teagan. Despite Teagan's tough exterior, it looked like it was working.

"Tell me, *human*," Maliya spat at her, "where can I find the locket?"

"I don't know." Teagan's voice shook.

Maliya's palm cracked across the side of Teagan's face. My stomach sank, but Teagan barely let it show it bothered her.

"She's telling the truth!" Fiona burst. "Ryland had the locket tonight, and you knocked him out."

"I didn't ask you, filthy fox!" Maliya roared.

Fiona flinched.

Maliya straightened. "I don't have all night to have my men search your entire house. So I'll give you three guesses on where you think the bear left the locket."

Teagan narrowed her eyes at Maliya. "Screw you."

This time, Maliya's hand missed Teagan entirely and exploded across Fiona's cheek. Fiona let out a cry. A red welt in the shape of Maliya's fingers grew on Fiona's skin. I winced. She was going to torture Fiona to make Teagan talk, and there was nothing I could do to help.

"One guess down, two to go," Maliya mocked.

"Stop it, Maliya," Venn demanded. I'd never heard him speak with such commanding authority before. "We'll give you the locket as soon as Ryland wakes. It's not worth any of our lives."

Laughter bubbled up from Maliya's chest. "Oh, honey," she sang in condescension. "You know how the rules go. I don't negotiate. We do this on *my* terms."

"We don't know where he put it," Venn growled.

Maliya smirked. "Then the girl better use her best educated guess."

Teagan tightened her lips, but she didn't speak.

"You're running out of time," Maliya mocked.

Teagan took a deep breath, as if fighting against her fury. "Try the room at the top of the stairs, in the black bag next to the dresser."

Maliya gestured to one of her cronies. He raced inside to check it out.

"I can't promise you it's there," Teagan said.

"Then you better make your next guess count," Maliya snarled.

Venn leaned over, closing the few inches between us. His warm skin touched mine. Though he didn't say anything, I knew what he'd say if he could.

It's going to be okay, Rae.

Except it wasn't. We were drastically outnumbered. It would take a miracle.

"It's not here." The vampire who'd gone inside returned, holding on to an empty black duffel bag. All the contents had been emptied, and the pockets had been turned inside out.

Maliya's face remained expressionless, like she was an expert at hiding her true emotions. She paced slowly in front of us until she stopped in front of Venn. She gazed down at him past her nose. With a sudden burst of energy, her knee swung up and clipped his jaw.

I let out a shocked cry as Venn's body whipped backward. I tried to get to my feet, but the vampire behind me held my shoulders down and twisted my arms around my back. My knees sank into the earth. The two vampires guarding Venn slammed their fists into his face over and over again. A foot sank into his ribs, and he cried out. I knew his ribs hadn't healed yet, so the blow must've hurt like hell.

"Stop it!" I screamed.

"Please don't!" Fiona cried.

"I told you I don't know where the locket is!" Teagan shouted at the same time.

"Then think harder!" Maliya screamed back at her.

The vampires beating Venn pulled away. His eyes swelled, and blood dripped down a cut in his lip. His head lolled to the side as the vampires dragged him to his knees and forced him back beside me. I ripped my arms out of the vampire's grasp and caught Venn before he face-planted into the dirt. The vampires behind me quickly yanked my hands off him and separated us. They held on tight to my wrists, securing them firmly behind my back. I struggled against their hold, but I couldn't fight two at once.

"Let go of me!" I shrieked, but it was no use. All I wanted was to reach out for Venn and pull him into my arms.

"Stop it, or you're next!" Maliya threatened.

I continued to struggle and got one hand free, but it was instantly restrained again in less than a second.

"She means it, Rae," Venn groaned.

I stopped struggling, not because I knew Venn was right, but because I didn't know why I was struggling in the first place. Even if I managed to get free, I couldn't save Venn—or anyone else, for that matter.

"Guess again," Maliya demanded of Teagan.

"I don't know!" Teagan repeated. "Try the top drawer in the dining room hutch."

"No!" Fiona objected immediately. "I was just in those drawers. The locket isn't there."

Maliya raised an eyebrow. "Any other guesses?"

Teagan drew in shallow breaths. "Go to hell."

Maliya scoffed. "Honey, I've been planning my trip to hell for decades. It'll be a blast. In the meantime, let's see what kind of hell I can make for you."

Maliya gestured to the men behind me. Before I knew what was happening, pain blasted through the side of my head. I caught myself a moment before my face smashed into the ground.

Screams filled the air around me, but I couldn't make sense of who was saying what.

Stop it!

You don't need to do this!

Hit her again.

That last one, I was certain was Maliya, but it barely sounded like her over the ringing in my ears.

"Stop! I have another guess." I thought for sure that was Teagan.

Fingers tangled in my hair and yanked my head back. The hand on the back of my head forced my face forward. It connected with the ground with a sickening *crunch*. A flash of red crossed my eyes, and hot pain spread across my nose. The breath left my lungs as foot after foot connected with my abdomen. I tried to protect myself by crossing my arms over my stomach, but the pain continued. Blow after blow after blow.

"Go check," I heard Maliya bark.

Everything around me faded. The sounds. The lights. Everything. All I heard was the blood pulsing in my ears. All I saw was the pitch black of the inside of my eyelids. All I felt was the fresh, tender bruises on my skin and the excruciating pain of a broken nose. Every inch of my skin the vampires beat ignited in sharp pains.

It will all be over soon, Rachel, I told myself.

As soon as the thought crossed my mind, I realized that I truly believed it. These were my last moments. And it honestly didn't bother me.

I closed my eyes, welcoming the pain. Soon, it would all be over. Soon, I would see my family again.

It'd been so long since I'd seen my dad's smile and felt my mother's embrace. I hoped it was nice where they were, that the sun was shining, that it smelled like my mother and tasted like my father's homemade apple pie.

I'm sorry I couldn't save you, Jenna, I thought, as if she might be able to hear me from wherever she was. I believed with all my heart she was still alive, and I'd failed her.

I hoped I was wrong. For once, I *wanted* to be wrong.

I didn't want to say goodbye to Venn or the rest of them. I'd enjoyed my time with them. They made me feel like I had a family again, if only for a brief moment.

The pain seemed to wash away. I hardly noticed it anymore as a positive energy consumed me. Whatever happened next, I was ready for it.

"Finally, we have it," a satisfied voice cut through my clouded mind. "Kill them all."

My stomach twisted. I couldn't have heard that right, could I?

It was one thing to accept my own death, but I'd be leaving this world with one regret. I'd let another family down. I hadn't been able to save them.

It's not over yet, a voice in the back of my mind said. *You still have time.*

The voice was right. Until my soul left this body, I still had a chance. *Venn* still had a chance.

I peeled my swollen eyes open. Two vampires loomed above me, still delivering blows to my abdomen in what felt like slow motion. Their faces contorted in anger. Did they even know what they were angry about? I felt sorry for them. They probably didn't know what love was. Their curse had stolen that from them, and now they were damned to eternal misery. It wasn't fair of the vampires to take everyone else down with them.

It took all the strength I had to move my lips and force my vocal chords to produce sound. Past the dry, scratchy ache in my throat, an incantation spilled out.

"*Ardeat ignis.*" I repeated the phrase I'd heard Genevieve use to ignite her candles.

I didn't know what I was expecting, but I wasn't ready for the sight that unfolded before my eyes. Red and orange flames engulfed the two vampires above me. The blows against my abdomen immediately stopped as they both stumbled backward, screaming in pain. Heat from the fires warmed my skin, and the smell of burnt flesh filled the air.

The other vampires on the lawn all stepped back, their eyes filled with utter shock.

"What the hell?" Maliya shouted. "Help them!"

The remaining vampires on the lawn rushed forward to help put out the flames, but this wasn't any ordinary fire. This was a witch's fire—*my* fire—and it wasn't giving up that easily. All of Maliya's cronies lit up like they'd been doused in gasoline, the flames spreading rapidly along their skin. It only took moments for the fires engulfing the first two men to fizzle out as their bodies disintegrated into a pile of ash.

Maliya screamed, calling attention to the vampires inside the house. I lifted my head to see a small group of them rushing toward the broken window in the living room to make it outside as fast as they could.

I muttered the incantation under my breath a second time. All throughout the house, red and orange light danced across the walls as Maliya's men burst into flame. Soon, the curtains caught fire, and smoke billowed out the windows. Glass shattered out a window on the second story, and a man alight with flames jumped out of it, screaming. He was already reduced to a pile of ash before he hit the ground.

Teagan and Fiona rushed over to Ryland, who was just regaining consciousness. Venn's swollen face came into view. He touched me gently, making certain he didn't hurt me.

"Rae," he said in a rush, helping me sit up.

That voice. That beautiful voice. I loved the way he said my name—

I didn't get enough time to enjoy it before a strong hand grabbed the back of my shirt and dragged me to my feet. Something sharp pressed to my throat. I glanced to the ground where the vamps had tossed the dagger, but it was gone.

I swallowed, but the fear had completely left my body. Instead, a sense of victory washed over me. Venn and his family were free to make a run for it now.

"What kind of trick are you and your friends playing?" Maliya spat into my ear, but she directed the question at Venn.

He'd shot to his feet. Fiona, Teagan, and Ryland all froze on the ground behind him.

"Let her go," Venn demanded. "You have the locket. You got what you came for."

Maliya laughed. "You know I don't work that way. All of my men are dead."

"Then kill me already," I said in a calm, collected tone. Even I was surprised by it.

"I want to know how you killed them," Maliya demanded.

"You forget…" Venn said as he took a cautious step forward. "We have a powerful witch on our side."

"Sondra?" Maliya asked. "She's not even here. There's no way she could—"

Venn didn't let her finish. In a precise, calculated movement, he leapt and shifted mid-air. His teeth sank into Maliya's arm.

She shrieked and dropped the knife at my throat. Her hold on me vanished as she stumbled backward. I whirled around just in time to see Venn's paws slam straight into Maliya's chest. She fell to the ground, and her arm instantly shot in front of her face to protect herself. The sleeve of her dress rode up her wrist, revealing a scar in the shape of a *V*.

"Wait!" I shouted before Venn could snap at her again.

He hesitated. I rushed forward and grabbed Maliya's wrist as hard as I could. I pulled her sleeve down to reveal the rest of the scar. It matched Cowen's perfectly. It was the same mark that had haunted my dreams for years.

"You're Soulless!" I accused.

Maliya laughed. "Does that surprise you?"

Venn looked up at me with a questioning expression in his eyes.

I ignored him and fixed my eyes on Maliya. A new hope filled my chest. The chance I'd thought had vanished had resurfaced.

"Where are they?" I demanded. "The Soulless. Tell me where they're hiding."

Maliya scoffed. "I left them years ago. Even if they're where they used to be, what makes you think I'd tell you?"

My grip tightened around her wrist, so much that her teeth gritted in pain. "Because if you don't tell me, I'll do the same thing to you as I did to your men."

Realization crossed her eyes when it clicked that I was the witch Venn had been talking about. My fist cracked across the side of her face. Her head twisted to the side, but her expression remained stone cold.

"Tell me where they are," I repeated.

She pressed her lips together.

I took a deep breath and leaned down to Maliya's level. My hands clamped around the blade at her feet. In a flash, my arm swung downward. The dagger stuck from her thigh, and a piercing scream ripped through the air.

"Rae," Venn's voice came from beside me. He'd shifted back to human form. "What's this about?"

I turned to him. "My sister."

Venn looked shocked. "Why didn't you tell me the vampires who took her were Soulless?"

"Because I knew you'd never let me go after them."

"No, I wouldn't," Venn agreed. "It's too dangerous."

I knew he was right, but I still burned to know where my sister had been the last two years.

"I need to know," I whispered.

"You'll just kill me," Maliya accused.

"I won't," I promised. It was worth letting her go if it restored my hope. I ripped the blade from her thigh, and she winced, biting back another scream. "But I have every intention of doing so if you don't talk."

Maliya's lips tightened, like she wasn't sure whether she believed me. "They're on Gregor Island," she admitted. "It's an island in the Great Lakes where Valkas served his prison sentence. It's been cloaked by magic for ages."

"How do I know you're not lying?" I asked.

Maliya smirked. "Because I'd like to see you try to take them on. And because I value my life."

As evil as Maliya was, something told me she wasn't bluffing.

Satisfied, I stood. "You know, you should really learn to read the contract."

"What do you mean?" Maliya snarled.

"I said *I* wouldn't kill you. I made no promises about you making it out of here alive."

I turned to Venn and stuck the handle of the dagger out to him. He glanced down at it momentarily and then took it. Maliya was Venn's demon. It was up to him to decide her fate.

"Wait!" Maliya cried, her voice shaking. She looked up at me with fear glistening in her eyes. "Who *are* you?"

"You know who I am," I said with a smirk. "I'm the Ravenite, bitch."

I turned away. Fiona reached an arm out toward me, and I slid mine around her shoulder. Teagan, Ryland, Fiona, and I faced the house, watching in sorrow as the flames consumed it.

A moment later, Venn's comforting fingers laced in mine. I glanced down to see the locket in his other hand. Behind us, Maliya's dress lay in a heap on the grass.

The sound of sirens blared in the distance.

"I think it's time to go," Ryland said in a strained voice.

Another beat passed as everyone stared up at the house that was once their home. They would never get their house back, but at least they still had each other.

And now I had a family, too.

24

I wrapped my arms around myself, trying to ward off the chill of the night. I was exhausted beyond belief, like all my energy had been sucked out of me with a straw. We'd driven an hour outside of Nocton and stopped in the parking lot of a public hiking trail. It was far enough away from any towns that we could set the bones in Ryland's arm without risk of anyone hearing his screams.

At least, we thought he would scream. It didn't surprise me that he was tough enough not to. He'd bitten down on a rolled-up t-shirt to silence the agony.

"You need to get yourself a pain-relieving spell," he'd told me after I cast the spell to speed his healing.

"Nah," I teased back. "It wouldn't be any fun if you couldn't feel it."

Though the car had already been packed half-full before the vampires attacked, I'd never gotten a chance to retrieve my things from my apartment. Even if I'd had a pain-relief spell copied down in my spell book—which I didn't —I wouldn't have been able to use it.

I stood on the bank of the river not far from the parking lot we'd stopped at. I stared out across the water that reflected the moonlight. Footsteps approached, and I knew without looking that they were Venn's.

"Ryland's feeling better," he said in a near whisper once he reached me.

A light weight settled on my shoulders, and my arms suddenly started to warm. I pulled the sweatshirt Venn had offered tighter around me and inhaled the scent. It smelled like cinnamon—like Venn. He stuck his hands into the pockets of his jeans and gazed to the tall trees on the other side of the narrow, rippling water.

A sense of relief washed over me. "That's good. It'll take a while until he's back to normal. I've found that the spell only increases healing by about a factor of ten."

"I don't know about that," Venn said. "He says it hardly feels tender anymore. Maybe with your practice casting the spell you've gotten better."

"Maybe," I agreed. "How are you feeling? How are your ribs?"

I looked to him. In the moonlight, I could see that the swelling on his face had significantly decreased. Even my own tender bruises didn't hurt anymore.

Venn gazed down at me. "I'm feeling better. Tired, but better."

I cracked a smile. "Me, too."

"You should get some rest," he suggested. "Fiona's already curled up on the back seat."

I could really use some sleep, even if I had to nap in the grass tonight.

"Once everyone's ready, we'll grab some food and then head to Matias's," Venn said. "It's about another three hours away."

Teagan had explained to me in the car where they'd found the locket. Ryland had been wearing it. When he shifted, it broke off his neck and flew beneath the coat rack in the hallway. The family had once again found their hope in getting Sondra back safely. I had my hope for my own sister, but at this point, I didn't know what to do with it.

A silence hung in the air between Venn and me.

"You're still going after her, aren't you?" Venn asked softly. "After your sister?"

I turned to him and wrapped my arms around his waist. My head rested on his shoulder. The warmth of his arms around me and his breath through my hair was unlike anything else. I could almost forget the world had gone to shit. In his arms, I felt safe. Everything felt perfect.

"I am," I whispered.

Venn's shoulder's fell. "Then I'm going with you."

Relief washed through me, even though I knew it was selfish of me to want him to come.

I sighed. "I don't know where to start. The Great Lakes are *huge*. We need to narrow it down."

"I think Sondra might be able to help," Venn said. "She may at least know someone who can point us in the right direction."

I buried my face deeper into his neck, contemplating my options. "Then I'm coming with you. After we reunite your family, we'll reunite mine."

Venn smiled that heart-melting smile of his. "We will. I promise."

He bent down and brushed his lips against mine. My chest ignited with fireworks. A warmth spread over my skin, washing away the last of the tenderness in my muscles. I wondered if he knew he had that effect on me.

Times had never been worse, but they'd never been better, either. With Venn, I could honestly believe that things were about to change for the better.

Hang in there, Jenna, I thought. *I'm coming for you.*

END OF BOOK ONE

RESILIENCE

BOOK TWO

1

Matias Vayne must've had a dick the size of a breath mint. That was the only explanation I could think of as I stood at the base of Vayne Tower, trying to take in its sheer magnitude. This vamp was definitely compensating for something.

The morning sun was hidden behind the clouds—or was it smog?—but still, the windows six hundred feet above my head seemed to reflect the light. It wasn't the tallest building in Chicago, but it certainly stood out in the forest of skyscrapers with its clean, modern architecture.

"Rae?" Venn's voice cut through my thoughts.

I tore my gaze from the massive structure and turned to him. He wore a navy button-down collared shirt over a clean white t-shirt and a pair of jeans. The sleeves were rolled up casually, showing off his toned forearms. His dark eyes traveled over me, sending a wave of butterflies to dance around in my stomach. I swore Venn got hotter by the day.

So unfair.

"Are you ready?" he asked.

"Yeah," I said. "I just didn't think it'd be... so big."

"I know," Ryland agreed from several paces ahead. "It's a little over-the-top, isn't it?"

"Maybe he needs it," Teagan mumbled. "You know, for his... ego."

Fiona stifled a laugh beside Teagan. She wore black slacks and a nice purple top, but she didn't have the heels for it. Teagan hadn't foregone her usual skin-tight cargo pants, but she'd put an olive-green cardigan over her black tank top and let her dark hair fall in waves around her shoulders.

After fleeing their burning home, none of us had many personal items with us anymore. Teagan, Venn, and Fiona had managed to pack a few bags in the

147

car before the fire consumed everything else, but Ryland and I had nothing. I still wore my ripped jeans, black tee, and boots. Ryland wore his usual enchanted clothing—jeans and a t-shirt. His left arm hung in a sling we'd picked up this morning, since the bones were still healing after the vampire attack.

Even with everyone else's attempt to look business-casual, we still stuck out in the sea of businessmen and women rushing to their next appointments. Luckily, most people didn't notice us. They were either preoccupied on their phones or staring straight ahead like robots. I had the urge to slap one of them just to see if they had feelings.

I already missed Nocton, where we only had a hundred thousand people or so to worry about. Cities packed to the millions weren't exactly my thing. But I had to face it for a few hours, because once we got inside and exchanged the Leora Locket for Sondra's safety, we'd finally be able to hunt down my sister.

As we approached the front doors, Fiona leaned over to me and whispered. "You're going to love Sondra. She once made Ryland believe he was a chicken for three days because he insulted her drawings. We fed him dry cereal just to watch him peck at it."

She giggled, lightening the mood. I couldn't help but laugh at the thought.

We stepped into a huge lobby. Tile floor stretched out in front of us, and the room bustled with foot traffic. The ceiling was so high and the room so long that I was pretty sure it was big enough to play football in. The tall windows were heavily tinted, blocking out most of the sun and casting a gray hue across the room. I noticed several pairs of silver eyes and realized the dark windows provided enough sun protection to allow vampires to roam the building during the day.

The lobby was empty of everything—even color—except for a long white desk situated opposite the door. There weren't even any seating areas—or God forbid, a plant. Eight elevators lined the wall beside the front desk, where people hurried in and out of them.

Ryland led the way across the lobby and stopped at the front desk. A thin woman in a dark blazer looked up from her computer. Her lips immediately turned down, showing the age lines around her eyes that she clearly tried to hide.

"Can I help you?" She sounded like she meant it, but there was judgement in her eyes. Apparently, we didn't look rich enough for her blood. She probably thought we were lost and needed directions or something.

"Yes," Ryland said in a confident tone. "We're here to see Matias Vayne."

The woman couldn't hide the scoff that escaped her lips. Her expression quickly fell so that I could barely read her face. Another robot. We wouldn't want genuine human interaction, would we?

No, I thought, *not when you work with heartless vamps.*

"I'm sorry," Robot Lady said, "but Mr. Vayne doesn't take walk-ins."

"He will for us," Ryland insisted. "Tell him we're here on behalf of Leora."

"I'm sorry," she repeated, "but your boss is going to have to call Mr. Vayne's secretary privately to set up an appointment."

I held my breath. We *had* to get in. There was no way we were leaving here without Sondra.

I wasn't going to wait around. I pushed past Ryland and leaned my elbows against the counter. "You have a phone right there. Call his office and let him know we're here."

"Ma'am," she said with a frown, like my demand only amused her, "if I called Mr. Vayne every time someone came in asking for him, he'd never get any work done. If this is an urgent matter, your boss can—"

"Is there a problem here?" A woman with flawless dark skin and silver eyes stepped forward. Even her vampirism couldn't strip away her dark skin tone. Her hair was pulled back into a tight bun at the base of her neck, and she wore a slimming red pantsuit and high heels.

"They want to see Mr. Vayne," Robot Lady replied. "On behalf of... what did you say your boss's name was?"

"Leora," Ryland told her.

"Right. And I told them—" Robot Lady started, but the vampire cut her off.

"Leora?" She looked at us in shock. "Please, come with me."

Robot Lady stared at us with her mouth agape as we followed behind her vampire boss. She led us away from the long line of elevators and to a hall at the far end of the lobby.

"Mr. Vayne has been eagerly awaiting your arrival," she said in a professional tone.

"We apologize that we couldn't make it sooner," Fiona said.

Vampire Boss stopped at the end of the hall and pressed a button beside the lone elevator that stood there. She folded her hands and turned to us. "Not to worry. You're here now, and that's what's important."

The elevator doors slid open, and Vampire Boss gestured for us to step inside. We all filed in. She pressed the button to the top floor, and the doors glided shut.

My gut twisted as the elevator ascended, and it wasn't because I was scared of cramped spaces. We'd just locked ourselves in a tiny room with a vampire who could eat us all if she wanted to. Not that she'd succeed, considering she was outnumbered, but I still felt uneasy in her presence. Instinct told me to stake a weapon through her heart, but even if it came to that, there were no weapons in the immediate vicinity. We'd all agreed Teagan should leave her blades in the car so we wouldn't provoke the vamps.

The elevator was eerily quiet, despite the tacky music playing softly from hidden speakers. Venn must've noticed my unease, because he grabbed my hand and squeezed it. Tingles spread across my skin at his touch. I laced my fingers through his and squeezed back.

The elevator doors opened, revealing an elegant waiting room. There were no windows, and the room was cast in soft lighting. Black carpet stretched from one gray wall to the other. Plush red couches that looked worth more than I made in a year sat around a burning gas fireplace. If Matias was going for *modern vampire lair*, he'd certainly hit the decor on the nose.

Beyond the waiting area, a blonde woman with breasts that bulged out of her top sat behind a long reception desk. She wore a pair of reading glasses, but I knew she didn't need them. Her silver eyes gave her away as a vampire. Along with flawless beauty and supernatural strength, vampires had perfect vision. Beside Blondie and straight across from the elevator sat a pair of double doors.

Blondie glanced up from her desk and smiled when she saw Vampire Boss leading us into the room. "What can I help you with, Veronica?"

"These ladies and gentlemen are here to see Mr. Vayne," Vampire Boss—Veronica—replied, stopping at the desk.

Blondie turned to her computer. "Do they have an appointment?"

"No, which is why I escorted them here personally," Veronica said. "They're here on behalf of Leora."

Blondie typed something into her computer. "Mm… Leora… I don't think—" Realization suddenly dawned. "Oh! I'll let Mr. Vayne know right away." Blondie quickly picked up the phone on her desk and punched in a number.

"Please, sit," Veronica offered, gesturing to the red chairs nearby. "Can I get you anything while you wait?"

I could've asked for a water, but who knew if they served anything but blood around here? They probably planned to add us to the menu.

"No, thanks," Venn said. "We're fine."

Everyone else nodded in agreement.

"Enjoy your visit to Vayne Tower," Veronica said kindly before leaving us alone and returning to the elevator.

Because I was *so* going to enjoy myself in a vampire-infested skyscraper.

I shifted uncomfortably in my seat. For expensive-looking couches, they weren't very comfortable.

"You okay?" Venn asked from beside me.

I nodded, though honestly, I felt uneasy. I preferred to kick vampire ass on the street, where there was an easy escape. Here, we were trapped. I hoped Ryland knew what he was doing.

From the chair beside Venn, Fiona grabbed a magazine off the end table and began flipping through it. Teagan sat close to her, looking distressed. Ryland stood near the fireplace with a hard look on his face. He wasn't about to try getting comfortable in a place like this.

Venn's thigh brushed against mine. My skin heated where he touched me, and all I wanted to do was scoot closer to him and wrap my arms around him. Freaking hormones. Now was not the time.

We were only alone for a moment before the double doors beside the reception desk swung open. I turned to see a man in his early forties step out of the room. He had a strong jaw, straight nose, and a five o'clock shadow that most women would swoon over. Like all vampires, his skin was flawless, and his eyes were silver. He wore a dark tailored suit that showed off his trim figure. Not a single one of his brown hairs was misplaced. Everything about him screamed *money*. Though the very sight of the vampire repulsed me, I couldn't deny that the guy was insanely attractive. What was it with rich, attractive men like him? He set off all sorts of *asshole* alarms.

I stood, mostly because I didn't want to let my guard down, but I suspected Venn, Teagan, and Fiona followed suit out of respect.

"Ryland," the vampire sang. He opened his arms wide, as if expecting a hug.

Ryland stood rigid. "Matias."

Matias dropped his arms. Up close, I got a better look at his eyes. I could've sworn I recognized him from somewhere. I racked my brain trying to remember, but I figured I'd just seen him in a TV commercial or something.

Matias's eyes scanned our group until they fell on me. "Who's the lovely new lady?"

He reached out his hand for mine. I swallowed hard but let him take it. This guy probably wiped his ass with hundred-dollar bills. I didn't want to find out what he'd use his money for if we disrespected him. His fingers were cold, sending a shiver down my spine. He brought my hand to his face and brushed his icy lips across it. I wanted to gag.

Venn stepped forward. "This is Rae, and if you know what's good for you, you'll keep your grubby little hands off of her."

Matias dropped my hand. Venn was officially my hero. I could kiss him right now. Then again, I always wanted to kiss him.

"I think the witch-shifter can speak for herself," Matias said, eyeing me curiously.

"I can," I replied through tight lips. "But you're lucky I didn't. How'd you know I was a witch?"

Matias smirked. "I didn't, but you've just confirmed it."

"You play dirty. I see how it is," I said.

Matias laughed. "Sweetheart, I'm a vampire. Dirty is all we know. I may be able to find a position here for you if you're in to that kind of thing."

Was he hitting on me? *Gross!*

Venn snuck his shoulder in front of mine protectively. Good thing, because if Matias kept looking at me that way, my knee would be all up in his royal jewels. My lack of self-control was a serious curse.

"Are we done yet?" Ryland cut in. He sounded completely unamused. "Let's cut to the chase, Matias. You know why we're here."

Matias's eyes lit up. "Yes, of course. I presume you have the item on you."

The way he said it suggested the family wouldn't dare enter this building without it.

"We want to see Sondra first," Ryland demanded.

"You'll see her as soon as I receive the locket," Matias said coolly.

"No," Teagan protested.

"I've got this, Tea," Ryland said under his breath as he placed a hand on her shoulder.

Teagan ignored him. "You'll bring her out here safe and unharmed, or you can kiss your precious locket goodbye."

Matias smirked, like he found Teagan amusing. He glanced between the five of us and must've decided we weren't screwing around.

"Fair enough." Matias turned to Blondie behind her desk. "Allison, call Walker and tell him to bring the girl."

"Yes, sir," Allison said as she picked up the phone on her desk.

The following silence was agonizing. Matias stood there with his hands folded in front of him. He held his head high, looking positively pleased. Though Ryland held his gaze, Matias's eyes kept flickering toward me. It made my skin crawl.

The sound of a door opening across the room caught all of our attention. A tall, muscular vampire in a suit stepped into room, dragging a woman by her wrist behind him.

"Let me go!" she protested.

"Do as she says, Walker," Matias commanded calmly. "She is, after all, our guest."

Walker dropped the woman's hand, and she straightened. She was tall, but so thin that it looked like they hadn't fed her in days. She looked at least thirty, and though she had dark circles under her brown eyes and wore no makeup, she was beautiful. Her facial structure was similar to Fiona's, but her chestnut hair matched Ryland's.

I couldn't explain it, but I could sense a goodness radiating off of her, like she was someone I could trust even though she was a complete stranger.

Her eyes fell on our group, and she instantly rushed forward.

"Hold on, Sondra." Matias held a hand up, and Sondra stopped in her tracks.

"What'd you do to her?" Venn demanded.

Matias shrugged. "Nothing. It's not my fault she refused to eat. I'll take the locket now."

"Do we have your word that we'll be allowed to leave unharmed?" Ryland asked.

"Yes," Matias answered. "I'm a vampire. I'm not a monster. I run clean business deals."

A muscle popped in Ryland's jaw. I wasn't sure how Matias could consider a hostage situation a *clean* business deal.

Matias held out his hand expectantly, and Ryland reached into his pocket and pulled out the golden locket. He placed it in Matias's hand.

"It's been a pleasure doing business with you," Matias said with a smile. "Half of the agreed amount will be deposited into your bank account within the hour."

"Half?" Ryland gawked.

"Yes, half." Matias was dead serious. "You were late on your delivery. Be glad

I'm generous enough to offer payment at all, considering your unprofessionalism."

Nobody said anything. I mean, Matias was right. He could've just had his vampire staff kill us all. Matias turned on his heel. Sondra ran forward, and Fiona pushed past the rest of us to reach her first. They fell into an embrace. Fiona buried her face in Sondra's hair.

"I'm so glad you're all okay," Sondra whispered.

Teagan stepped forward and joined in their hug. Venn stayed back and wrapped an arm around my waist. I leaned into him, welcoming his comfort.

Ryland cleared his throat and stole a glance at Matias, who'd stopped in front of the double doors to watch us. *Creep.*

"A lot has happened since you've been gone," Ryland said.

Sondra caught my eye. She tilted her head, as if trying to recall where she'd seen me before. I wondered if maybe she'd visited Bloodstone, the spell shop I worked at—used to work at.

"I can see that," she said. "I'm Sondra, but I guess you knew that already."

I shook the hand she offered and nodded.

"We can get to more formal introductions later," Venn said. "Let's get you somewhere comfortable."

"Agreed," Sondra said quickly.

Matias's eyes followed us all the way to the elevator. Every time I looked back, he was staring at me. Shivers tickled down my spine like a thousand tiny spiders crawling across my back. I itched for him to give me a reason to pick a fight. The guy was pompous as hell. Every instinct told me to run far, far away.

Or punch him in the nose. One of the two.

Venn must've noticed my discomfort, because he pulled me closer. "It's okay. We'll be out of here soon enough."

We filed into the elevator, and I whispered to Venn under my breath. "That guy creeps me out."

"I know," Venn agreed. "He creeps everyone out."

The hair on the back of my neck rose as we exited the building. It was as if Matias's eyes were still on me. Normally, vampires didn't scare me, but in that moment, an all-consuming fear hit my chest like a freight train. What if he *was* watching me?

"What do you think he's going to use the Leora Locket for?" I asked. I knew it could be used to tell the future based on a person's current intentions, but I couldn't help but wonder what his end goal was. Did he want the locket as a novelty item, or was there something bigger going on here?

"It doesn't matter," Fiona said as we descended the steps in front of Vayne Tower. "I told you it's pretty useless anyway."

"It depends on how you use it," Sondra mumbled under her breath.

"What do you mean?" Teagan asked.

Sondra hesitated and glanced around at the bustling street. "I have something to tell all of you, but we need to find somewhere safe to talk. I don't think —" Sondra cut off.

"Think what?" Venn asked.

"Does anyone else feel that?" Sondra whispered while quickening her step.

Ryland looked around to follow Sondra's flickering gaze. He glanced to the darkening sky. "Feel what? A storm rolling in?"

"No," Sondra said. "That tingle on the back of your neck, like—"

"Like you're being watched?" I cut in.

Sondra swallowed. "Exactly. We need to get to the car now. I think we're being followed."

2

"What the hell's going on?" Ryland demanded the second we were back in the car.

Fiona shifted into her fox form and curled up on Sondra's lap next to me in the back seat. It was the only way we'd all fit. Venn sat on my other side with his comforting arm around me. It helped slow my pounding heart that had followed me on the long walk back to the car.

Teagan turned in the passenger seat to face us. "They didn't hurt you, did they?"

"No," Sondra said in a rush. "Just start the car, and let's get out of here."

Ryland turned the key and shifted into drive. I had no idea where he was headed. I only knew that none of us wanted to hang around Vayne Tower. As soon as we were moving, I felt like I could finally breathe again. The tingle on the back of my neck had vanished, but there was still a feeling in the pit of my stomach that told me I shouldn't let my guard down just yet.

"So, Sondra, about Rae…" Venn started.

"We can talk about what happened while I was gone later," Sondra insisted. "Right now, we have more pressing matters. I overheard some things. I know why Matias wanted the locket. We have to stop him."

Every muscle in my body tensed.

Ryland glanced to Sondra in the rearview mirror. "I thought you said this was a harmless job. You said he wouldn't even know how to use the locket."

"And I also said the locket's power lies in how you use it," Sondra clarified. "I thought for sure he was going to use it to watch his competitors. The locket only shows a *possible* future. It's very hard to use it to predict someone else's intentions."

Ryland pressed the brakes as the cars in front of us slowed at a stoplight. "What's he going to use it for, then?"

"He's not going to use it to predict someone else's intentions," Sondra said. "He's going to use it to predict his own."

My brow furrowed. Did she mean he was going to use it to gamble?

"What does that even mean?" Teagan asked.

Sondra swallowed. "He's going to use the locket to predict the outcome of his decisions so that he can find the thing he really wants."

"Which is…?" Venn prodded.

"He just called it the Artifact," Sondra answered. "From what I heard, it's an ancient object that's been hidden for centuries that's capable of wiping out magic again—for everyone except the owner."

"Wait," I blurted, my whole body igniting in alarm. "Matias wants to be the *only* person who can use magic?"

Pompous ass.

Sondra nodded.

"That doesn't make any sense," Teagan pointed out. "He's a vampire. How's he going to use magic?"

"I don't know," Sondra admitted. "He could retrieve the artifact now and wait for reincarnation. That's what I'd do."

"Hold up," I stopped her. "Reincarnation?"

Why hadn't anyone mentioned this to me when they told me about Synchrony?

"Yes, reincarnation," Sondra confirmed. "It's the only reason Matias hired us to find the locket in the first place."

I stared at her, completely baffled.

"Sondra was the witch who created the Leora Locket," Venn explained.

"I thought the Leora Locket was centuries old," I said. "And Fiona told me the witch who created it was named Leora."

"Yes," Sondra agreed. "That was my name, in a past life."

I pressed my fingers to my temples. Holy crap! Past lives? It was a lot to wrap my head around, though I shouldn't have been surprised by anything these days.

I lifted my head, my curiosity piqued. "How'd you create it?"

Sondra glanced to Venn, as if wondering how much I already knew and how much she could trust me to share.

"Magic can be bound to everyday objects," Venn explained. "It usually happens over time when an object is long associated with strong emotions, which could be good or bad. That's why houses can be haunted or a rabbit's foot can bring luck. Things like family heirlooms or old wedding rings tend to have a lot of positive magic tied to them. A weapon used in murder would have a lot of bad energy surrounding it."

I shuddered thinking about it.

"That's not the only way to create a magical object," Sondra said. "Witches can infuse magic into things, such as by using them in a powerful spell. For most people, these magical artifacts will affect their emotions, depending on the energy they give off. For witches, they can be incredibly valuable. They can be used in certain spells or can amplify a witch's abilities. They can be very dangerous if the wrong witch gets their hands on them."

"When you say you created the Leora Locket in a past life and found it in this one… you just remembered where you left it?" I asked. "And if Matias finds the Artifact in this life, he'll remember in his next?"

Sondra shook her head. "It's not that easy. As a high witch, I'm able to remember bits and pieces of my past lives, but they're not as strong as my memories of this life. The memories come to me in in flashes or in dreams. It took us months of gathering clues from visions of my past life to find the locket."

"So, Matias would have to be born a high witch in his next life to even have a chance of using the Artifact?" I asked, relaxing slightly.

Sondra frowned. "That's not how it works. You aren't born a witch by chance."

What she said completely shocked me. If I wasn't a witch by chance, how did I become one?

"Excuse me?" I asked.

"Witch magic is connected to your soul," Teagan told me. "It's all about how closely connected you are to Synchrony. If you were a witch in a past life, you're more likely to be a witch in the next life. You don't get to become a high witch without lifetimes of practice under your belt. That's why, even though the rest of us understand magic, none of us are any good at it… yet. But we're all working on it."

"Anyone can become a witch?" I asked.

"Yes," Sondra confirmed. "The ability can be nurtured. The more a person studies witchcraft throughout their lives, the more powerful he or she becomes. It's easier with each lifetime. I think Matias used to be a witch before he became a vampire. It makes sense how he accomplished so much in the business world."

My head spun. "I'm guessing you know why vampires can't use witch magic. You seem to know everything else."

"Vampires are ruthless because the vampire virus damages their soul," Sondra explained. "But since witch magic is connected to the soul, they're unable to access magic. No one's quite sure how badly vampirism damages the soul, but I think that when a vampire dies, their soul is freed from their body's prison, and they start over in a new life."

"Killing them is doing them a favor," Ryland mumbled from the driver's seat.

Huh. You learn something new every day.

"Why don't all vampires want to die, then?" I asked.

"Because they don't all believe the same thing," Teagan answered. "And they don't want to lose their immortality. They'd lose any power they've already established and have to start over. Which makes me think Matias isn't going to wait around to be reincarnated to use this artifact. He's so rich, he could easily pay a witch to do it for him."

"Why would he do that?" I asked.

Teagan shrugged. "I can think of a lot of reasons. Maybe he wants to eliminate some of his competition. My guess is that he wants to control magic and sell it to the highest bidder."

Venn turned to Sondra. "Would this artifact allow him to do that?"

"It sounded like it," she replied. "I think that's what makes it so powerful, that the owner gets to pick and choose who keeps their magic and who doesn't."

"That's pure evil!" I blurted. "So essentially he'd be the most powerful man alive?" *And the richest, too.*

Who the hell did he think he was, trying to strip everyone of their magic? No more healing spells from me. No more shifting into a raven. No more super strength so I could protect humans against vampires. It felt like a personal attack. I shook in rage.

"No kidding," Sondra agreed. "That's why we have to go after it and destroy it. No one should have that kind of power."

Ryland's good hand tightened around the steering wheel. "We should've killed him back there."

"If we killed him, then what?" Sondra asked. "We'd just walk out of Vayne Tower? We all would've been executed on the spot. If the chance presents itself, believe me, I'll be the first to drive a stake through his heart."

Sondra was fierce. I liked her.

"Why couldn't you have escaped?" I blurted. "I mean, if you're a high witch."

Sondra sighed. "First of all, Matias's place is heavily enchanted. Second, even high witches have their limits."

Ryland floored the pedal as we turned onto the freeway ramp. "What if he uses the locket to watch us? He's at a huge advantage here."

"I know," Sondra admitted. "I haven't figured that part out yet. Either way, we have to find this thing before he does."

My jaw clenched. What about the promise Venn made to me?

"We're just going to drop everything to go after it?" I tried to keep the irritation out of my tone, but I couldn't help it.

"It's not like we have anything to go back to," Teagan mumbled.

Sondra sat straighter. "What do you mean?"

Everyone exchanged a glance. Fiona dropped her head. It was clear no one knew how to tell her.

Teagan's fingers tightened against the back of her seat. "I'm going to be blunt, because there's no other way to tell you... the house burnt down."

"What?!" Sondra exploded. She seemed like such a quiet, gentle person that it surprised me to hear her shout.

"We had a run-in with Maliya," Venn admitted. "She came to the house and... it was the only way we could escape. We were kind of hoping everyone would presume us dead in the fire."

Sondra pressed two fingers to her eyes. "It's okay," she finally said with a sigh. "What matters is that none of you were hurt."

"Where do we start?" Venn asked.

The breath left my chest. I stared at him in shock. He was just going to ignore his promise to me?

Of course—because he'd known these people a heck of a lot longer than he knew me. Why would he feel any loyalty toward me? Plus, it only made sense to go after the thing that would save a bunch of people rather than going after one person who may or may not still be alive.

She's alive, I told myself. *And I finally have a lead. I just didn't want to do this alone.*

I turned my gaze from Venn, hoping he wouldn't notice my expression. I couldn't tell him what I was really thinking. It was selfish.

"I want to stop for supplies," Sondra said. "Remember my friend Amalia? She helped us with a job last year. She lives here in Chicago and can help us get what we need. I'll run a spell that should help us figure out where to start. And for heaven's sake, can we please stop for a burger or something? I'm starving."

Venn pulled me closer and whispered in my ear. His hot breath rushed across the side of my face. It was almost enough to distract me. "What's wrong, Rae?"

"Nothing," I mumbled.

"Please don't lie to me," he said softly.

A heavy weight settled on my chest. I wonder how *he* liked being lied to.

"I'm not the only liar in this car," I snapped in a hushed whisper.

Venn's eyebrows drew together. "Rae..."

I spoke so quietly that only he could hear. "I just thought..." I hated feeling this way.

"That we were going after your sister?" he finished for me. "We will. We are."

"Are we?" I whispered.

I didn't know why I said that. All I knew was that my hopes had been crushed once again. My chest tightened, and my face heated. All I wanted was to shift into raven form so that he couldn't see my expression.

"Hey, Sondra," Venn said. "If it's cool with you, Rae and I have some unfinished business to attend to—"

"Venn, no," I protested under my breath. It wasn't fair of me to ask him to do this. I could do this on my own. I didn't *want* to, but I could.

Venn lowered his voice again just for me. "I promised I'd help you find your sister after we rescued Sondra. I don't break my promises."

My chest suddenly seemed ten pounds lighter, but it still didn't seem right to accept his generous offer.

"Where are you going to go?" Sondra asked.

Venn bit his lower lip. "I'm not sure, but we have to start somewhere. Rae's looking for her sister, and we believe she might be at a place called Gregor Island. Have you heard of it?"

Sondra thought about it for a second, then shook her head. Of course she didn't know. Not even the Internet knew anything about Gregor Island. Maybe Maliya had lied to us.

Filthy vampires.

"We believe it's where the Soulless are hiding," Venn said.

Sondra's eyes widened, and Fiona's pointed ears perked up. Even in her fox form, I could see the frown on her face. She looked terrified for us.

"You know you can't go," Teagan protested.

"We already talked about this, Tea," Venn replied. "Rae's stubborn, and she's going after her sister with or without us. I'm not letting her go alone."

Swoon.

"You know what you're getting into, don't you?" Sondra asked, as if in warning.

"Yes," I answered automatically. And it was worth it. For Jenna. I turned to Venn. "But you don't have to come with me. I don't want you to get hurt."

Who was I kidding? I definitely wanted him to come with me. But it was true that I didn't want to see him hurt.

Venn brushed a piece of hair behind my ear. "That's exactly why I'm going with you, Rae."

Out of the corner of my eye, I swore I saw Teagan roll her eyes from the front seat. Because she *totally* wasn't all over Ryland all the time.

"You're sure?" Sondra asked Venn. "I mean, if you—"

"I'm sure," he cut her off. "You need to get the Artifact, and we need to find Jenna."

I shot Venn a small smile.

"How are you going to get around?" Sondra asked.

"We'll rent a car," Venn decided.

Sondra raised an eyebrow. "And you'll stay in touch?"

Venn nodded. "Every step of the way."

Sondra pursed her lips—like she wasn't ready to tell Venn goodbye but knew she couldn't talk him out of this. "I don't want you going by yourself."

"But we—" Venn started.

Sondra cut him off. "There may be something else we can do."

My curiosity piqued.

"We'll split up for a few hours," Sondra said. "You can look for information on Rae's sister while we gather supplies. We'll meet up when we're both finished."

"I'm guessing you know where we should start?" Venn replied.

"I know a witch named Clarita who might have some information on the Soulless," Sondra told him. "Luckily for you, she's on the way."

3

The tension in the air was palpable the moment Venn and I stepped into the elevator at Clarita's condo. Venn pressed a button, and the doors slid shut, trapping us alone inside. We stood side-by-side facing the door, neither of us daring to steal a glance at the other.

Venn was close enough that I could smell his familiar scent. It made my insides go haywire. Every muscle in my body told me to turn to him and jump into his arms, to press my body against his and tangle my fingers in his hair. I wanted him to kiss me back like he meant it, to touch me in places I'd never been touched before. The surface of my skin heated just thinking about it. It was crazy what being alone with a guy for barely a second could do to your basic instincts.

Except Venn wasn't just any guy. He was *the* guy, the one I could picture giving everything to and spending the rest of my life with.

I'm going to have his shifter babies someday.

What the hell? Where did that come from? Behave, brain.

Venn broke the silence. "Are we ever going to talk about it?"

I glanced to him and tucked a loose strand of hair behind my ear. I willed myself not to blush, but my pale skin betrayed me. "Talk about what?"

Venn must've thought I was stupid, because the look in his eyes gave everything away. Couldn't we just make out and let the moment speak for itself?

"*You* know," he said with a teasing smile. "Don't you feel the crazy connection between us?"

Of course I did, but I wasn't about to admit it out loud. Except, with Venn, I almost *wanted* to talk about it. It was weird. I didn't like sharing my feelings with anyone, but there was something about Venn—about his whole family—that made me want to open up.

Venn inched closer to me until his chest was only an inch away from mine. If I breathed too hard, my boobs were going to touch him. Not that that'd be a bad thing…

There was plenty of space in the elevator for both of us, but in that moment, it felt as if the walls were shrinking in on us—and not in a claustrophobic I-need-to-get-out-of-here kind of way. More in a way that made me feel secure and safe, and freakishly hot. Why was my skin burning up?

"I think you know I feel it, too," I whispered.

What the heck? I wasn't supposed to say things like that out loud. But something about it felt *good*. It felt *right*. Nothing had felt right in years, so speaking the truth to someone I trusted was a relief.

Venn reached up to brush my hair from my eyes. His touch sent an electric tingle across my cheek. I dropped my gaze, hoping he couldn't tell that he totally took my breath away. I killed vampires for fun. I wasn't supposed to be brought to my knees by the simple touch of a drop-dead gorgeous guy.

Don't kid yourself. You'll be dropping to your knees eventually.

I bit down on my lip to keep from smiling. *Get your mind out of the gutter, Rachel.*

"What should we do about it?" Venn whispered. His hot breath rushed across my face.

I inched backward. I wasn't sure why, considering all I wanted to do was close that small gap between us. Venn followed until my back was pressed up against the wall. My lower back dug into the metal rail that lined the perimeter of the elevator.

I suddenly realized what I was doing. I *wanted* him to advance on me, because it meant he wanted me. By the look in his eyes, he wanted me as much as—if not more than—I wanted him. A shot of adrenaline raced through my veins, and my heart slammed against my rib cage as I waited for Venn to make the next move.

He wrapped his arms around the rail on both sides of me, trapping me in. I made no effort to escape, though. This position was hot as hell. I'd stay trapped between his arms as long as he liked, if the fool would just kiss me already.

The elevator *dinged*, pulling me out of my trance. Venn jumped and turned toward the doors as they slid open. Reality came crashing down on me, reminding me why we were here.

Damn it. We had to get serious now.

Venn looked as disappointed as I felt.

"We'll pick this up later?" I suggested.

"Yeah," he said with a shy nod. "Right where we left off."

Good, I thought in relief. I had something to look forward to.

My heart slowed as we stepped out of the elevator on the twelfth floor of Clarita's building. The long hall was lit with soft lighting, and the doors were spaced far apart. The spotless gray patterned carpet made the apartment building look like a luxury hotel.

When I heard the word *witch*, I pictured cauldrons and pointed hats, but I'd come to learn that they were as diverse as anyone. Some witches, like Genevieve, preferred the cobwebs-in-the-corner Halloween theme. Others, like Clarita White, opted for modern luxuries. Judging by the condominium she lived in, she hadn't let her powers go to waste.

We reached the end of the hall and stopped in front of a door marked *1212*. I took a breath and knocked.

A woman poked her head into the hallway. All I could see was her shoulder-length black hair with thick bangs that brushed the top of her cat-rimmed glasses. She glanced between Venn and me.

"You're the ones Sondra called about?" she asked before either of us had a chance to speak.

"Yes," Venn answered. "May we come in?"

Clarita swung the door open, and I finally got a good look at her. She was at least three inches shorter than me with a curvy figure that filled out the dark purple dress she wore. Long earrings with rainbow-colored feathers attached dangled from her ears. Gorgeous blue beads hung from her neck, and she wore all different kinds of rings on each of her fingers.

She shot us a friendly smile. Clarita had a vibrant glow about her that I instantly connected with. She gave off serious *cool aunt* vibes, like she was the kind of person you could say anything to and get the best advice in return.

"Can I get you anything?" Clarita asked as we stepped inside. "Perhaps tea or water?"

"Water's fine," I answered.

Clarita gestured for us to sit while she closed the door behind us and headed to the kitchen. Her condo walls were white, but the decor was accented in every color of the rainbow. Pink, green, and blue throw pillows filled the couch and matched the bright floral pattern of her area rug. A coffee table with a stack of books on it sat in the center of the room, and a large-screen TV hung on the wall opposite the couch. Glass doors with long drapes beside them led out onto a balcony, and potted plants dotted the room. The condo wasn't huge—Clarita only seemed to have as much as she needed—but it was nice enough that I was sure it cost more to live here than what I made in a month.

I sank into the couch next to Venn. The cushions were so soft I could've fallen asleep right then and there.

"Here you go." Clarita returned and handed us each a bottled water. It was cold in my hand and refreshing when I took a sip.

"What do you do for work?" I couldn't help but let my curiosity get to me.

Clarita sat in the plush armchair across from us. "I own a boutique shop not far from here. It's been my dream since I was a kid."

"You don't work in magic?" Venn asked. He sounded surprised, like every other witch he'd met used their magic for profit.

"I used to," Clarita said as she adjusted her glasses. "Now I only work with a select few clients. What is it that I can help you with?"

Venn and I exchanged a glance. This wasn't the type of conversation you approached lightly.

Venn leaned forward and rested his elbows on his knees. He spoke slowly. "Sondra said you might know something about the Soulless."

Clarita's right eyebrow twitched slightly, but apart from that, she didn't let her thoughts show. She took a long, deep breath and then let it out in a sigh. "I'm afraid I can't tell you much."

My body went so numb that my water bottle slipped out of my fingers and landed on the cushion beside me.

"It's true that I've had an interest in the Soulless for many years," Clarita said. "I, along with many other witches, am quite interested in learning what happened to them. We know how they came to be, but we don't know where they disappeared to when they went silent two years ago. Some suspect they're planning something big and that they'll be returning in full force soon."

"What do *you* think?" Venn asked.

Clarita straightened in her chair. "I haven't reached a clear conclusion yet. I've been trying to track them down for years, hoping that if we could infiltrate their nest, we might be able to figure out what they're planning. So far, I've only come up with guesses. Tracking spells, unfortunately, can be quite tricky without a starting point."

"Like how you need something that belongs to a person to track them?" I asked, remembering how we'd used Cowen's watch to track him.

"Exactly," Clarita confirmed. "But in this case, since we're looking for a hidden location, it starts with information. Unfortunately, we don't have enough of it."

"Information like what?" I asked slowly, wondering if what Venn and I learned from Maliya was enough.

"A general location would be a good start," Clarita said. "We know the Soulless are somewhere in the States, but reports are pretty widespread. We suspect their nest is located in the Midwest, but each time I perform the spell to narrow the location, I hit a block. It's like an ocean I can't cross."

Almost literally.

"That's because it is," I said in a rush.

She tilted her head in question.

"We believe the Soulless are hiding on an island somewhere in the Great Lakes," I elaborated. "But the lakes are so big that we don't know where to go from there. We were hoping you could help us figure it out."

Clarita pressed her lips together and shook her head. "We've tried the Great Lakes region, and nothing has ever come up."

I looked to Venn, my eyes widening. "Maliya lied to us."

Venn's lips tightened. "I don't know… I thought I could read her pretty well, and I believed she was telling the truth." He looked back to Clarita. "The island would've been cloaked by magic up until eight years ago, when Valkas escaped. It could still be cloaked."

Clarita stared into the distance in thought. "So Valkas is still in the same location he was imprisoned?"

Venn nodded.

"Mm…" Clarita mused. "Then why haven't *you* found him yet?"

"What do you mean?" I asked.

"You are a witch, aren't you?" Clarita responded.

I nodded, my heart rate spiking. "How could you tell?"

She smiled that soft, friendly smile of hers. "I'm a high witch. I can sense the magic around me, and you, sweetheart, radiate it. Perhaps I'm mistaken, but I sense you have a strong connection with the Soulless."

I looked to Venn, as if he might be able to explain what she meant by that. "I guess so. I mean, they kidnapped my sister, so I'm pretty motivated to find them and get her back."

"No." Clarita shook her head. "I meant a connection that spans many lifetimes."

Clarita stood and crossed around the mahogany coffee table to stand in front of me. She sat on the table casually, as if it were a chair, and held out an inviting hand. I hesitated.

"It's okay," she encouraged.

I glanced to Venn. He seemed relaxed enough, and I trusted his judgement, so I offered her my palm.

Clarita lifted her glasses and pulled my palm close to her face. She eyed it intensely, as though trying to burn a hole through it with laser vision. After studying my palm for what felt like a full minute, she closed her eyes and inhaled a deep breath. Finally, she opened them and dropped my palm.

Clarita readjusted her glasses. "It's very clear that your past lives are deeply rooted in history. I suspect you were among one of the witches to imprison Valkas."

I drew in a sharp breath. She was wrong. No way did my past lives involve powerful magic like that.

"I suppose you don't remember that yet, do you?" Clarita asked.

I shook my head. I couldn't seem to form any words in that moment. Clarita spoke so casually, like it wasn't a huge revelation. She had to be lying to me.

"You're much stronger than you think you are," Clarita said. "You have yet to realize your full potential in this life."

"That's what I told her," Venn chimed in.

I sat there dumbstruck. I was still trying to wrap my head around this whole past lives thing, let alone entertain the possibility that I'd been there to imprison the original vampire. It was clear I wasn't quite the low witch I'd always thought I was, but I wasn't powerful, either. Clarita was insane.

Clarita stood and crossed over to a cupboard set into the wall. She began shuffling through it while she spoke. "Is there anything else you can tell me about the location of the Soulless?"

"Yes," Venn answered confidently. "We were told the Soulless are residing in a place called Gregor Island."

Clarita's eyes lit up as she turned from the cupboards. She held a large roll of paper in one hand and a black marker in the other. She bounced on her toes in excitement. "That's excellent! You know the name! If it's true, pinpointing the location should be simple."

My heart soared in excitement. *One step closer.*

Clarita lowered herself to her knees and swept the books off the coffee table, as if they were unimportant. She unrolled the paper in her hand to reveal a large laminated map of the United States. I leaned forward to get a better look.

"Can you get the drapes?" Clarita asked.

Venn quickly rose to his feet and rounded the couch. He pulled the drapes shut, and the room was instantly blanketed in darkness. Only a small amount of light peeked through the edges of the curtain.

"The dark helps me concentrate," Clarita said to no one in particular. "Let's get started."

In the darkness, I could only see silhouettes. Clarita reached up and slipped a set of beads off of her neck. She held them straight out and dangled them above the map.

The cushion beside me sank in as Venn returned to his spot. I barely noticed him, though. Clarita had stolen my attention.

She closed her eyes and began muttering unfamiliar words under her breath. To my amazement, the beads in her hand began to sway, though Clarita hadn't moved an inch. The room sizzled with energy that only grew with each passing second. I could feel it brush across my skin, raising the hairs on my arms.

The beads swirled clockwise and increased their speed without expanding the small imaginary circle they were outlining. Clarita's eyes remained closed, and she continued to mutter words I didn't understand. Her hand opened, but the beads remained suspended in mid-air.

My heart hammered as I witnessed the magic unfold before my eyes. I'd seen spells performed before, but this was different. The beads seemed to have a mind of their own and moved as if gravity didn't matter. It was mesmerizing, and honestly a little freaky. This went far beyond the laws of physics.

The beads slowly descended through the air, as if they were connected to a wire. They stopped when the lowest bead touched the map, though they continued to hang there, circling a small area of blue in the northernmost part of Lake Michigan.

My breath ceased. Had we found it?

Clarita's eyes snapped open. Almost instantly, the beads fell into a heap on top of the map. She brushed them aside and popped the cap off her marker. She quickly drew an X right where the beads had been hovering and then looked to us in alarm.

"You must go." She spoke so fast that the words all jumbled together.

Clarita jumped to her feet while she rolled up the map. Venn and I both shot up from the couch at once. Tension suddenly overtook my entire body.

"What's wrong?" I demanded.

"Here, take this." Clarita shoved the map into my hands. "But don't use it yet."

I opened my mouth to demand an explanation of what was going on, but she was already ushering us to the door.

"Hold on," Venn insisted. "What—?"

"Go to your family," Clarita interrupted. "They need you."

"What do you mean?" I demanded. My body broke out in a sweat. Was Venn's family in danger? "What's happening?"

Clarita swung the front door open. "I cannot tell specifics, only that you need to return to them now."

Venn opened his mouth to say more, but Clarita grabbed a set of keys from the small table in her entryway and shoved them in his hands.

"Take my car," she insisted. "The parking garage is down the hall and to the left."

Venn and I both seemed to realize at the same moment how serious Clarita was. It didn't matter what she knew or how she knew it. It was clear there wasn't time for explanations.

Venn shot me one glance of horror and then grabbed my hand.

"Wait!" Clarita called before we made it too far.

I whirled around to face her, my heart hammering.

She stood in her doorway. "I mean it about the map, Rae. If you use it before helping your family with their current quest, you and your sister have no hope of making it off Gregor Island alive."

My blood ran cold.

"Now go," Clarita said in a rush. "Your family can no longer wait."

4

Heavy raindrops pounded against the windshield of Clarita's car, obscuring our view of the street in front of us. The wipers swiped as fast as they could, but it wasn't enough. People rushed off the streets to escape the downpour, and the traffic in front of us slowed.

"Venn—what if—what do you think—?" I couldn't get the words out as the possibilities raced through my mind. "There has to be a faster way."

Venn spun around in his seat, glancing up and down the street. His eyebrows were tight, but he didn't voice his worry like I had. In front of us, a vehicle pulled into traffic from where it had been parked on the curb.

"Hang on," Venn said in a rush. He pulled the wheel to the right and whipped into the parking spot.

He rushed out into the rain, and I quickly followed behind him. I was drenched in under a second, but I didn't care. All I cared about was making sure Venn's family was all right.

"How far?" I shouted.

Venn grabbed my hand and began sprinting down the sidewalk. "Not far!" he called back.

The crosswalk up ahead signaled *walk* as soon as we approached it, and we raced across the street. We hurried past shop after shop and weaved past groups of people. No one took notice to us, as we simply looked like a couple who had forgotten their umbrellas.

Venn turned right at the end of the block. The sidewalk was nearly empty here, since most people had already escaped the rain. We passed by a coffee shop, and then a café, before spotting a sign that read *Amalia's*.

"Venn, your car!" I pointed to the black car parked further down the street. It should've brought me comfort knowing we'd found Venn's family, but it only made my anxiety flare. What if we were too late?

Venn whipped open the door to Amalia's, and I rushed inside. I didn't know what I expected to find, but I was shocked by the quiet atmosphere. Neatly stocked shelves filled with books and herbs lined the outer walls of the small shop. Candles, crystals, essential oils, and various other items filled the tables in the middle of the room. The shop was bathed in natural wood tones and accented in earthy colors.

There were two women to our right who were soaking wet and looked as if they'd only entered the shop to get out of the rain. Another lady browsed the shelves toward the back of the store.

A blonde who looked around Sondra's age glanced up at us from behind the checkout desk. Venn rushed over to her.

"Can I help you?" she asked. There was a hint of recognition in her eye when she looked at Venn.

"Yes," Venn said breathlessly. "Sondra. Have you seen her?"

The blonde smiled. "Oh, that's where I know you from. I was trying to figure it out."

"This is urgent," Venn pressed.

The woman's eyes grew wide. "I'm sorry. I haven't seen her since—"

Venn cursed under his breath and whirled around before she could finish her sentence. I rushed behind him back outside into the pouring rain. Venn raced down the sidewalk.

"You don't think...?" I started, but I couldn't finish my sentence.

"I don't know what I think—" Venn's words died on his tongue as a scream cut through the air. He skidded to a halt once we reached the end of the block.

I stopped behind him. Down the next street, shadows moved through the thick rain. A deep roar met my ears, and a creature as big as a bear rose to its hind legs. *Ryland.* Three other female figures moved through the rain—Fiona, Teagan, and Sondra. At least four other guys retaliated against them.

The breath left my chest. We'd found Venn's family, and it wasn't good. At all.

Venn sprinted forward and shifted into a wolf mid-stride. I raced behind him. Venn slammed into the nearest vamp, who had Fiona by the back of the neck. He stumbled backward and released her. The first thought that went through my mind was to ignite a fire under his feet and watch him burn, but I knew even my magical fire wouldn't burn in this type of downpour. My gaze flickered upward, cursing the skies.

And that's when I saw the tiger. One story up on a metal fire escape, a massive orange cat peeked over the railing, watching Ryland's every move. He adjusted his legs, calibrating for attack.

Damn it. We weren't just dealing with vampires here. We were facing shifters, and this one might actually stand a chance against Ryland.

I didn't think about what I was doing. I just acted. My body shrank to the size of a raven, and I spread my wings. Rain hammered down on my feathers, and it took every ounce of strength I had to push against it and fly through the sky. A gust of wind caught my wings and hurled me off course. I quickly corrected my flight and continued on my intended path.

To my horror, the tiger shifter was already making the leap. I dove as fast as I could toward him. Disgust twisted in my gut as I felt my talons slice deeply across the skin between his eyes. A roar filled the street as the tiger fell through the air.

I landed on the closest fire escape and held tightly to the metal. The tiger landed on Ryland's back, but I could see that the roar had alerted him. Ryland spun around, and his jaws clamped upon the tiger's paw.

Lightning cracked through the street. But it hadn't come from the sky. I could've sworn it had come straight from Sondra's hands, blasting back one of the men. As fast as it was there, it was gone. I only paused a moment to take in the scene before I was swooping down to the street again. I glanced around frantically, hoping to find something to use as a weapon. I found nothing. I would have to fight with what I had: my talons and beak.

Before I had a chance to reach the fight, the man Sondra had blasted backward hopped to his feet. Freaking vampires and their immortality. Even through the downpour, I could see the fury in his eyes as he fixed them on Sondra.

I flew forward and dug my talons into the back of his neck. He cried out in pain and whirled around to fling me off of him. My small body whipped through the air and slammed against the side of the brick building. I sank to the ground and gasped for breath.

When I glanced up, Lightning Guy was sauntering toward me. Terror filled my chest when I realized his eyes weren't silver. They were blue. Which meant he wasn't a vampire. To survive the kind of shock Sondra had just given him, he must've been—

Lightning Guy raised his palms and muttered an incantation under his breath. I spread my wings, but I already knew I wasn't going to make it out of the way in time. A blast of dark green energy erupted out of his palms.

I flinched, but before I felt the blast hit me, a dark shadow crossed in front of me. I opened my eyes to see Venn writhing on the sidewalk in pain. Slowly, his arms and legs lengthened as his body shifted back into human form. He stared straight up into the sky while the rain pounded down on him. His body convulsed uncontrollably.

The blood drained from my face as I quickly shifted back into human form and knelt beside him.

"Venn, no!" I cried, leaning over him.

His gaze traveled straight through me.

I shot to my feet and narrowed my gaze at Lightning Guy. "Fuck you!" I screamed.

He only laughed as he gazed down at Venn in satisfaction.

"Ardeat ignis," I mumbled under my breath.

The hem of Lightning Guy's jeans caught on fire. It burned, despite the dampness of the fabric, but the rain had put it out before he even noticed.

Lightning cracked across the street again, pulling the guy's attention away from us. His face fell when he realized only he and the tiger shifter remained. The tiger shifter ran as fast as he could on three feet toward Lightning Guy. Ryland sprinted behind him, limping on his bad leg, and Lighting Guy took off running alongside his tiger friend.

I didn't watch to see how far Ryland chased them down the street. Instead, I fell hopelessly to my knees beside Venn. Boils had erupted across his face, marring his handsome features.

"Stay with me, Venn." I placed my hands on his shoulders, but he only shook more violently under my touch. I ran my fingers down his arm and squeezed his hand tightly. It was beginning to swell.

I was aware of several other figures kneeling down beside us, but I didn't quite register them until a voice spoke.

"We have to get him inside. Now." I recognized the voice as the blonde from inside Amalia's. She must've followed us outside.

Sondra stood beside the blonde and mumbled something under her breath. To my surprise, Venn's body elevated off the pavement, as if being carried on an invisible stretcher. My sobs ceased instantly, and I rose beside him. Venn continued to shake and stare lifelessly up at the sky.

"Is he going to be okay?" Fiona asked.

Sondra turned her eyes away and didn't answer. That couldn't be a good sign.

"He'll be okay," Teagan said softly, wrapping an arm around Fiona. "He has to be."

"This way," the blonde said in a rush, gesturing for us to follow her.

She led us down an alley, past various doors and dumpsters. We followed her inside a door that I could only presume led to the back of Amalia's. She glanced up and down the alleyway. Ryland rushed forward in human form and entered the hallway we stood in.

"They got away," he said through heavy breaths.

The blonde shut the door and whirled around. She rushed past each of us in the narrow hall. "You're safe here. My shop is heavily guarded with protection spells." She flung open another door. "In here."

"Oh my God," Ryland whispered, his eyes fixed on Venn.

Fiona responded, but I was too overwhelmed to hear what exactly she'd said.

Sondra guided Venn into a small room no bigger than my studio apartment. There was a small kitchenette against one corner and a big burgundy couch against another. The break room had similar decor as the main shop. I figured the soft lighting and earthy tones were meant to be relaxing, but I couldn't relax right then.

Sondra lowered Venn onto the couch, but he continued to convulse. I froze near the door and swallowed my emotions, pushing them down far into the pit of my stomach. My guts felt like rocks. I wanted to rush over to Venn, to cast a healing spell over him, but I knew my healing abilities wouldn't help.

I couldn't even combat the effects of vampire venom. I wasn't going to reverse another witch's spell.

"What do you have, Amalia?" Sondra asked.

"I might have something," the blonde responded, "but it's going to take three of us. We could call Clarita—"

"There's no time," Sondra insisted. "This curse will take over his body in minutes. Rae, get over here. We have to act now."

5

———————

"**R**ae!" Sondra repeated my name while Amalia hurried out of the room. I suddenly snapped to attention.

"They need three witches to run the spell," Fiona told me. "You can do it, Rae. You're good at healing."

"Regular injuries," I emphasized. "Not supernatural ones."

"Well, you're going to have to do your best." Teagan grabbed my shoulders and forced me forward until I was standing right beside Venn.

I turned my face away. I didn't want to remember him like that, the way he stared straight through me. It was terrifying.

"Why can't you heal him yourself?" I asked Sondra. "You're a high witch."

"Because," Amalia answered as she returned to the break room. She held a stack of glass vials in her arms and dumped them on the table nearby. "Breaking another witch's spell is almost impossible. Can you grab me a bowl from that cupboard?"

Amalia pointed above the kitchenette, and Fiona quickly crossed the room and retrieved a large mixing bowl. Amalia began pouring contents of the vials together in various amounts.

"In most cases, only the witch who cast the spell can break it," Amalia explained, "but this spell is weak enough that we might be able to save him."

I dared to steal a glance at Venn. Weak spell my ass. His eyes were swollen shut, and I was pretty sure he was on the brink of losing his breath.

"If you don't want your friend to die, I need your help," Amalia insisted.

She held out two vials, each full of a clear liquid. Sondra stepped forward and took one. Amalia stretched her arm out further, encouraging me to take the other.

I cleared my throat, willing my voice to stay strong. "What do I have to do?"

"Calm down, Rae," Sondra said in a soothing voice.

I couldn't understand how she remained calm at a time like this—or how she expected me to.

"Magic works best without anxiety or tension," Sondra said, as if she were coaching me. "Venn has a better chance of survival if you can let all that negative energy go."

If she thought that was a comforting way to put it, she was way off the mark. But the fact was, I was wasting time standing there. I needed to do exactly what I was told, for Venn's sake. Emotions be damned. I'd control them, not let them control me.

I snatched the vial out of Amalia's hand. Behind me, Fiona and Teagan stood beside Venn and did their best to comfort him. Ryland stuck his hands in his pockets near the door, looking shook. It seemed like he wanted to help but didn't know what to do.

"We'll save him," Sondra whispered reassuringly beside me.

I forced myself to believe her.

"When we're all ready, I want you to repeat these words with me while we all pour our oils together into the bowl, okay?" Amalia said in a serious tone. "*Sana carissimi nahil pati.*"

I repeated the words aloud, testing them on my tongue.

"Not until you're ready, though," Amalia warned.

We were running out of time. If I wasn't ready to perform magic in the next five seconds, I might lose Venn.

I didn't let myself think about that. Instead, I closed my eyes and pictured his sweet face, letting the warmth of his smile wash over me. Memories of the morning after I met him flickered through my mind, how he'd stayed in my apartment to clean my wound while I was passed out and had made sure I was all right. I recalled our friendly banter, how I teased that the first thing he'd tell his family about me was that I let him strip my pants off on our first meeting. I cracked a smile. I wasn't sure he'd actually told anyone that.

Venn better live, because he still needs to take my pants off and get in them this time.

I let out a deep breath, letting the tension in my shoulders melt away with it. Deep down, I was still a nervous wreck, but this was the best I could do.

"Ready?" Sondra asked, eyeing me with concern.

"Ready," I stated.

Amalia lifted her vial and began the incantation. Sondra and I joined in, repeating it over and over again until our vials were completely empty. The liquid mixture in the bowl swirled on its own accord, transforming into pink, then purple, before finally settling on dark blue. Amalia dipped her fingers into the potion. It dripped from her hand in a thick paste.

"Each of us will take about this much and spread it across his skin," she explained. "The rest he will have to drink."

I didn't ask how we were going to get the paste down his throat. Fiona and Teagan quickly stepped aside as Amalia, Sondra, and I approached.

"Each of you take a hand, and keep repeating the incantation," Amalia instructed as she wiped the blue substance across Venn's inflamed face.

I focused my attention on his fingers, which had swollen to the size of sausages. I rubbed a glob across his dark skin. It spread evenly and soaked into it like lotion.

Venn coughed violently, causing my anxiety to spring back to the surface. Amalia pulled the bowl away from his mouth. Blue goop the consistency of yogurt ran down his lips.

"He's choking!" I cried.

Sondra grabbed my wrist before I could reach his head and help him. "Hang on. It's working."

Just as she said it, Venn's coughing ceased. The thick potion slid down his throat, and the convulsions stopped.

"He's going to be okay?" I asked, glancing between Sondra and Amalia.

Amalia placed the bowl back up to Venn's lips and forced more of the potion into his mouth. "It'll take a couple of hours before we know for sure. We've done all we can."

To be honest, I didn't feel like I'd done anything. Boils still covered his face, and his eyes were still swollen shut. At best, we slowed down the curse's progress, but I wasn't sure we'd reversed the effects.

"We just need to give him time to recover now," Sondra said somberly as she stepped away from Venn. "He's a fighter. He'll be all right."

I wanted to believe her. I had to.

I sank to the floor next to the couch and leaned my head against one of the cushions. I held on to Venn's hand and stroked his skin, praying to every god I'd ever heard of that he would survive.

At some point, I closed my eyes, and my consciousness drifted away.

I gazed down at my hands. I knew they were mine because they were attached to my body, but they didn't look like my hands. The fingers were longer and the nails the wrong shape, but the abnormalities didn't seem to register in the moment.

"I need your hand," I instructed in a voice that sounded familiar, as if I'd been hearing it my whole life. But at the same time, it was like I'd never heard it before. I spoke with a thick British accent. It felt perfectly natural, like I'd been born with it.

A hand came into view, though I didn't look up to see who the hand belonged to. Somehow, I knew it was a man, despite the smooth skin and neat fingernails. I grabbed on to his wrist and held his hand over a wooden bowl.

"This is going to hurt," I warned him.

"I know," the man replied in an equally thick accent. "I'm prepared."

My heart hammered as I picked up a dagger sitting on the table beside my bowl. Somehow, I knew it was the man's dagger. I gazed down at the embellishments on the handle, knowing I'd never be able to afford something like this on my own.

I placed the blade to his palm. My hands shook, and I hesitated.

"Do as you're told, witch," the man snarled. He said the word witch *like it was poison on his tongue.*

I swallowed hard and then dragged the blade across his skin, cutting deeper than I needed to. I wanted the man to hurt. I wanted him to suffer. Every instinct told me that he deserved it.

Blood poured out of the wound, filling the bowl with a crimson liquid. The man didn't make a sound, as if he was immune to the pain.

"I hope this is what you truly want," I said.

"It is," the man growled. "I will not let the fate of man claim me."

I jerked awake. The details of my dream began to slip away the moment my eyes opened. I mentally clamored to hold on to the memory, though I wasn't sure why I bothered. It was only a dream.

I blinked, trying to remember where I was. I stared up at a white ceiling bathed in soft lighting. The surface beneath me was hard and uncomfortable.

"Have you heard of it?" a female voice asked from across the room.

I pushed myself up. I'd been lying on the floor in Amalia's break room beside the couch. Venn lay there with his eyes closed, his chest rising and falling slowly. The boils on his face had completely disappeared, though there was still swelling around his eyes. His hands had slimmed and looked like his again. I ran my fingers across the soft skin on his cheek. It felt like he was running a fever of a hundred degrees.

"Rae."

Fiona's voice caught my attention. I jerked away from Venn as if I'd been caught doing something wrong. I looked up to see everyone else seated at the break table.

I rubbed the sleep from my eyes. "Why didn't anyone wake me up?"

Ryland shrugged. "You looked peaceful. Plus, Tea said you'd probably stab my eye out if I woke you."

I couldn't argue with that.

"What's going on?" I asked.

"Why don't you come sit by us?" Sondra suggested, gesturing to the empty chair beside them.

I glanced between it and Venn. I didn't want to leave his side.

"Venn could use some space," Amalia said. "He needs to heal."

No way, bitch, was my first reaction. I almost let it slip out, too.

"I'm fine here, thanks," I said instead. "Can someone fill me in on what happened? Who were those guys?"

"They were some of Matias's men," Sondra answered. "I recognized one of the guys from his security team. He must've sent them to follow us to make sure we weren't trying to double-cross him or something. We noticed them following and confronted them."

I nodded in understanding.

"Amalia was just going to tell us what she knows about the Artifact." Fiona sounded excited.

I sat with my back to the couch and draped Venn's limp arm across my chest. My fingers laced in his. I placed a light kiss on the back of his hand while I listened.

"It sounds like the artifact you're describing is the *Sapiens noctua*, otherwise known as The Wise Owl," Amalia said. "I remember my great aunt saying something about it before she passed. She was the only other witch in my family."

Sondra leaned forward. "What'd she say about it?"

Amalia shrugged. "Just that it was very old. It was created centuries ago by a group of witches who wanted to block another witch's powers, one who was using magic for all the wrong reasons. I don't think it was ever intended to be used on a mass scale, only for the greater good."

"Did your aunt ever say what the object actually was?" Teagan asked.

Amalia shook her head.

Ryland shifted in his chair. "Did she mention where to find it or how to destroy it?"

"No," Amalia answered in a regretful tone. "All I know is that when magic returned, my aunt became very interested in it, to the point where her kids thought she'd gone completely off her rocker. She became very involved in the magical community and taught me most of what I know, though her magic was a lot more advanced than mine. I think she got a lot of her information from her past lives. I have yet to remember anything from mine."

"You believe in reincarnation?" I asked. "And Synchrony?"

How did everyone I meet just know this stuff when the rest of the world still thought we were in the middle of the apocalypse?

"Yes," Amalia replied, "but only because my aunt told me. Most witches can perform magic but don't actually know how it works."

It sounded like my boss, Devin.

"So, your aunt remembered The Wise Owl?" Fiona guessed.

"No, actually, she read about it in a book," Amalia said. "A few years ago, my aunt got her hands on a book that explained a lot of the truth about magic and had chapters on known magical artifacts and their history. If you want to learn more about The Wise Owl, I think your best bet is finding that book."

"You don't know where it is?" Sondra asked.

Amalia's lips tightened. "No, unfortunately. My aunt left it to me, but her kids ignored her wishes and sold it instead."

"You never tried to track it down?" Sondra asked.

"Of course I did!" Amalia sounded slightly offended. "But it's loaded with protection charms."

"Is there anything else you can tell us about the book?" Teagan asked.

Amalia shook her head. "All I remember is that it was a good six inches thick with a leather binding. It had images of the sun, moon, and stars on the front cover. That's all I can tell you."

Venn stirred next to me. I immediately whirled around and knelt beside him. Everyone else in the room stilled.

"Venn, talk to me." I stroked my fingers through his curls.

He grunted. It sounded like he was trying to speak, but I couldn't tell what he was saying.

"What?" I demanded. "Venn..."

"Genevieve," he managed to croak out.

Excuse me? It's Rachel, your girlfriend.

"No, Venn. It's me. Rae. You're going to be okay." I was practically on the verge of tears just from hearing his voice.

Venn's eyes opened into slits. "No, the book. Genevieve."

Fiona drew in a sharp breath beside me. I hadn't even realized she'd crossed the room. "Venn's right. I remember a book like that at Genevieve's."

Sondra stood beside Fiona and looked down at Venn, concern for him etched in her eyes. "I think you might be right. I didn't pay any attention to it before, but..."

Ryland sighed. "Well, we can kiss that big paycheck goodbye."

I looked at him still seated beside Amalia and Teagan across the room. "What do you mean?"

Teagan crossed her arms and leaned back in her seat. "We have a bit of debt with Genevieve."

Ryland scoffed. "A bit."

"And she's not going to help us without payment," Teagan said.

"She helped us before," I pointed out.

"That's because I wasn't there," Sondra said. "My old mentor... isn't fond of me."

My eyes nearly bulged out of my skull. I couldn't imagine a pure-hearted witch like Sondra working with someone dark like Genevieve.

Teagan stood from her chair. "When do we leave?"

Sondra glanced back to Venn, who had gone still again. I pressed my palm to his forehead. He was still burning up.

"We have to stay here overnight," Sondra said. "Venn's still healing."

"Tea and I will take the car," Ryland suggested.

"No," Sondra replied almost instantly. "I want us all to stick together. We'll get a hotel for the night and all rest up. We'll head to Genevieve's in the morning."

"You think she'll help us?" Fiona said softly.

Sondra hesitated. "God, I hope so."

6

Venn was hotter than cement on a summer day, and I meant that in a literal sense, though his body was smoking hot as well. I lay beside him on the queen-sized bed in our hotel room. Heat radiated off his skin like a furnace. He was running a fever hotter than any human should. But Venn wasn't exactly human.

"Are you going to give the guy space or what?" Ryland lay on the bed beside us, leaning his back against the headboard and flipping the channels on the TV.

"No," I answered automatically.

Fiona flung a pillow at Ryland while she made up the sofa bed for her and Sondra across the room. "Give her a break. It's not like you wouldn't be doing the same to Teagan if she'd been cursed."

"Whatever," Ryland said with an eye roll.

"Don't kid yourself, babe," Teagan teased from beside him. "You'd be all over me."

Ryland shot her a glare.

The door to our hotel room opened, and Sondra strode in carrying two pizza boxes and a bottle of citrus soda.

Ryland sat up straight. "Seriously, Sondra? You know I'll eat a whole pizza by myself."

She placed the boxes at the foot of his bed and shrugged. "I'd like to see you try."

A sly smile crossed Ryland's face. "Challenge accepted."

Teagan slapped his arm when he pulled a whole pizza box into his lap. "You can share."

"Fine," he said begrudgingly as he opened the box and offered her a piece.

Fiona and Sondra were already digging into the other box.

"Aren't you hungry, Rae?" Fiona asked after taking a bite.

I shifted uncomfortably on the bed. "No. I'm okay."

Sondra eyed me with concern. "When was the last time you ate?"

Honestly, I couldn't remember, but my stomach had twisted into enough knots that I didn't feel hungry.

"Please come and eat something, Rae." Sondra spoke softly, but there was a mother-bear tone to her words that told me she would force feed me if she had to, just so I wouldn't starve to death.

I sighed and rose from the bed. It broke my heart to leave Venn's side, even though I was only a few feet away from him. Fiona scooted over on the foot of the bed so I could sit beside her. I grabbed a piece of pepperoni pizza and took small bites. Even though I wasn't hungry, I couldn't deny that it was delicious. Everyone went silent while they ate and watched an old cartoon play across the TV.

Everyone except Sondra. She sat in the chair in the corner and kept her eyes locked on me.

Finally, I couldn't take it anymore. "Do I have something on my face?"

Sondra sat up straighter. "No. I was just trying to figure out where I know you from. I thought I recognized you when we first met, but I think I finally know where I've met you before."

I glanced to Fiona, who looked intrigued but didn't say anything.

"I'm pretty sure we've never met," I said, though I couldn't deny there was something familiar in her eyes, too. I figured she just had one of those faces.

"Not in this life," Sondra agreed.

It took me a moment to realize what she was saying. I initially wrote it off as one of those things people say, but then it hit me that she could very well be serious.

"You—you think you remember me? From a past life?" I asked. It seemed weird to talk about it so casually, but something about past lives just made sense.

Sondra nodded. "And I think I know who you were."

My curiosity suddenly piqued. I finished my last bite of pizza and wiped my fingers across my jeans. "Who was I?"

Sondra finished her pizza and leaned forward in her chair. "I believe you were Abigail Williams."

Fiona inhaled a sharp breath. Someone else—probably Ryland—hit *mute* on the remote.

Abigail Williams. Where have I heard that name before?

The memory suddenly clicked. She was one of the faces on the wall back at Venn's house—before it'd burnt down. Sondra had drawn her face, like all the others. Venn had said she'd remembered the faces, which made complete sense now that I knew Sondra could remember bits and pieces from her past lives.

I racked my brain, trying to remember what Venn had told me about Abigail. She was a witch, I remembered that. But which one?

"You were still *you*," Sondra explained, misinterpreting my silence. "Just a different version of yourself. It was the same soul."

"What do you mean?" I asked. "What's a soul, anyway?"

"Your soul is what makes you... you," Sondra said. "It houses your empathy, your thoughts, and your most important memories."

"What does a soul look like?" I was completely intrigued. "Like a spirit?"

"Your soul isn't really a physical *thing*, more of an abstract idea, but I suppose you could visualize it as a ball of energy," Sondra said with a shrug. "When you die, your soul continues to exist on a separate plane. A spirit is the soul of someone who is between death and reincarnation. They can roam the earth, observe, and communicate with psychics, but a soul needs a body to exist physically."

"What happens to a soul once their body dies?" I asked.

"Those who have unfinished business might stick around," Sondra said. "Others will live again in another body."

"How does that work?" I glanced between Fiona and Sondra. "Reincarnation, I mean."

Fiona was the one to answer. "Synchrony assigns souls to bodies based on whatever will bring balance."

"Where do souls come from?" I questioned for my own curiosity.

"Synchrony creates new souls as new life blossoms," Fiona explained. "But so far, no one knows how to destroy a soul. The most you can do is trap them with a spell. Only Synchrony itself can destroy souls."

"Actually destroy them?" I asked in shock.

"It's only a theory," Sondra clarified. "Some witches believe that Synchrony's balance tips in favor of goodness, of positive energy. So when a soul turns evil, it is destroyed to maintain that balance."

Sondra sounded skeptical.

"What do you believe?" I asked.

She took a long breath before answering. "Look around you. There's evil everywhere. Greed, abuse, hatred... I'm not sure that story isn't just a scare tactic..."

Silence settled over the room before Sondra spoke again. "It doesn't pay to worry about it. Just focus on bringing your own goodness into the world. Life is easier that way."

I sat there silently, absorbing all this information. It was strange how for the first time in my life, it felt like I was listening to the truth rather than just another bogus theory.

"So, I'm Abigail?" I asked slowly, testing out the concept.

"Mm..." Sondra mused. "It's a little more complicated than that. You *were* Abigail, but now you're Rae."

"But you just said my soul is the same from one life to the next," I pointed out.

"Yes, it's the same soul," Sondra agreed, "but a different person, if that makes sense."

It didn't. Not really.

"The person you are in this life is shaped by both your soul and your experiences," Sondra explained. "Your past life experiences have some effect on you, but it doesn't mean you'll be the exact same person."

"Okay," I said slowly. "I think I get it. So, Abigail... who was she exactly?"

"She's the witch who created shifters," Fiona reminded me.

"Right," I said in realization. "She was married to that Charles guy, who fused his body with a wolf's so they could track vampires."

"Yep," Fiona said. "Which makes total sense, because—"

"Because souls are drawn to each other from one life to the next," Sondra finished for her.

"You mean soulmates." I smiled, amused.

"Yes," Sondra confirmed, "but it's not just souls connected by romance that are drawn to each other, though that is the strongest bond. It can also happen with friends or family members, like a mother and child."

Everything they said made so much sense. I felt a sense of peace wash over me now that I knew the truth.

Venn's voice cut through the brief silence.

I quickly hurried to his side and took his hand. "What is it, Venn?"

"Eyes... window... soul," he managed to force out.

I looked to Fiona, like she might be able to translate for me.

Venn cleared his throat. "Eyes are the windows to the soul."

"Eyes are the windows to the soul?" I repeated.

Venn nodded.

"What does he mean?" I asked Sondra.

Sondra stood and crossed to the foot of the bed. "He means it quite literally. If you're magical enough—or if you had a very strong connection with that particular person in a past life—you can recognize a person's soul through their eyes."

A memory of Venn's words flashed through my head. *There's something in her eyes...*

He'd said that to Ryland when he'd brought me home with him. He was trying to convince Ryland I could be trusted.

And *his* eyes... Venn's soft brown eyes... maybe it hadn't been lust that drew me to him to begin with.

"It's true," Venn croaked. "Sondra told me ages ago that I was Charles."

Shock riveted through me, though I don't know why I was surprised. It made a lot of sense after just hearing that I was Abigail, his wife.

"So, you were the first shifter?" I asked.

Venn nodded.

"Ironic that you were a wolf shifter back then and a wolf shifter now," I thought aloud.

"Not really," Sondra said.

I looked to her for explanation.

"Shifter genes are genetic," she explained, "but you could end up *any* type of shifter once that DNA is in your blood. I personally believe that you shift into whatever animal matches your personality."

"Huh." I'd never thought of it that way before.

Beside me, Venn finally peeled his eyes open. My heart swooned under his gaze.

"You're okay," I said breathlessly as a smile spread across his face.

He nodded, but it sounded like it pained him to speak. "When I met you, I saw something in your eyes, Rae. The way it felt when I first saw you... it was like we'd lived a whole life together."

My insides danced, and the rest of the room faded away. I understood now why I was so comfortable around him, why I didn't mind spilling my secrets.

"I think I know what you mean," I whispered.

"Ugh," Teagan gagged. "Get a room."

"If you don't like it, you can leave," Venn teased back.

His eyes returned to mine, then traveled down to my lips. Oh, God. He was going to kiss me now, right in front of his whole family. Not that I didn't want him to, but the look in his eyes told me I didn't exactly want his family to see what he had in mind.

"You're feeling better?" I felt his forehead, which was still hot but had cooled down several degrees.

"A little bit," Venn said with a forced smile.

I smirked. "Then I can tell you what an idiot you were?"

He faked offense, but it was quickly replaced with a smile.

"You shouldn't have run in front of me," I scolded.

"This is the thanks I get?" he teased. "Rae, I'd run in front of you a thousand more times to make sure you don't get hurt."

I swore my heart skipped a literal beat. "You don't have to do that, Venn. I'd just reincarnate anyway."

Sadness filled his eyes. "That doesn't matter. I still don't want to see you hurt. And I don't want to wait to spend another lifetime with you."

Fair enough.

Venn reached up and brushed a strand of hair behind my ear. Then, in what felt like slow motion, he lifted his head and pressed his lips softly to mine. Fireworks exploded in my chest. My head spun, and I could hardly breathe.

Cheers filled the other side of the room, reminding me that there were other people watching us. My cheeks flamed red, but I kept my head down so that only Venn would see it.

"Shut up, you two," Fiona snapped at Teagan and Ryland, who were *whooping* and hollering at our expense. She hopped up from the bed to pour herself some soda. "I think it's sweet."

A hint of a smile crossed Sondra's face. "We should all get to bed. Everyone needs sleep."

She crawled into the pull-out bed, and Fiona climbed in beside her. It suddenly occurred to me that the only spot left to sleep was next to Venn. I didn't just stop breathing this time. I literally died.

Well, not literally, but close to it, I swear. I got to spend all night snuggled up next to this amazing creature? Sign me up!

Venn realized the same thing, and a grin spread across his face. He placed a chaste kiss on my nose and then pulled the covers away so I could crawl beneath them with him. I was still in my jeans as usual, but that didn't seem to matter. All that mattered was Venn's warm body pressed against mine. His cinnamon scent filled my nose, and his breath rushed across the back of my neck. His arm wrapped across my chest, and his legs curved around mine, as if our bodies were made to fit together like puzzle pieces.

I held my breath so he couldn't hear my heavy breathing. My heart thumped against my rib cage, as if it were trying to escape. That, I couldn't help, even though I worried Venn could feel it through my skin. My stomach danced with butterflies, and my body became so alive that I didn't believe there was any way in hell I was falling asleep tonight.

Which I guess was fine by me. It'd give me plenty of time to enjoy Venn's soothing embrace and the warmth of his body pressed closely against mine.

I couldn't remember the last time I was this happy. Probably never. The only times that ever came close were when my family was still alive...

Reality came crashing down on me all in a single instant. In my world, happiness was forever short-lived. This peaceful feeling would be gone as soon as we went back to slaying vampires and searching for the Artifact.

Tonight, I was going to enjoy Venn's company while I could. Tomorrow, it was back to my cruel, harsh reality.

7

"I 'll be damned." Genevieve stood in her doorway with a smirk on her face. "You're alive."

"You think I'd go out that easily?" There was no hostility in Sondra's tone, despite the dark look Genevieve gave her.

"No, I suppose not," Genevieve said, raising her head slightly. Her dark pixie cut lay flatter today than the first time I met her, but she still looked like she'd stepped out of a middle-aged women's fashion magazine. "What are you doing here? You know I refused to work with you again after—"

She cut off when Sondra shoved an envelope in her hands.

Genevieve raised a curious manicured brow. "What is this?"

"It's the debt I owe you," Sondra said simply. "All of it."

"Sweetheart, where could you possibly have...?" Genevieve trailed off when she opened the envelope and saw the number typed out on the cashier's check. She only let her surprise last a second before her face fell again. "I assume this isn't all you came for?"

"No," Sondra said. "We need your help."

Genevieve pressed her lips together. "Of course you do. Right this way."

She turned on her heel and left the door open for the rest of us to follow. The six of us filed down the hallway. I expected Genevieve to lead us into the door on the left like she had the last time I was here, but instead, she gestured to the room on our right.

We stepped into a sitting room dotted with Victorian-style furniture. A long red couch with a curved back sat opposite a large fireplace. Two matching black chairs sat on either side of that. The room was bathed in dark tones and lit only by two small lamps on end tables. An antique piano was situated next to an old

185

grandfather clock. Large framed photographs and two huge mirrors hung from the walls.

"Please, have a seat." Genevieve sounded strangely pleasant. It was probably thanks to the giant check she'd just received. I resisted the urge to roll my eyes.

I sat between Venn and Fiona on the couch, while Sondra and Teagan claimed the chairs and Ryland sat on the piano bench. He no longer wore his sling, but he favored his left arm like it was still quite sore.

Genevieve stood in front of the empty fireplace. "Can I get you anything? Tea, perhaps?"

"Tea is fine," Sondra answered for everyone. I personally didn't care either way.

"Perfect." Genevieve snapped her fingers. "It should be ready shortly. Now, what can I help you with?"

Sondra leaned forward in her seat. "We're looking for information on an item called *Sapiens noctua*, or The Wise Owl. Have you heard of it?"

Genevieve nodded. "I have, but I must say I'm shocked to hear that you have. Most people haven't heard of it, and those who have tend to write it off as myth."

"We hear you're in possession of the book that explains it," Teagan said.

Genevieve's lips twitched. "Who told you that?"

"That doesn't matter," Sondra said. "It's true, isn't it?"

Genevieve held Sondra's gaze for several seconds before motion by the door caught her eye. A pleasant expression washed over her face. "Ah, here's the tea."

A silver tray floated into the room. A teapot with seven cups sat upon it. We all watched as the tray slid onto the table in the corner by itself and the teapot began pouring tea into the cups. When the first finished, it floated through the air over to Sondra and landed gently in her hands. Sondra took a sip. It wasn't until we all had steaming cups of tea in our hands that Genevieve finally spoke.

"It's true. I am in possession of such a book, but it's not for sale."

"We're not here for the book," Ryland said. He hadn't even touched his tea.

I glanced to Venn, who was sipping his. I shot him a questioning glance, as if to ask if it was safe. Genevieve totally could've poisoned it. He gave a light nod, letting me know I could trust it. I took a sip. It was the most incredible tea I'd ever tasted.

"We're just here for the information in the book," Ryland clarified.

"Of course," Genevieve said, taking a sip of her own tea. "But with information this valuable, I must ask what you intend to use it for."

Sondra sighed. "You know me, Genevieve. Even *you* wouldn't use something like this for evil."

"Of course not," Genevieve scoffed. "Look around you. I have everything I could ever need. I have a beautiful home, more clients than I could ever dream of, and more wealth than you have in your pinky toe. And don't even get me started on my husband. He's a total dreamboat." Genevieve wiggled her eyebrows.

The gesture was weird, to say the least. Not to mention I was a little surprised to hear she was married. She seemed like the kind of person who would murder all four of her husbands for the money.

"If I wanted such an object," Genevieve said, "I would've found it by now. There's a reason I haven't divulged the information of its whereabouts."

"Why's that?" Fiona asked. She'd already finished her tea. She held her cup in her lap like she was hoping for more.

Genevieve took another sip. "Considering you know about The Wise Owl, you must know what kind of power it holds. No witch would want anyone else using that power on them. I have not gone after it because it is safest right where it is."

"That's exactly why we need to find it," Sondra insisted. "There's a vampire after it, and we believe he intends to use it to control who gets power and who doesn't. We hope to destroy it."

Genevieve's face fell. She dropped her teacup, but it hovered there in midair and glided back to the tray.

"Why you?" Genevieve asked skeptically. "Why should you be the ones to destroy it?"

We all exchanged a glance. No one knew how to answer the question.

"Why *not* us?" I blurted.

All eyes turned to me, including Genevieve's piercing stare.

"We've lost everything," I said. "Everything except each other. Our magic is one of the last things we have left. It's part of who we are. Come hell or high water, we're going to protect that—for everyone."

Sondra shot me an encouraging smile. She approved of my speech.

"You have a good point." Genevieve turned to Sondra. "I believe you will not use The Wise Owl for your own personal gain. What I do not know is if I can trust your colleagues and if you have enough power to retrieve the object on your own."

"You can trust us," Sondra promised. "All of us."

Genevieve pressed her lips together. "And what will you do with it once you find it?"

"Destroy it," Sondra said simply.

Genevieve sat there like a statue, contemplating our offer. "Okay. I will tell you, but should you fail, this is on *your* head. There's no going back."

"I know," Sondra said with confidence.

Venn ran his fingers across the back of my hand. I hadn't realized my hands had clenched around my teacup until then. I hadn't been sure we'd make it out of here with an answer.

From across the room, Genevieve snapped her fingers. The sound of a wooden chair against the hardwood floor reached my ears, and a chair immediately flew in through the door and stopped behind Genevieve. She sank into it casually, the skirt of her black dress lightly billowing around her. She snapped her fingers a second time. A leather-bound book floated in through the door, following her command. I remembered seeing the book sitting open on a table in the other room the last time I'd visited. I wrote it off as decoration. I was sorely mistaken.

Just as Amalia had described, the front leather cover was stamped with an image of the moon eclipsing the sun and the stars scattered all around them. The book was huge, at least a foot and a half across and thicker than a stack of pancakes. The book floated gently into Genevieve's outstretched hands. She opened it to the index and began scanning the page, using her pointer finger as a guide.

"Mm…" she mused. "Let's see… ah, there it is."

She opened the book to the middle and flipped a few more pages until she found what she was looking for. We all held our breath, waiting to hear what she had to tell us.

Genevieve scanned the page. "The last known location of The Wise Owl was at a history museum in Minneapolis."

"That's it?" Teagan asked in disbelief. "That's the safest place for it? Out in the open?"

"That does seem strange," Sondra agreed skeptically. "Matias would've known where to find it by now."

"I assure you, it's not that easy to retrieve," Genevieve warned. "You will have to undergo grueling obstacles before it is yours."

Fiona leaned forward in her seat. "What exactly is it we're looking for? I mean, what *is* The Wise Owl?"

Genevieve blinked several times, like it was obvious. "It's a literal owl."

"Like, a stuffed owl?" Ryland asked.

Genevieve shot him an unamused glance. "No, a carving of an owl. You will know when you see it."

"Is that it?" Sondra peeked at Genevieve's book.

Genevieve snapped it closed. "That is all you need to know. When it comes to power like this, you can rest assured I would not lead you astray."

"I want to see the book for myself." Sondra wasn't demanding it. She was merely stating a fact.

Genevieve stood. "Sweetheart, this book has more secrets in it than you have past lives. Nobody touches the book but me."

"A book like that should belong to the public," Sondra argued.

"Not when there are people out there who would use it against others." Genevieve held her head high, confident in her reply.

It shocked me a little that Genevieve had a sense of morals. Venn had implied she was in to dark magic. She didn't seem like the kind of person to worry about others.

Genevieve snapped her fingers, and the teacups in everyone's hands rose and returned to their tray. I *had* to learn how to do that.

"That is all I can provide you at this time," Genevieve said. "If there's nothing else—"

"There is." Sondra rose from her chair. "I need to purchase some supplies for a protection spell."

Genevieve frowned. "Sweetheart, there are over a dozen different places in this city where you can buy protection spells. Why do you need me?"

"Because it's not just any protection spell," Sondra clarified.

Genevieve pressed her lips together. "Very well. Follow me."

It was clear in the look she shot us that the invite was only for Sondra. The rest of us remained seated and exchanged uncomfortable glances.

I was the first to speak. "Why does Genevieve care so much about protecting secrets? I thought she was a dark witch."

Venn leaned casually against the armrest of the couch. "I told you, even dark witches have to believe in their cause to perform magic. I don't think she cares about protecting anyone else. I think there are things in that book that she's keeping secret to protect herself."

"Protect herself from what?" I asked curiously.

"Who knows?" Teagan asked rhetorically. "She's kind of had a shitty life. A lot of people have taken advantage of her. I can see where she might be paranoid."

"That's why she works in dark magic?" I asked. "Because she thinks it will protect her from…"

I wasn't sure I wanted to ask what would drive her down that road.

"From poverty, neglect, abuse…" Teagan shrugged. "Yeah, I guess."

Fiona opened her mouth to say something, but she stopped dead in her tracks when Sondra and Genevieve returned. Sondra held a small felt bag in her hands no bigger than her fist. We all stood. Venn was so close to me that I could feel the heat of his skin on mine.

"Thank you for your help, Genevieve," Sondra said genuinely. "And for trusting us."

Genevieve nodded, but a cold expression remained on her face. "Just be careful, okay?"

"We will," Sondra agreed.

"Excellent," Genevieve said. "Because this is not going to be an easy journey. Good luck."

8

The clouds darkened above us when we arrived in the Twin Cities, casting an ominous glow across the entire landscape. It was evening, but the darkening sky made it seem several hours later than it actually was. Teagan and Ryland seemed completely relaxed as they walked across the museum parking lot in front of me. Fiona practically skipped along next to them, and Venn's hand was loosely tangled in mine. Beside me, Sondra looked nervous as she stared up at the building in front of us. The museum was the size of my high school with a long staircase leading up to Roman-inspired pillars at the entrance. The look on Sondra's face sent a wave of anxiety through my body.

"We have an hour until the museum closes," Ryland said, checking the clock on his phone. "Think we'll find it in time?"

Sondra took a breath. "We better. Because I'm not leaving here without it."

I like her attitude.

We climbed the steps and entered through the front door. The lobby was vast, with a ceiling that reached two stories high. A woman behind the front desk with wild curls and black framed reading glasses sold us our tickets, but not before warning us that the museum would be closing soon and that they didn't issue refunds. Venn just shot her a smile and assured her we'd be out by closing time.

"This way," Sondra hissed under her breath as soon as we had our tickets in hand. She led us out of the main lobby and into an exhibit hall on the right.

"How do you know where we're going?" I asked. "Shouldn't we split up to look for it?"

Sondra shook her head. "I can definitely feel something powerful in this building. Can't you?"

Apart from the footsteps following beside me, the hall was quiet. I concentrated, trying to feel the power she spoke of. Energy sizzled through the air. It was reminiscent of static electricity, but it was different. It was magic.

"I think I feel it," I admitted in a whisper.

"I don't feel anything," Fiona said.

"No," Sondra replied simply. "You wouldn't unless you were a witch."

Fiona frowned. "I'm working on it."

"I know," Sondra said with a smile. "A few more years and you'll be able to call yourself a low witch."

Fiona smiled back, like she was perfectly happy to settle with being a low witch. It seemed there was a lot I could learn from Fiona and her positive attitude. I had to make it a point to spend more time with her and soak up some of her positivity.

We wove through an endless maze of hallways and small rooms, each dedicated to a different era of history. Everyone went quiet as our eyes danced from display to display, looking for any signs of The Wise Owl. It felt like a half hour had passed, but I hadn't thought the museum was that big.

"I think we're getting close…" Sondra said as we entered a maze of rooms on the outer edge of the building. Each room was about the size of the hotel room we stayed at, with a window on one side and displays dotting the walls.

Sondra stopped in her tracks, and everyone paused behind her. She stared ahead through a doorway that led to the next exhibit hall. Past that, about fifteen yards from us, another doorway opened to a larger room. A life-sized stone carving of an owl sat perched atop a display pedestal.

Ryland furrowed his brow. "That was… easy to find."

"You're right," Sondra agreed. "This magic… it doesn't feel…"

My attention remained fixed on the Owl, so much that I barely heard what they said. My breath grew loud in my ears. The stone owl radiated magical energy. It danced across my skin in waves.

All that power… I could take it for myself. I sensed the thought go through my head, but it didn't feel like my own. I'd never wanted that kind of power. I just wanted to be me. If I was capable of more than I thought I was, that was something I would work for, not just steal from others.

No one should be able to take that hard work away from me… away from anyone, I thought. *We have to destroy it.*

The scent of smoke hit my nostrils, pulling me back to the present.

Teagan sniffed the air. "Does anyone else smell that?"

"Yeah—" I started to say.

Before I could finish my sentence, a shrill alarm cut through the air. The noise was so loud that we all jumped. I immediately brought my fists up, my eyes darting around the room. Teagan's hands flew to her waist, even though she'd had to leave her knives in the car due to the building's security regulations. The sprinklers on the ceiling opened up like the skies, raining water down on us. Ahead in the next room, orange light flickered across the walls.

A fire.

Ryland shouted something, but it was hard to hear him over the alarm blaring through the air.

"What?" Sondra screeched at Ryland.

"This must be one of the obstacles Genevieve mentioned," Ryland shouted. "We have to go through!"

"I don't know," Sondra screamed back with uncertainty. "I don't know that—"

"I'll go!" Fiona volunteered.

"No, Fiona!" Venn protested before she could shift.

Only a few seconds had passed, and the room in front of us was already engulfed in flames. They stretched into the air higher than my head, and dark smoke hit the ceiling and billowed out into the room we stood in. Heat radiated from the other room, and we all took a collective step backward.

"I'll shift into a fox," Fiona offered. "I'm small and can make it through."

"You could get hurt, Fiona," I objected. "I'll go through. I can fly."

"Everyone just calm down," Sondra demanded. "I think—"

"I can do this," Fiona argued. She shifted and darted between Ryland's legs and ran straight for the doorway and into the fire. Her red fur disappeared. Concern for her whipped through my body, and my heart hammered a million beats per minute.

"Fiona! No!" Ryland sprinted forward, with me, Venn, and Teagan close on his heels.

Sondra stood rooted in place and began mumbling an incantation under her breath.

We reached the doorway, but a blast of fire kicked into the room. A searing hot pain spread across my body as the flames touched my skin. I stumbled backward and nearly tripped over the feet behind me, but Venn caught me.

Sondra cursed. "The fire's working against me. That's not supposed to happen."

My eyes darted out the window for a second, but I didn't think anything of the darkening clouds until I did a double take.

"Oh my God," I whispered, horror filling my chest.

While Ryland and Teagan were preoccupied with finding a way through the fire and Sondra began a second incantation, Venn stepped forward to gaze wide-eyed out the window with me. Debris rushed past the glass. Things that shouldn't be flying through the air flipped across my vision: loose bits of concrete, entire tree branches, and a garbage can. In the middle of the debris, a funnel cloud had formed. It twisted and grew longer. All around us, the building began to shake.

I backed away from the window slowly and glanced to Sondra. "Is this another obstacle?"

Her eyes darted to the tornado beyond the window. She nodded and spoke breathlessly. "Yes. We need to destroy the Owl. Now."

"Forget the Owl!" Ryland shouted above the rattling of the building and the on-going fire alarm. "We need to save my sister!"

"She'll be fine!" Sondra cried. "The only way out of this is to get to the Owl."

The deafening sound of shattering glass exploding around us filled the air. I ducked. Venn was in front of me in a second, his strong abdomen pressed to the side of my head as he blocked me from the glass that sprayed across the room. The water raining down from the sprinklers had stopped, but strong winds swirled around us, whipping my hair in every direction. The flames seemed unaffected by the wind, but they continued to climb higher. Between the blaring fire alarm and the air pounding at my ears, I couldn't hear what Ryland shouted. When I lifted my head, all I saw was him run forward, disappearing into the wall of flames. Teagan followed behind him.

My eyes widened, and I sprang up out of Venn's protective hold. There was no way in hell they were entering that room without me. It was too loud to hear if Venn protested.

I shifted and flew into the air. I kept myself high, out of the reach of the flames, but visibility was nearly non-existent near the ceiling. I held my breath, knowing that if I inhaled, I wouldn't get any oxygen anyway. Heat seared my skin, making it feel as if my feathers were going to burn off, but I ignored it. There were more important things in life than feathers.

Glancing down, I saw nothing but orange flames through the thick smoke. I swooped lower, but I couldn't go far before the flames reached me. If I didn't get out of here soon, I was going to cook and be served on a platter for Christmas dinner. My lungs ached as I ran out of oxygen. On instinct, I inhaled a breath. My nasal passages burned, and my lungs felt heavy. I squinted across the room, but I couldn't see anyone anywhere.

I'm no use to them dead, I told myself.

One last glance through the flames revealed nothing. Both doors on either side of the room were completely engulfed in flames. I didn't hesitate, because I knew that if I did, I was done for. I flapped my wings and swooped downward, propelling myself through the door opposite the one I came in through.

My body collapsed to the tile floor, and I inhaled deep breaths, greedy for oxygen. My whole body shook, which was weird because I'd already caught my breath, and—

The sound of cannons exploded around me. Above my head, the ceiling fractured, alerting me to the fact that *I* wasn't the one shaking. The entire *building* was.

I spread my wings and shot into the air not a moment too soon. Plaster fell from the ceiling and smashed to the floor right where I'd been lying a moment ago. More pieces of plaster continued to rain down, and I dodged around them. I landed beneath the lip of one of the display tables for safety.

I finally took in the room. It was at least five times bigger than the other rooms we'd walked through. All types of stone artifacts lined the displays, with the carved owl sitting at the center of it all. I prayed my eyes would land upon Fiona, Ryland, or Teagan, but I saw no one.

Another piece of plaster cracked into the ground just in front of me. I jumped. If possible, my heart pounded even harder. My breathing grew erratic as my eyes darted from the flaming doorway to the crumbling ceiling.

Where are you? I silently begged. *Please be alive.*

The building moaned as the fracture in the ceiling widened. My eyes darted upward. These obstacles were insane.

The only way out of this is to get the Owl. Sondra's voice echoed in my head.

If this was all due to the magic in the Owl, then destroying it should stop all of this. I surveyed the crack in the ceiling, trying to decide if it was safe to dart across the room, grab it, and then get back under the safety of my table without injury.

Before I could make a move, four figures burst from the flaming doorway and fell into the room. Ryland cradled Fiona in her fox form, though she showed no signs of breathing. Beside him, Teagan screamed in pain. Most of her flesh was blackened with burns. Venn sat up and knelt over her. He said something I couldn't hear. I expected it was meant to comfort her.

I darted from the safety of my table the moment I saw them. But I never made it across the room. A loud rumble echoed across the space between us. My eyes just barely caught Venn's before a heavy wall of debris knocked his face out of view.

Sheer hopelessness slammed into my gut like a freight train. The pile of rubble had consumed them all.

They were gone.

9

"**N**O!"

My scream echoed off the walls of the museum. I hadn't even realized the violent winds had died down and the building was no longer shaking. The fire alarm had stopped blaring, but the pulse of blood in my ears seemed just as loud. It felt as if someone had reached into my abdomen and ripped my guts out.

In human form, I jumped onto the pile of rubble and began clawing at any pieces of broken building I could move.

"Rae!?" Sondra's voice cut through the air.

I glanced up to see the room between us was still on fire, but I couldn't see her through it.

"They're hurt!" I called back. "All of them!"

"They'll be okay," Sondra promised.

She has no idea.

"I need you to stay calm," she yelled across the space between us. "Can you do that?"

"I..." I wasn't sure I could, to be honest. *Calm* wasn't exactly my middle name, but I trusted Sondra. If we were going to make it out of here alive, she was my only hope. "I can try."

"Okay," she said in that soothing voice she always used. "This fire is enchanted. I can't get through. Is there another entrance to the room you're in?"

"Yeah!" I shouted back, while continuing to move debris out of the way. "There's another door that looks like the one I came through."

"Stay right there," Sondra instructed. "I'm going to come around."

A sliver of hope filled my heart, but it quickly disappeared as I dug further and further into the rubble without any signs of survivors.

"Hurry up!" I cried.

I quickly reminded myself to stay calm. I might need to use magic, and I couldn't do that if I was a blubbering mess. I took a deep breath and pushed a piece of concrete the size of a couch cushion out of the way. I inhaled a sharp breath when I saw Venn's face beneath me. Blood coated his forehead.

"Venn!"

His eyes fluttered open, and my heart soared in my chest. *He's alive!* Between the small opening of rubble, I bent and placed a kiss on his lips. It barely lasted a second, and I was too overwhelmed to truly enjoy it. It was too soon for this. Venn and I hadn't even had a chance to indulge in that make-out session he promised me.

"I'm going to get you out of here." My voice was strong. I couldn't let Venn see me weak right now.

"Wait," he croaked, stopping me from grabbing the next bit of rubble at the top of the pile.

I leaned over him. "What?"

He grimaced, like speaking caused him pain. "You can't save me, Rae."

"Of course I can," I argued. "I'm strong enough to move all this debris, and then I can heal you."

"No," he replied hoarsely. "You won't get to me in time."

"Stop talking," I demanded. "You're wasting time."

Venn spoke while I pushed pieces of concrete and plaster out of the way. "I've been impaled."

My face grew hot, but I forced down the lump in my throat. I had to stay calm as Sondra instructed.

"I need to tell you something," Venn said. "Rae, please stop and just listen to me. It's about your sister."

My entire body tensed, and I froze as he'd asked. "What about my sister?"

Venn took a deep breath. "She's dead."

I immediately backed off the pile to look him in the eye. He was wrong. "My sister's not dead. I would know."

"No," Venn argued. "You just want to believe it so badly that you won't face the truth. Clarita told me our search for Gregor Island was pointless because your sister was already gone. Jenna died that night the Soulless took her."

"You can't know that," I said with certainty. Except... how could I be sure? *My heart tells me she's alive* isn't much of an excuse. Clarita clearly had some serious powers. It was possible she could see into the past. "When did Clarita tell you?"

"It doesn't matter," Venn whispered through pained breaths.

"Don't you dare give up on me," I warned him. "I'm going to get you out of here and heal you."

Tears pricked at my eyes. If what Venn said was true, then I'd already lost my sister. I couldn't lose him, too.

"Forget about me," Venn insisted in a gravelly tone. "Matias is on his way. You have to keep going. You have to destroy the Owl before he gets to it."

Venn's eyelids fluttered.

"No, Venn," I ordered. "You aren't going to die."

I leaned down and pressed my lips to his again. They were so soft and warm, but he didn't respond to my touch. A hole opened in my chest.

"No, no, no," I repeated again and again.

No matter how much I didn't want to convince myself of the truth, I knew that Venn was gone. There was no hope of unearthing Fiona, Teagan, or Ryland alive, either. In the blink of an eye, I'd just lost everyone. I was alone now.

"Rae." Sondra's voice cut through the eerie silence.

My head snapped in her direction. I was suddenly reminded of the fact that I wasn't alone. Not entirely.

I shot to my feet. "Sondra, they…"

I didn't know how to break the news to her, but I didn't have to. She stepped forward and gazed into the rubble, straight at Venn's lifeless face. A hand shot over Sondra's mouth, and her eyes grew red.

"I'm sorry," I whispered.

She dropped her hand, but her eyes remained on him. "It's one thing to picture your worst fear in your head. It's another to actually experience it."

I bit my lower lip and nodded in agreement. I didn't think I could speak without turning into a sobbing mess.

You have to destroy the Owl. I could still hear Venn's voice in my head. There wasn't time for grief, not yet. Sondra and I still had work to do. In the meantime, I had to pick myself up and push forward.

This is going to suck balls.

"How do we destroy it?" I asked, my voice sounding stronger than I felt.

"I'm not sure," Sondra said, "but we have to try something."

"Okay," I agreed quickly.

I raced to the center of the room and snatched the Owl off its display. It was heavier than I thought it would be, but I held it above my head and hurled it at the tile floor with as much force as I could. It bounced off the floor and went spinning across the room. The tile had cracked and indented at the point of impact, but the Owl remained unharmed.

Sondra took a calm step forward. I took note of this and forced myself to relax, mirroring her stance, despite the agony ripping away at my insides.

"It's going to take a lot more than that to destroy this thing," Sondra stated, like it was fact.

"Any ideas?"

Sondra nodded. "A couple."

She faced the Owl, but remained frozen as it rose into the air under her silent command. It hovered three feet above my head. In the blink of an eye, it darted through the air and pummeled into the nearest wall. When that didn't work, Sondra sent it flying across the room at lightning speed and crashed into the opposite wall. The stone owl didn't even chip, though it left a sizable dent in the wall.

"I don't think this is going to work," I said. "It's too powerful."

Sondra guided the Owl to the ground on the other side of the room. "Let me try this…"

She muttered a syllable under her breath, and bolts of lightning erupted from her palms like I'd seen earlier during the ambush. Electricity sizzled through the air, sending strands of my hair to rise around me due to static. I wanted to join in, but I didn't know the incantation for lightning and didn't know if I'd be able to conjure it even if I did. Sondra's lightning bolts struck the stone over and over again, but it wasn't enough to crack it.

Smoke from the other room filled the air and burned my lungs. The fire roared, consuming the museum at an alarming rate.

"The fire!" I blurted. "You said it was enchanted. Maybe it's strong enough to destroy this thing."

One last bolt of lightning cracked through the air. Sondra paused for only a moment before lifting the Owl into the air with her magic. She sent it floating across the room and into the heart of the fire.

We stood side-by-side, watching the stone owl. Heat waves washed over us, and sweat broke out across my forehead. I expected to see the Owl crumble or melt or burn, but even though the flames were large and the smoke thick, I could see it remained unaffected.

My stomach bottomed out. If enchanted fire couldn't harm it, then what would?

"It's going to take the fires of hell to destroy this thing," I stated.

"I know," Sondra agreed. "It's too powerful."

She didn't have to remind me. Beneath the heat waves, I could still feel the Owl's power moving across my skin. It called to me like a beacon, begging me to take ahold of its powers and claim them as my own.

An idea suddenly struck me. "What if we weaken it?" I suggested. "If we take some power from it, it will be less protected, won't it?"

Sondra's gaze remained on the Owl in the fire. She stared at it intensely, as if willing it to explode. "It's too risky."

"But it's the only way," I countered. Somehow, I knew she'd agree with me. "I'll take its power, and you can destroy it."

"No," she countered, bringing her gaze to mine. "I'll take it. You don't know what that kind of power could do to you."

At this point, I was willing to take the risk if it meant keeping this thing out of Matias's hands.

"How do I destroy it, then?" I asked. "Sondra, I don't have that kind of power… not in this life. You're the only one who can destroy it. The least I can do is help weaken its power and give you a chance."

Sondra grimaced, contemplating my argument. "Okay, but you have to understand what you're getting yourself into."

I didn't. Not really. But whatever happened, I'd handle it.

"Bring it on," I said confidently.

Sondra guided the Owl out of the fire. It landed unharmed on the tile in front of us.

She stared at me seriously. "Don't let the power consume you, Rae. Everyone else is gone. I'm not going to lose you, too."

She hid the emotions from her tone, but I could see the heartbreak on her face. I swallowed my heartbreak, too.

"You ready?" she asked.

"Ready," I agreed.

"You know what you're doing?"

I didn't know how I knew, but the magic contained in the Owl sculpture told me exactly how to claim its energy as my own. I took a deep breath and bent to one knee. And then my hands clamped around the stone.

Red-hot pain seared across my skin. And it wasn't just because the stone was still blazing hot from the fire. This was a different kind of pain, the stabbing, scalding pain of magic that wasn't my own pouring into my body through my palms. And I licked it up like a chocolate milkshake through a straw. My scream echoed through the hall.

"Rae!" Sondra cried in concern. She reached out and touched my shoulder, and shock of a million volts burst down my arm.

I could feel her magic. This wasn't the minute charge I imagined she felt around other witches. It was sizzling hot, electric pain that felt as if I was standing in the eye of a thunderstorm. I could feel them all. All the witches, all the shifters, all the artifacts in existence. And I knew that by my simple command, I could flip off the switch to any one of them at will. The Wise Owl was more than just an artifact to control. It was a direct line to Synchrony. Anyone with malicious intentions could wreak serious havoc with this thing. It had to be the most dangerous weapon in the world.

And *I* had access to it. The possibilities flipped through my mind at lightning speed, but they went so fast that I could hardly process them. One thought stuck: I could do anything... *be* anything.

It'd be so easy.

Which is why it felt so wrong. Life wasn't easy. Life was an endless roller coaster ride with no destination. Sometimes it made you want to laugh and smile. Most times, it made you want to vomit.

This was one of those times when life was forcing my guts back up my throat. Whatever this power was, it wasn't *me*. I didn't want it. But more than that, I didn't want anyone else to have it.

"Rae," Sondra repeated, concern laced in her tone.

"Destroy... it..." I managed through gritted teeth.

Sondra's eyes widened as the ground began to shake beneath our feet. She took several steps backward toward the pile of rubble.

The pile of rubble where Venn lay dead.

I squeezed my eyes shut, doing my best to push my grief down. I'd handle it later. Right now, I needed to focus on destroying this artifact before the magic in it destroyed me.

It should've destroyed me already, I told myself. There was a reason witches didn't try to handle magic above their skill level. But maybe this was different, since I was trying to harness the power rather than drain it.

An earth-shattering *crunch* filled the air.

"Rae!" Sondra cried to get my attention.

My gaze shot between us. A huge cavern had split the floor in two. I grabbed The Wise Owl and scurried backward, hugging the wall as the floor continued to crumble and the cavern grew. Above us, the crack in the ceiling widened to reveal the dark, clouded sky.

Sondra's eyes lit up. She shouted across the space between us. "Whatever you're doing, keep doing it!"

"I'm not doing anything," I assured her. Only trying to hold the magic in my body back.

"Yes, you are!" she called back. "We can do this together."

Sondra's lips moved, but I could no longer hear her over the sound of shattering earth around us. She continued to drift away from me as the rift between us widened. The rumbling of the earth was so strong that I was certain I was never going to hear again.

When it felt as if Sondra and I were miles apart, she caught my eye and yelled something at me. There was no way in hell I could hear her from here, so I tried to read her lips. I was a terrible lip reader.

She pointed to the Owl and then gestured to the cavern. Was she suggesting I throw it in? What would that do if smashing it hadn't worked before?

She continued to point at the cavern. It looked like she was encouraging me to gaze into it. Slowly, I got to my hands and knees, though it was difficult to maintain my balance as the earth rocked around me.

Daringly, I peeked over the edge. Dirt and rock stretched down for miles, ending in a red glowing pit.

Holy shit! The earth's crust had broken apart to reveal a layer of magma.

"Throw it!" I just barely heard Sondra's instructions carry through the wind.

I hesitated. I could keep The Wise Owl—keep all the power for myself.

No, I countered instantly. I wouldn't take that power from everyone else.

I heaved the heavy stone up in my arms and then hurled it over the edge of the cavern. I watched it tumble over and over again, until it became just a small dot and then disappeared from view completely. I knew the moment it hit the magma because I felt its power *whoosh* out of me.

And then everything went black.

10

I lay on my back. The earth was perfectly still, and the white ceiling above me had been untouched by any natural disaster. My head spun.

What the—?

I pushed myself to my elbows and glanced around the quiet exhibit hall. Five bodies lay sprawled on the floor beside me. The next room was pristine, as if it hadn't been burning just moments ago. I was so confused that I could hardly process the images in front of me.

The sound of clapping reached my ears. My head snapped in the direction of the opposite doorway just as a woman in a black dress stepped through it.

"Well done, Rae," she said. "I'm impressed."

Reality came crashing down on me. It took my breath away, and not because I was upset. I was beyond *relieved*. It wasn't real. None of it. Tears sprang to my eyes.

Beside me, everyone else began to wake. Venn sat up. Though confusion filled his eyes, they were full of life. Happiness swept through me and consumed the very core of my soul.

I sprang to my feet and tackled Venn with a hug. "You're okay!"

He squeezed me back so hard I thought he might crack a rib, but I didn't care. I just wanted to feel his arms around me.

He nuzzled his face in my hair. "Of course I'm okay. I thought I'd lost you!"

"Me?" I drew away in surprise.

"Yes," he said, tears brimming his eyes. "The ceiling collapsed on you. It felt so real."

I bit down hard on my lower lip and shook my head. "In my version, you were the one who died. All of you except Sondra."

Venn pushed my hair out of my face and stared longingly into my eyes. My heart cartwheeled around in my chest under his gaze.

"So, that thing you said about my sister...?" I asked. "It wasn't true?"

Venn's brow furrowed. "What thing?"

Thank God!

I whirled around, shooting daggers at Genevieve. "What did you do to us?"

She smiled and stepped further into the room. Her heels clicked against the tile. "Relax. You did exceptional."

"That was a nasty-ass prank," Teagan bit from behind me.

Sondra stood and spoke calmly. "It was a test."

Genevieve stopped in the middle of the room and crossed her hands in front of her. She smiled a knowing smile.

I glanced between Sondra and Genevieve. "You knew." It wasn't a question.

Sondra nodded, never tearing her gaze from Genevieve. "I suspected something wasn't right, but I didn't realize Genevieve was behind it. I tried to tell you, but when you didn't hear me out, I figured the best thing to do was go with it. The vision wasn't going to end until we destroyed the artifact."

Ryland helped Fiona to her feet and pulled her into a hug. It was like watching ghosts. The vision had felt so real.

"Precisely," Genevieve confirmed.

"At some point, our visions must've diverged, showing us each our worst fears," Sondra theorized as Venn and I stood.

Ryland leveled his gaze on Genevieve. "You better have a damn good excuse for doing this. That was beyond cruel."

Genevieve pursed her lips. "I may break the rules every once in a while, but I am not cruel. Not without purpose, at least."

Fiona crossed her arms. Even *she* wasn't taking any of this shit. "So, why exactly did you have to make us watch everyone we love die?"

"To test you," Genevieve said simply.

"Test us for what?" Teagan demanded. "You already know what we're capable of."

Genevieve shook her head. "The Wise Owl is a very delicate artifact. It requires much more than experience to get to. I had to know if your team was capable. If you couldn't make it through this, you'd never make it through the real thing."

"And we passed?" There was almost no emotion in Sondra's voice.

"Yes," Genevieve said proudly. "You were each shown your worst fears to test your resilience—how quickly you could bounce back from hardships. You're going to need it when you undergo the true obstacles. Only one of you failed."

She shot a look at Fiona, who dropped her head in shame.

"You were then each tested on your intentions, how well you could resist the power of The Wise Owl. Only one of you passed."

Genevieve looked at me. I glanced around, wondering if she was looking at someone behind me, but everyone was now standing side by side. Surely she didn't mean that I was the only one who could resist the power.

Genevieve pressed her lips together in thought and stared at me. "Strange, though. I designed the deception to replicate the powers of the true artifact. You shouldn't have felt as much connection to Synchrony as you did. You should've only had the power to block magic, not steal it."

I glanced to Sondra, wondering if she could explain what that meant, but she looked as confused as I did.

Genevieve waved her hand nonchalantly. "No matter. You were still able to resist the power. That's good enough for me, but it means that if I am to trust you in the location of the true artifact, you must all promise that Rae will be the one to retrieve it. The rest of you will act to protect her through the obstacles."

"Why trust us at all?" Sondra asked skeptically. "You never have in the past."

Genevieve pursed her lips. "Because I agree with you. This power should not exist. Everyone should have a right to their own magic. I would destroy it myself… if I thought that I could. But we both know I couldn't resist magic like that, not once it was in my hands. And so, I need you to do it for me."

Understandable, I guess.

"But next time, you need to be more prepared," Genevieve warned. "I guarantee that when you face the Artifact for real, the earth isn't just going to open up and swallow it whole."

"Does your book mention how to destroy it?" Sondra asked. "The real Artifact?"

"It'll take more witches than you have at your disposal," Genevieve said. "This artifact was not created alone, nor can it be destroyed alone. There is strength in numbers, and you're going to need a helluva good team of witches to disperse the power it holds."

Sondra jutted her chin out confidently. "We can work with that."

Genevieve nodded her approval.

"Is any of this real?" I asked, gesturing around the exhibit hall. "Or are we still sitting in your lounge with teacups in our hands?"

Genevieve's laughter reverberated off the walls of the museum. "Yes, this is real. I do not have the power to produce visions on my own. I needed a bit of… help."

Her eyes locked on something behind me. I turned to stare past the open doorways. A stone carving of a coiled snake sat on the display where the Owl had been in my vision. The strong tingles of magic I'd felt earlier danced across my skin.

"This is the artifact responsible for your visions," Genevieve explained. "I arrived an hour ahead of you to ensure you would only see what I wanted you to see. Obviously, you didn't all pass my test, but that would be nearly impossible. It's clear to me that you all care very deeply for one another, and I'm confident that you will make a good team."

She was right. We did care deeply about each other.

Genevieve sighed. "Having said that, it's time to tell you the truth."

11

I remained speechless the whole time Genevieve explained the truth to us.

"The true Artifact is hidden in a cave," she'd said.

Of-freaking-course it was. The top of a mountain or the bottom of the ocean, I was down with. Why did it have to be a cave? They were dark, damp, and creepy. Worst of all, they had very few escape routes, and that was the part that scared me most.

"A group of witches brought The Wise Owl to the States sometime in the early 1800s," Genevieve told us. "They wanted to make sure it wouldn't fall into the wrong hands but didn't want to destroy it in case they had to use it to protect the world from a vengeful witch. After years of hiding it and searching for the best solution, they laid it to rest in a cave that remains unexplored to this day."

She wanted us to explore the bloody cave.

I, apparently, was the only one bothered by the idea of a spelunking expedition. Who knew what could happen to us? We could get lost and starve to death. The whole thing could cave in and trap us there. We could suffocate.

I couldn't exactly back out now, though, not when Genevieve assured us that I was the only one who could resist its power and destroy it for good.

I worried about Jenna, and my mind continued to flicker to the map Clarita had given us. But I couldn't get what Clarita had said out of my mind, about how we had to finish our current quest first before going after my sister. Every fiber of my being told me to say screw it and race off to Gregor Island on my own, but another part of me—my intuition, perhaps—told me that I should listen to Clarita. Maybe it had something to do with being the only one who could resist The Wise Owl's power.

I didn't know. Frankly, I didn't know anything these days, and it put me completely on edge.

Genevieve was deliberately vague on the details, saying that the less we knew, the better. She offered to sponsor our journey, which meant booking us a five-star suite in the Twin Cities while she got the rest of our affairs in order.

"You need to rest," she'd said. It sounded like she honestly cared about our well-being. I was starting to think that Genevieve wasn't all that bad, that there was a good heart hidden beneath all the black lace and dark makeup.

And a crapload of money, too, I thought as the six of us stepped inside our hotel room.

Hotel room was a massive understatement. It was a freaking royalty suite. My jaw dropped to the floor. Fiona went bug-eyed beside me.

"Holy moneybags," Ryland muttered under his breath.

A vast room bathed in beige tones stretched out in front of us and met up with a row of floor-to-ceiling windows. On the other side of them, a balcony overlooked the city, which was hauntingly beautiful beneath the dark night sky. Two long couches faced a flat-screen TV that practically took up the whole wall. Another seating area surrounded a gas fireplace. Beside that, six chairs sat around a dining room table next to a full kitchen and bar.

I managed to tear my gaze from the main room and glanced into one of the bedrooms. A huge king-sized bed took up the space. On the opposite wall, a smaller TV hung above another fireplace. A private bathroom sat beyond an open door.

"Ohmigosh!" Fiona called from another room. "You have to see this."

I whirled around and almost slammed straight into Venn's chest. I stumbled backward. He stared down at me with a soft smile, like he wanted to say something.

"We get this room!" Teagan called, pushing past us and breaking our stare. She dropped her bag on the king bed.

"Rae, come look!" Fiona popped her head out of one of the doors and gestured for me to follow her.

I dropped my gaze shyly, wondering what Venn was about to say to me, but I stepped away from him and followed Fiona.

In the main part of the suite, Sondra held the small black bag Genevieve had given her. She pulled a pinch of a powdered substance from it and mumbled under her breath as she sprinkled it in the corner of the room.

"Come on," Fiona encouraged. She led me into a huge bathroom, complete with a glass-door shower with a rain-fall showerhead. Beside that sat a jetted tub fit for at least two.

Venn and I could fit.

Wait. Where had that thought come from? *Hold your horses, girl. You haven't even got to second base yet.*

Still, the tub looked inviting. I couldn't remember the last time I actually took a decent bath, considering my apartment only had a shower, sans tub. I longed to fill it and let the jets massage away all the tension I'd been bottling up these past few years. It wouldn't hurt to spoil myself, would it?

"Dibs on the tub!" I blurted.

Fiona laughed. "Come on. Let's go check out the other rooms."

The last room was a double queen suite. I did the calculations in my head, and unless Venn decided he wanted to sleep on the couch, we were going to end up in bed together again. Which I had absolutely *no* qualms about. I mean, it wasn't like we were going to *do* anything with Sondra and Fiona in the same room, but that didn't matter as long as I got to snuggle up in his arms again.

But first, I was getting in that jet tub.

"Genevieve said we could order anything from room service and charge it to the room," Sondra announced. She flipped through a menu on the coffee table. "Anyone hungry?"

"I'll eat later," I told her. "I'm really itching to get in that tub."

Sondra's eyes lit up. "That bathroom is amazing, isn't it? Oh, hey. When you get out, do you want me to do a cleansing spell on your clothes? It'll save you at least an hour on laundry."

"That would be amazing," I agreed.

I slipped into the bathroom while everyone else continued to explore the suite. Inside, I took a deep, calming breath. Tomorrow, I would worry about Matias, the Artifact, and the Soulless. Tonight, I was going to relax.

After a beat, I crossed the room and twisted the faucet. Warm water rushed out of the tap and filled the base of the tub. A neatly-arranged stack of toiletries sat on a washcloth on the ledge. I rifled through it and found a travel-sized bottle of bubble bath. After twisting off the cap, I turned the bottle completely upside down and let the whole thing pour into the water. Bubbles erupted under the flow of the water. Satisfied, I turned to the switch on the wall and dimmed the lights before stripping off my clothes. I would've started soothing music on my phone if I had it, but I'd left it at my apartment the night we fled Nocton.

I climbed into the hot water and leaned my head back against the edge of the tub. The warmth seeped into my bones and eased the tension in my muscles. When the water reached my chest, I turned off the faucet and started the jets. Bubbles grew higher and higher, and the jets massaged away the rest of my tension.

It felt like a sin to soak in the tub when the rest of the world was drowning in turmoil. I bet there were vampires roaming the city streets right now who deserved a stake to the heart. And it wasn't fair that I was sitting here warm in a tub when I had a lead on Jenna's whereabouts and wasn't doing a damn thing about it.

There's nothing you can do right now, I reminded myself. *Relax while you can.*

With that, I inhaled deep breaths, taking in the lavender scent of the bubbles. For once, my mind wasn't racing. I focused only on the rise and fall of my chest and the image of dark brown eyes—Venn's eyes—behind my lids. I couldn't remember the last time I'd felt this relaxed. It must've been years.

I stayed in the tub for what felt like at least an hour, but it still didn't seem long enough. I finally decided to get out when most of the bubbles had fizzled away and the water temperature had dropped to lukewarm. I lathered shampoo through my long dark hair, then added conditioner and scrubbed the rest of my body with soap before getting out. I was disappointed that I didn't get a chance to shave, considering my legs were starting to look like a gorilla's and my pits were in serious need of a razor. That *definitely* meant nothing could happen between Venn and me anytime soon.

After I'd dried off, I twisted the towel around my head and slipped into the plush white robe hanging from the back of the door. At the sink, I took a swig of complimentary mouthwash and swished it around in my mouth. Then I gathered my clothes from the floor and stepped out into the main room.

The suite was quiet and empty. I glanced into both bedrooms, but the beds were still neatly made, and nobody was in there. I spun around, wondering where they'd all gone without telling me, but then my eyes settled through the glass doors and onto the balcony. Sondra sat curled up on one of the patio chairs.

"Hey," I said gingerly as I stepped out onto the balcony and pulled up a chair beside her.

She looked up from the notepad she'd been doodling on. "Hey. You ready for that cleansing spell?"

"Yeah. Where is everyone?"

Sondra set her notepad aside. "They're down at the pool."

I couldn't help but steal a glance at her drawing. It was clearly just a quick sketch, nothing like the detailed drawings I'd seen on the wall back at her house, but she was amazingly talented. Somehow, she'd managed to capture the shadows perfectly on the face she'd drawn.

"That looks like Matias," I observed.

Sondra took my clothes and began shaking them out to fold them. "Yeah. I'm trying to see if I can remember him."

"Like, from a past life?" I asked while adjusting my robe to cover my knees.

"Yes. Sometimes, I think I recognize him, but I'm not sure. It's hard to tell with the silver eyes. But I think there might be something to my theory of him being a witch before he changed. It's like the memory of him is right on the edge of my mind, but I can't quite grab it yet." Sondra finished folding my clothes and placed them in a pile on her lap. "Drawing helps me with the memories."

I smiled. "You're really good, by the way. I saw the drawings at your house."

"Oh, you did?" she asked in a bright tone.

"Yeah, I thought they were great. I can't draw, so I'm not sure how I'll ever remember my past lives."

Sondra's brow creased. "It's not the same for everyone. Drawing helps me, but you'll find something else that'll help you."

"Like what?" I asked. "How does remembering this stuff work?"

Sondra shrugged. "It usually starts with some sort of trigger, like seeing someone you met in a past life, visiting a place you'd been in that life, or doing something that would've been significant to you."

"Shouldn't I remember my life as Abigail now that I've met Venn?"

Sondra shook her head. "Not necessarily. It's not normal to remember your past lives. It takes magic."

I frowned and mumbled, "Which I'm not very good at."

Sondra looked shocked by my attitude. "Don't say that. It just takes practice."

I sighed, knowing she was right. "How do you stay so calm and positive all the time?"

Sondra pressed her lips together and looked out over the city. "I guess I just trust Synchrony. I know that things will always work out, so it's easy to let go of worry."

"You worry about your family," I pointed out.

She smiled. "Of course I do. I don't want to lose them. Sometimes you just can't help but worry about the things that matter most to you."

My thoughts flew to Jenna, and a pang of guilt shot through my chest. I shouldn't have ever given up on her. I shouldn't have waited two years for a Soulless to show up on my doorstep and force me into taking action.

"I know what you mean," I whispered. "Could you maybe teach me? How to do magic, I mean?"

"I can teach you the basics," she offered, sending my heart soaring. "But the true magic comes from within you."

"I know," I said. "I don't expect you to do any of the work for me, just... I guess teach me how to stop doubting myself. Venn says that's what's holding me back."

Sondra nodded. "He's right. Doubt only breeds negativity. Synchrony reflects your intentions back on you, so if you doubt yourself, you will only see negative results."

"Venn explained that to me," I said, leaning further back in my chair. "I guess I'm just not sure how to do it, to let go of the doubt and be more positive."

Sondra and I stared at the city lights without saying anything for several breaths. Finally, she spoke.

"I wish I could tell you there's a secret to it, but I can't. It's something you have to figure out on your own, unfortunately." She scooted her chair around a few inches to look at me. "There are two things I've done to improve my magic. The first"—she held up a finger—"is to breathe." She inhaled a long, deep breath to demonstrate.

I raised an eyebrow. "That's it? Just *breathe*?"

Her lips turned down. "When you put it that way, it sounds silly, but I swear by it. With each breath I take, I release the tension from my shoulders and the negative energy with it. You just have to find what works for you."

"Well, the bath helped calm me, but I can't take a bubble bath every time I want to perform magic," I said.

Sondra nodded in agreement. "It's a lot easier said than done. Magic can be simple, but that doesn't mean it's easy. We'll have to figure something out for you. I suggest starting with a happy memory."

"Okay," I agreed, thinking on it briefly. "What's the second thing?"

"I don't do it as much anymore, only when I successfully execute a spell or potion I've never done before, but the second thing I do is take notes."

"Take notes?" Magic couldn't be this easy. If it was, everyone would be doing it.

"Yes," she said. "If you believe you're good at magic, you will see all the times you succeed. If you believe you're bad at magic, you'll see all the times you fail. I want to believe I'm good at magic, so I keep a record of my successes."

I considered it for a moment. "I think Fiona was trying to explain this to me before. She said I was good at healing because I'd already done it before. I already *believe* I can do it."

"Right." Sondra nodded. "Every success will make you believe that much more. Eventually, you won't need to remind yourself to believe in it. You'll have looked at enough evidence that you aren't just temporarily convinced; you'll truly have faith."

A sense of peace washed over me, though that could've been residual feelings left over from my amazing bath. I was starting to think I understood this. Enough to get a good start on practicing my magic, anyway.

"What do you want to believe?" Sondra asked curiously.

I kept my eyes on the city lights and didn't meet her gaze. What *did* I want to believe? I wanted to believe Jenna was alive. I wanted to believe Matias wouldn't get his hands on the Artifact. I wanted to believe that one day life would be better than it was now.

But I didn't want to say any of that. I sensed Sondra wasn't looking for me to dive that deep. Instead, I settled with, "I want to believe that I'm powerful, that I'm capable of more than just healing. I mean, healing is great, but I feel like I could do so much more."

A smile crept across Sondra's face. "Have you ever done a cleaning spell, Rae?"

I shook my head.

Her smile widened, radiating positive energy across the balcony. "Today's your lucky day." Sondra stood and gestured for me to follow her inside. "It's actually a really easy spell. We just need something that signifies cleanliness."

"Would a bottle of shampoo work?" I asked.

"That would be perfect," Sondra said.

She set my pile of clothes on the coffee table while I slipped into the bathroom to grab the shampoo off the lip of the tub.

"Okay," Sondra said, patting the couch cushion beside her to encourage me to sit. "You'll have to use a small amount of shampoo and rub it on your hands. Then you'll place them over the clothes and repeat after me."

"That's it?" I asked as I sat beside her.

"That's it," she replied simply. "I told you it was easy."

I followed Sondra's instructions and repeated the short incantation. I didn't even feel the magic buzz through me. By the end of the incantation, I wasn't sure the spell took.

"Did it work?" I asked. "I barely felt anything."

Sondra shrugged. "Do you believe it did?"

I hesitated. "I—I'm not sure."

"Check," she instructed.

I grabbed my jeans off the pile first. To my surprise, they were soft, like they'd just come out of the dryer, and they smelled of lavender. I unfolded them to see that the dirt on them was completely gone.

"Wow." I was practically speechless. I mean, I knew this spell wasn't very advanced, but still, I did it. A sense of pride washed over me.

I pulled the jeans to my chest and turned to Sondra. "Thank you so much! I should probably go get dressed. This robe is a little... airy. I don't need to be flashing my goods to everyone when they get back."

Oh, wow. I'd taken that a step too far. I barely knew Sondra, and here I was talking about my *goods*. Awkward.

I gathered the rest of my clothes, but I hesitated before I stood.

"What?" Sondra asked curiously.

I bit my lower lip. "You wouldn't happen to know any sort of hair removal spell, would you?"

Sondra held back a laugh. "No, but I know Fiona has a package of disposable razors in her bag and wouldn't mind you using one. I'll get one for you."

Sondra rose from the couch. As I watched her leave, I realized I had a question for her that I never got a chance to ask.

I shot to my feet before she left the room. "Hey, Sondra?"

She turned around, her hand on the door frame to our room, and stared expectantly at me. "Yeah?"

"I was just wondering... you don't have to answer if you don't want to. But why didn't you pass Genevieve's test?"

Sondra paused. "I guess even though I don't want anyone else to have the power... I feel like I could still use it for good."

With that, she left the room.

12

Ten minutes later, I returned to the bedroom with silky soft legs. I'd kept the white robe on because it was plush, comfortable, and I'd rather sleep in it than in my jeans, though I'd added clean underwear beneath it. Thank God. I no longer felt like anything was at risk of going on display. I ran my fingers through my damp tangles. Seeing as I didn't have a hairbrush with me, it was the best I could do.

The sound of the front door opening met my ears. Hopefully it was Fiona. I could ask if she brought along a hairbrush.

"Shut up, Ryland," I heard Teagan scold lightheartedly. "You need to watch less TV and read more books like Venn does."

"What's the difference?" Ryland retorted. "They're both fiction. My method is easier."

"It kills more brain cells," Fiona teased.

"And reading doesn't?" Ryland asked.

"Really?" Venn asked lightheartedly. "Of all the things you could make fun of me for, you choose to take a jab at *reading*. You're really stretching it there."

"What else am I going to tease you for?" Ryland asked. "Playing the guitar? Chicks dig that kind of thing. The only other thing I've got is the race card, and—"

"Don't you dare," Fiona scolded him before Ryland could say anything about Venn's skin color.

I stepped into the doorway to see Ryland holding his hands up in surrender.

"I wasn't going to," he said.

My eyes fell on Venn. I couldn't tear my gaze away from him even if I wanted to. He wore only a pair of black athletic shorts, which left his broad shoulders and defined abs exposed. Though he'd clearly dried off since leaving

212

the pool, several water droplets remained on his skin. I suddenly felt like my robe was tied too tight, like it was stealing the air from my lungs. I was getting *far* too warm wrapped in the plush fabric.

Fiona's eyes caught mine. "Oh, good. You're out of the bath. I'm next."

Fiona hurried into the open bathroom. She wore a black sports bra with matching athletic shorts. I guessed her swimsuit never made it into her luggage. Teagan was the only one dressed in a proper swimsuit, an olive-green bikini that suited her tan complexion and showed off every curve.

A pang of jealousy hit my gut at the sight of her thin legs, flat tummy, and generous bosom. Why Venn wanted pasty-white *me* when he lived with *her*, I'd never know. But he didn't even steal a glance her way. Which was weird, because even *I* was staring at her breasts and contemplating my sexuality.

When my eyes returned to Venn's strong, defined torso, Teagan's boobs completely fell from my mind. There was a good chance I was drooling at this point, but I didn't care. I could stare at him all night, entranced, and not get bored.

"Rae," Venn said as he approached me.

"Huh?" I asked in a daze, my eyes still greedily drinking him in.

"My eyes are up here."

At that, I instantly snapped out of it. Right. He was a human being, not some object on display.

My cheeks flamed. "Sorry. I just—"

"I was kidding," he said with a smile, stopping just inches from me in the doorway.

He reached out to sweep a strand of wet, tangled hair behind my ear. I gazed into his brown eyes, and my heart did that fluttery thing in my chest again. I stood there frozen, my cheek tingling in the spot where he'd touched me. My throat felt like sandpaper when I finally reminded myself to swallow.

"Seriously," Teagan said from the couch, pulling mine and Venn's attention away from each other. "Stop making googly eyes at each other and get a room already."

Venn gave her the side eye. "We have a room, thank you very much."

He stepped forward and pulled me inside the bedroom before shutting the door behind us. I stifled a laugh, but it quickly died when my eyes met his again. A single lamp between the beds lit up the room, casting shadows across his gorgeous face.

My God. What was it about looking this man in the eyes? The way he constantly gazed at me in wonder took my breath away. It was as if he had some sort of magic that stalled my heart but sent it beating a million times per minute all at the same time. My brain turned to mush around him, I swear. When he looked at me, nothing else in the world seemed to matter.

Which was dangerous as hell. Luckily for me, I liked danger.

But *this*? This love-sick, heart-on-fire girl wasn't me. Venn changed every-thing I knew about myself. He made me want to tear all my walls down for him. And for some strange, inexplicable reason, that didn't scare me when it should.

Venn smiled down at me, a seductive smile that sent my heart *pitter-pattering* against my chest.

Like I said, *so* not me.

"Now that we have a room, what should we do with it?" he whispered softly. He stood so close that I could feel his body heat, though he didn't touch me.

Which I was desperate to remedy. Without thinking, I reached out and placed my fingertips to his exposed chest. I studied his smooth skin, marveling at his even skin tone. Even the goosebumps that grew beneath my touch were beautiful.

I knew what *I* wanted to do with the room. My body screamed for it as certain parts I never used heated.

I bit my lower lip and lifted my gaze. He stared down at me with an expectant half-smile. He was waiting for me to say it out loud.

Ugh. Why did we have to use *words*? Wasn't it obvious? Couldn't he feel the heat sizzling between us? Or maybe it was just the robe. He'd have to help me out of it before I fainted from heat exhaustion.

Virgin, I teased myself. Seriously, what was *wrong* with me?

Venn was experienced. He'd never mentioned it directly, but the way he'd talked about being a blood slave hinted that there was more to that story. I wouldn't have been surprised if he'd lost his virginity long before that. I wasn't going to ask all the details, because I knew it would only resurface old, bitter memories. While it stung a little to think about him with other girls—with *Maliya*—it also made me want to make him forget about all of that. If I could, I'd kiss all the pain from his past away.

"We could… finish what we started in the elevator," I finally answered.

Oh, God. Why did he make me say it out loud?

"Mm…" Venn said in a tone that made my knees go weak. "I think that can be arranged."

In the blink of an eye, Venn swooped down and pressed his lips to mine. Butterflies danced in my stomach like a freaking rave party, and every inch of my skin came alive.

My arms slid around his neck as he deepened the kiss. I barely realized we were moving across the room until the back of my legs bumped up against the bed. I expected to tumble backward, but Venn caught me and twisted. He fell onto the mattress on his back and pulled me on top of him. My eyes roamed his body, and his dropped to my chest, where my robe had parted slightly.

"I can't believe how natural it feels to be with you," I said.

Why did I have to break the silence? We were doing fine without talking. Stupid mouth.

"You mean… almost like we're soulmates?" he asked.

A wide smile spread across my face. "Exactly."

The word *soulmates* hung in the air and permeated down into my bones. I couldn't explain it, but beyond a shadow of a doubt, I knew that Venn was it for me. It made no rational sense, but I didn't think it had to, as long as I trusted it was true.

Venn pulled me closer to him and pressed his lips to the sensitive skin below my ear. My back arched in response to his touch, and I held back a moan as his lips traveled down my neck, his breath brushing across my skin the whole way.

He drew away. "What do you want, Rae?"

You. All of you.

"I mean, I know it feels right to be with you," he said, "but we can take this as fast or slow as you want. I don't want you to feel rushed just because—"

I silenced his words with a passionate kiss. Heat pooled in my belly. We both drew a deep breath when we parted.

"Believe me," I said, "I'm not waiting for anything, except maybe a private room." I shot a glance at the door, which didn't have a lock on it. Anyone could barge in at any moment.

Venn's eyes widened. "I didn't mean—I just meant—"

"It's okay," I told him with a giggle. "I'm fine with just this."

Liar.

He stared up at me with desire and passion in his eyes. He pushed himself up briefly to place a kiss on my nose. "You're amazing. You know that? Has anyone ever told you you're amazing?"

The question was rhetorical, but I answered anyway. "I don't think so. I mean, besides my parents, but that was in, like, a totally different way. And, I mean, pretty much everyone who called me the Ravenite, but they thought I was some sort of super shifter or something."

Oh my God. You're ruining it with your rambling.

"I'll shut up now," I said quickly.

Venn laughed. "You're great."

The words sent a warm tingle to settle in my chest. I felt light and airy, carefree.

"So, uh…" I threw another glance at the door. "Sondra and Fiona aren't going to stay out there all night. I want to enjoy every second of alone time I have with you."

Venn wiggled his eyebrows. "Better get started then."

I beamed and accepted his invitation. My lips trailed from his mouth and down his jaw, then to his neck and finally to his collarbone. He shivered beneath my touch, and his hands tightened from where they rested on my hips.

I'm such a tease.

Tonight would take me further than I'd ever been with a guy, and I should've been terrified. But with Venn—with his kisses and his hands roaming over my backside—I wasn't scared. I didn't want to tease him. I wanted to take this further. Not all the way… but further.

I arched my back and pressed my pelvis into his. Slowly, I reached up with shaky fingers and tugged at the tie on my robe. The fabric fell away to expose my bare midriff and my bra. My breasts swelled as he gasped, his hungry eyes drinking me in. His hands moved over the bare skin of my legs and ran all the way up my abdomen until his fingers settled against the fabric on the underside of my bra. My mouth went dry, and my blood pulsed in my ears. What was he waiting for?

He couldn't wait any longer. He let out a deep growl, and he sprang on me. His arms were around me in an instant, dragging me into him until our lips connected. My mouth parted, letting him in. His tongue danced across mine, and I gladly welcomed the rush it brought. It was like conjuring magic, only a hundred times more powerful. Unlike magic, the tingle didn't shoot straight through me. It gathered into a ball in my chest, making me feel heavy and light all at the same time.

Venn spun me around, tossing me on my back. He paused a moment as his eyes roamed over me. My chest heaved in heavy breaths as I waited in unbearable anticipation for his next move.

Venn grabbed the sheets from beneath me, and we both climbed under the covers. He bit his lower lip as he hovered above me, straddling me. His gaze flickered down to my breasts. Desire burned in his eyes, reflecting back how I felt.

Now it was my turn to run my hands up his legs. Brazenly, I pushed the fabric of his shorts aside and ran my hands up to the skin at the apex of his thighs. The ends of my fingers just barely grazed him *there*. He was *so* ready for me.

"What do you want, Rae?" he whispered.

I thought about it for a moment. The part of my soul connected to him wanted it *all*. But the Rae part of me—the inexperienced part—begged for merely just a taste. We didn't have any protection on hand, which was kind of a deal breaker for me. But there was *plenty* we could do without it.

"I want you to touch me," I whispered back before wrapping my arms around his neck and pulling him closer to me. My chest heaved, and my nipples hardened beneath the fabric of my bra. "And kiss me."

Venn gladly took my invitation, claiming my mouth as his own once again. My legs wrapped around his middle, pulling him even closer to me, while my hands ran across the exposed skin on his back. His right thumb ran just below my underwire, teasing me.

Do it.

Venn wrapped an arm underneath me and pinched the sides of my bra clasp together. Suddenly, the fabric loosened, and cool air rushed across my exposed breasts. Venn pushed aside the fabric and ran a warm hand across my bare skin, sending fireworks to explode through my chest. My heart pummeled against my rib cage as my fingers tangled in his hair. Sweet, sweet adrenaline coursed through me, igniting every nerve ending in my body in a warm tingle.

"More," I moaned between his kisses as his hand roamed over my breast.

I hadn't even realized I'd said anything until his weight lifted off of me and he resituated himself to lie beside me on the bed. His lips stayed on mine, but his hand left my breast and trailed downward, running further beneath the sheets. His fingers stopped at my waistband.

No, don't stop!

I curled my fingers deeper into his hair and bit his lower lip, letting him know he was welcome. His hands slipped beneath the fabric. I let out a wavered breath. He paused for a moment, until I protested by deepening our kiss and digging my nails into his shoulder. He responded by kissing me back with equal passion. Then he slid his fingers further down my body until he was touching me *there*. My back arched, and a deep breath passed my lips.

His fingers moved across me in ways I'd never experienced before. The motion sent a fire to build up inside of me, until I was biting his shoulder just to keep the moans from escaping. And then that fire exploded, rushing through me like a blessing from the gods.

Venn pulled the covers up to my chin and wrapped me in his arms. I lay beside him feeling weightless. I couldn't think straight. He placed a kiss on the back of my neck.

"Good night," he whispered.

"What about you?" I mumbled.

"Shh…" he replied softly. "Don't worry about me. We'll have plenty of other chances."

Plenty of other chances. I liked the sound of a future together.

I took a deep breath, inhaling his scent and melting into his chest, before I dozed off into a peaceful slumber.

13

I stared into Venn's eyes—only, the face wasn't his. Still, I recognized him just the same. My fingers reached out to wrap in his. My skin was darker than normal, but only by a shade or two. His was paler than mine, in stark contrast to his usual midnight-dark skin. He dressed in clothing that didn't look to fit this century, and we stood in a thick forest where no one else could hear us. Somehow, I knew our home lay just on the other side of the trees.

"I think it's a good idea," he said, taking my hands in his. "But we don't have to do this, Abigail."

"Yes, we do, Charles," I countered. I barely recognized my own accent. "It's the only way to save everyone."

He dropped my hands and pulled me into an embrace. I leaned into him and rested my head on his shoulder.

"You know what this means, don't you?" I whispered. "If we do this, we will never stop hunting down the vampires."

"I know," he replied, "and I'm okay with that."

"Our lives will never be the same," I said.

"No, they won't," he agreed, "but our lives already changed months ago when they killed our daughters. No one should have to go through what we went through. We'll rid the world of vampires if it's the last thing we do."

"Get up!"

I startled awake, my heart thumping wildly against my chest. "Jesus Christ, Fiona!"

She bounced on her knees at the foot of the bed, shaking the springs all the way up by my head. Venn rolled away from me and rubbed the sleep from his eyes. Cool air that tasted a lot like disappointment rushed between us.

I forced my eyes open and glanced to the digital clock on the nightstand. "It's five a.m.!"

Fiona climbed off the bed. "I know, but we have to be at the airport in less than an hour. So, chop-chop."

I sighed and leaned my head back on the pillow as Fiona hurried out of the room, leaving Venn and me alone. My heart was still racing.

"Are you okay?" Venn reached out to touch my shoulder. Although his skin only made contact with my robe, my shoulder heated beneath his touch.

I raked my fingers through my hair and stared blankly up at the ceiling. "Yeah, I'm fine. I just... I think I had a vision."

Venn propped himself on his elbow, immediately alert. "A vision?"

"A vision, or a memory or something." My gaze met his. "It was us, Venn. In our past life."

The worried look on his face vanished. Intrigue replaced it. "Really?"

I nodded. "We were young and living in Europe. It was the mid-1700s. We had three daughters."

Venn opened his mouth to speak, but I cut him off.

"Don't ask me how I know all the details. I just remember."

He smiled. "We really had three girls?"

I nodded, but I knew the sadness was written all over my face. Venn's expression fell.

"They were the reason we started hunting vampires," I explained. "I mean, when we were Abigail and Charles. The vampires..."

My throat closed up. I knew the girls weren't *my* daughters, not in this life, but my heart still broke for them. A muscle fluttered in Venn's jaw.

I squeezed my eyes closed and shook my head, as if trying to rid myself of the memory. "We were discussing our options. You wanted me—Abigail—to perform the spell, the one that turned you into a shifter. You wanted to save everyone else from the vampires."

It didn't surprise me that Charles sounded so much like the Venn I knew.

Venn shifted beside me and pulled me close to his chest. He didn't say anything as he placed a gentle kiss on my forehead. Warmth spread across my skin, calming me.

I drew away. "That's all I remember."

"That's okay," Venn said gently. The look in his eyes told me he meant it. "The fact that you remembered anything at all from your previous life is amazing."

I lifted the corner of my lips into a smile. "Thanks."

Fiona stuck her head back in the room. "Come on, you guys. Breakfast will be here soon. You don't want Ryland to eat all your food, do you?"

She left the room again, and Venn and I exchanged an amused glance.

He groaned and rolled away from me, the muscles in his back rippling as he pushed himself up. "She's right. Ryland eats like a bear."

I stifled a laugh.

Venn rolled his eyes as he pulled a shirt on over his head. "Don't laugh at me. That was a cheap joke."

"What?" I asked innocently as I pushed myself up to sit on the edge of the bed. "I'm not allowed to find you funny?"

Venn pressed his lips together, like he was thinking hard. "I guess, if that's the kind of humor that entertains you. But in that case, we need to get you out more."

I crawled across the bed and rose to my knees beside him. My hands tangled in his shirt as I tugged on him, encouraging him to come back to bed with me. "I'd rather stay in."

Venn caved to my invite and parted his lips. My tongue grazed across his lower lip as his hands roamed my backside. Every nerve in my body came to life.

He drew away and took a deep breath. "Fiona was serious, you know. If we aren't out there by the time breakfast arrives, we won't get any."

I stuck my lower lip out in a mock pout. "Fine, but we need to make up all the cuddles we missed from being woken up so early."

Venn's eyes sparkled. "We'll have plenty of time for that on our flight."

Reluctantly, I dragged myself out of bed. Venn grabbed his shoes and left the room, closing the door behind him. I tugged at the tie on my robe and let the fabric fall to the floor.

Suddenly, I felt *extremely* exposed. The hairs on the back of my neck stood as if the air conditioning was blowing directly on me, but the vent was all the way across the room and it hadn't been turned on all night. I quickly scooped up the robe from the floor and held it close to my chest while I glanced around the room. The door was securely closed, and the curtains were drawn. I could hear everyone else talking out in the main room.

And still, something didn't feel right—as if someone was watching me.

I shook off the feeling and quickly pulled on my clothes. By the time I'd laced up my boots and tossed my hair into a ponytail with Fiona's brush and one of the hair ties she'd left lying on the dresser, the anxiety rushing through my veins had waned, but the strangeness of the sensation lingered. I exited the room, running my fingers through my hair, to see that everyone was seated around the dining table with plates of food in front of them. I slid into the chair beside Venn, my eyes darting around the room the whole time.

"You look worried," Sondra observed as she took a bite of pancake.

"No," I lied, picking up my fork. "I was just wondering about that protection charm you got from Genevieve."

Way to be subtle.

"What was it for?" I asked.

"This?" Sondra held up the small black bag from where it hung off her neck.

I took a bite of egg and nodded.

"It's a blend of herbs that's supposed to protect us from other magic," Sondra admitted.

"Does it work?" I asked hopefully. Maybe it was just my imagination getting to me.

"It should."

"And what if it didn't work?" I asked. "Matias has the locket. He could be tracking us."

I hated putting my fears out there in the open, but it was a very real possibility.

"Why would he track us?" Ryland cut in. "He's unaware we know about The Wise Owl, isn't he?"

"Well, those guys at Amalia's didn't attack us for no reason," I pointed out.

Ryland opened his mouth to say more, but Sondra cut him off.

"You're right," she said. "That's why we have to get on an early flight and follow Genevieve's coordinates."

"Do we know the coordinates yet?" Teagan asked.

"No," Sondra answered with a shake of her head. "She'll send the coordinates once we land."

Teagan's eyebrows rose. "Where are we going, exactly?"

Sondra swallowed another bite of food. "We won't know until we get to the airport. The reason Genevieve hasn't told us where we're going yet is in case Matias *is* watching us."

"And you trust her?" Ryland asked skeptically.

"Yes," Sondra said. "On this, I do. As long as we make it there before Matias does, everything should work out."

"*Will* we make it there before him?" Venn asked, sounding worried.

"I don't see how he would make it ahead of us," Sondra replied. "Don't worry. We're going to get this thing and destroy it. We'll figure out the rest from there. Any other questions?" Her eyes scanned the table.

Fiona's hand shot into the air. "Yeah, um... can I have a window seat?"

The car Genevieve provided was stocked with everything we needed for the plane ride: travel snacks, magazines for entertainment, and our plane tickets. What surprised me, though, was the sight of my I.D. sitting in the folder with the plane tickets.

I gasped and grabbed it, flipping it around in my hands to make sure it was real. How did it get there?

Inside the folder, a yellow sticky note read, *I figured you'd need this. The rest of your belongings are at my house for when you return. Genevieve.*

Genevieve must've gone to my apartment and taken the bag I'd packed before I left. I was relieved to know my stuff was safe, even though it was just my phone, my spell journal, and a few pairs of clothes. At least it meant my sketchy landlord didn't have his grubby hands on my stuff.

Almost an hour after we arrived at the airport, we boarded a plane to Nashville.

Fiona inhaled a sharp breath when she saw our destination. "Mammoth Caves," she whispered. "That must be where we're going."

She was the first from our group on the plane. She quickly found our row and settled in by the window, staring out it in wonder even though we hadn't even left the terminal. I sat beside her in the middle seat. Venn placed his bag in the overhead bin before sliding into the seat beside me.

I eyed Fiona curiously. "Have you ever flown before?"

She couldn't tear her gaze off the window. "No, I haven't. If Sondra ever has to travel for business, she always takes Ryland with her."

I glanced to Ryland, who was trying to find enough leg room to rest his feet. He was far too big for the plane and had to spread his legs so his knees didn't touch the back of the seat in front of him. I could see why Sondra took him along. He was a full security team shoved into one body.

"And you, Venn?" I asked. He threw a nervous glance at the window. "Have you ever flown before?"

"I—I did once," he said hesitantly. "When I was a kid, my family flew to California for my cousin's wedding."

"Me, too," I told him. "My family took a vacation to Florida when I was eight. I loved it."

Fiona leaned over and whispered, "Venn hates it."

My shocked gaze snapped in his direction. "You're afraid of flying?"

He nodded, and his hands tightened around his armrests as the plane began to roll away from the terminal. I felt bad for him. I couldn't imagine being afraid of flying. Granted, when I flew it typically wasn't in an airplane, and I usually had the wind whipping through my feathers to add to the thrill, but still…

"It's okay, Venn," I said lightly as I rested a hand on his. "I live for flying. I wouldn't let anything happen to you."

A ghost of a smile touched his lips. "Thanks."

When we reached the runway, his hand tightened around mine. He closed his eyes and took a deep breath as we picked up speed. I knew when the plane's wheels left the ground because my stomach flipped in my abdomen. Venn squeezed my fingers so tightly he could've crushed bone.

Beside me, Fiona gasped as the earth dropped out from beneath us. "Oh, wow! It's so pretty from up here. Venn, look!"

Venn didn't open his eyes. Ryland muttered something under his breath. I didn't catch it, but I figured it was some sort of insult. Teagan slugged him in the arm. My gaze darted to Sondra across the aisle, wondering what I should do to help Venn.

"There's no shame in being scared," Sondra said simply. "Most people see fear as a weakness, but it's how you use fear that matters."

This woman was freaking wise. I wanted to be her someday.

"What do you mean?" I asked, intrigued.

She leaned on her armrest and stuck her head into the aisle. "Fear is important to self-preservation. There's such thing as too much fear, so much that it keeps you from truly living. But if you fear nothing, you will almost certainly get yourself killed. A healthy amount of fear is a good thing. Venn's learned that and knows how to handle it."

He nodded, his eyes still closed. "She's right. I'll be fine. I just need a minute."

"I'm scared of things most people aren't, too," Fiona chimed in. "Vampires, for one."

I looked at her in disbelief. "You are not." I didn't want to say too much with other passengers around, but Fiona freaking slayed the bastards.

"No, really," she insisted. "I do what I have to do, but honestly, I've just been lucky. Hey, Ryland, remember that time when you threw up and that vamp slipped in it while he was coming after me? If Ryland hadn't been sick, I don't know if I'd be here today."

I briefly wondered why we were talking about vampires out in the open like this. Most people didn't take kindly to our vampire-slaying hobbies, considering the bloodsuckers still had rights. Then I caught a glimpse of Venn's face and saw that his expression had relaxed. Fiona was talking to distract him.

"I'm scared of the dumbest things, too," I joined in.

"Really?" Teagan's brows shot up from across the aisle. "Rae? Scared? No way."

"Yes way," I said with a laugh. "I'm scared of…"

What was I scared of? Certainly not vampires. I was scared of being alone again, of going back to my old life where I had no friends, no family. But this wasn't the kind of conversation that warranted diving that deep. I was supposed to be making Venn feel better.

"Maggots," I settled with.

"Maggots?" Teagan laughed.

"They're gross!" I argued. "I just don't want them touching me. When I was little, my sister and I found a dead mouse at the park by our house. It was full of maggots. She told me it was the mouse's insides coming to life and that he was going to become a zombie mouse. I ran home screaming."

Fiona snickered from beside me. The memory churned my insides. When Venn peeled his eyes open, everything I'd just said was so totally worth it.

He smirked. "And you believed her?"

I shrugged, holding back a laugh. "Of course I did. I was, like, five. Anything's possible when you're five."

"True," he agreed, relaxing his hands on the armrest. "I used to believe my toys came to life at night."

"I did, too," I giggled. "*Toy Story* was my favorite movie. I thought it was real."

Venn laughed. "I once apologized to a toy soldier because I stepped on him. For the longest time, I thought he'd died and the other soldiers had buried him, because I couldn't find him after that. I eventually found him in my brother's room months later."

"You guys had it easy," Fiona teased. "Ryland convinced me my dolls were evil. I couldn't sleep for weeks until Mom and Dad locked my dolls up in their closet. I only played with puzzles for, like, six months before I got a stuffed bear for my birthday." Fiona shot Ryland daggers.

Ryland looked up from the game he was playing on the screen in front of him. "Hey, I said I was sorry, like, a million times."

"Only because Mom and Dad made you," she shot back with a laugh.

I grinned. "So, what I'm hearing is that Ryland's always been a jerk."

Fiona wrinkled her nose. "Mostly. But he can be sweet sometimes."

"*Sometimes?*" Ryland repeated. "I'm a freaking jar of strawberry jam. I'm as sweet as they come."

"Oh, honey." Teagan patted his leg. "You're strawberry jam if they forgot to add the sugar."

Sondra chose that moment to take a swig from her water bottle. She nearly choked as she tried to keep from spraying her water all over the seat in front of her. She coughed to compose herself. "I've never heard anyone speak such truth before." She screwed the cap back on and high-fived Teagan.

The plane ride wasn't long, but Venn and I passed the time by tossing peanuts into the air and trying to catch them in our mouths.

I caught the first three, but the forth landed on the side of my cheek and shot out into the middle of the aisle. Venn leaned over and grabbed it. I opened my mouth, and he took aim. It hit me square on the end of the nose.

"Excuse me," a voice snapped. A steward with a bald patch stopped in the aisle next to our seats. He gazed down at us with judgement in his eyes. "But I'm going to have to ask you to stop."

Venn and I exchanged a guilty glance.

I cleared my throat. "Yes, sir. We're sorry."

I held back my laugh, clearly not meaning it.

The steward nodded and turned from us, his nose held high. I threw a peanut at the back of the guy's head as he walked away. Fiona and Venn both broke out into a fit of laughter.

Eventually, I lay my head against Venn's shoulder and stared out the window at the rising sun. I was enjoying the flight so much that I nearly forgot where we were headed until we landed.

"The car's this way," Sondra said with confidence once we stepped off the plane.

We followed her through the airport until we came to a parking garage.

Sondra stopped beside a silver minivan and glanced at her phone. "This is it. Genevieve says the keys are in the glovebox and there are supplies for us in the back."

Sondra headed to the driver's side door and opened it. She poked her head inside the van and came out holding a white slip of paper. She smiled and turned the paper to us. "Genevieve says good luck."

"Should we check out what she left us?" Ryland suggested, popping open the back hatch.

"Ooh. Fancy," Fiona said when she saw the six backpacks piled up behind the back seat.

Venn reached for the red one on top and unzipped the main pocket. "Looks like Genevieve thought of everything. Water, headlamps, food, first-aid kit, rope... do you think we'll need rope?"

Sondra shrugged. "We might. I don't know what to expect. We have to prepare for anything."

"Hell yes!" Teagan exclaimed, glancing into a black backpack she'd pulled off the top. She looked up with a wide smile on her face. "Genevieve scored me some throwing knives. I'm going to have to rethink my feelings on this lady."

"You can go through your bags in the car. We should get going," Sondra suggested. "I don't want to waste any time."

"How far is the drive?" I asked.

Sondra glanced down at her phone. "It looks like it'll take about two hours. I can get us there in one and a half." She smiled mischievously.

My brows shot up. "I didn't know you were a speed demon. I like it."

Teagan let out a light laugh while she climbed into the van. "You say that now."

Fiona rolled her eyes and opened the passenger-side door. "Because you're a *much* better driver."

"I never claimed that," Teagan laughed before turning her attention to Ryland. "Hey, babe. You wanna sit in the back by me? We can make out like lovesick teenagers."

Ryland's eyes lit up, and he eagerly climbed in and jumped over the seat to sit next to her.

Teagan held up her hands in surrender. "Jeez. I was joking."

"So, you don't want to make out with me?" Ryland leaned over her and stuck his tongue out, threatening to lick her with it.

I stifled a laugh while I slid into the middle seat. Venn sat beside me and closed the door behind us.

"Ew!" Teagan complained, placing a hand on Ryland's chest. "Get that thing away from me."

I knew now wasn't the time to be joking around and laughing, but I couldn't help but enjoy the moment. I'd become so serious over the past few years that I almost forgot there were still things worth laughing over. *And things worth loving,* I thought as my gaze roamed over Venn.

He didn't notice my eyes on him as he draped his arm around my shoulder and settled in for the long car ride. For just a few more hours, I would enjoy the warmth of Venn's embrace and the glorious sound of my new family bickering with each other.

Then it was down into the cold, damp cave, where anything could happen.

14

True to her word, Sondra pulled off a deserted road into a narrow gravel driveway an hour and a half later. The forest was thick around us, and the sun was playing peek-a-boo behind the clouds. Something about the wilderness made me feel free, like I could run for miles or fly high in the sky. Ahead, the trees parted to give way to a clearing where a small cabin sat. It looked old but well taken care of. There were no signs of human life on the property.

"Genevieve said we should park here off the main road," Sondra explained as she slowed the van to a stop. "Technically, we're trespassing, but it's a vacation home that no one's using right now, so we should be fine."

"How far away are the caves?" Venn asked.

"If Genevieve's coordinates are correct, it looks like we have a good three-mile hike ahead of us," Sondra said. "But she says the entrance isn't going to be easy to find, so we're going to have to keep a close eye out for it."

Sondra parked, and we all piled out of the vehicle and strapped our day packs to our backs.

"How are you doing?" Venn whispered under his breath as we entered lush green forest behind everyone else.

"I'm fine. Why?" It sounded like a lie, even to my ears, though I didn't know why. I hadn't realized I was lying.

"Because your sister is still out there," Venn answered. "I can see it in your eyes every now and then that you worry about her."

"I do," I agreed as I stepped around a thick tree and over underbrush. I slowed my pace to put distance between us and the rest of the group. I lowered my voice so only Venn could hear. "I should've gone after her years ago, but I didn't know where to start. I was hopeless. I think that's part of why I started killing vampires—because it gave me hope that the world might be a better place without them."

Venn cocked his head like he agreed with me.

"I miss her so much," I whispered.

"I know," Venn said. "As soon as we're done here, we're going after her. I promise."

I shot him a light smile. "I really appreciate that."

The longer we walked in silence, the more I thought about Jenna. My gut twisted as guilt assaulted me.

She can hold out another day, I told myself, but I wasn't an easy person to convince.

The fact was, thinking about Jenna was sending my anxiety into overdrive. There was nothing I could do right now for her out in the wilderness, and I knew I might need to access magic for whatever lay ahead. So, despite the guilt tearing through me, I pushed her from my mind. *Temporarily,* I told myself.

I took a deep breath and released the tension in my fists on the exhale. I focused on the calming sound of the wind rushing through the trees… until the wind began to pick up. A chill traveled down my spine. The sky began to darken, and the temperature seemed to drop a few degrees within a matter of minutes. Something in the air tasted different, but I couldn't pinpoint what. I hadn't even realized the air normally *had* a taste. I just knew something wasn't quite right.

"It looks like it might rain," Ryland said, glancing up at the sky. "How close are we?"

Sondra stepped around a tree. "Not far. Keep an eye out."

Fiona scanned the landscape. A short hill rose ahead of us, but other than that, the forest was fairly flat. "I don't see how we're going to find a cave around here."

"It could look like anything," Sondra said. "It might just be a hole in the ground."

Fiona's eyes darted to her feet in horror, as if wondering whether or not we were going to fall straight into a cavern.

A familiar tingle spread across my skin, raising the hairs on my arms. I might've written it off as static electricity in the air from the incoming storm if I hadn't been acutely tuned to my magical sense.

"I feel something," I announced.

"I do, too," Sondra agreed. "There's magic up ahead. We're getting close."

As we crested the hill, the energy sizzling across my skin intensified. The hill stopped abruptly at a rocky wall at least ten feet high. We stood at the top of it, overlooking the rest of the forest.

"It's here," I said confidently, though I couldn't tell exactly how I knew. Somehow, I could just *feel* an enchantment in the air.

"What are we waiting for?" Teagan asked. "Let's check it out."

Ryland walked to the edge of the short cliff and jumped straight down. Fiona inhaled a sharp breath, but he landed just fine at the bottom.

Show off.

"You okay?" Sondra called to him.

He better be, considering the guy was big enough to practically reach up his arms and touch our toes.

"Fine," Ryland said. "Are you coming or what?"

Teagan backed away from the edge. "I'll take the easy way down. I don't plan on breaking any bones today."

"Oh, come on, babe." Ryland held his arms out. "I'll catch you."

Teagan shot him the stink eye, like she didn't believe him.

"Catch me!" Fiona said quickly.

She bent her knees, and a look of horror crossed Ryland's face. She gave a small hop into the air but only came off the ground a few inches.

"You're so gullible," Fiona said with a laugh. She turned away from Ryland and followed Sondra down the side of the hill. "You should've seen your face."

The rest of us took the gentle slope down the lowest corner of the rock wall and climbed down easily. As soon as we reached level ground, I spotted an opening in the rock. It wasn't very big, only about the size of the window back in my apartment. But it sloped downward and stretched so far back into the hillside that all I saw was pitch-black darkness. The magical energy I'd felt earlier was stronger than ever.

I stood in front of the mouth of the cave and placed my hands on my hips, peering inside. Ryland's ass was going to get stuck in there. I was sure of it.

"So… who wants to crawl into the creepy tunnel of doom first?" I asked.

"I'd go first," Fiona offered, "but we have to find the creepy tunnel of doom first. Feel anything else?"

I furrowed my brow as she scanned the forest, totally oblivious to the cave mouth I stood in front of. "Yeah. It's called using my eyes."

"What?" Fiona asked, like I wasn't making any sense.

That's when I noticed everyone's eyes still roaming the rock face. Venn stared out into the trees, as if he might find the mouth of the cave a hundred yards out. Sondra was the only one who seemed to notice the opening.

"They can't see it?" I asked her.

She stepped forward and glanced into the cave. "Apparently not. You feel that magic emanating off the rock face?"

I nodded.

"The rock must be enchanted to hide the cavern," she theorized.

Teagan placed her hands on her hips. "What are you talking about?"

I ignored her and kept my attention on Sondra. "Why can we see it when they can't?"

Sondra thought about it for a beat. "The artifact was made for witches, by witches. The coven that hid it must've enchanted the entrance so that only a witch could find it. That must be why this cavern has remained undiscovered all these years."

"So, if we're the only ones who can see it, are we the only ones who can enter?" I asked.

Sondra shrugged. "Genevieve didn't say anything about an enchanted entrance. From here on out, we're on our own."

Well, shit. That meant *I* was going down the creepy tunnel of doom first. *Bring it on.*

"Now's not the time for games," Ryland warned. "Are you two being serious?"

"Yes," I answered. "You really can't see this?" I gestured to the cave entrance.

Venn stepped forward and ran his hands along the stone, eyeing it in wonder. "That's so weird. To us, it's just a flat rockface."

His hands ran flat across the opening of the cave, as if he were a mime. I wondered what it would look like to them if I entered it. Would I just disappear into the rock like a ghost?

"Let's see what happens if I go inside," I offered.

Venn stepped aside to give me room. I ducked my head and leaned forward, but before I could get my hands on the edge of the opening, the top of my head slammed into something solid. I recoiled, rubbing the area of impact and cursing under my breath. Ryland burst into a fit of laughter behind me. Teagan swatted at him, but she too was stifling a laugh.

"Very funny," I snarled once the curses died down. "I'm not making this shit up. There's a cave right here! It's just…"

I stretched my hand out. My fingers met a cold, hard material I couldn't see.

"Rock?" Ryland finished for me with a raised eyebrow.

Fiona crossed her arms and glared at him. "Well, *I* believe her."

"I didn't say I didn't believe her!" Ryland rebutted.

"Can you guys just chill for a minute?" Sondra insisted. "I need to think."

Everyone went silent as Sondra ran her hand over the invisible rock face and inspected the enchanted cave opening.

After what felt like several minutes, I dared to break the silence. "Didn't Amalia say that only the witch who created a spell can break it?"

"Usually, if the spell is strong enough," Sondra answered without looking up at me. She was on her knees now, inspecting the rock. "But this enchantment was meant to be broken."

"How do we break it?" Teagan asked.

"Genevieve should've known about this," Venn said with uncertainty in his eyes. "She didn't mention anything to you?"

Sondra tilted her head to look at the underside of the rocks jutting out from the wall. "No, which means there must be a clue around here somewhere."

Fiona joined Sondra on her knees to inspect the rock. She shot the rest of us a look of disapproval. "What are you all waiting for?"

Before we had a chance to join in, Sondra spoke. "Hold on. I found something."

Sondra gazed into the cave and stared at something on the rock ceiling. I squeezed in beside her to take a look. Beyond the invisible wall, a string of words had been engraved into the stone.

"*Witches rise, and witches fall, but a heart that's pure and clean will enter with revelare, three tears, and smoke of evergreen,*" Sondra recited. She stood and dusted off her knees. "This is our way in."

Confusion crossed Ryland's face. "What does it mean? *A heart that's pure and clean?* So, we need a virgin witch to get us through? Where are we going to find one of those?"

I glared at him and placed a hand on my hip. "Really? You're just going to assume I'm *not* a virgin witch?"

"Ryland," Teagan scolded.

"I was just—"

"We don't need a virgin," Sondra cut him off.

Ryland rose his eyebrows. "I suppose you're going to cast the spell? Your heart's not exactly pure and clean."

Sondra scowled at him. "I've made my amends, and you know that. Now, would you stop it and go find some pine needles?"

"Pine needles?" Ryland asked in confusion.

"Yes," Sondra emphasized. "Did you miss the part about *smoke of evergreen,* or were you too focused on sacrificing a virgin?"

Ryland held his hands up in surrender. "I heard it. I just don't know where I'm supposed to find pine needles. This isn't exactly a coniferous forest."

Teagan spun around and grabbed Ryland's huge bicep. "Come on. It's the least we can do to help."

Sondra shook her head and turned back to the cave opening once Ryland and Teagan walked away. "Cousins. I tell ya."

"Hey," Fiona dragged out in mock offense.

"Relax, Fiona. You're practically my sister," Sondra said with a smile.

"Aww…" Fiona blinked rapidly and fanned her face like she was touched.

"Keep that up," Venn encouraged. "We're going to need three of those tears."

Fiona smiled. "Always happy to help."

I shifted my weight between my feet. "So, we have the evergreen and the tears. What about that first part? *Revelare?*"

"That's the incantation," Sondra explained. "So once we have the pine needles, we should be able to get through. It's actually a really simple spell."

"Should we go help look—?"

I was cut off by the sound of a twig breaking in the distance. I whirled around, expecting to see Ryland and Teagan on their way back, but the forest was empty. Chills immediately danced up and down my arms, but I quickly realized it was just the cool breeze from the storm rolling in.

Just as I thought it, the first of the heavy raindrops fell. One splattered against the tip of my nose while another hit the back of my hand. I glanced up to the sky just as the clouds opened and it began pouring.

Fiona ducked and pulled her backpack up over her head. Within seconds, my hair was sticking to my face, and my shoulders were soaked. I instinctively hugged the edge of the rock, hoping the cliff would provide some relief from the rain, but there wasn't an overhang to protect us from the downpour.

I cursed under my breath. "How are we going to get smoke in this kind of weather? And what if Ryland and Teagan get lost?"

Venn was quick to act and pulled a small tarp out of his bag. He unfolded it and draped it over the two of us.

"Come on." He gestured for Sondra and Fiona to join us.

The tarp was barely big enough to cover the four of us, and we had to hold on to the corners tightly to make sure the wind whipping by us wouldn't steal it away.

"What do we do?" Fiona yelled to be heard over the strong wind. "Should we go looking for them?"

"There they are!" Sondra pointed, her finger getting wet beneath the rain.

Two shadows sprinted forward. I blinked away the water from my eyes and pushed my wet hair from my face. Teagan came to a halt in front of us and quickly threw the remaining corner of the tarp over her head. Ryland stood in the rain, using his backpack as an umbrella. It was so small compared to his large frame that it looked more like he was trying to keep dry with a soggy piece of bread.

"Here!" Teagan shoved a pile of pine needles and twigs into Sondra's hand. "Sorry they're wet."

"That's fine," Sondra said in a rush. She placed the pine needles on the small piece of rock that stuck out just beneath the cave opening.

Venn stretched his arm around me to hold the tarp over Sondra's workstation. My breath caught in my chest as his arm brushed against the side of my head.

"Who has tears for me?" Sondra asked.

"Working on them," Fiona said. Her lips turned down, and her eyes sparkled like a puppy dog's. She squeezed her eyes shut, trying to force the tears.

"Dead puppies," Ryland blurted.

"That's just cruel," Teagan snapped at him.

"You need tears," Ryland said. "I'm just trying to help."

"Babe—" Teagan started to scold, but Fiona cut her off.

"No, it's fine. The more horrible things he throws at me, the better chance I have of crying." Fiona blinked, forcing the tears out. Water dripped down her face, but I was ninety-nine percent sure that those were rain droplets and not tears. We were going to have to break someone's foot if we wanted tears on demand.

I could cry, I thought to myself. I mean, I hated crying, but I wasn't so emotionally detached that I couldn't shed a tear.

"Think of Mom and Dad," Ryland encouraged.

I knew the words were for Fiona, but I let my thoughts drift to my own parents. For the first time in what felt like years, I dropped my emotional walls and recalled the memories I'd pushed away for so long. My chest tightened as I thought back to my mother's soft smile and the way my dad's scruffy beard felt across my face when he kissed my cheek. I could still smell the scent of my mother's signature Summer Sunshine shampoo. I thought of the time she held me in her arms while I cried one night when I was twelve, the day Wendy Bolton punched me in the face for flirting with the guy she liked. I remembered the proud look in my dad's eyes the next day when he was teaching me how to defend myself. I'd knocked him off his feet on my third try. I remembered how Jenna had offered to kick Wendy's ass herself if she ever touched me again.

God, I missed my family. We weren't always perfect, but we always had each other's backs.

And now they're gone.

The words echoed in my mind. My parents were gone forever. And Jenna… who knew?

My cheeks heated. Tears welled in my eyes and poured over the lids. I quickly leaned over the pine needle pile and squeezed my eyes shut to let the tears fall. When satisfied that at least three tears had been added to the pile, I pulled away and wiped the rest from my cheeks. I opened my eyes to see everyone staring at me in shock.

"What?" I shrugged. "I have feelings, you know."

Sondra shot me a somber look, then pulled her attention away from me and to the pine needles. Venn wasn't as quick to dismiss my display. He wrapped his free arm around my shoulder and pressed his cheek to the top of my head. He didn't say anything, but he didn't have to. Already, I felt warmer, and the weight on my chest began to ease beneath his embrace.

"Let's speed it up," Ryland pressed. "I'm soaked."

Sondra muttered an incantation I recognized under her breath, and the wet pine needles ignited.

"*Revelare,*" she said as the fire quickly ate away at the needles and smoke rose into the air.

The smoke instantly changed directions, swooping into the cave mouth as if it'd been sucked into a vacuum. Everyone but Sondra and me drew a collective breath. I knew they could now see the deep, dark hole in the side of the rock.

"I'll go in first and make sure it's safe," Sondra said hastily, rising to her feet. "Ryland, you go last and make sure everyone gets through okay."

"I will," he agreed, dropping the childish demeanor from earlier. Clearly, he knew things were about to get serious.

Fiona followed behind Sondra, and I went in after her. I crawled in on my hands and knees, relieved that it was dry. The entrance wasn't much bigger than the covered slide at my old elementary school, and it sloped down at a similar angle. Ahead of me, Sondra's light cast shadows across the tunnel. Too bad I hadn't grabbed my headlamp. It felt like I was crawling into the belly of a beast that wanted nothing more than to eat me alive.

Good thing I had plenty of experience slaying monsters.

15

The tunnel widened, giving way to a cavern I could stand in. The space wasn't much bigger than the bathroom back in the suite we'd stayed in, but the ceiling was at least four feet higher. Under the light of Sondra's headlamp, I could see that three tunnels split off from the room in different directions.

I stepped away from the tunnel we came through to give everyone else room to stand. I swung my backpack off my shoulder and set it on a damp rocky ledge along the wall of the cave. I found a headlamp in the front pocket and strapped it to my forehead.

"This one's a dead end," Fiona announced as she peeked into one of the tunnels.

I stepped toward the opposite one and shone my light down it. All I saw was a rocky wall and muddy floor.

"This one, too," I said.

Venn emerged from the tunnel and stood, glancing around the cave in wonder.

"This one goes forward," Sondra said, gesturing the last tunnel. "It must be this way."

Teagan and Ryland reached the cavern.

"Can we maybe dry off?" Ryland asked, gesturing to his soaking clothes.

"We don't need Sondra using any more magic than she has to," Venn objected.

Ryland considered his words for a moment. "True. I suppose I'll survive."

"You better," Fiona said. "I'm not losing my brother in here."

Ryland cracked a smile, though I didn't think he realized anyone noticed.

"Aw, isn't that sweet?" Teagan feigned. "Let's get going."

235

We started down the only tunnel that led anywhere. It was cramped at first, barely allowing enough room for my hips and shoulders to squeeze through. We went single-file. Ryland had to go sideways so that his shoulders would fit. It felt like the walls were squeezing in on us. The farther we went, the less I felt like I could breathe. All I heard were the footsteps and the sound of everyone else's breathing around me.

After a good five minutes in the Suffocation Tunnel, the ceiling gradually dropped, but the walls of the cave widened until we could walk side-by-side. We came to a room that was bigger than the last one, but it appeared as if we'd hit a dead end. That was, until our lights passed across the five-foot-wide hole in the ground.

Sondra approached the pit cautiously and glanced inside. She sighed. "I'd get us all down there with telekinesis, but that's going to take too much out of me. I'd pass out by the time we were done. It looks like that rope Genevieve gave us is going to come in handy."

Fiona held on to Sondra for support and peeked over the edge. "Who wants to drop forty feet to their death first?"

Venn and I reached the rocky ledge and glanced inside the pit. Rock outlined the hole like an old-time well for about ten feet before a wide cavity opened below us. It looked like an acrophobic person's worst nightmare.

"No one's scared of heights, are they?" I asked.

Ryland took a look, shining his headlamp into the hole. "Pfft. That's easy. I could jump that far."

"Then I guess you're going first," Teagan challenged him.

Ryland stepped back from the edge. "Hell no."

"We'll go one at a time," Sondra cut in, taking charge. "Venn, you had the rope in your bag, didn't you?"

"Yeah." Venn swung his bag off his shoulder and pulled open the main zipper.

"How are we going to do this?" Fiona asked. "There's nothing around here to safely secure the rope to. We can't just leave someone behind."

"I'll go last," I offered. "I can fly, so I don't need the rope anyway. And you all know I'm strong enough to lower you down."

Ryland shrugged. "Good enough for me. I trust her."

"Then you're up first," Venn said with a smile as he tossed one end of the black rope into the pit. I heard it hit the bottom with a soft *thwack*.

"I'll assist as much as I can," Sondra offered.

"Nah, I got this," Ryland declined. "Don't tire yourself out. We don't know how much energy you might need later."

Venn, Teagan, and Fiona helped me hold the rope as Ryland climbed down. Sondra slid down the rope next, then Teagan.

"What's down there?" Venn called.

"It's a big cavern," Ryland replied. "About the size of our house. There's only one tunnel leading out, but we're going to have to climb. It's about fifteen feet off the ground."

"You go next," Fiona said to Venn. "I'm the lightest, so I'll go last. That way I can help Rae hold you up."

Venn nodded in agreement. "Just don't drop me."

"Then don't doubt us," I teased lightheartedly. "Or we just might."

"Would you now?" He smirked back at me.

"No," I admitted, "but we could."

"Stop batting your eyes at each other, and let's go," Ryland called up to us. "We're losing daylight here."

Fiona shook her head as she grabbed the rope and braced herself. "My brother's an idiot."

"We know," Venn agreed with a light laugh.

I planted my feet firmly on the ground and held on tightly to the rope wrapped halfway around my torso. Venn lay on his stomach and grabbed the rope, shimmying his way down. It vibrated in my hands as he descended. I felt when he touched ground because the weight on the rope vanished, and it went slack again.

Fiona stepped forward cautiously. "So... uh, how do I do this?"

"Lie on your stomach and dangle your feet into the hole," Sondra instructed. "Then grab the rope and plant your feet on the side of the rock to work your way down."

Fiona lay on the ground as she was instructed. "This, uh, doesn't seem safe."

Sondra hadn't heard her. "Once there's no more rock, you'll lock your feet around the rope and slide the rest of the way down."

"Can you help me just a little?" Fiona shouted. "With telekinesis, I mean?"

"I can assist," Sondra offered, "but don't rely on it completely, okay?"

"Okay," Fiona agreed. "I'm ready!"

Fiona barely tugged on the rope as her weight left the ground. Suddenly, her weight shifted. A collective gasp came from everyone else in the cavern below me. My heart lurched at the sound of rock against rock impacting and echoing off the chamber walls.

"What happened?" I cried. I could still feel Fiona's weight on the rope, so as far as I knew, she was safe, but my heart still hammered as if something had gone terribly wrong.

"It's okay!" Fiona called up to me. "I'm okay. I just dislodged a rock. Not much further to—"

"Shit!" Teagan cried.

"What the—?" Sondra cut off.

Everyone else's voices filled the air as the sound of rushing water met my ears. Fiona screamed, and I felt the rope rushing back and forth.

My stomach bottomed out. "What's going on?"

"Water!" Fiona called up to me. "The whole cavern's filling with water. Sondra, help me! I don't know how much longer I can—"

The rope went slack. The sickening crunch of breaking bone met my ears, and Fiona's shriek echoed throughout the cave.

My heart stopped as I rushed forward and fell to my knees at the side of the hole. "Fiona! Oh my God. What happened?"

Everyone surrounded Fiona, all talking at once so that I couldn't make out any of their words. They hovered over her so that I couldn't see what had happened. Fiona screamed out in agony.

"Is she okay?" I demanded, though I knew deep down that something had gone terribly wrong.

And it was only going to get worse. In the cavern below me, water rushed across the floor. It touched Venn's shoes, rising quickly.

"I'm sorry!" Sondra cried. "I was distracted by the water. I'm going to fix this, okay? Just lie back. The pain will only last another minute."

Venn turned his gaze up to me as Sondra began muttering an incantation under her breath. I shielded my eyes so I wouldn't be blinded by his headlamp.

"She broke her leg. The cavern's filling with water—and fast," Venn explained.

"We need to go back," Teagan insisted from where she knelt beside Fiona.

"It's just another obstacle—a booby trap," Ryland said. "Someone should take Fiona back to the car. The rest of us can keep going."

"We don't know what lies ahead!" Teagan countered. She shot to her feet and moved aside just far enough that I could see Fiona's leg bent at an odd angle. "What if this whole cavern fills with water and there's no way out through that tunnel over there?"

I was already stripping my backpack off. "I'm coming down!"

I didn't wait for anyone to respond as I dropped my bag and headlamp to the ground and shifted into raven form. Without hesitation, I dove into the cavern and landed beside Fiona. The water was halfway up my shins, and Fiona's body was hovering just inches above it as Sondra continued her incantation. Fiona's screams died down, and her eyes rolled back in her head.

"I can help," I offered. I forced my shaking hands to steady, thinking back to Sondra's lesson on controlling my emotions. It hadn't been much, but it was all I had. "That way you won't drain your energy so fast."

"Okay," Sondra agreed. "But we have to act quickly. She can't feel a thing right now, so we're going to have to set the bone."

"I'll take her back," Teagan offered. "The rest of you are more useful in this cave than I am."

"No, Tea—" Ryland started to protest, but Sondra cut him off.

"We don't have time to argue," she said in a surprisingly calm voice.

You need to stay calm, too, Rachel, I reminded myself. *Now's not the time to freak out. Remember what Genevieve said about resilience. You're going to need it today. So grow a set of lady balls and calm your tits.*

"Teagan will take Fiona back, and the rest of us will continue on," Sondra decided. "Ryland, hold Fiona's leg here. On the count of three—"

The sound of rocks clashing together rumbled above us. The water rising around us rippled. Alarm shot to everyone's faces.

"Did that just sound like—?" I started.

"A cave-in?" Venn's voice rose several pitches.

I cursed. "I'll go check it out. You help Fiona."

I shifted and shot into the air. There was no light to guide me through the tunnel and back to the entrance of the cave, but I could sense where I was by the sound of air coming off my wings and bouncing off the cave walls. The tips of my wings skimmed the edge of the tunnel several times, almost knocking me out of the air, but by some miracle, I managed to stay airborne.

I knew when I'd hit the first cavern because the air moved differently, sounded different. I landed and shifted back to human form, my chest heaving from the exertion. My eyes darted around the pitch-black cavern. There should've been a sliver of light cast through the darkness, even in the midst of the storm, but darkness completely consumed me.

I stepped toward the wall and ran my hands over a rocky ledge. I knew it was the same one I'd set my bag on earlier. Inching further along the wall, I felt my way across the cavern until my hands met nothing but air. It was the opening to the room I'd looked into before, the one that was nothing but a dead end.

Skipping over the dead-end room, I continued along the wall until I thought I was standing in front of the tunnel leading outside. My foot caught a rock, and my ankle twisted under me. I crashed to the ground and caught myself on a sharp rock.

Fear tumbled around in my gut as my fingers blindly roamed over rock after rock. In the quiet, I could just barely make out the sound of wind whistling through the rock. The storm outside raged on, but I would've preferred standing out in a thunderstorm to my new reality.

We were trapped.

16

I sprinted down the tunnel, back to Venn and the others. When I broke out of the narrow space and into the room with the hole in the ground, my eyes finally found a dull glow from a flashlight. But light wasn't the only thing I found. Fiona lay on her back, and Teagan leaned over her.

"I'm going to need you to shift, Fiona," Teagan demanded. "It's the only way I can carry you back."

"It hurts," Fiona cried, tears streaming down her face.

"Sondra shouldn't have wasted power getting you back up here," I said breathlessly.

"Rae?" Venn called up to me.

"Yeah," I shouted back.

"We need to leave now!" he cried. "There's a tunnel, but—"

I stuck my head over the top of the hole so I could see him. "The main entrance caved in. Teagan and Fiona are going to have to come with us."

Teagan shot to her feet. "What?!"

I whirled toward her. "I'm sorry, but we can't go back the way we came. Our only chance is to go forward."

"How are we going to get Fiona…?" Teagan glanced down at her somberly. She lowered her voice. "Sondra did a pain relief spell, but it's already wearing off. This isn't something you can just heal in a matter of minutes."

"I know," I said.

"We'll stay here—" Teagan started.

"And what if the water rises to this room?" I asked. "There's no other way out. Fiona, you can shift, can't you?"

"Not with a broken leg," she protested. "What if it doesn't heal right?"

Teagan bent beside her and stripped off her backpack. She pulled open the main pocket and began digging the contents out of it. "Your leg will heal fine. Sondra made sure of that. Now, will you please shift and get in the bag? I'll carry you the rest of the way."

I bent to scoop up Teagan's food and supplies, then put them in my bag that still sat beside the hole.

Fiona groaned and shifted into a small fox. She was careful not to put any weight on her leg as Teagan helped her into the backpack and zipped up the sides to secure her in, leaving nothing but her head poking out.

"What's going on up there?" Venn demanded. "I meant it when I said we had to leave now."

I picked up my headlamp from where I'd left it on the ground and adjusted it on my head. "Watch out. We're coming down!"

I glanced into the hole to see the water was high and the coast was clear. Without hesitation, I jumped.

Cold water hit my skin and swallowed me up. My feet touched the cave floor. I bent my knees and shot myself upward. I sucked in a deep breath when my head broke the surface, and I wiped the water from my eyes. When I opened them, my gaze fell on Venn, who was treading water several feet away from me. Reaching out my arm and kicking my feet, I swam over to him.

"You're okay?" he asked with concern.

I nodded. "I am."

"Tea?" Sondra called up to us.

"Coming!" Teagan shouted. "Hold your breath, Fiona."

Teagan leapt into the hole. Water splashed into my face when she landed. She came up for air a moment later, and Fiona sputtered in the backpack behind her.

"Let's go," Sondra ordered.

I swam behind her. Ahead of us, a tunnel was carved out high in the room. The water had already reached the base of the tunnel and was rising fast.

"This can't be the only way out," I theorized. "This water has to go somewhere."

"The water's enchanted," Sondra replied with certainty. "In fact, the whole cavern is probably enchanted. Can't you feel it?"

Now that she mentioned it, I could feel a tingle of magic if I focused closely.

"So, how do we know this is the tunnel we have to go down?" Ryland asked, making strong strokes through the water.

Sondra's hands curled against the edge of the tunnel, and she pulled herself onto a dry cave floor. She turned to give me a hand. "We don't, but we sure as hell don't have time to figure out if there's another enchanted tunnel around here. The water's rising too fast."

Ryland bent to pull Teagan from the water just as it hit the edge of the tunnel. The cavern we'd just been swimming through looked like a lake. I shivered from the cold. Venn's gaze roamed my body and settled on my goosebumps, but he didn't get a chance to offer me relief from the chill.

"What the—?" Teagan said.

The water rose higher and higher, but it stopped at the opening of the tunnel. It met up with an invisible barrier, as if there were a pane of glass between the tunnel and the lake.

Ryland breathed a sigh of relief. "Thank God. The tunnel's safe."

Sondra didn't take her eyes off the water surface as she stepped away from it. "Let's not make any assumptions. Come on. We don't know how far we have to go."

We hurried down the tunnel, leaving the water behind us. The lights from our headlamps bounced up and down against the rock on either side of us. Ahead, there was nothing but darkness, as if the cave stretched on for miles with no outlet.

I watched my footing so that I wouldn't trip over rocks jutting up from the cave floor or slip across mud. I quickly started to notice that the tunnel was dipping lower and lower, taking us further down beneath the surface of the earth.

"How far do you think—?"

Ryland was cut off by the roar of rushing water, as if a dam had just broken.

We all exchanged a quick glance before Venn cursed. "Run!" he yelled.

We all broke into a sprint. Water rushed by my boots, passing me. My feet slapped against the ground, spraying up water as I ran. Collectively, we picked up speed, but there was still no end in sight.

"Christ!" Teagan cursed. "How long is this freaking tunnel?"

"I can feel… another enchantment… not far ahead…" Sondra said through heavy breaths. "Just keep up the pace… and we should—"

Sondra's feet slipped out from under her, and I nearly went down behind her as my boot skidded along the slick cave floor. Venn quickly wrapped his arms under Sondra's and pulled her to her feet, but a second later, the wall of water caught up to us.

The water swept me off my feet like a giant beast swiping at my ankles. Within a split second, I was tumbling through the strong current. I couldn't see anything, even when I tried to open my eyes. My back slammed into the side of the cave before the water caught me again and sucked me downward like a sink drain.

My lungs burned in protest, and my hands instinctively shot out, as if I might be able to find some relief and control my momentum. But relief didn't come. Only pain as the skin on my hands skidded against sharp rocks. On instinct, my lungs opened to fill with air, but they were only assaulted by the sharp pain of water burning up my nostrils. I didn't know where Venn was. I didn't know where anyone was. For the brief time the current took hold of me like Mother Nature's beast, I was completely alone.

My stomach jumped up to my throat as the sensation of falling washed over me. Suddenly, the current was gone. I was suspended in the water, finally gaining control of my movements again. But I had no sense of which way was up or which way was down. Panic shot through my chest, sending my heart pounding so hard that I could hear it pulsing in my ears. I did all I knew I could to save myself. I kicked my feet and swiped my arms through the water, hoping beyond hope that I wasn't pushing myself deeper underwater.

My lungs were on the verge of imploding when my head broke the surface. I gulped in a greedy breath of air. Relief washed over me so fast that I thought I might cry.

Four headlamps shone back at me, and the tension in my shoulders immediately eased. We were all safe.

Spotting Venn, I swam forward as fast as I could. He'd wrapped me in his arms before I could even fling my hands around his neck. Water brimmed in my eyes, and it wasn't cave water, either.

"Thank God!" Teagan cried in relief as she swam toward Ryland and Sondra.

Ryland hugged her, but his eyes were on his sister. "Are you okay, Fiona?"

Fiona coughed, but she nodded her little fox head.

Venn reached out and wiped a long strand of wet hair from my face. I glanced around while we treaded water. Beyond the headlamps, there was nothing but darkness. Even when I looked upward, all I saw was black. A jet of water spewed out of a tunnel above us. All around us spanned an underground lake inside a massive cavern.

"I see shore," Sondra stated, pointing.

The shore was barely visible in the dim light. The closer we swam, the more I could make it out. There were only a few yards of shoreline before the ground met up with the cave wall, where six separate tunnels split off in different directions.

By the time we reached the thin beach, I was physically exhausted. I fell to my back on the cave floor, not caring that my pack was uncomfortable on my back. I inhaled deep, audible breaths.

"I need a quick break," I said as I pushed myself to a sitting position and pulled my pack onto my lap. I reached inside for a drink of water and a granola bar, hoping it wasn't soaked. I rifled through the contents, past a first-aid kit in a water-tight container and another rope, until I found a granola bar that looked safe to eat.

"We'll take five minutes," Sondra agreed. "But let's hurry, because this cavern is heavily enchanted, and—"

I never got to hear the rest of Sondra's sentence. My entire body gave a jolt of terror. Pain shot through my skull as cold fingers tangled in my hair and dragged me backward into the depths of the deep, dark tunnel behind me.

17

An earth-shattering scream ripped out of my lungs. "Venn!"

The light from my headlamp darted across the rock above me, but I was moving so fast that the cave ceiling was just a blur. My fingers dug into the dirt beneath me, and sharp rocks skidded along my lower back, biting at the skin between my shirt and jeans.

When I found no relief clawing at the ground, my hands shot above my head and clamped around damp, cold flesh. My fingernails sliced into the creature's wrist. It responded in a high-pitched hiss, but it didn't let me go. It continued to drag me by the hair, nearly tugging my ponytail out of my scalp.

"*Ardeat ignis!*" I shouted, but the fire I expected never came.

Shit. How am I supposed to let go of negative energy at a time like this?

I squeezed tighter on the creature's wrist, using all the strength I had, but it still didn't drop me. What the hell was this thing? Its wrists should be broken by now.

"Let go of me, you mother—" I kicked my feet off the ground and twisted. Hair ripped from my scalp, but I was no longer being dragged. I quickly sprang to my feet. All I saw was a shadow the size of a child as I kicked the creature with all my strength. It went flying across the tunnel.

Then my light caught it. It was less than half my size, with hairless, translucent skin the color of dirty dishwater. It was bipedal, with long nails growing from its human-like fingers. Its eyes were mere pin-pricks, and its ears were just holes in the side of its head. It had a flat nose and a row of sharp, razor-like teeth. My breath wavered at the sight of it.

A deep, guttural bark resounded through the cave. A moment later, the shadow of a large canine crossed my light's path. A low *thud* met my ears as Venn leapt forward in wolf form to fight off the creature made of nightmares.

The creature showed no fear. It leapt forward and sank its nails into Venn's snout. Venn shook his head violently, whipping the creature off of him. It slammed into the cave wall so hard that the rock above us shook. I expected it to fall to the ground unconscious, but it sprang right back up and lunged for Venn again as if it'd felt nothing.

Bile rose to my throat when I saw that the first creature was the least of our problems. At least fifty others crept into the light. Their muscles twitched unnaturally as they moved, making them look like something from a horror movie.

They can go straight to hell.

Venn let out a howl as the creature's sharp teeth tore at the flesh on his front paw. Bones crunched. Venn immediately lunged forward, his jaws snapping until they clamped around the freaky thing's throat. Though it let out a low sigh as it went limp, it didn't bleed.

The being vanished from between Venn's jaws upon its death. Which could only mean one thing. These creatures were made of magic.

Taking a deep breath in through my nose, I released the air out through my mouth. *This better work.*

"Venn," I whispered, holding out a hand cautiously.

He looked to me, his wolf eyes glowing back at me.

"Step away slowly," I instructed.

Venn followed my gaze and noticed the other cave creatures approaching us for the first time. His body tensed, but he retreated with careful steps. The beings eyed us with interest, inching closer and closer with each passing second.

"When I say so, get ready to run," I warned.

Venn nodded.

I waited until the creatures were only a few yards away. "Now!" I screamed just before shouting the incantation for fire.

Orange flames shot out of my hands like an explosion, assaulting the creatures. Heat touched my face. I just barely saw the beings scurrying away before I turned and ran behind Venn.

The light from three other headlamps bobbed in the distance. Venn shifted as soon as we met up with the others.

Sondra reached me first and placed her hands on my cheeks, looking me over with panic in her eyes. "Are you okay?"

"Yes," I said, glancing behind me to make sure we weren't being followed. "But Venn isn't."

I shrugged my bag off my shoulders as Venn shifted. Teagan was immediately at his side, inspecting his bleeding hand.

"What happened?" Ryland demanded breathlessly.

I pulled the first-aid kit from my backpack and stole another glance down the tunnel. It was completely deserted, but that didn't keep me from working quickly in case they were on their way.

Venn slumped against the wall and sank down to the ground. He sucked in a sharp breath and closed his eyes, looking weak and worn out. The cut was deep. He was losing a lot of blood.

I gently took Venn's hand and began wrapping gauze tightly around it. "We were attacked by these… things. I don't know what the hell they were."

"They didn't bleed," Venn said in a labored tone. "And one disappeared like a vampire when I killed it."

Sondra knelt beside him and whispered an incantation under her breath. I wasn't sure if it was to help with the pain or restore his energy, but as soon as she finished, he opened his eyes, looking more alert.

"Here," Sondra said, shoving a water bottle toward him. She gently lifted it to his lips, forcing him to drink. "How are you feeling?"

"Better," Venn admitted once she drew the water bottle away from him.

"What about you, Sondra?" I asked with concern. She was starting to look a little pale. "You look like you're exerting too much energy."

She waved a hand like it didn't matter. "I'm fine. I'm a high witch. I can handle a lot of magic."

Except something told me that despite her ability to cast complicated spells, she didn't have the stamina to cast them all at once.

"You said they disappeared?" Sondra asked, redirecting the conversation.

"Yes," Venn confirmed as he stood.

I shoved the first-aid kit back in my pack and rose to my feet beside him.

"I've heard of these things before," Sondra said. "They're the enchantment I felt back by the lake. I'm sure of it."

"What are they?" Teagan asked.

"Mongrels," Sondra answered. "Mongrels come in various forms and can look like almost anything. They're a physical manifestation of a spell that's used to scare people. The spell is usually used to protect something valuable, which definitely fits the bill in this case."

"Why haven't we ever heard of them?" Ryland asked.

"Because the spell is incredibly rare and difficult to cast," Sondra explained. "But they only appear in front of the scared and the weak."

"I was exhausted when we came out of the lake," I said. "Is that why it attacked me?"

Sondra nodded. "Yeah, that makes sense. I know how hard this sounds, you guys, but you can't let your fear get to you in here. The more scared you are, the more chance there is of running into the mongrels again—and who knows what else."

"I thought you said a little fear was a healthy thing," Teagan pointed out.

Sondra hesitated a moment. "I did… But this is not exactly a test of fear. It is a test of faith. We're safe by each other's sides. I promise you that. I'm going to get each and every one of you out of here. You have nothing to be afraid of."

Venn took a breath and nodded. "Agreed. I trust Sondra. I trust all of you. We've got this."

The weight on my chest lifted. "So, now that the mongrels are gone, where do we go? There were six tunnels by the lake. Do you think one leads to the Artifact?"

"Yes," Sondra said. "I don't feel anything down this tunnel anymore, so let's go back and see if we can feel something down one of the others."

We started down the tunnel back the way we came. After a good five minutes, I was starting to worry.

"This is the way we came, isn't it?" I asked. "I wasn't even dragged for a minute. Was the mongrel *that* fast?"

"No," Sondra replied, glancing around the tunnel. "We should've been back at the lake by now. I didn't see another tunnel. Did anyone else?"

Everyone shook their heads.

"Crap," Sondra muttered.

"What?" Venn demanded. "What's going on?"

Sondra's eyes remained locked ahead. I followed her gaze to see the tunnel widen into a small cavern no bigger than a bedroom. Five other tunnels broke off in all directions like the ones back at the lake. It was clear we were no longer in the right tunnel.

Sondra spun as we entered the cavern, taking it all in. "There's no telling where these tunnels lead. Be prepared to question everything you see down here."

"What are you saying?" Teagan asked.

Sondra let out a heavy breath. "We've just entered an impossible labyrinth."

18

"What do we do?" Ryland demanded, as if Sondra navigated changing labyrinths daily.

"The important thing is that we stick together," Sondra said. "If we end up down different tunnels, we may never find each other again."

Teagan peered into each tunnel. They were all equally dark and ominous. "What's the trick?"

"Trick?" Sondra asked.

"Yeah, the trick," Teagan replied with a wave of her hand. "How do we make sure the tunnels stop changing and always lead to the same destination? How do we decide which one holds the Artifact?"

"I'm not sure we *can* stop it from changing," Sondra replied. "This is just a wild guess, but I think what we're looking at is Synchrony on steroids."

"Huh?" I asked.

"Synchrony reflects your intentions back on you," Sondra explained. "Positivity breeds positivity. A labyrinth like this will do the same thing, but with different energy signatures."

"So you're saying fear will breed fear?" Venn theorized.

"Exactly," Sondra confirmed. "That's what the mongrels are. They will take any shape to scare you. But I have a feeling that's not the only thing we'll encounter down here."

"Examples?" Ryland pressed.

Sondra shrugged. "It could be anything. If all you're focusing on is how you'll never get out of here, you'll never find an exit. So I suggest you try to let go of worries."

Teagan scoffed. "Easy for you to say. You've had lifetimes of practice."

Sondra frowned. "I never said it was easy. Keep your thoughts positive and

248

we shouldn't have any issues. And if you *do* end up victim of the labyrinth, I suggest you find a way to turn your thoughts around. We'll start down this tunnel."

Sondra began toward the tunnel on the left side of the one we came through. Ryland and Teagan exchanged a glance before following behind her, putting Venn and me in the back.

"Sondra's very optimistic," I said as Venn and I fell into step side by side.

"She tries to be empathetic, but I think she forgets sometimes how hard it can be to control yourself," he replied.

I kept my eyes on Fiona's red fur in front of me. "I know what you mean about losing control. Put a vampire in front of me and a sharp object in my hand and you can bet he's not leaving except in a pile of ashes."

Venn laughed lightly. "You get a pass for vampire slaying. Nobody can resist a good fight." He shot me a teasing smile.

"Well, let's just hope we don't get split up because"—I glanced behind me to see the room we'd left was just barely visible in the distance—"I wouldn't want to be the sucker who has to navigate this labyrinth alone…"

I turned back toward Venn, but my light hit nothing except the rocky cave wall. As my light swept the tunnel, I found that I was completely alone. When I glanced back to the tunnel room, that was gone, too. It was nothing but a long, dark tunnel with no end in either direction.

I should've been scared shitless at everyone's sudden disappearance, and maybe I would've if Sondra hadn't just explained the nature of the caves. Instead, all I felt was annoyance sink in my gut.

"Well, shit," I muttered. "I'm officially a sucker. I always did hate mazes."

***

I continued the way I was originally headed, hoping I'd run into something worthwhile eventually. Maybe I'd stumble upon the Artifact. Or at least make it back to the lake or circle around to the tunnel room. Then I could wait until someone showed up again—hopefully.

But the fact was this tunnel led nowhere. It just went on and on without even rising or falling a degree. I was pretty sure I'd walked past the same rock jutting out of the wall fifty times. I'd stopped to rest three times and ate all my granola bars. I must've been walking half the day. My feet were starting to hurt, and I was in serious need of a nap.

I stopped walking and sank down the wall to the cave floor. What happened back there? Was Venn worried about me?

It's just one of the labyrinth's tricks, I told myself. I needed to focus less on how much I'd been walking, how much my feet hurt, and how freaking lonely this vast tunnel was. Like Sondra had instructed, I had to turn my thoughts around.

"Positive thoughts… positive thoughts…" I repeated, closing my eyes. "I *will* find Venn…"

I half expected to hear his voice calling in the distance. I peeked one eye open, but nothing had changed.

I squeezed my eyes shut again. "I will find the end of this tunnel. I will get out of here."

And when I do, the first thing I'm doing is ordering a juicy double bacon cheeseburger, because I'm starving.

This time when my eyes opened, I noticed a glimmer of light at the end of the tunnel. I shot to my feet, squinting to make it out. I turned off my headlamp just to be sure, and sure enough, the light continued to flicker across the cave walls like a flame.

I hurried forward, eager to finally escape this endless tunnel. The light grew brighter and brighter as I approached, until I broke free of the tunnel and stepped into a vast cavern with a tall ceiling. The cavern was the size of a gymnasium, with long wooden tables spanning the length of it. Each table was set with hundreds of flickering candles placed between plate upon plate of chocolate cake. My mouth watered.

"Very funny!" I shouted to no one in particular.

It was official. I was going insane. Could that happen after only a few hours? Or had it been longer? My stomach rumbled like I hadn't eaten for days. The endless chocolate cake stared back at me, tempting me to gobble it up like Thanksgiving dinner.

But I had more sense than to eat random pieces of cake inside an enchanted labyrinth. It'd probably poison me, or turn me into a frog or something. Still, I found myself stepping toward the closest plate. What would it hurt to take just a little bite?

My gaze caught a fork I hadn't noticed before, and I reached for it. Sure, I could resist one of the most powerful objects in the world, but when it came to chocolate, I was done for.

I'm not going to eat it, I decided. *I'm just going to smell it.*

My fork plunged into the cake, and I tore a moist corner off. Small white pebbles poured out of the cake from where I'd broken it. At least, I thought they were pebbles... until they started squirming.

Maggots!

The labyrinth was sticking up her middle finger at me.

"Nasty!" I stuck mine up right back and skewered the suckers with my fork.

The maggots I stabbed only broke apart and multiplied. Suddenly, maggots exploded out of hundreds of cakes around me. There were so many that they covered the tables and fell to the floor.

Disgusting!

I gagged and whirled around to race back toward the tunnel. It was just behind me when I entered the room, but now it was a good fifty yards away. I pushed forward, squashing maggots with my feet as I went.

Ew, ew, ew!

I trudged through the pool of maggots that were up to my knees now. Why did it have to be *maggots*? They were only second on my hit list after vampires. They were hands down one of the most disgusting creatures on the planet.

Suddenly, they started jumping, as if they were some sort of mutant maggots. I could already feel them squirming against my legs. No way in hell was I taking one up the nose.

The tunnel seemed farther away than ever, and my heart began to pound like I was never going to make it. These suckers were going to crawl inside my throat, choke me, then eat me before my body had a chance to cool.

Not on my watch.

Ignoring my instinct not to touch them, I pressed my hands to the nearest maggot-infested table. Their little bodies squished under my weight while others wiggled their way onto my skin. I pulled myself onto the table, freeing my legs from the swarm of maggots at my feet and shaking off the others. I quickly jumped up and raced down the table, kicking plates as I went.

The only thing that would make this worse is a...

I didn't get a chance to finish my thought before the cavern began rumbling. The table shook beneath my feet, and a pile of rocks crumbled down a tall slope in the wall to my right. Bile rose in my throat. I told myself to not look back, but I couldn't help it. I had to see for myself.

I dared a glance behind my shoulder as I ran. What I saw stole my attention, which sent me tripping over a plate and into the pile of maggots. I caught my fall, squishing guts out of their little white bodies and between my fingers.

But maggot guts were the least of my worries. Behind me, the holy mother of all larvae rose up. It was as big as a semi-truck. Its tall brown head nearly touched the ceiling of the cave. Six legs protruded from its fat, slimy white body and wiggled in the air. In the candlelight, it looked freaky and disgusting as shadows rippled across its body. It let out a deep roar akin to Ryland's. Which was totally weird, because I didn't think maggots made a sound. But maggots weren't exactly the size of semi-trucks, either. It must've been a product of the labyrinth's mind games meant to scare me. Which, by the way, was kind of working.

This is apparently what I get for being a Negative Nancy. *Control your damn thoughts, girl!* Except I couldn't just think away the giant vermin. God, this enchanted cave was confusing as hell.

I grabbed the first thing my hands could find, which happened to be a plate. I sprang to my feet and chucked it at the giant maggot's head. I didn't stick around to see where it hit. I whirled toward the tunnel I came through and took off sprinting—only, the tunnel wasn't there anymore. Worry ripped through me involuntarily.

You can't worry, Rachel! It'll only make it worse. Think positive thoughts. Rainbows. Butterflies. Sunshine.

Even my own mini pep talk was *so* not helping me right now.

I glanced behind me just in time to see the giant maggot lunging toward me, as if it was going to grab me between its pinchers and gobble me up for its next meal.

Oh, no you don't.

I quickly dodged out of the way, leaping over the pile of baby maggots on the ground and to the next table. Big ol' Mother Maggot crashed into the table I'd just been running down. It collapsed beneath her weight. I promptly leapt to the next table, and then the one after that, to put as much distance between myself and Mother Maggot as possible. My eyes darted around the cave, desperately searching for an exit.

Mother Maggot isn't getting her next meal. I'll fight to the death if I have to.

My eyes fell upon a tunnel on the other side of the room. Problem was, Mother Maggot was right between me and my chance of escape. She rose up again, showing off her size and staring down at me with eyes I was sure were there—but couldn't see. They must've been just pin pricks. Her jaws snapped at me. Taking a deep breath, I swooped down and grabbed a fork in each hand. She wasn't a vampire, and these forks weren't exactly knives, but this bitch was begging for a fight. And she was going down.

"Can't we compromise?" I said aloud, as if Mother Maggot could actually understand me. "You let me go free and I don't kill you?"

She didn't even hesitate. She threw herself forward again. I ducked and rolled out of the way, crushing hundreds of baby maggots. I felt the wind rush past her and the table buckle under her weight. She groaned. WTF? Maggots don't groan. What kind of freaky cave was this?

My gaze darted to where the tunnel had just been, but instead of finding it where I expected, it had moved. Even though Mother Maggot and I had changed directions, my escape tunnel was still on the opposite side of her.

Which only meant one thing. The labyrinth wanted a show.

I couldn't help but let out a low laugh. It was probably mostly because I was tired and hungry and a bit on the loopy side, but it felt damn good to laugh. "You're on."

Mother Maggot was already rising up again. I jumped forward and leapt onto her back. She was slippery, but her skin had ridges that I could hold on to. Pulling back my arm, I jabbed my fork into her skin. It did nothing but bounce off of her.

Okay...

Mother Maggot began thrashing her body from side to side, trying to throw me off of her. I held on tighter. In a last-ditch effort, she threw herself to the ground. The impact shook her whole body, and I could no longer hold on. I fell into a pile of baby maggots. Before I could jump back to my feet, Mother Maggot's body came into view. She was rolling over, and she was going to squash me!

I ignored the baby maggots and scrambled to my feet, digging them into the ground and diving out of the way. I just barely missed being pinned beneath her body. Glancing around for a weapon, I grabbed the closest thing my fingers could find—one of the flaming candles. Just as I turned around to use it on her, Mother Maggot's legs clamped around me.

I screamed in surprise as she lifted me into the air, but she squeezed me so tightly that my scream was cut off within a second. I lifted the candle to burn the closest area of flesh I could find, which happened to be one of her legs.

Mother Maggot cried out in pain, sounding a lot like a whale in labor—not that I was exactly familiar with that sound. She loosened the one leg and snapped her jaws at me again. My arm slipped free, and I jabbed the candle straight into her face between where I guessed her eyes would be.

She stumbled backward, loosening her grip on me just enough that I could get my hands on one of her legs and twist as hard as I could. The cry only grew louder, and her hold on me weakened, but she didn't let me go. Mother Maggot stumbled and twisted, until we both went crashing into the cave wall. She caught herself with her top legs, but it wasn't enough to keep the air from knocking out of my lungs.

As I sucked in deep breaths, my eyes fell upon the huge rock pile beside us. Just before she could right herself, I reached out and grabbed the closest rock I could find. To my surprise, it was a sharp, pointed rock. Just what I needed.

I smiled cunningly. Mother Maggot lowered her jaw, aiming her open mouth at my head. Now that I had my lucky rock, I wasn't even worried. I drew my arm back and plunged that sucker straight into her chest.

A high-pitched shriek echoed off the cave walls. She finally let me go, but I held on to that rock with dear life as I dropped to the ground. It sliced through her all the way down. Guts spilled onto the cave floor, covering me in a fresh layer of goop.

But I didn't care. Mother Maggot's body slumped against the rock pile. I was free. I smiled triumphantly, but I didn't stick around to revel in the victory. I dropped my rock and whirled around, sprinting straight for the tunnel before it could move again. I didn't slow down until I knew the room of rotten nightmares was far behind me.

When the light from the room faded and the tunnel was covered in pitch blackness again, I finally slowed. I took a knee to catch my breath and turned my headlamp back on. Now that that nightmare was over, I needed to figure something out—and fast. Frankly, I was already sick of this labyrinth and its little mind games. If I didn't learn how to play this game to my favor, I'd be trapped here forever.

The earth rumbled beneath me, and my eyes instantly darted around the tunnel. My heart hammered violently as I shot to my feet. If I thought Mother Maggot was bad, it was nothing compared to this. The cave walls were inching closer and closer together, the space around me shrinking right before my eyes like some sort of Scooby-Doo boobytrap shit.

My time to play my cards had run out. If I didn't figure out my move in the next twenty seconds, the labyrinth was going to crush me.

S ondra's words echoed in my head. *If you do end up victim of the labyrinth, I suggest you find a way to turn your thoughts around.*

How the heck was I supposed to turn my thoughts around? Panic settled in as my headlamp hit a rocky ceiling that was closing in on me inch by inch each passing second.

Run, instinct told me, but there was nowhere to go. The whole tunnel was shrinking, with no way out.

"No, no, no, no," I cried as I reached my hands to either side of the tunnel. Both of my hands touched rock, and I locked my elbows as if I could hold the rock back. Even with my super shifter strength, I couldn't hold back the freaking earth.

So instead, I closed my eyes, plugged my ears with my fingers, and squatted down, curling into a ball. All I needed was to take my mind off of the shrinking tunnel. The labyrinth reflected my thoughts and worries back on me, right? I just had to stop worrying.

Shit! This is hard.

My mind flickered through thought after thought as I forced myself to ignore the impending danger surrounding me. *Venn, Jenna, Fiona, ice cream, spell books, vampires, venom...*

Why the heck were these the first things to flicker through my mind? This wasn't working!

It was like trying to wish away the monster under my bed as a kid...

And that's when it struck me. That was all this labyrinth was. A maze of monsters of my own making. And there was only one way to get rid of the monsters.

I began singing. Though it was horribly off key, my mind slipped back to a memory I hadn't recalled in years. My mother sat on the side of my bed, running her fingers through my hair while I held the edge of the blanket up past my nose. Her beautiful voice filled my bedroom.

> *The full moon is shining*
> *The stars glitter above*
> *The wind whispers softly*
> *Goodnight, my love*

I repeated the lullaby again, rocking back and forth ever so slightly as the melody filled my heart and made me think of home. All my fears flashed across my eyelids in a split second: getting crushed to death here in this cave, standing in front of Jenna's gravestone if I ever made it out of here, hearing Venn tell me the family didn't want me around anymore, getting bit by a vampire and waking up with silver eyes and a thirst for blood...

But I pushed all of those fears away as the memory of my mother's eyes overshadowed them. I thought of my dad's tight hugs and the way he would tickle my feet to cheer me up, even when I was a teen and refused to smile for him. One time, Jenna joined in and they tickled me so hard that I kicked her in the face and she had to go to the emergency room. It turned out her nose wasn't broken, so Dad took us both out for ice cream afterward to celebrate her "miraculous recovery."

A tear fell down my cheek as I continued singing the lullaby. Not because I was scared anymore, but because I missed those times with my family. I missed them so badly it hurt. The best I could do now was be thankful for what little time I had with them and never let their memory die.

I am strong. I am resilient. I will make it out of here.

As the last line of the lullaby passed my lips another time, I suddenly realized that the walls of the cave should've crushed me by now. Slowly, I lifted my head and peeled my eyes open. A sigh of relief whooshed out of my lungs when I saw that the tunnel had widened back to its original size. I let out a nervous half-cry, half-laugh.

"Thank you!" I shouted to the labyrinth. I rushed over to the wall of the cave and kissed it. "Thank you for not crushing me!"

I started down the tunnel, feeling hopeful about what was at the end of it. Sondra had said I needed to find something that would work for me to calm me down to perform magic. I was pretty sure the lullaby from my childhood was it. Which was weird because I couldn't sing worth a damn, but hey, if it kept me from getting crushed in a booby-trapped tunnel, I was all for it.

"Okay, labyrinth," I said aloud. My voice echoed down the tunnel. "I've almost drowned, fought off your mongrels, got lost for hours, faced one of my worst nightmares, and just survived almost being crushed to death. I don't give up that easily. Bring on your next move! I'll take on whatever you've got until I find that artifact."

As if in answer, my headlamp caught a dark, open cavern ahead. I couldn't see what lay beyond the opening, but I rushed forward to find out. The closer I came to it, the more I could feel the energy from a strong enchantment buzzing through the air. Whatever was in there was powerful. I slowed when I reached the end of the tunnel.

As soon as I stepped into the room, a thousand candles lining the rocky walls lit up, as if I'd set off a motion sensor. I drew in a breath as my eyes spanned the cave. It wasn't huge, perhaps the size of a large bedroom, but the ceiling stretched up at least fifty feet above my head. The only way out was through the tunnel behind me. Layers upon layers of rock jutted out from the walls, creating flat surfaces for the candles to sit.

In the middle of it all stood a naturally formed rock pedestal. On top of that was the object radiating the magic I felt in the tunnel.

Sapiens noctua. The Wise Owl.

It wasn't like the marble carving in the Genevieve's test. It was an honest-to-God real owl skull. I stepped closer to it and reached out my hand cautiously, as if I thought it might burn me. As soon as my fingers clamped around the skull, a jolt of magic shot through me like a lightning bolt.

I crumbled to my knees, and though I was pretty sure I let out a cry, I couldn't process it. Magic pulsed through me at all angles like I was standing between two massive stereo speakers at high volume. It didn't hurt, really, but it was uncomfortable and overwhelming. The power I felt rushing through the Artifact was ten times that of what I felt in Genevieve's test.

Somewhere through my clouded mind, my thoughts broke through. *Do something, Rachel.*

What did I mean? What was I supposed to do?

Focus.

"*The full moon is shining...*" I started, but the words fell from my mind as the magic intensified, pulsing stronger through my body.

Shit. Where was I? What's going on?

I barely remembered I was in the cave at all. It felt like I was in a billion different places at once—that I was a billion different people with a billion different thoughts racing through my head. I couldn't differentiate my own thoughts from all the other voices whispering in my mind. A single thought stuck out in the sea of noise.

Control it!

This power was too much. If I didn't push back, it was going to rip me apart.

Except... how did I control it? I was only a low witch. I didn't have this kind of power.

You do. Everyone keeps telling you that you're more powerful than you think. It's time to start believing it.

"Gah!" I screamed as the magic pushed in on me, as if trying to crush me.

So much power. You could do anything. Be anything.

Yeah, another voice countered. *You could be dead.*

That thought immediately made me more alert, pushing all the other voices to the back of my mind. I was looking into the heart of Synchrony. Surely with the power to flip the switch on anyone's magic, I could find a way to dull my own, to control it.

But before I do...

I knew it was stupid of me to dive deeper, but the temptation was too great. Even if it killed me, I *had* to know.

I sifted through the voices, through the energy signatures I now had access to. I flipped through them faster than a computer could process data, searching for the one that was most familiar to me after my own.

Her energy felt like velvet and smelled of sweet apples. There was a roughness around the edges that I was unfamiliar with, but there was no doubt it was her. A sensation that felt a lot like my own shifter magic tingled through me, and an image of Jenna's face flickered across my closed lids.

She's alive.

That was all I needed from the Artifact. I had no desire to control the rest of its power, and so I pushed it away. It was like trying to push a thousand-ton boulder off a cliff, but slowly and surely, the power eased, and the voices softened. They were still there, but they were like whispers behind the brick wall I'd built in my mind.

I forced my eyes open. The cave floor swam in front of me, but my knees felt steady on the ground.

And then the sound of clapping met my ears. My heart leapt into my throat. I whirled around, my hands already curled into fists in front of me. The last person I expected to see stepped out from the shadows of the tunnel and into the candlelight.

Matias Vayne.

<h1 style="text-align:center">20</h1>

Matias looked exactly like he had the first time I saw him, all suited up with perfect hair and that damn attractive jawline. *It's just another trick*, I told myself.

"Well done, Rachel," he said, stepping further into the room.

"Nice one," I said, rolling my eyes. "But I'm not scared of this dude." I eyed him up and down. Even if he were really here, I figured I'd stand a chance against him.

Matias's eyebrows shot up. "You think I'm a hallucination? A part of the enchantment put on these caves?"

He took another step forward. I planted my feet firmly in place, leveling him with a challenging gaze.

"You are, aren't you?" I accused.

Matias gestured to himself. "I'm as real as they get, sweetheart. You know, the funny thing about these caves is that you can never quite tell which parts are real and which ones are only in your head. The mongrels, for example… those bastards will kill you. The rest… well, that's just for fun."

"And which are you?" I asked coolly. "Are you just for fun, or are you the killing type?"

Matias took another step forward but turned to a candle beside him. He ran his fingers across the top of the flame, as if he needed something to do with his hands. He laughed lightly. "We can have fun if you're in to that, but I assure you this is not the killing kind of visit."

He was *so* wrong. He was a vampire. Vampire visits were always the killing kind. Not to mention that he wanted the Artifact, which I was bound and determined to destroy, *and* he was standing between me and my only chance of escape. I only had one choice.

"Yeah, well," I countered, "it's the killing kind of visit for me."

I lunged forward, intending to clip him in the jaw, but he reacted quickly and dodged out of the way. The bastard was smart and kept himself between me and the tunnel, ensuring I couldn't just turn around and run. So I aimed a foot at him instead. He let out a grunt as my heel connected with his abdomen. In the blink of an eye, his hands shot out and clamped around my ankle before I could get it out of his reach. He squeezed tightly and twisted. I let the momentum take me, grabbing on to one of the long candles on the ledge behind me as I spun. My other foot connected with his cheek as I went crashing to the ground. He smirked in satisfaction when he saw me lying there, but it only lasted a split-second before I shoved the burning candle up into his face.

He reeled backward, giving me just enough time to jump to my feet. Clutching the Artifact in one hand, I rushed toward the tunnel. He had a hold of my wrist in under a second, and he whirled me around until he was between me and the tunnel again. I swung my knee up *hard*, sinking my knee into his royal jewels.

Damn, that was satisfying.

The vamp was too focused on baring his fangs at me to even flinch.

Seeing as I didn't have a weapon handy, I did the only other thing I could think of. I shifted, abandoning my backpack, and scooped up the owl skull with my talons. I flew high above his head and swooped down toward the tunnel. He spun away from me and raced toward the rock ledges, using them to gain height. Before I made it to tunnel, he was soaring through the air, reaching for me.

His hands caught my leg and tugged at my lower feathers as he dragged me out of the air and whipped me across the room. My body slammed into the rock walls, and The Wise Owl fell from my talons.

I shifted back to human form and grabbed the skull before he could get to it. I breathed heavily as I took a defensive stance. I kept my eyes on him, but I focused on my peripheral vision, hoping to spot a loose rock or something to use against him.

And then I realized… I was holding one of the most powerful objects in existence in my hand. I could just flip the switch on his vampire magic that was keeping him alive and kill him. Right? Was that how it worked? No harm in trying it.

"I just want to talk," he said, holding out a hand as if trying to reason with a wild dog.

"About what?" I demanded. "How can I even be sure you're real?"

Matias relaxed, standing straighter. "Do you really think I'd be anywhere else, that I wouldn't have found you?"

I hesitated. "I don't know how you did. The locket only works when—"

"Pfft," Matias scoffed. "I wasn't talking about the locket. I had eyes on you the whole time. As soon as I received the locket and saw that you were going after the Artifact, I sent my men after you. But my men you attacked on the street weren't the only ones watching."

I searched for his energy signature while he spoke, but his words halted me in my tracks. Now he had me intrigued.

"You let Sondra overhear you, knowing she'd find it?" I guessed.

Matias nodded. "I had a hunch. She always was easy to manipulate. I needed a witch who could find these caves and open the passageway. Luckily for me, you did all the work; I just had to follow and make sure you didn't turn back."

I drew in a sharp breath, though I tried not to let it show. "You're the reason the entrance caved in, aren't you?"

Matias smirked. "Guilty. I couldn't have you giving up when you were so close."

"Why go after the locket in the first place if all you ever wanted was this?" I sneered.

Matias leaned an elbow against one of the rock ledges, looking amused. "I never said it didn't come in handy. It is quite a useful object if you know how to use it. Imagine my surprise when you, Rachel Collins, showed up to deliver it."

Nausea hit my gut. "How do you know my name?"

Matias smirked. "I have an unlimited amount of resources. What would you rather I call you? Ravenite, perhaps?"

The blood drained from my face.

He must've noticed my expression, because he straightened and shrugged. "Like I said, unlimited resources, my dear. You have quite the reputation, don't you?"

My jaw tensed, and I spoke in warning. "Yes. I'm very good at killing vampires."

"Of course," he said with a nod. "You've spent many lifetimes cleaning up the mess you made."

"Excuse me?" I snapped.

My magic honed in on his energy signature. It felt rough like rock and smelled of burning oil. I was ready to cut off his magic at any point. But I couldn't bring myself to do it until I heard what he had to say. How did he know so much about me?

"Oh, you don't know?" His eyebrows shot up, and he clicked his tongue. "Rachel, Rachel, Rachel... I must say, I'm a little disappointed in you. I mean, if someone like *me* can remember my past lives before Valkas returned, I would've expected much more from you. Though you were... what? Ten or so when it happened."

"What are you talking about?" I demanded. "You couldn't have remembered anything before Valkas escaped. You didn't have the magic to remember."

Matias let out a fake sigh, as if amused. "Oh, sweetheart. You're like a child all over again. How about a history lesson?"

He didn't give me a chance to answer before continuing. "Magic never completely disappeared with Valkas. It only weakened. I mean, we still had psychics, healers, and things like that. We saw magic in a different way. Some people called it luck. Others called it miracles. I called it hard work and perseverance. How else would I have built the empire I have from the ground up?"

He began pacing in front of the tunnel entrance. "I was a strong witch in my past lives. I didn't know it in this life, but I was able to use my natural connection to Synchrony to find success. With each success, I could feel there was something bigger than me, something handing me everything I asked for. I found a diary from my past life that explained everything, about Synchrony, about Valkas—all of it."

My eyebrows shot up. "And you just stumbled upon it?"

He shrugged. "I was drawn to it. Ever have *déjà vu*, Rachel? Ever felt like a place was familiar when you'd never been there before, or recognized someone you'd never met?" He didn't let me answer, but I knew exactly what he meant. "I followed Synchrony like a religion, and the more I came to understand about it, the more I remembered. I was there when we trapped Valkas, and so I could break the spell. I knew how to free him."

I gasped. "It was *you* eight years ago! You're the reason he came back!" My hands curled tighter around the Artifact. As soon as he was done talking, he was dead.

Matias smiled. "Yes."

"Why would you do that!?" I shouted. "Do you know how many people he's killed?"

Matias dropped his gaze. "Yes, and for that I am truly sorry."

I scoffed. "You're a vampire. You have no empathy or remorse."

"I did," Matias shot back at me. "I've done more for this world in my life than you could ever imagine. Do you have any idea how much money I've given to fight poverty? The homes and counseling I've sponsored to save women from domestic violence? The foundations I've set up to fight childhood hunger? Vampires are the least of your problems. People were destroying each other long before Valkas came along."

"What does any of this have to do with freeing Valkas?" I questioned.

Matias's voice returned to a normal level. "It was never my intention to let him live. I only freed him to free magic. With it, I knew I could heal the world. But I made a mistake. You see, I thought that breaking a spell only took a piece of what was used to create it. And so, I tracked down the dagger used in the spell to spill Valkas's blood. I tried to kill him as soon as I freed him, but he only pulled the blade from his chest as if nothing had happened. That's when I realized that to break the spell, you didn't *only* need an object used to create it. You also needed the witch who cast it."

"So you freed Valkas, tried to kill him, but he changed you instead," I guessed.

"Yes," Matias said. "Luckily for me, his bloodlust got the best of him, and he wasn't thinking straight. I changed rather than died. I think Synchrony wanted it that way."

"Why? What's your plan now? Take the Artifact and control the world?"

"I wouldn't say control. I will... *improve*."

The way he said it sure didn't sound like it.

"How?" I asked.

"I don't need to go into the specifics," he said with a wave of his hand. "I will create a world with structure... with rules that will be followed without question. The world will finally be at peace."

"By taking away other people's free will." It wasn't a question.

"People don't know how to handle free will!" he shouted. "Look what they've done with it! They rape, they murder, they steal. I will use the Artifact to purify the world. Nobody else is willing to step up and do what has to be done."

Matias had a point, but he was talking about playing God, about using the Artifact as a judgement tool. With control over magic, he could choose who lived and who died. He could control everything...

It wouldn't fix the world. Far from it. It would only give the illusion until someone broke through his chains and decided to fight back. And that sorry sucker was probably going to be me.

That was why this Artifact needed to be destroyed. He wasn't getting anywhere near it.

I'd heard enough. If he wanted to get rid of the tainted hearts plaguing the world, his could be the first to go. I tapped into Synchrony through the Artifact, and I willed the magic keeping him alive to leave his body.

It pulled against me, protesting against my power. I tried again, but it was like running into a wall. And that was when I realized that vampire magic was different. This magic fed into him, whereas witches and shifters pulled from Synchrony at will. I couldn't use The Wise Owl to kill him.

"What's your plan with the vampires?" I asked, acting as if nothing was happening inside of me. "You'll never get rid of evil as long as they're around."

"You act like evil is a vampire trait, Rachel. It's not. It is and always has been a human trait. It only became a mark of vampirism when Valkas's own evil heart tainted the spell that created him. Anyway, that's where you come in."

"What do you mean?" I kept my voice calm, but damn it all if I wasn't burning for him to spill every last detail he knew.

"I told you only the witch who created the vampire curse can break it. It wasn't just luck that you stumbled into my office, Rachel."

I don't stumble.

"You still don't get it, do you?" he asked, eyeing my expression. "What do you know of your past lives?"

I hesitated. "Not much," I answered, feeling uncomfortable, like he was fishing for information.

"Oh, dear. It must be sad that I remember more about your past lives than you do. I recognized you the second I saw you, though it didn't all click until later." It sounded like he was telling the truth.

"I know about my last life," I said, refusing to give him so much satisfaction. "I know I was one of the witches who trapped Valkas with you."

"Of course," Matias said, "but you were so much more than that. Like I said, you've been trying to clean up your mess ever since. First, as Abigail. You created the shifters to fight the vampires. Then as Lily Gregor. It was Lily's idea —*your* idea—to gather us all together to trap Valkas. And now in this life, you fight and kill vampires, because you can't handle the evil you created."

"The evil I created? You're implying that I'm—"

"Elizabeth Martin," Matias cut in. "Precisely. You, Rachel, are the witch who created Valkas."

21

My knees went weak, and my mouth felt like sandpaper. *No way* was I responsible for all of this. He was lying to me. That... or none of this was real. It was the labyrinth toying with me again. Yet, a part of me couldn't help but believe him... like I'd already known it was true.

Matias reached into his jacket. Though I went rigid, I was curious as to what he'd pull out. Damn this intriguing, mysterious man.

"I need your help to make the world a better place," Matias said. Which sounded nice, until you considered his plan for power. He produced a small white towel and began unfolding it. "Will you, Rachel, do the honors of killing Valkas and finally ridding the world of this curse?"

It sounded like he was proposing to me or something. *Sorry, buddy. I'm already taken.*

Matias finished unfolding the towel. Inside lay a silver dagger. I recognized it from the dream I'd had at Amalia's. Which meant he was telling the truth. I'd already started remembering my life as Elizabeth. I'd dreamt of the night I'd used the exact same dagger to spill Valkas's blood and perform the spell that would change our world forever.

"I want you to have this, Rachel," he said. "It's the only way to kill him."

I didn't move. There was too much that didn't add up. Clearly, Matias wanted Valkas dead. Maybe it was out of revenge for changing him, or maybe he just wanted to rid the world of such evil. But it didn't make any sense.

"You talk a good talk," I said, "but you can't convince me that easily. What happens to you when I kill Valkas?"

Matias only shrugged. "I suppose it breaks the spell. Once that magic is no longer keeping me alive, I would die—just as would all the other vampires."

It made the idea of killing Valkas just that much more appealing. Except...

"You're asking me to sign your death certificate," I pointed out. "Why would you want that? What about your plan to cure the world?"

"Vampirism may seem like a blessing. I could do so much with my immortality. But there are far more terrible things about it. The constant bloodlust. The emotional disconnect. Oh, don't look so surprised. I'm very aware that I don't feel empathy these days. And that's a problem. There are human emotions I long to feel again... but just can't no matter how hard I try. Vampirism is truly a curse. Once I'm free of the curse, my successor will take my place and carry out my plan."

He sounded so noble, but I wasn't buying it. Maybe at one time he believed he could make the world a better place, but vampires just didn't talk like that... they didn't think like that. They didn't have the empathy he spoke of. I'd run across enough vampires to know there weren't exceptions to the rule. Which meant that whatever Matias's true motivations were went far beyond what he was telling me. He only talked about emotions to manipulate me.

"Come on, Rachel," he encouraged. "Don't you want to avenge your sister?"

My heart stopped at the mention of Jenna. How the hell did he—? *Unlimited resources.* This guy probably hacked into my email accounts and everything.

"Yes," I said slowly... but I couldn't let him go through with his plan. For a better world or not, no one deserved complete power.

First things first, I was getting that dagger. If what he said about it was true —and my gut was saying it was—then I'd need it to get rid of Valkas once and for all.

"I accept your job offer," I said, standing straighter and speaking more confidently.

"Excellent," he replied with a smile.

I stepped forward and held my hand out.

Matias pulled it away. "Give me the Artifact first."

I hesitated. I had no intention of handing it over, but I also needed a weapon if I was going to make it out of here with the Artifact in hand. My options quickly rushed through my head as I contemplated my next move. Chances were Matias had the locket tucked under his shirt and would be able to predict every move I made before I made it. So how the hell was I going to trick him into letting me get away with the owl skull and the dagger? By now he surely knew I wasn't going to let him have it. And if I handed it over and decided to stab him afterward, he'd know that was coming, too.

And so I had to make a choice—one of the hardest decisions I'd ever been asked to make. Would I kill Valkas, effectively destroying the rest of the vampires, and allow another power to rise up—perhaps worse than the last? Or would I let the world continue to spiral down the shithole it was already sinking into? It was a choice between two evils, one I didn't think I was fully prepared to make.

But the answer was obvious to me. I already knew what option I'd choose before I realized I'd decided. This was *Valkas* we were talking about, the man who orchestrated murderers of thousands of people, who wreaked havoc across the country for years, and whose men stole my sister and probably served her for breakfast, lunch, and dinner daily. They were the same men who murdered my parents. He deserved a fate far worse than death. I would trade anything for the chance to drive a dagger through his heart.

My hand stretched out, as if on its own, to offer the Artifact to Matias. In return, he handed me the towel-wrapped dagger.

As soon as the Owl left my hands and the pulse of magic disappeared with it, I realized what a horrible mistake I'd made. What if the world he created was worse than the one we were living in? I had no idea what someone could do if they knew how to leverage The Wise Owl's power.

He smiled. "Excellent. Now—"

I dropped to the ground and swung my leg out at his ankles, catching him completely off guard. His legs whipped out from under him, and he went crashing to the ground. His head caught on one of the rock ledges. I was on top of him in less than a second, my dagger raised and aimed for his heart.

His hand shot out and grabbed my wrist. Holy crap! This guy was stronger than he looked.

"I told you I run fair deals," Matias said as he fought against my arm that pressed toward his chest. "You would make a terrible businesswoman, Rachel."

He threw his hips upward and spun me around until I was flat on my back. Before I knew it, he was on his feet. His foot pressed down on my chest so hard that I couldn't breathe. I gasped for breath and tightened my hold on the blade.

He leaned down, looming over me as shadows flickered across his face. "I'm not going to kill you, Rachel, so let's stop with the theatrics. We made a fair trade. I'm going to walk out of here with the Artifact, and you're going to go in the opposite direction with the blade. We both get what we want. Understand?"

No way, dickhole!

He wasn't leaving with that artifact as long as I had something to say about it. Unlike him, I never claimed to run clean business deals. I did what was best, and right now, the chance to stop both Valkas *and* Matias looked pretty damn appealing.

In one swift motion, I kicked my foot upward and sliced my blade across his ankle at the same time. My toes connected with the owl skull, sending it flying across the cave. It landed several feet away with a clatter. All within the same second, the weight on my chest lifted.

I inhaled a deep breath as I sprang to my feet then dove for the Artifact. But before I could reach it, Matias's fingers came out of nowhere and snatched it right out from under me.

He took off running down the tunnel. Thinking fast, I grabbed my headlamp that had slid off when I shifted and sprinted behind him. My light bounced off his back as I chased him down the tunnel. The ankle wound had slowed him down, but not enough.

Next time, slice deeper.

Ahead of us, the tunnel split in two directions. Matias took the left path just as a scream of terror ripped through the tunnel on the right.

"Venn!" the female voice shouted.

Sondra.

The family was in trouble.

I skidded to a halt in front of the passageways, hesitating. Did I go after Matias, or did I help my family?

The choice was impossible to make.

22

M y hand squeezed tighter around the blade as I glanced from one tunnel to the other.

"Get off of him, you mother—" The sound of Ryland's roar cut Teagan off.

I didn't have time to stand around contemplating my options. In a split-second decision, I rushed forward and sprinted down the tunnel to my right.

When I broke out of the tunnel, I found myself back on the shore of the underground lake. A shining white orb—some sort of enchantment—hovered high above the lake close to the ceiling, so I could see the chaos in full force. Everything moved so fast that I could barely process it.

Six of Matias's men fought the family, and at least fifty mongrels were clawing at whomever they could get their hands on. Shifters, witches, vampires… it didn't matter to them. They were on no one's side.

I recognized the witch who'd hit Venn with the curse fighting a dozen mongrels alongside the tiger shifter who'd been with him before. Four other vampires were present, two of them taking on Venn in his wolf form. Ryland's jaw snapped at mongrels that were trying to bite him. Teagan sat on his back with Fiona still strapped securely in her pack. She aimed a knife at one of the closest vampires. It landed in his eye socket, sinking through the flesh and into his brain. He disappeared in a pile of ash. His clothes and the knife fell to the floor where he'd vanished.

Five mongrels jumped Sondra at once, dragging her to the ground. She threw her elbow into one of their faces and kicked a knee up into one of their groins.

I rushed toward Sondra since she looked like she needed the most help, but a half dozen mongrels scurried in front of my path. The first one bared its teeth at me and jumped forward, but I kicked that sucker straight out of the air like a soccer ball. He squeaked and went flying. The next one lunged forward with his teeth aimed at my ankles. The freaky little monster wasn't getting anywhere near me. I ducked and sliced my dagger across his throat. He disappeared like the imprint of a ghost washed away with the wind.

Another mongrel jumped on my back, his sharp claws digging into my shoulders. I reached behind myself and grabbed a fistful of the skin on the back of his neck. His claws sliced through my skin as I ripped him off of me, but I barely felt it. Rage and adrenaline shot through me like a flood in an open waterway. A battle cry ripped from my lungs as my dagger sank into the chest of the next mongrel, then sliced the stomach of the one beside him.

Finally clearing a path from me to Sondra, I sprinted for her. She'd managed to take care of most of them, but there was one left and on the verge of biting her face off. I didn't slow as I ran forward and swung my foot out. My foot connected with his gut as I punted him. His hands flew off of Sondra's shirt, and he went soaring fifteen feet into the air. I quickly offered Sondra my hand and helped her to her feet.

"Thank you," she breathed just before we both spotted another group of mongrels emerging from one of the tunnels and heading straight in our direction. "Go help Venn!" she instructed. "I've got this."

I didn't question her. I whirled around and sprinted toward Venn. Behind me, flashes of white light went off and electricity sizzled through the air as Sondra attacked the mongrels with her lightning power.

A vampire with dark hair held Venn down by his tail, while another with a ratface swung his knee up into Venn's jaw. Ratface's hands tangled in Venn's fur and forced his head back, his fangs heading for Venn's neck. Venn swung his good paw out, slicing his claws against the side of the vamp's face. Ratface pulled back just in time for his eyes to connect with mine as my dagger sank into his friend's back.

"Leave my boyfriend alone!" I snapped as Dark-Haired Vamp disintegrated into a pile of ash.

Ratface smirked. "Gladly. If it means I get you, Ravenite. I bet you taste wonderful."

He was in front of me in a flash. He threw his arm out, and his palm slammed into my chest. My body flew backward and crashed into the cave floor with a hard *thud*.

"Too bad you'll never find out," I said through labored breaths as I swung my leg around, aiming for the back of his knee.

Ratface caught my leg before I could knock him off his feet. I shoved my dagger up into his shin. At the same time, Venn's sharp wolf teeth sank into the vamp's wrist. Ratface let out a scream and dropped my leg. I ripped my dagger from his flesh and sprang to my feet. Venn clamped his jaw tightly around Ratface's arm and swung his head down, pulling Ratface to the ground. A moment of surprise caught his face a split second before my dagger entered his chest.

Venn dipped his head and brushed his fur against my hip, but we didn't have time to enjoy each other's company just yet. Witch Guy and Tiger Shifter had fought off their mongrels and were headed our way. The last vampire had abandoned his fight with Ryland and Teagan to join them. Mongrels flooded out of the caves behind us, most of them headed for the closest target—Ryland, Teagan, and Fiona.

There were too many mongrels to take on at once, not to mention the strongest of Matias's men remaining.

My eyes darted around the cavern, first to Sondra, who was still using lightning to fight off the mongrels. She looked pale and weak, and her lightning was barely visible now as it cracked through the air. She was quickly running out of energy.

On the other side of me, my eyes fell upon the dark lake. It gave me an idea, which was a heck of a long shot but also our only option.

Finally, my gaze fell upon Matias's men stalking confidently our way. Witch Guy's lips moved, though I didn't hear what he'd said. Suddenly, a glowing green ball of energy erupted from his palm, aimed straight for Venn. Venn ducked out of the way, and the spell exploded against the ground behind him. Witch Guy's eyes flickered toward me, but he quickly looked back to Venn, anger etched in his eyes. The vamp and tiger beside him also had their eyes trained on Venn, like they barely noticed me there.

"Get them to the water, Venn," I told him. "I have a plan."

Venn nodded once. I spun around, praying he'd be able to handle himself against them for a minute or two. I ran toward Sondra, where she was just barely holding off the mongrels surrounding her. Her magic was getting weaker, and the mongrels were closing in on her. I swung my blade outward, cutting three mongrels in one swipe, and jumped over two others until I reached her.

"What will lightning do to vampires?" I asked in a rushed breath.

"With enough power, immobilize them," Sondra answered quickly without looking at me.

"Great. How do I use it?"

The sound of the tiger's growl sounded behind us. *Please be okay, Venn.*

Sondra's gaze flickered to mine before returning to the mongrels in front of us. Sweat dripped down her forehead, and her face had drained of color. She looked on the verge of passing out. "Rae, you're not ready—"

"I am," I argued. At this point, it was do or die. I didn't have a choice.

I glanced behind my shoulder to Venn. The tiger was on top of him, both of them snarling at each other. We didn't have time.

Sondra hesitated before mumbling the incantation for me. "*Fulgur.* Focus the magic in your chest, then shoot it out through your palms."

She quickly demonstrated, but her lightning barely stunned the mongrels.

"*Fulgur...*" I tested the incantation on my tongue. A strong jolt of magic passed through my chest, startling me. I hadn't expected it to feel so powerful. The hairs on my arm rose as the magic passed through my body, but they quickly fell back into place as the magic dissipated. My muscles ached, as if I'd just finished benching a thousand pounds. This spell was not going to go easy on me.

"Fulgur," I tried again, this time honing in on that energy and guiding it down my limbs.

Blinding white bolts of lightning shot out of my left palm and connected with at least a dozen mongrels, knocking them off their feet. A deafening *crack* thundered through the cavern, echoing across the lake. Sondra's eyes widened, like she couldn't believe I'd actually done it.

"Get these mongrels into the water," I instructed, trying to mask my exhaustion. "And make sure Venn doesn't die."

Sondra nodded confidently.

I whirled around and shouted across the cavern. "Teagan!"

She kicked a mongrel off Ryland's back while Ryland's teeth sank into the throat of another one. Her eyes darted to mine.

I muttered the incantation again to show her my lightning. I took a chance and directed it toward the tiger shifter. It connected with his chest, stunning him enough that Venn gained the upper hand and sprang to his feet, dodging another spell Witch Guy threw at him. With my eyes on Teagan, I gestured to Venn then to the water. Behind her, Fiona's fox eyes widened in realization, and Teagan's quickly followed. Teagan patted Ryland's back and whispered something in his ear before he took off running toward Witch Guy and the vamp beside him.

I turned to the mongrels and repeated the incantation. I struck five at once, all of which disappeared upon their death. The others shied away, retreating slowly toward the water as I advanced on them on unsteady feet. Ahead of me, Sondra and Witch Guy were battling it out. She shot purple spells at him that looked like fireworks, while he threw green balls of energy back at her. Ryland barreled into the vamp, knocking him backward into the water.

One by one, the mongrels entered the lake, their feet splashing up water at the edge of the shore. One of them in the back must've found a drop-off, because I saw his head bob under the water before he started thrashing around, trying to swim.

Almost there… I gritted my teeth and forced myself to focus past the dizziness assaulting me. I watched the tiger shifter and the Witch Guy closely. All in one moment, the tiger swiped his paw at Venn's face, ripping into the flesh, while Witch Guy's spell finally struck Sondra in the chest. Blood poured from Venn's wound, and Sondra lay motionless on the ground.

The next second, their feet were at the edge of the water. I took my one and only chance and struck.

I never got a chance to see if my lightning hit the water and immobilized them. That last bolt was all my body could take before my knees buckled beneath me and the world faded to black.

<h1 style="text-align:center">23</h1>

I blinked my eyes open to a white ceiling. Soft lighting bathed the room. My body felt warm and comfortable, unlike the cool, damp caves we'd been in. My stomach twisted in hunger. Hushed whispers met my ears from across the room. *Venn and Fiona.*

I pushed myself to my elbows to take in more of my surroundings. I saw that I was lying on a queen bed. There was a long dresser on the wall across from me, with a TV on top of it and a desk beside that. The curtains on my left were drawn, but I didn't see any sunlight peeking in around the edges. It must've been late. To my right sat a matching queen bed with someone—I couldn't see who— lying under the covers. Beyond that, a short wall that didn't reach the ceiling separated the bedroom from the rest of the suite. I could hear Venn and Fiona talking from the other side of the divider.

A shadow crossed my bed, and a pair of soft but cold hands touched my shoulder. I leapt in surprise. My eyes darted upward to see Genevieve standing over my bed.

"Lie back," she instructed in a quiet voice. "You need to rest."

I sighed and did as I was told. "What's going on? Is everyone all right? How did we get out of the caves?"

"I think I hear Rae." Fiona's voice came from the other side of the room.

Before Genevieve could answer me, Venn and Fiona popped their heads past the corner of the divider. Half of Venn's face was covered in gauze and tape, but he smiled wide when he saw me. Relief flooded my body, and tears welled in my eyes.

Venn hurried past the other bed to mine. Fiona followed behind him, using a pair of crutches to stabilize herself.

Genevieve stepped aside when Venn reached me. He sat on the side of my bed and leaned down to me. His hands gently touched both sides of my face. I noticed tight gauze wrapping around his hand where the mongrel had bit him. My fingers grazed his good arm, just so I could touch him.

Venn dipped his head and pressed his lips to mine, a full, passionate kiss that sent a warm glow to settle in my chest. He pulled away far too soon.

"What happened?" I asked.

"Your plan worked," Venn answered. "You stunned everyone, and we killed the rest of Matias's men. We got out before any more mongrels attacked."

My head relaxed into the pillow. "How'd we get out? The entrance was blocked."

"There was another exit through the tunnels," Venn said. "Afterward, we called Genevieve. She got on the first plane to Nashville and helped everyone with their injuries. We should all be back to normal soon."

"Where are Teagan and Ryland?" I asked.

"They're fine," Fiona said, sitting down at the end of the bed. "They're bringing back dinner."

"Is Sondra okay?" I glanced to the bed beside mine.

Genevieve nodded. "She's recovering."

"So the spell that hit her…?"

"It was only meant to hurt her," Genevieve answered. "It will pass."

"What happened to everyone while we were separated?" I couldn't keep the questions from tumbling out of my mouth. "I have so much to tell you."

"One second you were there, the next you vanished," Venn told me. "We turned back to go looking for you, but the tunnel led us back to the lake. Then we were attacked."

I furrowed my brow. "How long did it take you to get back?"

Venn shrugged. "Maybe ten minutes."

"No." I shook my head. "I was gone for *hours*."

"The labyrinth screws with your perception of time," Fiona pointed out. "It may very well have been hours, but to us, it was just minutes."

"Matias found me in the caves," I blurted. "He got away with the Artifact. He gave me a blade and said—"

"We know," Fiona interrupted. "Genevieve figured it out when she saw it. You were Elizabeth Martin."

"Yes," I confirmed. "Which means only I can kill Valkas. Where is the dagger?"

Venn shot a glance at Genevieve. *Translation: Genevieve had it.*

My eyes darted between him and Fiona. "We're trusting her now? Like, fully?"

Venn's jaw tensed. "She didn't exactly give us a choice."

"I'm keeping it safe," Genevieve emphasized. "For now."

I lifted my head again, ignoring Venn's hand pushing my shoulder back down to the pillow. "I have to go after him!"

"Yes," Genevieve agreed, "after you rest up."

"No," Venn objected firmly. "You can't go after him."

"What are you talking about?!" I sat straight up, though my head spun. "We're headed to Gregor Island anyway. We know where to find him and have the tools to kill him. We *have* to do this!"

"Going after your sister is one thing," Venn said. "Trying to kill the *original* vampire is another. We'll die before we ever make it close to him."

I crossed my arms. "Are you doubting me? I'm the only person who gets to doubt me, and I'm done with it. I doubted myself as the Ravenite. I doubted myself in the caves. I doubted Synchrony. And I am *done* doubting. I can do this, Venn."

Venn shook his head. "I'm only saying that this is Valkas—"

"And I'm Rachel Collins!" I burst. "I created the damn guy! I need to get rid of him."

"How many lifetimes do you think that will take?" Venn asked rhetorically. "You've already *tried*, Rae. If something happens to you in this life, I wouldn't..." He trailed off.

"This isn't about you," I said sympathetically.

Venn stared back at me, his eyes glistening.

I sighed. "I just mean that this is bigger than any of us. Wouldn't the world be better with the vampires gone? Don't you want revenge on them for changing your brother?"

Venn hesitated, but he didn't get a chance to answer. The hotel room door swung open, and the delicious smell of Chinese takeout hit my nose.

"Dinner!" Ryland called.

"He ate half of it in the car," Teagan teased.

"I had *two* egg rolls!" Ryland clarified.

Fiona rolled her eyes then stood, balancing on her crutches. "You better have saved me a crab rangoon."

"Please," Ryland scoffed as he came into view. "I know better than to eat your food." Ryland's whole body went ridged the second his eyes fell on me.

Teagan appeared behind him, carrying a handful of plastic bags. "Oh, good. Rae's up. See, Ryland? I told you we'd need to order enough for her."

Fiona followed Teagan as she turned to the living area to unpack dinner. Ryland paused for a long moment, crossing his arms and narrowing his gaze at me. I shifted uncomfortably on the bed. What was his problem? Before I could ask, Ryland spun around and disappeared behind the divider.

I looked to Venn for an explanation. "What's up with Ryland?"

Venn hesitated, as if he wasn't sure whether to tell me or not. His shoulders dropped. "He's been acting like that since we learned you were Elizabeth Martin."

I furrowed my brow. "Why? Isn't it good news, since we know how to kill Valkas now?"

Venn chewed on his lower lip. "It is, but... he kind of blames you."

"What?" I asked in disbelief. "But Valkas made me—Elizabeth—do it! He threatened her family... didn't he?"

Venn nodded. "Ryland still says that's no excuse, that because of your decision—Elizabeth's decision—too many people have died. He says she should've chosen the greater good."

"She couldn't have known," I argued.

"I know," Venn said. "We've tried explaining it to him. It's not your fault, Rae. He'll come around eventually."

I groaned. Ryland didn't seem like the kind of guy to *come around* easily. Good thing he didn't know I'd given up The Wise Owl for the dagger; otherwise, he'd be furious at me. I was happy letting him assume Matias got away on his own—and not because of my impulsive decision.

I was starving, so I was going to have to face Ryland sooner than later. I started to get up, but Genevieve flicked her finger from the foot of my bed. An invisible force held me in place.

Holy crap! This lady had some serious magical skills.

"Stay," she instructed. "You need to rest. I will bring you some food."

Her hold on me vanished, and I relaxed back into the pillow.

"Dibs on an eggroll," I called after her before turning my attention back to Venn. "So, about Valkas?"

Venn's jaw clenched. "This isn't up for discussion."

My jaw dropped. "Who died and made you the boss of me?"

Venn took a deep breath and ran his fingers through his hair, the muscles in his biceps rippling. "I'm not trying to tell you what to do—"

"But you are!" I accused.

"I'm just trying to keep you from making a stupid decision."

I almost snapped back, until he pulled me into his arms. My head lay against his chest. I felt so warm and comfortable. It was like waking up in heaven. How could I argue with him when he felt this great?

"I care about you, Rae," he said softly, placing a kiss on the top of my head. Tingles spread down my body. "I don't want you getting hurt."

I ran the palm of my hand up his arm, enjoying the goosebumps that traveled along my own skin. "I don't want to hurt you, either."

It was the truth. As I said it, the strongest sense of guilt assaulted my gut, immediately masking any appetite I thought I had. Bile rose in my throat.

It didn't matter what Venn said or how much I cared for him. Once I was back on my feet, I was going to Gregor Island... with or without him.

That's where I'd finally find Jenna—and where I'd kill Valkas.

END OF BOOK TWO

RESOLUTE

BOOK THREE

Rachel Collins didn't know how amazing she was. It wasn't just that she was beautiful. I mean, she was. Her smile made my heart beat in an unnatural rhythm. At first, I thought there was something wrong with me, but Ryland assured me *That's love, bro.*

Rae's pale skin was flawlessly beautiful, and I constantly had to restrain myself from running my fingers through her sleek black hair just to feel how soft it was. Every now and then, I caught my eyes roaming over her trim figure. I didn't want to be *that* guy, but I couldn't help it. It was like she'd been carved from magic.

But all of that was superficial. She could look like anything and I'd still want to be with her. I mean, the girl killed vampires on the daily for fun. She was totally badass, and to be honest, I was a little jealous of her skills.

She was serious most of the time, but every so often, she'd make a snarky comment that made me laugh, or her eyes would twinkle when she was reminded of her family, and I knew—this girl was made for me.

I couldn't take my eyes off her. I sat on the couch in Genevieve's lake house half an hour outside of Nocton. Genevieve had offered for us to stay here while we all healed and she worked on finding a lead on Matias, who had escaped from our grasp with a very powerful artifact only days ago. Genevieve was a dark witch and a selfish one. I knew she'd drop the offer for a roof over our heads the second she was finished with us, but we were all involved in this now. We were in it with her until the Artifact was finally destroyed.

The cabin was the size of our house, with a high ceiling that stretched to the second level. There were two bedrooms and a bathroom up there, and a loft that overlooked the common area. The kitchen sat open to the living room, so I could easily see everyone else from where I sat. The entire cabin was bathed in natural textures and earthy tones, from the thick wooden beams above our heads to the marble countertop and stone fireplace.

Across the cabin, Rae and Ryland sat opposite each other at the dining room table. Their hands locked together, each of them resting an elbow on the table in an arm wrestle. Neither of them was making any headway to either side. Ryland's eyebrows knitted together. He was still pissed since he found out Rae was Elizabeth Martin in a past life, the witch who'd created the vampire curse. No doubt he'd challenged her to an arm wrestle to relieve some of his frustrations and show her up. And she gladly accepted, knowing he drastically underestimated her.

Ryland's face twisted in concentration. The dude was trying damn hard, which was hilarious considering he was the size of a school bus and Rae looked like a pixie compared to him.

I guess that was what happened when you dealt with shifter magic. Some shifters were naturally stronger than others, no matter what animal they shifted into. I wondered if Rae's strength had anything to do with the fact that she was a witch, like she was stronger because she had more magic running through her veins or something.

Her lips twisted up into a sly smile. God, I swear the twitch of those perfect lips stopped my heart right there. The book I'd been flipping through fell from my fingertips and onto the floor.

No one noticed my blatant gaping. Rae and Ryland were too preoccupied with wrestling one another, and Fiona and Teagan kept close watch, hooting and hollering for Rae. Sondra was nowhere to be seen, since she was in the other room on the phone.

"Go, go, go!" Fiona shouted, pounding her fist on the table in delight.

"You've got this, Rae," Teagan cheered.

"Seriously, babe?" Ryland asked flatly.

Teagan shrugged. "She's kicking your ass. I officially love her."

Me, too. I just didn't know how to tell her.

"Aww," Rae replied to Teagan. "That's sweet. What do you say, Ryland? Winner gets Teagan?"

"Done," Teagan agreed without so much as a glance toward her boyfriend.

"*Babe!*" Ryland objected. The muscles in his arms rippled as he tried harder to push Rae's arm to the table.

The three girls burst into a fit of laughter. Just seeing Rae smile like that sent tingles up and down my body.

I couldn't deny it. I was head over heels for this girl. She was smart… funny… and she wanted *me*. Not only that, but she treated me like a real human being. Before Sondra rescued me from Maliya's nest, most people in my life had treated me like they owned me. It took me a long time to realize not everyone was like that.

Guilt knotted in the pit of my stomach. Rae sure didn't treat me like a piece of property, but I'd been horrible to her these past few days. I thought girls were supposed to like it when guys acted all protective or whatever, but Rae wasn't like most girls. If she set her mind to something, she was going after it one way or another. Lately, she'd been talking about going after Valkas.

Yes, *that* Valkas, the original vampire—the guy who orchestrated the kidnappings and killings of thousands of people in the last decade. He was heartless, ruthless... the worst kind of being imaginable.

Of course, that was exactly Rae's cup of tea. The badder they were, the more driven she was to destroy them.

Which would've been fine... under normal circumstances. I'd follow her to the ends of the earth to help her. But things changed when I learned that Rae was the one who created Valkas in a past life. Which meant she was the only one who could destroy him in this life. Every time I thought about it, my throat turned to sandpaper and my chest felt as if a ton of bricks was sitting upon it.

It wasn't that I didn't think Rae could kill Valkas. I mean, it was a long shot, but she was strong and smart. She obviously had a chance if she played her cards right. But I feared what would happen to her if the cards didn't play in her favor. What if Valkas discovered who she was? I couldn't bring myself to picture the horrible things he would do to her if he found out *she* was the one thing who could destroy him.

Unlike other vampires, Valkas couldn't die via a stake to the heart, decapitation, or fire. He was the eye of the storm, and it took the witch who started that storm to end it. If she failed, her fate would be far worse than death. Valkas wouldn't just kill her. If he did, her soul would return in less than a century in another body with the chance to take him out again. Death was hardly the worst thing that could happen to a person. He'd find a way to trap her soul—or destroy it. It was the only way to ensure he could live forever.

I sighed, feeling completely heartbroken as I watched her. She smiled across the table at Ryland. She had no idea what kind of terrors lie ahead if she went through with this. The only reason I hadn't told her why I insisted she didn't go was because I was certain it would only drive her closer to Valkas. If there was ass to kick, she was right there to shove her foot straight up it.

Not only that, but I was selfish as all hell. I knew from the moment I saw her that we were destined to be together. I saw something in her eyes the night we'd met, something that looked so familiar it knocked the wind right out of me. There was an instant connection because we'd already lived a whole lifetime together... and I wanted to live every other lifetime with her, too.

"Surrender!" Rae demanded with a laugh, cutting through my thoughts.

Sweat had broken out on both her and Ryland's heads.

"No," Ryland objected. "I'm not losing to a girl."

Rae scoffed. "You're not winning to one, either."

Fiona doubled over in a fit of laughter. Even I snickered.

Shit, I couldn't let this girl go, not right when I'd found her. I'd waited years for her to show up. I didn't know I was waiting for *her*, of course, but I knew I was waiting for *someone*. I had the sketches from Sondra to prove it. They were tucked in the outer pocket of my duffel bag. I'd pulled them off the wall before our house burned down.

Sondra couldn't exactly tell the future. No witch could without a magical object to assist them. But they could get a sense of where Synchrony was leading you. Sondra knew Synchrony was leading me to Rae long before Rae ever stepped into my life. She'd drawn the sketches to give me hope.

Rae pushed with all her might, making headway. Ryland pushed back, but Rae had already gained the upper hand. He conceded before his hand ever hit the table.

Ryland dropped Rae's hand and crossed his arms. "Okay, I give, but only because I have a bad arm."

He scowled and rubbed his bicep, which wasn't even the arm that had been broken. Besides, he'd undergone enough healing spells that it should've been good as new by now.

Rae shot her fists into the air in victory. My heart danced inside my chest when I saw the overly excited look on her face. Most of the time, she was all business. It was nice to see her beaming for once. And lord, was it beautiful.

Teagan and Fiona both gave Rae a high-five before she stood from her chair and turned to me with a smile.

Slay. The girl effing slayed me. She was perfect.

She caught me staring, and I involuntarily blushed under her gaze. She didn't notice.

Rae wiggled her eyebrows. "Your turn to challenge the beast, Venn."

I sat up straighter and laughed. "Believe me, Ryland and I have had our fair share of show-downs."

Rae smirked. "Me, Venn. I meant *me.*"

I couldn't help but smile. Holy crap, was it a wide smile. I must've looked like I had a fork stuck sideways in my mouth. But that was the way she made me feel, like there was this light inside of me that had been begging to escape my whole life but was shadowed by all the darkness in my past... until she flipped the switch. All that light came pouring out all at once.

"Nah," I said, waving my hand like it was no big deal. "I think you've already crushed enough sets of balls for the night." My gaze flickered to Ryland, who shot daggers my way.

He scoffed and mumbled, "I'm sure she'll be doing more than that later tonight."

I had the sudden urge to punch him.

Rae crossed her arms and stuck out her hip. I wanted to kiss the pout right off those sexy lips of hers.

"I didn't realize this was the freaking patriarchy," Rae teased with a raise of her eyebrow. "They're not going to revoke your man card."

I shrugged. "They might."

Rae crossed the room and grabbed my hand from off the back of the couch. Fire tingled up and down my skin, but the good kind—the warm kind.

"Come *on…*" she begged. "We're just having fun."

How could I deny her of that? It'd been all business since we met, besides the few minor make out sessions that left us *both* wanting more.

I took a deep breath, pretending like I had to think about it. Finally, I stood and followed her over to the table. "Fine."

"*Whip-cha.*" Ryland made a whipping motion through the air.

"Shut up," I grumbled as I pushed him aside so I could take his seat across from Rae.

"Watch out," he warned as he stood. "This girl is stronger than she looks."

My eyes met hers, and I beamed. "I know."

She gazed back at me with challenging eyes, then took my hand, squeezing it tightly. My breath caught in my chest.

"On the mark of three…" Teagan stated. "One… Two… Three!"

Every muscle in my body tensed as I threw all my strength into the arm wrestle. Damn, this girl was strong. Most girls would go flying across the room under my shifter strength. But Rae was nothing like most girls.

Needless to say, she won the arm wrestle, but I was the lucky guy who won a red-hot consolation kiss.

1

The world had a way of raising you up just to slam you into the dirt the second you thought you were safe. I'd learned to roll with the highs and lows, but I also knew that perfection was only temporary. Which meant that the few days I'd had with my new family in Genevieve's lake house were coming to a close.

Venn and I lay beside each other on one of the big couches in front of the fireplace. We barely fit, but he pulled me securely to his chest to keep me close to him. My ear rested just above his heart. The hairs on my arm rose as I listened to the comforting *thump* of his heartbeat and felt the warmth of his breath across the top of my head. The fireplace crackled, and soft voices from the patio drifted in through the screen door with the cool night breeze.

My fingers ran over the back of Venn's hand, examining the skin that'd been sliced open just days ago. There were no signs of injury anymore, and when I pressed down, he made no indication that it bothered him.

I'd tested Ryland's arm earlier, and that was back to normal—though his attitude hadn't improved much. He didn't say anything when Teagan was around to keep him in line, but I caught him throwing death glares my way every now and then. He looked like he wanted to punch me for what I'd done in a past life. And maybe he would've—if he knew I wouldn't smack him right back.

Through the sliding glass doors, I could see Fiona standing next to Teagan, sipping on her soda and staring out across the lake. It was clear her broken leg was healed as well.

It should've been great news, but it only made me feel sick. I told myself I'd stay long enough for everyone to heal. Now that we were all feeling better, I had to go.

I didn't *want* this amazing mini-vacation to end. For the first time in years,

I'd felt normal. I cooked breakfast with Teagan and stayed up late talking with Fiona. We all went swimming in the lake and ate popcorn while we watched a dumb slapstick comedy that made me forget—if only for a moment—that I lived in a world of monsters.

And then there was Venn. Every moment with him was like magic. He took my breath away. It didn't matter the circumstances, whether it was the time I caught him staring while we were cleaning up after dinner, or the time he cornered me in the laundry room and we had the most amazing make out session. I was totally smitten by the guy.

Except for one thing. He didn't want me going after Valkas.

And I *had* to. For one, Jenna was on that island with the bastard, and I already knew without a doubt that I was going after her. But now I had the chance to kill Valkas while I was at it? It wasn't an opportunity I could pass up. Not only did it mean eliminating one of the worst terrorist threats in history, but Matias had said that killing Valkas would kill all the other vampires as well.

"What happens to you when I kill Valkas?" I'd asked him.

"I suppose it breaks the spell," he'd replied. *"Once that magic is no longer keeping me alive, I would die—just as would all the other vampires."*

I'd asked Sondra about it while we were sunbathing along the lakeshore a few days ago, and she agreed it made sense. If I broke the curse, all vampires would perish.

This *had* to be done, and I was the only person who could do it. I only wished I could convince Venn to come with me.

"Venn?" I cleared my throat.

"Yeah, Rae?" He let out a long, soothing breath.

Damn it. He was totally relaxed. I wasn't ready to have this fight with him again… but I couldn't keep putting it off. There was work to be done.

"We need to talk about what's happening next."

Venn's whole body tensed. He glanced down at me. "We're going after Matias. We have to destroy the Artifact."

My jaw clenched. "You know he's not the only threat out there. You promised we'd go after my sister."

Venn sat up straight, pulling his arm out from under me. I nearly toppled off the end of the couch, but I quickly righted myself and sat next to him.

Venn raked his fingers through his dark hair. "That was before. You don't understand how dangerous Gregor Island could be, do you?"

I stared back at him with a stone-cold expression. If he thought I didn't understand the dangers of going after Valkas, he seriously underestimated me. But it was because of those dangers that I had to go. No one had heard from the Soulless in two years, which only meant they were planning something… something *big*. And I had to stop them first.

"I know things changed when Matias gave me that dagger," I said, "but I have to go through with it. I couldn't do it in my past lives because I didn't have the dagger used in the spell that created him. Now I have it, so it's the perfect chance to strike."

Venn's fists tightened, and his gaze narrowed at the flickering flames in the fireplace. "Have you ever considered that maybe Matias was lying to you?"

Honestly, the thought had crossed my mind, but Matias sounded genuine. He truly wanted Valkas dead, so why would he give me a fake dagger? Not to mention I saw the same dagger in a vision—a memory.

"Matias could be working for Valkas," Venn pointed out.

My brow furrowed. "That makes no sense."

"It could be a trap to lure you to Gregor Island."

"Again, that doesn't make sense," I said. "I was already headed there anyway."

Venn's lips tightened, but he didn't respond.

"You know you can't talk me out of this, right?" I asked. "The only question is, are you—or anyone else—going to come with me?"

Venn finally lifted his gaze to mine, but he completely ignored the question. "You can't even go after him without the dagger, and Genevieve has it."

I crossed my arms. "So I'll get it from her. Just remind me again why we trusted her with it?"

Venn took a long breath. "So you wouldn't do anything stupid."

I stood. As much as I adored Venn, he was starting to get on my nerves. Was that supposed to happen with soulmates? The thought frustrated me even more. "This isn't stupid! This is what I'm supposed to do."

"You aren't *supposed* to do anything!" Venn shot to his feet beside me. He stole a quick glance at the patio doors. Fiona caught his eye but turned back to the lake a second later.

"But I *should*," I said in a softer tone. "The vampire curse is my fault. I have to be the one to stop it."

"It's *not* your fault, though," he argued. "You're different from the girl who created Valkas."

"Different how?" I challenged. "It was my soul. Maybe I was a different person at the time, but that doesn't matter. What matters now is that I'm the only one who can stop it. The laws and blood banks have only slowed the vampires down. They haven't stopped them. They're still out there murdering people and kidnapping them as blood slaves. They have no compassion or remorse and will do anything to serve their own purpose. Wouldn't you do something about that if you could?"

"Yes," he said, "but we have to stop Matias first. If he uses the Artifact before you get to Valkas, you'll lose your powers. You won't be able to defend yourself against Valkas. You said yourself that the Artifact doesn't work on vampires. You'll be up against him and his vampire strength without any powers of your own."

"That's exactly why I have to go. I'll never stand up to Valkas if I lose my magic. What if we fail and Matias uses the Artifact and blocks everyone's magic?

I have to get to Gregor Island, kill Valkas, and find my sister all before Matias strikes."

"Look, we won't fail. Valkas will be there when we get back."

"Will he?" I questioned. "What if the Soulless make a move before we get to Matias? What if this is my only chance? If I kill Valkas, we won't have to worry about Matias."

"And what about his successor?" Venn pointed out.

"You're asking me to sign your death certificate," I'd said to Matias. *"Why would you want that? What about your plan to cure the world?"*

"Vampirism may seem like a blessing," Matias had said. *"I could do so much with my immortality. But there are far more terrible things about it. The constant bloodlust. The emotional disconnect... Vampirism is truly a curse. Once I'm free of the curse, my successor will take my place and carry out my plan."*

"What if his successor is easier to beat?" I asked. "We could kill the vampires, then go after the Artifact."

"And what if his successor is worse?" Venn asked softly.

The room went quiet. It appeared we'd reached an impasse. He reached out to pull me into his arms, and I relaxed into his embrace, inhaling his sweet scent. My whole body shivered beneath his touch. There was no way in hell I'd ever want to abandon these strong, protective arms and the comforting smell of home. If he would just come with me...

Venn drew away slightly, and I tilted my head up to meet his dark brown eyes. His gaze flickered down to my lips, and my mouth went dry. Heaven help me. If he was going to kiss me again, I didn't know if I would ever make it to Gregor Island without him.

"Rae," he whispered, his eyes glistening. "I know danger is your thing, but this is too risky. What if Valkas finds out who you are?"

"He won't," I said with certainty. "I'll never give him the chance."

Venn sighed, still holding my gaze. "I know you think that, but—" His voice cracked, and he wrapped his arms around me tighter.

I laid my head on his chest, basking in the warmth of his embrace. Tears pricked at my eyes, and I cleared my throat. "This is a pointless argument, Venn. I know you think you can talk me out of it, but like you said, danger is my thing."

Venn paused a beat before speaking. "That's what I was afraid of."

"Besides," I said like it was no big deal, "if I don't get him this time, I'll come back in a few years and get another chance. You'll be drawn to me and recognize me and can tell me all about it."

Venn went rigid. "Rae, I don't think you understand—"

A door banged open down the hall, and Sondra rushed into the living room. "Get everyone in here. I just got a lead on where Matias is staying."

Venn's arms dropped from around me, and cold air rushed in to take his place. "How soon?"

"I'm still waiting for full details," Sondra said, "but we need to start packing. By the time dawn breaks, we're going after him."

There was no talking any sense into Venn. And I thought *I* was supposed to be the stubborn one. Which only left one option. I was doing this without him.

"Venn is going to be beyond pissed," Fiona said when I told her.

We were in the guest room we shared, packing up our stuff. I had all my belongings back since Genevieve had taken them from the apartment I'd abandoned. But I always knew our stay at her vacation home would be short-lived, so I only had to pack my hairbrush and a few dirty clothes I'd left lying at the foot of my guest bed. I'd plopped my bag on Fiona's bed and asked her to watch my stuff for me while I was gone.

Believe me, I didn't want to leave the family. They were going to consider me a flight risk until the day I died. But I would return for certain. I just had to let *someone* know so they didn't think I was kidnapped or dead or something.

"I know," I agreed with her. "I just need a head start. And I need you to make sure he doesn't come after me."

Fiona gathered her hair ties from the dresser and turned to me with a raised eyebrow. "Do you really think I can stop him?"

I sighed. "He's the one who claims this is so dangerous."

"It is!" Fiona hissed. "You should take all of us with you."

"Ryland doesn't even want me around, and you're all going after Matias anyway," I pointed out.

"Yes, because he's armed and highly dangerous." Fiona sat beside me on the bed. "He probably already has a witch lined up who's waiting on a big payday. Do you have any idea how dangerous it will be if he uses The Wise Owl? You wouldn't stand a chance against a vampire if you couldn't access your magic."

I frowned. "You've been talking to Venn, haven't you?"

"Well, yeah," Fiona admitted without shame.

"That's why you guys have to find Matias before he can use it," I said.

"Once we do, *then* we can go after Valkas. Together," she replied. "What's the rush, Rae? He's been hiding out for years. Why do you have to kill him *right now?*"

"There are a lot of reasons," I told her. I didn't think I could even begin to explain any of it. All I knew was I *had* to do it. Maybe Synchrony was pushing me toward it or something... I mean, why would I get the dagger right now, right when the threat to lose my magic loomed over my head? I just had a gut feeling that Gregor Island was where I needed to be right now.

Fiona shifted on the bed. "I don't know, Rae. It doesn't feel right, none of it. It was too convenient that Matias just handed over the dagger he spent so long searching for. You could be a pawn."

I shrugged. "That's exactly what I am to him, and I'm okay with that. I'll deal with his successor once I kill Valkas."

Fiona nervously ran her fingers through her silky red hair. "I think you should talk to Sondra."

"No," I declined immediately. "You're the only person I trust to let me go."

Fiona bit her lower lip.

"Speaking of which," I said, glancing to the dark night sky. "It's time for me to leave. Maybe you can tell everyone I went to bed?"

Fiona's eyes glistened with tears. "You're so stubborn, Rae."

I smiled, glad someone understood me.

"You're like my long-lost sister," she said, wiping at her eyes. "I didn't want you to go so soon."

I leaned over and pulled her into a hug. "Do me a favor and kick Matias's ass for me?"

Fiona gave a nervous giggle and squeezed me back. "I'll get a good one in if I get a shot."

I drew away from her and swallowed down the lump in my throat. "I'll miss you."

Fiona's voice cracked. "I'll miss you, too."

I stood from the bed and crossed the room to the window, taking nothing with me but the clothes on my back.

"Rae?" Fiona called in a small voice before I shifted.

I turned back to her, and a knot formed in my chest. "Yeah?"

"Come back in one piece, okay?"

I hesitated before answering. I wasn't about to make a promise I couldn't keep. "I'll do my best."

Then I turned to the window, shifted, and flew off into the night.

2

I'd never flown over such a long distance before, but it was easy to follow the roads to Nocton. Once inside the city limits, Genevieve's house was simple to find.

I landed at the edge of her lawn and stared up at the dark bricks that matched the night sky. The windows were dark, like the rest of the houses on her street. For some reason, I pictured Genevieve as the kind of witch who would still be up at an ungodly hour, brewing potions in her cast iron cauldron. But even witches had to sleep. She'd make an exception for me, right?

I spent far too long staring at her house, contemplating my options. Did I go up and knock on the door, hoping she was still awake? Or did I wait until morning?

The sound of scuffling footsteps in the grass caught my attention a moment too late. I'd been wrapped up in my thoughts and let my guard down because I thought this was a safe street.

My head snapped in the direction of the noise just in time to see a tall, muscular figure diving for me. My heart lurched, and I spread my wings, but I wasn't fast enough. Hands clamped around my throat, slamming my raven body into the grass. Judging by how hard he squeezed, I had to guess he was human or witch. A vamp or shifter would have a much tighter hold on me—but that didn't change the fact that it still hurt.

I shifted immediately, hoping to startle the guy. It worked. He loosened his grip on me. I got my feet beneath him and dug them into his ribs, then kicked outward. He went flying across the lawn and landed with a *thud*. He gasped for breath but jumped to his feet quickly, taking on a defensive stance.

In the light from a nearby streetlamp, I was able to make out his features. He had light skin and dark hair that was just beginning to gray at the temples.

There were age lines to his eyes that suggested he was in his late forties or early fifties. He had a straight nose and strong jaw, with a *successful businessman* vibe going on. Except for the plaid pajama pants and white t-shirt.

"What the hell?" I snapped. Did this guy seriously think he could take on a shifter?

"I don't take kindly to shifters hanging around my house," he growled. "Who sent you?"

His house?

Before I could answer, the sound of the front door opening met my ears. I was relieved to see Genevieve poke her head outside. Her short hair was tame, and she wore a silky black nightgown.

"Are you going to stay out there all night?" she called across the space between us.

I glanced to Business Guy. The look he gave me said he didn't know whether she was talking to me or him.

"You'll have to forgive my husband," Genevieve said. "If I'd have known you were coming, I would've warned him."

Business Guy glared at me. "You two know each other?"

I straightened my shirt. "As a matter of fact, yes. And I don't appreciate being attacked for it."

His lips tightened. "You were acting suspicious."

"I was *standing* here!"

"Suspiciously," he muttered.

"That's enough," Genevieve snapped. "Richard, leave our poor guest alone. Rae, come inside. I don't have all night."

I hurried up the lawn to the front door. Genevieve didn't say anything as she pulled the door open to invite me inside. Richard followed, looking embarrassed.

"I'll see you when you're finished, darling." He took Genevieve's hand and kissed it before turning down the hall.

Only when he was out of sight did I finally speak. "I'm ready for that dagger," I said, glancing around, as if I expected someone to come bursting into the house looking for me.

"I figured you'd come for it soon." She gestured to the stairs for me to follow her.

"You're just going to hand it over?" I asked, shocked. "Just like that?"

"Yes," she said simply when we reached the top. "Your family asked me to keep it safe. They didn't say safe from whom."

I let out a snort. Totally embarrassing. Genevieve cocked an eyebrow at me.

"Clearly, you know I'm doing this without their blessing," I said.

Genevieve shrugged and led me into the room at the top of the stairs. "You don't need their blessing, do you? I, for one, would like to see you kill Valkas. Together, you and this dagger are his biggest weakness."

We entered a large room lined with dark bookshelves. The drapes had been pulled over the two long windows at the other end of the room. Two plush black armchairs stood in front of a burning fire that cast shadows across the library.

Genevieve strolled over to the mantle, her nightgown billowing around her as she walked. "You'll have to excuse my husband," she said without looking back. "He's very protective and gets nervous about the kind of business I run. Please, take a seat."

I followed behind her and sank into one of the velvety chairs. My hands shook against the armrests. I couldn't believe I was going through with this. But at the same time, I never dreamed there was any other option.

Genevieve pulled a decorative box off the mantle and turned to me. It looked like a jewelry box and had a lock on the outside, though I didn't see a key anywhere in her hands. She sat across from me and waved her hand over the box. She muttered something under her breath that I couldn't understand, and the top popped open.

I inhaled a sharp breath when Genevieve turned the box toward me. The silver dagger sat on a bed of velvet material. I reached out, and my fingers curled around the handle of the blade. Warm tingles of magic spread up my arm. I felt powerful and unstoppable. *This mofo is going down!*

"Do you know how you're getting to the island?" Genevieve asked.

My grip tightened around the handle. "I was kind of going to wing it. I figured I could hitch a ride, then fly to the island."

Genevieve's eyebrows shot up. "You said it was in the middle of the Great Lakes, didn't you?"

I nodded.

"That's a long way to travel, considering you might miss it. I thought you said it was concealed by magic."

I shrugged. "I have pretty good endurance and a hell of a lot of determination. And it *was* concealed by magic—when Valkas was prisoner there."

Genevieve pressed her lips together. "If Valkas has even one witch on his side, it could very well still be concealed. The concealment charm won't be nearly as strong as the one that was on the island before he escaped, so it should be easy to break once you're close enough. The incantation *veritatem revelare*—reveal the truth—should work. The spell will be virtually undetectable since the island will only reveal itself to you and no one else. But the spell has a short range, so you have to know where you're going." She shot me a pointed expression, as if she didn't believe in me.

"I know where it is," I said confidently. I'd never forget where Clarita placed the mark on that map. It was my only connection to Jenna.

Genevieve stood. "Richard will drive you, then you'll take a boat as close as you can get to the island. You can fly the rest of the way. Remember the incantation."

"*Veritatem revelare,*" I repeated.

"Good," Genevieve said with a nod. "When would you like to leave?"

I hesitated. By now, Fiona had surely dropped the bomb on where I was headed. No doubt Venn was already on his way to stop me. What was his deal, anyway?

"As soon as possible," I answered.

"I'll have Richard get the car." Genevieve started toward the door, but she stopped halfway there and turned back toward me. "Oh, and Rae?"

"Yeah?" My throat tightened. I didn't like the tone of voice she used, as if she was about to break some terrible news.

Genevieve cleared her throat, but she held her head up high and confident. "You should know that there's always more than one way off an island."

I furrowed my brow. It sounded ominous, like she thought I might get trapped on Gregor Island. "I thought witches couldn't tell the future."

She shook her head. "I can't. I'm just letting you know that even when strong bridges crumble, there's always another path to take."

3

I stood at the end of the marina, staring out into the vast water. It was like standing at the edge of the ocean. Water stretched across the landscape as far as the eye could see, and waves lapped at the rocky shore. Unlike the beautiful blue skies and clear water I'd seen when I visited the ocean as a kid, Lake Michigan was covered in a gray haze, and the horizon was invisible behind a dense layer of fog. The early morning air was cool, and I couldn't see the sun behind a thick layer of clouds. I wrapped my exposed arms around myself and clutched the dagger tightly in my hand.

Jenna was somewhere out there. I was so close to her now… yet so far away.

"Time to go."

I turned to see Richard standing behind me. He gestured to one of the motorboats parked at the edge of the dock and held tightly to the keys he'd rented.

"You know where you're going?" he asked with a raised eyebrow.

I nodded. "If you have a map, I can show you exactly where it is."

"Follow me."

I climbed onto the boat behind him. It was the nicest boat I'd ever been on, with an enclosed cabin and fancy leather seats for sunbathing. It wasn't big enough to live on, but I could probably sell it and buy a house in a cheap neighborhood.

Richard let me inside, and I pointed out our destination on the navigation screen. He started up the boat and began the long journey across the water. I stood outside the cabin, clutching on to the metal railing and letting the wind rush through my hair. I barely registered the cold air since I was concentrating so hard on the water in front of me, searching for any signs of a hidden island.

After what felt like hours, Richard slowed the boat until we left no wake behind.

"We're close," Richard said, "but we have a large area to search."

I closed my eyes, concentrating hard on the energy around me. If there was magic concealing the island, I should be able to feel it. I felt nothing but damp air on my skin.

"Keep going," I stated confidently.

Richard didn't even question me. He increased our speed slightly, though not as fast as before.

After several minutes, the faintest feeling of magic tingled across my arms like static electricity. I took another deep breath, letting out all the tension in my shoulders. My senses were on high alert. I heard the water lapping against the side of the boat, smelled and tasted the humidity in the air, and felt the faintest of breezes across my skin.

"We're getting closer," I said.

The farther we went, the more I felt that magical tingle. It was barely there, not nearly as powerful as the magic that radiated off The Wise Owl. I wouldn't have even felt it if I hadn't been paying attention. But it filled my heart with a sense of hope. Jenna didn't have to wait much longer.

Richard slowed the boat again as the fog thickened, blanketing the water until we could barely see in front of us.

"We're here," I said, more to myself than to Richard.

He pulled back on the throttle and killed the engine. The boat gently cut through the water, propelled along by our momentum. Without the sound of the engine to distract me, the magic felt stronger. It tingled up my arms and down my spine like a hundred tiny ants crawling across my skin.

"*The full moon is shining, the stars glitter above, the wind whispers softly, good-night my love.*" I closed my eyes and whispered the tune to my mother's lullaby. I let it carry me to another place, a happy place, where all magic was possible.

In my head, her voice called back to me. *You can do this, Rachel.*

I was born to do this, I replied.

My eyes sprang open, and the incantation dropped from my lips. "*Veritatem revelare.*"

Straight in front of me, the fog parted, revealing huge boulders jutting out from the water fifty yards off the side of the boat. The boulders led like stepping stones to the edge of a rocky cliff. The cliff spanned hundreds of yards, but it barely covered the full length of the island. The island wasn't huge by any means, but it had to be at least fifty acres. Atop the cliff sat a lush green forest, full of all different types of trees, from deciduous varieties to evergreens. Just above the trees, I saw the peaks of a large building and several chimneys reaching up into the sky. It looked like it might be a mansion.

A sense of pride washed over me. I'd found it. I'd found Gregor Island!

I turned to Richard. "It's here."

His eyes continued to scan the water. He couldn't see it. The incantation Genevieve had given me only lifted the concealment charm for me.

"You're sure?" he asked.

"Yes. Please tell your wife thank you."

"Wait." Richard stopped me before I could leave. "Should I stay here and wait for you?"

I shook my head. I didn't know how long it would take me to find Jenna. "Your only job was to get me here. I'll find my own way back."

With that, I shifted and scooped up the dagger in my talons, then took off. I soared high above Gregor Island, trying to take in as much of the layout as I could. In the center of it all was a huge structure bigger than Maliya's mansion. It reminded me of a French chateau, with high towers stretching above the peaked roof. There were rows upon rows of windows set into the brick siding. A stone pathway led from the main doors and into the surrounding forest.

High above the island, I could see that the trees thinned into long, narrow strips that spiderwebbed away from the chateau. It looked like there were paths or roadways beneath me, but I couldn't see through the forest to the earth. One pathway led far away from the chateau, ending at a wide clearing that housed a cluster of small wood cabins. There must've been at least fifty of them. They reminded me of the single-room cabins we slept in at camp when I was a kid. There'd been enough room for two bunk beds and a small table in the corner to keep our stuff.

A sandy beach stretched out from the cabin community and down to the shoreline. Two figures sat on the beach, but other than that, the community was quiet.

The cabins intrigued me. Why would the Soulless bother building cabins on their island if they already had a beautiful chateau to live in?

The answer struck me the moment I questioned it. The cabins were the blood slaves' quarters.

I dropped lower in the sky, swooping down to land on a tree branch near the farthest cabin from the beach. I clutched the dagger in one talon and the tree branch in the other, spreading my wings out to keep my body balanced until the limb stopped shaking beneath my weight. Curiously, I peered into one of the windows, but all I saw was darkness. I jumped to the next branch over, closer to the window. Still nothing. It looked as if a pair of dark curtains had been drawn closed, blocking my view of the inside.

If Jenna was here—and I knew she had to be—she'd no doubt be in one of these cabins. *Time to finally see my sister again.*

Flying over to the next tree branch, I came in closer to the second cabin and looked inside. I saw that the curtains were open and the window cracked. The daylight spilled inside just enough that I could see a figure lying on a bed, the sheets pulled up to his or her chin. I couldn't see the person's face, though, just the shape of a body sleeping there.

It could be Jenna, I thought hopefully.

Then the figure shifted. A mop of blond hair came into view, and I noticed the broad shoulders. Definitely not Jenna.

Inching my way down the branch and closer to the buildings, I peered into the third cabin's window. This one was arranged differently than the last. I could easily see two beds from my perch outside the window. Both were occupied, and each person's chest rose and fell slowly.

I glanced to the sky. The sun was hidden behind the clouds, but it must've been the middle of the day already. If everyone was asleep, it meant the Soulless had them on a schedule, one that kept them awake at night with the vampires.

The sound of breaking twigs stole my attention, and my gaze snapped in the direction of the noise. A man with skinny arms and a long nose tore through the forest. He wore a tattered white t-shirt with jeans and black boots, and a pair of keys jingled in his hands. He threw frightened glances behind his shoulder.

I went completely rigid, hoping he wouldn't spot me high above him in the tree. A huge black bird holding a dagger was more than a little suspicious.

To my relief, he didn't notice me. His feet skidded in the dirt as he nearly missed his turn. He caught himself and raced between the first two cabins. The sound of a door opening met my ears. I inched down my branch until I had a better view inside the second cabin. The blond mop-headed guy I'd seen sleeping sat bolt upright in bed, frightened by the arrival of his roommate.

"What the bloody hell?" Mop Head snapped before lowering his voice, which carried through the open window. "What are you doing?"

"I'm done with this shit," Skinny Guy breathed. "It's time to go."

"What?" Mop Head replied in disbelief.

"I said *it's time to go*," Skinny Guy emphasized. "We're getting off this island." He dangled the keys in front of Mop Head's face, grinning.

Mop Head's eyes widened in horror. "Are you insane?"

Skinny Guy shrugged. "Maybe a little."

"Did you just steal the keys to the Soulless' boat?" Mop Head hissed. "Do you have any idea—?"

I didn't hear the rest of what he said as the sound of an engine roared through the forest. Not just one engine, I quickly realized. An entire fleet of them. And they were coming right this way.

I shrank further back into the trees to conceal myself, but I kept my eyes on the cabin window. Mop Head was out of bed now, his fists clenched tightly as he hissed in low whispers at his roommate. I couldn't hear what he was saying, but it did *not* look good. Skinny Guy tried to make a run for it, but Mop Head grabbed him by the collar.

"I'm *not* taking the fall for this!" he shouted.

Just then, an ATV came tearing through the forest at high-speed. It was just a blur on the other side of the cabins. The four-wheeler stopped abruptly in front of Skinny Guy's cabin. He'd left the door open, so I could see some of what was going on. At least six other ATVs stopped behind it.

Skinny Guy and Mop Head were engaged in a scuffle now, fighting for the keys that had fallen on the floor. Mop Head was telling him to give the keys back, while Skinny Guy was shouting for them to make a run for it.

"Do you know what you've done?" Mop Head demanded. "You've killed us both!"

I stared through the window and out the open door, my eyes locked on the large figure riding the first ATV. Every inch of his body was covered in black clothing. He even wore a long-sleeved turtleneck shirt, with leather gloves and a tinted black motorcycle helmet.

He swung his leg over the seat of his four-wheeler and stood, throwing his shoulders back confidently. He must've been at least six-foot-five, with broad shoulders and thick biceps. His footsteps were heavy, *thudding* against the earth as if in warning.

Skinny Guy and Mop Head both went silent. Their bodies trembled as they turned to look at him.

It wasn't until the guy stepped inside the cabin that he pulled his helmet off. He was hauntingly beautiful, with a straight nose, strong jaw, and piercing silver eyes. He had pale skin and dirty blond hair. Most girls would swoon over him. Me? I was already itching to drive my dagger through his heart.

Rage knitted in his tight eyebrows, and his jaw clenched. The man looked terrifying when he was angry, like he could snap a person in half in one swift, strong motion. Though he was conventionally attractive, there was *nothing* beautiful about him. It was like he brought a darkness with him when he stepped into the room. And I knew exactly why.

The man was Valkas.

I'd seen photos of him before. They always gave me an uneasy feeling, and my guts twisted at the sight of him. Seeing him up close was even worse. After everything he'd done, I prayed he would suffer a fate far worse than my dagger.

Valkas smirked. He didn't even glance at the men as he pulled the leather gloves off his hands, finger by finger. "Well, well, well... what do we have here?" There was a hint of a British accent to his tone, but it was muddled, like he'd been to enough areas of the world that no single accent had stuck with him.

Skinny Guy dropped the keys at Valkas's feet and backed up slowly. "We... we found these in the woods."

Valkas finally looked up, then cocked his head. "Is that so?" The words rolled off his tongue like poison. "Because my men say someone with your description stole them from the boathouse."

Mop Head dropped to his knees. "Please, sir. Spare me. I had no idea."

Valkas's arm swung out, and the back of his hand cracked against the side of Mop Head's face. I flinched, but I couldn't tear my eyes away.

"You'll speak only when spoken to!" Valkas roared. His face twisted in rage, and spittle flew from his mouth. "And I will be addressed as *Lord* for as long as you live on this godforsaken island."

Lord Valkas. Oh God. This guy was worse than I thought. And vain as hell.

I should've gone in there and killed him on the spot, but there were five other faceless guys standing behind him, their arms crossed. They all wore motorcycle helmets, so I couldn't see their eyes, but I guessed they were all vamps. There was only one man, a sixth one, whose skin was exposed. He was almost as big as Valkas, with tan skin and slicked-back dark hair. I was strong, but not strong enough to fight them all off at once. I had to attack Valkas when he was alone. And until then, I couldn't risk exposing myself... no matter what.

"*You*," Valkas snarled, turning on Skinny Guy.

"I-I'm sorry, sir—Lord," Skinny Guy stuttered, lowering his head. "It won't happen again, Lord Valkas."

Valkas smirked. "No, I don't imagine it will."

In the blink of an eye, Valkas's hand shot forward, slamming Skinny Guy into the wall as his hand sank into his chest. Skinny Guy's eyes went as wide as golf balls, and his mouth hung open, as if he was trying to inhale a breath that didn't come. My whole body gave a start. I thought my eyes were playing tricks on me, until Valkas pulled away, producing a deep red meaty organ the size of his fist. *A heart.*

It was like watching a scene from a horror movie, except it was playing out right in front of my eyes. I was beyond nauseous. Normally, I could handle this kind of thing, but my head spun, and I had to grip on tighter to the tree branch to keep from falling to the ground. The sick sensation that slammed into my gut only lasted a split second before rage bubbled up to replace it. Valkas was pure evil, and he was going straight to hell if I had anything to say about it.

Skinny Guy's limp body slumped down the wall and to the floor. Mop Head kept his head low and didn't make a sound, no doubt afraid that he'd be next.

Valkas didn't even spare him a glance as he strolled out the door, the warm, fresh heart still clutched in his hands. He didn't even bother placing the helmet back on his head to protect his skin from the sun. There was a thick enough cloud cover that I was sure he'd only walk away with mere first-degree burns.

"I know you're all awake!" Valkas boomed. "All slaves are to be out of their cabins by the time I count to five. One... Two... Three..."

All throughout the community, cabin doors began to swing open. People flooded out onto the dirt paths. I couldn't see most of them, but I could hear the scuffle of footsteps. Valkas paced along the dirt path and out of my view.

I hesitated. I didn't come all this way just to be caught. But the temptation was just too great. I *had* to see if Jenna was somewhere in that mass of people.

I spread my wings and lifted off my perch, landing on the roof of the cabin. I clutched the dagger tightly in one talon and hopped forward until I could see Valkas below me.

He held the heart high above his head for everyone to see. "Four... Five."

Men and women stood outside their cabins in their pajamas. I expected them to be clutching each other and crying in fear, but all emotion was hidden away. It was like they'd come to expect this level of violence from Valkas, like they knew they'd be punished for cowering in fear of him. One woman slid her hand into another lady's fingers, and a male had paled to the point where he looked like he might vomit. Other than that, the blood slaves swallowed down their disgust.

My eyes scanned the crowd, and my heart *pitter-pattered* in anticipation. I didn't see Jenna anywhere.

"*This* is what happens to people who steal from me," Valkas boomed. "See to it that it doesn't happen again."

Valkas flung the heart across the ground, snarling in disgust. He turned away before it finished rolling. It stopped at a woman's feet, coated in dirt. She took a step back, unable to hide the horror in her expression.

Valkas didn't even notice. He licked the blood from his fingers and turned to the guy with the slicked-back hair. He gestured to the cabin. "Clean this mess up, Rogers."

Stoically, he placed his gloves back on his hands, like the remaining blood didn't bother him one bit. One of his men hurried over with Valkas's helmet. Valkas snatched it from his hands and situated it on his head as he swung his leg over the seat of the ATV. The engine roared to life, and he sped off into the forest. Three of his men took off behind him, while the other three stayed to follow orders.

Everyone remained frozen like statues as Rogers stepped forward. He waved his hand, and the next thing I knew, Skinny Guy's body was floating out of the cabin like it was suspended by invisible ropes.

A *witch*, I realized in disgust. What kind of person would pledge himself to the Soulless? Valkas must've promised a very generous deal.

The witch dropped the body, slumping it over the back of one of the ATVs. My stomach twisted at the sight of Skinny Guy's eyes staring lifelessly toward the sky.

It wasn't until Valkas's men had disappeared into the woods behind him that the people below me finally moved. They all took a collective breath, as if they'd been holding it until now. Even I hadn't realized my lungs were about to implode from the pressure. I inhaled deeply through my beak, trying to shake off the uneasy feeling that had settled in my feathers.

For the first time since Valkas's arrival, emotions began to cross people's faces. The whole clearing broke out into whispers. People grabbed on to each other for comfort. One girl threw her hand over her mouth and raced behind a cabin to spew her guts. Another dropped to her knees and covered her face with her hands while she cried. Two guys came up behind her and settled gentle, comforting hands on her shoulders.

"We're here for you," one of them told her.

Three other women quickly joined them, surrounding the younger woman to make sure she was all right. At least six people entered the cabin I was perched on top of. I could hear their voices reassuring Mop Head.

"It's not your fault," a male voice said.

"We'll get this cleaned up," a woman added.

It struck me how much these people cared for each other. No one turned into their cabins to leave the mess for someone else. They acted like one big family, like a community.

It should've warmed my heart, but I was still shaking in rage. Valkas had aptly named his gang of vampires. *Soulless.* How could anyone with a soul be capable of such evil?

The young woman couldn't stop her sobs. The group surrounding her helped her to her feet and into a nearby cabin. My breathing grew ragged as the sound of her cries echoed in my ears.

This is what happens to people who steal from me.

Surely theft wasn't worthy of a death sentence. The man was an innocent captive; of course he wanted a way off this island. I didn't even want to think about what the Soulless had done to him to drive him toward risking his life like that.

Whatever it was, I couldn't sit around contemplating the possibilities. My gaze swept across the clearing again, but Jenna was nowhere in sight. Every fiber of my being told me that Jenna was somewhere on this island. If she wasn't here with the other blood slaves, that meant she must've been up at the chateau. I'd go there, find Jenna, and kill Valkas. Once he and his men were gone, I'd get all these people safely off Gregor Island.

Mind made up, I launched myself into the air in the direction of the chateau.

4

I swooped down at a back entrance to the building. The trees were close and concealed me, but since I didn't see anyone nearby, I shifted into human form. It'd be easier to navigate around the chateau that way. Glancing upward toward the tall windows, I saw that the curtains were drawn on all of them. After determining the coast was clear, I raced across the space between the trees and the backdoor, keeping the dagger clutched tightly in my hand.

The doorknob twisted easily, and I peeked inside. I breathed a sigh of relief when I saw that the hallway was empty. Quietly, I slipped in. I was careful to close the door behind me as softly as I could. As a shifter, the vampires wouldn't hear me coming by my heartbeat or my breathing, but they'd definitely hear a door banging shut and announcing my arrival.

I started down the narrow hallway, taking soft steps. Light flickered across the walls from the fire within the sconces on the walls. It definitely gave off a *haunted house* vibe, which only made me smile. Haunted houses were totally my thing.

The various doorways on either side of the hall were all closed, so I couldn't see where they led. I itched to peek into one of the doors just to see if Jenna was inside, but I wasn't too keen on waking a group of vampires. I'd scope everything out first to get a feel for where Jenna might be.

I reached the end of the hall and came to a second hallway. This one was wider than the last, with big arches cut out in the wall that revealed a huge seating area. The drapes were drawn, and a huge candelabra chandelier hung from the ceiling, lighting up the room. There were no lamps or overhead bulbs, no electricity of any kind, and that gave the place an even more unique, antique vibe.

I could hardly take in the grandeur of the chateau. Whoever had designed it certainly had good taste. The floors were all polished hardwood and the walls were plain white, but there was an architectural beauty to the place. In the large room beyond the arches, sofa upon sofa sat elegantly arranged in various seating areas, with a big grand piano in the corner. Had this really been where Valkas had been imprisoned all those years? I'd been picturing him hanging out in a deep, dark cave or something on a deserted island. This place was practically a castle.

A door banged loudly toward the end of the wide hallway, where I could see it opened up to a large foyer. I caught sight of a group of men in dark clothing and immediately crouched down low. Peeking around the corner, I saw Valkas's three men remove their helmets. As I predicted, they all had matching pale skin.

"Caleb, wake the girls and bring them to my room." Valkas's voice carried down the hall. "Punishing slaves makes me thirsty."

The girls? Blood slaves?

Jenna!

I shot up from where I was crouched but hesitated. My eyes followed the men as they dispersed. Valkas started up a grand staircase, while the other men went in opposite directions. I had no way of knowing which one was Caleb. Otherwise, I would've followed the bastard to find my sister.

There was only one other easy solution. Follow Valkas and wait for Caleb to bring Jenna back to his room.

One of the vamps was headed my way, so I crept back down the hall and crouched behind a long, decorative table. I held my breath as the vamp continued past the large sitting room with the grand piano in it.

As soon as I heard his footsteps fade, I was back on my feet, peeking out into the wider hallway. It was deserted, so I took my chance and hurried down it. My heart slammed against my rib cage, but not because I was scared. If anything, I was *excited*. I was going to see my sister again. These vampires were going to die at my hand. This was a freaking thrill ride!

When I reached the foyer, the sound of footsteps in the hall above the grand staircase met my ears. I glanced around quickly, but the foyer was empty. The only decorations were mirrors and paintings on the walls, unlike the rest of the chateau, where there was a sofa, table, dresser, or some other piece of furniture every few feet. I rushed into the corner beneath the stairs and held my breath, praying that whomever it was wouldn't see me through the darkness.

Who was I kidding? It was sure to be a vampire. If he took one look at where I stood, he wouldn't miss me. I held my dagger up, poised for attack if it came to that.

The man's footsteps pounded down the stairs above my head. When he reached the bottom, he slipped his motorcycle helmet back on and exited out the front doors.

I remained frozen in the corner, forcing my breathing to slow and listening to the sounds around me. The building was eerily quiet. Taking my chance, I rushed out of the shadows and hurried up the stairs with light footsteps.

When I reached the top, I found a maze of hallways, all veering off in different directions. I had no way of knowing which way I'd find Valkas. So I took a wild guess. I started down the hallway to my left, passing by door after door. Something told me Valkas's room would be a bit over the top and easy to spot, so I skipped all the plain doors and headed to the pair of double doors at the end of the hall. I pressed my ear to it and heard muffled voices inside.

"Lord Valkas does not like to be woken in the middle of the day," a gruff voice said.

Definitely not Valkas's. The way he spoke, it didn't even sound like Valkas was in the room, but I continued listening to be sure.

"This incident will reflect poorly on all of us," Gruff Voice continued.

"Yes, of course, sir," another man replied.

"This never should've happened in the first place," Gruff Voice said. "If you men down at the boathouse were paying the slightest bit of attention, it wouldn't have." He spoke in such a harsh tone that it made me flinch. "See to it that it doesn't happen again."

"Yes, sir. It won't."

"Excuse me a moment," Gruff Voice interrupted.

Silence followed for several seconds. I had no idea what was going on behind that door. Then the sound of the floor creaking just on the other side met my ear.

I leapt away instantly and took the first hiding place I could find—a large, decorative vase situated in the corner of the hall. I shrank to my raven form and hugged the wall, holding my breath. My dagger had fallen from my hand and lay at my feet.

I heard the door swing open. In the reflection from one of the mirrors on the wall, I saw a man stick his head out the door and glance around. Something in his features hinted at old age, but his skin had been smoothed out, and there wasn't a gray hair on his head. Freaking vampire curse turning them all into the most beautiful versions of themselves. It was like cosmetics on steroids.

He narrowed his silver eyes and pursed his lips, looking so angry it rivaled Valkas's terrifying features. The man gave me chills.

He stood there for what felt like a full minute, frozen in the doorway. If it weren't for his eyes scanning the hall, I might've mistaken him for a statue. He sniffed the air.

He can't smell me, I told myself as reassurance. It was true that he couldn't smell me the way he could smell humans, but perhaps he could sense me in other ways? The metallic smell of my dagger? The scent of laundry detergent on my clothes? Perhaps he could even sense the shift in the air when I breathed.

Usually by now I would've already staked the vamp through the heart, not giving him enough time to assess my presence, but I wasn't about to alert the whole house I was here. Killing him would be reckless and stupid and… *fun.*

He stepped out into the hall. I could see his polished black shoe from where I crouched behind the vase.

He doesn't see you. He'll give up, I told myself.

But I was a liar. Because he'd already seen me, and his hand was headed straight for me.

Instinct took over. I shifted just before his fingers touched my feathers. In a quick motion, I threw my hands upward to connect with his wrist as I ducked out of the way. I used my strength against his agility, following the momentum of his hand upward. And then I yanked down, causing him to flip through the air and land with a hard *thud* on the floor.

I reached for my dagger. Before I had my fingers around the handle, he'd already leapt to his feet. His knee swung upward, connecting with my nose. Pain shot out through my face, which turned out to be a blessing. He caught sight of the blood trickling down my face and paused momentarily. Hunger burned in his eyes.

It was just enough time for me to kick my leg out beneath him and knock him back on his ass. Before he could react, I was on top of him, shoving my dagger through his heart. He crumbled into a pile of ash beneath me.

I didn't even have a moment to relish in my victory. A split second later, the second guy was in the doorway. This man was younger than the last, though he had the same good looks. A moment of shock crossed his silver eyes.

I leapt to my feet and sprang on him. He reeled backward and slammed into one of the bookshelves in the room. He spread his arms out to catch himself. His fingers curled around one of the thick books, and he hurled it at me. The thick, pointed corner smashed just above my right eyebrow, making me see red.

I cursed under my breath, clutching my forehead, which was warm and sticky from blood. All he did was smirk.

"That freaking hurt, jackhole," I snapped at him.

"I've got plenty more where that came from." He wiggled his eyebrows and lifted another book. "Who are you, and what are you doing here?"

"Seriously?" I asked, totally unamused. "We're going to talk this out?"

He hurled the second book at me, but I ducked. It soared over my head and crashed into a shelf on the other side of the room.

I sprang back to my feet. "Hey, now. We don't want to wake everyone."

"Then tell me who you are," he demanded.

"So you can kill me?" I shrugged. "Nah, I'm not really one for talking."

He cracked his knuckles. "Have it your way."

He dove toward me. His shoulder smashed into my abdomen, and his arms curled around my middle. I didn't even try to dodge out of the way. I let him take me to the ground.

As his fingers clamped around my throat, I swung my dagger downward into his back. His eyes went wide, and he inhaled a sharp breath, then… nothing. His clothes fell on top of me as his body turned to ash.

I squeezed my eyes shut and closed my mouth to keep from getting it in my face. I felt the ash rain down on my skin, but I shook it off.

After I sat up, I used the guy's suit to wipe the blood from my face. Outside the door, I grabbed Gruff Voice's clothes, cleaned up as much ash from both of them as I could, and shoved their clothes into a drawer in the desk across the room. Surely, I didn't have long before someone noticed the two were missing, but I didn't need someone walking in on the evidence and launching a search party before I got Jenna out of here.

Once completed, I hurried out of the library and down the hall. When I reached the top of the balcony where I'd started, I decided to try the hall to the right. It was identical to the last, only mirrored. I got the strangest sense of *déjà vu.*

When I reached the pair of double doors on the end, they were open a crack. I tiptoed forward and peeked inside.

At first, I saw nothing but an empty four-poster bed. Thin red fabric draped across the canopy, and the sheets were crumpled up in the middle, as if the owner had just gotten out of bed.

Then I saw him. The blond hair, the broad shoulders... it was definitely Valkas. I couldn't take my eyes off of him as he paced around the room. He looked distressed as he raked his fingers through his hair, then curled his hands into fists at his sides. Just looking at him made my insides burn with rage. All I could think about were all the people he'd killed when he'd rampaged across the States eight years ago. All the people he'd changed into vampires and the ones that they'd killed and enslaved in turn. How he'd forced Elizabeth to cast the spell that changed him. He was a monster then, and he was a monster now.

But worse than all of that, he'd ordered his men to kidnap my sister. And I'd be damned if he didn't pay for that.

He was alone. No one was around. All that stood between me and him was a thin wooden door. All it took was one move, one stab through the heart.

Now was my time, before Caleb returned with the girls. I could hardly believe this was happening. All I had to do was slip inside and kill him. This would all be over soon.

Valkas sat on the bed with his back to the door. He reached for an unlit candle on the nightstand and tilted it to the one that was burning.

Now! Do it now!

I didn't second guess the little voice in my head. I pushed on the door, and it swung easily under my weight just enough for me to slip inside. I felt like a ninja as I tiptoed across the floor. My footsteps were so quiet across the carpet that Valkas didn't notice me. He was too preoccupied lighting his candles.

My heart pummeled against my rib cage as I lifted my dagger, careful not to make a noise. I held my breath so tightly it felt like my lungs might explode. But I barely noticed, because I was on Valkas's island, in his chateau, in his bedroom, and I was half a second away from killing him.

The world would rejoice. I didn't even care if anyone recognized me for what I'd done. All I cared about was getting rid of the vampires once and for all.

Goodbye, filthy vamps! No one will miss you.

I thrust my blade downward.

But my hand never made it to his back. Valkas whirled around and caught my wrist without half an inch to spare. My heart leapt into my throat. He yanked on me so hard it felt like my arm was going to rip off, spun me around, and pinned me to the bed.

Holy hell! Vamps were fast, but I'd never seen one move *that* fast! I probably had freaking whiplash from the bastard.

"Mm…" He straddled me, pressing my hips into the bed and leaning in so closely that I could smell the copper on his breath. "What's this?"

Hell! What have I done?

My mind instantly flickered to Venn. Maybe he'd been right.

Valkas's eyes roamed over me, and he inhaled deeply. Pleasure crossed his expression, and I thought I might throw up in his face. I tried to struggle out of his hold, but the vamp was holding on tight. He was even stronger than Ryland. He squeezed my wrist so tightly I knew it would bruise, but I didn't drop the dagger. I only curled my fingers around it tighter.

"A shifter?" he asked with a smirk, biting his lower lip like it pleased him. "And not one of mine."

"I'm not here to talk," I snapped, then I threw my head forward into his nose.

The top of my head throbbed from where they'd connected, but he barely reacted apart from tightening his hold on me. I writhed beneath him, trying to find a way free. But I'd already broken my one rule about vampires. *Never let them get the upper hand.*

Valkas laughed, a terrible laugh that made me nauseous. "Oh, you're a fighter, too?" he mocked.

"Go to hell." I spit in his face.

He didn't even bother wiping it from his eyes. Instead, he leaned down until his lips were at my ear. For a second, I thought he might bite me, which by the way was a total *never gonna happen*.

But he didn't bite me. All he did was whisper in my ear. And those words were enough to make my blood run cold.

"I'm going to have fun with you."

5

I thrust my hips upward. It bought me just enough space to turn to the side. I grabbed hold of one of the bed posts with my free hand and yanked myself across the bed. I managed to get one foot free, and I kicked it up under his chin.

He responded by tugging hard on my arm, throwing me back down on the bed. I held in my cry of pain as the muscles in my shoulder tore. I kicked my feet out again, trying to struggle free, but he knelt on top of my chest, looming over me. He pressed down so hard that I gasped for breath.

"*Ardeat ignis*," I muttered under my breath. I expected fire to come shooting out of my palms and burn his hand, but all that happened was the surface of my skin heated a little.

"*Fulgur*." I tested the incantation for lightning. Nothing happened.

Reality hit me like a ton of bricks. My magic wasn't going to save me this time.

Valkas laughed. "A shifter *and* a witch? Such a wonderful combination." Squeezing my wrists tightly with one hand, he wrenched the dagger from me with the other.

It was my one hope of making it out of here alive. If I couldn't fight him when he was alone and unarmed with the one weapon in the world that could kill him, how did I ever stand a chance? I felt all my hope drain out of me at once, and I began to panic. I clawed at anything I could: his face, his arms, and the leg pressing down on my chest. Every inch of my body felt alive with fire as a panicked rage tore through me. I would've screamed if I could catch my breath.

"Now, now, dear shifter," he said calmly, eyeing the dagger with interest. "If you don't start treating me with respect, I may just have to use your very own weapon on you."

Like hell you will!

I threw my fist so hard at his face that his body lifted off of me. I inhaled a greedy breath the same time my foot swung outward and connected with his hand. The dagger flew out of his grasp and slid across the floor toward the door. I immediately jumped off the bed and dove for it.

Mid-air, something caught my foot, and I fell to the ground with a hard crash. I caught myself, but I was a half an inch away from a second bloody nose. A split-second later, I felt my body being dragged across the floor, away from the dagger. I reached out for anything, clawing at the carpet. My hand finally found the foot of the bed, and I grabbed on tight.

To my surprise, Valkas dropped me. I sprang to my feet again, but he was in front of me in less than a second, blocking my path to the dagger and to the door.

I wasn't about to give up so easily. After a split-second to come up with a plan, I swung out my leg and my heel connected with one of the bed posts. The entire thing shattered, sending wood splinters everywhere. The top beam of the canopy sagged without its support. I grabbed the closest splinter—a big, thick one with a sharp, jagged end—and held it out in front of me.

Valkas stood still but looked ready for me, like I was some little puppy he was trying to corner. "Oh, darling," he sang. "It'd be a shame to kill you. You amuse me. That isn't going to kill me."

"It will certainly slow you down," I replied.

Valkas's lips curled up into an evil smirk. "You are quite the resolute assassin, aren't you?"

"*Resolute assassin?*" I repeated, narrowing my eyes at him.

Valkas waved his hand. "Yes, *resolute*. Determined. Unwavering. You'll do whatever it takes to fulfill your cause."

"I know what it means," I snapped. "And you're damn straight I'll do whatever it takes."

I lunged for him again. I swore I almost had him, but he dodged at the last millisecond and used my momentum against me. His palm slammed into my back, sending me smashing into the floor so hard it knocked the wind out of me.

Valkas reached for the red sheet on the bed and tore a chunk off so fast I barely saw it. He jumped on top of me again and pinned my wrists together. He tried to tie the fabric around them, but it only tore as I fought against it. I smirked a little. Even Lord Valkas couldn't keep this girl tied down.

The sound of footsteps in the hall caught my ears. Was that a glimmer of hope I heard?

"Out!" Valkas shouted before I could even turn to see who it was.

I heard the door click shut. *Well, crap!*

"You want to play rough?" Valkas growled in my ear. "We'll play rough."

His hand fisted in my hair, and he tugged *hard*.

"Ow!" I cried, cursing.

His palm cracked against the side of my face so hard my head spun. Then I felt the cool metal of the dagger touch my neck. I immediately went still. Valkas's face swam in front of my view.

"Why are you here?" he demanded.

"You killed my parents. Kidnapped my sister. Murdered thousands. Take your pick," I replied, disgusted.

Valkas smiled, like I wasn't listing off his crimes but rather his accomplishments. "I'll take them all, darling."

Ew! Was he going to keep calling me that? It sounded horrible on his tongue.

"Or you could just go to hell," I retorted.

The dagger pressed tighter against my skin. This was it. I was going to die. Somehow, I kind of always knew it'd happen at the hands of a vampire, though I'd always hoped it wouldn't. At least it would be quick. Better to die at the hands of a vampire than to be turned into one.

But he didn't. He just sat there looming over me, his nostrils flaring.

"Go on. Do it," I insisted. "Why aren't you killing me?"

He tilted his head. "And risk you reincarnating just to come after me again? I don't think so."

The blood drained from my face, and my breathing stalled. How did he know?

Valkas drew away from me slowly. It was almost like he was letting me go, but I couldn't just leave now. He stood and sat on the bed, leaving me on the floor. I pushed myself to a sitting position, but I otherwise didn't move. For one, I was dead if I did. And two, I had questions that needed answering.

"Funny thing about this dagger," Valkas said, like he was sitting down a child to tell them a story. "I've seen it before. It's the only thing that can kill me." His eyes darted from the dagger to me, and he stared at me with those evil eyes. "*But*, there's only one person in the world who can use it. Another has tried and didn't succeed. What makes you think you can?"

My jaw tensed, and I kept it locked tight. The way he asked the question suggested he already knew the answer.

Valkas stood and began pacing around the room. My heart pummeled against my rib cage. I was starting to question that whole haunted house thing. It wasn't as fun when the real monsters came out to play.

"I have a theory," Valkas announced. "I think that bastard who staked this dagger through my heart eight years ago realized his mistake. I think he went searching for the one person who could kill me." His eyes connected with mine. "And I think he found her."

Oh, shit! Nothing gets past this guy, does it?

I swallowed hard. "And what if he did?"

He leaned against the desk in the corner, looking amused. "Then I think I'm going to trap her soul. But first, I'm going to have some fun with her."

I clenched my jaw. "And what if she, say, kills herself before you could do that? Assuming you even *know* how to trap a soul."

Valkas smirked. "I have my ways. But I trust that she'll keep herself alive. Because if she doesn't do *exactly* as I say, I'll torture her sister to the point where it'll make the devil look like a fairytale hero."

My knees shook, and they weren't even holding me up. "You're bluffing," I accused. "I want to see her."

Valkas straightened. "Oh, darling. I *never* bluff when it comes to torture. I'll let Jenna know you said hello."

Time altogether stopped when he said my sister's name. What. The. Hell?

Valkas grinned and spread his arms out wide. "Shall we begin?"

6

I had to remind myself that there were certain things in life far worse than death. Death wasn't actually that scary once I thought about it. I'd certainly miss Jenna if she died, the same way I missed my parents, but at least she'd be free of captivity. At least she'd have a chance to reincarnate and start over again.

But if I didn't comply, Valkas would torture her. I couldn't even bring myself to think about the things he would do to her, considering he was the guy who just this morning had ripped a guy's heart fresh from his chest. What would Jenna endure if I didn't do as I was told?

My body shuddered just thinking about it.

"I want to see proof she's still alive," I demanded.

Valkas clicked his tongue. "I don't negotiate."

I didn't trust Valkas one bit, but I found myself trusting him on this. Jenna was here, and he *would* torture her to hurt me.

I wasn't the kind of girl who did as she was told. I went against all the rules if I thought it was the right thing to do. But right now, complying was the right thing. It was the only way to spare Jenna from Valkas's wrath.

But dammit, it was hard.

"On your knees," Valkas demanded.

I went rigid for a moment. My body didn't want to comply, even though my mind did.

Valkas stepped forward threateningly. "I'm not going to ask you again. On. Your. Knees."

I swallowed down the lump rising in my throat and pushed myself to my knees.

Valkas gave a triumphant smirk. It was clear his power over me brought him pleasure. It made me sick.

"Very good," he said as he paced around me. "Now shift."

I didn't. Not right away. I had to let him know that I wasn't going to be some mindless follower. I would fight. Not now, but once Jenna was safe, I would.

I held out just long enough for him to inhale another breath. Then I did as I was told.

As soon as my body shrank to my raven form, Valkas reached down and grabbed me. His fingers tightened under my wings, forcing them outward. He lifted me and looked me in the eye. I responded with a calm expression, mostly just to piss him off.

"Hold still, darling," Valkas whispered. "This will only hurt a little."

Before I knew what was happening, he tossed me onto the bed and pinned me to the mattress. I gasped for breath as my face pressed into the sheets. I pumped my wings in protest.

Valkas tugged *hard* at the end of my right wing, then pain shot up through it. Shortly after, the pain radiated up my left. It was a sharp, tender pain, as if he'd just ripped my fingernails from the nail beds.

Suddenly, Valkas's weight lifted off of me. I inhaled a deep breath and squawked. I flapped my wings on instinct to distance myself from him. I managed to kick myself to the edge of the bed, but I stumbled off of it and crashed to the floor.

What the hell? Why couldn't I fly? What had Valkas done to me? The calm, collected façade I'd put on only moments ago completely vanished.

"You can shift back now," Valkas offered.

I finally looked at him, and what I saw caused my stomach to bottom out. Valkas paced to the other side of the room with a large handful of black feathers clutched in his hands.

Mine!

I glanced to my wings to see that my flight feathers had been ripped out, making my wings look shorter and disproportionate. He'd done it so I couldn't escape the island! Evil didn't even begin to cover it. I'd never felt so violated in my life. Every fiber of my being told me to attack, to fight, but the little voice in the back of my head reminded me of Jenna.

So I didn't move. I lay there on the floor, letting the pain pulse through my wings and thinking about all the horrible things I'd do to Valkas when given the chance.

If given the chance, I corrected myself. I'd had my chance, and I'd screwed it up. Valkas wasn't like the normal vampires I fought. He was faster and stronger, not to mention he had an army of vampires *and* a witch to do his bidding for him.

"On second thought, stay in your shifted form." Valkas's voice cut through the silence. "I think you'll be more comfortable that way." The way he said it didn't sound the least bit comforting.

The pain in my wings disappeared as a numbness took over. *Hopeless.* That was the one word that went through my head. How had I strolled in here with so much determination and confidence only to end up here, a prisoner to the Soulless?

After dropping the dagger and my feathers on a desk opposite the bed, Valkas picked up a small metal object I didn't get a good look at.

He approached me again. I didn't protest as he reached down and lifted me by the neck. He held me away from him as if I was a piece of dirty garbage.

I just hung there, a million thoughts racing through my mind all at once. This couldn't be it, could it? There had to be a way out of here. A way to get that dagger back. A way to find Jenna. A way to get off this island.

Valkas left the room and turned down a hall I hadn't been down. The first thing I noticed was a thick black wire cage sitting upon a table at the end of the hall, surrounded by fake red rose blossoms. Dim light from the few wall sconces reflected off a mirror hanging above the table.

All throughout the chateau there were decorative arrangements placed on narrow tables, hung on the walls, or situated in the corners. At first glance, the bird cage looked like a beautiful decoration, until I realized his intention. This decoration just so happened to serve Valkas's purpose perfectly. My whole body tensed as Valkas opened the cage and shoved me inside. The cage was small and cramped. If I tried to shift, it'd squash me.

Valkas opened his hand to reveal the metal object he'd brought with him. A padlock. He placed the lock around the wire bars and shot me a devilish grin. "Sweet dreams."

Then he turned on his heel and retreated down the hall.

I sat there with a clenched beak, watching him go. He could enjoy my captivity all he wanted. I'd play his game for now, but one way or another, I was getting out of here.

<hr>

"Rachel." Venn wrapped me in his arms, pulling me close to him. The scent of home filled my nose, and my whole body warmed under his touch. I saw nothing as I buried my face into his shoulder.

"Venn, I'm so sorry. I should've listened to you."

"I missed you," he whispered, pressing his nose in my hair. "You have no idea how worried I was."

I drew away from him to look him in the eyes. His eyes were warm and welcoming. I became so lost in them that I didn't even register our surroundings. We could've been floating through space for all I knew.

"But I had to do it," I told him. "I had to at least try."

"But you failed," Venn argued.

"No." I shook my head, refusing to believe it. "This isn't over yet."

"It's fine." Venn pulled me back into a tight hug, and I relaxed into his embrace. "All that matters is that you're safe with me now."

"But I'm not, Venn," I stated. "Not yet."

The sound of a door slamming startled me awake. I hadn't even realized I'd drifted off. I squawked and spread my wings, but the tender ends hit the edges of the cage, sending a fresh wave of pain through my wings. The memory of my dream resurfaced, and my heart ached for Venn. I hadn't been gone long, but I already missed him. I wished he'd come with me.

A man walking through the hall turned to glance at me. He had pale skin and silver eyes. No surprise there. He looked confused by my presence but continued on down the hall. A few moments later, another door opened and a woman emerged from the room. She had the same silver eyes, but dark hair and young features.

"Hey, Kyle!" she called, catching up with the other vamp. She moved down the hallway quicker than any human and stuck her arm in the crook of Kyle's elbow.

"Hey, Penelope," he greeted back. "Did you hear what's happening tonight?"

"No," she replied, sounding interested. "Give me the deets."

"Well, let's just say we're going to see a show."

That was all I heard before the couple turned down the hall and their voices faded. I sighed and shifted around in my cage. If I was going to stay here for a while, I might as well try to get comfortable. Which was basically impossible, but hey, things could be worse, couldn't they?

I kept telling myself that.

In the silence, I tried summoning my magic. I'd never done magic in shifted form before, but surely it worked the same way, right? I focused on my body and honed in on my magic, but it was barely a tingle. Reciting the spell for healing in my head, I turned my focus to the end of my wings, which were still sore from the feather-plucking incident. The dull pain eased for a moment before it returned.

What the heck? When I couldn't perform magic back in Valkas's room, I'd assumed it was a *me* problem. But now here I was in the silence, all calm and ready to conjure magic, and it *still* didn't work?

A terrifying thought struck. Had Matias already used The Wise Owl?

No, not yet, I told myself. If he was blocking me, I wouldn't be able to shift.

Maybe I wasn't as calm as I thought I was, or perhaps I couldn't perform magic in shifted form, since I needed to speak the incantations out loud. Either way, magic wasn't going to get me out of this one.

Soon, more vampires emerged from the rooms lining the hallway, and I heard others I couldn't see and voices coming from the foyer. I didn't know how long I'd been in that cage, but judging by the sounds of the chateau coming alive, I had to guess that night had fallen.

After what felt like two hours since I woke, I finally saw a figure coming toward me down the hall. He had broad shoulders and took prideful steps.

Valkas.

He was flanked by three guards. I recognized the witch guy among them, but the other two were vamps. They all wore dark black, but their hands and faces were no longer covered. One of them had his sleeves rolled up, and I noticed the sign of the Soulless etched into his skin—a scar shaped like a V with two fang marks in the center.

Valkas stopped in front of me and peered down at me past his nose. "Well, shifter. I hope you're well rested. You have a big night ahead of you."

I didn't respond, seeing as I was in shifted form. But he probably would've slapped my head right off my shoulders if I actually spoke some snarky comeback.

Before I knew what was happening, Valkas grabbed the top of my cage, and I lost my balance. He swung the thing around as if there weren't a live being trapped inside. I slammed into one side of the cage only to be tossed to the other a split second later.

Take it easy, would ya?

Neither Valkas nor his men said anything. I was a little disoriented trying to stay upright in the swinging cage, but I saw enough to know we were headed down the grand staircase. About a dozen vampires stood in the entrance chatting. They caught sight of Valkas and immediately went silent, bowing their heads at him while he passed. He didn't even acknowledge them, keeping his head high and eyes on the front door, like they were mere decorations.

Just before we slipped outside, I caught the eye of one of the women in the foyer.

Brown.

Her eyes were brown. It suddenly occurred to me that only half the people there were vamps. I didn't even have to look at their eyes in the dim lighting to know which ones they were. All the vamps stood close to their respective blood slaves, laying claim to them as if they were some piece of property.

The door swung shut behind us, blocking my view of the people inside. Outside, the sky was dark, and the air was cold. I couldn't see the stars behind the clouds, but the moon peeked through just enough that I could see the shadows of the trees.

I thought that maybe Valkas was taking me to the slaves' quarters. Maybe he'd show me off and use me as an example or something. But he veered in the opposite direction down a narrow path that led up a hill and toward the cliff.

It wasn't long before I heard the sounds of chanting. I couldn't make out the words, since there were various chants all going on at once, but it sounded like a bunch of people all getting psyched up before a big football game or something.

Valkas turned down a trail even narrower than the one we'd been on, then stopped when we reached a small clearing. In the middle of the clearing was a long wooden table with all sorts of weapons on it. I saw various types of knives, along with a sword, an ax, a bow and arrow, and even one of those chains with a spikey ball on the end.

What was this? Were they going to hold me down and fillet me or something?

Valkas set my cage down on the grass. Or rather, threw it. The cage landed upright but tipped over and rolled a few feet when my body slammed into the bars. He removed the keys from his pocket and bent to unlock the cage. He didn't even set it back upright before standing.

"Choose your weapon," he said, then he whirled around and started back down the trail. His men followed close behind him.

I quickly scurried out of the open cage, using my wings to hoist me out, then shifted.

"Wait!" I called before he could get too far.

Valkas paused, but when he turned and his men stepped aside so he could look at me, he didn't look pleased. Valkas wasn't the kind to take orders from anyone. I was pretty sure the only reason I was still alive was because he was curious to know what I had to say. Beneath the turned-down lips and narrowed gaze, I thought I detected a hint of amusement.

"Aren't you going to tell me what this is all about?" I asked, gesturing to the table of weapons. "Do I get to know what I'm up against?"

Valkas smirked, bringing all that amusement to the surface. "No, but that's the fun part."

"I don't even get a hint?" I protested. "How can I choose an adequate weapon if I don't know what I'm fighting?"

Valkas was upon me in a second. Wind rushed by my hair, and he reached out to smooth it down.

Ew! Don't touch me!

I tried not to let my detest for the man show, for my sister's sake.

"Pick the weapon that will do the most damage," he said coolly. "I'd very much like to see you survive the night."

"What?" My whole body went rigid. I wasn't scared to die. Not really. But I was scared of leaving behind unfinished business. That simply wasn't an option.

"Yes, darling," he said, taking note of my fallen face. "You're going to want to choose wisely. This one's a fight to the death."

7

A fight to the death? Was he serious? Against whom? Him? Another vampire? His witch crony? His hint wasn't exactly helpful, though he strolled away looking positively pleased with himself.

I turned back to the table, surveying the weapons under the moonlight.

I could run, I thought to myself. No one was around to see if I escaped into the forest. But then again, where would I go? Valkas had made sure I couldn't fly away, and I couldn't exactly swim to the mainland. I'd drown before I made it. Chances were the boathouse I'd heard about was heavily guarded after what had happened earlier. I'd never make it off this island before I was found, and Valkas didn't seem like the kind of guy who would forgive such an incident.

Which meant I was still playing his game, whether I liked it or not.

My eyes fell upon the bow, which had two arrows sitting next to it. That would be helpful for a long-distance shot, but I'd never shot a bow before. There was a pretty good chance I wouldn't hit anything with it. I continued down the table, fingering the spear, then moving on to the sword. Most of these would kill a vampire, but what if I wasn't up against a vampire? Would I have to fight from close or far range? The chanting grew louder in the distance.

Just pick something, I told myself.

Without contemplating it too hard, I picked up the sword, which was heavier than it looked but would do a lot of damage. I grabbed one of the knives for good measure and slipped it in my boot.

Hey, Valkas never said anything about rules. He wanted a good show? I'd give him one.

A few moments later, I heard the sound of heavy footsteps approaching down the path. I whirled around with my sword held out in front of me, poised for attack.

A huge vampire stepped into the moonlight. He was at least six and a half feet tall with biceps bigger than my waist. He was shirtless, so I could see every hill and valley on his six-pack abs. I didn't care how much shifter blood I had in me. This guy would snap me like a twig.

He stopped at the entrance of the clearing and folded his arms over his chest. Interesting. I expected him to launch an attack right away.

"So, what's the deal?" I asked. "I attack, you rip my head off?"

Giant Vamp huffed and spoke in the deepest voice I'd ever heard. He spoke in a thick Russian accent, too. "If only it were easy. Come."

He turned back down the path, and it suddenly occurred to me. He wasn't my opponent. He was my escort. Clutching the hilt of the sword tightly in my hand, I hurried down the trail behind him. The guy's legs were super long, so it practically took me running to keep up with him.

"Any idea what I'm up against?" I asked, hoping for a little warning.

Giant Vamp scoffed. "Your opponent very fierce."

"Fiercer than you?"

The chanting grew louder as we walked. Up ahead, I saw lights flickering through the trees. *Torches*, I realized.

He smirked. "Nobody fiercer than Anton."

"Good to know. I'd hate to be the sorry loser fighting against you."

"Maybe one day," he said. "For now, you fight."

We reached a large clearing in the trees. I only had a moment to register the scene before me. Torches had been set into the ground, surrounding an empty square the size of a basketball court. The far end of the clearing met up with the edge of a tall cliff. I could barely see the water through the darkness, but I knew it was there. On either side of the torches sat people on raised bleachers, and beyond them, trees. The trees sloped down the hill, giving a wide view of the chateau.

There must've been at least two hundred people in the arena, which looked like a lot more all packed into the clearing. I couldn't tell if they were vampires or human, but my bet was most of them were vamps. Valkas sat in a big chair in the front row, like he was a king sitting on a throne, waiting for a jousting match to being. Rogers, the witch, sat at his side.

That was all I could process before Anton grabbed me by the back of the shirt and shoved me into the middle of the ring. I landed hard on my knees in the dirt, pinching my fingers between the hilt of my sword and the ground. I shot to my feet immediately, looking around for my opponent. Chants of *fight, fight, fight* filled the air, but I faced nothing but empty water at the other end of the ring. I whirled around to the trail entrance, but there was nothing there, either. Anton was already gone.

Valkas stood from his chair and held his hands up. The arena quieted without him having to give the command. It was eerily silent. The only thing I heard was the sound of the breeze rustling through the trees and the water against the rocks below the cliff.

"I'm sure by now you all know that we have a new shifter among us," Valkas said. He didn't speak loudly, as it was easy enough to hear him. I remained alert the whole time. "As with all our new recruits, she must be initiated."

Recruit? Is that what he was calling me? I didn't get any credit for finding this island when it was hidden beneath a cloaking spell?

I suppose not. He wouldn't want his loyal followers questioning his power.

"Only the strongest survive on my island." Valkas smirked at me. "So, without further ado, let the game begin!"

At his cue, a small creature flew out of the darkness as if someone had tossed it. It had gray fur and a long ringed tail.

A raccoon.

They thought I'd be afraid of this little thing? They obviously didn't know much about me.

It rolled across the dirt and immediately sprang to its feet when it came to a stop. An ax landed in the arena in the same manner, skidding to a halt beside the creature.

The raccoon lifted its gaze to mine, and an expression I couldn't quite read crossed its features. I thought I detected a hint of surprise, but it quickly turned to fury. Something about that look seemed familiar, but I couldn't place it. The raccoon didn't even shift and grab its weapon before it sprang on me.

I ducked out of the way. The image of its tiny little paws reaching out for my face would forever be seared in my memory. The shifter landed on the ground behind me, clawing into the dirt to stop its momentum. It landed only a few feet away from the edge of the cliff.

I didn't want to hurt him. Killing humans and shifters wasn't my thing. I was all about slaying vampires. But I didn't want to die, either. The raccoon bared its teeth at me. Damn, it looked vicious. I had to make up my mind. And fast.

It lunged for me again, all while people screamed from the bleachers.

"Get her!"

"I wanna see some blood!"

"Use your sword!"

This time, I threw my hand outward and thrust it into the fur on the raccoon's chest. I followed his trajectory and spun around. I bent to one knee, using his momentum to slam his body into the ground. It earned me a round of applause.

I thought maybe if I got the shifter in the right position, we could talk something out—fake a death or something like that. He could go free, and I didn't have to kill him. It was a win-win for both of us.

But the little sucker didn't even hesitate. He gasped at the impact, then lifted his head and sank his teeth into my hand. I let out a yelp but didn't let go. I curled my fingers tighter in his fur, and he bit back harder. I bent down to his level, where blood dripped out of my palm and onto his fur. He used his little paws to scratch me, sending stinging shoots of pain up my hand.

"I'm trying to help you," I hissed. "Maybe there's a way we can both survive. You game?"

Instead of clawing at my exposed arm, he swiped his paw out and sliced across the skin on my cheek. I reeled backward.

"I'll take that as a no," I snapped back. I could barely hear my own voice above the cheering.

The raccoon bit down again, and I finally jerked my hand away. It hurt a lot, but the pain barely registered as my opponent righted himself and readied to jump at me again.

"Shift, shift, shift," the crowd cried out. I wasn't sure if they meant me or the raccoon. Either way, they wanted us to fight in the same form. No way was I shifting into a raven without my flight feathers. I was staying close to this sword the whole damn time.

I was ready for the next attack, but what I didn't expect was for the raccoon to shift mid-jump. A human body slammed into me, knocking me on my back. Another chorus of cheers broke out from the crowd. I held my sword up, but the shifter was already running away, heading for the other side of the arena to grab the ax. I jumped to my feet to see that the figure had short hair but a slim middle and wide hips. A woman?

Aw, shit. I really didn't want to kill her.

If you don't, she'll kill you, I told myself. And then there was no hope for getting rid of the vampires. I was the only one who could do it, and I'd do whatever it took until that happened. Even take innocent lives...

The thought made me sick, but it was what had to be done... for the greater good.

I hated when the greater good screwed you over.

I raced up to the woman just as she bent to grab her ax. She whirled around at the last second and moved so fast I didn't even see her face. The head of her ax clanged into my sword, knocking it out of my hands. Less than a split-second later, her fist swung out and slammed right between my eyes.

I stumbled to the ground, and my elbows skidded across the dirt. Judging by the sting, a good couple layers of skin came off. My vision blurred from the impact, but I wasn't ready to give up just yet. The girl stepped forward, her face masked in shadows.

"*Ardeat ignis,*" I shouted, aiming my hands at her. But all that came out was sparks.

It took me by complete surprise. Since learning the spell for fire, I hadn't had trouble using it in a fight. Now I'd failed at the spell twice? The theories I'd developed earlier about my magic no longer seemed credible. My latest theory, and worst of all, was that something was blocking my magic, something beyond my control.

Just another obstacle, I told myself. *I'll figure it out.*

Says the girl who lost her magical dagger, lost her ability to fly, and now lost her magic.

A heavy shoe connected with my gut. I grunted, and my arms instantly came to my abdomen, protecting from another blow.

Time for my back-up plan. I swung my leg out to connect with the back of the girl's ankle, then grabbed the knife out of my other shoe. She landed on her back on the ground, and her ax flew from her hand. The crowd shouted all sorts of things I couldn't process. I quickly scrambled to my feet and loomed above her, shoving the blade of my knife up against her throat.

Her face finally came into view. Shadows flickered across it from the torches, but there was no denying that I'd seen that face a thousand times before. The straight nose, pale skin, blue eyes… they were all just like mine, only slightly tweaked.

All the air rushed out of my lungs. "Jenna?"

She smiled up at me. "Hey, sis."

I should've been overjoyed to see my sister, but all I could think was, *A raccoon! You never told me you were a raccoon!* Heck, I didn't even know she was a shifter! Then again, I'd never gotten the chance to tell her I was one, either. I guess I should've assumed as much.

"Jenna Bean?" I asked breathlessly.

Her hand shot out to grab on to my wrist, forcing the knife away from her throat. "What? You expected someone else, Rugrat?"

She spoke with such malice that I could hardly believe it was her. But there she was. Her hair was shorter, and she'd lost some weight, but it was definitely her.

"Yeah," I admitted. "I kinda did."

"Fight!" someone in the stands roared.

Jenna responded by slugging me hard on the inside of my arm, where she knew from many scuffles as children was my weak spot. I dropped the dagger on instinct. Mostly, I was just too shocked to fight back.

"What are you doing?" I demanded.

"Beating you up," she sneered. "What does it look like?"

Jenna's fist swung out again, connecting with the side of my jaw. The taste of copper filled my mouth. She jumped to her feet and readied herself for another blow.

"Jenna," I protested, still on my knees. "I'm not going to—"

Her foot slammed into my chest, knocking the air from my lungs. Seriously, what was her problem? Had the vamps messed her up that badly? Oh, God. What had they done to her?

That was all I could think as her fist connected with the side of my face again. Pain shot through my cheek, but I just couldn't bring myself to fight back.

Everything I'd done, all the vampires I'd killed, had been for her. Suddenly, it felt like maybe there'd been no purpose in becoming the Ravenite. Maybe I shouldn't have come to Gregor Island at all.

"Jenna, stop!" I cried.

Her hands flew toward me again, but this time she didn't hit me. Instead, she fisted her hands in my shirt and pulled my face close to hers.

"I waited for you," she hissed. "For two damn years. Do you have any idea how long that feels when you're trapped on an effing island?"

"Jenna, I'm sorry—"

"Why didn't you come sooner?" she snapped, delivering another blow.

I barely felt it this time. I didn't care. I deserved it, because she was right. I should've come sooner.

"Because I—"

"Because you're selfish," Jenna bit, tossing me across the ground.

The momentum took me a mere foot from the edge of the cliff. I stole a quick glance at the steep drop, but I could barely process it. I was still trying to take in the fact that my sister was standing right in front of me after all this time. Jenna reached down and grabbed my clothes again, pulling me to my feet. She had a strong punch, and my eye was starting to swell because of it.

"Are you going to kill me?" I whispered. I loved Jenna more than anything in the world, but this wasn't the Jenna I knew. It broke my heart.

She heaved my body upward and slammed me to the ground. The sound of cheers grew so loud around me that I hardly heard what she said when she bent to whisper in my ear.

"No, I'm not going to kill you," she said. "Just play along. They like a good show."

"So, you're not really mad at me?" I asked in a raspy whisper.

She smirked. "Oh, I'm pissed. But we can discuss that later. Wanna punch me?"

No, not really, I wanted to say. The fact was, I'd rather hug her. But hey, what are sisters for? I curled my hand into a tight fist and swung it at her face.

Jenna let the momentum take her. She rolled to the side, clutching her cheek.

I should've felt bad about punching her, but I grinned like a lunatic. That punch to the face was proof that she was here. My sister was alive, and we were together again!

I threw myself at Jenna just as she was getting to her feet. My arm locked around her neck, and I held her in a headlock.

"What now?" I whispered in her ear while she clawed at my arm. "I won't kill you."

"Knock me out," she hissed.

"What? No."

"You want this to be over? Kick me in the face."

Punching her was one thing. Knocking her out was another. I didn't want her to end up with a concussion or something.

"I'll fake it," she said. "Do it now!"

Apparently, Jenna had developed a thing for pain since the last time I'd seen her. I swung my knee up just between her eyes, and her whole body went limp. I let her body fall to the ground, and the crowd went crazy. People shot up out of their seats, clapping and hollering.

I stared down at Jenna, horrified. For a moment, I thought I'd truly knocked her out. That kind of blow from a shifter could kill a human being, but surely Jenna would be okay. Right? *Right?*

She opened her eyes for a mere split second to wink at me. Relief flooded through me. I wanted to kneel beside her and drag her into a hug, but Valkas was already strolling out into the ring. He grabbed my hand in his—*shudder*—and held it above my head.

"Ladies and gentlemen," Valkas called, causing the crowd to quiet. "I give you your champion!"

The vampires went ballistic again.

"So, that fight to the death thing..." I said to him. "Just a rumor?"

Valkas smirked, as he always did. I was starting to wonder if it was a permanent expression. "Something like that. I'd have liked to see what would've happened if you took it seriously."

Valkas started toward the trail, and I had no choice but to follow him, seeing as he was still holding on to my hand. He gestured to Rogers, who immediately stood and followed behind us.

"What now?" I asked, glancing back at Jenna. She hadn't moved an inch. All the other vamps were starting to get up out of their seats, leaving her forgotten. "What about my sister?"

"Relax," Valkas said with a wave of his hand. "I wouldn't waste good shifter blood. She's too... sweet."

Repulsive! There was no doubt by the way he said it that he'd fed on her before. My heart ached for my sister. How was I going to get her away from here?

"Where are you taking me?" I demanded.

He tugged on my arm. "You ask too many questions, darling. From now on, I'll be the one asking questions."

"What kind of questions?"

I didn't even realize the irony until Valkas reacted. In the blink of an eye, his hand left mine, and it shot toward my throat. Instinct overtook, and I threw my arm up to block him. His face contorted with anger, and his other hand clamped around my neck as he shoved me hard up against a tree. My shirt rode up, and the bark skidded along my lower back, sending a raw pain across my skin. I couldn't breathe, but I didn't fight back, either.

Rogers just stood there observing, his hands folded in front of him. He didn't speak a word.

"I will not tolerate you taunting me," Valkas snapped. His face was only inches from mine, sending my heart pummeling against my rib cage. He lowered his voice and spoke in warning. "Your sister's blood can turn bitter *real* fast. So I suggest you don't make this a habit."

He wasn't lying. That much was clear. My sister's shifter blood couldn't protect her forever.

"Yes," I said in a raspy voice. It barely sounded like anything.

Valkas dropped me, and I inhaled a gulp of air. He grabbed me by the hand again and dragged me behind him before I could find my footing.

"Come," he snarled. "We must celebrate."

My stomach bottomed out. I didn't know what *celebrating* entailed, but there was something in his voice that suggested I didn't want to find out. Which meant I was still useful to him… for now.

I had to make sure it stayed that way.

9

Valkas led me back to the privacy of his room. The bed had been made, and the dagger he'd left on the desk was no longer there.

Rogers entered the room behind us and stood to the side. I swore the guy was just there for decoration. Which was crazy, considering he wasn't even that pretty. I mean, sure, he had the tall, muscular thing going on, but slicked-back hair was so not my style.

Valkas forced me to sit beside him on the bed. You'd think when a guy brought you back to his room, he'd be gentle about it and treat you like a lady, but it wasn't like that with Valkas. He practically yanked my arm out of the socket.

All I could think about was Venn, how he'd act like a gentleman if this were him.

Except Venn would never be in this type of scenario. He was too kind to run any sort of shifter fight club. And he *definitely* wouldn't bring a girl back to his room without asking.

Venn. I didn't know how much more heartbreak my body could handle, but I missed him so much.

Valkas leaned over to me, pressing his lips to the soft spot under my ear. My skin crawled, and nausea rolled around in my gut. All I wanted to do was pull away, but I didn't. There was still the whole *stay on his good side* thing... no matter how disgusted it made me feel. I'd never felt so sick in my life.

"Now that you've earned your place on this island," Valkas said, "there's something you should know about me."

You can't get it up? Let's hope to God, because if things went in that direction tonight, I didn't think Jenna and I were making it out of here. I'd die before I let the devil take my virginity. The greater good be damned.

I wasn't an expert on how vampire magic worked, but judging by some of the horndogs I'd run across during patrols, those parts still worked fine and dandy.

"Is he going to watch?" I gestured toward Rogers, who stood as still as a statue. His eyes were hard and looked untrustworthy. He took a job with the Soulless, for heaven's sake. I never trusted anyone with a heart black enough to side with vampires.

"What did I say about questions?" Valkas snarled.

"Right. Forgive me."

Valkas scoffed, like that was never going to happen. "No, darling. He's not here to watch. In fact, he's here to help."

I almost asked him to elaborate, but I clamped my mouth shut at the last second. Surely, that couldn't mean what it sounded like.

"You see, I'm very *particular* about my meals."

Meal? Well, that was better than other types of torture, but it still wasn't exactly a good thing. Being feed on was like being administered drugs you didn't want. It wouldn't kill you, but it was still a violation of your body.

Valkas pressed his lips to the underside of my jaw again. This time, I actually did shudder. "I don't like my women… squirming."

At that, Rogers muttered the first words I'd ever heard come out of his mouth. "*Quod dico facies.*"

My whole body went rigid, and panic tore through me. I tried to move, but my muscles wouldn't comply to my demands. It was like my whole body had gone to sleep, like my limbs weren't getting the signals that my brain was sending. What had that bastard done to me?

"Lie back," Valkas commanded.

Even if I wanted to, I couldn't move.

"Um…" Good to know my voice was still working.

"Shh," Valkas said, like I was some pet that needed soothing.

Rogers flicked his wrist, and I fell backward onto the bed. Fear ignited in my chest. If I had control of my body right now, I'd be shaking unlike ever before. For the first time, I wanted to beg for my safety. It was my last resort. Rogers had put me under some type of spell that turned me into his own personal marionette. How powerful was this creep?

"Don't worry, darling," Valkas said, looming over me. He reached up to brush a dark strand of hair out of my eyes, as if that was supposed to comfort me. It only made my heart pound harder—and definitely not in the good way. "This won't hurt a bit."

Valkas's fangs elongated, catching in the light of the burning sconce next to the bed.

"No, please—"

I gasped as Valkas's fangs sank into my neck. A sharp pain shot out across my skin, but was quickly replaced by a sense of euphoria. My heart rate instantly slowed, and a comforting warmth spread over my extremities like a soft blanket. My muscles relaxed, like I'd been immersed in a tub of calming potion.

I'd been bit once before, but that had lasted only a few seconds. It was easy to forget what it felt like after just the slightest taste. When Valkas fed on me, I felt so calm that I altogether forgot a vampire was stuck to my neck. I didn't think about the fact that I was trapped on this island. I didn't think about Jenna or Venn or my family. All that mattered was this feeling overtaking my body, like nothing could ever hurt me again.

I lost all sense of time. Valkas could've been feeding on me for a minute, or he could've been feeding on me for an hour. When he pulled away, I felt light-headed and tired. I noticed him licking his lips but saw that there was no blood on them. He apparently wasn't a messy eater.

That was the only thought that went through my head before the reality of what had just happened hit me like a landslide. As soon as it registered, all the calmness I'd felt vanished. It was replaced by a dirty feeling beyond anything I'd ever felt before. I wanted to dive into a vat of chlorine and wash all the ickiness off of me.

I regained control of my body, and my hand slapped up to my neck. I wiped at the liquid there and pulled my hand away, expecting to see blood. But it was only saliva. Vampires could heal the wounds they inflicted with their saliva so that their prey didn't bleed out. I felt so woozy that I nearly forgot that tidbit of information.

I wanted to yell at Valkas, to tell him how wrong it was that he'd done that. But judging by the satisfied smirk on his face, he already knew how wrong it was.

I started to sit up, but Valkas placed a hand on my shoulder and pressed me back into the mattress. How could I have been so calm when he fed on me? This mattress felt like a rock.

"But darling," Valkas said. "We've only just begun."

Dear Lord. Don't tell me he was going in for another round. I didn't think I could handle any more blood loss. I felt like puking as it was, but maybe that was just from Valkas's close proximity.

Valkas lay beside me and propped himself up on his elbow. He twisted my hair around his finger while he spoke.

Gag.

"You are very sweet," he said. "Sweeter than your sister, even. It's a shame we hadn't met sooner."

Yeah, a real shame. I kept my lips sealed.

"Where were you that night?" Valkas asked, like we were old friends catching up.

"I don't know what you're talking about," I replied, careful not to phrase it as a question.

"That night your sister came to us."

My whole body tensed, and it wasn't from some puppeteer spell, either. He said it so casually, like he actually believed she made a choice coming with them. Maybe in his own twisted way, he did believe it.

"Oh? The night your men murdered my parents?" I couldn't help the question this time as my body shook in anger. Why would he bring that up? Was he trying to piss me off?

The thought of my parents punched an invisible hole through my gut. For so long, I'd avoided thinking about them. I pushed down the memory of their screams and their lifeless faces when I found them that night.

"My men?" Valkas asked innocently. "I think you mean *me*, darling."

He smiled as the blood drained from my face. There wasn't much left to begin with, so I could only imagine how pale I looked.

"You were there?" Another question. Dammit.

"Oh, yes." He gave me a cunning grin. "Who else could have murdered your parents in such a way?"

I squeezed my eyes shut, trying to shake the image from my mind. It'd been brutal and bloody beyond belief. I couldn't bear to recall the memory.

Now I was lying in bed with the man who'd murdered them. This couldn't be happening. I knew the Soulless had killed them, but I'd never known Valkas had been with them that night. I'd dreamed so many times of facing the man who murdered them, but in my mind, he always had a different face. In my head, it was always the guy with the scar above his eyebrow, the one who'd rampaged through my room while I hid in my raven form. I never truly thought I'd meet the vamp responsible.

"It's ironic," I said through clenched teeth, unable to keep my anger from rising to the surface.

"What is?" Valkas asked curiously.

I couldn't look at him. Instead, I stared straight up at the ceiling. "That you would be the one to take everything from me when I'm the only one who can kill you."

I finally looked at him, only to see his eyes narrow at me and his nostrils flare.

"It wasn't an accident," he snapped. Clearly, he didn't like being reminded that I was one of his biggest threats.

"I've been looking for you for a long time. As you know, you pose a threat to my existence, and I don't like feeling threatened." He leaned down to whisper in my ear, clipping each word. I held my breath. He pulled away a moment later, but it didn't seem soon enough. "Finding someone from an old life can be... tricky."

"I didn't know it was possible."

"Possible, for sure. But tricky. Luckily, Rogers here"—Valkas gestured to him in the corner—"came to the Soulless several years ago. He helped me track down the *young girl who could kill me*."

"You must've offered him generous compensation." It was the only reason I could think of why a human would go along with this.

"One doesn't need compensation when they believe in the cause," Valkas drawled.

"And I suppose that cause is world domination."

"Ah, see?" Valkas said. "You already know me so well. We could get along, if only you wanted to be on the winning side."

"Oh, I do," I replied, finally looking him in the eyes. "I just don't intend for that side to be yours."

Valkas chuckled. "So naïve. I like it. And how do you intend to kill me when I have your dagger?"

I shrugged, feigning disinterest. "I haven't worked that one out yet."

Valkas grinned. "Excellent. Just what I like to hear."

"You tell a great story," I said, "but it doesn't make a lot of sense."

Valkas stiffened, like he was offended. "And how's that?"

"Well, you found me, but you took my sister instead."

Valkas drew away from me and pushed himself to a sitting position. I finally felt like I could breathe again. As soon as he stood, I sat up. Valkas passed by Rogers and headed to the table in the corner, where he poured himself a glass of an amber-colored liquid. I figured it was whiskey or something, but I didn't know why he was drinking it. It took a lot for a vamp to get a buzz. I think he just liked to hold the glass for something to do with his hands, like he thought it made him look intimidating or something.

Valkas took a sip and leaned casually against the table. "I don't admit to many mistakes, darling, but in my four hundred years, I have to say that was my biggest."

Before I could figure out how to phrase my question as a statement, Valkas continued.

"The fact is, we took the wrong girl." Valkas wore a pained expression, like it killed him to admit it.

I scooted myself to the edge of the bed so my feet hung off. It made me feel a little safer, like I could run if I had to. "So you tracked me down. You could've come after me again."

Valkas shrugged. "I could have, but Rogers counseled me to stay put, that you would come for me one day. And it seems he was right."

My gaze flickered to Rogers. "Witches can't see the future." Not without a magical object, at least. He couldn't have one, right?

Valkas took another sip, then gazed down into his glass, like there was something interesting in there. "It depends on how you look at it. Can they see a play-by-play of real events? No. But can they see generalities? Sometimes, if they're strong enough."

Answers to questions I'd been asking myself for years began to fall into place. "The Soulless disappeared two years ago, shortly after you took Jenna. Which means..."

I purposely let my statement run open-ended. I wanted him to confirm my suspicions without me having to ask.

Valkas spread his arms out wide. "Which means, it's all been for you, darling. I pulled back my men so that you'd come looking for me. I didn't know who you were until you conveniently showed up in my room."

So when he first mentioned Jenna, he was taking a wild guess, I theorized. It wasn't exactly hard to figure out we were sisters, considering our resemblance.

I swallowed down the lump in my throat. "Why are you telling me all this?"

Valkas crossed the room slowly, silently. He stopped in front of me, then his hand snapped out to crack across the side of my face. I let out a cry and brought my hand up to protect my cheek. It burned.

"What did I tell you about the questions?" he snarled. "You are such a curious shifter. The fact is, darling, honesty goes a long way."

That was saying a lot coming from the most morally corrupt man on the planet.

"You must figure that if you're honest with me, I'll tell you something in return," I guessed.

Valkas smiled, but it was one of the most gut-wrenching smiles I'd ever seen. I took that as a yes.

"You shouldn't have been so quick to show your hand," I said with a shrug. "Considering I don't have any secrets."

Valkas leaned closer to me, running a chilling finger down the side of my face. "Oh, but you do, darling."

"Funny," I deadpanned. "I don't seem to recall any."

Valkas sat beside me, and the mattress dipped under his weight. I could smell the alcohol on his breath. "I want to know what matters to you. *Who* matters to you."

I kept a stone-cold expression on my face as I looked him in the eye. "That's not a secret. You already know I care about my sister. I wouldn't be here if I didn't."

Valkas took another sip of his drink, then clicked his tongue. "But two years, darling. That's a long time to be alone. I should know. I spent more than a century on this island. Didn't you meet anyone?"

"I met a handful of vampires," I said coolly. "But I never really got the chance to chat with them."

Valkas's lips turned up at the corners. "None of mine, I hope."

"None of your current followers, unfortunately."

Silence followed for a beat, then Valkas spoke. "So, what's your weakness, darling? A boy, perhaps?"

Venn! My body went rigid. I realized too late and hoped it didn't give me away.

"I have no one," I lied. The fact was, if I'd come here months ago, that would've been true.

"Darling," Valkas pouted, like he thought I might actually feel sympathy. "I was honest with you. It's only fair that you're honest in return."

"Fair?" I asked in disbelief. "You murdered my parents and kidnapped my sister. You want to talk about *fair?*"

I snapped my mouth shut. I didn't mean to snap at him, and it was probably a huge mistake. Soon, Valkas would get annoyed with my big fat mouth and shut it for me.

"You're right," Valkas said with a wave of his hand. He stood and set his empty glass on the nightstand. "There's no point in trying to be fair with you."

Valkas gestured to Rogers. Rogers reached into his pocket and pulled out a small vial with a clear liquid inside. He took a step forward and popped the top off.

"Whoa!" I cried, scurrying back across the bed. "Don't tell me you intend to give me that… whatever it is."

"Oh, I absolutely do," Valkas said with an evil smile.

Rogers reached out for me, but I pulled my arm away.

"But you didn't tell me what's in it," I protested.

Valkas raised an eyebrow. "I'm not obligated to. You'll take the potion, or I'll force you to watch as I carve your sister's skin off."

For a moment, I had forgotten how cruel Valkas was. He was playing nice with me, which made him almost seem… human. But he was only doing it to manipulate me, and when he realized that wasn't working, he was right back to his devilish antics.

"What is it?" I asked.

Big mistake. Valkas was *so* done with my shit at this point. He jumped on the bed and slammed his hand into my chest. I fell back onto the mattress, and he climbed on top of me, holding me down. I squirmed beneath him, trying to break free. What if it was some sort of poison that would kill me? Or a potion that would prevent my soul from reincarnating?

I threw my hands up to his face, but he grabbed on to my wrists and squeezed tightly, holding them above my head. I fought against him, but I was so weak from the loss of blood that it didn't do anything.

"Now!" Valkas roared.

Rogers reached out for my face. I snapped at his hand with my teeth and tasted blood. Valkas readjusted his hands to squeeze the corners of my jaw and force my mouth open. Rogers tipped back the vial, and a tasteless liquid entered my mouth. I planned to spit it out, but Valkas forced my jaw closed, and Rogers pinched my nose shut. My lungs felt like they were going to implode. Basic instinct took over, and I swallowed the liquid against my will.

My body went still. It wasn't like when Rogers tried to go all *puppet master* on my ass. Nor was it like the calmness that overcame me when Valkas fed on me. This was more or less like I'd given up fighting. Which was *so* unlike me. Whatever they'd given me acted quickly. Rogers returned to his post at the door, and Valkas sat beside me on the bed.

He spoke slowly. "I'm only going to ask one more time. Besides your sister, what other weaknesses do you have?"

"My family," I admitted. I had no idea where the words came from, but I felt them slip out of my mouth, heard them come in my own voice.

Truth potion! The bastard.

"Ah," Valkas said in interest. "Tell me more."

I found myself spilling every last detail about Venn, Fiona, and the rest of them. I told Valkas about how I'd met them, what their powers were, and how I felt about each and every one of them.

Truth be told, I couldn't remember much of what I said beyond that. I wasn't sure if I was still feeling woozy from the blood loss or if it was part of the potion that made my head fuzzy. Either way, secrets tumbled out of my mouth that I never would've told Valkas otherwise. Eventually, he took my hand and guided me up off the bed. My knees shook, and the room spun around me. I felt drunk, only without the urge to vomit. Which was weird, because Valkas constantly made me nauseous.

He led me toward the door, but before he let me go, he leaned over to whisper in my ear. "In case it wasn't clear, darling, that's how I expect you to act every time I ask you a question. I'm done giving you second chances. I expect nothing but respect from now on." Valkas straightened and turned to Rogers. "Deal with her."

Valkas let me go, and it was enough to send me falling to my knees without the support. A pair of hands reached out and caught me, then I felt my body being tossed upward. It took me a second to realize I was slumped over someone's shoulder and already headed down the hall.

"Where are you taking me?" I thought I asked the question, but I didn't hear the words come out.

"Shh..." It was hard to pinpoint the voice, but I thought it was Rogers. "You mustn't worry."

He was dead wrong about that. Worry was all I did these days.

It certainly wasn't going to end now.

10

It was dark when I blinked my eyes open. I shot to a sitting position, but the top of my head slammed against something hard. I rubbed the goose egg on my head and cursed.

"Rachel," a familiar voice called out from the darkness.

"Jenna?"

My eyes adjusted to the darkness to see that I was in one of the log cabins the blood slaves stayed in. Light from an oil lamp cast shadows across the room. I was lying on a lower bunk, and Jenna was eyeing me from the bunk opposite mine. Two other girls who looked a few years older than me gazed down with sad eyes from the bunk above Jenna.

Everything that had happened since I arrived at Gregor Island came rushing back. My skin crawled at the memory of what had happened in the privacy of Valkas's room. All I wanted to do was take a shower. My stomach rumbled, and I realized I was starving. My arms shook as I pushed myself up to sit on the edge of the bed.

"I'm glad you're okay," I said.

Jenna forced a smile. "For now. As long as they think they can use me to manipulate you."

Of course. That's why Valkas hadn't let her die in the ring.

"What happened?" I asked.

Jenna cleared her throat. "Rogers dumped you at our door, said you were our new roommate. This is Andi and Bri, by the way."

I looked up to the girls on the top bunk. One had long blond hair and a small nose, and the other had dark skin and tight curls. Judging by the way they were sitting, they looked close, like being on this island had brought them together.

"Hey," the blonde waved.

"Hi." I gave a non-committal smile.

"Are you okay?" Jenna asked, eyeing me with concern, a look I'd seen so many times throughout the years.

"Just hungry," I lied.

"What happened to you?" she asked.

I dodged around the question. I'd rather talk to her in private. "Is there anything to eat around here? Or anywhere to shower?" I added.

Jenna stood. "Follow me."

"Hey," the dark-haired girl said softly, stopping her. "You want us to come with?"

"We'll be fine, Andi," Jenna answered. "But thanks for the offer."

Jenna and I stepped out of the cabin into cool night air.

I turned to her. "So, you've still got some of that softness in you?"

Jenna frowned. "A lot has changed since we last saw each other, but I'm not a monster."

"Huh. Could've fooled me," I said, recalling her fist flying toward me in the ring.

Her shoulders dropped. "Come on, Rachel. Don't be like that. I didn't mean what I said. I was shocked and overwhelmed. I wasn't sure I actually believed it was you."

I was just about to shoot back some snarky comment, but then I looked her in the eyes. All my snark vanished as tears rose to my eyes. Out here alone under the moonlight, it felt like I was seeing her for the first time since the night she was taken. And I lost it.

Without ceremony, I threw my arms around her neck and dragged her close. She still smelled like I remembered… subtle tones of fresh linen mixed with a light strawberry scent. Memories of us as kids rushed through my mind—playing in our treehouse pretending we were pirates, talking about boys at our late-night slumber parties, baking cookies with Mom at Christmas, and grilling out with Dad in the summertime. Tears rolled down my cheeks. Once they started, I couldn't turn them off. Jenna hugged me back, and for the first time since I'd lost her, I felt that hole inside my chest shrink ever so slightly.

"I'm so sorry," I whispered, my voice cracking. "I'm sorry I didn't come for you sooner."

Jenna drew away from me and wiped at her eyes. The tough exterior she'd put up earlier in the night had completely crumbled. "Where were you, Rachel? I waited for you. I thought they'd killed you that night. I kept telling myself they didn't, that you were alive and coming for me. But I-I—"

I sniffled. "I tried, but I didn't know where to start. I was hopeless. Once I had enough money, I turned to a witch and tried to track you down, but the spell didn't work. I didn't know what else to do, so I gave up. I'm a horrible sister. I didn't think I had a chance of finding you until I saw this vampire with the mark of the Soulless on his wrist. That changed everything. I finally found out where you were, but then… shit hit the fan."

Jenna took my arm and led me toward a large building at the end of the rows of cabins. A few people passed by, but the cabins were mostly quiet. "Why don't you tell me about it inside? Let's get you cleaned up."

We stepped inside a dark building with rooms going off in all different directions. It was stylized in the same way as the cabins, with smooth wood floor and thick wooden walls. Jenna led me into one of the first rooms. I could hardly see anything until she turned to a table next to the door and lit a match. She placed it to the wick of an oil lamp, and the room became cast in a soft glow. I looked around to see three separate tubs, the kind on claw feet, with hand-pump faucets over each of them.

"No running water?" I asked.

Jenna walked over to the nearest tub and set the lamp down on an end table next to it. "Unfortunately, no. The island is completely cut off from the mainland. Valkas has a few generators here and there, but he saves them for himself. Get in. I'll pump your water for you."

I stood at the head of the tub and hesitated.

"Come on," Jenna encouraged. "We're sisters. We used to take baths together as kids. It's nothing I've never seen before."

True. I stripped down and climbed into the tub while Jenna worked on the pump. Icy cold water rushed over my toes, and I screamed, almost jumping out of the tub.

Jenna laughed. "No electricity, either. Remind me again what a warm shower feels like."

"A lot more pleasant than this." I settled back down into the tub, trying to ignore the coolness surrounding me.

When Jenna looked at me with her soft blue eyes, I could see the sister I used to know. She spoke quietly. "Do you want to tell me about it now?"

Yes! I wanted to tell her everything.

I took a calming breath, then dove into everything that happened after I found out about Gregor Island. I told her all about being the Ravenite, about Clarita's warning, about our journey to the caves and my encounter with Matias. I told her about the dagger, my past lives, Synchrony, Venn—all of it. By the time I'd finished, I was clean and had been soaking in the tub for what felt like an hour.

"Wow," Jenna said, dragging out the word. She sat on the lip of the next tub, her elbows rested on her knees. "That's... a *lot* to take in."

I bit my lip. "I know. I think I know what Clarita's warning meant now."

She tilted her head in question.

"Her warning was all about the dagger. If I hadn't gone down into the cave, I'd never would've faced Matias. I never would've gotten the dagger that could kill Valkas. But now..." I dropped my head. "I messed up, Jenna Bean."

She sighed, like she didn't know what to say. She had no words of comfort to offer me.

"You're a big help, sis," I stated flatly.

Her shoulders fell. "What do you want me to say, Rachel? That you can't give up? That you'll make it off this island alive? I've been here a long time, and I've never seen anyone escape. This is our reality now."

My stomach felt hollow. This couldn't be it, could it?

But Jenna had a point. We didn't have a way off this island. My one chance had already come and gone, and I didn't know what to think about that. *Hopeless* was the best way to put it.

To take my mind off it, I asked Jenna, "So, what's up with this island anyway? How'd a chateau end up out here? I mean, if this place was hidden for over a century..."

"As far as I've heard, the mansion was here before Valkas was imprisoned. The cabins and stuff only came after he escaped. His cronies run off to the mainland all the time to bring supplies back."

"So, the Soulless... are they all here, then?" I'd honestly expected there to be more of them.

"God, no," Jenna answered. "The Soulless are everywhere, stationed at different places around the world. This is just their headquarters, where Valkas keeps the strongest of them and the ones he trusts most."

"Oh, okay." It made sense.

"Anyway, about the mansion... rumor has it one of the witches who trapped him here—Gregor, obviously..." She shot me a knowing look, since I'd told her all about my past lives. "Lily Gregor owned the island and lived here on and off. She offered it up as the place of his sentence. As the legend goes, the mansion was symbolic to his imprisonment. It was supposed to make him reflect on what he'd done, to look at all the empty rooms and think of the people he'd killed."

I laughed lightly.

"What?" she asked curiously.

I shrugged. "That sounds like something I'd come up with, even if it was in a past life."

"I still can't believe you're all those people." She spoke so softly I barely heard her. "It's crazy that my sister is such an important part to all of this."

"It's not like I chose it," I said.

"I know, but..." Jenna left the sentence hanging. The following beat of silence made me a little uncomfortable.

"I still can't believe you're a raccoon," I subbed in, laughing.

Jenna smirked. "What did you expect? A dragon?"

I smiled. "I guess I always knew you'd be a shifter. I mean, since it's genetic and all of that. But I just couldn't ever picture you as an animal, you know? I mean, you're *Jenna*."

"Jenna the Fierce Raccoon," she teased. "And don't you forget it."

"Oh, I won't be forgetting that anytime soon."

"And you're a raven?" She raised her eyebrows, like she was impressed. "Can't say I'm surprised. I think it suits you."

"Does it?" I asked. I didn't know what that meant, but I supposed it did, in a way.

Another beat passed, but I spoke to break the silence. I was dying for more details. "What happened to you these last two years?" After a pause, I added, "Only if you want to talk about it…"

Jenna shrugged, like she didn't mind sharing. It was weird. I looked at her, and she was my sister, but there was definitely something tougher about her than I'd ever seen before. I guess that was what being a blood slave did to you.

She laced her fingers together in front of her. "What's there to tell? I was kidnapped, fed on, and forced to fight other shifters for the vampires' sick entertainment."

My stomach dropped like a bag of rocks. I hated that she'd gone through all of that. "That's how you got so good at fighting?"

"I had to," she answered coolly. She barely sounded like my sister when she talked about it. "They care about shifter blood around here—for feeding—but they care about watching a good show, too. Some of those fights end in death, Rachel."

I knew they had to, but hearing it from her mouth made me shudder.

"I've done what I had to do to survive," she said, not meeting my gaze. "I didn't always want to, but…"

"But what?" I regretted asking the question as soon as it left my lips. I didn't want to make Jenna say any more than she was comfortable with. I understood how hard this kind of thing was to talk about.

"But I wanted to survive. To see you again."

Tears rose to my eyes again. She endured all that for me?

"I love you, Jenna," I whispered.

"I love you, too, Rach. Now finish up." She stood and turned away from me, but I heard her sniffle as she paced across the room. It was like she didn't want me to see her cry. Wow, how she'd changed.

I scrubbed down a second time to give her a moment of privacy. She handed me a towel when I got out, but didn't say anything. I dried off, enjoying the warmth that came with it, then wrapped the towel around my body and secured the corner under the pit of my arm. I gathered my clothes and folded them into a neat pile, then took a bar of soap. Jenna eyed me curiously.

"You know how I told you I was a witch?" I asked.

"Like I could forget that." She rolled her eyes playfully.

I smirked. "Do you want to see me perform magic?"

Genuine interest crossed her features. "Yes!"

Jenna and I settled on the floor on either side of my pile of clothes. I held the bar of soap above the clothes and whispered the cleansing incantation Sondra had taught me.

"Did it work?" Jenna asked when I finished.

"Wasn't very fantastical, was it? It's one of the only spells I know." I grabbed my shirt off the top and sniffed it. It had a hint of the soap scent hidden beneath a layer of sweat, as if the spell had only half worked. My shoulders fell. "This worked perfectly the last time I used it."

Jenna sniffed my jeans. "Ew, Rachel."

My eyebrows knitted together. "I know. This spell is simple. It's like ever since I stepped foot on this island something's been blocking my powers."

Jenna pressed her lips together in thought. I could barely see her expression in the shadows.

"What?" I asked, seeing the gears turning in her head.

"I'm just thinking about what you told me about Synchrony. You talked about positive and negative energy."

"I do have positive energy," I countered. "I've been getting a lot better at casting spells. How can all of that just go away?"

"Because that's how life works," Jenna said. "Nobody's positive all the time, Rachel. Sometimes, it takes just one thing to set us back ten spaces."

I snorted. "One thing? Like Valkas."

"Exactly," Jenna agreed. "Magic isn't a linear progression. It's a rollercoaster ride of loops and turns and ups and downs."

A light smile crossed my lips. "When did you become the expert in magic?"

Jenna shot back a smirk. "I'm not. I just know how life works. I've been through enough shit to know that one."

I dropped my gaze, really contemplating what Jenna was saying. "Maybe you're right. I have been holding on to a lot of anger lately." I closed my eyes and took a deep breath, trying to force out some of the tension in my shoulders.

"Believe me..." Jenna reached out and placed her hand on mine. I opened my eyes to look at her, and the rest of the tension melted out of me. Her words were like an energy of their own, reminding me that I wasn't alone. "I know how hard it is to stay positive in the roughest moments."

Silence settled over the washroom as Jenna and I stared at each other. The knot in my chest softened, and I felt my lips twitch into a smile. I turned my hand over to hold on to hers. Jenna didn't have to say anything else. Just her presence here and the familiar look in her eyes restored a sense of peace within myself I realized I'd let slip away.

"Can you try the spell again?" she asked.

"Okay." I grabbed the soap bar and repeated the incantation. This time, my clothes smelled fresher, though they still had a few dirt stains on them.

Jenna shrugged. "Good enough, I guess."

I changed back into my clothes and ran my fingers through my hair. Before Jenna and I left the building, I stopped her. "Hey, Jenna?"

She paused with her hand on the doorknob. "Yeah?"

"Don't let me forget what you said, okay? About the ups and the downs. I need a reminder about that every now and then."

She draped an arm around my shoulder and opened the door. "Me, too, sis. Me, too."

11

I laid my head back in the sand and closed my eyes, focusing on the sound of the waves lapping against the shore. The sun was hidden behind a thick layer of clouds, as it tended to do here on Gregor Island. I thought that maybe the sounds of nature would take my mind off everything, but it did nothing to shrink the gaping hole in my chest where all the hope and determination I'd had once resided. Now, there was nothing.

Several days had passed, but it felt like months. I still wasn't any closer to figuring out how to find that dagger, kill Valkas, and get off the island. At this point, I didn't think I ever would.

On the bright side, I hadn't seen Valkas again, which was both a good and a bad thing. On one hand, I didn't *want* to see him again. On the other, it made me a little suspicious. I'd stayed alive that first night because he was having fun with me. Now he was totally ignoring me? It didn't sit right with me, but I decided to look at it as a blessing.

Blessings these days were few and far between. I spent my nights forced into slave labor in the chateau, cleaning chimneys and fireplaces or polishing baseboards. That part wouldn't have been so bad if it weren't for the uniform, a tight-fitting outfit that my butt cheeks hung out of. At least once an hour some sicko would pass by and whistle at me. I'd even been slapped in the ass a few times—and I just took it, because what was the point in fighting back now?

During my downtime, I'd been trying to channel more positive energy, but it wasn't helping with my magic. It was nigh on impossible to stay positive after everything I'd seen.

I watched a female vampire grope her male blood slave in front of his cabin, squeezing so tightly that tears rose to his eyes. Then she criticized him for showing any emotion, saying he should be pleased because they "always had a good time." I listened to a woman cry in the next cabin over after she returned from a feeding, and I saw a man beg a vamp for a feeding, just to get that high from it he'd become addicted to. The vamp refused and looked positively pleased when the man fell to his knees and begged for a hit.

One guy even went into shock from blood loss on his way back from the chateau, and a group of blood slaves had to carry him back to the cabins and nurse him back to health. His master forced him back on his feet the next evening.

The second night I was here, I listened to the story of how Andi had been snatched the night before her wedding a few months ago, straight from the hotel suite her maid of honor had booked for the bridal party. I felt sick each morning Jenna returned from the chateau after being paraded around and fed on. The life in her eyes left for a good two hours afterward until she finally felt like talking again.

I tried not to let it all get to me, but I couldn't force the nausea out of my gut. Instead, I figured I could use it to fuel my power, shaping the anger and resentment I felt toward the vampires into love and compassion for their slaves.

"*Ardeat ignis.*" A blast of flames shot up out of my palm, but as soon as it came, it was gone.

All my efforts were futile. I rolled over in the sand and pulled my knees up to my chest, curling into a ball. This wasn't the first time I'd ever given up, but somehow, it felt like it would be my last. Valkas was planning something for me. I was sure of it. Soon enough, he was going to get bored of keeping me around. I'd already lost so much. I didn't have long before I'd lost absolutely everything, including Jenna.

"That fire was sweet."

I started at the sound of the voice behind me and sat up. "Jenna."

She plopped down in the sand and bumped her shoulder against mine. "It was really cool. You should do it again."

I shook my head. "It's not working right. I don't know if it's me, or if it's something about this island. Probably me."

It was like Synchrony had forgotten about me, like I was no longer needed and Synchrony wasn't willing to respond to me anymore.

"Nothing's gone as planned," I continued. "It feels like I'm just sitting around waiting for Valkas to sink my teeth into me."

Jenna laughed. "Aren't we all?"

I shrugged, totally not feeling the laughter right now. I dropped my gaze to the sand and curled my arms around my knees. It felt like I had to shrink into a ball just to hold myself together, like if I stretched out, my guts would fall right out of my abdomen.

"What are you doing out here?" I asked. "Shouldn't you be sleeping?" The whole island went to sleep during the day.

Jenna rolled her eyes. "Screw that. It's the only time any of us get to ourselves."

I looked away without responding.

Her expression turned serious. "Are you okay?"

Tears pricked at my eyes, and my throat swelled. I bit my lower lip to hold it all back, but I couldn't keep it from Jenna. "No," I admitted, my voice cracking. "I'm not. I—"

I wanted to explain it all to her, but the words wouldn't come out. Instead, tears began rolling down my cheeks. I buried my face into my knees, letting the tears soak into the jeans Jenna had leant me.

"Rachel," she whispered.

She placed a gentle hand on my shoulder, and I lost it. My shoulders heaved against my will, and I turned into a blubbering mess. Once it started, I couldn't turn it off. Jenna scooted closer to me and wrapped an arm around my shoulder. She didn't say anything. She just stroked her fingers through my hair, then ran a comforting hand across my back.

I leaned into her and cried until my tears dried up. Soon, my sobs turned into dry heaves.

It'd been up to me to rid the world of the vampire curse, and I'd let everyone down. All the terrible things the vampires did… the murders, the feedings, the abuse… it would all go on without any way to stop it. Is that what Synchrony wanted?

If so, Synchrony was stupid.

Then there was Venn, Fiona, and the rest of them. I'd never see them again. They'd never know what had happened to me. I wished I could tell them how sorry I was.

"Do you want to talk about it?" Jenna finally whispered.

I buried my face deeper into her shoulder and shook my head. Even though I objected to her invitation, I found myself speaking anyway. "I feel like such a screw-up."

"You're not a screw-up," she argued.

"I am," I cried, lifting my head. I wiped at my face. "I was the key to making the world a better place, but I totally screwed it up. I don't have a chance of getting that dagger back. I'll never kill Valkas, and we'll never make it off this island."

Jenna's eyes glistened with tears. Damn it. I was going to start bawling again if she cried.

"I can't stand to see you like this," she whispered.

"Then go away," I offered.

"No! I'm not leaving you alone at a time like this."

"It's fine, Jenna. I'll be all right." It was a total lie. All I wanted was to be next to her.

"You're my sister," she said. "And what should sisters do?"

Her words caught me off guard. It was something Mom always said when Jenna and I were fighting. She'd force us to look each other in the eyes and would say those exact words.

"Sisters shouldn't fight," Mom would tell us.

"Yeah, yeah," we'd reply in unison.

Mom would come back in a stern voice and say, *"What should sisters do?"*

"Love each other," I answered.

Jenna nodded. "That's right. You better believe it when I say it. I *love* you, Rachel. And I'm here for you."

I forced a smile. "Thanks, Jenna."

"For what?"

"For your positive energy. I don't know how you've kept it all this time. I wouldn't be nearly as strong as you if I went through what you have these last couple of years."

"Kept it?" she repeated. "Rachel, I *make* my own positive energy. You don't survive long on this island without it. No one's going to hand that to you here. You have to go make it yourself. Ups and downs, remember?"

I considered her words for a moment, then said, "When did you get so wise?"

Jenna laughed. "I've always been this wise, dweeb. It took you long enough to notice." She got to her feet and held out an inviting hand. "Follow me. I want to show you something."

All I wanted to do was stay here and shrivel up, but Jenna had me intrigued. Curiously, I took her hand and followed her into the woods.

"Where are we going?" I asked as we stepped over fallen logs and underbrush.

"It's not very far," she replied, but she didn't answer my question.

After a short hike, Jenna came to a stop beside a large rotting stump. A thick log lay on the ground beside it, which was covered in a large pile of sticks and other debris. She sat on the ground beside it and looked up at me.

"What is this?" I asked.

She patted the dirt next to her. "I've never shown anyone this before, so you'll have to keep it a secret."

"Who am I going to tell?" I lowered myself beside her.

She shrugged. "True."

"So, what's the secret?"

She took a deep breath. "You asked me how I stay positive. The truth is, it's not easy. Honestly, I'm not sure if I'd even use that word—*positive*. The fact is, I gave up a long time ago. I resigned myself to the fact that the Soulless had taken everything from me and there was no way to get any of it back."

Sounds familiar.

"About four months in, someone said something to me. He told me, *'The Soulless can take everything from you—except for who you are.'*"

She paused for a moment to let the words sink in. Honestly, I wasn't quite sure what she meant. It sure seemed like the Soulless could strip you of everything if they wanted to.

"That stuck with me, but it wasn't until I made this that I started to understand what it meant." Jenna pushed the debris aside and pulled out a hand-made wreathe from beneath the pile. "I couldn't change what the Soulless did to me. I could only change how I reacted to it."

I took the wreathe in my hands to examine it. It was made of twisted evergreen boughs, with pinecones and acorns attached. "You made this?"

Jenna nodded. "For Mom. I know it's silly, but I just had to make her one."

"For Mother's Day," I said breathlessly. Jenna and I always made one together for her.

She pulled out a second one to show me. This one was bigger and more intricate and had dried flowers scattered throughout.

"I can't believe you still make her a wreathe every year."

Jenna smiled shyly. "I made you something, too."

"You did?" I looked up at her in shock.

She pulled out a long, hollow stick that had a line of holes cut out along its length. "It's supposed to be a flute."

I took it and handed her back the wreathe. I could hardly find the words. "You really made this for me?"

"Yeah, for your eighteenth birthday. I never thought I'd get the chance to give it to you, though. I thought that maybe I could use it to play that lullaby Mom used to sing to us."

"The full moon is shining. The stars glitter above," I sang softly.

"The wind whispers softly, 'Goodnight, my love,'" Jenna finished.

Now my eyes were tearing up for an entirely different reason. I brought the flute to my lips and blew through it. Nothing happened.

Jenna giggled. "It didn't work out like I'd hoped."

My lips lifted at the corners. "Thank you anyway. It's a really sweet gift."

Silence passed between us, but it was anything but awkward. It felt good to just sit here with my sister. It'd been so long. I forgot how nice it was.

Finally, Jenna took a deep breath and spoke. "Anyway, I came down to the beach because I wanted to talk to you about something."

"Oh?"

She took the flute back and placed everything beneath the debris pile again, where it was hidden from view, then turned to me. "I've been doing some thinking. For so long, I honestly thought I'd never see you again, and now here you are. You know what that tells me?"

I shook my head.

"Even when we've given up hope, there's still a chance. I'm starting to think that maybe this isn't the end."

"Really?" I asked, my heart lifting slightly.

"Really."

My stomach dropped. She was talking crazy.

"How am I going to get the dagger back?" I asked. "I don't even know where it is."

Jenna pressed her lips together in thought. "I think I know someone who can help us. Are you up for a party?"

"A party?" That sounded like something we'd get in trouble for.

Jenna waved her hand nonchalantly. "The vamps don't care what we do as long as we're at their side when they say so. Personally, I think they let us have our little bits of freedom because they know we'll comply easier with it. The feedings aren't as bad if you have something to look forward to afterward. Not to mention healthier blood slaves taste better."

Ew! The thought made me cringe.

"I swear it's the only thing that keeps me from going crazy," she said. "And I'm sure that's why they let you room with me. So… are you up for it?"

I hesitated. "What kind of party?"

"Just some people getting together down at Eagle Rock."

"Will there be booze?"

Jenna laughed. "Do you think the Soulless wouldn't supply alcohol? Alcohol-infused blood is the best kind."

"It's stupid and reckless," I told her.

"Yep." She patted my knee for show. "And that's one good thing about me that hasn't changed. What about you, Rugrat?"

I guess it wouldn't hurt to let loose a little—since I was stuck here anyway. "I do reckless shit all the time. What do you think brought me here?"

"Awesome. Is that what you're wearing?"

I tugged at the hem of my shirt. "Is there a dress code?"

Jenna stood and held her hand out to me. "Come on. Let's go find you something."

12

"**D**amn, you look hot!" Jenna whistled from across the cabin.

I twirled around to show off the black bikini from all angles.

"When did you get boobs?" she teased.

I swatted at her. "Shut up. I've always had them. Where'd all these clothes come from, anyway?"

She shrugged, glancing to the dresser at the foot of her bed. "I don't know. The vampires supply them. They're all enchanted to shift with us, too."

"That's weird," I said. "It's almost like they care."

She rolled her eyes. "Don't be so naïve, Rachel. Would you let *your* pet run around in rags all the time?"

I frowned at the word *pet*. It was sick that that was all she was to them.

"How does it work?" My tone shifted, becoming soft, and I sank down onto the bottom bunk beside her. "With the vamps, I mean. Do they… share you?"

"No," Jenna replied with a shake of her head. She dropped her gaze and picked at her fingernails. "Each of the Soulless has one or two blood slaves specific to them. The higher up in the rankings they are, the more they get. Of course, Valkas gets his choice of any of us, but he cycles through his favorites."

"And you…?" I started hesitantly.

"I used to be one of his favorites," she answered with a frown. "But he gets bored easily. I've been with Silas for about a year. He's gentler than Valkas, but…"

"But what?" I pressed.

She sighed. "But it's unpleasant."

"Yeah. No one's exactly begging for vampires to go around biting them."

"Oh, believe me," Jenna said, "some people do."

An uncomfortable silence hung in the air. I quickly changed the subject. "So, that day I came here, when Valkas ripped that guy's heart out, where were you? I thought I'd find you up at the chateau, but…"

"No, I was actually down on the beach. I was lucky enough not to witness that."

"The beach?" I suddenly remembered seeing a couple sitting down there while I was flying over the island. Jenna's hair was shorter, and she'd put on some muscle since the last time I saw her, so I hadn't recognized her from above. "Who was that guy you were with?"

She shot me a confused expression, as if to ask how I knew. Then she stood and started for the door. "Come on, Rach. There's someone I want you to meet."

I followed behind her in bare feet along one of the trails. Laughter broke through the trees, and I heard the sound of water splashing in the distance. It wasn't long before the forest opened and I saw a group of people gathered where the trail ended. Jenna and I stepped out onto a wide, rocky surface that rose about fifteen feet out of the water. Moss and grass covered the ground, and a tall tree hung over the edge of the rock, where a guy in swim trunks was swinging from a rope. He let go and flailed his arms as he plummeted toward the water. People around him cheered and clapped.

"Hey, Jenna!" A guy holding a beer approached us. He had six-pack abs, long blond hair tied into a bun at the base of his neck, and a small amount of facial hair on his chin. He looked like a hippie, but a sexy hippie.

"Hey, Ronark," Jenna greeted, gesturing to me. "This is my sister, Rachel."

"A pleasure," he said, extending his hand out to me.

"Call me Rae," I said, shaking his hand. "So, Ronark? That's an interesting name."

"It's a surname," he said. "Elijah just doesn't sound as cool, you know?"

"I think Elijah is a good name," I told him.

Ronark laughed. "You wanna take your chances on the rope, Rae?"

I glanced over to the girl doing a backflip off of it. It actually looked kind of fun.

I shrugged. "Sure, why not?"

"You have to play the game, though," he insisted.

"Okay, I'm intrigued. What's the game?"

"It's a variation of Truth or Dare," Jenna explained. "If you step up to the rope, you have to do whatever challenge the person behind you gives you, or you don't get to go again. We go until there's only one person left."

I smirked. "Challenge accepted."

I stepped up to the line behind a girl with dark skin and shoulder-length black hair. Ronark took the spot behind me, with Jenna behind him. The dark-haired girl glanced back at me after grabbing the rope.

"You have to give her a dare," Ronark explained.

"Um, okay…" I thought about it for a moment. "No using your legs?"

She smirked. "Easy."

She held high up on the rope, took a running start, and jumped off the end of the rock. She went soaring through the air and pencil-dived feet-first into the water.

The rope came swinging back to me, and I grabbed it out of the air. "What's my challenge, Ronark?"

He eyed me up and down, thinking. Then he threw back a gulp of beer and said, "No splash."

"Are you kidding me?" I complained.

"Hey," he said, spreading his arms wide. "No one said the challenges had to be fair."

"Fine. I've got this."

At least twenty pairs of eyes were watching me. Holding firmly on to the rope, I kicked off the rock. As I reached the peak of my swing, I pulled my legs upward and aimed my head toward the water. Mid-jump, I shifted into a raven. Cool water rushed over my beak, then my feathers. I spread my wings out under water, and for a moment, it felt like I was flying again. I quickly shifted back to human form and kicked my feet. My head broke the surface of the water, and I took a deep breath.

All around me came a chorus of *oohs* and *ahs*.

"Did that count?" someone in the water asked.

"It totally counted," someone else replied.

"Is that allowed?" another person responded.

I looked up to Ronark on the rock, beaming at him. It sounded like I'd completed the challenge.

He sighed, but there was a smile on his face. "I'll give it to her."

A few girls in the water cheered for me.

"What's my challenge, Jenna?" Ronark asked.

She crossed her arms and smirked. "You know."

He dropped his shoulders. "Seriously? Again?"

"If you didn't want to do it, why'd you stand in front of me in line?" she challenged.

Ronark rolled his eyes and handed her his beer. "Fine. Hold my beer."

"Famous last words," she teased.

Ronark sighed and reached for the waistband of his swim trunks. Before I could look away, his trunks had fallen to his ankles and his package was out there in the open for everyone to see. He was seriously blessed in that department. People all around us whistled and hollered.

"Ronark the Magnificent, everyone!" Jenna announced, gesturing to him like he was a trophy prize.

"Yeah, yeah," he said sarcastically, flipping her off. Then he sprinted to the edge of the rock, jumped to grab the rope, and flipped into the water. He broke the surface a second later, while people continued to cheer. After pushing wet hair out of his eyes, he held up two middle fingers to everyone. "You all can go screw yourselves!"

"With that image in my mind?" the guy closest to him joked. "No way!"

Ronark started swimming toward him, and the guy quickly made a beeline for the edge of the rock, where there was a slope leading back up to the top.

"Ew!" he cried. "Keep your dick away from me, man."

Ronark climbed out of the water and started chasing after him. His bare butt was on full display. I couldn't help but laugh. Even in the midst of everything that these people had gone through, they found a way to make the most of a bad situation.

Jenna took a swig of Ronark's beer, then jumped for the rope and did a flip into the water. Once she broke the surface, she made her way over to where I was treading water.

"Having fun?" she asked.

"It's the most fun I've had all week," I replied, stating the obvious. The last time I'd gone swimming was at Genevieve's lake house. The thought instantly made me think of Venn, and my heart sank. I missed him so much. I wished he was here right now—or rather, that I was with him.

"You okay?" Jenna asked.

I nodded to reassure her. "Yeah, I just miss my boyfriend."

"Aww," she said genuinely, like it was sweet. "Come on. We have work to do."

"Work?" I asked.

"I didn't drag you out here just to catch a glimpse of Ronark's manhood."

"Oh, but it was a fun show," I joked.

"I know." She smiled mischievously before leading me back to dry land.

Ronark returned from out of the trees, snatched up his swim trunks, and slipped them on. A guy in the water groaned in jest.

"Show's over, Brad," Ronark snapped playfully.

A few girls laughed and splashed Brad. He quickly retaliated.

Ronark grabbed his beer from off the rock and downed the rest of it, then made his way over to Jenna and me. "You drank my beer," he accused her.

She shrugged. "You put it in my hand."

"I should've known better," he admitted. "I'm going to grab another one."

"When you're done, we need to talk," Jenna said.

"Ooh," a guy sang as he passed by. "*Someone's* in the doghouse."

"Shut up!" Ronark snapped back. "It's not like that. You want one, Rae?"

"Nah, I'm good," I replied.

"Jenna?" Ronark asked on his way to the cooler.

She shrugged. "Might as well."

Ronark returned and handed Jenna a beer. She cocked her head, and we followed her into the woods. We walked until we were far enough away from the swimming hole that we could hardly hear the hoots and hollers anymore. Jenna sat on a fallen log and took a sip of beer. I sat beside her, while Ronark leaned against a tree.

"What's up?" he asked casually.

Jenna got straight to the point. "We need your help."

His eyebrows shot up. "I'm intrigued. Go on."

"Out of everyone on this island, you've been here the longest. You know Valkas best. If we wanted to…" Jenna exchanged a quick glance with me. I didn't like where this was going. "If we wanted to steal something valuable from him, you'd know where to find it."

Ronark smirked and nodded. "You girls are entering dangerous territory."

"He's right, Jenna," I said. "I don't know about this."

She kept her eyes on Ronark, ignoring my statement. "If it works, we all go free."

His face lit up, but it quickly reverted to normal. "Nobody goes free on this island, sweet cheeks. There's only one way off, and it ain't pretty."

"Unless you happened to have access to the one thing that could kill Valkas," she replied.

Ronark pressed his lips together, looking skeptical. "And what might that be?"

I could tell he didn't believe her. As far as anyone else knew, Valkas couldn't be killed. Jenna glanced to me. Even though I could tell she trusted Ronark, she was deliberately vague.

"That's for us to know and you to find out," she said.

Ronark laughed and tipped his bottle to his lips.

"It's true," Jenna snapped.

He went completely still and slowly lowered the bottle. "You can really kill him?"

She nodded. "He has a dagger that can be used to stop him. Do you know what he would've done with it? Hidden it? Destroyed it?"

"Destroyed it, maybe…" Ronark said in thought. He began pacing back and forth in front of us. "But how do you destroy a dagger? You could break it, but the shards could still kill you. Or melt it down, but where would he find the means on this island? Besides, if it's infused with magic, it might not be able to be destroyed. He might send it off the island, but… no, I think I know exactly what he'd do with it."

He stopped pacing and turned to look at us, a bright expression on his face.

"Well…?" Jenna pressed.

"It's not going to be easy to get," Ronark said. "Nearly impossible, even."

It was like he could read my mind.

"Just tell us," Jenna insisted.

He sighed. "He's got it on him."

"Of course," I muttered.

It sounded so much like him. *Keep your friends close but your enemies closer* kind of thing. Valkas wouldn't trust that weapon anywhere else but where he could keep a constant eye on it.

I turned to Jenna. "Look, this party was fun, but that's it. At some point, I have to accept that I'm a blood slave now and I'm never going to see my friends again. This plan is never going to work."

"You don't know that," she countered. "The least we can do is try."

"Our odds are next to none," I pointed out.

"I thought the same thing about seeing you again, Rachel. I never thought I would." Jenna's eyes pleaded with me.

"Yeah, but this…" I shook my head.

"What's the worst that could happen?" she argued.

She had a point. I could die trying, but what did that matter? Valkas had to be planning worse for me anyway. Might as well go out with a bang.

"I… I guess it's worth a shot," I admitted. "As long as you realize it probably won't work."

"Don't say that," Jenna insisted sternly. "If Ronark's right, all you have to do is get him alone."

I pressed my lips together in thought. "I guess that's pretty easy if he decides to feed on me again."

Ronark scoffed. "Not unless you want to get yourself killed. Where do you think he's keeping it? On his belt? In his boot? On a sheath strapped to his thigh? You only get one guess, sweet cheeks—"

"Don't call me that."

"And if you don't guess correctly, it's game over," he concluded.

Jenna glanced between the two of us nervously. Her plan was already starting to crumble. "So, what do we do?"

Ronark turned and gazed off into the forest, taking another sip of beer. "Wait for the end?"

"Oh, don't even with me!" Jenna shot to her feet and stomped over to Ronark. She grabbed him by the shoulder and forced him to turn around and look at her. "You have *not* given up."

"What makes you say that?" he challenged. "I've been here eight years, snatched during my first shift before anyone even knew what shifters were! I never got to finish college. I don't even know what the outside world is like now, except what I've heard from the rest of you. What's there to go back to?"

"Come on, Ronark," Jenna pleaded. "I know you don't truly feel that way."

"Oh, yeah? And how come you think you know me so well?"

Jenna stared him in the eyes and softened her tone. "Because we wouldn't be having this conversation if you thought that. You're always telling me there's more than this."

"Those are just hopes and dreams," he said.

"Exactly," Jenna replied. "You're the one who told me I get to choose how I react. This is it. This is my decision."

Ronark's shoulders fell. "When'd you become the smart one, Collins?"

She smiled. "The day I met you, Eli."

"Oh, come on," he complained. "You know I hate it when you call me that."

"Okay, okay." She held her hand up in surrender. "I'll drop the pet name for good, but you have to help us."

Ronark pressed his lips together. "You two really think you can do this?"

"No." Jenna looked to me. "I *know* we can."

Her confidence in me was astounding.

Slowly, a grin spread across Ronark's face. "Now that's the kind of attitude I'm talking about. But you're going to need at least four or five shifters to take him on."

"Why?" I asked. I couldn't believe we were actually going to go through with this.

Ronark shrugged. "Conservative estimate. He's strong. A good shifter or two might be able to take him on, but you need more than just a distraction. You need to immobilize him."

"So we gather a team and sneak in during the day while everyone's asleep?" I guessed.

"No, no." Ronark quickly shot my idea down. "Too risky. There are guards stationed in every hallway."

I furrowed my brow. "Not the last time I was in there."

"When was that?" Ronark cocked an eyebrow.

"Um… the day of the incident, the one where that guy died."

Ronark scoffed. "You got lucky. Valkas corralled his guards to deal with that security issue. On any given day, you'd run into at least four guards before you hit Valkas's room."

"So we create a distraction," Jenna offered.

"No. I think I might know something that could work better." Ronark sat on the log beside me, and Jenna joined him on his other side. We both leaned in close while he whispered, "Valkas's Awakening Ball is coming up in just under a week."

"Awakening Ball?" I asked.

"It's a celebration he holds every year to honor himself," Ronark explained. "Dumb, really, but the Soulless eat it right up. It's the anniversary of the day he escaped the island."

"How's that going to help us get close to him?" Jenna asked.

"Each year, he puts on this grand march ceremony where blood slaves carry him into the ballroom on one of those big carriage-like things with the poles. You know what I'm talking about, right?"

Jenna nodded. "It's called a litter."

"Right. I just so happen to know the vampire who coordinates the whole thing." By the way he said it, it sounded like he was her blood slave. "I can make sure we're on that list to carry him in."

Jenna smiled mischievously. "And we strike before he ever makes his grand entrance."

"Bingo," Ronark confirmed.

"Are you sure that's going to work, though?" I questioned. "That he'll actually be alone?"

"Darling, I've been watching these things go down for years. Valkas is so vain he wants everyone to witness his grand entrance. I assure you we can get him alone beforehand."

"What about me?" I asked. "Valkas knows I'm a threat. He's not going to let me alone with him without his witch bodyguard present to play puppet on me."

"Good point," Jenna agreed. "And Rachel has to be there. She has to be the one to do it."

Ronark didn't ask why, like he trusted Jenna without question. "We could disguise her…"

"Too obvious," Jenna said.

Ronark turned to me. "Then I guess, princess, you're going to have to find a way into that litter on your own."

I didn't like what he was suggesting. Not one bit. But if I was going along with this, I had to make some sacrifices.

It was time I made my first one.

13

My opportunity came that night when I was summoned to the chateau. Anton came to my cabin to collect me and led me to a fancy dining room I hadn't seen before. There was a long mahogany table set for twelve, with a big chandelier hanging over it and a fireplace beside it. The red drapes had been pulled back so that moonlight spilled through the tall windows.

"You must wear this," Anton said, gesturing to a dress that hung from a sconce on the wall.

I eyed the silky black evening dress and matching high heels. "I'm comfortable in this, thanks."

"No choice. Lord Valkas requires it."

I pressed my lips together. If I wanted to have a civil conversation with Valkas, I might as well do as I'm told.

"Fine," I agreed, "but I'd like some privacy."

Anton nodded and turned out of the dining room, leaving me alone. I glanced toward each of the doors leading out of the room in various directions while I pulled my pants and shirt off and slipped into the dress. It was a perfect fit, but the neckline plunged so far that the girls were practically playing peek-a-boo with each other. At the base of my cleavage was a feathery beaded brooch that I might've liked if it wasn't just there to draw Valkas's nasty eyes.

Just as I was pulling on the shoes, the door farthest from me opened. I kicked my clothes and boots under the decorative table in the corner and straightened.

Valkas entered with a smile on his face. He wore a black suit with a red tie, looking like some sort of stockbroker or something. "Rachel," he greeted, like we were old friends.

"Valkas," I said coolly as my spine stiffened.

He stopped at the head of the table opposite me. "What is it, darling? You don't like the dress? I thought it would suit you quite well."

"It does," I lied. "I just didn't know you knew my name."

He waved his hand nonchalantly. "Darling, nothing stays secret for long on this island. *Especially* from me." He leveled me with a challenging glare that sent a shiver down my spine. "Please, take a seat."

I sat where he gestured at the opposite end of the table from him. The long table was like a football field between us, which I suppose was a good thing, but it also felt highly impersonal.

Valkas sat, then rang a bell that was set next to his glass.

"To what do I owe the pleasure?" I asked, placing my napkin in my lap—only because that felt like the proper thing to do.

Just then, a line of servants came through a swinging door, which I presumed led to the kitchen. *What does a vamp need a kitchen for?* I thought briefly.

The woman in front pushed a cart to my end of the table and set a plate of steaming food in front of me. The scent of garlic, onions, and a mix of spices filled my nose. My mouth watered at the sight of a juicy steak and roasted potatoes. I reached for my fork immediately, but I slowed when I remembered who was serving it to me.

The woman leaned over and filled my glass with water without a word. Across the table, another servant poured a thick red liquid into Valkas's glass. Between us, a different woman threw another log of wood in the fire, then they all turned in unison and headed back to the kitchens.

Valkas took a sip of blood, then smacked his lips before responding to my question. "I just thought we could have a nice dinner together."

"You must forgive my caution," I said flatly.

"Go ahead, Rachel," Valkas insisted. "It's not poisoned. If I wanted to poison you, I would've done it in the dining hall in the slave quarters. Actually, I wouldn't have even waited that long."

That was very true. I lifted my knife and cut into the steak. Its savory flavor filled my taste buds with so much pleasure that I might've stayed on this island just for the food.

"Delicious, isn't it?" Valkas said with a smile. "It will give your blood a nice... *juicy* flavor."

I immediately slowed my chewing and set my knife down. "Is that why you brought me here? To feed on me again?"

"Oh, no." Valkas spoke slowly and took another sip of his drink. "That is merely a perk of the meeting."

"What am I here for?" I suddenly remembered how much Valkas hated questions. He didn't seem to notice this time, though.

"I want to make you a proposition."

I poked a potato with my fork and glanced up at Valkas across the table. The look in his eyes told me he was serious. I contemplated how to phrase my next question without asking directly, '*And what makes you think I'd agree to that?*'

"A girl like me doesn't often negotiate," I said before popping the potato in my mouth.

"That's because a girl like you doesn't know what she wants." A shadow passed across Valkas's silver eyes, making them look even darker.

He was wrong. I knew exactly what I wanted. *Safety.* Safety for my family. For my friends. For the world. And that was never going to happen as long as there were vampires alive. I didn't care what the government thought about their *rights*. Vamps thrived off evil tendencies and didn't care who they hurt in the process.

"What is it that you think I want?" Woops. Another question. Though this time, his eyes brightened, like he was more than happy to answer.

He leaned back in his chair and gestured around himself. "What does *everyone* want, Rachel?"

I went silent, not sure if he actually intended for me to answer.

"Power," he said. "Wealth. There is nothing else."

Maybe to him there wasn't. But to me, there was family. There was happiness. His power couldn't earn him that.

"When you have those two things," he continued, "you don't need anything else."

"But if everyone's powerful, no one is," I countered, taking another bite of potato.

Valkas smirked. "Not everyone gets what they want, darling. Only the best of the best can achieve greatness. Everyone else follows because they think they can experience greatness vicariously through their master."

Bingo! That was exactly how he'd amassed a following of Soulless. They wanted a piece of the winning pie. I was sure it was the same with Rogers, too.

"So this proposition… it would provide me with power."

"Oh, yes," Valkas replied with a greedy look in his eyes. "More power than you can possibly imagine." He stood and began pacing toward me, slowly running his fingers across the back of each chair as he went. "Can you imagine it, Rachel? A world where we controlled the wealth, where people complied to our every demand, where we were worshiped as gods?"

He stopped behind the chair next to mine and stared down at me with a hungry look in his eyes. I felt like I might puke up my steak.

"You want me to join you," I said without emotion. Right now, it was best if I masked it. I wasn't going to get anywhere by ramming my steak knife through his hand, which I was honestly considering.

Valkas held his head up proudly. "You are a powerful witch, Rachel. With some training, you could be the best."

"And only the best deserves to be at your side." I smiled, playing my part, as if the thought of running the world pleased me.

I didn't have to ask him why he would propose such a thing. *Keep your friends close but your enemies closer* never rang truer than in this moment.

And that's when it hit me. Valkas had been bluffing about trapping my soul. He didn't know how. That, or he didn't have the means. The next best option was getting me on his side, where he could keep a close eye on me. In his eyes, he surely thought he could manipulate me into giving up the fight—as long as the reward was worth it. And if I had all of that, all the power and wealth he'd promised, he might think he had a chance at convincing me to change for him. That way, as an immortal vampire, I'd never come after him again in a reincarnated form.

That was never going to happen, but it just so happened to be the very cover I needed right now.

Valkas stepped behind my chair and brushed the hair from the back of my neck. I shivered beneath his cold touch, but I otherwise remained calm. He bent to whisper in my ear.

"I strive for the best in all areas of life, Rachel. And I always get what I want."

I turned my head to look up at him. "That's a very generous offer."

"Yes, well, I'm a very generous person," he said proudly.

I resisted the urge to snort. "What about my sister?" I couldn't seem too eager to accept his offer. That would only arise suspicion.

Valkas rounded my chair and sat in the chair to my left. "What about her?"

"Correct me if I'm wrong, but I believe this is a negotiation."

He thought about it for a moment before answering. "Yes, I suppose it is."

I almost let a smug smile find its way across my lips. "If I were to go along with this… to join the Soulless… then I have one request."

"Your sister's freedom," Valkas guessed.

"Yes," I answered. "She gets full immunity from any harm. Your men shall not touch her or harm her in any way."

He pressed his lips together in thought. I could tell it was hard for him to accept a negotiation. He liked to be the one in charge. But he also *really* wanted me by his side, where he could keep watch over me for eternity.

"I think that can be arranged," he finally agreed. "I have to say, I thought you'd take more convincing."

I almost panicked, but I shrugged for show. "Like I said, it's a generous proposal. All I want is for my sister to go free. Then I'm more than happy to enjoy the power and wealth you've offered."

Valkas's lips curled into an evil grin. "You're a wise woman, Rachel."

Ha! *Woman*. No one had ever called me *that* before.

"So, you will join me?" he asked.

I took a sip of water. "I thought we already established that."

"I need to hear you say it, darling." Valkas took my hand in his and stood from his chair. Then he lowered himself onto one knee. Definitely not how I pictured my first proposal. "Rachel, will you do the honor of becoming my right-hand woman and helping me conquer this world?"

Pushing down the bile rising to my throat, I answered in the softest, sweetest tone I could muster. "I will."

Valkas pressed his slimy lips to the back of my hand, then flipped it over so it faced palm-up. His fangs elongated.

"Whoa." I pulled back slightly, but not enough to escape his grasp. He held on to my wrist tightly, and it became very apparent why Ronark cautioned me against doing this alone. He was *strong*.

Valkas looked up at me, and darkness crossed his eyes. "I thought it was apparent what would happen next. I must give you the mark of the Soulless to secure our deal."

"Fair enough," I said, though I really, *really* didn't want the mark of the Soulless on my wrist. "I just thought…" I paused for dramatic effect.

"Thought what?" Valkas growled, clearly starting to get annoyed.

"I thought there'd be a big ceremony or something. We could announce this in front of the entire island. It would mark the beginning of a new era for the Soulless."

Valkas paused for a moment. "And when would we do this?"

"Your Awakening Ball, perhaps?" I suggested, holding my breath. If this didn't work, I was going to crap diamonds. All hope would be lost.

Valkas dropped my hand and stood. "You make a fair point. We will announce it in a week's time. That will give me plenty of time to coordinate our first strike in the new war against humanity. And you, my darling, will fight alongside me as my queen."

He pressed his lips to the exposed skin on the side of my neck, his fangs trailing along my skin without breaking it. My breath wavered momentarily. Convincing Valkas I would fight alongside him had been far too easy.

That's when I realized a horrifying truth. There were likely things about Valkas's plan he had yet to reveal to me. He could very well be playing me for an even greater purpose.

I just had to beat him at his own damn game.

14

I was counting down the days until the Awakening Ball. Five days had passed since my meeting with Valkas when Ronark invited Jenna and me into his cabin to discuss the plan.

"Be careful what you say," I warned in a low voice. "I think I'm being watched."

I knew how guys like Valkas worked. He pretended like I was nothing more than the dirt on his shoes, inviting me to fancy dinners with him only to put me on the menu for dessert—and yeah, it had happened more than once this week, and I'd had to stomach it for the sake of our plan—only to toss me back to the slave quarters when he was done with me.

But I think he did it because he thought I was more comfortable in the slave quarters and around my sister than I would be up at the chateau. It was his way of luring me into a false sense of security. But I couldn't shake this feeling—the one that made the little hairs on the back of my neck stand up—that I was being watched. Which didn't surprise me in the slightest. It just meant I had to be cautious.

"We're all shifters here," Ronark said, glancing from my sister to me, then to the shades that were drawn over the window. "They can't hear us."

"Still, keep your voice down," I said. "What kind of shifter are you, anyway?" He looked like he might be something small and gentle, like a hamster or something.

Ronark held up a hand to stop me. "Believe me, sweet cheeks, you don't want to know."

"So, did you get us on the list?" Jenna cut in.

Ronark smirked. "Yep. I've got Andi and Brad on the list, too, and they're all for taking Valkas down. I trust these shifters with my life."

361

"And me?" I asked. Valkas and I had agreed to make our big announcement during the Awakening Ball, but he never agreed to have me ride in the litter with him. One way or another, I had to get to the staging area, where he'd be alone and it'd be seven against one.

"I'm still working on that, sweet cheeks," Ronark replied. "It's hard to convince my mistress without admitting I know what's going on. I have to make her think it's her idea."

"Or I need to convince Valkas," I said. "He's not the kind of guy who would want to share the spotlight."

"Which is exactly why I think we need a Plan B, C, and D," Ronark said. "We have one shot at getting this guy alone. We can't screw it up."

My stomach twisted. I still wasn't sure this would work.

Just then, voices came from outside, more than I expected to hear this early in the morning. Usually, the slaves came back from the chateau one by one, not in a huge group, and we still had an hour until sunrise. Jenna and Ronark exchanged a quick glance, and they both frowned.

"What?" I asked in alarm. "What's going on?"

Jenna pushed away from the wall where she'd been leaning. "New recruits."

I hated the way people used the word *recruits* around here… like they had a choice.

"Come on." Jenna turned toward the door. "We should go help them find their cabin assignments. Tonight's been rough enough for them as it is."

The three of us stepped outside to see a group of fifteen people surrounded by half a dozen vampires. Other blood slaves had emerged from their cabins and were whispering among themselves.

"Jackson," one of the recruits hissed at the guy beside him, elbowing him in the ribs. He looked young, but he had a long brown beard. The guy beside him—Jackson—was the spitting image of him but with a shorter beard. They wore matching plaid shirts and reminded me of lumberjacks. "Shh…"

"You!" one of the closest vamps said, pointing toward the three of us at the cabin door.

My heart jumped a little until Jenna stepped forward.

The vamp handed her a piece of paper. The mark of the Soulless peeked out from under the sleeve of his leather jacket. "Get them to where they need to go. Their initiation begins tonight."

"Yes, sir," Jenna said confidently.

He turned on his heel and started for the trail leading back up to the chateau. The other vamps followed behind him. The new blood slaves huddled together, throwing glances this way and that.

"I know how hard this must be for all of you," Jenna started, but I didn't hear the rest of her speech.

My gaze fell upon one of the faces in the back of the group. The guy's eyes connected with mine, and he looked at me like I was the only girl in the world.

All the air whooshed out of my lungs, and my knees went weak beneath me. Time stood still as I tried to make sense of what I was seeing.

Dark skin… tight curly hair… I'd know those brown eyes anywhere. What was he *doing* here? Was I hallucinating or something?

Relief momentarily washed over his features. It was quickly replaced by a glistening in his eyes, like he might burst into tears at the sight of me.

Seeing Venn standing in front of me was like the moment you reach the top of a rollercoaster. You feel your heart lift in your chest, and you hold your breath until you think your lungs might burst. For a moment, everything is quiet and still. Then *Bam!* You reach the edge, and your heart flies up into your throat. Every inch of your body pulses with adrenaline. A moment later, the track levels out, and you realize you were never in any danger at all, but still… you can't tame the pounding of your heart and the quaking of your fingers.

Emotions I couldn't even put names to whipped through me so fast that it left me lightheaded. My whole body lit up in desire for him. It was like I could feel every nerve ending come alive, leaving me shaking and on the verge of tears. All that mattered was running into his arms and holding him again. I'd missed him so much.

I started toward him, prepared to rush into his arms, but Ronark grabbed hold of my wrist and pulled me back. I just about clocked the guy in the jaw, but then I caught the look in his eyes.

He lowered his voice. "You're being watched, remember?" He glanced around like he might spot a sniper somewhere in the trees. "If you recognize one of them, the last thing you want to do is let the vamps know."

Good point. My heart ached as I stood there, staring out into the small crowd at Venn. My knees shook, as if they wanted to make their way over to him despite my commands for them to stay put. Venn's expression was full of pain, sorrow, and relief, but he remained still. I knew he did it for the same reason that I continued to stand at Ronark's side. But I spotted something soft in his eyes—something I'd seen so many times throughout my lives that it spoke to me in a way words couldn't.

I bit down hard on my lower lip to keep my emotions at bay. He was like a magnet drawing me to him, and keeping my distance was literally causing me physical pain.

Jenna helped guide the newcomers to their respective cabins, separating them by numbers like livestock. When I saw that Venn was headed our way to fill the empty bed in Ronark's cabin, I nearly toppled over right then and there. My heart pounded so wildly in my chest that I thought the vamps might be able to hear it from the other side of the island.

"In, you two," Ronark instructed.

I couldn't get into the privacy of the cabin soon enough. As soon as Ronark shut the door behind us, I fell into Venn's arms.

"You're here!" I cried. I stood on my toes and pressed my lips to his before he could get in a word. Heat pooled in my belly, and my heart pummeled against the inside of my chest. My hands roamed all over him—up his arms, over his back, and in his hair. I had to check that he was there in flesh and blood, that he was real. And by the hands of all that were holy, he was.

I gasped when he drew away, trying to catch my breath. Venn gazed down at me as tears rolled down his cheeks. He looked at me like he was staring into the eyes of a deity—like he couldn't believe I was standing there in front of him.

"God, Rae. I missed you so much it nearly broke me." Venn's voice was like a song, a beautiful, wonderful song. He pulled me back into an embrace and buried his face in my hair, inhaling my scent like he craved it more than anything else in the world. We rocked from side to side as he held on to me with such tender loving care. "I was so worried about you."

I let my tears soak into the front of his t-shirt. "I can't believe you're here."

"I can't either," he whispered in my ear, his voice cracking. My spine tingled, but in a good way. "But it's really me. I swear."

"I don't mean to interrupt your... reunion," Ronark said. I'd barely remembered he was there. "So I'm going to go."

I heard the door creek open and then shut, but I didn't take my head off Venn's chest. I just wanted to hold him until the end of time.

"You shouldn't have come," I finally said. "It's dangerous here."

"I know." He drew away from me to look me in the eyes again. Tears stained his cheeks. "That's exactly why I had to come."

Swoon.

"Why?" I whispered. "Now you're stuck on this island with the rest of us."

Venn took a deep breath. "I know. It was reckless and impulsive."

I chuckled, mostly because the emotions tearing through me had left me overwhelmed. "It sounds like some of my personality is rubbing off on you."

Venn smiled. "Yeah, it might be. I just couldn't handle not knowing what had happened to you."

We stood there in silence for several minutes, just wrapped in each other's arms. Finally, I spoke.

"Do you have any plans for getting off the island?" God, I hoped he wasn't as stupid as I was. "Because clearly my plan didn't work."

Venn dropped his gaze. "I'm still working on that."

"Yeah, me too. How'd you get here?" I asked.

He shrugged. "I ran into some trouble along the lakeshore."

"When you say *ran into trouble,* you mean *sought out the Soulless,*" I accused lightly.

Venn smirked. "It was the only way to find you. I traveled from bar to bar until I found a guy with the mark on his wrist. I had a little bar fight and... let them take me."

"Venn," I said breathlessly. "You shouldn't have. Did they hurt you?" He looked okay, at least.

He shrugged. "They got a couple of good punches in, but that was almost a week ago already."

"A week? Where have you been all this time?"

"Detained," he answered vaguely. "Until they put us all on a boat and brought us here."

My heart sank. "They don't know who you are yet, do they?"

He shook his head. "No, I don't think so. As far as they know, I'm just some random guy."

I hugged him tighter, even though all I wanted to do was yell at him for being reckless. Then again, I shouldn't exactly be the one to talk. What he did was incredibly noble, and I was glad he was here with me now.

"I'm sorry," I whispered after a brief silence.

Venn ran his fingers through my hair. "Sorry for what?"

"For leaving."

He pressed his lips to the top of my forehead, warming my skin. "I'm just glad I found you."

I wiped the tears from my eyes. "Why did you come?"

Venn's eyes searched mine, like he couldn't tell what I was feeling. "I came for you."

"But... aren't you mad at me?"

His eyebrows knitted together. "Mad?"

I nodded. "For leaving without telling you."

Venn sighed and led me across the cabin to sit on the lower bunk. "Honestly, Rae, I was upset and a little hurt when you left."

I knotted my hands together in my lap. "I'm a terrible girlfriend, aren't I?"

"No," he answered.

"But... we're supposed to be soulmates. And I just... left."

Venn tilted his head in question. "I don't think you understand. Being soulmates isn't an easy way into a relationship. It doesn't mean we'll be perfect. It just means that we have a strong connection. It's what we do with that connection that matters. The connection dies if we don't nurture it."

He wrapped an arm around my shoulder, and I leaned into him, absorbing what he said. I'd never had to work on a relationship before. I'd just assumed they either worked out or they didn't.

"We're a team, Rae," Venn whispered. "Being part of a team takes a lot of work."

I nodded as what he said began to sink in. "I'm glad we're part of the same team."

"Me, too." Venn drew away from me to look me in the eyes.

Slowly, he leaned down until his lips were hovering just millimeters away from mine. That split second before the kiss, all the anticipation leading up to it, was everything. My breath caught in my chest, and my heart lifted until it felt like my entire body was floating.

Then his lips connected with mine, and I completely forgot I was on Gregor Island, surrounded by hundreds of the most ruthless vampires in the world. All that mattered were Venn's lips on mine and his words echoing in my head. *We're a team, Rae.*

I'd be damned if I let my team fall apart.

For the first time, I was starting to get a sense of what Jenna meant when she said that even when we've given up hope, there was still a chance.

"Venn." I drew away, panting. I pressed my forehead to his and gazed down at our entwined fingers.

"Rae," he whispered back. I loved hearing him say my name.

"Are you scared?" I asked.

"Absolutely." He wasn't even afraid to admit it, and that, I felt, took a level of courage I didn't have. I admired him so much for it. "Every day I was without you, I was terrified."

"Me, too," I whispered, closing my eyes. A knot formed in my chest. It was harder to admit than I thought. "I know I'm the Ravenite and I'm not supposed to be afraid of anything, but I am, Venn. I'm just as scared as everyone else."

"Hey," he said lightly, pulling my chin up. "That's okay. Remember what Sondra said? It's okay to feel fear. It's how you use it that matters. I know you, Rae, and I know you'll use it to fuel your determination."

Determined. Resolute. Hell yeah, I was!

I nodded as the knot in my chest began to loosen, as if his words had the power to unravel my unease. All the hopelessness I'd been collecting suddenly seemed irrelevant.

In that moment, Genevieve's words came back to me. *You should know that there's always more than one way off an island.*

Did she know this was going to happen? She couldn't have.

But there had to be something to what she said. Jenna had been trying to convince me of it for days. There *was* another way off this island. There *was* a chance to retrieve the dagger again. We could do this. Together.

"I'll use my fear wisely," I promised.

Venn took my face gently in his hands, guiding my gaze to his. "I know you will."

I lifted my chin to brush my lips across his mouth again. It felt so good, like being in his arms was where I was meant to be—like we were meant to face all of this together. I just wished I could show him how much I loved him.

My hands found their way under his shirt, and I ran them up the bare skin on his back. His fingers tangled in my hair, and he pulled me in until I crawled onto his lap. My whole body shook against him. In that moment, it was as if Venn and I were alone in the world—like there weren't any vampires outside our cabin and we weren't facing a war with impossible odds.

Just us, I repeated to myself, feeling as if time had come to a standstill and the statement was irrevocably true.

I tugged at Venn's shirt until he drew away from me just long enough for me to pull the shirt up over his head. A moment later, his lips were on mine again as my hands roamed his body. I lifted my arms and grabbed hold of the top bunk to steady myself. Venn took my shirt off and tossed it onto the floor. Gently, he wrapped his arms around me and lowered me to the bed. I grabbed for the sheets and pulled them down as we both kicked our shoes off.

Venn's hands found the skin above my waistband and began inching their way up my body. His lips left mine to trail down my neck and to my bra strap lying across my collarbone. I gasped as tingles of excitement spread their way across my skin. Heat pooled between my thighs, and my heart pounded so hard I could feel it shaking my entire body.

"Are you sure about this?" Venn whispered against my shoulder.

I'd never been surer about anything in my life. Yeah, most people might've waited until all of this was over, until they were sure they were safe, but for me, safety was a luxury. Somewhere between all the vampire slaying, I had to live my own life… which I hadn't allowed myself to do in years. I might as well start sooner than later.

"Yes," I breathed, pulling him in closer to me and planting a passionate kiss on his lips. "Venn, I love you."

"There's no rush," he said.

I couldn't help but smile. No one had ever treated me with such tender care before. "I know."

"There will be plenty more opportunities when we make it out of here," he continued. "If you're only doing this because you think we won't—"

"I'm not," I assured him. "I *want* to do this. My life is crazy, Venn. That's not slowing down anytime soon."

He smiled.

"Unless you don't want to…" I started.

"Rae," he said like I was being ridiculous. "I've never wanted to be with anyone more than I want to be with you."

Tears pricked at my eyes again. How'd I find such a wonderful man? My voice came out a mere whisper. "Then be with me."

Venn's lips came down on me again, and I inhaled a sharp breath. Reaching his hand beneath me, he undid my bra and tossed it aside. My chest heaved as his hand roamed over the swell of my breast. I wanted more. So much more.

My fingers trailed down to undo his belt. He kicked his pants off, then unbuttoned mine beneath the sheet. Venn's bare legs were warm against mine, and it only made me want him more. I didn't even know that was possible. My thighs burned for him.

"Please," I begged in his ear.

"Please what?" he asked, teasing me.

I could hardly get the words out past my shallow breaths. "Please. I want to be yours forever."

"You will. I promise."

He sealed the promise with a kiss, then relaxed into me. We gasped in unison. I thought it would hurt, but it didn't. It felt warm and comforting… and *right.*

"Venn," I moaned as he moved against me. Fire raged through my veins.

He pressed his lips to the sensitive skin just below my ear, sending a wave of pleasure down my spine. My breath caught as he pressed into me faster. I squeezed my eyes shut tightly and sank my teeth into his shoulder to keep quiet.

Venn took shallow breaths as his lips roamed over me. His fingers fisted in my hair, and he claimed my lips for his own. His tongue slid inside my mouth, and he kissed me with a passion I'd never felt before. My fingers clawed at his exposed back. He pulled away to kiss my neck, then nipped at my breast.

"Oh my God," I whispered. I couldn't help but let the words slip out of my lips. Being with Venn was unlike anything I'd ever experienced before. It felt like I'd stumbled upon a magical object capable of harnessing all the pleasure from the world and channeling it into myself. It felt so good I thought my heart might burst into a million tiny little stars. Nothing—and I mean *nothing*—could compare to the way I felt when Venn touched me. His skin on my skin... it was like Synchrony itself had blessed me with all the magic in the world.

Venn's hand moved up my side, to my breast, and then down again, until finally landing between my legs.

"Oh *God!*" I cried into his shoulder as he gently massaged me.

My chest heaved beneath him as that magical force built within me until it burst, sweeping through my body like strong waves crashing into a rocky shore. I barely took a breath before he was thrusting against me in a way that made those waves stronger and fiercer. Holy hell, it made it even better.

Venn fell onto his back beside me, panting. Curling up, I rested my head on his shoulder and snuggled into him.

"Venn?" I asked through shallow breaths.

He wrapped both arms around me. "What?"

"After that, I feel like I can do anything."

15

I woke up several hours later in Venn's arms. I hadn't even realized we'd fallen asleep. I rolled over and scooped my clothes up from the ground and began putting them back on. Venn shifted on the bed beside me. I looked over at him and beamed.

He smiled back. "Hey, beautiful."

"Hey."

He reached for me to drag me back into bed, but I just squeezed his hand and said, "Your roommates probably want to get back in here at some point to sleep."

Venn nearly jumped out of bed at the mention of his roommates.

I chuckled. "How much you wanna bet Ronark took one look at the pile of clothes on the floor and headed straight back outside?"

"My bad," Venn said.

My eyes roamed over him as he pulled his pants back on. Images of what we'd done just this morning flickered through my head, and I couldn't help but smile even wider.

"Ronark?" Venn asked. "Is he that guy from earlier?"

"Yeah," I said. "He's friends with my sister. He's going to help us get out of here."

Venn slipped his t-shirt on and turned to me. "How is she? Your sister?"

"Alive and healthy," I answered, which was all I could ever really ask for. "You saw her last night."

"The one with the short hair?" he asked as he sat down beside me.

"That's her."

"She kind of looks like you," he observed.

I shrugged. "Yeah, well, we *are* related."

He laughed and wrapped an arm around my shoulder. "I'm glad you found her."

I leaned my head against him. "Me, too."

"Should we let my roommates back in now?"

I nodded and stood, then headed to the door. When I swung it open, I found Ronark sitting just outside. He turned to gaze up at me.

"Sorry," I said.

"Nah." Ronark stood and waved a hand like it was nothing. Then he leaned in close to whisper, "I would've done the same thing."

"Uh, thanks. Hey, Venn, do you want to grab something to eat?"

Ronark's eyes went wide. "Wait. That's not what you were doing in there?"

I slugged him in the shoulder. "Shut up."

Venn chuckled from behind me.

"Watch this girl," Ronark said lightheartedly, holding on to his shoulder. "She's one tough cookie."

"Hell yeah, I am. Now get some sleep." I waved to Ronark as Venn and I started down the dirt path.

"Hey," he called. "If you see Brad or Dawson, let them know they can come back."

"Will do," I told him. "Thanks for standing guard."

Ronark gave me a salute, then turned inside his cabin.

"He seems nice," Venn said once we were alone.

"Yeah. I can see why my sister likes him." I quickly changed the subject. "How's everyone else doing? Fiona's all right, isn't she?" I missed her.

"Yeah, last I heard."

I opened the door to the bathhouse, which had a kitchen off one of the rooms where we could grab food whenever we wanted. I lowered my voice in case anyone was inside. "Last you heard? When was that? Have they made any headway on finding Matias or his successor?"

"I'm not sure. Remember, I ran into the Soulless not long after you left. I've had no way to contact everyone."

My shoulders fell. "I hope they're okay."

We entered the kitchen, which was basically a bunch of cupboards and countertops with a hand-pump sink in the corner. There were multiple coolers, but otherwise no stove or refrigerator. I pulled a loaf of bread from the corner and began working on sandwiches.

"It's not pretty, but they keep us fed," I said. "Anyway, it won't be long now before we can make our move. But we should probably wait to discuss specifics."

Venn nodded in agreement, then held his palm up when I handed him the sandwich. "I'm actually not very hungry."

I shoved it toward him. "I don't care. You have to eat. You need your strength."

He eyed the sandwich curiously, then took it. "Strength for what?"

I hated that I had to be the one to break the news. "For your initiation ceremony tonight. They'll test your strength to see which vampire you should belong to."

Venn frowned. "That doesn't sound good."

"No, it isn't. My advice? Knock your opponent out. They'll move on to the next fight if it's not entertaining them."

Venn looked nervous.

"With me, Valkas only wanted a source of entertainment. For you?" That wasn't something I wanted to think about.

"For me?" he pressed.

"For you, it's going to be an actual test. And you have to make sure you pass."

Venn will be fine. He's a wolf shifter. He can handle anything.

And I meant it.

As night fell, blood slaves began making their way up to the chateau, and the "recruits" were rounded up. I didn't know if I was invited to watch, but I figured no one would notice a cleaning maid missing from the chateau on a night like this.

In the light of the moon, I followed the trail toward the fight ring I'd been thrown into my first night here. Several couples—vampires and their slaves— walked ahead of me on the trail. As they took their seats in the stands, I slipped around the back of the bleachers and stood in the shadows. The hair on the back of my neck stood. It felt like I was doing something wrong, like I wasn't supposed to be here without a vampire to escort me.

Screw that. I wasn't letting Venn face this fight alone.

I watched as more and more couples flooded into the arena and took their seats. My eyes fell upon Jenna as she and her vampire—Silas—emerged from the trees. The sight of him knocked the air out of my chest like a punch to the gut. He was tall, with broad shoulders and thick arms, and he had a scar above his eyebrow.

He was there the night my parents were killed!

Why hadn't Jenna ever mentioned it? She always talked about her vampire so vaguely—when she talked about him at all.

I urged to rush forward and pick a fight with him right then and there. After everything he'd done to Jenna—kidnapped her and forced her to give up her blood for him—he deserved it. But I swallowed down my fury and stayed put. Picking a fight with a vamp on a cliff *full* of vampires wasn't exactly the best idea. I was reckless, but not *that* reckless.

Jenna's expression was unreadable as she followed her vampire into the stands. She acted like a robot. Which I guess was the only way to survive as a blood slave. It was that or show your true feelings and get yourself killed.

Chatter filled the arena, and soon, the chanting took over.

Fight. Fight. Fight.

I knew Venn and the other recruits were picking their weapons right now. I just hoped he picked a good one.

Soon, the entire island was seated in the stands. Valkas walked out of the trees, with Rogers in tow, and the chanting turned to cheers. Valkas held his hands above his head and spun around with a huge smile on his face. He craved the attention, like he was a king. It made me sick.

Sit down already, asshole.

Valkas dropped his hands, and the crowd went quiet. "I won't bore you with a lousy introduction tonight," he called across the ring. "Let's just have some bloody fun, shall we? Let the games begin!"

The crowd erupted into cheers again. From out of the trees, I saw Anton push a girl into the ring. She stumbled but quickly righted herself before placing an arrow on the bow she'd picked. She'd shoved the second arrow in the back of her jeans pocket.

She whirled around and drew the bow just as a guy twice her size stepped into the light of the torches. He was one of the lumberjack twins, the one with the longer beard, and he'd brought a mace as his weapon of choice.

I was already nervous for her. She was such a petite little thing, and he was huge. If she wasn't a shifter, she didn't stand a chance.

Her arms shook as she anchored the bow to the corner of her lip, then let go of the string. She changed her mind at the last millisecond and pulled the bow to the side just as the arrow went flying off the rest. It interrupted the arrow's trajectory, and the arrow went flying off to the side into the woods.

She realized what she'd done a second later, and her eyes went wide. Lumberjack lifted his ball and chain and swung it at her. She jumped out of the way just in time for the spiked ball to land in the dirt where she'd been standing.

Her mouth moved, but it was impossible to hear what she said over all the cheering. The look on her face suggested she was pleading with him. A heavy weight settled in my stomach like a bag of rocks. The Soulless didn't care whether they pulled innocent people off the streets or not. They'd make sinners out of them one way or another.

Lumberjack swung his weapon at her again, and she ducked out of the way, somersaulting until she was on the other side of him. She placed her second arrow on the string, then drew back a second time. I held my breath for her.

She let go of the string just as the ball connected with her head. Everything happened so fast that it was hard to process it all. The girl fell to the side the same time the arrow struck the guy in the shoulder. Blood began pouring out of his wound and onto his white t-shirt.

While he was momentarily distracted by the pain, the girl shot to her feet again.

Definitely a shifter, I concluded. There was no other way she could've survived that blow.

Using her bow, she swung it at Lumberjack's head. It connected with such a hard *thwack* that I heard it above the cheers. The crowd screamed even louder at that. The guy stumbled backward, disoriented, and landed on his elbows.

The girl rushed forward to grab the weapon that had flown from his hands. She swung it high above her head, then brought it down straight on his face. I flinched and turned my face away from the scene, but I wasn't fast enough. The image of blood squirting everywhere would forever be seared in my memory.

The crowd went wild. I slowly peeled my eyes back open to see that vampires were on their feet now, cheering for the shifter girl's victory. Meanwhile, she stood in the center of the ring, staring down at the man's mangled features. Her whole body shook.

Valkas stood and made his way over to her. The crowd didn't quiet long enough for him to announce her as champion, but he clapped her on the back and whispered something in her ear. Whatever he'd said didn't seem to soothe her as her shaking legs carried her back toward Anton at the entrance to the trail.

Valkas whirled back around and took his seat on his throne again, then said something to Rogers. Rogers mumbled an incantation, then Lumberjack's body lifted from the ground as if it were attached to strings. Rogers guided it over to a group of vamps in the front row, who all were happy to drape the body across themselves and dig in like it was a Thanksgiving smorgasbord.

What the hell was wrong with them? Couldn't they at least show some respect?

Of course not. They were vampires.

Moments later, another figure stepped out of the trees and into the ring. He was as big as the last guy with the same look and muscular build. It was the second lumberjack twin, the one named Jackson. His eyebrows were tight, and his lips pressed together in a thin line. His eyes fell upon his brother, and I noticed his grip tightened on his sword.

He'd just watched his brother die, and they wanted to see how he'd handle it. I was beyond disgusted.

Jackson glanced around frantically, as if calculating how he might be able to escape. Before he could take in his surroundings, Anton grabbed another recruit and threw him into the ring. My stomach sank when I saw it was Venn. I didn't want him fighting anyone, let alone a guy who wasn't even in the same weight class.

Venn took a defensive stance, holding a dagger out like he was ready to strike if Jackson came too close.

I didn't know if I could watch this. What if the strategy to knock his opponent out backfired? What if Jackson gained the upper hand? Sure, Venn had killed vampires before, but never another human being. I didn't think he'd do it just to save himself.

Survive, Venn. That's all I ask.

I held my breath as the fight began. Jackson swung his sword out, aiming it straight for the side of Venn's neck like he was going to decapitate him. Venn ducked out of the way and jabbed his dagger toward Jackson's arm, where it would do the least damage. It barely nicked him, just enough that I could see a spot of blood, but not enough that Jackson reacted. Jackson spun toward Venn, looking like he was about to shoot fire out of his nose.

Come on, Venn. You can do this.

Jackson took another swing at him, this time at his legs. Venn jumped, just barely making it over the top of the blade. Jackson quickly tried another method. He jabbed the sword toward him like he was going to impale him. I flinched, but when I opened my eyes, Venn had dodged out of the way and spun toward the guy. He grabbed on to Jackson's wrist and yanked him forward, then sliced his dagger across the back of his hand.

The crowd cheered, and Jackson dropped his sword. Venn quickly bent to retrieve it, then tossed both weapons toward the edge of the cliff. The dagger flew into the darkness, while the sword teetered on the edge, then slipped off into the water.

Jackson's eyes went wide as he realized his weapon had vanished. Venn didn't waste any time. He immediately threw a punch at the guy's jaw. He stumbled backward a bit, and Venn took aim again. Jackson regained his composure a moment later and lunged for Venn.

I gasped when Venn slammed into the ground, over two-hundred pounds of muscle squashing him. Jackson drew back his fist and shoved his other hand into the collar of Venn's shirt. He hesitated, then his eyes flickered to his dead brother's body. A moment later, his fist pummeled Venn's face.

My hands shot over my mouth, and my knees shook beneath me.

No! My mind screamed. *Fight back, Venn! I need you. You have to survive.*

I wanted to rush in and help him, but I knew the vampires wouldn't allow it. I'd die right there with him.

That's how it should be, I thought.

My feet moved beneath me before I gave them the command. I was just about to run into the ring, but I stopped myself when I saw Venn's face morph into a black wolf's. Half the crowd shot to their feet in excitement. Meanwhile, Jackson paused as he realized he was no longer holding on to Venn's clothes but on to his fur. Venn's powerful jaws snapped at the guy's hand, and a pained scream broke out above the noise of the crowd.

Jackson scurried off of Venn, distancing himself from him. Venn rolled onto his feet and curled his lips back over his teeth, growling at him.

"Venn, don't," I whispered to myself.

Of course, he couldn't hear me. He lunged forward, and his paws slammed into his opponent's chest. I thought for sure he would rip his throat out, but he only stood on top of him, growling. Jackson's eyes darted around the arena—to the vampires on either side, to his brother's body, and finally to Venn's eyes. His lips moved, but I couldn't tell what he said.

Without ceremony, he shoved Venn off of himself, scurried to his feet, and sprinted to the edge of the cliff. The whole crowd gasped, including me, as Jackson hurled himself into the rocky water below.

Several vamps at the edge of the bleachers rushed over to the edge of the cliff and peeked over. They must've liked whatever they saw, because they turned back to the crowd and began cheering.

Venn had gone as still as a statue, staring out into the dark water like he couldn't believe what had just happened. Relief flooded through me. It was horrible, considering Jackson was as good as dead. If the rocks below hadn't killed him, the water would. No way could he swim back to the mainland without drowning, even if he was a shifter with super endurance. But I was so happy Venn was alive.

Valkas hesitated for a moment, then stood and made his way out into the middle of the ring. "Ladies and gentlemen… our second champion of the night!"

At the sound of the crowd cheering, Venn blinked and seemed to come back to reality. His lips curled back over his teeth, like he wasn't at all pleased by the outcome. He looked two seconds away from ripping Valkas's head off, but we all knew how that would go.

Still in wolf form, Venn's shoulders dropped, and he slumped back toward the other recruits in the trees, appearing more worn out than I'd ever seen him before. Looking at him made it feel like someone had punched a hole straight through my gut. I just wanted to hold him and tell him everything would be all right, even if it was a lie.

I quickly abandoned my hideout in the shadows of the bleachers and raced into the forest after him.

16

"Venn!" I cried, rushing through the trees toward him.

I saw his silhouette shift from wolf to human form. He reached out and steadied himself against a nearby tree. I was almost to him when an arm swung out of the darkness and swooped me out of the air.

I instinctively swung my elbow backward, but my assailant ducked out of the way. My elbow met nothing but air.

"Where do you think you're going?" a deep voice asked in my ear. *Anton.*

I relaxed until he set me back on my feet, but he didn't let go of me. I looked up into his silver eyes behind me. "He's the champion of his round, and he needs medical attention. I would hope the vampire he's assigned to would want him in top shape for his first feeding."

Anton finally released his hold on me. Venn's gaze flickered to mine through swollen eyes. Blood dripped from a large gash on his cheek. His eyes pleaded with me, like he thought it was best if I let him be instead of fighting with the vamps.

I turned back to Anton and spoke through gritted teeth. "May I take him back to his quarters?"

Anton glanced between me and the latest fight in the ring. He huffed. "Fine, but do not make it habit, Raven Girl."

"Yes, sir." I rushed over to Venn and draped his arm over my shoulder, helping support him on our way down the trail. He barely let me help him, but he seemed a little disoriented. "That was quite a beating."

Venn blinked a couple of times, as though he was still trying to process it. "It... it all happened so fast."

"How's your face?" I asked. The blood had reached the bottom of his chin now.

Venn shrugged. "He had quite a punch."

"Yeah, I can see that. He might've given you a concussion, too."

Venn shook his head, still looking dazed. "No, I just..." He pressed his fingers to the raw skin on his cheek and came away with blood-soaked fingertips.

"We'll talk about it once we get you to the bathhouse," I said.

Venn didn't say anything the rest of the way there. I led him inside the bathroom and instructed him to get into the tub. I handed him a wash cloth to wipe his face, then took a towel and headed to the kitchen, where I wrapped ice from one of the coolers in it. When I returned to the bathroom, Venn was lying in the tub with his head leaned back and his eyes closed.

"You okay?" I asked.

His eyes sprang open, and he started. "Yeah, I'll be fine. A healing spell might help, though."

I frowned. "My magic isn't working lately."

"Ice is fine, then." He took the ice pack from me while I turned and lit the lamp in the corner. I rounded the tub and placed the plug in the bottom, then began pumping the water for him.

"What the vampires do to *initiate* their prisoners is horrible," I snarled in disgust.

Venn shivered as cool water rushed over him. "When they told us what we were going to do—that we had to choose a weapon and fight—most of us thought they were joking. I might've too if I didn't already know how ruthless vamps were. I mean, why would they bring us here if they were just going to kill us?"

"It's their form of entertainment around here."

Venn sighed. "I know. I was being rhetorical."

"It's sick, if you ask me."

Venn scoffed. "Yeah, it's sick you if you ask me, too."

Several quiet moments passed. The only sound came from the water rushing out of the tap. I dared to break the silence.

"What did Jackson say to you, right before...?" I couldn't finish my sentence.

Venn slowly pulled the ice away from his face until his eyes met mine. "That's the crazy part. He sacrificed himself so I could win."

"Sacrificed himself?"

"Yeah. He said, '*I won't become a killer for them.*'"

"He didn't want either of you giving up who you are," I whispered. It reminded me of what Jenna had said to me, how she couldn't choose what the Soulless did to her, but she could choose how she reacted to it. Jackson chose not to play their game. "He wasn't willing to sacrifice his character."

Venn nodded solemnly. "I don't know if I could've done it. Killed him, I mean."

I stopped pumping the water and sat on the floor beside the tub. Reaching out, I took Venn's hand in mine. "I'm so sorry."

After a beat of silence, Venn spoke so softly I barely heard him. "I don't know if I can do it again, Rae."

"Do what?"

"Be a blood slave."

"Venn…" I wished I could find the words to reassure him, but there was nothing I could say to make this better.

"When you've been a blood slave long enough, feeding becomes a drug. That high you get from it… it screws you up, Rae. I've spent a long time trying to heal after what Maliya did to me."

My stomach twisted at the mention of the horrible woman.

"But…" Venn stared at me with such sorrow in his eyes that my heart tore in two. Tears welled in my eyes for him.

"But what?" I squeezed his hand tighter.

"I'm scared I'll forget all of it if another vamp feeds on me."

The bathhouse went eerily silent as his words hung in the air. A lump rose to my throat as I thought about him going through all of that again.

"It's not going to happen," I heard myself say.

Venn eyed me curiously, as if to ask what I meant by that.

"Tomorrow night is the Awakening Ball," I reminded him. "If everything goes as planned, there won't be any vampires left to feed on you."

Venn's lips lifted at the corners. "I hope you're right."

"Hey," I teased. "Don't ever underestimate the Ravenite."

Venn chuckled, but it sounded pained. "Never."

17

Breathe in… and out. In… and out.

The night of the Awakening Ball had arrived, and I was practicing deep breathing exercises like Sondra had suggested to me weeks ago. I'd been working on calming myself and preparing for tonight since I woke several hours ago.

I can do this, I told myself. *Tonight, Valkas will die. Tonight, the vampires shall perish with him.*

Unless he's not carrying the dagger, a little voice in the back of my head replied.

And let me tell you, I squashed that little sucker with my mental hammer faster than you can say *screw yourself.*

"I am strong," I whispered to the walls of my cabin. "I am powerful. I believe in myself."

On the exhale, I pictured all the negative energy leaving my body. I slowly peeled my eyes open and held my palm up.

"*Ardet ignis.*" Flames erupted from my palm, shooting a foot into the air. They were gone as soon as they came, but the test proved to me that the meditation exercise was working. My powers still weren't as strong as usual, but I felt more in tune with Synchrony than I had since I'd arrived on the island.

The cabin door creaked open, and I looked up to see Jenna arriving back from the kitchens carrying a handful of snacks.

"Hey, Jenna Bean," I said, smiling up at her.

"You hungry?" She held out a granola bar.

"Not really," I replied.

She rolled her eyes. "Eat, Rachel. Nightfall is in less than half an hour. You need to keep up your strength."

I took the granola bar from her, but I didn't open it. Instead, my eyes roamed her features—the angle of her dark bangs across her face, the shape of her straight nose, the paleness of her cheeks. For so many months, I'd dreamed about what it'd be like to see her again. Nothing had gone like I'd hoped, but I was still glad she was here with me right now.

Jenna furrowed her brow, like I was creeping her out. "What?"

"Nothing." I shook my head. "I just can't get over how much I missed you. You're so different than I remember, but the same. You know?"

She smirked and sat beside me on the bed. She wrapped an arm around me and laid her head on mine. My heart warmed beneath her touch. "I know exactly what you mean. You used to be so sweet, and now you... kill vampires for a living."

"Kill first, ask questions later," I teased, stealing Teagan's motto. God, I missed Teagan—and Fiona and the rest of them. I hoped they were figuring things out on their end.

"See?" Jenna teased. "Old Rachel never would've said stuff like that."

"Yeah, well, old Jenna would've laughed more and would've played pranks on her cabin roommates."

Jenna shot me a glance, like she couldn't believe I was bringing that up. "This isn't summer camp, Rachel. Are you saying I'm too serious for you now?"

"No, just more... grown up, I guess."

Jenna snorted. "I'm not *grown up*, Rachel. I'm... I don't know the word for it."

I wrapped my arms around her. "Strong, Jenna. The word you're looking for is *strong*. You've been through so much here, and you've learned how to deal with it."

"Yeah, because I had to in order to survive."

I drew away to look her in the eyes. "Don't downplay this. You deserve credit for everything you've been through. Everyone on this island does. After tonight, it will all be over and you're going to get the chance to take your strength out into the world and make a difference."

Jenna's eyes brimmed with tears. For a moment, I saw a glimpse of the sensitive sister I used to know. "No one has ever called me strong before."

"They didn't have to. Because you already know it's true."

She smiled, but I could tell she was holding back.

"You don't have to be afraid to show your emotions, Jenna Bean," I assured her. "It doesn't make you weak."

She pulled me into a hug so hard it knocked the wind out of me. Her voice cracked when she spoke. "I know. It's just been so long since I've been around someone I felt I could share my emotions with."

I rubbed her back. "Well, I'm here. Always, from now on."

Jenna pulled away from me and wiped her eyes. "It's just about time for me to head up to the chateau."

"Me, too. Valkas wants me *dressed like a queen*, he said." I rolled my eyes.

She chuckled. "Do me a favor, will you?"

"Anything," I promised.

Jenna sniffled. "Make me proud tonight."
I nodded. "I will."

"You look gorgeous," Bri raved.

I turned to the mirror in the private suite I'd been assigned to get ready for the ball. Bri had been waiting there with an endless supply of makeup and a black dress that had more feathers on it than fabric. Apparently, Valkas had personally assigned her to help transform me for the ball.

I gasped when I saw my reflection. I didn't look gorgeous. I looked like a freaking monster.

My eyes were rimmed in dark black makeup, and my lips were a dark shade of red I'd never worn before. Bri had twisted my hair up into an elegant bun, which was the only good thing about the whole ensemble. The dress would've been okay if it weren't for the fact that it was so poofy I could hardly move in it. It had a corset top with lacey straps and beautiful beading I actually liked, but then there were the feathers... so many feathers. They completely covered the skirt and trailed up my back, ending just below where my wings might be if I could semi-shift.

Valkas was mocking me. *You're a raven, but you're* my *raven. And as long as you're mine, you will never fly.*

Maybe I was looking into it too much, but that was the kind of message I was getting.

I fingered the corset. "Do you think it's a little... much?"

Bri stood behind me and smiled at my reflection in the mirror. "Not at all. Valkas is a very flashy person. I hope I did enough."

"Oh, I think it's enough," I said before turning to her. "He didn't happen to say anything about how tonight would run, did he? He never clarified for me when I'm to arrive at the ball."

Bri started cleaning up the makeup spread out across the vanity. "No, sorry. He didn't say anything to me. I'm just here to make you pretty."

"Thanks."

"No problem," Bri said kindly. "Now if you'll excuse me, I need to get ready myself. My master is waiting."

Bri exited the room, but I caught the door before it swung shut and poked my head into the hall. Two guards stood on either side of my doorway, staring ahead like Secret Service agents.

I cleared my throat, and the guy to my right glanced over at me. He was super tall and all muscle. The other guy was short and stocky.

"Excuse me, but do you know how I'm to arrive at the ball? When can I leave to go down there?" I tried to sound as innocent and curious as I could.

"Don't worry," Muscles said in a gruff voice. "We'll escort you there ourselves."

"I was kinda hoping to arrive in time to see Valkas make his big entrance," I said. "I heard it's really amazing. I would hate to miss it."

The guards exchanged a look at each other, as if I made a good point.

"So, will I be arriving before him?" I pressed.

"No," the first guard said. "You're not to make your entrance until Valkas announces you."

"That's fine. Whatever he thinks is best. Thank you." I retreated inside the room and shut the door behind me. That act was so totally *not* me that it was embarrassing.

I paced around the room, thinking about what the guard had said. I knew how to get to the staging area and when I was supposed to arrive—Ronark had briefed me on that much—but he'd left the *how* up to me. How was I going to get past the guards unseen? My eyes fell upon a statuette of an angel on the nightstand.

Ironic, I thought. A symbol of purity in the middle of a vampire nest.

My fingers trailed over the outstretched wings. They came to a sharp point, and I decided it was as good a weapon as any. I turned to the bed and took the corner of the sheet between my hands, then tugged as hard as I could. A long piece of fabric tore off, and I used it to secure the statuette to my thigh. The dress was thick enough that it hid the weapon nicely.

I smiled. For the first time in… forever, I was actually going into something with a plan.

A knock came at the door, and Muscles stuck his head inside the room. "Time to go, love."

I held my head high and stepped toward him confidently. Neither me nor the guards spoke as they led me down the hall and to the grand staircase. The chateau halls were dead silent until we reached a wide hallway that ended at a pair of double doors. Chatter, music, and the sound of clinking glasses spilled out into the hall.

From this distance, I could barely see into the ballroom. It was beautiful, with a high ceiling and velvety gold curtains hanging from the tall windows. Everything glittered, from the flames burning in the chandeliers high above everyone's heads to the champagne in everyone's glasses. Most of the vampires were dressed in black, but their blood slaves were in all different colors. Some wore long silky evening gowns, while other were in big ball-gowns like mine. I searched the ballroom for signs of Venn, but I didn't see him.

Damn it! He was supposed to meet me out here.

The guards stopped me at the end of the hall so we wouldn't be seen. We stood there in silence. Each passing second, I became more and more worried for Venn. I didn't have the time to wait for him. Where was he?

Maybe he'd been assigned to a mistress and couldn't get away from her. *Yeah, that sounds about right*, I told myself, though I wasn't entirely convinced.

After several minutes of watching the doors with no sign of Venn, I decided that I was going to have to go along without him. We only got one shot to get Valkas alone, and I couldn't miss it—Venn or not.

"It's too bad you don't get to see Valkas's grand entrance," I said to the guards, like I actually cared.

"Nothing we haven't seen before, love," the guard on my right said.

And it won't be something you'll ever see again.

"Would it be okay if I went to the bathroom beforehand?" I asked sweetly. "There wasn't a bathroom in my room, and well… I'm still human."

The guards exchanged a glance.

"Can't you hold it?" Short and Stocky asked.

I gave a fake grimace. "No, not really."

Muscles looked nervous, like the very thought of human bodily functions made him uncomfortable.

"There has to be a bathroom around here somewhere." I turned and started down the hall in the opposite direction, gazing around curiously.

The guards hurried up behind me, like I'd hoped. "Ma'am, you are not permitted—"

"I just don't want to interrupt the ceremony, you know?" I said. "Best to deal with this now." I turned down a narrow, isolated hallway.

"Hey!" Muscles grabbed my hand and spun me around. "You're not to go wandering off."

"Oh, I'm sorry," I said innocently. "I just thought… no, it's okay." I waved my hand like it was no big deal. "I'll hold it. Can I fix my shoe first, though?"

I leaned down to lift the skirt of my dress, and that's when I struck. I slipped the angel statuette from its makeshift sheath and swung it at Muscles. He realized what was happening and ducked out of the way. Staying alert, I saw that the second guard was already lunging for me. I aimed the statuette at the center of his forehead, and it connected with a sick *crack*. The angel's head snapped off and went flying. Short and Stocky stumbled sideways.

Meanwhile, Muscles reached out and grabbed hold of my dress. I yanked away from him, and a satisfying tearing sound filled the hallway. A weight fell from my hips as the top layers of fabric dropped away. I ripped off the last few remaining threads, leaving behind only the thin bottom layer. I suddenly felt like I could move again.

I quickly swung my leg up. The heel of my shoe connected with Short and Stocky's face. Muscles jumped me from behind, wrapping his arm around my neck so tightly I couldn't breathe. Gripping the statuette firmly in my hand, I swung it backward into his face. He cried out, and I spun around to see the angel's wing was poking into his eyeball.

Woops.

The second guard was already on top of me, tackling me to the ground. He might've been shorter than Muscles, but his biceps were thick, and the guy was strong. So I took to playing dirty. I shoved my fingers in his hair and pulled as hard as I possibly could. I felt the strands disconnect from his scalp as he let out a cry of pain. It was enough to distract him so that I could punch him in the throat. He rolled off of me.

Beside him, Muscles had pulled the angel statuette from his eye. His face contorted in fury, and his growl echoed down the hall as he came at me.

I ducked just in time for him to stumble into one of the wooden benches that lined many of the chateau hallways. It crumbled beneath his weight.

I glanced behind me. Any moment now, someone from the ball would rush out here to see what all the racket was about. Thinking quickly, I reached for one of the broken bench legs.

The guard rolled over and looked at me with his one eye just in time to see the shattered piece of wood headed toward his heart. That was the last thing he saw before his body withered away into a pile of ash.

Short and Stocky lunged for me again. "Bitch," he snarled in my ear as his hands clamped around my throat.

My throat felt like it was on fire as I gasped for breath. The broken pieces of bench dug into my skin beneath me. But in his rage, the guard hadn't realized I still held my weapon in my hand. Smirking, I shoved the stake straight into his heart.

Ash rained down on me, and I sprang to my feet. The hallway was a total disaster, but I didn't have the luxury of cleaning it up. Footsteps were approaching.

I had to get out of there. *Fast.*

I turned in the opposite direction of the ballroom and sprinted down the hall. I rounded a corner at the end and hid in the shadows as I peeked back to see who had come for me. At least six vampires had stopped in front of the scene.

I noticed Rogers there, too. He looked calm and collected, like he wasn't at all surprised by this turn of events—as if he expected such a thing from me. He lifted his gaze and glanced around, but I snuck into the shadows before he saw me.

I hoped.

I hurried down a dark hall lit only by the occasional sconce. Breathing deeply, I tried to picture in my mind Ronark's map he'd drawn me in the sand a few days ago. I was at least two hallways away from where I was supposed to be, but I could make it there without turning back the way I came.

Watch out, Valkas. I'm coming for you.

18

My heart hammered as I raced down the hall. At the end, I found myself in a wider hallway with more sconces lighting up the path. I glanced both ways and saw a long stretch of marble floor that met up with the grand staircase. I hurried toward the main foyer, but the sound of a deep voice stopped me in my tracks.

"Walk faster!" Valkas barked. "I can't believe how incompetent you are."

Shit. I was late.

Valkas came into view. Four shifters walked into the foyer toward the ballroom, carrying the poles of the litter on their shoulders. It looked like a small carriage without wheels. There was the main box with a bench where Valkas sat, with four tall pillars rising toward the ceiling like a canopy bed. Long red curtains draped over the top and wound around the supports. The poles the shifters carried stuck out from each corner parallel to the floor.

Valkas wore a pointed crown and a fur-lined cape. He stared down at the shifters in front of him like they were nothing more than slave animals meant to take care of a king.

"Immortality doesn't make me any more patient," Valkas complained. "Sometimes I swear it's a goddamned curse."

Ronark shot Jenna a nervous glance. Yeah, yeah, I got it. *Where is that Rachel bitch?*

"You know," I blurted. "I can help end that curse."

Valkas whirled around, and his expression shifted. His eyes burned with more rage than I thought one person could hold, and his upper lip curled back over his teeth to display his long, sharp fangs. Four other pairs of eyes turned to look at me, and relief flooded their faces. The shifters took my presence as their signal. They dropped the litter to the ground and sprang on Valkas all at once.

385

He leapt upward and grabbed hold of the litter supports above him, swinging out of reach of the shifters aimed for him.

Ronark shifted mid-air. He was large, nothing like the hamster I'd been envisioning. He had blond fur and a thick mane, with strong, powerful jaws he snapped at Valkas.

A lion.

Valkas kicked the heel of his foot into Ronark's nose, then dropped back into the litter to knock Andi's and Brad's heads together. Jenna reached up and wrapped her fingers in Valkas's hair the same time Andi shifted into a black jaguar and sank her teeth into Valkas's ankle. Jenna yanked his head backward, and he let out a rage-filled scream. It didn't sound like one of pain, more like of warning.

Brad rubbed his head, like he was a little disoriented, but quickly blinked the world back into focus. He shifted, and his body grew to over three times its normal size. Huge antlers unlike any I'd ever seen before sprouted out of his head.

An elk.

I reached Valkas just as his foot swung out to connect with the side of Andi's face. His crown slipped off his head and into Jenna's hands. My body slammed into his, knocking him out of the litter and onto the marble floor. Before he could right himself, I shifted into raven form and snapped my head toward his face. My beak connected with bone, and I tasted the salt from his skin in my mouth. He screamed again, this time in pain.

Damn it. That was satisfying.

But I didn't get to peck him again before his hands were on me. He pulled me off of him, and I saw that my beak had left behind a deep gash just above his nose.

"You think I'm that stupid, darling?" he drawled. "I knew you'd come for me eventually."

Ronark lunged for Valkas in lion form, but Valkas shot to his feet and threw his hand out. He shoved his fingers into Ronark's mouth and pulled upward, forcing his jaw open. To my horror, he shoved my body straight into Ronark's open mouth.

Panic sent my heart pummeling against my rib cage. The first thing that crossed my mind was to not hurt Ronark. I tilted my head backward and tried to keep my beak from skidding along his tongue. Complete darkness enveloped me, and I couldn't breathe. When I tried, no air filled my lungs, only the smell of cat breath.

Jesus, Ronark. Do you ever brush your teeth?

Speaking of teeth, the sharp bastards were digging into my skin. Ronark coughed, and I went shooting out of his mouth. I spread my wings to slow my momentum, but I still slammed into the wall like I'd been hit by a truck.

Ronark was already on the move, joining Brad and Andi to help drag Valkas down. But Valkas wouldn't be knocked down again without a fight. Somehow, against a jaguar, lion, and giant deer, he remained on his feet. Jenna had frozen up, still clutching the crown and staring straight ahead.

Valkas became so enraged that color began to fill his face, which I didn't even know was possible with vampires. His eyebrows came so close together that they nearly touched, and he bared his teeth and hissed. All at once, he stopped clawing at Andi's fur and reached out to wrap his fingers around Brad's antlers. He twisted, and the sickening crunch of breaking bone filled the foyer.

Brad slumped to the ground, and his body shrank back into human form. His neck was twisted at an odd angle, and his eyes stared lifeless up at the ornate ceiling. Valkas stared down at him with a satisfied smile as he grabbed hold of Andi's jaws and yanked as hard as he could. He swung her around and let the momentum take her. Her body slammed into the bannister of the grand staircase so hard that the wooden rungs crumbled.

At the same time, Valkas kicked Ronark in the gut with so much force he went flying toward the second level. He bounced off the railing at the top of the stairs and went limp as his body plummeted back toward the hard marble floor below.

It all happened so fast that I'd barely taken a breath before Brad lay dead in front of me and the other two struggled to their feet in pain. My blood boiled as I shifted back into human form. My dress shifted with me, but my hair hung in loose waves around my shoulders since the pins had fallen out.

I threw myself at Valkas. He didn't even stumble as I jumped, wrapped my legs around him, and pummeled his face like my own personal punching bag. His elongated fangs cut into my skin, but I didn't care. Hearing the sound of his nose crunch beneath my fist was so satisfying.

Ronark righted himself and jumped Valkas from behind, digging his sharp claws into his back. Valkas merely swung his elbow backward. It connected with Ronark's face, shooting him off Valkas's back. Meanwhile, Andi had gone for his ankles again, but he kicked her aside like she was nothing more than a kitten playing with his toes.

"Screw you, you son of a bitch!" I cried as my fist raced toward his face again.

But it never made it. His hand shot up to block me, and he grabbed hold of my wrist so hard that I thought he might crush bone. He twisted, and my scream echoed off the walls of the foyer.

Valkas grabbed my ass and shoved me up against the wall, pressing his hips into me. His wild eyes roamed my face, and he inhaled my scent. I used my free hand to claw at his face, but he grabbed that one too and held it above my head. When I dropped my legs from around his waist, I just hung there, gasping for breath as his chest pressed against mine.

"So feisty," he said in amusement. "Just the way I like it, darling. You would've made *such* a nice queen if you'd meant anything you said."

"I suppose you didn't either." I caught Jenna's eyes for a moment, and I knew I had to keep him talking.

Valkas shot me that evil smirk he was so famous for. "Of course not, my dear. I always planned to change you myself. I'll let you rot away in my dungeons. Without blood to sustain you, you'll be as good as dead, but death will always be just out of reach."

The thought twisted my guts. No doubt he'd make sure I couldn't kill myself, either. Unless I ripped the bars off my cell and sent them through my own heart, there'd be no escape. But I'd have to be strong enough to do that first, and I didn't think Valkas would allow me to become that strong.

He leaned in close, sending his cold breath to rush across the corner of my jaw. "I did plan on waiting until we were in the ballroom, to make a spectacle out of it. So symbolic. The anniversary of the night I escaped this island would be the same night I escaped my one and only threat. It's the only reason I've kept you alive this long. But I'm done waiting. Let's get this over with."

His lips connected with mine, as if he owned me, as if he wanted me in *that* way. His tongue felt like a creature from hell inside my mouth, and he tasted like the dirt at the bottom of a sewage drain.

Suddenly, his body went still. His mouth left mine, and he slumped to the ground, freeing me. I breathed a heavy sigh of relief when I saw Jenna standing there, the point of the crown embedded in Valkas's back.

I spit and wiped my mouth. "Really?" I complained to her. "You couldn't have stabbed him sooner?"

She stared at me with wide eyes. "I-I froze up."

We didn't have time to waste. I dropped to Valkas's side and began patting him down. Jenna quickly joined me in the search for the dagger, while Andi and Ronark ransacked the litter. I pulled off his shoes, and Jenna checked his hips for signs of a sheath. We checked every inch of his body, but it wasn't there. We both looked at each other hopelessly.

I cursed under my breath. "How long will he be out?"

"I don't know," Jenna said in a rush. "Usually when you ram a sharp object through a vampire's heart, they don't bounce back from that."

"Not long, I reckon," Ronark said, wiping blood from his nose and coming up beside us. "He heals faster than the other vamps, too."

"Well, the dagger isn't here!" I cried, patting him down again.

Andi's shoulders dropped, like we were hopeless, and Ronark looked completely confused.

"But I thought—" Ronark started.

The sound of several pairs of footsteps down the hall reached our ears.

"Oh, shit," Jenna said, glancing behind herself. "We have company."

I looked down the hall just in time to see the six vampires from earlier, along with Rogers, sprinting our way. Jenna and I shot to our feet beside Ronark and Andi, ready to take them all on, just the four of us against seven.

But we never got the chance. Rogers pulled a small round glass vial out of his pocket and chucked it into the foyer. It shattered at our feet, sending a puff of red smoke straight up at our faces.

That was the last thing I saw before a putrid scent entered my nostrils and everything went dark.

19

I blinked my eyes open to see thin red fabric draped above my head in a dimly lit room. I blinked rapidly, trying to remember how I'd gotten there. It all came back to me in a rush, and I shot upright in the bed I was lying on.

The sound of someone clicking their tongue came from across the room. I glanced around frantically for signs of my sister, Ronark, or Andi, but I was alone in Valkas's room. I didn't know how long I'd been out, but it felt like less than an hour.

Valkas stepped forward out of the shadows. "Rachel," he said with a frown. "I can't tell you how disappointed I am that you ruined my Awakening Ball."

"Where are my friends?" I demanded. "What did you do to us?"

"The potion?" Valkas asked with a shrug. "Just a little magic to knock you out. It's a complicated little concoction, but it sure comes in handy." An evil grin spread across his face.

"Where are my friends?" I repeated in a calm tone, letting him know he couldn't intimidate me.

Before I could process it, Valkas's lips curled over his teeth, then he jumped forward and landed at the edge of the bed. He pressed his palms to the mattress and loomed over me.

"What did I tell you about asking questions?" he spat.

"I want to know where my friends are," I rephrased.

Valkas's hand cracked against the side of my face. "You will show me respect!"

Despite the burning ache across my cheek, I forced my breath to follow a calm, steady rhythm. I couldn't let my impulsive emotions get to me right now. My friends depended on it.

"You should just kill me already," I suggested coolly. "Get it over with."

Valkas straightened his spine and cracked his knuckles. "Kill you? I don't run a charity, darling. Killing you would be an act of mercy."

Yeah, and then I'd just be back for him in my next life.

I chose my next words carefully, trying to draw information out of him. "I don't get what I'm doing here. I thought you wanted to change me."

Valkas smiled proudly. "Oh, I will, darling. But there's something I want to show you first. Something that won't have quite the impact after the change."

Before I could respond, Valkas grabbed me by the wrist and yanked me off the bed. Pain shot through my shoulder, but I bit down my cry.

"On your feet," Valkas snarled, tugging me upward.

I got to my feet as fast as I could and stumbled after him. Valkas moved quickly down the hall, so fast that I had to sprint to keep up with him. I thought we were headed for the main foyer, but instead, he pulled me down another hall and to a door at the end. The door opened to a dark, narrow stairwell. I used my free hand to grab on to the railing to keep from falling down the stairs, while Valkas dragged me by the other wrist.

I didn't know how many stairs we descended, but eventually, we came to a stop at the bottom. The air was cool and damp.

Valkas led me into a long, narrow hall lit by the occasional sconce. Stone walls rose on either side of us, making me feel closed in, like I was walking through a cave. The sound of distant groaning filled the air. I wanted to ask where he was taking me, but I kept my mouth shut.

We reached a T at the end of the hall, and he pulled me to the right. I gasped when I saw what lay on the other side of the wall. A single sconce lit up rows upon rows of bars that ran from the floor to the ceiling. There must've been at least a dozen cells, each one barely large enough for a person to lie down in.

And most of them were filled with people.

"Come," Valkas commanded.

We moved by the cells so quickly that all I saw were shadows inside. I heard gasps from the prisoners, but I couldn't place their voices.

Valkas stopped at the end, the one where the pained groans were coming from. He grabbed the back of my shirt and shoved me forward. I caught myself on the bars and stared into the cell, trying to make sense of the shadow I saw curled up in the corner. A man clutched his stomach, writhing in pain. He wore only jeans. Through the darkness, I could see the long, straight wounds on his back darkened by blood, as though he'd been whipped.

Suddenly, the man threw his head back and let out a piercing shriek. My heart crumbled into a million pieces as the sound of Venn's anguished cry echoed off the walls of the dungeon. It felt as if someone had ripped into my chest, pulled my heart out, and smashed it with a meat tenderizer. I didn't think I'd ever felt so horrified in my life.

I whirled on Valkas. My hands fisted in his shirt, and I shoved him up against the stone wall. "What did you do to him, you bastard!?"

At the sound of my voice, Venn went wild in his cell. He let out a loud *howl* like a wolf and jumped at the bars, shaking them violently. His eyes caught in the light, and I just barely spotted the silver in them before he fell into a ball at the floor of his cell and went silent.

I couldn't feel my limbs as reality struck me like a cold, piercing stab to the gut. Venn was changing. Into a vampire. I didn't want to accept the truth, but it was sitting right there, staring me in the face.

When I finally began to feel my fingers again, I turned my gaze back to Valkas. He wore a proud smirk on his face.

"Do you want to kill me now?" he challenged with a smile. "Now that your boyfriend is a vampire? He won't reincarnate. All vampires are damned."

My hands shook in the collar of his shirt. "You asshole," are the only words I managed to get out.

I wanted to lash out, to punch Valkas in the face and drive a stake through his heart and do whatever I could to show him just how angry and upset I was… but I knew it wouldn't do me any good. There was no way to make Valkas pay for what he'd done.

I stared at Venn lying on the cold floor, shaking. I urged to wrap him in my arms and tell him that everything was going to be all right. But I knew it would be a lie. There was no coming back from vampirism.

My breath wavered as I dropped Valkas's collar and stepped toward Venn's cell. "Venn," I whispered lightly, reaching out for the bars. "Venn, I'm so sorry."

He just lay there, curled in a ball and taking heavy, shallow breaths. It was like he couldn't hear me.

"Venn," I whispered again.

"That's enough," Valkas snarled.

He grabbed the back of my hair, pulling so tightly that I felt several strands pull loose. He yanked my head backward and dragged me away from Venn's cell. It was only when he forced my eyes off Venn that I had a chance to look at the shadows in the other cells. My stomach bottomed out as various familiar faces took shape. What were they all doing here? Was this some sort of sick illusion?

"In you go," Valkas sneered. He swung the door open to the cell beside Venn and shoved me inside.

My palms slapped against the floor. By the time I scurried to my feet, Valkas was already securing the lock on my cell.

"Have fun watching the show." Valkas laughed maniacally as he started back down the row of cells.

As he distanced himself from me, my gaze scanned the dimly-lit dungeons in horror. Across from Venn's cell, Sondra hung from the wall in shackles. Her face was covered in bruises and dry, crusted blood, and her head hung to the side with her eyes closed, unconscious.

In the cell next to hers, a girl with long red hair knelt at the bars of her cell, staring at me with sad eyes. There was dirt caked in Fiona's hair, and her clothes were tattered and torn. Her usually bright eyes looked hollow, and her lips were dry and cracked. Ryland sat on the floor of his cell with his arms crossed, leaning up against the wall and looking furious. Beside him, Teagan paced her cell with her hands balled into fists. They had the same worn look to them as Fiona had, as if they'd been starving down here for days.

I looked to the cell next to mine and saw my sister shooting me a sympathetic expression. Ronark was locked up in the cell beyond hers, and Andi was in the one next to his.

Everyone was here, and it was all my fault.

"You guys—" I started, but Fiona cut me off.

"You don't have to say anything, Rae."

"Bullshit!" Teagan snapped.

A lump rose to my throat. "Tea, I'm sorry."

"Don't call me that," Teagan growled. "I'm so not in the mood."

I glanced to Ryland for explanation, but he just narrowed his eyes at me. It was like he was so mad he couldn't even speak to me.

"Rachel, are you okay?" Jenna reached through the bars between us to take my hand.

I squeezed hers back and glanced to Venn. The sight of him shivering on the floor next to me was unbearable.

"I'm fine," I told her, because it was my go-to response. Honestly, it felt like someone had poured red-hot coals into my chest cavity.

From across the dungeons, Teagan scoffed. She threw her hands up. "Of-freaking-course you are."

"What's that supposed to mean?" I asked, growing irritated. Shouldn't she be happy I wasn't dead by now?

Teagan walked to the end of her cell and gripped the bars, staring daggers my way. "Ryland was right about you."

"Excuse me?" I gaped at her. After everything we'd been through, she was turning on me?

Ryland growled and shot to his feet. "Don't you *dare* talk to her like that. This is all your fault."

"I never meant for any of this to happen," I said honestly. I dropped Jenna's hand and rose to my feet.

"That doesn't matter," Ryland insisted. "*You're* the reason the Soulless came after us. You told them about us and where to find us. We didn't even get *close* to Matias before they captured us and dragged us here."

I felt like I could hardly breathe. "How long have you been down here?"

"A week, maybe," Fiona said calmly.

I gasped. "Have they fed you anything?"

"A little." The way Fiona said it suggested it wasn't much.

"And Sondra?" I asked, gazing toward her unconscious body. "What did they do to her?"

Fiona dropped her gaze. "They beat her so she couldn't use her magic, then put some sort of spell on her to keep her unconscious. She's been like that for days."

I pressed a hand over my mouth as hot tears rose to my eyes.

Fiona looked at me sympathetically. "It's not your fault, Rae."

"How can you still be on her side!?" Teagan yelled at her.

"Ladies, ladies—" Ronark tried to cut in, but Fiona started speaking.

"Because I trust her," she snapped back at Teagan.

"How can you?" Ryland asked, his nostrils flaring. "She was the one who created the vampires. She came here despite the rest of our objections. It's her fault we're in this mess!"

His accusation stung like a slap to the face.

"How can you say that?" I asked in a hurt tone. "I'm here to kill Valkas. I'm here to save everyone."

"Because of the mess *you* made," Ryland pointed out. "If you weren't so damn powerful, the spells you cast in your past lives would've died with you."

"I can't control how powerful I am," I retorted.

"You *can*," Teagan replied. "That's the whole point of magic."

"Then why aren't I so powerful in this life?" I challenged.

"Because you haven't worked on it in this life," Teagan said. "You're too impulsive."

"What's wrong with being impulsive?" I snarled.

"Rachel," Jenna said, as if begging me to calm down.

Ryland cut in. "Look around you!"

At that, Fiona cracked. She shot to her feet and turned on her brother. "We knew the risks going into this! We knew from the start that Rae's sister was her priority. Killing Valkas to stop Matias makes sense!"

"But she *didn't* kill him," Ryland shot back.

"Blaming her for her past lives is bullshit, Ryland!" Fiona continued. "She can't control that any more than you and I can control what *we* might've done in past lives. Who knows what shit we stirred up?"

"Fiona—" Teagan started, but she cut her off.

"Don't try to defend him."

Teagan gaped at her.

Fiona turned back to her brother. "The fact is, neither of you are mad at Rae. You're just looking for someone to blame. You're mad because we couldn't fight off the Soulless when they came for us. Christ, what did you expect? They had us outnumbered five to one! You both need to grow a set of balls and admit that to yourselves instead of turning your anger around on your friends!"

The dungeons went silent for a moment. My skin heated and my heart raced as a plethora of emotions rose within me all at once. Words couldn't describe how sorry I was for everything that happened to all the people I loved.

"I'm sorry, everyone," I whispered.

"Sure you are," Ryland grumbled.

Fiona, Jenna, and Andi all yelled at him at the same time that I couldn't make out what they'd said. The dungeons went quiet again, and I retreated into a corner of my cell, watching in utter despair as my friends turned on me and Venn transformed into the one monster I despised.

20

Hours passed.

Every now and then, Fiona shot me a sad look. I was so glad to see her, but with Ryland and Teagan angry at me, I never got a chance to speak to her.

Jenna sat beside me in her cell and held my hand through the bars. I sat with my knees curled to my chest and my head dipped low. My mind raced with all the things that went wrong, all the things I should've done differently.

"If I never told Valkas about my family, he never would've found them," I whispered to Jenna, so low that only she could hear me. "If I never came here, they wouldn't have ever been put in danger. Venn never would've come after me and been changed. If I never created Valkas in the first place, vampires wouldn't even exist. The whole world would be a different place, and none of you would be hurt."

"That's not true," she whispered back, but I didn't believe her.

I replayed so many situations through my mind, trying to think back to the one moment where it all went wrong. Should I have walked away from Venn the first night I met him? Should I have pushed harder to find Jenna sooner? I thought about how I'd come to this island, how I fought Jenna in the ring, when Venn showed up and how happy I was to see him, how much I loved him.

And now I'd lost him. I'd lost Teagan and Ryland, and I was about to lose Sondra, Jenna, and Fiona, too. Even Ronark and Andi would perish in my name. Valkas would make sure of that.

I pressed my face into my knees, making my voice muffled. "After all the time you spent on Gregor Island, I never wanted you to die here."

Jenna rested her head on the bars between us. "Are you giving up?"

"What kind of a question is that?" I asked, raising my head. "There's nothing more we can do."

The only thing we *could* do was wait—wait for Valkas to torture my friends and family in front of me. It had to be the only reason they were still alive. Then wait for him to change me. Wait to rot down here for the rest of eternity...

"Maybe there *is* more," Jenna suggested. "If we put our heads together."

I shook my head as tears rolled down my cheeks. "It's over, Jenna. We tried, and it didn't work—again. We don't get a third chance. We're going to perish down here with Venn."

"No," Jenna insisted with tears in her eyes. "No, I won't accept that."

"Forget it. The Soulless have taken everything from us."

"You're wrong," she countered. "I still have you. I didn't get you back just to lose you again." Tears fell from her eyes when she blinked, dripping down her face and into the fabric of her dress.

"It's inevitable," I argued. "The Soulless have proven time and time again that they're stronger than we are."

I just wanted to spend my last few moments holding her, knowing that the last days of my life were spent in her presence.

"You've been given an opportunity to make this right again, Rugrat."

"How?" my voice cracked. It felt as if a hole had been carved out in my stomach and was only growing bigger each passing second.

"Every moment in your life has led you right here. Do you ever wonder if maybe that's what Synchrony wanted for you?"

I shook my head. "I had my chance, and I failed."

"But what if we got out of here?" she pressed. "Would you give it another shot?"

"There *is* no getting out of here," I argued. "Sondra's knocked out, my magic isn't working, and these bars are too close together for any of us to fit through in shifted form. Besides, don't you think Fiona, Ryland, and Teagan would've tried everything possible by now?"

Jenna lowered her voice, though we were already speaking in hushed whispers. "I have an idea."

My eyes darted to Venn, who lay curled up on the floor of his cell. He'd barely moved since I'd been locked away. My gut twisted in agony.

What about what Valkas said? I questioned myself.

Do you want to kill me now?

If I killed Valkas, I killed Venn. But if I didn't kill Valkas, the rest of my friends would perish. The decision was almost impossible to make. I loved Venn so much, but if what I'd heard about Synchrony was true, his soul was being destroyed right in front of me. What if I never lived another life with him? Was I willing to give him up, not just in this life, but every life to come?

I honestly didn't know.

"Rachel, he's a lost cause," Jenna whispered lowly, but her words cut deep into my heart like a knife.

My chest compressed. "What if there's another way to break the curse?"

Jenna shook her head. "I don't think there is."

"Jenna." My voice cracked. "I don't know if I can do this. If Venn's soul is damned because of me…"

"Rachel," Jenna said softly. "I'm not saying you don't care, because I know you do."

"You're damn right," I said.

"All I'm saying is that when a hard decision comes along, you have to put aside your emotions."

As much as I wanted to retaliate and tell her she was wrong, I couldn't help but think that Jenna had a point.

"Well, that's… a hard pill to swallow," I said. That was the understatement of the year.

Jenna gazed down at our entwined hands. "I want the best for you, Rachel."

A lump rose in my throat as I gazed at my sister's teary eyes. "I can't tell you how sorry I am for everything that happened to you. All I can say is that I'm glad that through it all, you found yourself."

I reached through the bars and pulled Jenna into a hug. It was a little awkward and wasn't the best hug we'd ever shared, but it didn't matter. All that mattered was that my sister was here in my arms.

"Clearly, my big sister still has so much to teach me," I said.

She pulled away and wiped at her eyes. "And you me. I just want to know one thing."

"What's that?"

She took a breath. "Where's the Ravenite you told me about?"

I gaped at her. Was she implying I'd lost everything the Ravenite stood for? *Had* I?

"What happened to all the fight in you?" Jenna asked.

I shrugged. "I guess that's another thing the Soulless took from me."

"No," she insisted. "They can't take that from you unless you let them. I know, because I used to think the same thing. But you can reclaim it, Rach."

"Jenna, you gave me this pep talk days ago, and look how great that turned out. This time, our odds are even worse."

"So you admit we still have odds?" she asked.

I stared at her blankly. I didn't know how to answer. Was I starting to actually believe what she was saying?

"We're going to get out of here, but you have to accept that it may not be on your timeline. One way or another, we'll make it off this island. Together."

"You really think so?" I asked.

Jenna held her pinky finger out to me. "I pinky swear."

I looked down at her finger, unsure if I truly believed her. But the fact was, Jenna had a point. If she felt—in the wake of everything—that there was still a chance, who was I to tell her she was wrong? The least I could do was stand beside her until the moment my soul left my body.

I twisted my finger around hers. "Pinky swear."

"Let's get started," she said before hopping to her feet and raising her voice. "Okay, guys. It's time to put our heads together."

Ryland groaned, but Fiona, Ronark, and Andi all perked up.

"I don't know about the rest of you, but I'm not ready to die down here," Jenna said. "We still have work to do."

Fiona stood. "Whatever it is, I'm in."

"Me, too," Andi said.

Jenna turned to Ryland and Teagan. They exchanged a wary glance.

I pushed myself to my feet and stood at the front of my cell. "I know how hard it must be to trust me after everything I've put you through. I haven't always acted out of everyone's best interests, but I want to make things right. I've always had a rule about death. If I ever end up facing it, I will fight until my last breath. And while my views on death might've changed since meeting you, the principle remains. You don't have to forgive me, but I do ask that we can put our differences aside—at least for tonight—and finish this mission."

"I'm with you," Ronark said.

I turned back to Teagan and Ryland. Teagan dropped her gaze to him, where he still sat on the floor with his arms crossed.

Ryland shot me a skeptical expression. "We've spent a week down here going over every scenario to get through these bars. What's your plan?"

"We need everyone's help," I said. "Ronark, what's our best bet?"

"We go after Rogers," he replied. All eyes turned toward him. "Think about it. Who's the one person Valkas trusts?"

"Um… Valkas," Andi stated like it was obvious.

Ronark sighed. "Besides himself. The only reasonable explanation I can think of for why we didn't find the dagger on him is because Rogers had it. He's the only person Valkas would entrust with it. It's not like Rogers can use it against him, and the guy would do anything to protect it."

"Are you sure?" I asked. Valkas didn't seem like he'd trust anyone.

"Valkas suspected you might come after him," Ronark pointed out. "But he wouldn't have expected you to go after Rogers."

"True," I agreed. "And even if I did, he wouldn't expect me to have a chance against him. Something on this island has been blocking my magic."

"It has to be Rogers," Ronark theorized. "He's cloaked the island from outsiders. I'm sure he can do something to limit another witch's magic, too."

Fiona and Teagan shared a wide-eyed glance.

"What?" Jenna asked. "What is it?"

"That would explain why Sondra had trouble with her magic when we got here," Fiona said. "But it only weakened her."

"Me, too," I said, thinking about the few times I'd gotten fire to rise from my palm.

"That's why they beat her to unconsciousness and put the spell over her," Teagan told us. "So she couldn't use her magic to get us out."

I pressed my lips together, thinking. "If Rogers can block witch magic, why not block shifter magic, too?"

"It probably affects the way we taste," Andi theorized.

Ronark nodded. "That, or they don't find it necessary. Rogers is only barely a high witch. His powers look impressive, but he has trouble maintaining them. He has the strength but not the endurance. He has to renew the spell cloaking the island every day, I know that much. A more powerful witch should be able to break down his spells."

"How do you know?" Andi asked.

Ronar smirked. "I've been around a long time, sweet cheeks."

"I thought only the witch who created a spell could break it," I said.

Ronark shrugged. "Depends on how powerful you are. Like I said, Rogers' magic is a little... touchy. His spells wouldn't last long after his death if he weren't around to maintain them."

"How would one break his spells?" I asked. "I mean, if I wanted to lift the spell that's keeping me from using my magic?"

Ronark breathed a heavy sigh. "Do you want the fast and easy solution or the slow and tough one?"

"Fast and easy," I answered automatically.

"You'd have to kill him."

Of course. I wasn't at all surprised.

"Okay," I said with a deep breath. "We'll get to Rogers, get the dagger, and then kill Valkas. Any objections?"

Teagan was the first to respond. "Ryland and I are in, but how are we getting out of here?"

"Is anyone good at picking locks?" Jenna asked.

Andi raised her hand. "I can."

"Perfect." Jenna turned to me with a smile. "Rach, your corset. It can get us out of here."

I glanced down at my dress in realization. Valkas could mock me all he wanted, but it was our ticket out of here. I reached for the bottom of my corset and tore the fabric, then grabbed on to the wire boning and pulled it out. I handed the wire to Jenna, who passed it along to Ronark and then to Andi.

"Once we're all out, I'm going to stay here," Teagan announced.

"No, babe," Ryland disagreed immediately.

"I'm human," Teagan pointed out. "I don't have the strength that the rest of you have, and I don't have my knives on me. There are hundreds of vampires up there. I would rather stay and make sure that no one comes down here and harms Sondra."

A weight settled in my gut when I glanced to Sondra. I could see her chest rising and falling; otherwise, she hadn't moved since I'd arrived. I didn't want anything to happen to her, either.

"I think Teagan has a point," I said. "Sondra can't come with us. If someone comes down here to see we're gone, they might hurt her even more."

"I'm with you, Teagan," Ryland said.

"But we need you," Fiona objected. "You're the biggest, strongest shifter here."

Ryland smirked. "Thanks for the vote, sis, but I'm not leaving Teagan and Sondra alone. In fact, I have a better idea. We'll head for the boathouse we saw when we came in. We'll get a boat ready in case all hell breaks loose."

Ronark checked an imaginary watch on his wrist. "By my estimate, the Awakening Ball is still going on. Security at the boathouse should be pretty thin."

"That's fine," I said to Ryland. "We don't want to be seen, so we should start with a small group anyway."

"Well, I'm going with Rae," Fiona insisted.

"Me, too," Jenna chimed in.

"I'm not breaking us out of here just to stay down here," Andi said as the lock on her cell disengaged. She quickly rushed out of the door and started on Ronark's lock.

"If anyone's going after the vampires, it's me," Ronark stated.

"Yeah, we need you," I replied. "You know this place better than any of us."

"Where will we find Rogers?" Jenna asked Ronark as Andi started fiddling with the lock on her cell.

Ronark stepped out of his open cell. "Rogers is part of Valkas's security team, so he should be monitoring the perimeter of the ballroom. We should have no problem getting to him."

Andi finished with the lock on my door and turned to Fiona's cell. I rushed out of my cell and stood outside Venn's. Seeing him lying on the floor, shivering in pain, sent another wave of emotions to rise within me. I placed my hand over my face and steadied myself against the wall. My breath wavered, and a hot tear streaked my cheek.

"What are we going to do about Venn?" I asked in a shaky tone.

Andi finished the lock on Fiona's cell and started on the next one.

Fiona stepped forward to place a comforting hand on my shoulder. "I don't know if there's anything we *can* do for him anymore."

An involuntary sob broke out in my chest. I knew it was true. It was just hard to hear it said out loud. I couldn't stand the thought of just leaving him.

"I know how hard this is." Fiona's voice cracked. "I don't want to say goodbye to him, either."

I reached for the bars of his cell and lowered myself to my knees. I felt another hand rest on my back to join Fiona's and tilted my head up to see Jenna at my side.

I looked back to Venn, my heart breaking all over again. His back moved quickly to the beat of his breath.

"It's like watching him slowly die right in front of me," I whispered.

A sudden, horrible thought occurred to me to put him out of his misery, but

I knew I'd ever be able to go through with it. The only thing I could do was kill Valkas. And with him, Venn would perish as well.

I couldn't bear to think about it like that, as if Valkas and Venn were connected as one. It made me sick.

"Venn." My soft whisper cut through the silence in the dungeons.

At the sound of his voice, Venn's breathing slowed, and my heart lifted. Was he still in there somewhere?

"Venn?" I said in a stronger voice this time.

He lifted his head, and it was like another shot straight through the heart. His eyes looked straight through me. Silver eyes. Not Venn's deep brown eyes I loved so much. It was like he was already gone.

I took a breath to calm my racing heart, but no amount of deep breathing or relaxation exercises could calm me right now. The love of my life was withering away before me, and I felt as if my heart was crumbling right along with him. This couldn't be the end for us.

But it was. In this life, it was. And if his soul was damned, then we'd never live another life together. I barely had any time with him. I'd give anything for just a few more moments.

"Rae."

A sharp breath crossed my lips as Venn spoke my name.

"Venn, are you still there?" I asked desperately. "I'm so sorry. You don't deserve this."

He pushed himself to a sitting position, and I thought for a second that I saw a light cross his eyes. I reached out for him, but Jenna pulled me back the same time Venn shied away into the corner of his cell. He curled his knees to his chest and turned his face away from me, like he was ashamed.

"You can't save everyone, Rae," he whispered so lightly that I barely heard him.

"Venn…"

He looked at me again, but his eyelids twitched, like it was difficult to meet my gaze—like it pained him. "Fiona's right. You can't help me anymore. The venom…" He gritted his teeth and sucked a deep breath.

My eyes went wide. Venn bit his lower lip, and I noticed for the first time his canines seemed longer than normal. Tears rushed down my face faster.

Venn forced the words out through shaky breaths. "The venom has already done too much damage. I can already feel the bloodlust setting in. I'm a danger to all of you now."

"You just hold on," I told him, but I didn't know what for. I didn't have a solution to this. And that ached to the very core of my soul.

Venn scooted himself closer to me, eyeing my fingers around the bars. I bit down hard on the inside of my lip to keep from bawling like a child. He was just within reach, yet so far away.

"You have to go, Rae," Venn said softly, looking me in the eyes. "I don't want you to see me like this."

"But Venn, we don't have long before—"

"Exactly," he cut me off. "We don't have long. You need to go get that dagger."

"He's right," Ronark cut in. "Someone's bound to come check on us at some point."

Fiona wiped at her eyes, then reached for my hand, but I pulled away from her. Venn was so close to me now, and I wasn't missing my chance to give him a proper goodbye.

Goodbye. This couldn't be it, could it? I wasn't willing to believe that... yet deep down in my heart, I couldn't deny it.

"Venn." I squeezed my eyes shut, letting the tears stream down my face. Without thinking about it too hard, I reached through the bars, grabbed on to him, and pulled him toward me. "I love you."

My mouth connected with his. It felt like kissing him for the first time. Fireworks went off in my chest, and a sense of peace surged through me. Yet it felt so comfortable, like we'd done this a thousand times before.

A split second later, his teeth clamped around my lower lip. Pain shot through my mouth, and the taste of copper rushed over my tongue. I screamed. Suddenly, at least three pairs of hands were on me, dragging me backward.

I forgot all about the blood in my mouth as Venn threw his head backwards and groaned in agony. Muscles rippled across his chest, like there was a power trying to escape out of his skin.

"Go," he forced between clenched teeth. "I. Can't. Control..."

Ronark dragged me to my feet. "We need to finish this."

Venn's heavy breaths filled the dungeon. He leaned forward and rested on his palms. He lifted his head, and I could just barely see the last bits of the Venn I knew staring out at me through those silver eyes.

"Go, Rae," he whispered. "And know that I will *never* stop loving you."

"I love you, too," I called back as Jenna and Fiona began leading me down the hall. Teagan and Ryland turned to Sondra's cell, and I added, "We'll see you soon."

We raced down the hall and turned toward the stairs. Just before we reached the end, Jenna grabbed my shoulder and stopped me. She threw her arms around me and squeezed me tight. Ronark, Andi, and Fiona all stopped to wait for us.

"I'm so sorry about Venn," Jenna said.

I hugged her back, but it didn't feel like I could squeeze hard enough to show her how much I appreciated the thought.

"Thank you," I said before drawing away.

My eyes fell on Fiona's sad expression, and I gestured for her to join us. Fiona stepped forward, and I wrapped an arm around her as she wiped the last remaining tears out of her eyes.

"I love you guys," I said.

"We love you, too," Fiona replied.

Finally, I drew away from them and stood up straighter. I'd cried just about as many tears as I possibly could, and my eyes had gone dry. I swallowed down the lump in my throat and took a breath. "Let's go slay some vampires."

21

Music from the ballroom spilled out from open doorways when we reached the top of the stairs. Quietly, we snuck out into the hallway. Ronark led us down a narrow hall and peeked around the corner. He threw his arm out across Andi's chest and pressed her back to the wall. The rest of us followed suit. I held my breath and forced my heart rate to slow.

Ronark placed an index finger over his lips, then peeked out around the corner again. Silently, he gestured for us to follow.

Halfway down the hall, we heard a pair of footsteps approaching. Ronark shoved us into a dark room. Judging by the shapes I could just barely make out through the darkness, it looked like some sort of study. Ronark stood at the door and peered through the sliver into the hallway until the sound of footsteps disappeared.

"Come on," Ronark hissed, leading us back out into the hall.

Fiona kept close to my side, her eyes darting this way and that. As we stopped the end of the hall, a collection of voices reached us.

"He's bluffing," a man accused.

"Am I?" another challenged.

"Just fold already." I recognized Rogers's voice.

"Poker?" I whispered in disbelief. Valkas was hosting the celebration of the year, and his security team was out here playing poker.

Ronark shrugged. "Makes things easy for us."

He looked around the corner, and I poked my head out beside him. I saw that we were in the hallway that led to the big sitting area with the large arches and the grand piano. Four guys sat around the couches with cards in their hands.

"What do we do?" Andi asked. "I can create a distraction if you need it."

405

"I think we can take them," I said. "It's one human and three vampires against five shifters."

"No, no," Ronark replied. "I think Andi's right. A distraction will give us a better advantage. They're less powerful if we split them up."

"So are we," Jenna pointed out.

"Jenna's right," Andi whispered. "We'll take them all at once. But we have only one shot to catch them off guard. I'm going to distract them, so get ready to strike."

Ronark turned to me and grabbed on to my shoulders, staring me in the eyes. "You take Rogers, Rachel. He's not as powerful as he seems. You can break through his spells. I know you can."

"You've never seen me perform magic," I pointed out.

"Doesn't matter. Every witch has something worth fighting for. Just make sure your reason is stronger than his."

I nodded.

"That a girl." Ronark patted my back, then turned to Andi. He dragged her into a hug and placed a kiss on the top of her head. "Be careful, baby doll."

"I will."

"What's the signal?" Fiona asked.

"You'll know." Andi winked.

Andi padded softly down the hall in her jaguar form, not making a single noise. She kept close to the wall and ducked under tables and around other decor to keep from being seen.

When she reached the first wide archway, she waited until she saw all the men had their eyes on their cards before hopping forward silently and ducking behind a couch.

Rogers glanced up from his cards and looked out into the hallway. He went rigid, as if he was on high alert. I could barely see him from this angle, but he seemed to relax a moment later and looked back down at his cards.

Andi lowered herself onto her belly and slid along the hardwood floor, her fur helping to muffle the noise. She cocked her head at us just before disappearing out of view.

Ronark led the way, sneaking out into the wide hallway as we all followed behind him. We kept close to the wall where the vampires couldn't see us, then stopped just before we reached the first arch. We were only mere feet away from the couches.

"Full house," a vampire with a bald head announced.

Just then, the sound of the piano filled the hall. It was a soft, beautiful melody. All four of the security guards' eyes widened as they looked to the corner of the room where Andi was playing. Three of the men—all but Rogers—shot to their feet.

"Hey!" Baldy called. "What are you—?"

"Now!" Ronark hissed.

The four of us jumped out at them while they were momentarily distracted by Andi's music. Ronark shifted and slammed into one of the vamps facing away from us. Fiona took the other, while Jenna jumped on the arm of the couch and kicked off, using her momentum to soar over the other two guys. She shifted mid-air and landed in raccoon form on Baldy's shiny head.

Meanwhile, I went for Rogers. I aimed straight for his eyes, but it was like he knew I was coming. He swung his arm out, and it connected with my chest so hard that when I gasped, no air came. My body flew across the room and slammed into the small section of wall between the archways.

Holy hell! Rogers is strong. Way stronger than any human should be, I realized.

I pushed past the pain in my chest and jumped to my feet before Rogers could reach me. Andi had abandoned her act on the piano and had joined Jenna in wrestling her guy onto the couch. Fiona grabbed a plant and swung the heavy pot at one of the vamp's head.

"A shifter, huh?" I shot at Rogers.

"Valkas would only pick the very best for his team." He smirked before throwing a fist in my direction. I ducked, and his knuckles connected with the wall behind me, sending crumbled pieces flying everywhere.

I kicked my leg out at him, and it sank into his abdomen. He let out a satisfying grunt, but it barely fazed him. He grabbed for me and caught me by the wrist, then spun me around until I was pinned to his chest.

"What's in it for you?" I asked. "Money? Fame?"

Rogers scoffed. "None of your business. How'd you get out of your cell?"

"None of your business," I shot back at him. I threw my arms downward with all my strength, breaking free of his hold. I dove toward a vase on the end table to use as a weapon and held it above my head.

But before I could bring it down on him, he muttered the words, *"Quod dico facies."*

My whole body stopped as if I'd been turned to stone, but my eyes still moved freely. I glanced over to my friends to see that Fiona had taken care of the first guy was helping Ronark with his. Any second now, they'd come to help me, too. Come hell or high water, we were getting our hands on that dagger.

Rogers stepped closer to me until his face was just inches from my own. "If you must know, I want to be on the winning side."

"You sure you chose the right one?" I asked rhetorically.

Rogers reached down and clamped a hand around my jaw. When he touched me, something like a small electric shot traveled across my skin. It was like I could feel his magic in his touch, and I knew that everything Ronark had said about him was true. Rogers's magic was strong, but it was without purpose. He was driven by fear and greed, and that was why he had to renew his cloaking spell every day. His magic was weak.

"Valkas is stronger than any witch alive," Rogers asserted. "You're the only thing standing in his way of eternal glory. And *I'm* stronger than you. Together, Valkas and I can rule the world."

"And what about when you die?" I asked. "If you become a vampire to live forever, you'll lose your magic. You don't think Valkas will toss you aside the second you're no use to him?"

Rogers hesitated to answer the question.

"Besides, if you're so strong, how come your spell stopped working on me a good ten seconds ago?"

Rogers's eyes went wide and darted up to the vase I held above his head. I'd been totally bluffing, but the second I said it, he lost his focus. His spell eased on me just enough that I found control over my fingers again. I opened my hand, and the heavy vase clunked into his forehead.

He was barely distracted for a second, but it was enough. I brought my knee up and pressed my foot firmly into his abdomen, then kicked with all my strength. He went flying backward and crashed into a table next to the couches. It crumbled beneath his weight. I was on him a second later, patting him down in search of the dagger.

His arms shot out and grabbed on to my wrists, so I threw my head forward into his nose. My head throbbed, but I was satisfied to see blood dripping down his face and onto the hardwood floor. Still, he didn't let go of me.

I pulled a move I'd seen in a movie once. I threw my arms outward, giving me enough momentum to break his hold on me. I grabbed his wrists with all my strength and tugged so that they crossed over his chest. I pressed my knee right where his arms met and again felt around for the dagger.

Relief flooded through me when my hands ran over a sheath secured to his hip. I pulled hard on his suitcoat, tearing the buttons and a corner of fabric.

I'll be damned. Ronark was right. Beneath the fabric of his coat, the silver handle of the dagger poked out of the sheath.

The moment I reached for it, Rogers let out a deep, angry roar from beneath me. He gathered all his strength and threw his arms out, tossing me off of him like a rag doll. My cheek slammed into the corner of the couch several feet away, but I ignored the pulse of pain and whirled around.

Rogers was already coming at me again, his fist flying at my face. I ducked, but I didn't get out of the way in time before a pain shot out through my other cheek. I stumbled backwards into another end table. I grabbed the legs and held the whole thing high above my head, swinging it at Rogers.

He threw his arm up to protect himself. The table snapped in half against his forearm, and the legs went flying in different directions. I was left with two legs in my hands and half a table top. So I swung it again.

This time, Rogers caught it mid-swing and twisted, ripping it out of my hands. I didn't let myself get distracted. Jumping onto the arm of the couch, I kicked off to gain height, then twisted in the air to land on Rogers's back. I curled my arm around his neck and squeezed tightly, but he was just as fast as I was. He grabbed on to my arm and threw his body forward, using the momentum to flip me over his head and slam me onto my back on the ground.

The air stalled in my lungs like the whole room had just been sucked of oxygen.

"You think you're so tough," Rogers drawled as he loomed above me. "You will *never* amount to anything as long as the Soulless are around."

I finally caught my breath and managed to choke out, "We'll see about that."

In a split second, I kicked off the ground, spun and grabbed the dagger out of Rogers's sheath, then sliced the hand racing for my throat. I jumped backward just out of his reach. My ankle met up with the wall behind me, and I held out the dagger in defense.

Anger ignited across his eyes, and his nostrils flared. He aimed his good fist at me, but I easily ducked and dodged it. What I didn't expect was for him to go straight for the sconce behind me, ripping it off the wall. Before I could react, a hot, burning pain seared my shoulder as he shoved the burning candle into my exposed skin.

My scream echoed above the breaking glass and grunts coming from the other side of the room. Rogers took the opportunity to reach down and tear the dagger out of my grasp.

That was it before he made a run for it.

"Rachel!" I heard Jenna calling my name, but I didn't listen. No way was I letting Rogers get away with that dagger.

I sprinted after him, down one hall and around a corner, until we reached a back door and broke out into the night. I ran after him as fast as I could, but he kept a steady pace ahead of me. He raced around the chateau and to a familiar trail, the one that led to the fight ring. My chest ached with shallow breaths the harder I pushed my body to keep up with him.

What the hell is he up to?

Rogers didn't slow until he reached the arena at the top of the hill. When I finally caught up to him, he was standing at the edge of the cliff, dangling the dagger over the water.

Dread slammed into my gut so hard that the air *whooshed* out of my lungs. I stopped in my tracks. It felt like I'd been punched in the stomach by Thor's hammer.

"Don't!" I cried, holding my hands out in front of me, as if I could reason with him.

But there was no reasoning with the Soulless. He'd already made his decision.

Rogers opened his fingers, and the dagger dropped out of sight. All of my hope fell with it, crashing into the waves below.

Instinctively, I shifted and flapped my wings, as if I might be able to catch it before it hit the water. But my wings failed to lift me into the air. I'd almost forgotten Valkas had ripped out my flight feathers. I shifted back to human form, feeling completely hopeless.

Maybe if I had a spell to stop it, or something to drag it up from the deep lake bed below… But I didn't have any of that. All I had was tonight, and my final chance had vanished in the blink of an eye.

Before I could really process what had just happened, Rogers's features started changing. His head ballooned as his body grew hundreds of pounds heavier. His skin transformed into a dark gray color, and it looked dry and rough. His nose elongated into a long, sharp horn.

A rhino! He was a freaking rhino shifter.

I quickly glanced around for a weapon and spotted a sharp rock at my feet. I knelt down and curled my fingers around the cool stone. My mind raced with possible solutions. A sharp rock against a rhino didn't give me the best odds. I needed magic.

Ronark's words instantly came back to me. *Every witch has something worth fighting for. Just make sure your reason is stronger than his.*

Rogers scuffed his foot in the dirt and lowered his head, aiming his horn at me. But for whatever reason, it didn't ignite a sense of fear within me like it should've. I remained calm.

As Rogers stood there threatening me, I turned my focus inward. I felt for the magic I knew was there, but instead of digging deep into my own magic, I searched for the barrier Rogers had placed over the island. My magic slammed against an imaginary brick wall. I pictured my magic spreading out across it, looking for weaknesses in the spell.

"Want to know the difference between you and me?" I asked boldly.

Rogers tilted his head to the side, like I'd piqued his curiosity.

"I have a family worth fighting for," I said.

This one's for you guys.

Rogers huffed and took aim, sprinting for me like he was going to impale me through the heart. But I raised my hand in defense.

Suddenly, my magic tore through the wall like a stick of dynamite blasting through brick. All at once, the power inside of me that had been held back erupted out of my palms. Air blasted backward with the power of a hurricane, leaving me safely in the eye of the storm. The bleachers crumbled, and trees bowed over as Rogers's body flew backwards at the force of my magic. He tumbled through the sky over and over, letting out a terrified whine. Then he was gone, thrust over the side of a cliff toward the rocks below.

In the blink of an eye, the storm was over. Trees righted themselves, and silence settled over the arena. It was almost like it hadn't happened at all. I stood there for a moment, dumbstruck. All that power… and I hadn't even muttered an incantation?

The sound of distant screams reached my ears, bringing me back to attention. I looked out over the trees toward the chateau, and my hand shot over my mouth. From this vantage point, I could see into the tall, wide windows that lined the ballroom. All throughout the room, blood slaves had shifted and vampires were going wild. The entirety of the island had turned on the Soulless. The sound of shattering glass was barely audible in the distance as two shifters threw a vampire through a window and glass rained down around him.

This isn't over yet, I realized. My family needed me.

I started toward the trail, knowing that I had to get down there and help them. But just as I reached the trees, a tall, dark figure stepped out of the shadows, blocking my path. My heart leapt my chest.

"Well, well, well," a voice came from out of the darkness. "You really should've stayed in your cell, darling."

My blood ran cold as the figure stepped out of the trees and into the moonlight.

Valkas had come for me. Judging by the evil sneer on his face, he was finally done playing games.

"How does it feel?" Valkas mocked, taking another step into the arena. "Knowing this is finally the end? Without that dagger, you'll never kill me, not unless you dive into the lake to retrieve it. The rocks at the bottom will kill you first." He smirked in satisfaction.

"There are other ways to stop you," I said confidently.

"How's that?" He feigned interest. "Trapping me on this island again? Darling, you don't have the manpower. Besides, look at how well that worked out last time." He gestured to himself, like he was living proof that my magic was weak.

The honest truth was that I didn't know how to stop him. I didn't even know how to slow him down.

Valkas took another step toward me and reached out to brush my hair over my shoulder, exposing my neck.

I slapped his hand away. In my other hand, my grip tightened on the rock I'd been holding. "Don't touch me."

"Darling," he snarled, leaning in close. His breath brushed across my face, sending shivers through my cheek. "I own you."

The next moment passed in the blink of an eye, but I saw it as if it were in slow motion. Valkas's hands shot out to wrap around me as his fangs elongated and headed toward my neck. He threw my body backward like we were a couple dancing on the clifftop and he was dipping me romantically. But there was nothing romantic about the moment.

As I felt the ground swoop out from under me, I shoved my rock upward—straight into his ribs. It was a last resort, one that I thought might slow him down... but it didn't.

Valkas's teeth sank into my neck, sending a needle-sharp pain across my skin. A split second later, that peaceful euphoria set in. Somewhere in the back of my mind, I knew this was not something to enjoy. This was a sign of the end.

I stared up at the night sky as strong emotions welled to the surface, overpowering that feeling Valkas's bite gave me. For so many years, anger and frustration were all I knew. But this was different. It was heavier. The weight pulling on my chest was full of regret and sorrow. Somewhere along the way, everything had fallen to pieces, and it pained me to the very core to know that I wouldn't get a chance to make things right again.

I thought of Venn, withering away to nothing in that cell. I thought of Sondra, how she'd been beaten to unconsciousness because of me. Jenna, how she'd been kidnapped and kept prisoner here all these years. Fiona, Teagan, Ryland, Ronark, Andi... all the other blood slaves on this island.

I'd come here to save them. And I didn't.

As I thought of them, one thought broke through all the others.

At least they knew I loved them.

The weight in my chest eased at the thought, and a sense of peace washed over me. It wasn't from Valkas's bite, either. This peace came from inside of me.

At least if nothing else came of this, my family knew I loved them. Maybe I wouldn't kill Valkas, and maybe the vampires would live on. They could take this world from us, destroy everything we held dear and rule as they had planned. But they would never take the moments. They would never take the feelings. They would never take *us*.

It was in that moment that I realized with unwavering certainty that Jenna was right. The Soulless couldn't break me unless I let them.

At the thought, a power rose within me, a strong tingling of magic I'd never felt before. It was unlike the fire or the lightning I'd conjured in the past. This magic was hundreds of times stronger, like a nuclear bomb about to go off inside my body.

Love, I realized. This was what it was like to love someone with so much passion that you thought your heart might explode.

You should know that there's always more than one way off an island. That's what Genevieve had said. I didn't know why those words came back to me in that moment, but I knew it meant something. Only... what?

Was she talking about the island in a literal sense, or was it a metaphor? And if it was a metaphor, then what did it mean?

A red-hot, searing pain entered my veins as Valkas released his venom. It felt as if someone had placed burning hot coals on my neck, turning my blood to flames. My body went completely rigid, and I longed to scream, but the cry of agony caught in my throat, unable to escape.

And that was when Genevieve's meaning hit me.

Even when strong bridges crumble, there's always another path to take.

She meant it as a mental island, the feeling of being stuck, alone, and hopeless. *The feeling of no escape.*

She was trying to tell me that magic had loopholes, that even though I'd lost the dagger, there were other ways to break the vampire curse. That had to be it.

I struggled through the pain clouding my thoughts, trying to think of what I knew about magic. A curse like this could only be broken by the witch who cast it through an object used in the original spell.

The dagger wasn't the only thing there when the spell was cast, I suddenly realized. I recalled the vision I'd had of Valkas, how I'd sliced his hand open with the dagger and watched his blood stream into a bowl.

It took everything I had to force words out between clenched teeth. "*Quod. Dico. Facies.*"

At my command, Valkas went rigid. I could barely sense it over the searing venom pulsing through my body, but I saw his muscles stiffen as I spoke the incantation for the puppeteer spell I'd seen Rogers use.

Drop me, I commanded in my mind.

Suddenly, my body fell from his grasp, and I landed hard in the dirt at his feet. Valkas stood above me with wide eyes filled with fright. He otherwise looked like a statue.

I pointed my hand at him and forced him to stand straight up. Blood dripped out of his open mouth. I could see in his eyes he was struggling to close his lips, but he couldn't.

I got to my feet. I pressed one hand against the wound on my neck and kept the other pointed at him. Rage burned behind his motionless eyes. I quickly whispered the incantation for healing, then wiped the blood from my neck.

"I remember slitting your palm," I said. "The dagger was the obvious option, but it never was the only one, was it?"

Valkas's eyes grew wider the more I talked.

"All I need to break this spell is something used when the spell was created. The dagger isn't the only weapon that can kill you. You, Valkas, were there," I stated as it became clear to me what I needed to do. "Which means you're a weapon against yourself."

I forced him to pull the sharp rock from his side, then let him take control of his mouth again. His scream echoed over the cliffside like a creature howling at the moon. He brought the rock to his chest under my command. Images of all the terrible things I'd seen the Soulless do flashed through my mind, but I settled on just one...

The day I came here, when Valkas had ripped that man's heart from his chest. After all the horrible things he'd done, Valkas deserved to know what it felt like to be one of his own victims.

"Stop it, Rachel!" he shouted. "You don't underst—GAHHH!"

I made him press the rock into his skin. It tore through his flesh and scraped along the bone like a blade cutting through ice. It carved out a deep, long wound surrounded by raw skin running from his collarbone all the way down to his sternum. Nausea hit me at the sight of it, but I forced the bile down my throat to concentrate.

Valkas screamed like I'd never heard anyone scream before. The sound of his voice carried over the empty water like a banshee in the night.

Drop the rock, I commanded in my mind.

He did, still screaming like he couldn't bear the pain any longer.

By the simple twitch of my finger, Valkas shoved his hand into his open chest cavity. He removed it a moment later and held up a dry, black heart.

His features contorted in a mix between disgust, fury, and terror. "You evil bit—"

The vengeance I felt toward Valkas melted away. This wasn't about revenge anymore. This was about saving the people I loved.

I curled my hand into a tight fist, forcing him to do the same. Valkas squeezed as hard as he possibly could.

It was ironic. The same hand that gave blood to create him would be the same to destroy him.

"*Biiiiitch!*" he roared.

The heart turned to ash in his hand.

I released my hold on him as the ashes drifted away in the wind. Valkas gasped and took a step toward me, but his legs began to crumble beneath him. He fell to the ground, and I watched in peaceful satisfaction as the spell broke before my very eyes. Valkas reached a hand out toward me, but his fingers washed away in the wind like sand upon a beach.

He shot me one last pleading look, as if begging me to reverse the spell, to keep him alive. But I could see it in his eyes—he already knew it was over.

"How does it feel?" I asked calmly, throwing his words back at him. "Knowing this is finally the end?"

He gaped at me as his body crumbled away. It took his arms and legs first, then his body, before finally wiping away the wide-eyed expression on his face. And then he was just... gone.

Valkas's clothes remained in a pile at my feet.

The pain of the venom rushing through my veins eased as the vampire curse broke. Relief so strong washed through me like a tidal wave hitting shore. Tears sprang to my eyes before I even knew they were coming and streamed down my face. My whole body shivered, and I dropped to my hands and knees, curling up into a ball with my forehead pressed to the grass. Deep breaths passed in and out of my lungs as I tried to regain my physical strength and process what had just happened. I couldn't believe it.

Never again would I give up, no matter how bad the situation. Tonight proved to me that anything was possible.

Against all odds, I had finally beat Valkas.

23

"Rachel!" The sound of Jenna's voice carried through the trees and over the cliff.

I didn't know how long I'd been kneeling there, staring down at Valkas's empty shirt, unable to believe he was truly gone. Eight years ago, he'd escaped from this island and the whole world changed. Now things could go back to normal.

I didn't even know what that looked like anymore. It felt like magic had been part of the world my whole life.

Magic. We still had magic. Of course things wouldn't go back to the way they were. Witches and shifters were still out in the open. But maybe now that the vampire curse was broken, magic wouldn't be so feared. We could embrace it, give it a different face than the horror vampires had put to it. We could use it for good.

"Rachel!" Jenna's voice came again, pulling me out of my thoughts.

"Rae!" Fiona's voice quickly followed.

"Up here!" I called.

"Rachel, oh my God." Jenna rushed out of the trees and fell to her knees beside me. She lightly reached out to touch the tender bruises on my face, but she pulled away at the last second. "What happened?"

"I... I killed him," I said, glancing between Fiona and Jenna. They were banged up and bruised themselves, but I didn't notice any major injuries. "I killed Valkas." I wasn't sure I truly believed it until I said the words out loud. "What about you? Did Ronark and Andi make it?"

Jenna dropped her gaze. "We fought off the vampires in the hall, but when we tried following you, we lost you in the chateau. We thought Rogers had led you to the ballroom. Only... when we got there, you weren't there."

"A fight broke out," Fiona said. "Before we knew it, all the blood slaves had joined us—shifters, human, all of them."

"Are Ronark and Andi okay?" I repeated.

Jenna took a long breath. "Andi didn't make it. A vampire got ahold of her—"

"I don't want to know how it happened," I interrupted.

Jenna nodded in understanding. "Ronark is fine. He's leading everyone in rounding up the Soulless."

I instantly became more alert. I lifted my gaze and looked down the hill toward the chateau. Windows were smashed, and bodies were strewn here and there. From what I could see through the windows, people walked slowly. Everything seemed so quiet and somber compared to when I'd seen the place in an uproar earlier.

"You mean, the vampires aren't dead?" I asked. When I killed Valkas, all the vampires should've died with him. The magic keeping them alive should've disappeared. "I thought I broke the vampire curse."

Fiona shot a glance at Jenna, like she didn't know how to tell me what came next. She placed a gentle hand on my shoulder and said, "You did. They just didn't die."

"What do you mean?" I asked, bewildered. "What happened?"

"It happened all of a sudden," Jenna explained. "We were losing people left and right, then suddenly... we just weren't. It was like the vampires lost their strength. We started winning, and they began surrendering."

"We all kind of realized what was happening at the same time," Fiona said. "The silver faded from their eyes, and..."

"You mean they're human again?" It didn't seem possible.

Jenna nodded. "Yes. It doesn't excuse their crimes, but—"

Before Jenna could finish, a shot of adrenaline jolted through my chest. I sprang to my feet so fast I nearly lost my balance. I clutched on to Jenna's and Fiona's shoulders to steady myself. "Oh my God! Do you know what this means?" I didn't wait for their response before answering my own question. "Venn!"

I sprinted down the trail and back toward the chateau. Fiona and Jenna were close at my heels. Inside, we navigated through an endless labyrinth of hallways until we found the door leading to the dungeons. I ran down them so fast that I almost lost my footing and slid all the way down. I caught myself on the railing and didn't stop running until we reached the cells.

I skidded to a halt to take in the scene. Teagan and Ryland were long gone, and Sondra's shackles hung empty. The wire used to pick the locks lay on the ground beside them. Venn stood with his hands on the bars of his cell, looking like it took all his strength to stay upright. His soft brown eyes met mine, and relief flooded through me. Venn looked down at himself in confusion. It was like he couldn't process what was going on.

"Venn!" I rushed over to him, grabbed the wire, and began fiddling with the lock on his cell. My fingers shook so badly that I couldn't get it in the hole.

"What happened?" Venn asked, sounding a bit disoriented.

Jenna grabbed the wire from me and began working on the lock so I could focus on Venn.

I reached out to take his hands. "I did it, Venn. I killed Valkas."

He looked beyond relieved. "How did I survive? The transformation must've not finished."

I shook my head, choking back the tears. "No, it only killed Valkas. Everyone else survived, but the spell is broken now."

The lock clicked free on Venn's cell. I yanked the door open and fell into his arms.

"I thought I'd lost you," I whispered.

His lips met mine, and I knew without a doubt. It was Venn—my Venn. Valkas had failed to take him from me.

My chest came alive, sending a rush of happiness through my veins like a strong ocean current whipping me off my feet and pulling me out to sea. I'd never felt such an emotion hit me so fast and so strong before. He cupped the sides of my face and tilted my head back. His tongue slipped inside my mouth, sending that ocean current to take me faster.

He drew away and spoke through shallow breaths. "I thought so, too. I'm glad everyone's okay."

I relaxed into him for a mere moment, until I remembered Sondra was still hurt. Now that Rogers was dead, she'd be waking any moment—if she wasn't awake already.

"Sondra," I said quickly.

Fiona gave me a wide-eyed look, like she just realized something. "Your magic's working. You can heal her!"

"Then let's go," Jenna insisted.

Venn took my hand, and the four of us hurried out of the chateau and to the boathouse. When we arrived, we found Teagan and Ryland preparing an expensive-looking boat for the journey home. It looked even fancier than the one Richard had brought me there on. The boathouse itself was just as nice as the chateau, with three stalls for different sized boats. It looked like a fancy garage, only with docks for flooring and open water where the boats sat. Several piles of clothes covered in ashes lined the dock, presumably where Ryland and Teagan had killed the boathouse guards.

"Nothing's going to happen to them," Teagan was saying to Ryland. "They'll be fine—oh my God!" She caught sight of us and jumped off the boat onto the dock. "You're okay!"

Teagan stopped in her tracks when she noticed Venn with us. Slowly, she backed away. "What's going on?"

"Rae did it!" Fiona exclaimed. "She killed Valkas and broke the curse."

Teagan's eyebrows came together. "Vampires are… human again?"

"Apparently," Fiona answered, shooting a smile in Venn's direction.

"What happens to their souls?" Teagan asked. "I mean, are the Soulless still... soulless?"

"We're not sure yet," Jenna said. "Venn could be different since the transformation wasn't finished. All we know is the others are still alive."

Ryland poked his head out of the cabin. "If they're still a threat, then we have to go."

"I don't think they are," Jenna admitted. "The blood slaves outnumber them, and they surrendered as soon as the spell broke."

"Let's heal Sondra," I suggested. "Then we can figure out how we're getting everyone off this island."

"This way." Ryland gestured to me to follow him.

We stepped inside the cabin to see Sondra lying across one of the bench seats. Her chest rose and fell slowly, but she otherwise didn't move. She looked so frail.

I knelt beside her and placed a gentle hand on her shoulder. Everyone went quiet while I took several long, deep breaths, trying to channel my power.

But the familiar tingle never came. That couldn't be, considering Rogers was dead and his spell had been broken. Had the fall not killed him? Was he still blocking my magic?

No, that didn't seem right. This seemed stronger... like my entire connection to Synchrony had been severed.

That's when it hit me.

Matias hadn't been misinformed about what would happen to the vampires when I broke the curse. He hadn't just taken a wild guess when he told me all vampires would perish with Valkas. He told me exactly what I wanted to hear—exactly what he knew would drive me toward this very ending.

"What's wrong?" Venn asked.

I looked up at my family in horror. "This was Matias's plan all along. There never was a successor. He wanted me to kill Valkas to release his own soul, so that he could access his witch magic again and use the Artifact. You guys..."

I could hardly breathe as the cold, dark reality of what had just happened hit me. "I played right into Matias's hands. And now he's taken all our magic."

END OF BOOK THREE

RETRIBUTE

BOOK FOUR

1

When you've been stripped of everything, the only thing left to hold on to is your free will. Matias Vayne was trying pretty damn hard to rip that away from us, too. No one should have that kind of power.

Even Valkas, the most ruthless vampire in history, hadn't stooped that low. When he'd imprisoned blood slaves on his island, he gave them time to do as they pleased. Valkas knew how valuable free will was—and that even slaves needed a bit of it to comply to bigger demands.

Matias thought this was the only way to cleanse the world. He thought he was the only one who could handle free will, that everyone else would only use it against each other. But when you take it away from someone, you strip them of their humanity—of what makes them unique.

Everyone had a choice, and Matias was making the wrong one.

I paced back and forth in Genevieve's living room, my hands fisting at my sides. The room was just as lavish as the rest of the house, with dark walls, velvety red couches, and a black chandelier hanging over the coffee table. The news played on the big-screen TV across the room, but I could hardly process what the newscasters were saying.

"He's holding our magic hostage!" I growled under my breath.

With The Wise Owl in his hands, Matias had the power to block magic from every witch and shifter on the planet. I wasn't sure what I was madder about—the fact that the heartless bastard had done it, or the fact that I'd let him.

I didn't know, I kept telling myself—but I couldn't shake the guilt settling like heavy rocks in the pit of my stomach.

"Rachel," Jenna sighed. She turned to me from where she sat on one of the dark red couches. "Take a breath and sit down."

How could I breathe at a time like this?

It'd only been a day since we escaped Gregor Island, freed the blood slaves trapped there, and returned to Genevieve's. We left the Soulless up to the Department of Magical Regulation after calling in an anonymous tip. The vampire curse was broken now, which was exactly what Matias had wanted all along. He used to be a vampire, unable to perform magic. Now without the curse holding him back, he had access to his witch magic again, and he was using it to manipulate a powerful artifact that severed any supernaturals' connection to Synchrony at his command. He was now the most powerful man alive.

Jenna's eyes pleaded with me, causing me to pause. Words she'd spoken to me on Gregor Island came rushing back. I could wallow in my regret all day, but it didn't change what Matias had done. The only thing we could do was decide how to handle it going forward.

I inhaled a deep breath and sank into the empty spot beside Venn. He reached out and curled his warm fingers around mine. I felt that weight in my stomach ease slightly.

Venn didn't look good. We all looked like crap, but he looked particularly rough. I guess that was what nearly being turned into a vampire did to you. His eyes looked hollow, and his lips were dry and cracked.

He almost looked as bad as Sondra, who sat curled beneath a blanket on the couch opposite us. She'd been beat unconscious on Gregor Island and still had the bruises across her face to prove it. I'd managed to administer a healing spell on myself before Matias struck. But by the time I got to Sondra, I could no longer access my magic to help her—and she hadn't been conscious enough to do the spell herself.

Everyone else was here: Jenna, Fiona, Ryland, Teagan, Ronark, and Genevieve. Even Genevieve's husband, Richard, was here. They'd come to help as soon as we got back to the mainland and found a phone. Genevieve had been helping us locate Matias, and we didn't know who else to call. Too late to locate him now, I suppose.

"A number of theories have surfaced for the unexplained events," the newscaster was saying. *"As of now, we are still waiting to hear from the Department of Magical Regulation to confirm exactly why vampires have mysteriously reverted to their healthy human state. Is this a trick from the magical community to lure us into a false sense of security, or have we finally found a cure for the magical plague that swept across our nation eight years ago?"*

"What are we going to do?" I asked. My eyes scanned each of theirs, waiting for someone to give the answer, as if they were all holding back a secret.

"What *can* we do?" Fiona replied, chewing her bottom lip. "I mean, we can't exactly go up against Matias without magic of our own."

She was right. It was hopeless. But if I'd learned anything in the last few days, it was that anything was possible. I'd killed Valkas when I thought for sure I'd failed. I watched my boyfriend undergo the transition from human to vampire —something I once thought was irreversible. Yet here he was, sitting right next to me with blood pumping through his veins and life flourishing in the clear brown eyes I'd come to cherish.

Anything was possible. We just had to find our loophole—but I had no idea what that might possibly be.

I glanced from Sondra to Genevieve. If anyone knew a loophole, it'd be one of them. Sondra stared forward blankly, like she wasn't really with us. I'd never seen her like that before.

Genevieve, on the other hand, looked well rested and alert. She sat at the edge of the chasse and kept her eyes on the TV, like she was trying to absorb everything the newscasters were saying. She ran a manicured index finger along her lower lip, as though she was concentrating hard.

"I don't know, Fiona," I finally said. I couldn't stand to let the statement hang without a response. "All I know is that the longer we wait, the more powerful he'll become."

"He can't actually use the Artifact to take more power, can he?" Teagan asked. Even she looked pale beneath her normally tan skin. "He can only block magic, right?"

Genevieve nodded, though she didn't speak.

"True," I said. "But if he's the only one with magic, he can use it against everyone else. No one will be able to defend themselves anymore. He'll build an army and ensure only his followers have access to magic."

"Okay, but if magic is illegal anyway, he can't get away with it, right?" Jenna offered.

I frowned at her. "We'll have an army of guys with guns up against an army with magic. Which are you gonna bet on to win?"

My money was on the magic.

"Besides," I said before she could answer, "magic shouldn't be illegal to use in the first place. It's people like Matias that give it a bad name. If the government wasn't so scared of it, then maybe we could use it for good on a large scale. I mean, think of all the people I could heal! Matias has stolen that from me—from all of us—and it's not okay."

Ronark shot to his feet, like he couldn't take it anymore. "This is bullshit. I didn't spend eight years on that island to come back to a world where I couldn't shift anymore. It's part of who I am, and I'll be damned if someone keeps me prisoner any longer. I say we go after the bastard!"

"I agree." Ryland stood beside Ronark and crossed his huge arms. "I've spent years using my shifter magic to protect people. I'm not letting that go without a fight."

Genevieve finally tore her gaze from the TV. "I think we can all agree this is wrong. If Matias builds the army he's planning, he could force anyone to comply or die. Innocent lives are on the line. But we're going to need time."

"We don't have much," I said. "He's no doubt already started building an army."

Venn's fingers tightened around mine, and his jaw clenched. His eyes glossed over, like he was thinking of something else entirely.

"You know," I said, feeling that anger bubble up inside me again, "the vampire curse might be gone, but we're still fighting a vampire. He's sucked our magic dry just as he used to suck his victims dry!"

"We don't know if he ever actually killed anyone," Fiona pointed out.

"No, but I wouldn't put it past him," I replied. "He told me himself he would kill to get the world he wants—a place where he decides who lives and dies so that peace can reign. His idea of peace, anyway. According to him, the rest of us can't handle free will. I can't see a world where stripping people of that leads to peace."

Just thinking about it made my blood boil. Matias might've thought he was doing the right thing, but he was going about it in all the wrong ways. His plan would only lead to bitter anger and resentment—because that was exactly what his plan was built on. Synchrony didn't work that way. It would backfire just as it had in his past life.

It'd been nearly two centuries ago when a group of witches teamed up to imprison Valkas. Matias and his followers had planned to double cross them and twist the spell in their favor. They wanted to steal other witches' powers, but it didn't work. Their spell backfired so hard that magic was wiped out for over a century, until Matias freed Valkas in this life and broke the curse holding magic back. On his search for power, he lost it.

Why couldn't he see he was making the same mistake all over again?

Fiona tucked a strand of red hair behind her ear. "Vampire or not, Matias seriously needs to get his ass kicked."

Ryland nudged his sister and chuckled. "You gonna do the honors?"

She punched him in the arm playfully. "If I have to."

"Not without me, you won't," Ryland argued. "If we're going after him, we're going together."

Venn let go of my hand and knotted his fingers together in his lap. His breathing increased, like he was agitated. His gaze locked across the room, but it didn't look like he was focusing on anything in particular.

"You okay?" I asked. It was a stupid question. Something was obviously bothering him, and it went far beyond the current conversation.

Venn snapped out of it and looked at me. Emotions I couldn't quite place—perhaps sadness and sorrow—swam in his eyes. He shook his head, then promptly stood and left the room.

The room fell silent, apart from the TV. Teagan and Fiona both shot me confused expressions, like I could explain his sudden disappearance. I gave them an equally shocked look back.

"What's wrong?" Jenna asked.

"I don't know," I said in a rush before jumping to my feet and following Venn down the hall.

"Venn," I called, but he didn't slow.

By the time I caught up with him, he'd already made it to the guest room we shared. Genevieve's house looked modest from the outside, but it was laid out like a maze, with endless rooms I hadn't even realized were there. I'd probably only explored half of the house.

I found Venn sitting on the dark black comforter with his head in his hands. My stomach sank. Quietly, I shut the door behind myself and tiptoed across the carpet to sit beside him. He didn't move, as if I weren't even there.

"You don't have to say anything," I whispered, "but I want you to know that I'm here. Whatever it is."

Venn nodded, though he didn't speak. When he pulled his hands away from his face, I saw that his eyes were bloodshot, like he was struggling to hold back tears. Which only made me want to cry. I couldn't bear to see him like this.

Testing his limits, I reached out to place a hand on his shoulder. When he let me, I wrapped the arm all the way around his body and held him in an embrace. He melted into me, then shifted until his arms were around me, too. He leaned back and pulled me onto the bed with him.

For the next several minutes, we lay there in silence, staring up at the ceiling. As I waited for him to speak at his own pace, I listened to the sound of his heart. It was the only thing keeping out the deafening silence and the worrying ache entering my chest. What could've caused him to walk out of the room like that? What was bothering him so much?

Finally, after several agonizing minutes and at least a hundred scenarios rushing through my mind, Venn spoke. "I can't stop thinking about him, Rae."

I lifted my head off his chest to look him in the eyes. Water brimmed across his lower lids.

"Your brother?" I asked softly. I understood the feeling all too well.

Venn nodded. "After Tyson was changed, I couldn't save him. He was already gone. But now…"

"He's cured," I finished for him.

Venn nodded solemnly. "I need to find him."

A gaping hole opened up in my chest. It reminded me all too much of what it felt like to lose Jenna. A silent beat passed between us before I swallowed down the lump in my throat and spoke again. "You said he was attacked by a vampire and changed. Do you know where he ended up after the attack?"

Venn shook his head without meeting my gaze.

"Do you have an idea of where to start?" I asked.

"I might know some people I can talk to," he admitted.

Before I could ask him about that, quick footsteps sounded outside the door, then a heavy knock came.

"Come in," I called.

Fiona whipped the door open, and her wide eyes connected with mine. "It's Matias. You need to come see this."

2

Venn and I jumped off the bed and rushed down the hall behind Fiona. I came to a dead stop in the doorway as I caught sight of Matias's eyes on the screen. Everyone in the room had gone silent, but they were more alert than ever. Sondra had snapped out of her daze and sat at the edge of her seat. She leaned forward with her gaze locked on the TV. *Breaking News!* scrolled across the bottom of the screen.

My heart hammered as the camera zoomed out to show Matias hovering above the streets of Chicago, showing off his magic. Dark clouds rushed by above him, and lightning crackled out of his hands, connecting with the sky scrapers. Violent winds whipped through the street, though not a hair on his head moved.

All around him, onlookers were trying to keep hold of their belongings. Couples clung to each other, and people crouched behind cars to protect themselves from the violent winds. Newspapers and litter tumbled down the street. The traffic had come to a complete stop as Matias floated casually above each vehicle.

Behind him, a group of half a dozen men followed like soldiers flying behind their captain. They all wore the same black tailored suit and shiny shoes. They each had a look of anger fixed to their faces, though they held their heads up high in confidence. One guy even smirked to the crowd, like he thought being at Matias's side automatically made him better than anyone else—as if the rest of them were mere dirt on his shoe. Each of them showed off a different type of magic. One guy made flames shoot up from his palms, and another used his telekinesis to manipulate a deck of cards in his hands—like a real magician.

"I have full control of magic!" Matias shouted to the crowd below him. "Join me, and you will see your magic restored. You can be a part of something better

—a powerful force stronger than any that has ever lived before. Together, we can overthrow the government and establish a world built on peace."

Several people stepped forward.

"No!" I cried. "You idiots!"

Couldn't they see how flawed Matias's plan for power was? Couldn't they see they were volunteering as his pawns? Matias didn't even *look* peaceful. Everything about him screamed *evil*!

Matias shouted above the strong winds. "Join, or surrender!"

The camera switched back to the newsroom, where an old man with a white mustache sat beside a younger woman with dark brown hair and a red pantsuit.

The man faltered with his words. "This confession is… quite shocking."

"Yes, it is," the woman agreed. "We are currently waiting on the Department of Magical Regulation to comment on this turn of events. We'll be back at nine o'clock with an update on these details—"

The sound instantly cut off, and the screen went black. All eyes turned to Genevieve, who was holding the remote.

"I can't stand to watch any more," she snarled. "Something needs to be done straight away."

"Who were those guys with him?" Fiona asked.

Genevieve's lips pursed tightly. "His first followers, I suppose. My guess is they're all witches he gathered before he ever used the Artifact."

"Did you recognize any of them?" Sondra asked.

The magical community wasn't very large, and Genevieve had all kinds of connections.

"Just one," she said. "The man directly behind him on his right, the one who was playing with the cards. His name is Tobias Ellwood. We've crossed paths a few times, but I refused to work with him."

Ellwood… Where had I heard that name before? I repeated the name several times in my mind, flipping through my memory for where I could've possibly heard of him. Maybe it was just one of those names…

Suddenly, it struck. Maliya had mentioned him to Cowen when I'd been locked up in her dungeon, right before she'd tried to carve me up like a Thanksgiving turkey. *"This shouldn't take long, Cowen. You'll have plenty of time to make your flight to Seattle. You can tell Ellwood all about the raven bitch once you get there."*

"I heard Maliya talk about a guy named Ellwood when I was in her mansion," I blurted. "Cowen was planning to meet up with him in Seattle for something. Do you think it's the same guy?"

Genevieve thought about it for a moment. "Very possible. Ellwood is a witch who's heavily invested in the blood slave trade. His work specifically specializes in shifter slaves. Cowen was probably headed to do some consulting with him. I suppose that business is no longer viable. If I know anything about the man, he ran straight to Matias's side the second he mentioned magic. He's only a mid-witch, and he probably thought Matias could give him more power."

"But he can't give him more power," Teagan said. "Only as much power as he had before."

Genevieve nodded.

"What are Matias's chances of rounding up enough high witches to go through with his plan?" Ryland asked.

Genevieve shook her head. "I don't know. High witches are rare, but there are enough of us that he could very well build an army, even if only a fraction join."

Ronark frowned. "He makes his cause sound noble, too, so I bet a handful of them *will* join."

"And it doesn't matter how many we get on our side," Jenna pointed out. "Since we can't use magic to fight against him."

"No," Sondra agreed, "but at least we can try to *keep* them from his side. If we talk to people, get the word out about what he really wants to do, then maybe we can keep him from getting too strong. He *is* giving people a choice, after all. We just need to get people to reject his offer."

"How are we going to do that?" Ryland asked. "Get up on national TV and announce he can't be trusted?"

"No," Richard spoke for the first time. "That's a good way to spark the spread of misinformation. We need to go directly to the community."

"You need to go to the Department of Magical Regulation," Venn suggested.

All eyes turned toward him.

"Magic like this, so public… the Department of Magical Regulation is going to be all over it and ready to stop it by any means necessary," he explained. "But they don't know what they're up against. We should tell them what we know, so they can use their resources to stop him before this gets out of hand."

"It's already out of hand," Fiona mumbled. "But I get what you mean."

"I think Venn makes a good point," I said. "Like Jenna pointed out, we don't have the magic to fight him. The DMR at least has resources we don't. If we tell them about the Artifact, they can target it and stop this."

"What happens when they get their hands on it, though?" Ryland asked. "What if they start using it?"

Fiona cocked an eyebrow at him. "Really? The DMR hates magic more than any other person or agency alive. You think they're going to use the Artifact?"

"Yes," Ryland said. "*Because* they hate magic. It's the lesser of two evils for them. Use magic once to stop it forever."

"And the Department of Magical Regulation is the lesser of two evils for us," Venn pointed out. "Matias is going to kill people for this. The DMR won't."

My mouth felt like sandpaper, even though I'd chugged a liter of water an hour ago. I was so torn. Everyone was making good points here, but I was leaning toward Venn's side. If we lost magic for good, we might as well go with the option where fewer people died.

Unless… there was a loophole.

"We could offer them a trade," I said.

Genevieve leaned forward, looking interested.

"We offer to destroy the Owl for them once it's in their possession," I proposed.

"So they can throw you in jail?" Jenna argued. "Won't admitting you're witches capable of destroying this get you in trouble?"

"You can't get in trouble for what you are," I pointed out. "Only for what you do—just as it was with vampires. We negotiate immunity on this act of magic. Once it's destroyed, our magic will return, and we can show them that magic can be used for good. It could be the first step in making better laws for the magical community by forming an alliance with them."

My gaze flickered to Sondra, who looked deep in thought. I hoped she would agree with me. Just the prospect of getting the chance at forming an alliance with the DMR made my stomach flutter in excitement. I couldn't believe we hadn't thought of it sooner.

"I think it's worth a shot," Sondra finally said. "We're all registered as witches, so it's not like we're telling them anything they don't already know. I think Venn's right that this is the lesser of two evils."

Genevieve stood. "I will schedule us a meeting. I want Rae and Venn to accompany me."

Ryland dropped his shoulders. "I miss out on all the fun?"

Genevieve frowned at him. "Rae was the one who spoke to Matias about his plan, and frankly, I trust Venn and Sondra the most. But Sondra needs to rest."

"How come you're in charge?" Ryland complained.

Genevieve crossed her arms. "If you'd like to sleep out on the street tonight, you're welcome to. Otherwise, you're just going to have to trust me."

Ryland sank down into his seat, looking totally defeated. Genevieve breezed out into the hall, and the room broke out into chatter.

I turned to Venn. "What about Tyson?"

"I don't want to delay going after him—"

"Then don't," I said. "Someone else can go to the DMR instead of us."

Venn's gaze fell, and he looked deep in thought. "No, we should go. It will take me a few days to track down some people to talk to so I can get a lead on my brother. And I don't want you going to the Department without me. They're on high-alert, so we don't know how they'll react. This meeting has the potential to be very good for us—or very bad."

I wrapped Venn in a hug. "I don't like the sound of that. I really hope it goes well."

3

The Department of Magical Regulation was like any fancy office building—
reception desks, waiting rooms, long hallways with endless doors...
except it was insanely busy today. It'd been less than twenty-four hours since
Matias made his big announcement, and the department was in a total uproar.
Phones were ringing off the hook, and people were running this way and that,
trying to deal with all of it. And this was only a branch of the department, a rela-
tively small building that only reached five stories. I hated to see what the headquarters in Washington, D.C. looked like today.

The drive to the Chicago office took forever, and we'd been sitting in the
waiting room for three hours past our scheduled appointment. I basically spent
the whole time twiddling my thumbs and staring at a large picture hung on the
wall that showed the department heads from D.C. I knew the face of Matthew
Robertson, the president of the department. He'd been in the news a lot when
the department opened a few years ago. But I couldn't place the blonde who
stood beside him. She was much younger than him, probably in her forties, but
there was something about her that tugged at a memory I couldn't place. Had I
seen her on TV before? Or had I met her in a past life?

Finally, a woman in a navy-blue pantsuit stepped through the door.
"Genevieve Morgan? Mr. Cavanaugh will see you now."

Genevieve stood, and Venn and I followed. I smoothed out my black dress
and kept close to Venn. Pantsuit Lady opened the door and gestured for us to
enter. A man of at least fifty sat behind a large mahogany desk opposite the
doorway. He was conventionally attractive, with dark brown hair, bright blue
eyes, and a strong jaw, but he didn't look up from his computer when we walked
in the room.

Such a warm, welcome greeting.

His assistant quietly slipped out of the room. The sound of ringing phones and chatter died as the door closed behind her.

Genevieve cleared her throat, and Leon Cavanaugh finally lifted his head. He gave the four of us a smile that didn't quite reach his eyes, then gestured to the chairs in front of him. I sat in the middle, and Genevieve and Venn claimed either end.

"Mrs. Morgan," Cavanaugh said. "My secretary tells me she had quite the interesting phone call with you yesterday and that this meeting couldn't wait."

"No, it couldn't," Genevieve said with a friendly smile, "but that didn't keep us from sitting in your waiting room for the last three hours."

Oh, snap! Genevieve was throwing some serious shade. She was *so* not having it with this guy.

"I apologize," Cavanaugh said, though it didn't sound like he meant it. "As you can see, we're quite busy today. Recent events have given the Department a lot to handle."

"Yes, and we're here to help," Genevieve said.

Cavanaugh straightened in his chair.

Genevieve continued. "We have information about Matias Vayne that could help you stop him."

Cavanaugh tilted his head to the side, but he didn't blink an eye. "Stop him?"

I gaped at him. "Aren't you the least bit concerned? Haven't you seen the news reports? Don't you know what he's up to? He's in your jurisdiction!"

Cavanaugh shot me a cold smile. "I'm well aware, and I have the best team on the case. But the Vayne case is simple. I'm merely wondering what information you might possibly bring to the table. In the meantime, we have endless unsolved cases that are finally getting some light shed upon them now that magic has been contained."

Cavanaugh's meaning was clear. No new information was coming out about these cases. They were simply prosecuting magic users in full force now that they couldn't defend themselves.

"Contained?" I asked in disbelief. I quickly adjusted my tone and spoke in a more professional manner. "Sir, I don't think you understand the gravity of the situation. Matias Vayne isn't doing you any favors."

Cavanaugh shifted in his seat, looking amused. "That may be true, but I also know that in the last two days, we've freed twice as many blood slaves as we did in the last quarter."

"That's great," Venn said genuinely, though I could hear the irritation in his tone. "But Matias has nothing to do with the vampires. You can take him out and rescue blood slaves all at the same time."

Cavanaugh shrugged. "We can't know that for sure. All we know is that he somehow gained control of magic at the very time vampires returned to human. He could very well be controlling the vampire virus."

His unspoken words were clear in his tone. *And we need it to stay that way.*

He *did* think Matias was doing him a favor! He was *so* wrong.

"That's what we're here to discuss with you," I said firmly. "Aren't you at least curious what we have to say?"

Cavanaugh suddenly seemed more interested, but he quickly relaxed. "I've met with at least a dozen people just today who have offered up their own theories on recent events. What makes your theory more credible than the others?"

I leaned forward and leveled my gaze with his, making sure he knew I wasn't screwing around. "Because Matias Vayne told me himself."

Cavanaugh raised his eyebrows, looking impressed. "I'm listening."

"Matias Vayne is in possession of a magical artifact called The Wise Owl," Genevieve explained. "It was created centuries ago by a powerful group of witches. They infused magic into it that allowed the owner to block anyone's connection to Synchrony."

Cavanaugh narrowed his eyes, like he wasn't quite following. "Synchrony? Never heard of it."

"It's the powerful force most witches believe fuels their magic," Genevieve said. "With this artifact, Matias can flip the switch on any witch or shifter's magic so they can no longer access it. That's why magic has disappeared, and why he's offering to restore it to anyone who joins him."

Cavanaugh nodded slowly, like he was absorbing the information. "So, how does that explain the vampires? He just flipped off the switch to their magic, too?"

"No," Venn said. His gaze flickered over to mine and Genevieve's. "The vampire curse was broken through other means. It was only after that happened that he was able to use the Artifact. Otherwise, he was unable to use his magic in vampire form."

Cavanaugh took a deep breath and finally straightened in his chair. "Okay, say this is all true. What exactly is it that you're proposing?"

Genevieve held her head high. "We're telling you this information so that you can retrieve the Artifact. Once it's out of Matias's hands, we'd like to offer to destroy it for you."

Cavanaugh nearly choked on his own saliva. "Destroy it how?"

"An object like this can only be destroyed through magic," Genevieve said. "It'd have to be powerful magic, more powerful than the witches who created it."

Cavanaugh smirked. "I supposed that means you, Mrs. Morgan? I'm aware you're registered as a high witch. You haven't been dabbling in any magic on the side, have you?"

"I would never!" Genevieve lied, rather convincingly. "But this issue is bigger than that. We don't have the means to retrieve the Artifact, which is why we need your help. But you need a group of witches strong enough to get rid of it, and that's where we come in. We can gather a team and destroy it, in exchange for full immunity on this magical task, of course."

I held my breath, waiting for his response.

Cavanaugh nodded. "A reasonable trade, for sure. But if the Department managed to retrieve such an object, why would we want to destroy it? Our procedures require us to catalogue and save all magical objects we come across."

"Have you ever come across an object powerful enough for a single person to build a magical army?" Genevieve cocked an eyebrow. "The Wise Owl is very dangerous in the wrong hands. It was created for noble purposes, but only to prevent people from Matias Vayne from rising to power. Now that he has it, everyone is at risk. You wouldn't want to repeat that, would you?"

"No, certainly not," Cavanaugh said, like the mere suggestion was preposterous. "So, this Wise Owl. What is it, exactly?"

"It's an ancient owl skull," I said. "I've seen it myself, even felt its magic. I can personally attest to how dangerous it is."

"Felt its magic?" Cavanaugh sounded intrigued. "How did you come across it?"

I swallowed. Perhaps I'd said too much. "Like I said, Matias showed me. I'm a low witch. I can't control when I feel magic. I didn't use it, if that's what you're implying."

"I'm not," Cavanaugh said. "What exactly is your relationship with Mr. Vayne, Miss...?"

"Collins. Rachel Collins." I shot Venn a quick glance. It was time to come up with a quick lie. I'd broken at least two dozen magical laws getting into that cave to find the Artifact, then following through with killing Valkas on Gregor Island. Cavanaugh didn't need to know about any of that. "Matias offered me a spot in his army. I didn't take it."

Cavanaugh looked like he believed me, so I relaxed.

"Thank you very much for this information," Cavanaugh said as he stood. "I will be sure to pass it on to my team. Unfortunately, I have many more meetings to get to today, so our time is up. We will contact you if there are any developments with retrieving this artifact."

Cavanaugh rounded his desk and opened the door to escort us out of his office. Or more accurately, *force us out.*

In that moment, one thing became very clear. Cavanaugh didn't see Matias Vayne as the threat he was. He was choosing to ignore it to fit how he wanted to see the world, rather than to see it as it was. He would hold off his men as long as he could so that his department kept the upper hand in the other cases they were pursuing. They would only strike at the last minute—and by then, it would be too late.

The three of us exchanged a wary glance, then stood. There was clearly nothing more we could do to convince him.

Cavanaugh reached for Genevieve's hand as she left the room. She shook his hand firmly, but she wore a scowl on her face. "I fear you're making a serious mistake, Mr. Cavanaugh."

He pursed his lips. "As I said, Mrs. Morgan, we'll contact you if anything comes of this situation." He was totally skirting around her statement.

Cavanaugh took my hand next, but the handshake was anything but the kind gesture it was meant to be. His hand was cold and uninviting. As he began to let go, I grabbed on tighter and leaned closer.

"You can't change that this world has magic, Mr. Cavanaugh," I said. "You can only change what you do about it."

The blood drained from Cavanaugh's face. He stared at me with such shock that he didn't seem to notice Venn shake his hand on his way out the door. Venn placed a gentle, protective hand on my shoulder and guided me down the hall until I could no longer see Cavanaugh's eyes on mine anymore.

"Just keep walking," Venn whispered under his breath. "We don't need to piss off the guy who has full authority to throw all of us in jail."

"He's completely ignoring us," I snarled under my breath. "He knows our story has merit, and he's choosing not to see it."

Genevieve pressed the button on the elevator at the end of the hall, and the doors slid open. We stepped inside the privacy of the empty lift.

Genevieve's lips pressed into a thin line as the elevator began its descent. She was *pissed*. "Cavanaugh is a fool. And that's exactly why from here on out, we'll be taking matters into our own hands."

"How?" Venn asked. "We don't have magic."

Genevieve stared straight ahead and took several shallow breaths, as if contemplating the question.

Finally, she turned to us. "Maybe we don't need it."

4

Several hours later, we were back at Genevieve's, breaking the news of our useless meeting with Leon Cavanaugh.

"It's almost like he *wants* Matias to take over," Fiona fumed.

We sat in Genevieve's sitting room, the one with the Victorian-style furniture, piano, and grandfather clock. Fiona was too agitated to sit.

"I don't think that's the case," Venn said. He leaned against the armrest of the couch with his fingers to his chin, like he was thinking hard. "I think he's milking the situation while he can."

"That's exactly what I thought!" I chimed in.

"Milking the situation?" Teagan asked from beside me on the couch. "What do you mean?"

"The DMR is using the situation to their advantage," I snarled in disgust. "They're cracking down on magical misuse while they can. Which is great for the blood slave trade. I'm glad they're helping people out of those situations, but it's not going to take him any extra resources to stop Matias. He already has a team allocated to the case."

Sondra scoffed and rolled her eyes. She rested an elbow against the armrest of her chair. She looked better than she had in days, though her bruises were still healing. "Sounds like typical political nonsense."

"Which means we're screwed," Fiona said. "If we don't get their help, we're not going to stand a chance against Matias and his Magical Merry Men."

Jenna placed her hands on her hips and sighed. "So, what happens now?"

"Maybe we should just take a step back," Ryland suggested from the piano bench. "The DMR will handle it eventually."

My jaw dropped. How could he suggest such a thing?

437

Ryland exchanged a glance with Teagan that I couldn't quite read. "I mean, why does it have to be us?"

"Seriously?" I snapped. "You're always up for a fight, but as soon as you're not the big bad bear anymore, you're backing down? Wow."

"It's not like that—"

"The better question is why *not* us?" I said. "We gave Matias the locket and led him to the Artifact. It's kind of our fault."

Ryland scoffed. "Finally you admit something's your fault."

The room burst into a chorus of voices coming to my defense. I couldn't even make out what each of them said.

Fiona slapped her brother hard in the shoulder. "I thought we agreed you were over that."

Ryland rubbed his shoulder and scowled at her. "Yeah, well…"

"What are you suggesting?" Jenna demanded of him. "We just give in? Let Matias take over and kill anyone who opposes him?"

Ronark shook his head. "We can't do that."

Ryland opened his mouth to respond, but Venn stood to face him before he could. "Rae's right. We've been a part of this from the start, and we're not backing down now. The fact is, no one else is going to step up."

"Agreed." I got to my feet beside Venn. "Magic or not, we have to do something about this. This isn't about a personal vengeance anymore. This is about speaking up for those without a voice, for saving the people he's hurt and the ones he will hurt. I believe we're here for a reason, that we've all survived for a reason. Synchrony has chosen us to restore the balance. We will retribute just punishment for Matias's crimes."

Ryland held his hands up in surrender. "Okay, but what's your plan? Because right now, it doesn't look like we stand a chance."

"It didn't look like we stood a chance against Valkas, either," I shot back. "We beat him against all odds. We can do the same with Matias."

Ryland looked to Teagan again. This time, I caught a softness in his expression, like he was worried. "We could get ourselves killed. Is it worth it?"

"Hell yeah, it is!" I replied. "What kind of a question is that?"

"Look, Ryland," Venn said sympathetically. "If you don't want to do this, you don't have to."

"It's not that I don't want to fight," Ryland insisted. "I believe in this cause as much as the rest of you. I'm just trying to think realistically here. If we're willing to put our lives on the line, fine, I'm all for it. Just as long as we all understand the risks. Because right now, I just don't see how we stand a chance against Matias."

Genevieve took a long, deep breath. "I think there's a way to level the playing field a bit."

Sondra immediately perked up. "How?"

Genevieve stepped forward and stopped behind Sondra's chair. "If you don't mind, I'd like to give a quick demonstration—an experiment, if you will. Do you trust me?"

Sondra hesitated. I knew the two of them had a long history together. Genevieve had been Sondra's mentor years ago as she learned magic. When Sondra went out on her own, Genevieve had loaned her money that she'd been struggling to pay off—until we forfeited the Leora Locket to Matias in exchange for Sondra's safety. He'd paid her enough to repay her debts. Even though the debt was resolved, I could still feel the tension between them.

"Y-yes," Sondra said. She cleared her throat and spoke more clearly. "Yes, I trust you."

Genevieve pulled a small vial of purple liquid from the folds of her black dress and held it out to Sondra. "I'd like you to drink it."

Sondra took the vial and eyed it curiously. "What is it?"

"It's a healing potion I whipped up months ago," Genevieve explained. "It's as good of a potion as any to see if my theory is correct."

"You think… potions could still work?" Sondra asked.

Genevieve nodded. "I don't think The Wise Owl is capable of removing all magic, only from allowing another person to access new magic. Anything we've created in the past should still hold its magical properties—potions, magical artifacts, that sort of thing."

Sondra pulled the cork out of the vial. "I guess we should test that theory, then."

Sondra put the vial to her lips and tilted her head back. The purple liquid slid down her throat. It felt as if the whole room was holding a collective breath.

Several seconds passed, and nothing happened. No one even made a sound. Then suddenly, the potion took effect. The swelling on Sondra's eye shrank to normal, and the bruises slowly faded. The cut above her eyebrow knitted itself back together right in front of our eyes. I'd never seen any sort of healing spell work so quickly.

"Wow," Jenna whispered, breaking the silence.

Sondra brought her fingers to her face and pressed on the areas that'd been affected only moments ago. A look of amazement crossed her eyes, then she turned her gaze up to Genevieve. "That was a really powerful potion. It must've been really complicated. You didn't have to waste it on me."

Genevieve smirked. "Yes, well, unless you wanted me to give you fear-inducing hallucinations for the next five hours, I figured this was the safest bet for testing the theory. Now that we know potions will work, we can use them against Matias."

"What do we have available to us?" Sondra asked.

"Not much," Genevieve replied. "I have guns and a few magical weapons, potions that will act like bombs when poured out of their container."

Sondra shot her a questioning glance, as if to ask why she would keep such a thing around. Genevieve didn't seem to notice.

"But I'm hoping to gather more," Genevieve said. "If we can get other witches on our side, we can bring in more potions and artifacts so we stand a better chance against Matias."

"So we build a magical army of our own," I said, thrilled with the idea.

Genevieve nodded. "Precisely. It will take time, but I think we can do it."

Sondra stood, looking hopeful. "I think it's a brilliant idea."

"What happens after we have our army, though?" Venn asked. "We can't just walk straight up to Vayne Tower and steal the Artifact back."

"We lure him out," Genevieve said simply.

"We're forgetting something," Fiona pointed out. All eyes turned to her. "The Leora Locket. He still has it. He'll be able to anticipate our moves."

"You let me work out those details," Genevieve said. "I'm trained in mind manipulation. I can misguide him. When the time comes, we will take any and all measures to retrieve that artifact. I don't care if we have to kill Matias and his men to do it. He's not going to win."

I stepped forward. "Let's do it."

A chorus of agreement traveled around the room, before all eyes finally turned to Ryland and Teagan for their answer. Teagan chewed on her lower lip and looked to Ryland. It was so unlike her. She'd never had any magic, and she'd always been willing to go up against supernaturals with five times her strength and speed. What was holding her back now?

Finally, Ryland breathed a sigh. "We're in."

Just then, the doorbell rang.

Sondra furrowed her brow. "You already called in some favors, didn't you?"

I already knew the answer. Genevieve had called them in the car, and I'd heard most of their conversation.

Genevieve smiled. "Yes. Though we haven't gotten along in the past, we've agreed to put our differences aside for now."

"Who?" Sondra asked.

Genevieve turned to the doorway. "Friends of yours. I believe you're familiar with Clarita White and Amalia Taylor."

5

I followed Genevieve out into the hall. She opened the door to two familiar women. Clarita wore a baby blue 1950s style dress that showed off her curves. Her dark bangs were clipped back, but she had on the same cat-eye glasses as when I first met her. Amalia had long blonde curls and wore high-heeled boots over skinny jeans. They both carried luggage bags with them.

"Thank you for coming," Genevieve said before the other two could get in a word. She swung the door open wider to invite them inside.

"Thank you for calling us," Clarita said as she stepped into the hall.

Genevieve bent down several inches, and the two exchanged kisses on both cheeks. It was meant to be a friendly gesture, but it felt stoic, like neither of them felt comfortable in each other's presence.

I didn't get why no one liked Genevieve. Yeah, she looked kind of scary with the dark hair, pointed look, and black lace, but she'd been helping us this whole time without asking anything in return. I didn't know where we'd be without her.

Clarita's eyes met mine as Genevieve moved on to greet Amalia. "Rachel!"

Clarita dropped her bags and rushed to me with her arms out. She pulled me into a hug, and I squeezed her back. I'd only met Clarita once, but I already felt like I knew her.

"How'd the island go?" she asked.

My shoulders fell. "Well, it's kind of the reason we're in this mess now."

"Nonsense. It's not your fault."

"I killed Valkas, so it kind of is." I bit my lower lip.

Clarita frowned. "Did everyone make it off okay? Your sister?"

I smiled. "Yeah, I found her. She made it."

My eyes turned back to the sitting room, and I spotted Jenna, Venn, and Sondra in the doorway watching us.

"This is my sister, Jenna," I told Clarita, gesturing to her.

Jenna stepped forward and shook Clarita's hand.

"Jenna, this is Clarita. She helped me find you."

"It's nice to meet you," Jenna said. "Thank you for your help."

Clarita waved her hand like it was no big deal. "My pleasure. Sondra, how have you been? It's been awhile."

Clarita moved on to greet Sondra, while Amalia approached me.

I gave her a hug and said, "Thank you, by the way. For helping Venn when that guy cursed him."

"That's what I'm here for." Amalia smiled and turned to Venn. "You're looking great."

"Thanks to you." Venn hugged her.

Suddenly, it felt a little claustrophobic in the hall as more and more people stepped out of the sitting room and into the hallway. Venn and I slipped into the door behind us to make room for everyone else. The room we entered was dark and quiet, with black curtains covering the windows. Bookshelves lined the walls, with all sorts of tomes and potion vials everywhere. The leather-bound book that had been lain across one of the tables last time I was in here was nowhere to be found.

Venn took a deep breath and began pacing around the room slowly. He reached out his fingers to touch the spines of the books as he passed.

"Are you okay?" I came up behind him and slipped my fingers into his. "You look deep in thought."

Venn dropped his hand and turned his gaze to mine. "Yeah. I'm just thinking about what Genevieve said, how we can use different types of magic against Matias. I'm wondering if maybe there's an artifact out there that can counteract The Wise Owl's effects."

I scanned the old books in front of us, but none of them had words on the spines. "Genevieve has so many books. Maybe there's something in one of them."

I glanced toward the hallway, but no one was watching us. "Do you think she'll be okay with us looking through them?"

I reached for the book closest to me and pulled it off the shelf. It was a thick hardback, at least five-hundred pages. When I opened it, the smell of old pages hit my nose. I thumbed through the pages to find endless words and diagrams on different types of spells. The whole book seemed to be about how to summon spirits.

"Mm…" I mused. "I've never done a séance before. You?"

Venn gently took my hands and closed the book. "No, and you don't want to try. Séances are dangerous. You never know what kind of spirit you might accidentally summon. It's not exactly considered a form of white magic."

I returned the book to its spot, feeling a little disappointed. It'd be cool to talk to the dead. My mind instantly went to my parents, but I quickly pushed the thought away. It would only tempt me.

"Hey, guys!" Fiona practically danced into the room, looking chipper as always. "What are you up to?"

"Making out," I teased.

"Oh, no. I wouldn't want to interrupt that," she replied, playing along.

Venn chuckled. "Relax. We're just talking about magic. Maybe there's something in one of Genevieve's books that can help us with Matias—like information on an artifact or something."

"Good idea. Mind if I help?" Fiona reached around us to grab a book off the shelf and began flipping through it. "Oh, cool! Necromancy."

"Not cool." Venn grabbed the book out of her hand before she could read anything out of it. He slammed it shut and grabbed another book. He quickly flipped through it, then handed it to her. "Try tarot card reading. A lot less dangerous."

"Come on," Fiona complained. "You don't want to have a little fun raising the dead?"

"A little fun could get you killed," Venn said. "You know that falls into the realm of black magic."

Maybe that's what we need, I thought.

"Okay." Fiona gave in. "No raising zombies. Not like I could even if I tried."

"Who's raising zombies?" Genevieve breezed into the room.

Fiona threw her book back on the shelf, like she was a kid who'd got caught with their hand in the cookie jar.

"No one," Venn said sternly.

"Shame." Genevieve frowned. "I always wanted to try that spell."

"Hey, Genevieve," I said. "Is it cool if we look through your books to see if there are any potions or artifacts that might help us against Matias?"

She shrugged. "Have at it. You'll do best to start at the bottom. The top two shelves cover rituals and spells, which won't be very useful now that our magic is gone."

"Cool." I bent and pulled a pile of books off the shelf, then plopped them on the table in the middle of the room. "Well, Venn, Fiona. I hope you guys like reading."

Venn smirked and sat in the chair beside me. "I was born for this."

"I'll grab some sticky notes to bookmark pages," Fiona said. "And maybe some popcorn?"

I sat beside Venn and opened the first book off the pile. "Definitely some popcorn. It's going to be a long night."

<hr>

I didn't know how late it was, but I knew we'd been sitting here for hours. Venn had taken a phone call at least an hour ago and hadn't returned since. I wasn't sure if he was still on the phone or had fallen asleep. Since he left, the room had been pretty quiet as both Fiona and I dove into the endless books. I'd been reading so long that my eyes were starting to water. Which was weird, because I was parched and didn't feel like I had an ounce of water left in my body.

I closed my book and looked up at her with heavy eyes. She'd tied her hair up in a messy bun and looked about ready to pass out from exhaustion.

"Maybe we should call it a night," I suggested. I ran my finger over the sticky notes sticking out of the book I'd been flipping through. "I've bookmarked over half a dozen spells that sound interesting, but none of them are going to help us. You find anything yet?"

"I found a piece of popcorn in my cleavage," she replied with a hopeless sigh.

"Not really the kind of thing we're looking for."

"Oh." She sounded both tired and disappointed. "I was just reading about these types of artifacts. They're just called trinkets in the book, but they can suppress a person's magic if they're a threat."

Fiona turned her book to me. All across the page were pictures of various trinkets, like jewelry, keys, and broaches. These artifacts could be anything.

"I think we sold trinkets when I worked at Bloodstone," I said thoughtfully as I scanned the page. "Devin never called them that, though. We just called them protection charms. This could work…"

I looked farther down the page. "Never mind. It says here they don't work on other artifacts."

"But if we got one close enough to Matias, it might affect his ability to use the Owl," Fiona pointed out.

I pressed my lips together. "Good point. Do you think we can get our hands on one?"

Fiona shrugged. "The book makes it sound like they're pretty common. Creating them doesn't take a lot of magic, but it also means they're not super powerful. Witches used to use them as sort of protection charms. If they wore a trinket, it kept other witches from casting curses on them. But it wouldn't completely suppress another witch's powers. Only weaken them a bit."

"Maybe weakening Matias is all we need," I said. "Let's talk to Genevieve and Sondra in the morning and see if they know anything about trinkets. In the meantime—"

I was cut off by the sound of a door slamming down the hall, followed by a string of curse words. First came a woman's voice, then the muffled sound of a man's.

"Screw you, Ronark!" Jenna yelled. "You don't know shit about me."

"You think I don't know how it feels?" he shouted back.

I left my books on the table and rushed out of the room. I turned down the hall to the guest rooms and stopped in my tracks.

Jenna stood outside Ronark's door, looking like a total wreck. Her short dark hair was in disarray, and her face was red and blotchy.

"Jenna?" I stepped toward her cautiously. "Are you okay?"

Her bottom lip quivered, like she was trying to hold her emotions back. Suddenly, she cracked, and tears began streaming down her face. "No, Rachel. I'm not okay."

6

───────────

I wrapped Jenna in my arms as worry for her knotted in my gut. "What happened?"

Jenna drew away from me and shook her head. She wiped the tears from her eyes, but they only kept coming. "I don't want to talk about it."

The door beside us opened, and Venn poked his head out. He looked to Jenna, then to me, as if to ask if she was all right. Jenna buried her face back in my shoulder as she sobbed. I just looked back at Venn hopelessly. I had no idea what was wrong, and it killed me that I couldn't fix it.

"How'd the phone call go?" I asked him.

"I'm closer to finding out where Tyson might be," Venn said softly. "Do you two want some privacy?"

Venn opened the door wider and stepped out of the way. "I'll go help Fiona."

"Thanks," I told him.

Venn placed a kiss on my forehead as he passed, then continued on down the hall. He threw back several worried glances before he finally disappeared.

"Jenna," I whispered, "let's go sit down in my room."

She didn't move until I began guiding her. I closed the door behind us and led her across the room to the bed. We both sat, but she wouldn't lift her gaze. She buried her face in her hands and continued crying.

"Are you sure you don't want to talk about it?" I asked softly.

She sniffled, but otherwise didn't respond. My guts twisted, and I was on the verge of crying myself. I hated seeing her like this.

I put my arm back around her. "Jenna Bean, I can't help you unless you tell me what's wrong."

She finally lifted her head and dashed the tears away. "It's nothing."

"It's not nothing," I insisted. "Did Ronark hurt you?"

"What? No!" She sounded shocked. "No, he'd never touch me. It's not like that."

I frowned. "There are other ways to hurt a person."

"No, look." Jenna's voice came out stronger. "We just had a fight. It wasn't his fault."

"What did you two fight about?" I asked, hoping she'd open up to me.

Jenna bit her lower lip. "I'm thirsty."

I reached for my plastic water bottle on the nightstand and handed it to her.

"Thanks." She opened the cap and threw her head back. I stared wide-eyed as she chugged the whole thing. She handed me back the empty bottle and sighed.

"Do you ever feel so thirsty it seems like you're going to shrivel up and die?" she asked.

The question almost sounded rhetorical, but I considered her words. The last few days, I'd felt parched beyond belief, no matter how much water I drank. Most of the time, I tried to ignore it. It was probably just from stress or something. But now that she pointed it out, I couldn't take my mind off how dry my throat felt.

Jenna looked at me with sad eyes. "You've been feeling it, haven't you?"

"A little," I admitted.

"Now imagine that, only a hundred times worse," she said. "It feels like I've spent a year crawling through the desert with nothing but sand to satiate me. It won't be as bad for you since you were only fed on a few times. But for me... for Ronark... it's unbearable."

Jenna ran her fingers over her neck as it dawned on me what she was saying.

"This is what the addiction feels like?" I asked, though I already knew the answer.

Vampire feedings were addictive, far beyond that of most street drugs. After just a few seconds of being fed on the first time, I already wanted more. But it wasn't enough for withdrawals to set in. But now, after being fed on several times while I was held prisoner on Gregor Island, I was starting to feel it. That was how fast the addiction set in. I couldn't imagine what Jenna and Ronark were feeling right now, not after being fed on night after night for years.

It was a cruel side effect of the vampire curse. If their victims left, they'd feel just how the vampires felt without blood. It created a dependency between the two of them and ensured the vampires would always have a fresh supply of blood.

It didn't matter that they didn't exist anymore. The effects of their feedings lived on. If we'd destroyed all the drugs in the world, addicts would still come looking for more. It was just like that.

"I used to think being fed on was one of the worst things that could happen to me," Jenna said without meeting my gaze. She looked so out of it that it was like she wasn't even talking to me. "Now I know that there are worse things out there."

"Jenna..." I didn't know what I could possibly say to her. My heart broke into a million pieces to watch her break apart like this. My throat began to close up, as if someone was squeezing my neck with a rope. The invisible force tightened with each passing second. "That's not true. You *hated* being fed on. I saw it in your eyes every night you returned from a feeding."

"I did," she admitted. "But it was better than this. At least with Silas I felt like I controlled myself in my own skin. Now there's just this… this *thirst*. I can't stop thinking of my master. I just want him to bite me again, to take this agony away from me."

It would be nice. Just one more wave of euphoria to take away the cravings. The sight of Valkas's fangs flashed through my mind.

What the hell was I thinking?

"Look at me." I grabbed Jenna's face and forced her gaze to mine. "People have gotten through this before. You can, too."

Jenna shied away from me, and tears began to fall down her face again. "I don't know that I can, Rachel. You don't actually know anyone who's overcome it."

"I do," I told her sternly.

Her eyebrows shot up, but her expression quickly fell. "I guess they were stronger than I am."

"Don't say that, Jenna." I reached out for her, but she shrugged me off.

"You don't understand. The one person who would understand—who I *thought* I could talk to about this—is being an asshole!" Jenna shouted the last few words to make sure Ronark would hear through the wall.

"Please calm down," I begged. "This isn't you talking."

She raked her fingers through her hair, making it stick up at all angles. "Sure it is. The withdrawals are just giving me the courage to say it."

"Look, you and Ronark are both irritable because of this, but you can break through it," I assured her. "What happened to positive Jenna from the island? Don't you remember what you told me? You can't change your circumstances, only what you do about them. You can get through this."

Jenna curled her knees to her chest and turned away from me on the bed. Hopelessness sank in my gut. What could I possibly say to help her at a time like this?

"That's not helping, Rachel," Jenna mumbled. "You must've forgotten the other thing I said to you."

I scooted closer to her. "What was that?"

"It only takes one thing to set us back ten paces. But this… this is like a hundred steps back." Jenna threw herself onto the mattress and buried her face in the pillow. "I don't think I have another hundred paces left in me."

Her shoulders began to shake, and in that moment, I knew there was nothing I could possibly say to her. The only thing I *could* do was show her that I was here for her, that she didn't have to go through this alone.

I lay down and wrapped an arm around her. She curled into me as tears began to soak my shirt. I didn't know how long we lay there like that, but it didn't matter. I'd sit beside Jenna until the end of time if I thought it would help make her feel better.

Jenna went still, and I thought she'd fallen asleep. I continued to brush my fingers through her hair because I couldn't bring myself to fall asleep, in case she needed me. Eventually, she stirred, and she drew away from me.

"Feeling any better?" I asked.

Jenna shook her head. "Not really."

"Maybe you need to take your mind off it," I suggested. "Do something to make you forget."

She frowned. "Like what?"

I shrugged. "I don't know. What's something fun we used to do as kids?"

Jenna thought about it for a moment. "I don't know. Tell scary stories?"

I bit the inside of my lower lip. "That's a little too real right now."

She frowned. "You're right. Honestly, it's late. Everyone's asleep. We should probably get to bed, too."

My eyes scanned the room, searching for ideas on how to get her mind off the cravings. I sat upright in bed when my gaze hit the nightstand and I remembered the flashlight I'd found in the top drawer. I reached over and threw the drawer open, then held up the flashlight for her to see.

"You sure it's too late for some fun?" I grinned.

Jenna's lips turned up into a half-smile, which I found encouraging.

"Come on," I pressed when she didn't answer. "It'll be fun."

"Okay," she caved. "Hold on."

Jenna jumped out of bed and hurried out the door. I followed. She entered her guest room beside mine and flipped the light on. Ronark rolled over in bed and threw his arm over his eyes.

"I thought you were mad at me," he complained in a tired voice.

"Get up, sleepyhead." She tugged at his feet under the covers. "We're going outside to have some fun, and I'm not going without you."

"What are you talking about?" he groaned.

"You. Me. Right now. Under the stars."

Ronark glanced to me, as if searching for an explanation.

I beamed at him. "We're going star-tipping!"

7

A few minutes later, Ronark was dressed, and the three of us were headed toward the back door. I caught sight of Fiona and Venn still flipping through books in the room off the main hall.

"Hey." I popped my head in the room. "You two up for a little adventure?"

Fiona shot a quick glance to Venn, suddenly looking more awake. "What kind of adventure?"

"Just a little game Jenna and I used to play as kids," I said. "You up for it?"

Fiona shrugged and stood. "I'm up for anything."

Venn looked tired, but he joined her. "What are we doing?"

I smiled. "Star-tipping."

Fiona hopped. "Ooh, sounds like fun! I'm going to see if Ryland and Teagan want to join us."

Venn followed me out the back door. "What's star-tipping?"

"It's simple," I explained. "One person looks up at the sky. You focus on a star, then spin around in a circle in the dark. After a few seconds, another person will shine the flashlight at you. That's your cue to stop spinning and start running toward the light. You get so disoriented that you can't help but fall over. It's hilarious."

We stepped out into Genevieve's back yard. It was dark, with only a soft glow from the city illuminating shadows around the yard. There was a high fence around the perimeter, which met up with a thick line of trees. Various trees and flowerbeds dotted the landscaped yard. In the farthest back corner was a brick fire pit with patio chairs all around it. The rest of the yard was wide open.

"I'll go first!" Jenna offered, looking excited.

She turned her head to the sky and spread her arms out wide, then spun

450

around as fast as she could. I clicked on the flashlight and shone it in her eyes. She didn't make it another step before she stumbled to the side and fell to the ground, laughing hysterically.

"Oh my God!" she cried between laughs. "I forgot how fun that was. Ronark, you go!"

Ronark looked reluctant, but he uncrossed his arms and took Jenna's place. He spun around, then came the light. Ronark tried to stay upright as he moved toward it, but he stumbled with each step. It was like watching him fall to the side in slow motion.

"Oh, fuuu—!" he shouted.

When he landed on the ground, Jenna rushed over to him to try to drag him to his feet, but he was laughing too hard to stand.

"Okay," he said through laughs. "I get it now. I've never felt that dizzy in my life. It's a bit of a rush. Venn, you should try it."

Venn glanced to me.

"Go ahead," I encouraged. "It doesn't hurt to have a little fun."

Venn sighed and stepped forward to the middle of the open lawn. "Okay, here goes nothing."

He spun faster than Jenna or Ronark did, and I let him go a little longer than the other two. When I clicked the flashlight on, his arms went still out on either side of him, like he was trying to stay balanced, but it didn't work. As the world spun around him, he tried to correct it with his footing, which only sent him tumbling to the ground. His laughter filled the yard.

I shoved the flashlight in Jenna's hands and ran over to Venn. Before he could get to his feet, I threw myself on top of him and held him down with a kiss. His laughter instantly died, and he relaxed into it. For the first time in what felt like weeks, the tension melted out of my body. For just tonight, I wanted to forget about Matias—about magic, vampires, all of it. For just one moment, I wanted to act like a normal girl with normal friends and without any cares in the world.

"Get a room!" Teagan's voice called from toward the house.

I drew away from Venn, blushing. He smiled back at me.

"Forget her," he said as he dragged me back to him. I wanted to kiss him back, but I could hardly manage it through the giggles.

"See?" I said when we finally parted. "It's fun, isn't it?"

Venn nodded as he gazed at me with soft eyes that melted my heart.

"My turn!" Fiona hurried across the lawn to Ronark and Jenna, who had moved to another area of lawn to star tip.

I lifted my head to see that she'd rounded up Ryland, Teagan, and Sondra. The three were already gathered around the fire pit, and Ryland was starting a fire. Sondra sat in one of the patio chairs and pulled out her sketch pad.

"Hey, Tea!" Venn called over to her. "You should try star-tipping. You'll love it."

"Nah," she replied as she snuggled up beneath a long cardigan beside Sondra. "I'm good. You go have fun."

"Her loss," I said as I got to my feet. I reached out my hand and helped Venn up. "Want to go again?"

He shrugged. "Sure."

Venn and I joined the others. Fiona had managed to stay upright for a few steps before she fell onto all fours and tried to stand up again. This time, she totally fell on her ass. She blinked a few times to get the world to focus again. I clutched my stomach as I burst into laughter.

"Whoa!" She shook her head. "That was not what I expected at all. That was fun."

It was my turn next. I turned my chin toward the sky and focused on the brightest star I could see. I held my arms out and spun... and spun... and spun. I was already laughing. It felt so carefree, like being a kid again.

Suddenly, a bright light cut through the darkness, and the whole world flipped upside down. I couldn't tell where my friends were standing, only that my feet felt as if they were no longer on the ground. The ground flew up to meet me, and though my body had stopped moving, it still felt as if the world was spinning around me. Only a moment later did I realize that I'd fallen over, as if some invisible force had taken over my body for a moment.

Fiona barked in laughter, and I started laughing so hard that I couldn't hear anyone else. Venn tried to drag me to my feet, but I was still a little dizzy that I stumbled against him.

"My turn again!" Jenna volunteered, shoving the flashlight into Ronark's hands.

This went on for what felt like another half hour. Eventually, I went so many times that it started to lose its effectiveness. Venn and I agreed we were done and went to sit by the other three near the fire. The fire was warm and inviting, but not as inviting as Venn's arm around me.

"What's going on over here?" I asked as we sat.

"Telling embarrassing stories," Teagan said. "And trying not to fall asleep."

"You can go to bed if you're tired," Venn offered.

Teagan shook her head. "No, you guys are all having fun. I want to be out here by you. It's been a long time since I heard you all laugh."

"Hey," Ryland said. "I laugh all the time."

Teagan rolled her eyes. "Yeah, babe. At other people's expense."

Ryland propped his feet up on the chair beside him. "Not my fault if other people's misfortunes make me laugh."

Teagan shook her head at him. "Why do you have to be such an ass all the time?"

"You didn't think I was being an ass earlier when we were—"

"Oh, God!" Teagan threw her hands over her ears. "People do *not* need to know what we were doing."

Venn scoffed. "Because we don't have *any* idea what you two do in your alone time."

"Well, you certainly don't need the details!" Teagan cried.

Venn shot Ryland a glance. "Trust me, Tea. I already know more than I care to admit."

Teagan's jaw dropped, and she widened her eyes at Ryland. "What did you tell him?"

Ryland rolled his eyes. "Relax. It's not like the tattoo on your ass is a secret. I personally find it sexy."

"You have a tattoo?" I asked.

Teagan looked embarrassed. "I got it when I was sixteen. It's just a heart on my right hip. It's nothing. Can we drop it?"

Respecting her privacy, I leaned over to Sondra beside me. "What are you sketching?"

Sondra snapped out of her daze to look at me. She quickly flipped the sketchpad shut before I could catch a glimpse of the picture inside. "Oh, it's nothing. I thought I'd draw you guys having fun, but…"

She didn't finish her sentence. I had no idea what she was about to say, but she never got the chance to finish.

Teagan quickly came to her rescue. "So, have you ever thought of getting a tattoo, Rae?"

I shrugged. "I used to think about getting a raven tattooed on my wrist, but then I realized it was a little conceited and obvious. I mean, I didn't want to be walking around advertising I was the Ravenite. The government still doesn't know I'm a shifter, so it's probably best if it stayed that way."

"Good call," Ryland said.

Venn leaned over to me and whispered, "I think a tattoo would look kind of sexy on you."

I looked to him in surprise. "You think?"

He eyed me up and down, like he was hungry for me. Butterflies danced in my stomach.

"Not a raven, though. Maybe a wolf…" I said. "For you."

Venn smiled, and it sent my heart hammering against my rib cage. I wanted to kiss him to make it slow. Suddenly, I felt very hot, and it definitely wasn't from the fire.

"I'd like that," he whispered.

The way he stared into my eyes was unlike anything else. I wanted him—right here, right now. Images from the first time we'd shared together flashed through my mind. I'd been dying to do it again, but with everything happening, we hadn't had the chance. Now…

Every nerve in my body came alive just at the thought. What were we waiting for? If he was waiting for a signal, he was sure as hell going to get one.

8

"Maybe we should go get that room," I said in a voice so low only Venn could hear.

He shot out of his seat like a bullet. He took my hand and started leading me away from the fire pit. Teagan's and Ryland's laughter followed behind us.

"You two have fun!" Ryland called.

"We will!" I shot back.

I was so excited about what was about to happen that I practically raced through the hall and to our room. Venn chased behind me, snickering. I'd never seen him act so carefree before. I loved it.

I locked the door behind us. By the time I turned around, Venn already had his shirt off and was tossing it to the side. I stood on my toes to kiss him, and a warmth spread all throughout my body. My heart felt as if it was trying to beat its way out of my chest.

Venn backed up until his knees hit the edge of the bed. I pressed on his shoulders, and we tumbled back onto the mattress together.

"Tonight… was… fun…" he said between my kisses.

I pulled away from him to place my index finger to his lips. "Shh…"

Venn ran his hands over the fabric of my jeans. "I just wanted you to know before we did this that I really appreciate what you did tonight. We all need to let go sometimes. I needed to laugh."

I smiled. "You're acting like that was the best part of the night."

He smirked. "So far. We still have time to change that."

Hell yeah, we would! I wasn't sure where my confidence came from, but I knew with certainty I was going to make it a night he wouldn't forget.

I ran my hands up his chest and over his shoulders. He shivered beneath my touch.

"What's wrong?" I asked as I kissed the sensitive skin beneath his ear.

His hands roamed over my back, pushing my fabric out of the way. My pulse quickened beneath his touch.

"Nothing," he said with a blissful sigh.

I couldn't take the suspense anymore. I placed another gentle kiss on his lips, then drew away and held my arms above my head. Venn bit his lower lip as he took my invitation and pulled my shirt up over my head. Cool air brushed my skin, but my insides felt like fire. My hands shivered as I took his in mine and guided them to my breasts. Venn beamed as he gently slipped a finger beneath the fabric and ran it across my skin, teasing me.

If he wasn't going to take initiative, I would. I reached behind myself and undid the clasp, then let the fabric fall away. Venn couldn't take his eyes off me as my breasts came out in the open. Warmth rippled across my skin. I felt so exposed, like showing him my body was akin to opening my heart.

And damn it. It felt amazing. I never thought I'd find someone I could share myself with wholeheartedly, but every touch, every moment with Venn, made me question why I'd ever thought that way in the first place. It was clear to me now that there'd always been someone out there waiting for me. I needed him. Without him, I was the bitter, lonely girl with a death wish. Now I was loved, with a purpose.

"Rae," Venn said breathlessly. "You're so beautiful."

I blushed and gazed down at his muscular chest. "You are, too."

A thought suddenly struck. "Oh, shit. Do we have protection?"

Venn smirked and reached over toward the nightstand. He opened the top drawer and pulled out a condom. "Ryland gave it to me as a joke. Look who's laughing now."

Venn gave it to me, then placed his hands on my breasts and squeezed gently. My nipples hardened beneath his palms. I closed my eyes and relished in the glowing feel of his hands exploring my body. They slipped beneath my jeans as he dragged me closer to him. Heat pooled between my thighs as he cupped my butt.

I couldn't get my pants off fast enough. My fingers shook as I undid the button, and my legs quaked as I kicked the jeans off and onto the floor.

Venn took one look at my bare legs and tossed me onto my back. I beamed as he knelt over me and pulled my panties down my legs. For a split second, I lay there fully exposed as his eyes drank me in. Instinct told me to shy away, but I mentally threw my instinct aside. I was his now. He could look at me all he wanted.

"Your turn," I whispered.

I reached for Venn's waistband and undid his belt, then the button. My skin heated as I pulled down the fabric to expose all of him. Venn gasped as my fingers curled around his erection.

Damn! Venn and I had only been intimate a few times before and had only gone all the way once. Touching him there felt like the first time. I still wasn't prepared for the shot of adrenaline and pulse of heat passing over my body.

I helped Venn get the condom on, then dragged him back on top of me. His lips connected with mine, and they didn't stop moving. He kissed me with such a passion that I never thought possible. Emotions I'd never felt before swept through me with such force that I wanted to cry just to let them out.

"I love you," I whispered breathlessly beneath his kiss.

"I love you, too," he said before returning his lips to mine.

His hand traveled down between our legs, making me shiver. He positioned himself and gently pressed down. I gasped as he moved inside of me. My legs wrapped tight around his hips. I wanted to drag him closer to me, as if we could melt into one being, one soul. We fit together like two pieces of a puzzle. He completed me, and I him.

Venn's hands ran over my hips, then down to the sensitive area between my legs. I fisted my hands in his hair as his fingers gently roamed over me.

Gentle. He was always so gentle. He treated me like a queen, always making sure I was comfortable and that I felt the pleasure of these moments as much as he did.

But I wasn't a gentle kind of girl. I wanted him unlike I ever wanted anything in my life. And I was going to have him. All of him.

I pressed my heels into the mattress and lifted my hips, forcing Venn to roll over. He looked up at me with shock as I took the lead. It only lasted for a moment before the shock melted off his face and he grinned at me. I laced my fingers through his and pinned them to the mattress above his head as I experimented with the movement of my hips. With every movement, Venn's body hit something inside of me that sent a wave of pleasure over my entire body. I increased my speed until I couldn't go any faster.

"I should've known you'd want to take control," Venn said in amusement.

"You know me so well," I replied with a smile.

"Yeah, I do." Venn's demeanor instantly changed. It was like watching him shift into wolf form. He went from the gentle, caring guy he started out as when we entered the room into a predator who'd just caught his prey.

It was. So. Freaking. Hot.

Venn flipped me over again, taking control. He looped his arm beneath my leg and pressed into me faster and faster. That pleasurable sensation I'd felt on top of him with each thrust was ten times stronger when he was on top of me like this.

"Oh God, Venn," I cried.

"Good?" he asked.

"Yes," I moaned. "Venn, I—"

I cut off as a strong sensation took over my body. I could no longer find the words. Pressure built up inside of me. I bit into his shoulder to keep the moans from escaping. Like an explosion, the pressure released in a glorious array of sparkling light, sweeping through my body like the blinding sun on a warm summer day. Venn's body tensed above mine as he reached his peak with me.

The room spun around me as we melted side-by-side on the bed. I closed my eyes and tried to hold on to the wonderful blissfulness before it drifted away. Venn had made me feel amazing things before, but never like that. That was... there were no words.

"That was even more fun than the first time," I told him when I finally caught my breath.

"It was," he panted.

I opened my eyes to see his beautiful face hovering over me, a hopeful look in his eyes. My heart melted. I didn't think I'd ever seen anything more wonderful in my life. I reached my hand up to caress the side of his face. "I never want this to end, Venn."

"It won't," he whispered. He bent to place a warm kiss on the top of my head. If possible, I relaxed even more.

"Venn?"

"Mm?" He pushed my hair out of my face and gazed down at me like I was a goddess he was seeing for the first time. There was such warmth and love in his eyes.

"I want to try everything with you."

Venn clicked his tongue. "Not so fast. We have plenty of time for that."

I bit my lower lip. "Well, the night's not over. Maybe we could try... one more thing?"

His eyes lit up. I grinned and rolled over so that my backside pressed against his front. He curled an arm around me and pulled me close to him. I tilted my head back to look him in the eyes. I felt so safe and secure in his embrace.

"Can we try it like this?" I asked.

Venn put his fingers in my hair and tugged back slightly to expose my neck. He trailed kisses down it and to my shoulder, then pressed his lips against my skin as he spoke. "For you, Rae, I'd do anything."

***

I woke the next morning to warm sunlight brushing across my eyelids. The normally dull colors of Genevieve's house seemed brighter today than normal. I lifted my head from Venn's chest and gazed at him. His eyes were closed, and his chest rose and fell softly. He looked so peaceful, and I didn't want to wake him. I quietly dressed and grabbed a fresh pair of clothes Jenna had loaned me, then tiptoed to the bathroom to shower.

The water was warm and refreshing. It felt like I could finally breathe, and I kept replaying the night over and over again in my mind. I wanted more nights like that, where I could laugh with my friends carefree and enjoy my time with Venn without interruptions.

I returned to our bedroom with a clean change of clothes and wet hair. Venn was sitting upright in bed, looking sexy as ever with a bare chest. He had his new phone to his ear. Genevieve had gotten us each one after we returned from the island—in case something went wrong and we had to contact each other.

As soon as I walked in the room, Venn's face fell. He didn't even look at me, as if the news on the other end of the line had pulled him out of reality and placed his mind somewhere else entirely.

The blood drained from my face, and I rushed over to him. "Venn, what's wrong? Your brother?"

Venn didn't say anything as the guy on the other end spoke, though I couldn't hear what he was saying. Slowly, Venn focused on the world again, and his gaze turned to mine. My heart sank in response to the worried look on his face. The seconds ticked by slowly, each one pounding like a drum in my ears.

"Thank you, Cory," Venn finally said. "Let me know how I can return the favor."

"No problem, man," I heard Cory reply. "What are friends for?"

Venn pulled the phone from his ear and pressed the screen to end the call. He stared down at it for several seconds, his fingers shaking, until he finally lifted his gaze.

"Is your brother okay?" I asked softly as I placed a hand over his.

"I'm not sure," he replied in a shaky tone. "But I know where to find him."

"That's great!" I exclaimed.

"Cory's an old friend from high school," Venn explained, almost like he didn't want to go into the more important details. "We had a bit of a falling out when he got into some bad deals with a group of vampires."

The room went silent for a beat before I spoke. "Did he... did he ever change?"

"Cory?" Venn shook his head. "No. He's a shifter—gorilla, and a big one, too."

I snickered. "A gorilla?"

"Ever seen a gorilla? They're scarier than you think. He worked with some vampires on some gambling deals, nothing like blood slaves or anything. But it still wasn't a good situation. They kept him around for intimidating their debtors. I think it was more than that, too."

Venn's meaning was clear. The vampires never changed Cory because they liked the taste of his blood.

"Anyway," Venn continued, "with his connections to different vampire gangs, I thought he might know something about my brother. He had to put in a few calls for me, but it sounds like he's found him in Detroit."

Venn's expression slowly shifted, like it had taken him this long for it to sink in. He was going to see his brother again. Nothing could replace the feeling of getting to see your sibling after so long, after you'd given up hope of ever seeing them. His lips twitched at the corners and finally spread into a hint of a smile. He looked like he could hardly believe it.

"Venn, I'm so happy for you," I said genuinely. "When do we leave?"

A moment of shock crossed his features. "Rae..."

He didn't have to finish his sentence. I could tell by the look in his eyes what he was about to say.

"You don't want me to come with?" I asked. The hurt was evident in my tone.

"Everyone else needs you here," he said softly.

"No, they don't," I argued. "They can figure out what to do about Matias without me. Besides, I don't want to be separated from you again."

Being imprisoned on Gregor Island and feeling like I'd lost Venn had nearly broken me. I couldn't imagine what I'd do if something happened to him.

Venn reached up to brush dark strands of hair from my face. He blinked back tears as he stared deep into my eyes. "I don't, either, but I think this is something I have to do alone."

A hole tore through my chest. My voice came out small and fragile. "You don't want my help?"

"It's not that," he said, his voice cracking. "I feel like two different people—the guy I was before my parents died and my brother was changed, and the guy I am now, the one I am with you and the rest of our family. I can't explain it, but I feel like I need to find my brother as the guy I used to be—the one I was when we were together."

He took a deep breath and raked his fingers through his hair. "I'm not explaining it well. It has nothing to do with you. Please try to understand that."

I nodded, though it still felt a bit like a rejection. More than that, though, I worried for him. I knew he could handle himself, but I still wanted to be there for him. "Is it dangerous?"

His voice was so quiet I barely heard it. "I don't know."

I chewed the dry skin on my lower lip. I really didn't want him to do this alone. What if his brother was working with a group like Maliya's? The vampires may be cured, but that didn't make groups like that any less dangerous.

"Are you sure you have to do this alone?" I whispered. "You didn't let me go after Jenna alone."

Venn's gaze dropped to mine, and he ran his thumb across my shoulder. "This is different."

"Is it?" I asked. "You don't know what you could be getting yourself into."

Venn closed his eyes and took a breath. "Rae, please. I need to do this alone."

My stomach knotted. I didn't know if he truly meant that, or if he was afraid I couldn't handle myself without my magic—like he was trying to protect me. But I didn't want to fight with him, and I wouldn't be the girl who kept him from his brother.

I took his hands in mine. It hurt to say it, but I wanted him to know I supported him no matter what he decided to do. "Then go. Your brother is more important than anything right now. You need to find him."

God knows I felt the exact same way about my sister. Screw whatever threats we were facing. Family was everything.

Venn wrapped me in a tight hug, and for a moment, I felt that hole in my chest begin to close. Then I thought about being separated from him, and it tore even wider.

"How will you get there?" I asked.

"I've already talked to Richard and Genevieve," he said. "They're going to let me borrow one of their cars. I'll have my phone on me, so you can call whenever you want."

It was probably best if I didn't. I'd talk to him the whole time and slow him down.

"Just promise me you won't get hurt, Venn," I whispered.

He kissed me softly, then drew away to look me in the eyes. "I promise. I love you, Rae. Always and forever."

"Always and forever," I repeated.

I relaxed into his embrace once more as silence settled over the room. I couldn't help but think of what it must've been like for him to lose his brother. It had to be on par with losing Jenna.

"What happened that night?" I found myself asking. "When Tyson was attacked?"

Venn stared up at the ceiling without answering. He shook his head lightly and closed his eyes, like he was trying not to go back there. His heartbreak ricocheted through me. I knew exactly how it felt to revisit old memories. I still hadn't told him all the details of what happened the night my parents died.

"It's okay," I whispered softly. "You don't have to tell me."

"I will," he promised. "Eventually."

9

VENN ~ FOUR YEARS AGO

I remembered it like it was yesterday. I'd spent years of endless nights replaying the events over and over again so that each detail could never escape my memory. I suppose I tortured myself because somewhere deep down inside of me, I had hoped I could go back and change it. But no matter how much I replayed it, nothing would ever change. Each morning I woke, I was still alone. My brother was gone.

Gramps had been drinking that night. I wished I could say there was a reason for it, like he was trying to drink away the memory of Grams, but he'd picked up the whiskey bottle long before Grams died. The fact was, the man was trash, and there was no reason for it.

"Give me the damn remote," he muttered under his breath as he snatched it from Tyson's fingers. He plopped down into his old, tattered recliner and took a swig of whiskey straight from the bottle.

My brother and I exchanged a glance from where we sat beside each other on the couch. You never argued with Gramps, especially when he got in these moods. He'd never hit us or anything, but you sure didn't want to hear the old man yell. The neighbors five doors down could hear it through the walls. I was sure of it.

Gramps clicked the remote, and the TV switched from cartoons to boxing. "Ya damn kids and your stupid cartoons," he grumbled like we couldn't hear him. "I don't know why I waste the cable bill on ya."

Tyson's hands curled into fists as Gramps continued to mumble under his breath about how much of a burden we were. It was like he blamed us for our parents' deaths and that we didn't have anywhere else to go.

Three more years, I told myself. Three more years until I turned eighteen and could legally get out of this hell hole. Tyson and I did our best to stay out of

461

Gramps's way and to clean up after him, but we could never get the smell of vomit out of our mattresses that had been there since we'd moved in, or the mysterious rotting stench that came from the kitchen drain. Our clothes were all hand-me-downs, and Tyson was in serious need of a new pair of shoes. They were ready to fall apart. We had to scour quarters from Gramps's recliner to do laundry, and only managed to find enough to do a load every two or three weeks. Gramps didn't care if his own clothes smelled like garbage and had ketchup stains on every white beater he owned. All he cared about was his boxing.

I placed a gentle hand on Tyson's shoulder, shooting him a glance that begged him to calm down. At thirteen, he was still trying to get the whole anger management thing down. Heck, I was no expert, but at least I knew to keep my cool around Gramps.

Without a word, Tyson stood and crossed in front of Gramps to head to our room.

"Get out the goddamn way!" Gramps yelled.

Tyson all but sprinted down the hall to avoid him. He shut the door quietly, but Gramps heard it.

"Don't you go slamming doors around here, boy!" he shouted.

I heard Tyson groan from the next room and decided to join him. I'd much rather be with him than out here with Gramps.

Slowly, I got to my hands and knees and inched my way across the carpet so I wouldn't interrupt Gramps's programming.

"Where you going?" Gramps demanded.

I stopped dead. "Uh, to my room."

"Microwave me a pizza pocket, will ya, Jason?"

I was used to Gramps calling me my father's name. At this point, I hardly noticed. I made it past the TV and got to my feet. The kitchen was small and cramped. I held my breath as I opened the freezer, hoping we weren't out. I breathed a sigh of relief when I found a single pizza pocket in the door.

"What's taking so long?" Gramps demanded. "It's just a pizza pocket!"

I rushed to grab a plate, then shoved his food in the microwave. Two minutes later, I was back in the living room, handing him his dinner. He took one bite and spit it back out, straightening in his chair.

"Goddamn, that's hot!" Gramps yelled. "You trying to burn my tongue off?"

I stepped away on shaky feet. "N-no."

"Get outta here," he snarled. "And take your goddamn disgusting pizza pocket with you."

Gramps shoved the food into my hand. I was dumbstruck. I didn't know what else to do, so I just turned away and headed down the hall to my room.

Tyson was curled up beneath his blanket, pretending like he was asleep. I placed a hand on his shoulder and shook him lightly.

He groaned. "Go away."

"Are you hungry?" I asked.

Tyson sniffed the air and sat up at the smell of food.

"You want to split it?" I asked.

"Gramps won't get mad?"

The last time we'd snuck food into our room, he threw a fit for hours—said it would attract mice.

"Doesn't matter," I said. "Are you hungry?"

Tyson gazed down at his hands. "Yeah, I guess so."

I ripped the pizza pocket in half and gave him the bigger chunk. He nibbled on it quietly.

"I'm sick of living here," Tyson said, breaking the silence.

I sank onto my bed across from him. "I know. I am, too. Once I turn eighteen, we can leave. I'll become your guardian or something."

Tyson remained quiet for several moments. "What if... what if we left tonight?"

I just stared at him, unsure if I heard him correctly. "You want to run away?"

He lowered his voice so that even if Gramps was standing outside the door, he wouldn't be able to hear. "This isn't a life, Venn. Mom and Dad wouldn't have wanted this for us."

I frowned. "Mom and Dad are gone. They don't have a say anymore."

"Well, *we* should," he argued. "We should have a say in our own lives."

"It's not that simple," I said.

Believe me, I'd thought about leaving Gramps's place plenty of times, too, but I knew it wasn't realistic. As soon as someone found us, we'd be right back where we started, and Gramps would never forgive us for putting him through that. And if we told the state what a hell hole this was, we could end up somewhere worse.

At least Gramps never laid a hand on us. That was what I kept telling myself. To be honest, it didn't make my life any less miserable.

"The only person who has a say is the state," I pointed out. "If they want us here, we have to stay. It's the law."

Tyson finished off his pizza pocket and crossed his arms. "Not if they don't find us. If you want to stay, fine. But I'm done."

Tyson threw the covers off himself to reveal he was already fully clothed, with his tattered shoes on and everything. He reached beneath his bed to pull out his backpack, which was so full that it got stuck for a second.

"You can't be serious," I hissed.

"Yes, seriously." Tyson stood and swung the strap of his bag over his shoulder.

I caught him by the wrist before he could reach the window. "Where are you going to go? Do you have any idea what kind of monsters roam the streets at this time of night?"

Tyson scoffed and pulled a pocket knife from his jeans. I had no idea where he'd gotten it. Probably traded it with one of his buddies at school. "I'm not afraid of a vampire. I can handle myself. Besides, we've been out at night plenty of times and been fine. It's like the vamps don't even know we're there."

"You *should* be afraid," I snapped. "These aren't the city streets we grew up on, Tyson. Nocton isn't safe at night."

"Well, I can't exactly run away during the day," he shot back, ripping his arm from my grasp. "Are you coming or not?"

"Tyson, you can't go," I said firmly, putting my foot down.

He raised an eyebrow at me. "Watch me."

He flung open the window, but I sprang forward to catch him around the waist. He threw an elbow back and caught me in the corner of the eye. I longed to cry out, but I knew that would only get Gramps's attention. He didn't need to know what was going on in here.

"Let me go," Tyson demanded, squirming out of my grasp.

I clawed out at him, but my vision was still blurry from the blow. I couldn't hang on.

Tyson slipped from my grip and hurried out onto the fire escape. I blinked the world back into focus and rushed behind him, but he was already racing down the rickety metal stairs.

"Tyson!" I hissed, but he kept going. I made a split-second decision. Screw the rules. Screw what Gramps might think. I had to go after my brother.

I crawled out the window and sprinted down the fire escape. Tyson reached the bottom level and jumped onto the pavement below before I'd made it down one story.

"Tyson!" I called again. I tried to stay quiet to avoid attracting any attention. The dark street below us was empty, but there was no telling what kind of monsters lurked in the shadows.

"Come on, Venn!" Tyson spun around, his arms wide out, like he was on the top of the world.

I reached the bottom level of the fire escape, which ended a good ten feet above ground. The ladder that was supposed to descend to let you all the way down was broken off. Gathering my courage, I took the leap.

My ankles ached as they twisted under me, but I caught myself with my hands and hurried back to my feet.

"This is great!" Tyson exclaimed again. "Let's go."

"Tyson, get back—"

I never finished the sentence before a figure leapt out of the shadows. It all happened so fast that I never saw it coming. One second Tyson was standing there with his arms spread proudly, and the next he was on the pavement, writhing beneath a vampire with a newborn bloodlust in his silver eyes.

My blood ran cold, and for a second, I just stood there. Looking back on that night, I always wondered what would've happened if I hadn't frozen up. Would I have reached him in time to keep the vampire venom from entering his veins?

It felt like an eternity had passed, but that eternity had lasted a mere millisecond. When I caught sight of those pearly-white fangs glistening under the light of the street lamp, I sprang into action. No bloodsucking parasite was going to touch my brother!

A primal urge to protect rose up inside of me, and a strong tingle like I'd never felt spread across my skin. The buildings around me seemed to grow taller as I fell onto all fours, but I couldn't make sense of the different proportions around me or the way colors swam differently in my eyes. All I could focus on was my brother and the vampire rolling around the pavement with him, trying to get a shot at his neck.

I didn't realize at the time how strange it was that Tyson was able to fight back, that the vampire didn't just snap his bones under his supernatural strength. I wouldn't realize it until hours later that that was the moment Tyson's shifter genes switched on and he came into his own supernatural strength. I didn't even realize the same thing was happening to me—my first ever shift into a wolf.

Protect. Protect. Protect.

That was all that went through my head as I sprinted forward and slammed into the vampire. He rolled across the pavement, but he sprang to his feet a second later, like he hadn't felt a thing. Blood covered his fangs and dripped down his chin as he curled back his lips to snarl at me like some wild animal.

Anger unlike anything I'd ever felt before swept through me when I realized that the blood dripping down his chin was my brother's. He'd managed to get a bite, and I hadn't even noticed.

"Venn," Tyson's voice called to me through the darkness.

Relief washed over me, but I couldn't take my eyes off the angry vamp facing me, looking as if he was about to attack. A deep growl bubbled up from my throat, and I bared my canines at him.

In the blink of an eye, the vampire lunged, taking me down from all fours and onto my back. I yipped and howled as he squeezed, as if trying to break bone. I kicked my wide wolf paws at him, trying to use my sharp claws to tear at anything I could find.

I swiped at the guy's face, barely able to make out the black fur coating my body. I knew *something* was different, but I didn't have the luxury of questioning it at the moment.

The vampire reeled backward and hissed. It was enough to allow me the upper hand. I pressed my back paws against his chest and kicked outward. The vampire flew through the air and landed with a *thud* beside my brother.

I realized my mistake a moment too late. Tyson was lying on the ground, clutching the bleeding wound on his neck. The vampire took one look between us and decided to go for Tyson—the weakest of the two.

Faster than I could process, the vampire grabbed Tyson and tossed him over his shoulder like a ragdoll.

"Venn!" Tyson cried as sheer terror swept across his features.

I sprinted after them as the vampire disappeared into the dark alley with my brother. I ran as fast as I could, trying to follow the sound of my brother's voice.

Even long after the footsteps faded, after my brother's cries were no longer anything more than an echoing in my own mind, and after my legs started to ache and my chest started to burn, I still pressed on.

I must've been wandering the streets of Nocton for hours, but it felt like years. Thick fog had settled over the streets, so much that the street lamps above my head seemed almost invisible. It was like walking through a dream. The streets were so quiet, so lonely. It didn't feel real.

"Tyson!" I tried to call out, but it only came out as a wolf's howl. It was like an ominous chord cutting through the night, signaling death.

He can't be gone, I told myself. *I will find him. I will find him.*

I must've repeated those words to myself a thousand times before they seemed to lose all meaning. My limbs felt so numb that it was as if they'd fallen off my body. I tried to push forward, but eventually, I could no longer move my feet. I curled up at the side of a brick building I didn't recognize and began to weep. I had no idea where I was and no idea how long it'd been. How had I lost him?

"Tyson," I whispered, but again, no words came out. It sounded like a whimper.

That was when I heard a whimper return, one that wasn't my own. I sprang to my feet immediately and forced myself to follow the sound of the voice. It sounded so familiar. Could it be...?

I turned down an alleyway between two tall buildings. Another whimper came, and I was certain this time that it was real. I rushed forward toward the noise, and a lone figure began to take shape.

A child sat curled up beside a dumpster. His chest rose and fell quickly, and little sounds kept escaping from his lips like he couldn't control the agony inside of him.

My heart turned to water in my chest. As it did, my limbs grew, and I finally stood upright again. The cool night air brushed across every inch of my naked body, but I didn't care. I'd found my brother.

I knelt beside him and placed a gentle hand to his shoulder. "Tyson?"

He started when I touched him, and his gaze darted to mine. Silver momentarily flashed across his irises before they returned to their normal dark brown. He blinked a few times, as if trying to process whether I was truly there or not. The wound on his neck had healed from the vampire's saliva, but his skin had paled, as if he'd lost a lot of blood.

When my brother looked at me—like he was part my brother and part something else entirely—I felt as if my spirit left my body. My limbs moved without my command, and all I could feel was an icy coldness enter my chest. It was like I was watching the scene from up above.

"Venn?" Tyson asked through labored breaths.

"It's me," I whispered. "Are you okay?"

Stupid question. Of course he wasn't okay. He was lying there shivering in the cold after being attacked by a vampire. No one would be okay after that.

Tears rose to Tyson's eyes. "It hurts, Venn. It hurts so bad. Like fire…" He bit down on his lower lip, like the pain was too much to allow him to finish the sentence.

I wrapped him in my arms and pulled him close to me. "We need to get help."

Tyson shook his head. "I'm too far gone, brother."

I knew it was true. I'd heard stories about the transformation before, but I wasn't willing to believe it was something that would ever happen to us.

"No," I protested. "We'll get you to a hospital, get the venom out of you."

Tyson went into a coughing fit, and it felt as if my heart was breaking into a million pieces. I pulled him tighter, like I could wish the venom away with enough love. But even I knew spells didn't work that way.

Finally, Tyson found his voice. He gazed up at me. "I'm sorry. I'm so sorry I dragged you into this."

I shook my head as tears streamed down my cheeks. "It's not your fault."

"You warned me." He sucked in a deep, pained breath as silver flashed across his eyes once more.

My shoulder shook in sobs. "No, Tyson. Stay with me!"

"You have to go, Venn," he cried.

"I'm not leaving you." I buried my face into his shoulder.

"I don't want to hurt you," he insisted in a groggy voice.

"You won't hurt me," I told him.

"You know how new vampires are," he said. "You've heard all about the bloodlust. There will be nothing I can do to stop myself."

"You will." I only said it to try to convince myself. I wasn't ready to lose my brother, the true only family I had left.

Tears streamed down Tyson's face, and he shook his head. "I won't. You have to leave me. Please."

The pleading look in his eyes was almost too much to bear. It was like he was asking me to let him suffer and die alone. I couldn't do that.

"I'm staying right here," I promised.

Tyson's brows knitted together in anger. "I will bite you, Venn. So help me, I will."

This time, I couldn't convince myself otherwise. Tyson was telling the truth. He'd use his new fangs just to get me to leave, to protect me from himself.

Now who's the one protecting who?

In that moment, I'd never hated myself more. I was the big brother. I was supposed to protect him… and I'd failed.

"Venn, I'm a goner," Tyson groaned. "Just let me have one last wish. Go."

I could hardly believe he was asking such a thing from me, but I also knew what would happen if I stayed. I'd be right where he was, vampire venom pumping through my veins, pain unlike anything imaginable—or so I'd heard.

Against my will, I decided to follow my brother's wishes. Slowly, I lowered him back onto the pavement and stepped away.

Of all the details I remembered from that night, the one thing I could never recall was what it felt like in that moment. It should've been the single thing that stuck out above all else, but it didn't. I used to wonder if maybe I was just so numb from everything that had happened that I felt nothing when I let my brother go, but I'd come to realize it was the exact opposite.

All the emotions I'd felt tore through me like a black hole, ripping me apart from the inside. There was so much pain and so much sorrow that my mind had blocked it all out. It was just too much for one man to bear.

I remembered crying. I bawled like the ocean itself was trying to push its way out my eyes. But everything else… everything else was darkness.

"Venn," Tyson whispered before I was out of earshot.

I turned back to him, hopeful that he still wanted me by his side while he made the transformation. "Tyson?"

He sucked in a sharp breath, like the venom was doing something bad to him again. "Don't come after me. I don't want you getting hurt."

I hesitated. "I won't."

"Promise?" he asked.

I didn't know how I could manage to make such a promise. I felt like the worst brother in history, leaving him to suffer alone just because he asked me to. I should've stayed. I should've comforted him when he needed it the most. But instead, I followed his wishes.

"I promise."

I barely remembered the walk home, when I knocked on Gramps's apartment door early in the morning and he answered with a string of curse words, only to find me naked and covered in dirt at his doorstep.

It was the first time Gramps laid a hand on me, after I'd told him what had happened. For whatever reason, I remembered every blow, every shot of pain that radiated across my skin. I drank all that in and seared it into my memory. I supposed that was because I thought I deserved it. When Gramps said it was my fault, I believed him.

10

The morning seemed to darken as we gathered in Genevieve's kitchen for breakfast and Venn said his goodbyes. Like the rest of the house, the kitchen was bathed in dark tones and soft lighting.

Genevieve, Jenna, and Ronark were already seated around the long mahogany table, while Teagan stood behind the island at the stove cooking eggs. Clarita, Amalia, and Richard hadn't made it down for breakfast yet. The rest of us—Sondra, Ryland, Fiona, and me—were all crowded around Venn.

"Don't be gone too long," Fiona said as she hugged Venn.

Venn hiked his backpack up on his shoulder. "I won't."

"Stay safe," Teagan said, as if in warning.

Ryland took Venn's hand and gave him a one-armed hug. "You sure we can't come with you?"

"Guys, I'll be fine," Venn insisted. "You have bigger things to worry about in the meantime."

Sondra wrapped him in a hug. "That doesn't mean we won't be worrying about you. Our intuition is crap these days. If something goes wrong—"

"Nothing is going to go wrong," Venn assured us. "I'm going to find my brother and bring him back. That's it."

"Maybe you should wait until you have more information," I suggested nervously, even though I knew there was nothing I could say to stop him from going.

"It's not like Tyson's location is plastered all over the Internet," Ryland said. "With groups like this—"

He cut off when Venn elbowed him. The meaning was clear. Tyson was hanging out with a dangerous, secretive group of ex-vampires. And Venn was walking straight into their nest. It was all too familiar. If he was anything like me, the more I pushed him to take precautions, the more reckless he'd be.

But I knew Venn wasn't like me, and that was the only thing giving me solace at the moment and keeping me from following after him. He would take precautions. He would think things through. He would take care of himself.

Right?

Venn pulled me close to him. "I'll be fine, Rae. You do your planning against Matias. I'll be back with Tyson before it's all over."

"You better be," I said. "I love you."

"I love you, too."

He gave me a kiss on the lips, then that was it. I watched at the window as he got into Richard's SUV and drove down the street. I didn't look away until he was long gone. Teagan's voice pulled me out of my daze.

"You hungry?" she asked. She stood at the table with a spatula full of scrambled eggs hovering above my plate.

I shook my head but sat anyway. "I'll eat later."

Jenna took my hand under the table and gave it a light squeeze.

"Venn can take care of himself," Sondra said reassuringly, though she didn't sound convinced.

"I know," I replied as I stared down into my full glass of orange juice. I wasn't sure I could stomach it right now. "It's just that he came after me when I went to find Jenna alone. I wanted to help him."

"He'll be back," Genevieve said from the head of the table. "In the meantime, we have work to do."

"What's the plan?" Ronark asked as he dug into his eggs and sausage.

"I know a few locals I'd like to approach to help us," Genevieve said. "There's a man who runs an underground spell shop. He might be willing to supply protection charms and potions."

Oh, God. I hoped she didn't mean Devin, my old boss at Bloodstone. I hadn't heard from him since I quit so I could go after my sister. If I knew him at all, he was already in Chicago cozying up to Matias. Asking for his help wouldn't be my first choice. His spells never were great to begin with.

"What's this guy's name?" I asked, finally taking a sip of orange juice.

"Alexander Morris," Genevieve replied.

Huh. Never heard of him. Wait…

"Alexander, as in Xander?" I asked.

I'd heard of the guy before, but I'd never met him. Devin had talked about him when I worked at Bloodstone. He always complained the guy was his biggest competitor. He even joked about doing some questionable things to him, though he never followed through with any of it. I always got the impression that Devin was a little intimidated by Xander's magic. The guy was at least a mid-witch bordering on a high witch.

"I've tried to reach him, but he hasn't been answering his phone. I want

Sondra to visit him today to see if he'll help us." Genevieve handed Sondra a set of car keys.

"You're not going?" I asked, a bit surprised.

She shook her head. "Clarita, Amalia, and I will be going through our inventory today and cataloguing any potions that might be useful to us. Besides, Xander and I haven't exactly gotten along in the past. He likes Sondra."

"I'm coming, too," I said immediately. No way was I sitting around here all day without getting in on some of the action.

"Me too," Fiona chimed in.

"And me," Ryland insisted, puffing up his chest.

Genevieve frowned. "You might scare him off."

"Yeah, he's pretty paranoid," Sondra said. "I think it should just be us three girls. He won't be as intimidated by us."

"But what if—?" Ryland started.

"We can handle ourselves." Sondra shot him a pointed expression.

Ryland gaped at her. "But without your magic…"

"Babe." Teagan placed a gentle hand on his shoulder. "They'll be fine. No one else has magic either, remember?"

"Maybe Tea should come with us, too," Fiona suggested. "She's been fighting vamps for ages without any magic."

Teagan poked at her food. "I'm actually not feeling great today."

"Can I come?" Jenna asked. "I'd really like to get out."

"Sure," Sondra said.

While they spoke, I eyed Teagan curiously. She had been acting weird lately —like she didn't want to fight anymore. Had something happened on Gregor Island that scared her? Something she hadn't told us about?

"You okay, Tea?" I asked.

"Yeah," she assured me. "Just a stomach bug. I'll start on the next pile of books you guys were reading through, see if I can find something."

"Well, girls," Sondra said. "Should we get going?"

Jenna, Fiona, and I got to our feet.

"Hold on." Teagan rose and started for the door. "Before you go, I think you should have some weapons on you. No one has magic anymore, but that doesn't mean they aren't dangerous. Follow me."

The four of us exchanged quick glances as we followed Teagan down the hall and to her guest room. Her room was almost identical to mine, but she had a pile of knives spread out on the bed. There must've been at least two dozen of them, all in different shapes and sizes.

Fiona gasped and reached for the closest one, running her finger along the blade to test how sharp it was. "Where did you get all these? I thought you lost yours."

Teagan smirked, looking proud beside her display. "Genevieve has been very generous after I told her I'd lost the ones she'd given me."

"Wow," Sondra said, like she couldn't believe it. "She really has changed, hasn't she?"

"What did she used to be like?" I asked, reaching for a dagger with a rose-petal design etched into the blade.

"She seems really nice to me." Jenna grabbed a large pocket knife and flipped it open. The blade was at least an inch wide and as long as my hand. She beamed, then closed it and slid it in her pocket.

"Let's just say she wasn't the best mentor to work with," Sondra admitted. "She was very hard on me."

Fiona crinkled her nose. "She wasn't exactly kind when I first met her, either. She wasn't even willing to mentor me because apparently fox shifters are weak. Like that has anything to do with witch magic."

Teagan held up a belt to Fiona, which had multiple sheaths built in for throwing knives. Fiona took it and began securing the belt around her waist.

"Honestly, I think meeting Richard has helped," Teagan said.

"They haven't been together long?" Jenna sounded surprised. "I assumed they'd been together forever."

Sondra shook her head as she secured a sheath onto her hip. "A lot has changed in her life over the past few years. She didn't have Richard or the house until later. It was all around the time I finished mentoring with her a few years ago. Her business took off, and everything just sort of fell into place for her. That was when she loaned me the money to start my own business, but that only hurt our relationship even more."

I slipped the dagger into my boot. "It sounds like she finally figured out magic."

"I think so," Sondra said. "I'm happy for her. I'm glad she changed."

Teagan handed Fiona her leather jacket. "Here. This will hide the knives."

Fiona put it on and grinned. She turned to the mirror above the dresser and spun around to take in her new look. She always looked so sweet in her jeans and flowery tops. Today, her red hair was piled on her head instead of down in waves. In skinny jeans, a deep green tee, and Teagan's leather jacket, she looked totally badass. It was like she'd aged five years in a matter of days.

"Wow," I said, coming to stand beside her. "You look awesome."

She smiled into the mirror nervously. "Do I?"

Teagan patted her on the shoulder and whispered in her ear. "You're a vampire slayer. Embrace it, girl."

Fiona grinned. "Can I still call myself that now that there are no vampires?"

Sondra raised her eyebrows. "You've killed a vampire before, haven't you?"

"Yeah," Fiona admitted. "Tons."

Jenna wrapped an arm around her and looked at Fiona's reflection in the mirror. "Then you're a vampire slayer."

I couldn't take my eyes off the mirror as I looked at our group of five. We were all dressed in dark colors and tight clothing. We kind of looked like a team of assassins. Maybe Xander *would* be intimidated by us.

"Should we go see what kind of trouble we can get ourselves into?" I asked. Excitement sizzled in my bones.

"Hopefully not too much," Teagan said as we all started for the door.

Ryland was already on his way down the hall when he caught sight of Fiona stepping out of the room. He stopped dead in his tracks.

"What?" she feigned.

Ryland looked gobsmacked seeing Fiona dressed in anything but her usual attire. "You look… different."

Fiona crossed her arms. "You mean I look like Teagan?"

"Well, that *is* Teagan's jacket, isn't it?" He eyed it like he wasn't quite sure.

Sondra stepped forward and draped an arm around Fiona's shoulder. "I think she looks great."

"You sure I can't come with? Help protect you?" Ryland begged.

"It's sweet you're worried about your sister," Sondra said, "but I think she can handle herself."

Ryland's jaw tightened. "She's only seventeen."

"And I've been fighting alongside you for years," Fiona shot back. "Why the sudden change of heart?"

Ryland gaped at her. "Because…"

"Because I don't have my shifter strength?" Fiona's irritation grew with each passing second. "I don't need it."

Ryland looked her up and down. He opened his mouth like he was about to protest, but before he could, she sprang on him. Fiona had a knife out of her belt in under a second. She pressed her forearm against Ryland's huge chest and shoved him up against the wall. Her arm came down to stab the knife into the wall just inches from his face before he could even blink.

Ryland's eyes went wide, and he held his hands up in surrender.

"Holy shit, Fiona!" Teagan cried proudly.

Jenna clapped and whooped, while Sondra tried to stifle a laugh. My jaw dropped, and my hand slapped over my mouth.

"You go, girl!" Jenna exclaimed.

Fiona smirked at Ryland. "Tell me again how you don't think I can handle myself."

He stumbled over his words. "I-I guess I was mistaken."

"Damn right you were." Fiona ripped the knife from the wall and turned to us to hide the look of utter disbelief written across her face from Ryland.

I held my hand up and gave her a high-five.

Sondra started down the hall, swaying her hips and snapping her fingers. "And that, cousin, is how a girl gets 'er done."

Jenna, Fiona, and I followed, swaying our hips in the same manner.

Jenna laughed. "You tell him, sister."

Fiona turned toward Ryland, walking backward to keep up with us. "Love you, brother!" she said as she kissed the ends of her fingers and blew the kiss to him while simultaneously flipping him off.

Teagan elbowed Ryland in the ribs. "Oh, don't look so surprised."

That was all I saw before we turned the corner and headed outside.

Fiona jumped down the front porch stairs and hopped excitedly on the side-walk. "Wow! That felt good."

"It should," I said. "Your brother's an asshole."

Fiona rolled her eyes. "Only sometimes."

Sondra led us to the garage, where we found a black sedan waiting for us. "I'm proud of you, Fiona, but we're all going to have to tone it down once we get to Xander's. He's not expecting us, so we have to tread carefully."

"What do you mean by that?" I asked as I slid into the passenger seat. Fiona and Jenna took the back.

Sondra started the car. "It means he's a great witch, but it's going to take some convincing to get him to join our side."

11

Fifteen minutes later, we pulled up to a three-story brick building. It looked old, with shop windows on the lower level and apartments on the upper. I'd only been in this part of town a few times before, but I'd never seen much vampire action around here.

We stepped out of the car. The air was chilly for a summer day, and clouds were rolling in. A few people walked along the street, roaming in and out of shops, but in general it was quiet and felt a bit ominous.

I glanced to the shoe shop on the lower level, but Sondra cocked her head toward the alley.

"This way," she whispered.

The three of us quietly followed behind her. I was acutely aware of the dagger in my boot, prepared to use it if something bad happened. The path between the buildings reminded me of the many alleyways I'd killed vampires in. I half expected one to jump out from behind the dumpster and attack us. But there was nothing except an old newspaper tumbling across the pavement in the wind.

Sondra stopped dead in her tracks and held a hand out to stop us. Warning bells went off in my head, sending my heart thumping. I followed her gaze to see the door we were headed for was cracked open. It creaked as we approached, giving way to a dark descending staircase. Tingles spread across my skin.

"Should my intuition be going haywire right now if I don't have any connection to Synchrony?" I whispered.

"It's not just you," Jenna said, stepping cautiously toward the door.

"Intuition or not, this is a little creepy," Sondra said.

Fiona shrugged. "Eh, we've dealt with worse. Let's check it out."

Sondra opened the heavy metal door wider. When we saw what lay at the bottom, she started sprinting. "Xander!?"

I was right behind her, my heart racing. The door at the bottom of the stairs had been knocked off its hinges. Beyond it, the spell shop had been completely ransacked. Shelves were knocked over, and empty potion vials lay everywhere. Pages had been ripped out of spell books and littered the floor. Most of the merchandise was missing. The fluorescent lights above our heads flickered on and off.

"Xander?" Sondra called again as she climbed over the shelving and tried to avoid the broken glass shattered everywhere.

I could hardly take in the horrifying scene as I followed behind her. Jewelry cases that once held trinkets and charms were completely empty, as were the bookcases along the far wall. The only sign Xander once sold herbs was the bag of sage busted on the floor.

"Who would do this?" Fiona asked breathlessly.

Jenna looked around to take it all in. "You think whoever did this got him?"

Sondra opened her mouth to say something, but a muffled voice cut through the momentary silence.

"Help!"

I immediately raced toward the back room to the sound of the voice.

"Sondra, is that you? Help!"

The back room was just as bad as the main shop. A heavy bookcase had been knocked in front of a closet door, where the voice was coming from.

"Xander!" Fiona called.

"Who is that?" he called back.

I reached for the case and began lifting it. Damn, I was really missing my shifter strength right now. This thing felt like two hundred pounds. Jenna and Fiona rushed over to help.

"I'm here," Sondra said. "You just hold tight. We're going to get you out of there."

We pushed the bookcase upright. Sondra kicked old books aside and yanked open the door. Inside, an old man with white hair shivered in the corner of the dark closet. He put his hand up to shield his eyes from the light. Xander?

He looked so frail—so afraid.

Sondra reached down to help him to his feet. His whole body shook as he took in the destruction of his shop. I grabbed a chair that had been knocked over and set it upright for him. Fiona rushed out of the room and came back a few seconds later with a paper cup full of water.

"Here you go, Mr. Xander," she said as he sank into the chair.

He took it with shaky hands and sipped the water.

"Xander, what happened here?" Sondra asked.

His eyes glossed over, like he couldn't believe what happened. "The Department of Magical Regulation found me."

We each shared a collective gasp.

"But your protection spells," Sondra pointed out. "They should've held, right?"

Xander shook his head regrettably. "I thought so, too. But they broke through it somehow. When the spell broke, it was like a bomb going off. Potion vials shattered, and shelves fell over. I drank a chameleon potion and hid in the closet. Then they came in and took everything. I heard all of it. By the time they left, the door was blocked."

"How long have you been in there?" I asked breathlessly.

Xander raked his fingers through his gray hair. "I don't know. A day, maybe…?"

"What's a chameleon potion?" Jenna asked.

"It basically renders you invisible," Sondra explained. "It's not true invisibility. It's a type of hypnosis spell. If someone looks at you while you're under the influence of it, they'll be compelled to look away. It's like putting a blind spot in someone else's mind. Lasts about twelve hours. What I'm more concerned about is how the DMR broke through your protection spell. It's supposed to keep any threats out of your shop."

Xander shook his head. "I don't know."

"The DMR must be using magic," I said in thought.

"What do you mean?" Fiona asked. "Like Matias is working with them?"

"I don't think so," I said. "Leon Cavanaugh told me the DMR keeps and catalogues all magical artifacts they confiscate. They must have loads of potions and artifacts that they're using to serve their purpose."

Jenna crossed her arms. "Well, that's just sick. Using the magic they despise to fight magic? A little ironic, don't you think?"

I rolled my eyes. "It's like Ryland said. It's the lesser of two evils for them. At least they can control the magic they have their hands on."

Xander seemed to relax now that he'd had a drink of water. He looked up to Sondra. "What are you doing here?"

"We came to ask for your help," she replied. "But we can talk about it later. Let's get you something to eat."

Xander stood to follow Sondra's lead, but he looked a little disoriented, like he was still trying to take it all in. Sondra helped steady him while I stood on his other side and helped him over fallen shelves and to the door.

He finally seemed to steady himself as we ascended the stairs. "Thank you so much for helping me. I didn't know how long I was going to be stuck in that closet."

"I'm glad we came when we did," Sondra said.

Xander stepped into the alleyway and glanced around with squinted eyes, as if the daylight was blinding.

"There's a café two doors down," Sondra said, pointing out of the alleyway. "Is that okay?"

"Yes, of course," Xander replied. "I'll eat anything right now."

We left the alley and entered a small café. The place was quiet, and there was only one other couple there. We claimed a corner booth far away from them so we could talk in private.

Our waitress arrived as soon as we sat, and she handed out menus. She pulled a pad and pen out of her pocket. "Welcome. I'm Terry, and I'll be your server today. Can I start you folks off with some drinks?"

"Water for me, please," I said. I still wasn't hungry since breakfast.

"You guys can order whatever you want," Sondra offered. "I'll pay."

"Ooh!" Jenna's eyes lit up, and she flipped to the back of the menu. "Do you know how long it's been since I've had a soda? And French fries!"

Fiona glanced up to the waitress. "I'll have a water, too, thanks."

Sondra stuck with water as well, while Jenna ordered soda and Xander ordered coffee. His fingers continued to shake as he tore open the sugar packet and poured it in his cup. No one spoke until the waitress took our food orders and disappeared back into the kitchen.

"What can I help you ladies with?" Xander asked without meeting any of our gazes.

Sondra leaned her elbows on the table from where she sat next to him. "You've heard about Matias Vayne?"

Xander took a sip of coffee. "I've been stuck in a closet for a day. I haven't been living under a rock."

"We plan to go after him," Sondra admitted. "We're looking for witches willing to join us."

Xander set his coffee down. His hand shook as he pressed his fingers to his lips to steady them. I was starting to wonder if his shaking was a normal tick and not due to being locked in a closet for the past twenty-four hours. "I fail to see how I can help, seeing as my magic is useless now."

Sondra frowned. "You know that's not true. You said yourself you used a chameleon potion just yesterday. Your potions and charms still work."

Xander shook his head. "No, no. I'm afraid I can't. The DMR took everything."

"Everything?" I asked breathlessly. There was nothing left in his apartment? Nothing he'd kept secret from his patrons?

Xander shot me a pointed expression. "Yes, everything. I can't help you."

He started to stand, but Sondra's hand shot out to grab his wrist. "Xander, please. We need you."

He hesitated. His gaze traveled around the table, taking in each one of our pleading expressions. We needed all the help we could get.

"Also, you need to eat something," Fiona pointed out.

Xander glanced to the kitchen, then relaxed back into his seat. He took a sip of coffee again, as if it might steady his nerves. "What exactly do you want from me?"

"Whatever assistance you can offer," Sondra said. "I know there's more to your spell shop than you keep out in the open."

Sondra had said Xander was a paranoid man. He must've had protection charms galore in hidden corners of his shop. Which meant whatever the DMR used to break through them was powerful.

"And none of that would be any use to you," he snapped. He crossed his arms over his chest, like he was protecting himself from something.

"We could use information," I added. "You could join us and help us find other people willing to support us."

"No," he answered immediately, sounding bitter about it. "I'm done. My shop is ruined, and my protection spells broken. I'm going into early retirement."

"You don't have to follow us," Fiona said gently. "We're just asking for any potions, charms, or trinkets that could help us face Matias and get our magic back."

Xander gaped at her, then hugged himself even tighter. "I told you. The DMR took everything."

"Do you know of anyone else who might be willing to help?" I asked, feeling hopeless. This guy clearly wasn't willing to get involved in any of this.

"I can't give out names," he insisted. "I won't put any other supernaturals at risk."

"That's not what we're asking." Jenna sounded offended. "No one will be at risk. We'll give them a choice."

Xander's voice became more aggressive. "It would be a breach of my clients' confidentiality!"

Just then, our waitress returned, and the whole table went silent. She placed a burger and fries in front of Jenna and a plate of pancakes in front of Xander. The rest of us hadn't ordered anything.

"You folks enjoy your meal!" Terry said kindly before heading to check on the other patrons across the café.

"Look, Xander," I said as softly as I could. I felt for the guy. I really did. But I also had a feeling he was hiding something. "What happened to you yesterday never should've happened. The DMR is abusing their power now that the magical community is vulnerable. We plan to change that. If we can restore magic, you can set up your protection spells again. All of us will get back a piece of ourselves that we lost when Matias took it. So if you know anything that could help us defeat the guy controlling magic, then please... help us."

My throat began to close up. If the magical community wasn't willing to step up against Matias with us, we would never defeat him. We couldn't do it on our own.

Xander's arms slowly relaxed, and he dropped them to his side. He shot a quick glance at Sondra, who was gazing at him with a pleading expression.

"You really think you can defeat him?" he asked skeptically.

"Yes," Fiona and Sondra answered in unison. I nodded, while Jenna was barely paying attention as she dug into her burger like she hadn't eaten in two years. Which, to be fair, was pretty close to the truth. She hadn't had a decent meal in that long, at least.

"And what happens when you do?" Xander asked. "Everything goes back to normal?"

"Yes," Sondra said, but her answer rubbed me the wrong way.

I didn't just want things to go back to normal. I wanted them to be better. I wanted things to change. I didn't want to keep hiding who I was, performing magic in secret and always watching my back when I shifted to make sure no one was watching me. I was a witch. I was a raven shifter. I'd embraced that, and it was time the Department of Magical Regulation embraced that, too.

Xander took several bites of his pancakes, then set his fork down. He inhaled a deep breath, like he was thinking hard about it. "All right. I will help you. But you must understand that I'm putting myself at great risk to do so."

Xander began reaching into his pockets. He dropped a handful of all sorts of random objects on the table: hair barrettes, jewelry, coins, even a small pencil eraser. Then he dug into his other pocket to pull out even more. My jaw dropped as I watched the pile grow taller and taller. To the normal eye, it all looked like junk, but I knew better. They were trinkets, the type of protection charm Fiona had found in the book we'd read. They'd suppress another supernatural's powers.

Xander reached up and pulled three different necklace chains over his head, which had been tucked into his shirt. He left one remaining for himself.

"Trinkets," Sondra whispered under her breath. "I thought of those, but they're not very strong."

"Not on their own," Xander agreed. "They won't win you any fights against Matias, but they can give you a bit of an edge."

"That's very generous of you," I said.

"Yes, well, it's all I have," Xander replied.

"It's more than enough," Sondra told him, staring down at the pile in fascination. "There will be enough for each of us to have one."

"Well, go on." He gestured to the pile. "Take them before I change my mind."

"Thank you, Mr. Xander." Fiona reached across the table and began gathering the trinkets into her jacket pockets.

I gathered the few she couldn't fit and put them in my own pockets.

"Just one thing." Xander leaned across the table and pointed a finger toward each of us as he spoke. "If this doesn't work out, I want the trinkets back. Every. Single. One."

I swallowed hard, acutely aware of the trinkets in my pockets. His words echoed in my mind. *If this doesn't work out.*

It had to…

Right?

<h1 style="text-align:center">12</h1>

"I knew trinkets were a good idea," Fiona raved proudly as we pulled into Genevieve's driveaway. A maroon sedan that wasn't there earlier was parked beside our spot.

"Is that another one of Richard's cars?" Fiona asked.

Sondra's eyebrows came together, as if confused. "No, I don't think so. I think I might recognize that car, but—"

Her eyes traveled to the front door, where a pretty blonde stood. She looked vaguely familiar from the back, but I couldn't place her.

"Oh my God!" Sondra exclaimed. She shoved the vehicle into park and cut the engine, then kicked her door open.

I quickly followed behind her. By the time I reached the front door, Genevieve was standing in the open doorway and inviting the girl inside.

"Zoey!" Sondra called, holding her arms out wide like she was going in for a hug.

The blonde turned, and a wide smile spread across her face. "Sondra!"

The girl hurried down the stairs and into Sondra's arms. And I. Stopped. Dead.

Instinct overcame me, and I suddenly had the urge to reach into my boot and stake my dagger through the girl's heart.

The shape of her nose, the Cupid's bow shape of her lips. I'd met Zoey before… except then her skin was paler, and her eyes were silver.

Fiona rushed up to greet Zoey like she was her long-lost sister, but I took a step back, completely dumbfounded.

Jenna stopped next to me. "What's wrong, Rach? You know this girl?"

I swallowed the lump in my throat, then finally found my feet. I grabbed

Jenna's wrist and pulled her down the walkway so we couldn't be heard. "I met her in a bar once. She tried to flirt with me."

Jenna shrugged and gazed at Zoey like she wasn't at all a threat. "So? Flirt back."

"Jenna." I swatted her shoulder. "It was a *vampire* bar."

Realization crossed Jenna's face. "She was a vampire?"

I nodded and shot a disgusted look at her. Fiona and Sondra were raving over Zoey like they were best friends. Ew.

"Okay," Jenna said, like it was no big deal. "So she's cured now. Why are you acting like she's still cursed?"

The question hit me like a slap in the face. I didn't have an answer.

"Come on," Jenna said, tugging at my arm. "Let's not be rude."

Jenna walked straight up to Vamp Girl and stuck her hand out. "Hi, I'm Jenna. I'm Rachel's sister. She's the one who killed Valkas and broke your curse."

The blood drained from my face. Jenna grabbed on to my shoulders and shoved me in front of her, forcing me to take Vamp Girl's outstretched hand. Her fingers were cold—just like a real vampire's.

"Hi, Rachel. I'm Zoey." She tilted her head, as if trying to remember where she'd seen me before. "We've met, haven't we?"

I cleared my throat and lied straight through my teeth. "I'm not sure."

"We have!" she cried. "I remember you. It was at Red Whiskey. We danced together for a few minutes."

I shifted my weight between my feet uncomfortably. I didn't talk to vampires. I slayed them. This whole encounter left me feeling uneasy. And they were just going to let her into Genevieve's house?

"Oh," I said, pretending to remember. "Yeah, I guess so."

"Is it true?" she asked. "That you broke the curse?"

"Yeah," Fiona said, draping a casual arm around my shoulder. "She was totally badass."

Vamp Girl smiled. "Well, thank you."

I gaped at her. I'd gone completely speechless.

"I'm happy to be back," Zoey said, then she turned and followed Genevieve into the house.

I whirled on Fiona and Sondra immediately. "You know Vamp Girl? She's a *vampire.*"

The two shared a look I couldn't read.

"Her name is Zoey," Fiona said, "and she *was* a vampire."

"How… how do you know her?" I asked. How had they ended up becoming friends with a vampire? They were supposed to kill them.

"Zoey and I were both students of Genevieve's," Sondra said. "Before she changed."

"Exactly. She changed," I pointed out. "Which means she's dangerous now."

Sondra crossed her arms and frowned at me. "Honestly, Rachel. The way you talk about vampires, you make it sound like they're an entirely different species."

"You of all people should know that," I stated.

"They're cured, though," Fiona argued. "I, for one, am thrilled to have Zoey back."

"But—" I started, but Sondra cut me off.

"Give Zoey a chance, Rae. I think you'll like her." Sondra turned and headed toward the door, and Fiona followed.

I just stood there dumbstruck, trying to take in the new information.

Jenna waited for me. "I'm not too keen on this vampire thing either, but I think Sondra's right. Zoey looks harmless."

I gaped at her. Shouldn't she be siding with me—after what the vampires had done to her?

I forced my feet to move beneath me, and I started up the steps and followed everyone else inside. Voices traveled into the hall from the kitchen. I found everyone gathered around the table, where Clarita and Amalia were exchanging greetings with Zoey. Only Richard, Ronark, Ryland, and Teagan were missing.

I lowered myself into a chair on the other end of the table, keeping a close watch on Zoey. I couldn't help but picture her with elongated canines. Yeah, she looked normal, and her eyes were no longer silver, but I couldn't shake the feeling that she shouldn't be here.

"How'd it go with Xander?" Amalia asked, turning to Fiona.

"Great!" she replied. "He gave us these trinkets to help suppress Matias's abilities."

Fiona dug into her pockets and spread the trinkets out on the table.

Clarita picked up a golden ring with a red stone to examine it. "A good idea. Not the strongest magic by any means, but we can use whatever we can get."

"Rachel," Jenna prodded, gesturing to the trinkets at the other end of the table.

Sighing, I stood and added my trinkets to the pile.

"Oh, wow!" Zoey gasped. "That's a lot. There must be dozens."

Genevieve pursed her lips, like she was thinking hard. "I want everyone to take one and keep it on themselves at all times. If Matias is using the locket to watch us, it should keep his visions fuzzy."

I took the golden ring and slipped it on my finger.

"So, Zoey," I said, trying to force my voice not to waver. "Will you be staying with us?"

Zoey glanced to Genevieve. "No. I heard all the guest rooms are full. I'm just here to help. No point in taking up extra room anyway. I'm only a few minutes away."

I didn't need a reminder of how many vampires roamed these streets... or used to roam them. Damn it. I was really itching to go out on patrol. Those days were over, though.

Sucks to be me.

"What can I help with?" Zoey asked, sounding enthusiastic to be on the team.

"We're still finishing up some cataloguing." Genevieve gestured for them to follow her. "I have a box of potions you brewed while we were working together, but they're unlabeled. I was wondering if you could help identify them."

"Sure thing." Zoey followed behind Genevieve and gave a little hop.

Ugh. She was way too bubbly for her own good.

As soon as the other witches were out of the room, Fiona turned on me. She crossed her arms and furrowed her brow. What the hell? She'd never looked at me like this before.

"What?" I demanded.

"Why were you being so rude to Zoey?" she asked.

"I wasn't!" I insisted.

"You were," Sondra argued.

Okay, maybe I was being a little cold.

Jenna stepped toward the door nervously, like she didn't want to get in the middle of this. "I'm, uh, just going to check on Ronark." She slipped out of the room without so much as another glance my way, leaving me to face Fiona's and Sondra's narrowed gazes.

I let out a huff. "I'm sorry. What do you want me to say?"

"You don't even know Zoey," Sondra said.

"I know she was a vampire," I shot back.

Sondra grabbed my hand. "Let's go talk in private."

I ripped my arm away. "Talk about what? There's nothing to talk about."

Fiona pursed her lips. "Yes, there is."

I gave in and followed the two to their guest room. Theirs was laid out differently than mine, with two twin beds in either corner and a long chest of drawers between them. I fell onto one bed, while they both sat on the other to face me.

"I feel like I'm being interrogated," I grumbled.

"You are," Fiona snapped.

"Jeez. Calm down," I snarled back. "What's your problem?"

"Zoey and I were close for a long time," she said in a harsh tone. "When she changed, it was like losing a sister. You realize vampires are gone, right? Zoey is human again. She's not going to hurt you."

Sondra held her hands up. "Okay, Fiona. You *do* need to calm down. We can have a civil conversation here."

Fiona took a breath but didn't respond.

Sondra turned to me and spoke softly. "Rae, what's going on?"

I sat up straighter in the bed, unsure how to answer that question. "I... I guess when you see someone as a heartless vampire, you can't really unsee it."

"Heartless?" Fiona asked in disbelief. "Did Zoey hurt you?"

"No," I answered immediately. "I just..."

"You just what?" Fiona raised an eyebrow. She was taking this way too personally. Zoey obviously meant a lot to her.

I switched gears. "We don't know how this curse affected people. What if the vampires are still…? I don't know, evil?"

Sondra looked like she was considering my words. She didn't get all defensive like Fiona did. She just sat and listened. "You think the curse could've damaged their souls permanently?"

I hadn't realized that's what I'd been thinking until she put it into words. "Yeah, I guess so. I mean, we don't know for sure, do we? Look at Matias. He's still out to kill anyone who doesn't agree with him. Maybe we should just be cautious."

Sondra shifted on the bed to sit closer to the edge. "I don't think that's the case, Rae. Everything I know about souls says that a soul only leaves a body upon death. Vampires were never truly dead."

"Yeah, but we don't know if this curse was an exception to that rule," I pointed out.

"We've always known the curse affected souls somehow," Sondra said. "It's why witches who changed couldn't use their powers—since witch power is connected to the soul. But I never once believed that vampires had lost their souls completely."

"You can't know that," I pointed out. "It could've damaged them somehow."

"Cool down," Sondra said. "I'm just trying to explain what I believe. I'm not trying to get into a debate."

I shut my mouth and let her talk.

"I've always believed that the vampire curse was powerful enough to overshadow a person's soul. It took their basic instincts and pushed them to the surface, while pushing their humanity down, the empathy and caring that made them human. But I believe they still had a choice in everything they did."

"Which makes them bad," I pointed out. "If vampires were willing to kill people or enslave them, doesn't that make them bad? If they *chose* that, rather than having it forced upon them through a curse?"

"Not all vampires did those things," Sondra responded. "They didn't all join up with the blood slave trade. Some of them never even tasted human blood outside a blood bank. Occasionally, the good would come out."

"I *never* saw that," I told her.

"How hard were you looking?" Sondra spoke softly, like the question wasn't a slap to the face.

"If you truly believe that, then why did you kill them?" I asked.

"We killed the ones who deserved it," Fiona replied, calmly this time.

What if they all deserved it?

"And what happened to them?" I challenged. "The ones you killed?"

"Their souls would've been released from their bodies, and they would reincarnate," Sondra said. "We know their souls were there all along now. Their souls have been restored. Otherwise, Matias wouldn't be able to perform magic."

"So he just gets a free pass?" I asked. "Once he dies, he'll be reincarnated to start his work all over again?"

Sondra shook her head. "We don't know that. With cases like Valkas and Matias, where the person is truly evil, we believe that Synchrony will destroy their souls to keep the balance. But that's not for us to judge."

"Then who *does* judge?" I asked.

"*Synchrony*," Sondra emphasized.

"Who's to say Synchrony isn't asking for our help?" I said.

Fiona shot to her feet, like she couldn't take it anymore. "This is ridiculous, Rae. You're just scared to admit that the vampires ever kept a trace of their humanity, because that would mean you've actually killed somebody!"

Fiona stomped out of the room, leaving me staring at her with my mouth agape. My blood boiled.

I glanced to Sondra. "She stands up to her brother once, and suddenly she's grown a pair of balls?"

Sondra stood, though far less dramatically than Fiona had. "Zoey was our friend. You of all people should know what it's like to get back someone you thought you lost."

With that, she strolled out of the room after Fiona, leaving me to consider her words.

13

Three days passed, and I spent most of it holed up in my room with piles of books I'd dragged out of Genevieve's spell room. Fiona and I hadn't talked, and I'd only spoken to Venn once. He'd made it to Detroit, but it turned out his brother was no longer with the group of vamps he started with. He was still trying to track him down. Jenna and Ronark were getting into more and more arguments, and I had to step in a few times to calm them down. The only thing that seemed to calm Jenna's nerves was an Aspirin and a tall glass of water. The withdrawals were getting worse with each passing day. I kept telling her things would get better, but I didn't know for sure. I just had to hope that was the case.

"This is kind of cool," Jenna said on the fourth night since Venn had left.

I was lying on my stomach on my bed and thumbing through a book on psychic energies. The words on the pages were beginning to blur together. I slammed the book shut and rolled over on the bed, staring up at the ceiling. The mattress shifted under Jenna's weight as she sat up and pulled the book she was reading closer to her.

"Anything useful?" I asked.

She shrugged. "Probably not. This one is all about incantations to control the weather. I just thought it sounded neat."

"Eh." I groaned from where I lay. "Maybe we should take a break."

"Should we get something to eat?" Jenna suggested. "Honestly, I could use another Aspirin."

I wasn't very hungry. I hadn't had much of an appetite these last few days, but my limbs felt a little shaky, and my throat was scratchy. "Yeah. I should probably get something in my stomach."

Jenna and I set our books aside and headed to the kitchen. The house was quiet, but when I entered the room, I found Sondra sitting at the table with a blank sketch pad in front of her. She looked deep in concentration with her pencil to the paper, but she didn't make a stroke. She heard our footsteps approaching and looked up.

"Hey," I said lightly as I headed to the fridge to grab a yogurt, then helped myself to a spoon from the drawer. "I thought everyone had gone to bed."

"Fiona's snoring, and I needed a quiet place to think," Sondra said.

Dishes clinked as Jenna reached into the cupboard for a bowl, then into the next cupboard for a box of cereal.

I took the seat beside Sondra. "How's it been going? Rounding people up, I mean. Teagan said yesterday didn't go too well."

Sondra frowned. "No, it didn't. I went to visit some friends about an hour away, but they refused to help us. They were afraid just associating with me would get the DMR's attention. They basically burned any evidence that they ever practiced magic in the first place."

I frowned. "We need more people, more weapons."

Sondra sighed. "I know. They at least gave me the names of some of their friends who might be able to help—but I think it was just to get me to leave. I've been trying to get ahold of them, but everyone's on high alert these days, especially anyone involved in magic."

Jenna caught my eye. She cocked her head toward the door to let me know she was headed back to her room to eat, then left me and Sondra alone in the dimly-lit kitchen.

The silence left me a little uncomfortable. I took a scoop of yogurt, then turned to Sondra's sketch pad. "What are you drawing?"

She shook her head and set her pencil down. "Nothing."

"Nothing?" I asked in shock.

Sondra dropped her head. "I haven't drawn anything since we've been here."

"But you always have your sketchbook with you. What about the other night around the fire?"

Sondra started fiddling with her pencil. "I was just pretending to draw. I couldn't manage it."

I couldn't wrap my head around it. "But that's your thing."

"It was," she said regrettably.

Her chestnut brown hair fell in front of her face, shielding it from my view. It was like she was trying to hide her pain from me. She sniffled, then pushed her hair back to look at me. When she did, she looked totally fine.

"The truth is, I don't know who I am without magic," she admitted. "I used to draw to make sense of the magic, to remember things from my past lives and sort through all the incantations in my brain, but now... it's like drawing has no purpose."

"Don't say that," I insisted. "You're more than just your magic, Sondra. You haven't even had magic all your life. Who were you before?"

She shrugged, and her lips turned down at the corners. "That's the problem. I don't know. I found myself through magic. It was like a compass guiding me to where I needed to go. Now… I don't know which direction I'm supposed to walk."

"Draw me," I suggested before I realized I'd even come up with the idea.

She furrowed her brow. "What?"

"You said you don't feel like your drawing has purpose. Well, give it purpose. Use me as your inspiration."

"I don't know, Rae." Sondra looked down at her sheet of paper, as if already mapping out the lines of my face on her sketch pad.

"How's this?" I asked, striking a pose with a faraway look.

Sondra looked like she was holding back a smile.

"This?" I threw my head back and bit the tip of my finger, giving her a *come-hither* look.

Sondra chuckled. "Okay, I'll try. Just relax. No sexy poses."

I sat up straight and got comfortable. Sondra shifted in her seat and bit the end of her pencil, studying me.

"You have really good bone structure," she said.

I smiled but held my pose. "Thanks."

"Your eyes are pretty, too."

I fluttered my lashes at her. "You think so?"

She laughed and took my chin to guide my face back where she wanted it. "Sit still."

Silence settled over the kitchen. The only things I heard were the sounds of my own breathing and the scratch of Sondra's pencil moving across the page. I glanced to her every now and then, and she looked deep in thought, like she was lost in another world while she was drawing.

At least an hour passed. Occasionally, she'd sigh, like she wasn't pleased how it was turning out. She held the pad up so I couldn't see the drawing.

Eventually, I broke the silence. "How's it going?"

Sondra chewed her lower lip. "It's getting there. I think maybe we should take a break. I can finish this up later."

"Can I see it?" I asked.

Sondra pulled the sketch pad protectively to her chest. "It's, uh, not done. I'll show you later, once I fix all the shadows and stuff."

"Okay," I said slowly, eyeing her. Sondra wasn't usually so protective of her art. I was starting to worry, but I didn't want to push her, either. I stood. "Goodnight."

"Night."

The bed was cold when I returned to my room, as if reminding me of the days that Venn hadn't been there with me. I thought he'd be back by now. The fact that he wasn't sent a chill through my body.

After changing into pajamas, I curled under the thick comforter and pulled out my phone. I found Venn's number in my contacts and held my breath as the other line rang.

"Hello?"

My breath came out in a puff of relief. I couldn't read Venn's tone, but I was happy to hear his voice.

"Hey, it's me," I said quietly so I didn't bother anyone in adjoining rooms. "Did I wake you?"

"Rae," Venn sighed, like he was relieved as well. "No, you didn't wake me. I couldn't sleep anyway."

"So… how's it going?" I didn't know what else to say. I just wanted to hear his voice and make sure he was all right. "Will you be home soon?"

"I don't know," he admitted sheepishly. "It's taking longer than I thought."

"Do you think Tyson's okay?"

Venn paused for a moment. "I don't know right now. I'm trying to get a private investigator to help, but the process is slow. It might be a few more days before we find anything."

"Maybe you should come home," I suggested. "Let the detective do his job."

Venn sighed. "I can't, Rae. Not until I know for sure."

I wasn't sure what he meant, but I didn't like the way he said that.

"Venn, are you sure you're okay alone?" I asked. My heart ached for him.

"I'm fine," he insisted, but he didn't sound fine. He sounded scared, agitated, and lonely all at once, though I knew he'd never admit it.

"I'm here for you," I told him honestly. "Don't be afraid to ask for help if you need it."

"I know," Venn whispered, like he couldn't find his voice.

After a beat of silence, he perked up. "How has the studying been going? Find anything useful?"

"Some," I admitted. I sat up and pulled one of the books off the nightstand. I opened it to one of the pages I'd bookmarked. "Most of it requires new magic, though. The good news is I've been reading so much that I'm starting to memorize some of these incantations, not that it's much help to us now."

Venn chucked. He knew all too well how much I sucked at remembering spells. I was glad to lighten the mood.

"I know," I said. "Can you believe it?"

"Of course." Venn sounded like he was smiling. "You're amazing."

My heart lifted in my chest. "You, too."

Venn sighed. "I miss you."

"I miss you, too," I whispered back.

Silence settled as I listened to the sound of his breathing.

"It's getting late," he said. "You should get to bed."

"What about you?" I teased. "It's later where you're at."

"I'll try," he told me, but it didn't sound hopeful.

My gut sank. "Are you sure you're okay? You don't sound well."

"I'm just stressed," he admitted, but something told me it was more than that.

I didn't press, but I couldn't help but feel like he was hiding something from me.

14

The next morning, I went upstairs to Genevieve's library. I hadn't been in there since the night I'd come to Genevieve for the dagger. The room was all polished dark wood and endless bookcases along the walls. We'd pretty much exhausted all the spell books downstairs, and I wanted to see if she had anything else we could use. My eyes passed by each spine, reading the titles, but none of them hinted at magic. They were all encyclopedias, textbooks, or books on finance.

"Rae?"

I turned to the door to see Fiona standing there. She held a few loose sheets of paper in her hands.

She took a step into the room. "Is it cool if we talk?"

I sighed. "Sure."

Fiona sat in one of the chairs in front of the fireplace. I took the other one.

"First of all, I wanted to say I'm sorry," she said. "I didn't mean what I said about you. I was just upset how you took meeting Zoey, but I get now where you're coming from."

I relaxed. "I'm sorry, too. I know Zoey is your friend."

I still felt uneasy about her, but I shouldn't have said those things in front of Fiona.

She gave a timid smile. "Thank you. I just don't want to keep fighting. We have bigger problems. If we're going to fight Matias, we need to work together."

It took setting all my pride aside to agree with her, but I knew she was right.

"Friends?" Fiona asked.

"Friends," I agreed. I glanced down to the papers in her hands. "What's that?"

"Research." She handed me the top sheet. "I went online to broaden our search, and I found a list of known artifacts. I don't think we have time to search for any of them, but—"

"Oh my God!" I stopped dead in my tracks when my eyes landed on a sketch of cufflinks in the shape of a lion's head. "I know these artifacts!"

"You do?" Fiona straightened in her seat.

"My old boss from Bloodstone, Devin, wore ones just like these all the time. I always thought it was weird because he wasn't exactly a classy guy. He always wore these dirty button-down shirts. I thought the cufflinks were sentimental or something. But what if they were *magic*?"

Fiona's eyes lit up. "Do you think he'd sell them to us?"

"For the right price? Absolutely. Devin's all about the cash." I looked back down at the printed web page. "What exactly do these cufflinks do?"

"They enhance your strength," Fiona answered.

"So we could actually stand up to any shifters Matias is recruiting," I said thoughtfully. "Now Devin's stupid can-crushing trick he always did makes sense. I always suspected he might have some shifter blood in him or something."

"Can-crushing trick?" Fiona asked.

"It was this stupid thing. The guy drank soda like it was candy. Whenever he'd finish a can, he'd crush it against his forehead and toss it out. Some stupid thing about asserting his dominance."

Fiona chuckled. "He sounds like a prick."

"A total prick," I agreed.

The room went silent for a few moments before Fiona changed the subject. "There's another reason I wanted to talk to you. I'm worried about Venn."

"Me too," I admitted. "I wish he would've let someone go with him."

"Have you talked to him lately?"

I nodded. "Last night. He still hasn't tracked Tyson down. He says he's doing fine, but I'm not sure I believe him."

"Maybe he's just—"

My phone began to buzz in my pocket. I shot out of my chair so fast that I nearly knocked it over. The name on the screen sent a shot of adrenaline coursing through my veins.

"Venn?" I asked desperately when I answered.

"Rae." Venn sounded relieved, but there was also a heavy sadness in his tone.

"Venn, what's wrong?"

"I just… wanted to hear your voice." His tone was low, so broken. I'd never heard him sound so down before.

"I'm here. What's going on?" The phone shook in my hands as a worry beyond anything I'd ever felt for him tore through me.

"I'll tell you when I get back."

"Tell me what? Venn!"

"I just wanted you to know I'll be home tonight," he said.

"Did you find Tyson?" My whole body was shaking now. Somehow, I already knew the answer.

"I have to go. I love you."

"I love you, too." Tears rose to my eyes.

The line went dead.

Fiona rose so slowly from her chair that I didn't hear her approach. "What happened? Is everything okay?"

I shook my head. "I don't think so."

My mind raced through all the possible scenarios Venn could've gone through the past few days. I couldn't read or talk about artifacts. I couldn't even eat. I sat at the kitchen window for hours, staring out over the front lawn even though I knew Venn wouldn't be back yet. People passed through the kitchen every now and then, but if they said anything, I didn't hear them. Jenna sat beside me the whole time, but she didn't talk. She just stayed for emotional support.

It felt like I'd been sitting there for days. The sun had fallen low in the sky when a pair of headlights finally pulled into the driveway.

I shot out of my chair and raced out the front door. Fiona was passing through the hall just then, and she quickly followed behind me. I heard Jenna's footsteps as well.

"Venn!" I cried as he stepped out of the vehicle.

Venn looked like hell. There were bruises across his face, and the skin on his lip was broken open, as if he'd been in a fist fight. His eyes looked hollow, like he hadn't slept in days. He looked at me, but it felt as if he was looking *through* me.

"Venn!" I threw my arms around him and stood on my toes to kiss him.

He kissed me back, but the kiss was cold, unfeeling.

I drew away from him, my eyebrows knitted. It was at that moment that I realized my worst-case scenario was real. Tyson wasn't with him.

"Your brother...?" I whispered. My eyes darted between his, trying to find the emotion. But it wasn't there. Venn was just... numb. It was like he'd totally given up.

"He's dead," he whispered so softly that I barely heard him. But the words were like a knife through my gut. I didn't even know Tyson, and I felt for him. It was only a fraction of what Venn must've been feeling, but it was enough to make it feel as if a hole had opened up in my chest. Venn had lost him... for good.

I wanted to help him, to heal him of the pain I knew he was feeling, but I knew nothing could fix this. I drew him into a tight hug, because that was all I could do in the heartbreaking moment. I couldn't bring his brother back, but I could at least show him I was here for him.

I was vaguely aware of several other arms wrapping around us. They weren't just Fiona's and Jenna's, either. Sondra, Teagan, and Ryland had followed us out of the house, and I hadn't even noticed. They all joined in on the hug, cocooning Venn in a safe embrace.

It was then that the tears began to fall from his cheeks. He curled into me, his face pressed into my shoulder. All the emotions he'd held back came out all at once like a broken floodgate. His shoulders shook, and sobs echoed in my ears, but it was like I was seeing the whole thing in slow motion—like the scene was playing far away.

"We're here for you, Venn," I whispered.

"Always," Sondra assured him.

Venn's breath shook against my neck. "I love you all."

"We love you, too," Fiona said.

"With all our hearts," Teagan added.

Ryland looked on the verge of tears. I'd never seen him like that before, but it was clear he cared for Venn's well-being. "Whatever you need, man. We've got your back."

Venn didn't want to talk about what happened to him in Detroit. Fiona had asked him what happened to his face—where the bruises had come from—but he just went silent, like he hadn't heard her. I was dying to know as well, but the more I pushed it, the more he would pull away. I knew it because I'd been in similar places, too.

It was painful not to ask him what was wrong. I wanted to help. But I decided to let him come to me at his own pace. I helped him into a warm bath and gave him a healing potion. Hours later, we were snuggled up in bed together, but he still wasn't talking. It hurt a little that he didn't want to confide in me.

At his own pace, I kept telling myself.

All I could do right now was hold on to Venn. He curled up on the bed with his knees to his chest, while I wrapped an arm around him from behind. At some point, I must've drifted off, because I woke up a few hours later to find the bed beside me empty and cold.

I shot upright and glanced around the room, my heart racing. Where was Venn?

I kicked the covers off myself and raced out into the hallway. My pounding heart began to slow as I heard the sound of his voice coming from the room beside ours.

"You should've seen the vamp," he was saying. "Twice the size of Ryland, and Teagan took him out with one strike."

The door was open a crack, so I pushed it wider. Ronark and Jenna were sitting on the bed laughing at Venn's story, and Venn was sitting in a chair in the corner, looking relaxed. I hadn't seen any of them look this chill since we left the island, not even the night we went star-tipping. What was going on?

The floor creaked under my weight, and three sets of eyes darted toward me. I swung the door open wider and stepped inside.

"What's going on?" I asked.

Their laughter died the second I stepped into the room. Ronark shifted on the bed, looking guilty about something.

"Nothing," Jenna said, though she shot a glance I couldn't read in Venn's direction. "Venn's just telling stories."

I sat beside her on the bed, feeling a little hurt that he was willing to talk to them and not to me. "Mind if I join you? I don't think I've heard this one yet."

Venn dropped his gaze. "It's a long story. And it's really late. I was going to head back soon anyway."

"Oh, okay," I said flatly.

Suddenly, I was twelve years old again, trying to hang out with my sister and her friends at their sleepovers, only to be told I was "too young." Except this time, it was worse, because it was my boyfriend pushing me away.

"Am I missing something?" My cheeks heated as I glanced between each of them. They all stared back blankly, like they were trying to hide their true feelings.

"No," Ronark said. "Nothing at all."

Ronark sounded genuine, but he was a hard guy to read.

You're just being paranoid, I told myself. If something was actually going on, Venn and Jenna would let me in on it.

"Well, we should probably get back to bed, then," I said.

Venn stood and shot Jenna and Ronark a frown. "Rae's right. I'll see you guys later."

Back in our room, I asked, "What was all that about?"

Venn shrugged as he crawled into bed beside me. He kept his back to me so I couldn't see his face. "I couldn't sleep, and I heard them up. They helped me relax."

"Did you tell them about Detroit?"

"No," he replied honestly, but something still didn't sit right with me.

"I don't like being lied to, Venn."

"I'm not lying," he insisted. "I'm not ready to talk about it yet."

"Okay. I just wanted to make sure we're clear on that."

Venn rolled over to look me in the eyes. "There are things you don't know, Rae, but it's not because I don't want you to know them. I'll tell you when I'm ready."

He took my hand and kissed it. It was all he was going to give me, and it wouldn't be fair of me to ask for more.

"Okay," I said. "I'll be ready whenever you are."

Except, I didn't know if he'd ever be ready.

15

VENN ~ FIVE DAYS AGO

Four years had passed since the night I lost my brother. Four years since I promised him I wouldn't go after him. And I was finally saying screw it to that promise.

The vampire curse was broken. My brother was human again. Whatever promise I'd made that night was under the assumption that he'd remain a vampire forever. Now, everything had changed.

I'd been thinking about it since the night the curse was broken, but I hadn't planned to mention it to Rae until we'd had a chance to rest. She'd just killed the most powerful vampire in the world. She deserved a moment to breathe before I told her I was running off on my own.

I knew she'd fight to go with me, but I couldn't let her. I had no idea how dangerous it might be, and I didn't want to put her in more danger than she already was.

But more than that, I had to make amends with my brother. Alone.

The fact was, I was still ashamed. I still blamed myself. The closer I got to my brother, the more questions she would ask. And eventually, I would break. I would tell her how I walked away from him that night, how terrible of a person I was. She wouldn't want to be with me anymore, not once she knew that I could walk away from someone I loved so easily. But if I fixed this with my brother, if I did it on my own without her help, maybe she'd see that I had changed—that I could love just as hard as if I had stayed.

Truth be told, I didn't know where to start. I'd spent years in the vampire crowd. After Tyson had changed, I ran away—for good, just like he wanted. Scared and with nowhere to go, I had no choice but to follow the vampire who had found me scouring dumpsters for scraps of food. Maliya had promised me a

496

warm bed and fresh meals, as long as I pledged myself to her. Years, and never a single mention of a Tyson Michaels.

So I turned to the one guy I could, someone who knew more about the vampire community than I ever did. Cory Reid, a gorilla shifter I knew from high school. He fell into the vampire crowd long before Tyson ever changed. He was the only guy I thought might know how to find him—the only one who would help me, anyway.

It took a while to track Cory down, considering we hadn't spoken in years.

"Venn?" he'd asked in surprise when I'd finally got ahold of him. "Venn Michaels? It's been forever. How are you, man?"

"Not great," I admitted. "You remember my brother, Tyson?"

"Your sidekick? Sure I do. How is he?"

"That's what I'm calling you about," I admitted. "I need to find him."

"Oh." Cory's voice flattened. "He changed, didn't he?"

I didn't like that word. *Changed.*

"Yeah," I said, my throat going dry. It wasn't from the withdrawals, either, but damn it, that was getting to me, too.

I'd been fed on while on Gregor Island, which sent all the cravings rushing back. I'd spent the last two years, all my time with Sondra, trying to get over that. I didn't want to have to go through it again… so I'd ignore it as long as I could.

I didn't know how he did it or who he had to talk to, but Cory managed to track Tyson down to Detroit.

The drive was brutal. Eight hours alone in the car. It gave me way too much time to think. What would it be like to see his face again? Would he be happy to see me?

A horrifying thought kept pushing its way in. Or would he hate me for breaking my promise?

I won't know until I get there, I kept telling myself.

I got more than I bargained for when I arrived. Cory warned me to be careful, that the group my brother had fallen into was ruthless. It sounded a lot like Maliya's nest.

I decided to scope the place out, see what I was up against. The address Cory gave me led me to an old warehouse. I parked the car several blocks away.

Night had fallen, and I slipped through the shadows and tiptoed to a back door I hadn't seen anyone use. Inside, I navigated endless hallways, following the sound of voices until I came to a huge room with a tall ceiling. It was practically the size of a football field, with endless rows of shelving.

"What is this?" a male voice snarled.

I peeked around a dark aisle to see a group of a dozen men in an adjoining room. They were gathered around a small table beneath a dim light. Tyson was nowhere in sight.

The guy in charge threw a bag of white powder to the guy across the table from him. "I asked for a *strong* batch of chrysanthemum, not this weak ass shit."

The blood drained from my face. Chrysanthemum? It wasn't just a beautiful flower. It was a slang term for a type of drug made with magic. Everyone who knew anything about magic knew that all the magical drugs were named after flowers. Cory hadn't told me my brother was involved in a magical drug cartel. My pulse quickened. This was definitely dangerous.

"The price of this stuff has gone up tenfold in the last week," the boss snarled. "Supply is down, and demand is higher than ever. But we need the best if we want to charge these kinds of prices. Tell your sorry excuse for a witch that we won't accept such a disgusting insult."

"Yes, Maverick, sir," the man replied in a shaky tone.

"Don't come back without the quality we expect," Maverick spat. "You don't get another shot at this, kid. Don't screw it up."

The guy huffed and left the room. I sank back into the shadows, only to back into something solid. My heart pounding, I turned and looked up to what I'd run into. A pair of blue eyes stared back at me from several inches above my head. Thick biceps twice the size of mine crossed over the man's chest.

I had only a split second to make a decision. It momentarily crossed my mind that without my shifter magic, I stood no chance against this guy. Before I knew it, my feet were moving under me, and I was making a run for it.

"Hey!" he barked. His footsteps echoed through the warehouse behind me.

Suddenly, a dozen voices were screaming and shouting as I raced toward the nearest door. I was almost there—

Arms tangled around my legs as I went crashing to the ground. I rolled over and caught a glimpse of the guy's face a split second before I slammed my foot into his nose. Blood spurted everywhere, but it only made him smirk.

"Big mistake," he said in a deep voice.

His fist connected with my face, and everything went dark.

I didn't know how much time had passed. All I knew was that my head hurt like hell when I came to. A dark room came into focus, and I noticed three figures standing in front of me, though I couldn't make out their faces past the blinding light shining in my face.

I tried to lift my hand to shade my eyes, but I couldn't move them. They'd been tied behind my back. My throat burned with more thirst than ever. Had these guys still been cursed, I might've begged for a hit.

I hated myself just for considering it.

The guy in the middle stepped forward until he was beneath the light. *Maverick.*

"Well, well, well, what do we have here?" He clicked his tongue and narrowed his eyes. "Do I know you?"

"No," I answered quickly, but I wasn't sure that was the right answer.

"He looks a little like Michaels," one if his cronies pointed out.

"Michaels?" Maverick spat. "You better start making sense, Cal."

"The little vampire shifter you recruited a few years ago," Cal clarified.

Every muscle in my body tensed. Tyson!

"Remember the coyote Remy used to pick fights with just to watch him squirm?" Cal glanced to the big dude who'd knocked me out—Remy, I assumed. Remy and Cal both chuckled, but they stopped dead when Maverick turned to glare at him.

"We don't talk of traitors around here!" Maverick snapped. "That kid left us for Diego's gang across town. Took our trade secrets with him, too. If I ever see that son of a bitch again, so help me I will slit his throat myself."

I tried not to let my surprise show. I came all this way, and Tyson wasn't even here? If he had truly betrayed them, they'd kill me just for being associated with him.

"Don't ever bring up that traitor's ass again," Maverick snarled, glaring between the two of his cronies.

"Look," I said, forcing my voice to stay calm. I was anything but calm. My strength was near non-existent, so there was no way I was getting myself out of these ropes without talking my way out.

"I don't know any Michaels," I lied. "I got your name from a friend. I'm here to buy some flowers."

Maverick turned back to me with a smirk. "Is that so? We don't tend to do business with people who *sneak* around our warehouse."

"Could be one of Diego's spies," Cal suggested.

Maverick's face lit up, like he approved of the suggestion.

"What should we do with him?" Remy asked, cracking his knuckles. "Send Diego a message?"

"No, I'm not Diego's," I said quickly. "I've never even heard of him. Honestly. I'm from out of town. I just need something to get me by while I'm here."

"Maybe we should—" Cal started, but Maverick cut him off.

"We don't want to be turning away good business, boys." Maverick leaned so close to me that I could feel his breath on my face. "Who sent you?"

I hesitated. I could give them Cory's name, but I didn't want to get him into trouble with these guys. The only other name I could think of was a guy Cory had mentioned he worked with. I jumped on it.

"Brent from Chicago," I lied.

Maverick relaxed, then scoffed. "Brent from Chicago. I should've known. Show us the money, kid."

"In my wallet." I lifted my hip the best I could and nodded toward my back pocket. I'd visited the bank before I left Nocton and pulled most everything out of my account for this. I was grateful I'd left some of it in the car. These guys wouldn't hesitate to clean house; then I'd be left without anything to get back home on.

Remy snatched my wallet out of my pocket and flipped it open. He pulled the bills out and tossed the wallet back to me without digging through the rest of it. The wallet bounced off my stomach and landed several feet away on the concrete floor. Remy handed Maverick a wad of cash. Maverick flipped through it with a satisfied smirk on his face. There was at least a few hundred dollars there.

"Let him go, Remy," Maverick ordered.

Remy drew a blade from his hip and cut the rope restraining me. I quickly grabbed my wallet, then followed behind Maverick as he cocked his head toward the door.

"What exactly is it you're looking for, kid?" Maverick asked as we started down a dark hallway.

I said the first thing that came to mind. "Magnolia."

"A great choice," Maverick said. "One of my favorites. Have a seat."

Maverick gestured to an open doorway leading to the room I'd seen him in before, though we came in on the other side. I took a seat at the end of the table. My hands shook as I waited, but I forced them to remain steady. All I had to do was get out of here with my limbs intact.

Maverick sat across from me. Remy and Cal stood behind my chair with their arms folded in front of themselves, like they were standing guard.

"Tell you what, kid." Maverick laid my money out on the table, then leaned back in his chair. "What you've got right here will buy you an eight ball of magnolia."

"That's it?" I balked before I could stop myself. In Nocton, that amount of cash would buy at least three times that.

Maverick shrugged. "Prices have gone up. You're not going to find a better deal in these parts. Are you going to take it or leave it?"

I heard the threatening sound of Remy's knuckles cracking. I didn't want the drugs, but I knew that if I didn't accept their offer, I'd be walking out of here with nothing in my pockets. At least if I took it, I could resell it and get my money back.

"I'll take it," I said, wanting nothing more than to get out of there.

Maverick smirked and pulled a small baggie filled with a light pink powder out of his jacket pocket. He set it on the table between us, then scooped up my cash. "It's been a pleasure doing business with you."

I grabbed the bag of magnolia and started for the door. Remy and Cal followed behind to escort me out.

"Oh," Maverick said before we got far. "And tell that son of a bitch Brent he knows the drill. He better not screw up next time."

A shiver ran down my spine. I hadn't meant to get anyone else in trouble. "Yes, sir."

I increased my pace as soon as I left the building. The door clanged shut behind me. I kept throwing quick glances over my shoulder to make sure I wasn't being followed. These weren't the kind of guys I wanted to mess with. I reached into my pocket and clung tightly to my keys, just in case some bastard jumped out of the shadows.

I breathed a sigh of relief when I made it back to the car in one piece. I quickly climbed inside and hightailed it out of there as fast as I could. Every muscle in my body tightened and remained on high alert.

"Stupid, stupid!" I screamed to the silence, slamming my hand against the steering wheel. How could Tyson have been so stupid to join up in a drug cartel? And how could I have gone in there so unprepared, with no weapon or anything?

On second thought, a weapon would've only made things worse. They would've found it and never bought my story.

All that mattered was that I was out of there. I had a general idea of where Tyson was, and I was one step closer to finding him.

It took one call to Cory, and I already had the details of where to find Diego and his men.

"Bro, I'm sorry," Cory had said. "You gonna bust up Diego's on your own, too?"

"That's the plan," I told him. All I needed was to get a glimpse of Tyson. Once I knew for sure he was there, I'd find a way to get him out.

"Man, you're crazy," Cory had said.

I approached a two-story home the next day. It wasn't much smaller than ours back in Nocton—the one that burnt down. I knocked on the door.

Silence.

I glanced up and down the street. It was quiet... and a little eerie. I already had a bad feeling about this. The door popped open a crack.

"Yeah?" A guy at least ten years older than me peeked out through the door.

I hesitated a moment. He had an angry look in his eyes that made me want to run. But I stood my ground.

"What the hell do you want?" he snapped.

"I need a fix," I lied. "Just one. I'll pay whatever you want."

His lips tightened. "Who gave you this address?"

I huffed, playing my part. "I dunno, man. He never said his name."

I tried to peek past him and into the house, but he took up the whole doorway. *Come on, Tyson. Hear my voice.*

"You ain't gettin' anything without a name," he growled.

"Okay," I caved, quickly modifying my story in my head. "Truth is, I don't remember. It was Ty... Ty-something. He didn't give me the address. I followed him."

The guy scoffed. "Ain't no one by that name here. Get lost."

"Wait!" A hand shot out to grab the door before the guy could swing it all the way shut. The door swung open to reveal another man in a tattered white shirt and scruffy beard. "You talking about Tyson?"

Hope surged in my chest. He recognized his name!

I played it cool and shrugged. "Could be. Don't know for sure. Bring him out here and I'll let you know."

"You kind of look like him," he said thoughtfully. "You some sort of relation?"

I hesitated.

The man swung the screen door open so hard that it nearly slammed into my face. I jumped backward, but his hands were already on me, fisting into my shirt. He shoved me up against the porch's support pillar. His rotten breath rushed across the side of my face.

"I asked you a question," he spat.

I shoved him off of me and ducked beneath his arm. "Get off me!"

"Diego!" one of the men called.

Diego kept a firm hold on my shirt as I tried to struggle out of his reach. My foot slipped on the top step, and we went tumbling down to the sidewalk together. He landed on top of me, then drew his fist back and slammed into the side of my face. At least six people had flooded out of the house to watch. Their cheers filled the otherwise quiet street.

"What the fuck, man?" I screamed. I shoved him off of me, but I didn't punch him like I wanted to, not if it meant they'd hurt Tyson because of me.

He stumbled back, then ran for me again when I righted myself. His fist clipped my jaw.

I held my hands up. "Whoa—"

He took another swing at me, but I dodged around it. His fists tangled in my shirt again. I ducked and slipped out of my shirt. He looked at me with fury in his eyes.

"No one comes 'round here like this!" he screamed. "You hear me? You're looking for Tyson? That asshole sold us bad secrets! You want to find him? Join him in hell."

He lunged at me again, and this time, I fought back. My fists slammed into his gut, but it couldn't have felt any worse than the gaping hole opening up in mine. Tyson wasn't here.

Good God, brother. What had you done?

The men on the porch quickly came to the aid of their friend. Suddenly, fists were flying at me from all angles. I aimed my foot at one of the men, and he went stumbling backward, then I swung my elbow out to connect with another guy's nose.

But there were too many of them. Their hands were all over me, dragging me to the ground until I couldn't stay upright anymore. Their feet slammed into my ribs, my legs, my face—anything they could reach. Pain radiated all across my muscles. I tried to block their blows, but they just kept coming.

Get to your feet! A voice sounded through my head. I tried to do as the voice said, but each time, I was just knocked down again.

Get up! You're going to die!

That sent a wave of determination through me. I brought my knees to my chest, then kicked them outward. They connected with one guy's abdomen. At the same time, I caught one of the feet aimed at my head, then twisted. The guy stumbled sideways into his friend beside him.

It was just enough to give me an opening. I scrambled to my feet and took off running as fast as I could. Hands reached out to grab me again, but they couldn't hold on.

I raced across the street and jumped into my vehicle, quickly locking the door behind me. The first guy slammed his body against my door, going wild like a rabid dog. I hastily started the car, my heart racing, then shifted into drive and shot out into the street. Two of the men had raced in front of my vehicle, like they could slow it down, but they jumped out of the way when they saw I wasn't screwing around and would run their asses over if I had to.

My heart finally slowed when I returned to my hotel room. I called Rae that night because I missed the sound of her voice. She sounded worried, and I just couldn't bring myself to tell her what had happened. She'd demand I leave, and I couldn't do that until I knew for sure where Tyson was.

I met with a private detective the following day, seeing as I'd run into a dead end. It was going to cost a fortune, but I'd do anything to find my brother. I didn't care about the cost.

After giving the detective everything I could possibly think of, he assured me there was nothing more I could do and suggested I go back to my hotel and get some rest.

That day stretched for an eternity and into the night as I waited to hear back from the detective. The next day, the eternity continued. It felt like the waiting would never end, like I might never know where to find him—like he'd be lost forever.

I tried to drink away my worries that night, but if anything, it made it worse. Time seemed to slow to a crawl, stretching out that eternity even more. It didn't help quench the aching thirst in my throat, either.

Rae called me that night. The sound of her voice was the one ray of sunshine in an otherwise dark set of days.

The next day, the call finally came.

"Did you find him?" I asked the detective hopefully.

"I'd like you to come in," he said.

I didn't know if that was a good or bad sign. I decided to take it as neutral to keep my hopes up. But the second I walked into his office, all hope had vanished. I could see the sorrow and regret in his eyes.

"Please, Mr. Michaels," Detective Olson said, gesturing to the seat beside his desk. "Take a seat."

"It's not good, is it?" I asked, already feeling it in my bones.

Detective Olson sat and shook his head. "I'm afraid not. Your brother... he's dead."

I didn't hear much after that over the ringing in my ears. If I weren't already sitting, I would've surely collapsed.

"When a vampire dies, almost all evidence is wiped away, including DNA evidence," he said. "Most vampire deaths are identified through the IDs left in their clothing, but your brother never applied for one. What I did find..."

Detective Olson turned his computer screen toward me. He hesitated with his finger over the keyboard. "Are you prepared to see what I'm about to show you?"

"Yes," I lied.

My hands shook in my lap as the video began to play. A surveillance video overlooked an alleyway. Tyson's terrified face came into view as he retreated into the narrow space, looking on high alert. He didn't look a day older than the last time I'd seen him. Five men pursued him, looking like they were speaking to him. I recognized the build of the man in the middle.

It was Diego and his men—the ones who'd tried to beat me to death.

"Is that him?" the detective asked.

I couldn't take my eyes off his face. I felt magnetized to the screen. I ran my finger across his moving figure, like I might be able to touch him through time and space.

"Yes," I said, my voice cracking. "That's my brother, Tyson."

Diego raised his arm, aiming a gun straight at Tyson's head. All it took was a blast of light, and my brother was reduced to nothing but a pile of ash.

Detective Olson sighed, then turned the screen back toward himself.

I blinked back the tears, and my hands formed into tight fists. My gut twisted, and I thought I might hurl. I shot to my feet and started for the door.

"Mr. Michaels." Detective Olson stopped me.

I paused with my hand on the doorknob.

"We can get the men who did this," he said.

I hesitated a moment. Hell, yeah, I was going to get these men—but not in the way Detective Olson was talking.

I shook my head. "I didn't come here for revenge. I came for my brother."

And he's gone.

The words echoed in my mind on the way to the car. Once in the driver's seat, I finally let my frustrations out. I slammed my hands against the steering wheel and let out a rage-filled scream. My anger melted into heavy sobs. I couldn't believe he was gone. I didn't *want* to believe it.

I'd never be proud of what I did next.

I waited outside of Diego's house, watching. I called Rae while I waited, because I thought the sound of her voice might help right my unsteady world. But then I saw Diego coming out of his house, and I knew I was going to pursue him. I told her I had to go, and I followed him on foot. I wore my hood up to conceal my features and keep my skin dry from the misting rain.

Diego came to a large park and glanced around before ducking into a thick patch of trees. I figured he was working a drug deal—and he wasn't going to finish it if I had anything to say about it. I quickened my pace and entered the trees behind him.

"You're late—" he started, but he cut off when he saw it was me.

"You murdered my brother, you son of a bitch!" I growled.

I was on him in under a second. He fought back, but I barely felt the pain. I was so pumped up on adrenaline that I felt ten times stronger than normal. Diego managed to get hold of me and shoved me hard into a tree. The back of my head cracked against the trunk. It only fueled me more.

He drew a gun and pointed it at me, but I lunged for him. The gun fell from his grasp as we tumbled to the ground. Over and over, my fist pummeled his face, until he was so swollen and bloody that he was hardly recognizable. I grabbed his gun from the ground and stood, pointing it at him.

He held his hands up in surrender. "Don't shoot! I'll give you anything you want."

You can't give me Tyson.

I could've done it. I was so enraged that I had it in me. But as my finger curled around the trigger, it really hit me. Even if I did this, it wouldn't bring Tyson back. Nothing could.

A moment of hesitation was all it took for me to know that this wasn't who I was. This wasn't what Tyson would've wanted.

I dropped the gun to my side, and Diego breathed a sigh of relief. "Consider yourself spared," I snarled. "But know this. The next person you piss off won't be as merciful as I am. Your days are numbered, Diego. Have fun watching your back."

I left the trees fuming, but I was glad I hadn't gone through with it. I tossed the gun in the bushes. I couldn't stand to hold on to it.

My hands shook when I returned to the vehicle. I leaned my head against the steering wheel and let the tears flow until they could flow no more. When I finally lifted my head, it was pounding, and there was a large hole widening in my stomach. It felt like I was falling apart, and I didn't know how to hold myself together right now—not without Tyson.

I reached into my pocket to pull out my key, but my hand found the little plastic bag of magnolia. I pulled it out and examined the pink powder. The thirst in my throat never seemed worse than in that moment.

A thought took root, and once it did, I couldn't get it out of my mind.

Maybe this will help me forget.

I already knew how stupid it was, how much I'd regret it later, but I also knew how much everything hurt—and how magnolia would help numb that pain.

Even if it were only temporary.

16

"Fiona found something," I told Genevieve over breakfast the day after Venn returned. "I think Devin has it."

She cocked an eyebrow at me. "Devin, as in the guy who runs Bloodstone?"

I didn't miss the look of disgust on her face. "Yeah, I know. That place is a shithole, but Fiona found an artifact I think he has, and it might help us."

Fiona already had the stack of papers in her lap. She reached across the table to hand the paper to Genevieve. Genevieve glanced over all the images on the page.

"I recognize the cufflinks," I said. "The website says the owner can increase his strength tenfold just by possessing one of them. We can buy them off him."

Genevieve pressed her lips together. "That sounds useful. Take whoever you want with you. Give Devin whatever price he asks for them."

I gaped at her. "You want me to arrange my own party?"

Genevieve shrugged. "Why not? You're the one who knows him. I guarantee he'll not be interested in doing business with me. He always saw me as a competitor. Was very bitter about it, too."

"If he doesn't like you, is he going to trust your money?" I asked.

She shrugged. "He doesn't have to know it's mine. I'll send you with the cash."

I nearly choked. Genevieve's house was nice, and she and Richard had a lot of cars, but it wasn't like she was living in a castle. If she had the kind of cash lying around that I knew Devin would ask for this sort of thing, she was living well below her means.

"Okay. I want Sondra…" She was always my first pick.

I was about to say Venn, but he still looked a little out of it, and I needed my team at the top of their game. Devin was the kind of guy who would release a poisonous airborne potion if he felt threatened.

"Fiona…" I decided next, because she was eyeing me eagerly, and also because she was the one who'd found out about the cufflinks in the first place.

I glanced around the table, looking for more eager eyes, but Jenna and Ronark were both staring down at their food. Ryland and Teagan shared that look again, the one I was still struggling to read. What was going on with them lately?

"What about you, Tea?" I asked. "Ready to get back out there?"

She froze. "Oh, uh, I—"

"I'll go," Clarita offered.

Amalia looked relieved beside her, like she was glad she didn't have to volunteer.

"Do you know Devin?" I asked Amalia.

She bit her lower lip. "A little. He was my mentor for a few months when he lived in Chicago. A useless mentor, honestly. He doesn't know half as much as he claims."

I knew exactly what she meant. Devin was an idiot.

"Well, it looks like I have my team. Should we get going?"

Fiona stood and bounced on her toes, looking eager. She already had Teagan's knives strapped to her waist. She caught me eyeing them. "Teagan's been teaching me. I've been practicing."

"Good," I said as I stood. "Let's hope we don't need them."

I wrapped my arm around Venn and kissed him on the back of the head. "I love you, babe."

He rubbed my hand. "Love you, too. Stay safe."

"I will," I promised.

<hr>

Bloodstone was hidden in the back of a bakery. When we pulled up outside, it was like stepping back in time to my old life. I hated working here, but it'd paid my rent.

"That's weird," I said, eyeing the front window. The lights were off, and the sign on the door read *Closed*. "Devin was never late for work. It was the one good thing about him."

"Maybe he shut down with the DMR investigations?" Fiona suggested from beside me in the back seat

I shook my head. "He'd still keep the bakery running, even if he got rid of all his magic in the back."

"Unless he was caught," Sondra said thoughtfully.

"There's only one way to find out." Clarita opened the passenger-side door and climbed out of the car. The rest of us followed.

I cupped my hands around my face and peered into the dark shopfront. The case beneath the counter that held donuts and bread was empty. I could see part of the kitchen from this view, but I spotted no movement.

I pushed away from the window. "This is just too weird. It isn't like Devin. He likes money too much to just shut everything down."

"What are you suggesting?" Clarita asked.

"I'm suggesting we investigate," I replied. "Follow me."

I started around the side of the building toward the small parking lot. It was squeezed between the bakery and a coffee shop next door and fit only eight cars.

"Breaking and entering?" Fiona hissed.

"It's not breaking and entering if you have a key," I said with a smirk.

Devin always left a spare beneath a pile of landscaping rocks near the side door in case he ever got locked out. I'd told him it was a good way to lose the key, but when he challenged me to find a better place for it, I couldn't.

I glanced around the street, like I might see Devin's little red sports car, but I didn't know why I bothered. He always parked it around the block to save the other parking spaces for patrons.

I found the key where I expected and unlocked the door. The hall was dark and looked ominous. I held a finger to my lips to signal everyone to be quiet. I tiptoed inside, remaining on high alert the whole time. The hall smelled mostly like a mixture of herbs, but there was also the slight hint of decay in the air. Was Devin dealing with another mouse infestation? I'd told him last time that if he didn't deal with that quick, the inspector was going to shut him down and both the bakery *and* Bloodstone would be out of business.

"Devin?" I called down the hall.

No answer.

"Devin, it's Rachel. You around?"

I was met with only silence.

I reached the door to Bloodstone. It wasn't anything fancy, just a backroom where we kept crystals, herbs, charms, and other magical objects. Devin had torn down the wall between two rooms so that Bloodstone was almost as big as the front of the bakery and looked like a shop of its own.

The door was left open a crack. All I could see was a sliver of red carpet and the dark black display cases along one wall. My hands shook as I reached for the door and pushed it open.

I leapt backward in horror at what I saw. My hand slapped over my mouth to keep from spewing my breakfast all over the floor. Three equally horrified gasps came from behind me.

Devin's body lay sprawled across the floor in a pool of his own blood. A hole larger than my fist went straight through his chest and to the carpet below, as if something had burned through it. His eyes were clouded over and stared lifelessly toward the ceiling. His round face was so pale that he barely looked like himself, but there was no denying his signature buzzed hair, thin beard, and slight pot-belly.

"What happened here?" Fiona asked breathlessly.

I finally found my feet and took a step into the room, being careful to avoid getting too close. I shook my head. "I have no idea. Devin worked with some shady people, but he was smart enough to never piss them off."

Clarita knelt close to the body to inspect the wound.

"Are you thinking what I'm thinking?" Sondra asked her.

Clarita didn't take her eyes off Devin's chest. "If you're thinking this was done with magic, then yes."

Fiona furrowed her brow. "There's no way he's been here long, so this couldn't be just any magic. An artifact, maybe?"

Sondra pressed her lips together. "It would have to be a very powerful one."

I looked around the room. Everything was in its proper place. Even the cash register at the counter hadn't been disturbed.

"What do you think they wanted from him?" I asked.

Fiona walked around the room, inspecting it for clues. "You knew him. Maybe someone had a grudge against him."

I shook my head. "I don't think so. He was an asshole, but not enough to get him killed. The only thing I can think of is they wanted something from him, something magical. But in that case, why not take the rest of this—the potions and everything?"

I thought back through the days of running inventory and tried to think back to the most powerful thing he sold. Devin never did sell anything you couldn't find in any other underground shop. Mostly herbs, spells, and charms. They were harmless on their own.

I stared down at the body, and my eyes caught something on his wrist. *The cufflinks.*

I knelt beside Clarita, who was still looking him over for clues. "Look. He still has the cufflinks. If someone killed him for an artifact, why didn't they take these?"

"Maybe they didn't know they had power," Sondra theorized.

"Or *maybe* it was for revenge," Fiona said again.

I reached out for the cufflinks, but Clarita grabbed my wrist.

"We don't want to tamper with anything," she warned. "We don't have magic. We won't be able to cover it up."

"This is what we came here for," I reminded her. "Who's going to notice them missing?"

Sondra looked conflicted, then finally dropped her shoulders. "Rae's right. We're preparing for a war. We don't have the luxury of leaving here without our arms full. We'll take whatever we can get."

"Fair enough," Clarita said. "But we have to be careful."

"There are plastic bags behind the counter." I pointed. "Fit whatever you can in them."

Clarita was careful not to touch anything but the plastic bags. She turned the first one inside-out and used it as a sort of glove to gather potion vials so she wouldn't leave any fingerprints behind. Sondra and Fiona followed her lead.

"Make sure to get those clear potions in the corner," I told them. "They're healing potions. And those yellow ones? They enhance the senses. We might want some of those."

I pulled the cufflinks off Devin's wrists, but as I drew away, my hand brushed by something cold. The phone in his pocket shifted and fell out another inch.

An idea suddenly hit me, and I was too curious not to investigate. I didn't care if I got my fingerprints all over everything. I had to know what happened here.

I pulled Devin's phone from his pocket. The screen came on when I touched it, but the battery was only at seven percent. It prompted me to enter a PIN. I held my breath and tried the one I'd seen Devin enter a thousand times before —5262.

To my relief, the screen unlocked. Devin was so predictable.

It opened up to the camera right away. I was about to go to the home screen and check his messages when a circle in the corner caught my eye, where the phone showed the last picture taken. It was blurry, like it'd been taken in motion.

I clicked on it, and a video started playing.

"Thank you for the offer, but I'm going to have to decline," Devin's voice came through the speaker. The screen went dark, like Devin had been hiding the phone while he recorded.

Clarita gasped from behind me. "What are you doing?"

She rushed over to me, but I hit pause and pulled the phone away from her.

"I think this might give us a clue to what happened," I said.

"I said not to touch anything," she hissed.

I shrugged. "Too late. Do you want to know what happened, or not?"

Clarita couldn't hide her curiosity.

"I want to know," Fiona said, coming up behind me.

I looked up at Sondra. "And you?"

"Yeah," she admitted. "I do."

The three gathered around me, and I hit play on the screen again. Another voice came over the speaker, lower than Devin's and slightly familiar.

"You owe me, Devin," the man snarled.

My heart started to pound violently in my chest. That couldn't be who I thought it was, could it?

"We settled that debt a long time ago," Devin shot back. "Look, I have a teenage daughter. I can't leave her now."

"Does she have magic?" the other man asked coolly.

Devin hesitated. "She… Lana's practicing."

"Then bring her."

My face paled. I didn't look up to see how the others reacted, but they must've been thinking the same thing I was.

Matias Vayne.

"No," Devin objected. "I won't get her involved in this."

"She's been involved since the day I gave you that loan," Matias growled back at him.

It was clear as day. It was definitely Matias. What was he doing in Nocton, trying to recruit Devin of all people? Was he that desperate for allies?

"I paid you back!" Devin shouted. "I don't owe you anything."

"Then come because you want to," Matias pressed. "You never could resist a good magic trick. Come join the greatest one of all."

"I told you," Devin said. "My daughter… she's still in school, and—"

Matias's tone turned hostile. "If you don't join me, you will die. Only the best can survive in the new world I'm creating."

A moment passed, then Devin said, "I guess you're just going to have to kill me, then."

Matias chuckled. "With pleasure."

A loud blast sounded through the speaker, then came the *thud* of a falling body. My hand shot over my mouth, and my whole body trembled.

I thought the recording would end there, but it didn't. Matias's voice continued. "It's a real shame. I do hate wasting good magical blood."

The sound of heavy boots followed, then the creaking of hinges as the door swung behind him, then… silence. Nothing but silence.

After several long seconds, I lifted my head and glanced between the three other women with wide eyes.

"Matias," Sondra whispered, like she didn't quite believe it yet.

I was so shocked I could hardly speak. "I-I can't believe he didn't go with him. I would've thought Devin… I forgot about Lana."

Fiona's voice wavered. "Matias isn't screwing around. If people don't take his side, he'll kill them."

Clarita looked deep in thought, but she snapped out of it a moment later and got to her feet. "Let's get out of here."

"Are we just going to leave him?" I asked.

"We don't want anyone to know we've been here," Clarita said. "Let's hope whoever finds him thinks Matias robbed him."

"What about security tapes?" Fiona asked.

"He doesn't use them," I assured her. "He doesn't want that kind of record of the type of business he runs."

Clarita started pulling more items off the shelves. "Rae, wipe your prints off the phone, then come help us fill these bags."

"I'll bring the car around," Sondra said quickly.

I was still trying to wrap my head around it. I knew Matias was bad, but this? It was clear Matias was worse than I initially thought. And it was going to take a hell of a lot more manpower than we had to defeat him.

17

The sound of screams met us when we pulled into Genevieve's driveway. I shot a quick glance at Fiona, who wore the same shocked expression as I did. I kicked my door open before Sondra had shifted into park, then grabbed the dagger out of my boot and raced up the front steps.

"You're being an asshole!" Jenna shouted.

I ran through the kitchen and toward the sound of voices in the living room, where the TV was playing loudly. Three pairs of footsteps followed behind me.

"And you're being a *bitch!*" Ronark snarled back.

"You're both acting like little bitches," Venn snapped. He grabbed for the remote in Ronark's hand, but Ronark pulled back so they were both fighting to take it from the other. Their expressions were hostile, like they'd burst into a shifter fight at any moment of they could.

Ryland shoved himself between them, trying to wrestle the remote out of their hands. "You jackasses are going to hurt each other."

Teagan brought her knees to her chest and screamed, "Everyone just shut up!"

Nobody did. They all just kept shouting obscenities at one another.

"What the hell is going on?" I demanded.

No one even looked my way, as if I weren't there.

"You dirt bag," Venn growled at Ronark. I'd never seen such an angry expression on his face.

"Douche!" Ronark snapped back.

Venn let go of the remote with one hand to slug Ronark in the shoulder. Ronark's eyes blazed with fury, and he yanked back as hard as he could. He wrenched the remote out of Venn's and Ryland's hands and reeled backward

512

onto the couch. The remote went flying out of his grip. He landed on top of Teagan, and his elbow slammed into her cheek.

Teagan screamed. Immediate rage burned in her features. She drew her arm back and punched Ronark in the side of the head. "Dick!"

She went to punch him again, but Ryland got there first. His hands fisted in Ronark's shirt, and he dragged him to his feet. "You're going to pay for that, asshole."

Ronark flinched as Ryland drew his arm back, but Jenna leapt forward. She let out a high-pitched battle cry and jumped on Ryland's arm, practically wrapping her whole body around him.

"Leave him alone!" she screamed.

I was about to jump in and call a stop to this madness, but I suddenly didn't know whose side to take. One second Jenna was cursing at Ronark, and the next she was defending him. All this over the remote? This was so not normal.

Venn tried to peel Jenna off Ryland, all while her legs flailed and she screamed.

"Guys! Guys!" Fiona tried to get their attention, but it was to no avail.

Sondra pushed past us and grabbed Venn and Ryland by the ears.

Venn whirled around and slapped her hand away. "Get off me!"

I returned the knife to my boot, then rushed across the room and scooped up the remote. I hit the power button, and the TV went silent. Everyone froze. All eyes turned to me.

"What. Is. Wrong. With. You?" I demanded.

Ryland looked to Venn, who looked to Ronark, who looked to Jenna.

Teagan was the one who answered. "They're all being a bunch of pricks."

"Yeah, I got that," I snapped. "The question is why."

"Ronark wants to watch the report on the DMR crackdowns, and Jenna wants to watch the ones on Matias," Teagan answered.

"The reports on Matias are more useful to us," Jenna insisted.

"That's not a reason to turn on each other," I said. "For God's sake, you're acting like children. You're supposed to be on the same team."

I looked to each of them to see a guilty expression fall across their faces. My eyes settled on Venn. His eyebrows were tightly knitted together, and his jaw was tightly clenched. He held my gaze for several seconds before huffing and storming out of the room.

What the hell? Venn had never looked at me like that before.

Anger bubbled up inside of me. "Grow up. All of you. Then come help us unload the car. We have shit to talk about."

We unloaded our bags at the dining room table. Genevieve looked completely shocked. "He sold you *all* of this?"

"Not exactly," I said.

Her eyes brightened. "He agreed to help?"

I bit my lower lip. "Uh, no."

Genevieve looked suspicious. "What happened?"

"When we got there…" Sondra took a deep breath and dove into the story of what happened at Bloodstone.

Everyone around the table went speechless. We were all here except Venn, Ronark, and Jenna. Those three were all still salty about what happened earlier —whatever that was—and had gone to hide away in their rooms. I wanted to talk to Venn, but I couldn't get the look he'd given me out of my head. Something told me he wasn't interested in my company right now. Besides, I had plenty of other things to worry about.

Okay, maybe *I* was salty about earlier. Might as well admit it.

"Do you want help cataloging these?" I asked Genevieve after our story finished and people started to disperse.

"That'd be very helpful," she said. "You're familiar with all this?"

"Most of it," I replied. "I worked there long enough. Most of it's labeled, but I can help you determine the potency of the potions and things like that."

Genevieve glanced into one of the bags. "Healing potions?"

"Yes," I said. "They're not nearly as potent as the one you gave Sondra, but they're better than an Aspirin."

"Perfect," she responded. "Fiona, do you mind taking these upstairs with the others?"

"Not at all." Fiona took the bag and left the room.

By now, Genevieve and I were alone in the kitchen. She sat across from me and started going through the bags. "Ooh, a sensory enhancement potion. I definitely want this one."

"I also got these." I took the cufflinks from my pocket and set them on the table between us. "I was thinking Ryland should take one since he's already so strong. It'll give him a bigger boost. And the other one could maybe go to Fiona, since she's—"

"Weak?" Genevieve cocked an eyebrow at me.

"I was going to say fragile." That sounded just as bad. "All I mean is that I care about her. I don't want her getting hurt thinking she can take on someone bigger than herself."

"She's stronger than you think, Rae. She's been doing this a long time."

"I know, but…" I trailed off.

"But what?" Genevieve prodded.

I paused. I shifted in my chair and picked at my nails. "I guess you're right. I underestimate her. I've been known to be a bad judge of character from time to time."

I immediately thought of Zoey.

"That's something you can work on," Genevieve pointed out as she dug through the bags and set things upright on the table.

I gave her a slight smile. "People are wrong about you."

Genevieve chuckled. "Is that so?"

I joined her in organizing the items in front of us. "Everyone makes you out to be scary. I don't think you're scary."

"Darling, you don't know a thing about me." She sounded amused.

"I know you're helping us," I said. "I know you're a very powerful witch. Would someone with a heart as black as they say be capable of what you are?"

She scoffed. "A black heart? Is that what they say about me?"

"No," I replied quickly. "No one's actually ever said that."

Wow. I was totally sticking my foot in my mouth. That was meant to be a compliment.

Genevieve smiled. "I know what people think of me, and they have every reason to think those things. I have a very dark past, Rae. It's only been recently that I've been trying to turn that around."

"Trying?" I couldn't help but fixate on the word.

She started on a new bag, ignoring my eyes on her. "It could take a lifetime or more to make up for what I've done."

I hesitated. I wanted to know what she meant, but I didn't know if I could ask.

"Do you want to know the truth, Rachel?" She could totally sense my curiosity.

"If you're willing to share," I said.

"You're sure? It could very well ruin your perception of me," she warned.

My mouth went dry. How could I resist this information? "I'm sure."

Genevieve leaned toward me and folded her arms across the table. "I lie. I cheat. I steal. Worst of all, I kill."

My body froze, and a chill ran down my spine. My voice shook when I spoke. "We've all done those things, haven't we?"

She shook her head. "I'm not talking about little white lies and petty theft. I'm not talking about killing vampires. I'm talking about human beings. No mercy."

Genevieve was starting to scare me, but a part of me still trusted her.

"I'm sure they deserved it," I said in a shaky tone.

"Did they?" she asked curiously. "I think they did, but who am I to judge?"

"What... what did they do to you?" I asked.

Genevieve got a blank, distant look on her face, as if she was traveling back to a painful past. "Horrible, horrible things. It started with my father, and then my husband."

"Richard?" I asked, unsure what she meant.

"No, not Richard," she said. "My first husband. When magic returned, I turned to dark magic as a means to escape. I tortured people to get to the men who hurt me, Rachel. Innocent people."

I swallowed hard as bile rose to my throat. I wasn't sure I wanted to hear the rest, but she continued anyway.

"I made my father watch as I tortured his new wife and children," she said,

dropping her gaze. "I burned him alive in his own house. And my ex-husband…
well, he suffered a far more painful death. He went mad before his body finally
gave out."

I shuddered at the thought.

Genevieve shook her head, like she was trying to push aside the memories. "I
started mentoring others shortly afterward. I was hard on my mentees. Sometimes I'm shocked they learned anything from me at all."

"Why are you telling me all this?"

"Because it's not a secret, Rachel—not among those who know me, anyway.
Part of healing involves admitting what happened, asking for forgiveness, and
moving on instead of hiding from it."

Her words hung in the air for several moments.

"How did you change?" I finally asked, cutting through the silence.

"Mostly magic," she answered simply.

"Is there, like, a spell for it?"

"No. Not even magic can change a person who doesn't want to change. Not
permanently, anyway. I stopped trying to *force* my magic and started *trusting* my
magic. Suddenly, magic became easier, and I knew it was working."

"Magic isn't that easy," I argued. That's why I preferred killing. Killing was
easier.

"Magic is one of the easiest things in the world," Genevieve replied.
"Attuning yourself to it, on the other hand, is one of the hardest things to do."

"Isn't that the same thing?"

Genevieve didn't get a chance to respond as the sound of footsteps entered
the kitchen.

"Venn!" I shot to my feet eagerly.

He wore a dark hoodie with the hood pulled up over his head. His gaze fixed
on the ground, and he continued through the kitchen like he didn't hear me. He
headed to the refrigerator, pulled out a bottled water, and chugged the whole
thing.

"Venn?" I stepped toward him cautiously.

He wiped water from his lips and looked to me with tight eyebrows.

"Do you want to talk?" I asked softly.

"No," he replied in a clipped tone that stung more than it should've.

"I just want to help," I told him. "I know things are hard right now. You don't
have to tell me everything, but at least—"

"I said I didn't need your help," he snapped. It was so unlike him.

I reached out for him. "Venn, I understand—"

"You don't understand shit!" he roared, swatting my hand away.

I stepped backward as tears rose to my eyes. Why was he shutting me out?

"Then help me understand," I insisted.

"You barely understand magic," he snarled. "How can you understand this?"

My stomach turned hollow as Venn whirled around and stomped out of the
room.

18

I shot a desperate look at Genevieve, like she might be able to explain Venn's erratic behavior. She looked just as shocked as I felt. A split second passed before I rushed out of the room after him.

"Venn!" I called. "Wait."

The door to our guest room slammed behind him. When I tried to open it, the door handle wouldn't twist. What the hell? He'd locked me out!?

"Venn, please," I said through the door. "Let me in."

He didn't respond. Anger swept through me. I got that he was upset, but he didn't have to make it personal.

"Venn!" I screamed.

The door beside me swung open. Jenna stepped out with her hair a mess, looking like she'd just woken from a nap. "What's going on out here?"

"Venn's shutting me out," I told her.

Her expression became more alert. She shifted into big sister mode and pushed me out of the way to bang on the door. "Venn Michaels, you open this door right now, or so help me I will break it down!"

"Jenna, that's not necessary," I said.

She turned to me with a stern expression on her face. "Nobody hurts my Rugrat."

"Thanks, but—"

"Venn!" She pounded on the door again.

"Go away!" he called back.

"You can't shut her out forever!" Jenna snapped.

"Go. Away!" he repeated.

"Venn, please," I begged. "I love you, but this is starting to get out of hand. If I did something wrong, please tell me so I can fix it."

"I told you," he shouted through the door. "You don't understand."

I just about snapped. What made him think I didn't understand trauma? Had he not listened to any of the stories I'd told him?

"Seriously? Seriously!" I yelled at him. "You think I don't know what it's like to lose someone I love?"

"No!" Venn shouted. "You don't. You found your sister. I lost my brother!"

All the blood drained from my face. My knees shook as I absorbed the weight of what he'd just said.

Jenna turned to me. "Rach, he didn't mean it."

I barely heard her. "Venn… Venn resents me?"

"No," she assured me, but I didn't believe it. "He's just going through a lot."

"Then why would he say that?" I snapped. "People don't say things like that unless they mean it."

I turned back to the door and softened my tone. "Venn."

He didn't answer.

"This is hurting our connection," I said. "Remember what you told me on the island? Being soulmates isn't easy. We're not perfect. We just have a strong connection. The connection dies if we don't nurture it."

I was paraphrasing.

Still, he said nothing.

I gave a light knock at the door again, but I was met with nothing but silence. Worry and anger knotted together in my gut, twisting everything around until I thought I might puke.

"Venn!" I shouted. "Jenna wasn't kidding about breaking this door down."

I thought I heard motion behind the door, but I couldn't be sure. I reached for the handle and shook it, but it was still locked. I was ready to knock this door down myself. With all my strength, I kicked at the door, and it gave way.

When I saw Venn, it was like the world was at a standstill yet shifting from side to side all at the same time. I couldn't move or breathe. I only stared.

Venn froze in place as he brought the back of his hand to his nose, where he was about to inhale a pink powder.

The world seemed to move again. Anger flooded through me. So much anger. I didn't even know what to do with myself in that moment. It felt like I was watching myself outside my body as I marched across the room and slapped his hand away from his face. The pink powder rained down to the floor.

"Drugs!?" I exploded. "You're doing *drugs*!"

Venn shot to his feet. His face came only inches from mine. "I told you that you wouldn't understand!"

I threw my hands up. "Congratulations. You were right. I don't understand how you can be doing drugs and didn't even tell me about it. Do I even know you at all? How long has this been going on?"

"Rachel," Jenna tugged at my arm, but my feet remained firmly planted in place.

"I knew you were hiding something from me," I accused, shoving my finger into his chest. "I knew it!"

"Rachel, calm down," Jenna begged. "It's not as bad as you think."

I turned on her. "This shit is dangerous, Jenna!"

"Stop it, Rachel," Jenna said. "Venn's right. You don't get it. You don't know what the withdrawal is like."

I drew in a sharp breath. "*You*! You've been doing this, too? That night you were all *just hanging out*, you were—"

"Yeah," Jenna admitted with gritted teeth. "So what? It helps us deal with it."

"This is not how you deal with it!" I screamed. "It's just one more thing to get addicted to."

"You don't know what it's like to be addicted to a vampire's bite," Jenna argued. "This isn't half as bad as that."

"It's still clearly a problem," I growled back. "You've all been so irritable lately. This is going to ruin relationships. Is that what you want?"

"That's not what—" Venn started, but I cut him off.

"Is. That. What. You. Want?" I repeated.

"Rachel, stop it!" Jenna yelled.

"No, Jenna," I shot back. "Ever since we got off that island, you've changed. What happened to the girl who was all about making the best out of a bad situation?"

"I *am*!" she shouted. "I'm dealing with it. Just because it's not in the way you think I should be doesn't mean I'm not doing something about it. It's going to take time."

I pressed my fingers to my temples. "I can't believe we're seriously having this conversation. I know what it's like to hit rock bottom, but I was *never* stupid enough to turn to drugs to deal with it."

"Really?" Venn asked. "So we're stupid now?"

"No, I just—"

"You just what?" Venn growled. "You just want to control everything. You want life to be a perfect place where you can slay your vampires and save the day and everyone bows down at your feet at the end of it. Is that it?"

"This is what I'm talking about!" I yelled. "This isn't you, Venn!"

"Well, it sure as hell isn't the drugs talking," he snapped.

I was so angry I wanted to stab something. Couldn't he see how reckless this was? How dangerous it could be for him?

"Forget it." I whirled around and stormed out of the room. I didn't know where I was going, but I had to get out of there before I hurt somebody.

Venn's voice followed me down the hall. "So that's it? You're done nurturing that connection?"

"No. That one's on you."

My legs carried me outside to the back yard, where I found Teagan and Fiona flinging knives at a target set up beside the long fence. Sondra and Ryland sat at the firepit close by, though there was no fire in it. They were snacking on potato chips. It was already past lunch. I hadn't eaten, but my stomach twisted just thinking about food.

I stomped over to Teagan and Fiona, fuming. "I need a knife."

Teagan raised her eyebrows. "Who won the fight?"

"You heard that?"

"Not really," Fiona admitted. "Enough to know you and Venn are fighting. Not enough to hear what you said."

Teagan handed me a knife. Before she could demonstrate how to use it, I hurled it at the target. It bounced off and landed in the grass.

"Another," I demanded, and Teagan handed the whole pile over to me.

I vented, accenting each word when the knives left my fingers. "Venn thinks it's *cool* to start doing *drugs* and to share with my *sister* and hide it from *me*. How stupid can he be? Doesn't he know how that shit messes with his body?"

I ran out of knives, and not a single one stuck.

Fiona's eyes widened, and her hand shot over her mouth. "Venn's been doing drugs? How long?"

"I don't know," I said. "Since he came back from Detroit, I guess. Maybe even since we got off the island."

Teagan froze and blinked a few times, like she was trying to absorb it. "I knew he'd been acting strange, but I thought it was from losing his brother."

"Look, I get trying to deal with the pain, but why didn't he come to me?" My anger began to melt into pain. The three of us started toward the target to retrieve the knives. "I know he's been going through withdrawals, too. I can tell by the way he's been acting. But I don't get it. I was fed on more while we were on Gregor Island, and I feel fine now."

"But Venn had been fed on for years," Fiona pointed out. "If a vampire bit him on the island, all of that would come rushing back. He'd have to go through the whole recovery process over again."

"The whole thing?"

"It wouldn't be as bad as last time," Teagan said, "but it'd be worse than what you've experienced."

We all just stood there in silence for several moments, like we were waiting for someone else to say something. Fiona's eyes were beginning to brim with tears.

"Come on," I said.

We returned to our spot in front of the target, and I started throwing the knives again. The first one stuck in the target, and I felt a small surge of victory.

I sighed. "I'm just conflicted. I think he's right that I don't know what he's going through, but he's not even giving me a chance. We're supposed to be a team, and I don't think we can do that when he's hiding things from me."

I bit my lower lip. "The truth is, I'm worried about him."

"I think we need to get you out of here," Sondra suggested. I hadn't even realized she'd come up behind me, or that she'd been listening. "You and Venn both need to cool down, then you can talk once you're both in a better mindset. How does that sound?"

"It sounds great," I said honestly. "But Venn…"

"We'll talk to him," Teagan offered.

"Yeah," Fiona agreed. "You don't have to worry."

"What are we going to do?" I asked Sondra.

"I'm still unable to get ahold of those friends of a friend I was telling you about. I'm starting to worry. I'd like to visit them in person. Are you up for a drive?" Sondra asked.

If this was anything like our last two visits, there was no way I was missing out. I had to burn off some of my energy if I was going to face Venn with a clear head.

"Absolutely."

19

The car ride was under an hour, but it seemed longer. Teagan insisted Ryland come along because she knew he'd only make things worse if he spoke to Venn about the drugs. Ryland agreed because he was *sick of missing out on all the fun.*

"And here I thought you were just scared," I teased.

"Hey," he joked back. "You want a rematch on that arm wrestle?"

"No thanks."

Ryland would crush me.

Genevieve also came along. We thought she'd be able to help us convince these people to join us.

It was late afternoon when we exited the highway. We drove another twenty minutes past endless farm fields. I was starting to think we might be lost, but then Genevieve pulled off the road and down a long country driveway. We stopped at a large house nestled in a small cluster of trees. It was large and looked only a few years old. It had multiple peaks made of different colored bricks and a large porch on the front. It looked like it belonged in some sort of architecture magazine.

"You're sure this is it?" Ryland asked.

"This is the only address listed for Carla and Adrien Bell," Sondra said. "So it better be right."

The air was unusually cool for the end of summer when we stepped out of the car. It was quiet, too, like the family had abandoned the property. I glanced around for signs of a vehicle, but I didn't see any, though that didn't mean no one was around. There was a two-car garage attached to the house.

Sondra knocked on the door.

"Maybe they're not home," I suggested while we waited.

"Or maybe they're just being cautious," Sondra replied.

I glanced to Ryland. Yeah, he'd definitely send off alarm bells. He was kind of scary.

Sondra knocked again. I continued to scan the property. As my eyes roamed over the porch we were standing on, I noticed movement in the nearest window. As soon as I spotted it, the curtains returned to their proper place, as if nothing had been there at all.

"They're home," I whispered lowly.

Sondra frowned, then raised her voice. "Carla and Adrien? We're sorry to drop in like this. I'm friends with Jordan Chase. She gave me your names. I've been trying to get ahold of you for a few days. When I didn't hear back, I wanted to check to make sure you were okay."

The front door opened a crack. A man in his forties peeked out at us. He was dressed casually and had a sort of *dad* vibe going on. The screen door remained closed between us, like it would protect him if we were unfriendly.

"You're Sondra?" he asked.

"Yes," she said kindly. "These are my friends, Genevieve, Rae, and Ryland."

"Adrien." A woman's voice came from behind the door. "Let them in. We need them."

Adrien hesitated, then opened the screen door.

The woman came into view. She looked Adrien's age, with dark blonde hair and a friendly smile. "Any friend of Jordan's is a friend of ours. Please, come in."

We stepped into the house, and the woman extended her hand out to each of us. "I'm Carla, and this is my husband, Adrien."

Greetings traveled around the entryway as we introduced ourselves, then Carla gestured for us to sit in the living room. Their house was filled with warm tones and family pictures, making me feel right at home. Sondra, Genevieve, and I took the couch. Ryland crossed his arms beside us like he was standing guard. Carla and Adrien both took a seat across from us in individual chairs.

"You'll have to forgive us for not getting back to you," Carla said.

"I understand," Sondra said. "None of us can be too careful with the way things are right now. Jordan didn't tell me you had children."

Adrien's face went white, but he quickly recovered when he glanced to where Sondra was looking. A family picture hung above their mantle. In it, Adrien and Carla sat in a pile of autumn leaves with a son and daughter who looked around the ages of five and seven.

Carla folded her hands over her knees. "Yes. Jordan said you might be contacting us, but with the kids, we were just afraid it'd be too much."

"We're glad to see your family is okay," I said. "Sondra was really worried."

"We should've called back," Carla admitted. "Things have just been really stressful around here lately."

I shifted uncomfortably on the couch. The way she said it made me uneasy.

An immediate look of concern crossed Genevieve's face. "Is your family in trouble?"

The couple exchanged a glance.

Adrien leaned forward to rest his elbows on his knees. He glanced down to his hands, like telling the story was difficult. "About a week ago, the Department of Magical Regulation came to our house with a search warrant."

I gasped. "Did they find anything?"

Carla shook her head. "No, thank heavens. But you can understand our caution."

"Of course," Sondra replied. "But you do… practice magic, don't you? Jordan said you did."

Adrien looked to his wife with concern, but he turned back to us with a sigh. "Yes, we do, but we don't profit off any of it. It's more of a hobby. We meet with a group of local witches about once a week, and we use our magic to bring fortune to our lives and others', but that's it. We're not actually sure how the DMR found out about us."

"We think maybe one of our group members exchanged our names for a reduced sentence," Carla theorized. "We haven't heard from most of them since everything changed, so it's impossible to know who."

"Jordan wouldn't," Sondra said with certainty.

"No, of course not," Adrien said. "We trust Jordan with our lives. In fact, she was the one who suggested we get rid of all our evidence before the DMR arrived. She basically saved us."

"The investigation is still ongoing, though," Carla told us. "Look, the reason we're telling you this is because Jordan said you might have an offer for us. She said you could help."

Genevieve sat up straighter. "We actually need *your* help. As Matias has been building an army, we've been building our own. We have over a dozen groups in the local area who have either donated potions or magical objects to help us or who have agreed to help us go up against Matias."

"You intend to get your magic back from him?" Adrien asked with raised eyebrows, like it was impossible.

"Precisely," Genevieve said confidently.

Carla narrowed her eyes, looking skeptical. "How exactly are you going to do that?"

Genevieve held her head up high. "Through any means necessary."

"Yes, but *how*?" Adrien pressed.

"I'm working out those details," Genevieve said confidently.

Carla sighed. "Look, we'd really like to help you, but this sounds dangerous. With the kids… we just can't commit to something like this."

Carla shot Adrien a glance, and he nodded back.

"However, we have something that might be of use to you." Carla stood and unclasped the bracelet on her wrist. "This is the only thing we kept since the DMR crack-downs."

She held it out toward us. Since I was closest, I took it and examined the bracelet. It wasn't anything spectacular, just a silver chain with fake diamonds embedded along it.

"Adrien is a therapist who works with victims of domestic violence," Carla explained. "We were working on designing artifacts that would protect women in these situations. This was our prototype. If the wearer is in danger, it will send a strong blast of air back at their command. It disorients their attacker to help them escape a dangerous situation."

"Are you sure you want to give this to us?" I asked.

Adrien nodded. "If you can defeat Matias and we get our magic back, we'll be able to make hundreds more artifacts just like this one."

"That's very generous of you," Sondra said. "Thank you."

"No," Carla replied. "Thank *you*. What you're doing is very—"

Carla cut off when the sound of tires came from outside. More than one set, too.

Adrien rushed to his feet and raced toward the window. Ryland was at his side in less than a second, and they both peered out past the curtain.

Adrien swore under his breath. "It's the DMR! What are they—?"

"Everybody down!" Ryland shouted.

Before I knew what was happening, Ryland flung himself away from the window. He spread his arms wide and knocked the three of us on the couch to the floor. My head narrowly missed being smashed against the corner of the coffee table. Carla immediately dropped to the floor and covered her head.

A second later, the sound of shattering glass filled the room. Something hard bounced across the floor. Then came a sharp hiss. The room began to fill with visible gas.

"Everybody run!" Adrien shouted.

Carla's face went stark white. "Adrien, the kids!"

Ryland dragged Carla to her feet. "Where are they!?"

I shot to my feet as fast as I could and raced after them down the hall. Gas was starting to fill the house. I could hardly breathe. Carla raced into the kids' room, and Ryland followed close behind. I paused outside the door to make sure the other three were behind us. Sondra and Genevieve stumbled down the hall, covering their faces.

"Adrien!?" I cried. "Where's Adrien?"

He rounded the corner and pushed past the other two to get to the kids. Ryland burst out of the room carrying both of the children. They were each wrapped in a blanket.

Carla grabbed clothes out of the basket near the door and shoved them at the children. "Cover your mouths! Don't breathe it in."

Both children had a look of terror fixed to their faces. The boy had frozen up, while the girl was crying and reaching out for her father.

Adrien leapt into father mode and took his daughter from Ryland's arms, cradling her. "This way!" he shouted.

Just as we all took off down the hall again, the front door burst open. My heart leapt into my throat. I stole a glance toward it as I rounded the corner into the kitchen. All I caught was the sight of men in gas masks and holding guns flooding into the house.

"Everyone on the ground!" one of the soldiers shouted, but we were already moving far back into the house.

My eyes burned, and my lungs felt like they were on fire. Adrien threw open the door to the garage and ushered his wife and Ryland through. I was next, but I paused when I looked behind me to see that Genevieve had stopped to catch her breath beside the kitchen island.

Sondra backtracked to take her hand. "We have to go!"

Genevieve took another deep breath, but she looked a little disoriented. I ran back to her and looped her arm over my shoulder. Whatever gas they'd fired into the house was seriously messing with Genevieve's respiratory system, because she was hacking up a lung.

"Genevieve," I said sternly, "there's no time—"

"ON THE GROUND!" a harsh voice sounded behind us.

Genevieve, Sondra, and I all froze up at once.

"Go," I mouthed to Adrien, who the soldiers couldn't see from the doorway.

Adrien's eyes went wide, but one look at his daughter, and he knew what he had to do. He turned and swung the door shut behind himself.

"I said on the ground!" the soldier demanded.

I twisted my head to see at least a dozen guns pointed in our direction. My heart slammed against my rib cage. I'd never had to go up against guns before.

"This residence is hereby found in violation of DMR regulation three," one of the men said.

"Please," Sondra said as she held her hands up in surrender. "We don't even live here. We're just visiting—"

"Arrest them," another deep voice commanded.

As three men with guns stepped toward us, instinct kicked in. Suddenly, I was back on the streets, surrounded by a group of vampires who'd like nothing more than to suck me dry. No way in hell was I going down without a fight.

Anger and fear rose within me. I could feel the strong emotions sweeping across my body like the tingle I used to get from shifting into raven form. My whole body felt like it was alive with fire, as if for just one moment, my magic had returned. I didn't know exactly what was happening. All I knew was that I had to run.

Arrest this, you asshole!

Boom!

Everything happened so fast. One moment, I could feel the magic from the bracelet tangling with my emotions and offering to save me. The next, the air in front of me exploded, blasting back all the soldiers. Fire shot out of one of their guns, and the deafening sound filled the kitchen.

A split-second passed in which I had to process everything that had just happened. It all sank in in a flash.

"Let's go!" I took Genevieve's arm and dragged her behind me.

She stumbled, like she couldn't quite find her footing. It felt like she was fighting me, but we were in too much of a hurry. I didn't slow.

Sondra, Genevieve, and I ran through the door to the garage to find a minivan waiting there for us.

"Get in!" Ryland shouted from the open side door. He gestured frantically for us.

We stumbled inside and fell across each other in the second row of seats.

"Go!" Ryland yelled to Adrien in the driver's seat. The children sat in the back, huddled up against their mother.

"Everyone hold on," Adrien warned.

He clicked a button above his head, and the door to the garage slowly opened. I didn't even catch a glimpse outside before the door to the house burst open and a soldier in the doorway was pointing a gun at the window.

"Drive!" Ryland shouted.

Adrien didn't wait for the garage door. He slammed his foot against the gas, and we went flying backward. The minivan tore through the door, and Adrien wrenched on the wheel. Six big DMR vans were parked in the driveway, and another line of soldiers were pointing their guns at us.

He shoved the shifter into drive, but hesitated a moment.

"Go!" Carla snapped.

The car jerked as Adrien floored the pedal and swerved around the soldiers. I ducked my head as bullets rained down on us from the back. The children sobbed.

Suddenly, three different vans were following behind us. Adrien shot a glance in the rear-view mirror.

"Faster!" Carla demanded of him. "They must have evidence against us. Otherwise, they wouldn't be here. They aren't going to give us a fair trial. This is our only chance!"

Adrien turned the wheel once again, and the van jolted as we sped over the side of the driveaway and into the field behind their house.

"Let's see how well they keep up with this," Adrien challenged.

I tried to sit up, but we were bouncing around so much that it was hard to stay upright. Beside me, Genevieve was starting to wheeze. I was concerned she might've been allergic to the gas, but when I looked over to her, I saw she was clutching her stomach.

"Oh my God!" I cried.

I didn't see the blood staining her dark dress right away, but then I noticed the liquid seeping around the wound.

"Genevieve's been shot!" I yelled.

I threw my shirt up over my head so that I was only in my bra. I balled it up and shoved it against her abdomen.

Sondra immediately jumped to Genevieve's aid as well.

"It's going to be okay," she said while she tried to get Genevieve in a comfortable position against the seat. She sounded calm, but she had worry written all over her face.

Tears streaked Genevieve's cheeks, and she stared up at the ceiling, like she couldn't quite focus on our faces.

"I'm sorry, Genevieve," I said desperately. "I shouldn't have used the artifact."

"No," she said between labored breaths. "You had to. The DMR would prosecute you, and—"

She gasped in pain as we went over another large bump.

"Stay with us!" Ryland reached over Sondra to help keep Genevieve's head up.

Genevieve groaned.

"No. No!" I screamed. "Genevieve!"

Genevieve kept one hand pressed firmly to her abdomen and lifted the other to take mine. She squeezed it tightly. She looked straight into my eyes and said, "Don't let the DMR get you. You *have* to defeat Matias."

My throat closed up, like invisible hands were trying to choke me. "Don't talk like that."

"You're going to make it," Sondra assured her. "We have those healing potions back home."

Genevieve shook her head and blinked tears away. The strong, determined expression she usually wore had melted away. She looked so frail. My chest felt heavy as I watched her. It felt as if a cinderblock were sitting on it.

"I'm sorry for everything I did," Genevieve whispered to Sondra. "I'm ready for a new start."

"No!" Sondra sobbed. "We need you!"

Genevieve didn't seem to hear her. She turned to me and never took her eyes off mine. She reached into the folds of her dress and placed her phone in my hand. "The passcode is 7427. Matias is coming. Make sure you're ready for him."

Another breath passed through her lungs, then she went still. Her hand went limp in mine, and her eyes glossed over. My stomach had never felt so heavy as I wrapped my arms around Genevieve's lifeless body. It all happened so fast. I could hardly process it.

Genevieve was dead.

20

Hours must've passed, but it felt like seconds just as equally as it felt like days. I couldn't process the time. All I knew was that it had gotten dark out and I hadn't slept yet.

We'd lost the DMR, thank God. I didn't think I could handle those bastards after what happened today. I vaguely remembered Sondra calling Fiona and explaining what had happened.

"You need to pack everything up and get out of there as fast as you can," Sondra instructed. "The DMR has Genevieve's license plate. They could be on their way now."

"Where are we going to go?" I'd heard Fiona ask. "The lake house?"

"No," Sondra said. "The house is in her name. The DMR might suspect that."

"What's going on?" Teagan yelled in the background. "Is Ryland okay?"

"Yes," Fiona said. "Just give me a second."

"Put Sondra on speaker," Teagan barked.

"I'll call Zoey," Sondra said. "In the meantime, get everyone to help you pack the cars. We need all the potions, trinkets, everything. I'll keep you updated. Can you put Richard on the phone?"

I basically didn't process anything after that. All I could do was relive the moment over and over again in my mind. I tried to shut it out—to stop feeling anything at all—but I couldn't. The feel of Genevieve's hand in mine, the look in her eyes as her soul left her body… it would all be seared in my memory forever.

An emptiness akin to the days following my parents' murder tore through me. I'd seen too much death in my lifetime. Now that I'd seen it again, it brought everything else back. It was like a black hole of death had opened up in the pit of my stomach and was trying to swallow me whole.

At some point, we arrived at Zoey' house in Nocton. It was a small one-story ranch-style house with an attached one-car garage. I barely saw the neighborhood as Ryland wrapped me in his arms and guided me to the front door.

I sat with a blanket around my shoulders in the living room, staring at the carpet but not really seeing anything. I wore Ryland's shirt he offered me and still held Genevieve's bloody phone in my trembling hands.

My hands. I tried to pretend those didn't exist, either. Because if I admitted they did, if I felt their existence in any way, I'd have to acknowledge the blood dried onto them.

I didn't really know what was going on other than Richard was dealing with the police and coroner—making up some elaborate lie that would keep the rest of us out of it, I was sure. Carla and Adrien had taken their family to a hotel, but I didn't know what their plans were after that. Would they help us fight Matias? Would they go on the run from the DMR?

I didn't know. Honestly, it didn't seem to matter right now.

"Rae." Zoey stepped into the room with a pile of clothes in her hands.

She gently set the bundle beside me on the couch. I shied away from her, turning to Ryland, who still had his arm around me. It was totally platonic and didn't really help, but I appreciated it nonetheless. Ryland always put up a tough guy front, but I knew he actually cared.

"I brought you a towel and a change of clothes for when you're ready to clean up," Zoey said.

"I'm good," I declined, but it was clearly the biggest lie I'd ever told. Genevieve had just died in my arms. I wasn't going to be *good* for a long time.

"Maybe you should clean up," Ryland encouraged. "Everyone else will be here soon."

I sighed. He was right. Nobody else had to witness the blood on my hands. It would just be cruel to shove the aftermath in their faces.

I looked up to Zoey. "Thank you."

I took the pile of clothes in my hands and stood on shaky feet. The blanket around my shoulders fell away, and cool air rushed across my skin. A chill ran down my spine.

"It's okay," Zoey assured me. "You'll all be safe here. You don't have to worry."

I shot a nod her way, but I couldn't find my tongue to speak. I *never* stopped worrying.

I carried myself to the bathroom and shut the door behind myself. I set the clothes and towel on the counter, along with Genevieve's phone beside mine. I slipped Ryland's massive t-shirt over my head, then stripped down the rest of the way and climbed in the shower.

Warm water rushed over me, but I sank down to the bottom of the tub and curled my knees to my chest. Genevieve's blood dripped off my body and swirled down the drain. I couldn't bear to look at it, so I didn't. I closed my eyes and forced myself to breathe, but it was like I kept forgetting how.

I didn't know how long I sat there, but I finally gave up on trying to breathe when the water started to get cold. I rose to my feet and scrubbed off with the shampoo and soap I found on the lip of the tub.

When I stepped out of the shower, I heard Jenna's voice from the living room, though I couldn't make out what she was saying. Some of the weight in my stomach seemed to ease. I dried off and dressed quickly, shoved Genevieve's phone in my pocket, and then hurried out into the living room.

Teagan sat on the couch next to Ryland, and Fiona sat on her other side. Jenna and Ronark stood and both fidgeted, like they couldn't sit at a time like this. Venn paced around the room, listening to Ryland's long-winded explanation of what had happened. Zoey stood watch next to the small dining room. I didn't know where everyone else was.

Venn's eyes immediately connected with mine. He rushed forward and scooped me up in his arms. I buried my face in his shoulder, as if our fight from earlier had never happened. He set my feet back on the ground and took my face in his hands. A split second later, his lips were on mine. I melted into him.

He drew away to look me in the eyes. "I was so worried after I heard…"

"I'm fine." It was mostly true. I hadn't been hurt. I just felt… sick.

Venn pulled me to his chest again. "I'm sorry about earlier."

Ugh. I didn't even want to think about that.

"Yeah, yeah, lover boy." Jenna shoved Venn out of the way and threw her arms around my neck. "You're officially no longer allowed out of my sight."

"Stop, Jenna," I said. "I'm fine. Genevieve…"

I choked on her name.

"I miss her already, too," Fiona said softly. She stood and came to my other side to offer a hug of her own.

I nodded and wiped at my eyes. If I spoke, I knew I'd start crying again.

"Why don't I show you where you'll be sleeping?" Zoey offered.

I lifted my head and nodded.

Zoey led us to the basement. It was wide open and completely finished. A couch and fifty-inch TV with endless gaming consoles sat against one wall, while a large computer desk took up another corner. In the middle of it all was a pool table. There were two other doors, one that I could see led to a bathroom and the other I assumed was a storage room.

Zoey walked over to the couch, which was piled with stacks of pillows and blankets. "I'm sorry I don't have extra beds, but there should be enough blankets for everyone."

Teagan stepped forward and took a dark navy blanket off the top. "This is more than we could ask for. Thank you for letting us stay."

"We're in this together, aren't we?" Zoey asked. "You guys take your time. We can unload everything in the morning. Feel free to raid the kitchen if you get hungry."

The thought of food made me want to hurl.

Zoey went back upstairs, and the basement fell silent. I liked the silence… but I couldn't stand it at the same time.

I took a blanket and pillow off the top of the pile. I spoke just to break the silence. "What took you guys so long to get here?"

"Ugh, don't ask," Fiona said as she grabbed her own pile of bedding. "Jenna, Ronark, and Venn were out, and we had a helluva time getting ahold of them. Basically Amalia, Clarita, and I had to load everything up ourselves."

That weight in my stomach returned. I avoided anyone else's gaze as I started to make up my sleeping spot near the computer desk. Venn was setting his up beside me.

"Where were you guys?" I prodded, though worst-case scenarios were already racing through my head. I felt betrayed.

"We were just out," Jenna said with a shrug. "It's not a big deal."

"If it's not a big deal, then you can tell me," I snapped.

"Chill, Rae," Ronark said. "It's not what you think."

I turned toward all of them, my face flaming. "How can I even trust you three after you *lied* to me?"

All three started talking at once.

"Stop it, you guys," I growled. "I don't want to hear it."

Venn reached for my arms to help calm me, but all it did was piss me off. I swatted him away and shot to my feet. He stared up at me with sad eyes before standing beside me.

"All we did was go get a cup of coffee," he assured me.

I tilted my head at him. "Is that code?"

"No! You're overreacting," he insisted.

"I'm not!" I cried. "You're acting like it's not a big deal, but it is, Venn. We aren't supposed to keep things from each other!" I lowered my voice and grumbled. "You should probably sleep on the other side of the room tonight."

"Everybody timeout!" Teagan threw herself between us. "Can't we talk this out without tearing each other's faces off?"

I crossed my arms and stared at Jenna, Ronark, and Venn.

"It's not a big deal," Jenna insisted.

"It is!" I shouted. "Because we're family, and we care about each other. We can help you."

"No, you can't," Ronark shot back. "There's nothing that can fix this but time."

"Then stop doing drugs!" I screamed.

Jenna's eyebrows knitted together, and her lips tensed. She looked about ready to slap me, but there were too many people between us. Venn's hands clenched into fists, and Ronark looked like he was about to explode.

Ryland shook his head, like he still couldn't believe it. "Venn, you said you'd never..."

Teagan pressed her fingers to her eyes. When she lifted her head, she was fuming, nostrils flared and everything. "Are we seriously going to go through this again?"

"Again!?" I exploded as pieces began to fall into place. "That's how you got over the addiction last time, isn't it?"

Venn gaped at me, like he didn't know what to say. What a jackass.

"Tell me the truth!" I demanded.

Venn raked his fingers through his hair, looking more distressed than I'd ever seen him.

I sucked in a sharp breath. "It *is* true. Why didn't you ever tell me?"

"Because it wasn't important," he insisted. "It's not who I am anymore."

"Clearly, it is!" I shot back. "Because you're doing the exact same thing."

"Well, it worked last time, didn't it?" he snapped.

Oh, hell no. Was he seriously trying to justify this? It was dangerous! I wasn't going to let him do this to himself.

"And what if it doesn't work this time?" I challenged. "We've already lost Genevieve. We don't need to lose you, too!"

The room went dead silent as everyone absorbed my words. Slowly, Venn's shoulders fell, and he took a step forward. His tone softened as he looked me in the eyes. "I never meant to keep anything from you, Rae. I just wanted to get through this on my own. I didn't want to burden you."

Was he serious right now?

"I don't believe you," I stated. "I think you're just trying to salvage your story."

Venn tried to take my hand in his, but I pulled away. "Rae, I mean it when I say that I love you with every fiber of my being. Some things are just too difficult to face—too hard to talk about. That has nothing to do with you. I told you there were things you didn't know, and I wanted to open up. But I just… I didn't mean to hurt you. I never want to hurt you, so from here on out, I'll tell you everything."

A warm, soft feeling settled in my gut. I knew he was telling the truth, but it was difficult to accept. He'd acted like he didn't trust me.

"I'm sorry," Venn whispered. "If this ruins your trust in me, I understand. But you should know that I'd give up anything to be with you."

I sniffled as I took in his words, but I didn't know how to respond. I was still mad, and I wanted to yell at him, but I also wanted to kiss him and tell him everything was forgiven. I didn't want to keep dragging this out. I just wanted to make up already.

"I'll prove it," Venn said, mistaking my silence. He reached into his back pocket and pulled out a small baggie with pink powder inside. "I'm giving it up. Now."

"Venn!" Jenna protested.

"Seriously, dude?" Ronark sounded horrified.

Venn whirled around and stomped past both of them.

I quickly followed. "What are you doing?"

He stopped in the bathroom beside the toilet. "I'm getting rid of it. It's hurt you, and I can't have that. I'd rather suffer through the thirst for a thousand years than lose you."

Venn looked to Jenna and Ronark in the doorway behind me. "I suggest you two do the same."

Venn threw his baggie into the toilet and flushed. Ronark let out a small whimper, like he couldn't bear to see it go. Jenna threw her hand over her mouth.

The moment the drugs were gone, Venn breathed a sigh of relief. It was as if they'd been weighing him down.

It seemed as though a minute of silence passed as I processed what has just happened. Venn had been right. I could never comprehend the full weight of what he'd been going through. But I knew one thing. Venn had just made a huge sacrifice for me.

I stepped forward and wrapped my arms around his neck. His body was warm and comforting. He pulled me closer to him and buried his nose in my hair. It felt like coming home after a very long time away.

"I love you, Venn," I whispered.

Tears rolled down his face and into my hair. "I love you, too. I'm sorry. I'm so sorry—"

His words cut off as I pressed my lips to his. For the first time all night, I felt like I could breathe again.

When Venn and I finally parted, I turned to Jenna. She looked on the verge of tears as she stepped forward into the small bathroom. She looked at me a moment, then threw herself forward and pulled me into a hug.

"I'm sorry, too, Rugrat," she said. "I made rationalizations I shouldn't have. I shouldn't have hidden it from you. I just thought..."

"You thought what?" I asked.

She shook her head and wiped her eyes. "Nothing. I don't want to hurt you, either, so I'm getting rid of my portion, too. I'll find a different way to get through this."

She reached in her pocket and tossed her baggie into the toilet, then turned to Ronark with expectation in her eyes.

He hesitated in the doorway, then sighed. "Believe me, I want to find another way through this, too, but..."

"We can do it, Eli," Jenna said, holding her hand out to him.

"You know I hate it when you call me that," he grumbled.

She took his hand and pulled him inside the room. It was started to get far too cramped in here, and everyone else was still watching from the doorway.

"You survived eight years on that island," Jenna pointed out. "That's a helluva lot worse than what we're facing now. It's going to be hard, but we're going to make it through."

Ronark took his baggie out of his pocket and stared down at it. "I was just hoping it would be easy..."

"This isn't an easy button, Ronark," Venn said softly. "It's a pause button. Sooner or later, you still have to walk through the fire. I know."

Jenna's hand closed around Ronark's. "We'll walk through that fire together. And get this over with as soon as we can."

Ronark took a deep breath. "Okay. Together."

Jenna and Venn spoke at the same time. "Together."

Ronark tossed his baggie into the toilet, and Jenna flushed it. She smiled as the drugs disappeared.

I took her hand. "See? I told you you were strong."

She took a deep breath. "We'll see."

"Guys!" a terrified voice came from the top of the steps. It sounded like Amalia.

"We're all down here!" Ryland called up to her.

She pounded down the steps until she was standing at the bottom where we could all see her. "It's Matias again. Something's happened."

21

We all raced upstairs and gathered in the living room, where Sondra, Clarita, and Zoey sat.

"What's going on?" I asked breathlessly. My heart pounded in preparation for whatever bad news they were about to say.

Sondra's hands shook. "Matias has attacked the DMR branch in Chicago."

The TV played footage of the destruction. The entire building had been leveled to the ground, and buildings all around it were in shambles. It looked as if a tornado had gone through the area. The images were dark, with nothing but nearby city lights to illuminate the scene. The TV anchor spoke, but I could barely process what she said as the images flashed across the screen.

"How do they know it's him?" Jenna asked. The color had drained from her face.

Clarita pursed her lips. "Keep watching."

"At this time, fifty-seven are confirmed dead, and another twenty-four have been severely injured," the anchor said.

The TV flashed to a cell phone video from earlier in the night. The five-story Department of Magical Regulation building was still standing, but high-speed winds whipped through the parking lot. The camera panned to a group of three dozen men in suits looking confidently up at the building.

Matias stood at the front of the group and looked directly into the camera. "The Department of Magical Regulation has overstepped their power, and they shall pay for it. The magical community will not stand this persecution."

Matias waved his hand like a signal to his followers. Magic of all colors swirled out of people's hands, while others looked to the skies to control the clouds. The magic wound together and swirled around the building, increasing speed until the colors blurred into streaks.

At Matias's command, the magic exploded outward in a flash of white light. The camera whipped backward, and the feed cut out.

I gaped at the TV. This was straight-up terrorism. How could Matias still think he was in the right?

"What the hell?" Teagan exploded.

"I can't believe he's killing people like this!" Fiona said at the same time.

Ryland scoffed. "I can."

"Yeah, okay," Fiona said. "I don't agree with what the DMR is doing, but those people in that building are just doing their jobs. It's the *system* that's the problem. Those people were innocent."

So was Devin.

"This is what Matias does," I growled. "He's determined to build this new world and will kill anyone who gets in his way."

"This is getting out of hand," Venn said. "We can't wait any longer. We have to end this now."

"What are our options?" Jenna asked.

"Genevieve was in contact with Matias," Clarita said. "She was trying to lure him here, to bring the fight to home field and try to get him away from the majority of his army."

"Without her..." Zoey hesitated. "Without her, we're doomed."

"No," I stated sternly. "I don't believe that."

"Then what do we do?" Fiona asked. "Take the fight to him?"

"That's too risky," Sondra said. "His army is bigger than we can take on."

"What if we partner up with the DMR?" Teagan suggested. "By now they have to take this threat seriously. Maybe they'll actually consider our offer."

"We can try again..." Sondra said, but she sounded skeptical.

Amalia stepped forward. "I'll be honest. I don't think *any* of us are in the right mindset to make a decision right now. Why don't we all get some rest and we'll reconvene after Genevieve's memorial in the morning?"

"We're having a memorial?" I asked.

"Just something for us," Amalia said. "In the back yard."

"We don't have time for this," Ryland said. "We have to fight—"

"Nothing is going to happen overnight," Amalia argued. "Besides, if we're going to fight, we need to be at the top of our game."

Sondra stood. "Amalia's right. Let's take the night to each give it some thought and we'll figure out what to do in the morning. It's been a long day."

Everyone agreed, and the group dispersed.

Downstairs, Venn and I lay next to one another on the floor. I snuggled tightly under my blanket and faced him. His face was only inches from mine as we talked in low whispers.

"Venn, is this mission hopeless?" I asked.

He thought about it for a moment, then shook his head. "No. I don't think so."

"Maybe this whole thing was a bad idea," I said, though I wasn't sure I truly believed that. "Going after Matias, I mean. The DMR will take care of him, right?"

Venn frowned. "His men just leveled a DMR branch."

"Yeah, but the DMR has a whole freaking SWAT team behind them," I pointed out.

Venn shrugged. "What's that against magic? If they can't stop him, we need to be ready."

"How are we going to do that without Genevieve?" I asked desperately. "She was orchestrating this whole thing."

Venn brushed his fingers across the side of my face. I realized I was on the verge of tears as her face flashed through my memory.

"Can we talk about something else?" I suggested.

"Yeah, of course," Venn said. "I think I'm ready to tell you about what happened in Detroit."

I sat and listened as he whispered lowly so only I could hear. He spared no detail. The thought of what he'd been through sent my stomach into knots, and for the first time, I was starting to understand why he'd turned to drugs.

I reached out and wiped the tears from his cheeks. "Tell me something happy."

Venn laced his fingers through mine. "Do you want to hear about my brother?"

His eyes brightened, like he was already thinking back to happy memories.

I nodded. "Yeah. I would."

Venn and I stayed up talking for hours. Eventually, my eyelids became heavy, long after everyone else had fallen asleep. Venn couldn't keep his eyes open any longer.

"Thank you," I whispered.

"For what?" he asked.

"Making me feel better. Tyson sounds great. I wish I would've met him."

"You would've liked him," he said.

"I think so. We should probably get to sleep."

Venn leaned over and kissed my nose. "Goodnight, Rae."

"Goodnight."

Venn closed his eyes and was out in an instant. I had to use the bathroom so badly that I crawled out from beneath my secure blanket cocoon and tiptoed across the room.

It was only when I was in the privacy of the bathroom that I realized I still had Genevieve's phone in my pocket. I pulled it out and cleaned it off, the whole time contemplating why she'd given it to me. There must be something important in it.

I sat on the toilet lid and turned on the screen. I closed my eyes, trying to remember the passcode she had given me. Five... seven... were there two sevens? No, it was two fours, definitely two fours. I entered 5474 into the screen. It buzzed once and prompted me to try again. What was the number again?

"Matias is coming. Make sure you're ready for him," she'd said to me.

Why couldn't I remember what she'd said right before that?

7454?

7427!

The code suddenly clicked, and I entered it in. The screen unlocked.

I just stared down at it for at least a minute until the screen timed out and shut off again. Where did I even start?

I opened the screen again and started with Genevieve's call history. She'd made a lot of calls in the last few weeks. A few were names I recognized, like Zoey and Clarita, but others I didn't know. It all had to be part of our plan to round people up. Should I call these people?

The thought sent a wave of nerves through me, so I closed the phone app and opened the messenger app. My heart stalled in my chest.

At the top of the screen was a conversation with Matias's name on it. With my heart pounding, I opened the conversation. The most recent message was from Matias and read, *"Okay. Let's meet. When and where?"*

I quickly scrolled up to read through the whole conversation. Each text message came days apart, like Matias couldn't be bothered by Genevieve.

> G: It's Genevieve. I want to meet.
> M: Genevieve who?
> G: Genevieve Morgan. You've heard of me.
> M: Of course.
> G: Can we meet?
> M: Meet?
> G: I'm considering joining you.
> M: Come to Chicago. We'll talk it over.
> G: I unfortunately have business in Nocton. Can you meet me here?
> M: I don't make house calls.
> G: Do you want me on your side or not?
> M: Okay. Let's meet. When and where?

With each text message, my fingers trembled more and more. Was Genevieve trying to double cross us? Or was she doing this to lure Matias away from Chicago? I didn't know. It was hard to tell the tone of the text messages.

She was on our side, I told myself. Deep down inside, I knew it. If Genevieve truly wanted to join him, she wouldn't have ever helped us. Besides, Clarita had said this was part of her plan.

And Genevieve had placed it right in my hands.

22

I didn't know what to do. I shivered the entire night, contemplating it all. Genevieve had left the choice up to me. Did I bring Matias here right now? Or did I wait until we had more people on our side?

You can't waste any more time, I told myself. *We have to do this now—with whatever we have.*

Before I could make a formal decision, I drifted off to sleep.

I woke the next morning to an empty basement, all except for Venn, who was sitting up against the wall watching me sleep. I rubbed my eyes and sat up beside him.

"Where is everyone?" I asked in a groggy voice.

"They're about to start the memorial," he said.

I was instantly awake. "The memorial. We can't miss it!"

I took Venn's hand and shot to my feet. The house was quiet as we hurried up the stairs. French doors led out of the dining room and to a patio in the fenced-in back yard. It was dark and dreary outside, like it was about to rain.

I slowed as we approached the doors. Sondra and Clarita stood inside, looking out over the lawn. I could see everyone else outside sitting in folding chairs with their backs to us. They whispered amongst themselves, but I couldn't hear what they said.

"Rae. Venn," Sondra said. "We've been waiting for you. Are you ready?"

I started to nod, but I found myself taking a step backward. Images of my parents' funeral flashed through my mind. It was a day like this one—dark, dreary, and cold. My mom's friend, Kathy, had planned the whole thing. I'd told her I didn't want to say anything because I was afraid I'd cry the whole time, but I didn't. Not one tear.

In the months that followed, my sorrow turned into anger. I went from grieving my parents' death to obsessing over my sister's return. When that hit a dead end, all that was left was a burning desire for revenge. Now that seemed futile.

I didn't want revenge for Genevieve's death. I just wanted my chance to grieve.

"You don't have to do this, Rae," Venn said.

I took a deep breath. "No, I want to. Genevieve deserves this."

We stepped outside and took a seat in the back row. I kept my head down to avoid everyone else's sad gazes. Richard took a cue from Clarita and stood to say a few words. He had a hard time finding his voice.

"Thank you all for being here," he said, choking up as he spoke. "Genevieve would've wanted you all here like this. The other night, she rolled over to me and said, 'You know what, Richard? I'm glad this happened.' I asked her what she meant, and she told me, 'I'm glad we lost our magic. It brought me closer to so many people. I got to tell them I was sorry. Whatever happens when we face Matias, at least there's that.' I didn't know what she meant at the time, but I get it now. Genevieve was ready to lay down her life for the rest of you, because through you, she finally found peace."

Dry sobs bubbled up in my chest. Once they started, I couldn't shut them off. Venn noticed and wrapped me in a hug, but that only made me shake harder. The image of her blood all over my hands entered my mind again. As soon as I saw that, I saw everything. Genevieve's lifeless stare turned into my parents' eyes. I was standing in their bedroom again the night the Soulless attacked, staring down at their bodies. Blood soaked my nightgown at my knees from where I'd sunk down into the pool of blood, too shocked to stay on my feet— too shocked to speak or move.

I pushed away from Venn and raced toward the back door into the house. His footsteps were close behind me. I buried my face in my hands and sank onto the couch in the living room.

Venn wrapped me in his arms and kissed the top of my head. "It's okay. You can cry."

I didn't want to cry. It made me feel weak. The Ravenite never cried.

But I didn't want to be the Ravenite right now. I just wanted to be Rachel Collins. I wanted to mourn the loss of my parents and my friend. Was that too much to ask?

Soft footsteps padded across the carpet, but I didn't look up to see who they belonged to. I already knew by the cadence that it was my sister.

"I've got this," Jenna said softly to Venn.

"I'm not leaving her," Venn replied in an equal tone.

"I'd like to speak to her privately," Jenna whispered.

He hesitated, then turned to me. "Is that okay, Rae?"

I nodded without looking up.

Venn headed back to the yard while Jenna took his spot on the couch. I leaned into her and sobbed.

"I miss them all so much," I cried.

She rubbed my back. "I know, Rachel. I miss them, too."

"Mom, Dad, Genevieve… none of them deserved this."

"Rach, did you ever talk to Mom and Dad after they died?" Jenna asked gently.

"What do you mean?" I sniffled. Was she suggesting some sort of séance or something?

"Did you ever just talk to them… like pretend they were there and they could hear you?"

"Jenna, that's ridiculous."

"Is it?"

I drew away to look her in the eye. She shot me a pointed stare.

"No. I never talked to them," I admitted.

Jenna rose from the couch. "Give me a minute."

She stuck her head out the door and gestured to Zoey, who rose from the last row and came to talk to her. They whispered a few things back and forth I didn't hear, then Zoey placed something small and metallic into Jenna's hand.

"What's going on?" I asked when she returned.

She grabbed my hand. "Come on. I need to show you something."

I pulled against Jenna as she dragged me toward the front door. "Where are we going?"

"You'll see," she pressed.

"We're in the middle of a memorial service!" I hissed.

"You need help," she insisted. "I think you really need this right now."

Jenna led me outside and to Zoey's car in the driveaway. The keys jingled in her hand as she opened the driver-side door.

"Jenna, we can't," I objected. "I have something important I have to—"

"Whatever it is, it can wait," she said, cutting me off. "Come on."

Jenna was already in the driver's seat and had started the engine.

I sighed and slid into the passenger seat.

"Close your eyes," she instructed.

I placed my hands over my eyes. "This better be good."

"Jenna, where are we going?" I asked in a rather irritated tone. "Can I open my eyes yet?"

I'd had them closed for half an hour already.

Jenna helped me out of the car. She held my arm and guided me across what felt like a soft lawn. "Not yet. Keep walking."

"I'm going to trip over something," I argued.

"You are not. We're almost there."

Jenna came to a halt, and I stopped beside her. She grabbed my shoulders and turned me to my left.

"Okay," she said. "You can open your eyes now."

My stomach bottomed out when I saw where she'd brought me. A long stretch of grass spanned in front of us, dotted with evenly-spaced headstones. Just feet in front of me were two matching marble headstones with my parents' names engraved on them. Dean and Marissa Collins.

My legs became numb as the weight of where I was slammed into me like a ton of bricks. I fell to my knees, shaking. I hadn't been here since the funeral.

I forced my gaze away from my parents' death dates and up to Jenna. My voice cracked when I spoke. "How did you know where to find them? You weren't at the funeral."

"I looked into it when we got back from the island," she said softly.

"Why would you bring me here?"

She knelt beside me. "Because I think you need to talk to them."

I closed my eyes and turned my head away. "This is cruel, Jenna."

She reached for my hand, and I let her take it. "I'm not trying to hurt you, Rachel. Please understand that. Can you just try... for me?"

A silent beat passed before I whispered, "I'd do anything for you, Jenna."

She squeezed my hand. "Tell them how you feel."

My throat closed up as I turned back to my parents' graves. "I... I miss them."

"Don't tell me," Jenna said. "Tell *them*."

Tears began to well in my eyes. I squeezed them tightly shut, until my eyes could no longer take the weight of the tears. Without a single sound, they began to trail down my face. I opened my mouth to speak, but my breath wavered.

"Take your time," Jenna encouraged.

"Mom. Dad." I dashed the tears away. "I miss you."

I expected Jenna to say something, for her voice to cut through the momentary silence, but she didn't. It was all up to me now.

"I miss the sound of your voices. You sang so pretty, Mom. And Dad... you always knew what to say. When you weren't there, I didn't have anyone to tell me what to do anymore. I felt lost. All I wanted was those Thursday game nights back. I wanted to bake cookies with you again and help you on that old car I always told you was a lost cause. I wanted Mom to hug me again and tell me to eat my vegetables or whatever. I regretted not watching that cheesy horror film with you guys the Friday before it happened and not going to that Home and Garden Show Mom asked me to come to with her that past spring. I wished I would've made you breakfast in bed more often and told you just how great of parents you were. You guys did everything for Jenna and me, and I absolutely know with every fiber of my being that you loved us. I loved you, too. It's just that sometimes... sometimes I'm not sure you knew it. And I wish you did."

Sobs broke out in my chest, and my head was starting to hurt.

Jenna placed her arm around my shoulder and whispered, "They knew, Rugrat. They knew."

Memories of that night pushed their way into my mind again. This time, I didn't shut them out. This time, I relived every moment until I curled into a ball at my parents' graves and wept until I could weep no more.

It was the summer after my Sophomore year of high school, just days after the school year had ended. I was looking forward to our mini vacation that weekend. Mom and Dad were planning a surprise stay at a waterpark resort for Jenna, to celebrate her graduation. I'd been dreaming about it when the sounds of screams jolted me from my sleep. I'd completely frozen up as my body trembled in fear. I sat straight upright in bed and pulled the blanket close to my chest, as if it could save me from the monsters like it did when I was a kid.

Heavy footsteps pounded up the stairs. I glanced around frantically for a place to hide. Under the bed wasn't an option, since it was too low to the ground to fit under. I raced over to my closet.

"No, she's mine," a deep voice said from my sister's room beside mine.

"Rugrat!" Jenna shrieked. "Run!"

My heart leapt into my throat, and my whole body quaked. A warm tingle rushed down my spine, and the room seemed to grow around me as my pajamas fell to the ground. It was the first time I'd ever shifted. Instinct I couldn't understand at the time kicked in. I flapped my wings and landed atop my bookcase. I crouched low in the darkness, hiding in the small space between the top shelf and the ceiling.

My door burst open, sending my heart pounding a million miles per hour. I held my breath and watched as a huge silhouette stormed into the room. He grabbed for my sheets on the bed but only found them empty. The man growled and flipped my mattress, then angrily stomped over to my closet. He yanked on the sliding door so hard that it came off its track.

"There's no one here!" he barked to the other men.

"Look harder," the other snapped back. "Search everywhere!"

The man in my room stepped into the dim moonlight coming from my window. It was only then that I noticed his pale features and silver eyes. Sharp, threatening fangs protruded from his mouth. I could even see a deep scar above his right eyebrow, which was weird, considering vampires had incredible healing abilities. Someone must've done some serious damage for that scar to stick around.

I crouched down even lower, trying to flatten myself against the shelf as his angry eyes scanned the room. I feared he'd seen me when his eyes flickered upward. My tiny raven heart hammered as he reached up toward me. In the light of the moon, I caught sight of the Soulless mark on his wrist.

He let out a primal scream and knocked all the books off the shelf below me, then stormed out of the room.

"Forget it, Silas," a voice said outside my doorway. "We have the girl. Let's go."

"Let me go, you son of a—" Jenna's words fell dead, as if someone was covering her mouth. It was in that moment that I realized I'd made a terrible mistake. I shouldn't have hidden. I should've fought.

I swooped down from my perch atop the bookcase and flapped my wings as hard as I could. I nearly rammed into the wall across from my room, but I corrected my flight on instinct. The men's footsteps had already faded down the hall and were at the front door.

I flew down the stairs and toward the front door, but it had already closed behind them. I quickly shifted back into human form and wrenched the door open as fast as I could. I raced outside in nothing but my birthday suit, only to find a large windowless van already pulling away down the street. My stomach bottomed out.

My sister was gone.

I could hardly process any of it as I turned back inside, my limbs shaking. I was in so much shock that I barely noticed the broken glass everywhere. I didn't know how long I stood there, trying to understand what had just happened. It was like I wasn't even in my own body anymore, like I was watching it all from above and just going through the motions. It struck me to call the police, but my throat was so tight that I didn't think I could speak.

Mom had left a pile of clean clothes in a basket on the couch. When I saw it, a little voice in the back of my head told me to put something on. It was the easy thing to do right now. I grabbed one of Mom's nightgowns and slipped it over my head.

I didn't want to go to my parents' room. I didn't want to see the damage. But I had to check on them—just in case.

My legs carried me down the hall, but it was as if my mind was elsewhere, like it was stuck the moment before I'd heard the screams. None of this felt real. It was like I was living my worst nightmare. But the nightmare only got worse.

In my parents' room, the moonlight illuminated their bodies. They were both slumped on the floor next to the bed. Blood pooled out from their bodies, mixing together between them. It was like a scene straight from a horror movie, where the blood was slashed all over the walls, on their clothes, the bed... everything.

I suddenly couldn't feel anything at all. My vision clouded over as I sank to my knees in their blood. Long wounds were slashed across their necks, as if the vampires had ripped their throats out with their teeth.

I was still shaking in a pool of their blood when the police arrived. I didn't know who had called them, but I assumed it was a neighbor who'd heard the screams. I vaguely remembered answering some questions and being told "everything would be all right."

All I could remember thinking was, *You're wrong. Nothing will be okay every again.*

Jenna held me while I cried at the foot of my parents' graves. I didn't know how long we sat there, but it must've been at least an hour of silence. With each passing breath, it felt like I was removing that ton of bricks weighing me down one at a time. When my tears finally dried, it felt like a huge weight had been lifted off my chest. I raised my head and wiped at my face. Jenna's eyes were red like mine, though she hadn't made a sound. I didn't realize until now that she'd been crying.

"Thank you, Jenna," I whispered.

"Do you feel better?" she asked.

I didn't feel like I should. Visiting my parents' graves should've left a hole inside of me the size of a bowling ball. That's why I had avoided coming here for so long. But instead, it was as if that hole had been stitched up.

I nodded honestly. "Yeah. I think I've held those feelings in too long."

"Me too, Rach."

I pulled Jenna into a hug. "I'm glad you brought me here."

"Should we get back?" she suggested.

"Yeah—" I started, but I cut off when I suddenly remembered something. "Oh my God, Jenna! I didn't get a chance to tell anyone this morning."

I reached into my pocket and pulled out Genevieve's phone. The battery was on the verge of dying, but it had just enough juice left that I could show Jenna the text messages. Her jaw dropped when she saw them.

"Genevieve said we had to defeat him," I told her. "We should respond, shouldn't we?"

She looked speechless but said, "Yes, of course we should, but maybe we should consult everyone else first. We don't want to rush anything."

"Right," I agreed. "But I don't think we can wait any longer."

I stood and took a deep breath, feeling more confident than I had in weeks. "Jenna, I think it's time."

23

When we returned to Zoey's house, we called everyone together in the basement to discuss our options.

"I know what we have to do," I announced. "Genevieve planned to lure Matias here. In her last breath, she handed me this and said, '*Matias is coming. Make sure you're ready for him.*' Sondra, can Matias use the locket to see that Genevieve's dead?"

She thought about it for a moment. "I don't think so. If he was watching her, his visions would go blank. He could guess she's dead, but he'd more likely assume she hadn't made a decision yet."

I held up the phone for everyone to see. "Good. We've been given the option to choose when and where this fight will take place. So, what will it be?"

"We're as ready as we'll ever be," Sondra said. "I say we do this as soon as possible."

"Agreed," Ryland said.

"Somewhere out of the way," Clarita added. "We don't want any casualties."

"Right," Fiona said. "But it also can't be somewhere that will raise his suspicions. Matias is smart enough to know if we're conning him."

"Let's put ourselves in Genevieve's shoes," I suggested. "If she were really going to enter into this deal, where would she meet him?"

"Her house?" Teagan theorized.

"No." Richard stepped forward. His eyebrows were tightly knitted together, like he was deep in thought. "Genevieve never met new clients at the house— only those she trusted."

"Matias wasn't a client, though," Zoey pointed out.

"No, but she would've taken the same steps to protect herself," Richard said.

"What about Bryant Park?" Fiona suggested. "It's just outside of town and almost no one ever goes there. Some of us can hide in the trees."

"Is that going to arouse suspicion, though?" I questioned.

"Not if we frame it right," Richard said in thought.

"I think it's a good idea," Amalia chimed in. "Fewer people will get hurt."

"When do we want to do this?" I asked.

Venn spoke up for the first time. "Tonight."

Nods of agreement traveled around the room.

"The sooner, the better," Fiona agreed. "It's time to get this over with."

I took a deep breath and opened Genevieve's phone to the text messages. "Okay. Here goes nothing."

Tonight. Bryant Park. I'll need space for my audition.

My fingers trembled as I hit *send*.

I held my breath. Moments later, the phone chimed.

I'll be there.

I stared down at the phone in disbelief. All eyes turned to me eagerly. "We're going to need more guns."

"It looks like everyone gets one healing potion," Fiona said as we organized the potions, trinkets, and artifacts we had gathered.

Sondra was upstairs, getting in touch with everyone Genevieve had convinced to help us. The rest of us were sitting on the ground in the basement, trying to divvy up the magic so everyone stood a fighting chance.

"I want Ryland to have one of these," I said, handing him one of the cufflinks.

"This is supposed to make me stronger?" he asked, eyeing it.

"Yes," I said. "I figure making you stronger will give us more of an edge over some of Matias's men."

"We don't know how many men he'll bring with him," Venn pointed out.

"I couldn't exactly tell him to come alone," I said. "It would've been super suspicious."

"If they outnumber us, then they'll go after our weakest members first," Venn said.

"Venn's right." Ryland stretched his hand across the pile of stuff in front of us and dropped the cufflink into Fiona's hand. "I think you should have one."

She scrunched up her nose at him. "Are you calling me the weakest member?"

"I'm saying I want to protect you," Ryland stated firmly. "You can fight bad guys. I know you can. We just need to level the playing field a little."

He turned to me. "Rae, you should take the other one."

"What about Teagan?" I asked.

Teagan's face paled. "Oh, I might—"

"Sensory enhancement!" Jenna exclaimed. "I call one of these potions."

My stomach sank. It was the same thing Genevieve had said when she'd seen those potions. I felt awful. I still hadn't had a chance to give a proper goodbye to her.

"Chill," Amalia said. "There's enough for most of us to get one."

"Hey, have you guys seen these?" Clarita held up vials of glowing blue liquid. "These ones are nifty. They give you a range of superhuman powers. The effects are totally random, but I once saw a guy turn invisible from one of these."

Ronark drew a sharp breath and shouted, "Dibs!"

I stood.

Venn reached out for my hand to stop me. "Where are you going?"

"I just need a moment alone," I told him in a low voice.

He dropped my hand, but he looked worried. "Okay. Let me know if you need anything."

"I will," I promised. I left him with a kiss, then climbed the stairs and headed out the back door. My stomach rumbled since I hadn't eaten all day, but I didn't know how much I could stomach right now anyway.

The sky was dark even though it was only mid-afternoon, and it was sprinkling out, but the rain was so light that it only felt like mist. I didn't care as I took a seat in the front row of fold-up chairs that were still sitting out on the lawn. It felt appropriate.

This seemed as good of place as any to talk to Genevieve. I pictured her standing in front of me as a spirit—caught somewhere between life and reincarnation. I didn't have all the details on how the afterlife worked, but I had a feeling she was still around, watching over us.

"Genevieve," I whispered into the damp air.

A light breeze passed through the yard.

"I didn't know you that well, but I know you were a good person. Even after the stuff you told me about your ex-husband and your father, it doesn't change what I think of you. I don't judge you for any of that, even though I know you think that makes you a bad person. All I know is that you've helped me time and time again. I don't think you would've done that if you didn't have a good heart. You changed, Genevieve, and I hope you knew just how good you were before you left. I hope you forgave yourself, because the rest of us have."

I closed my eyes and took a deep breath. The cool mist on my face felt like fingers caressing my skin, as if Genevieve were here telling me she was listening.

"We're going to miss you, but we're going to make you proud," I told her.

Silence settled over the lawn. In this dark, dank weather, it would usually send a shiver down my spine, but now it felt peaceful.

I sat there for several minutes, inhaling deep breaths through my nose and exhaling them through my mouth. I dedicated my thoughts to Genevieve, thinking of all the encounters we'd had—like when she led us to the caves to find The Wise Owl and healed us after we faced Matias there. Or when she let us stay in her lake house, then gave me the dagger that would kill Valkas. People often questioned her motives, but she had been our friend all along. She'd said it was for selfish reasons, but I didn't believe that. I think she truly wanted to help us.

The sound of creaking hinges sounded like a gunshot to my ears. I jumped to my feet and whirled to the side, where a door to the wooden fence surrounding the yard was slowly swinging open. The fence was so high that I couldn't see over it. A dark silhouette stepped through the fog and into the yard. As he came forward, I saw he was wearing a business suit and carrying a briefcase. It was so surreal, like some sort of dream. This guy *definitely* didn't belong here.

"Who the hell are—?" I stopped in my tracks when he took another step forward and I could finally make out his features.

"Leon Cavanaugh?" I balked.

Cavanaugh cleared his throat. "I don't have much time, Rachel. I'm here to make a deal. Would you like to hear it?"

"Why would I want to make a deal with you?" I spat. "You wouldn't take the one we offered."

"Because I'm prepared to offer you something better," he asserted, offering me a chilling smile. "What will it be… Ravenite?"

My blood ran cold. How did he know?

I wasn't registered as a shifter. No one but my friends knew I was the Ravenite. Unless one of those creeps on Gregor Island knew and spilled the beans…

"I don't know what you're talking about," I lied.

Cavanaugh gestured for me to follow him. "Let's not make a scene. I know exactly who you are, Rachel Collins. And I can help you."

"Help me with what?" I demanded.

Cavanaugh turned and started for the fence door again. He slipped around it where no one would see him if they glanced out the back window.

I couldn't resist my curiosity. I joined him at the door, but I didn't step through it. I let it hang open, where I could slam it in his face if I needed to.

Zoey lived on a corner lot, so this edge of the fence faced the street, as did the front of her house. There was a shiny black sedan parked next to the curb. It was easy to guess who it belonged to.

"How did you find me?" I demanded. Seeing as Cavanaugh was here, I was just waiting for the DMR to break down our door.

"I've been keeping a close eye on you and your friends," he admitted.

My entire body tensed, and I spoke in disgust. "Did you *follow* us to the Bells' house?"

Is that why the DMR had attacked us when we met with Carla and Adrien?

"Are you admitting to being on the premises?" he challenged.

"No," I said quickly.

"The situation at the Bells' house had nothing to do with you." He waved his hand like it meant nothing.

My blood started to boil, and my hands clenched into fists. Genevieve had died! One of his men had killed her. How could he just wave it off?

He started speaking like we were in a business meeting. "I looked into your files after you visited my office, Rachel."

He set his briefcase in the damp grass and opened it, then pulled out a thick yellow envelope. "The more I looked into you, the more I suspected something was missing from your file. I did some digging, some cross-referencing, and I found these."

My heart hammered as I reached into the envelope and pulled out large photographs. They seemed to come from various security cameras. All of them were in black and white, and each of them showed me fighting some asshole vampire. They never showed my face, but it was clear by the hair and height that it was me.

"This doesn't prove anything," I said, shoving the envelope back into his hands. "That's not me."

"We'll see what a jury has to say about that," Cavanagh challenged. "According to my files, the Ravenite is guilty of at least eighty-seven murders that we know of, along with multiple breaking and entering charges and one account of grand larceny."

My eyebrows shot up. Eighty-seven? Wow. I didn't know my count was *that* high. Then again, the grand larceny charge was definitely not me, so I was guessing they'd attributed a few unsolved crimes to my name.

I shrugged. "I don't know who did those things, but they weren't me. Besides, they were all vampires, weren't they?"

"Doesn't matter," he said. "In the eye of the law, they're still human. That defense won't work now that vampires have proven their humanity was inside them all along."

Cavanagh flipped through his papers. "Let's forget about the Ravenite for a second and focus on these other charges. I have your friend Sondra Thompson on at least three murder charges and illegal operation of a magical establishment. Fiona Thompson… no murders that I know of, but definitely illegal shifting. Ryland Thompson, multiple accounts of illegal magic use, and I'm sure a few murders I can get a jury to convict him of. Teagan Perry, accessory to magical misuse. Venn Michaels—"

"Okay!" I shouted. I quickly lowered my tone and threw a quick glance at the house. "What's this deal you want?"

Cavanaugh looked pleased. "The Department of Magical Regulation has attempted to go after Matias Vayne, but each attempt has been unsuccessful—"

"Why haven't we heard about any of this on the news?" I asked before he could finish.

He frowned. "We want people to feel they're safe, Miss Collins."

Which meant they'd been desperately trying to cover up their failures.

"I know you intend to go after him," Cavanaugh said. "Perhaps you will have more luck than we have had."

"What does any of this have to do with that file in your hands?" I snapped.

"I want the Artifact," he stated in a clipped tone.

"So that the Department can control magic?" I asked in disbelief. The thought made me sick. "You're going to use magic to stop magic. Sounds a little ironic, doesn't it?"

And predictable. I knew the asshole wouldn't be able to resist the temptation. He was almost as bad as Matias—stealing people's free will to get the world he wanted.

"I admit, it goes against everything I believe in," Cavanaugh said, "but I do think this is what needs to be done."

"You want me to bring it to you instead of destroying it," I stated. It wasn't a question.

Cavanaugh nodded and waved the file at me. "You retrieve the Owl and give it to me, and I can make all of this go away."

I narrowed my eyes at him. It *was* an attractive offer. He had enough evidence against me and my family to put us away for a long time.

"How can I trust you?" I asked. "What's keeping someone else from digging up the same information and putting us on trial?"

Cavanaugh pulled a sheet of paper from the file and handed it to me. "This is the contract you would sign with the Department of Magical Regulation. In exchange for the Owl, we would agree to grant you and your friends full immunity in your previous crimes *and* allow you to keep access to your magic."

"So that you can just ding us when we use it?" I snarled.

"No," Cavanaugh said. "If you read through the contract, you will see that you'll be free to use your magic, barring any harm to others."

I hesitated. "And if I don't hand over the Owl?"

"Then this information goes to the courts," Cavanaugh threatened. "You only have one choice in this matter, Miss Collins. Give us the Owl, or you and your friends will spend the rest of your lives in prison. I'll give you a few days to think it over."

Cavanagh left me with the contract in my hands as he turned back to his vehicle. Before he slipped inside, he turned back to me. "Oh, and Miss Collins? You tell anyone of this deal, and the offer's off the table."

I knew instantly what he was getting at. He couldn't have anyone persuading me not to hand the Owl over. With all the research he'd done, he knew I was his best shot at getting his hands on the Artifact. He also knew my family was my weak spot.

And he knew I was actually considering the deal.

24

Cavanaugh left me standing in the lawn, feeling completely torn. How could I pass up this deal if it meant protecting my family? But at the same time, how could I accept if it meant stealing magic from innocent supernaturals?

"Rae?" The sound of Venn's voice came from the back door. "You out here?"

I quickly folded the paper in my hands, shoved it into my back pocket, and hurried toward the door. "I'm here. Just needed a moment to myself."

Venn stood in the doorway looking at me. "I just wanted to check on you."

"I'm fine," I lied. My knees shook as I entered the house. I wanted to immediately tell him—tell anyone—about Cavanaugh's visit, but I knew I couldn't. I still hadn't made up my mind about it, and I knew the second I told anyone, the deal was over.

We started toward the basement, but my mind was racing. There was so much to deal with right now—losing Genevieve, facing my parents' graves, the contract with Cavanaugh... All I really wanted to do was forget about it all for a moment, to find just one ray of sunlight on this dark and dreary day. Jenna had been a huge help earlier, but not in the way I needed right now. I needed to know that once this was all over, everything would be okay. *We* would be okay.

Before I realized what I was doing, I pulled Venn down the hall. I pinned him against the wall and kissed him with everything I had in me. The weight in my abdomen melted away, and my shoulders relaxed. Warmth rushed in to replace all the cold in my bones.

I drew away from him, beaming. God, that kiss was everything. It might be the one thing that would keep me holding on tonight.

Venn smiled, looking pleased. "What's this about?"

I shrugged. The truth was, I didn't know where this came from. I was conflicted about everything right now. I just wanted to be with Venn one last time before we faced Matias.

I wrapped my arms around him and rested my head on his chest. "I just need to be with you right now."

He hugged me tightly and kissed the top of my head. "I'm here. Whatever you need."

I glanced both ways down the hall, then took his hand and dragged him into the privacy of the bathroom.

"In here?" he hissed.

He could take me anywhere he wanted and I wouldn't care.

"Where else are we going to get a little privacy?" I asked.

Venn quickly agreed by pulling his shirt up over his head.

I couldn't believe this was happening again. We'd been through so much these past few days. But I needed Venn right now as much as he needed me. I could see it in his eyes.

We wasted no time. Venn and I were on each other in seconds, our hands roaming over each other's backsides. He grabbed my ass, where I'd tucked the contract into my pocket.

Worry hit me, and I jumped back. He couldn't know I had that on me.

He shot me a confused expression, but then I stripped my pants off, and he relaxed. I tossed my shoes and jeans aside, then lifted my shirt up over my head. I stood in nothing but my bra and panties.

I helped Venn strip down to nothing, then he helped me. Our bodies pressed together as we kissed each other over and over again.

I drew away to catch my breath, then stole a quick glance in the mirror. Before, the sight of my own naked body used to disgust me. I wasn't skinny enough. I wasn't tall enough. My hair was too dark and my skin too pale. But now that I was standing next to Venn, it was like looking at a different girl. She was beautiful, and he was... there were no words.

He caught me staring at him in the mirror. "You like this view?"

"Yeah," I admitted breathlessly. My gaze flickered down our bodies, and I realized I *really* liked this view. Maybe the bathroom wasn't such a bad idea after all.

"Protection?" I asked him.

"Already on it." He smiled as he pulled a condom from his jeans on the floor. "Figured it'd come in handy eventually."

After he put the condom on, Venn guided my shoulders so I was facing the mirror. He pressed himself up against me from behind. I gasped at the feel of his warm body on my back.

"Is this okay?" he asked.

I couldn't take my eyes off us in the mirror. "Absolutely."

I bent over the counter, and Venn pressed into me. He held on to my hips, and I moaned as I watched him move against me. At the sound, Venn reached between my legs from the front and began massaging me. I moaned again. It felt so good that I couldn't help but close my eyes and simply bask in the glory of his hands on me. My breasts pressed against the cold countertop, which I liked even more. Everything felt more sensitive.

Venn rubbed harder, faster, until I couldn't take it any longer and grabbed the hand resting on my left hip. I brought it to my mouth and bit down on his hand to keep from making any noises. Venn increased his speed, until we both finished in a glorious display of mental fireworks.

We both went weak in the knees and fell the ground. The plush rug in front of the sink was warm against my back.

I struggled to catch my breath. "Venn… That was amazing."

He looked to me from where he lay beside me. "You're telling me?"

I chuckled. "I'm glad we're not fighting anymore."

Venn kissed me lightly. "Me too. I'm sorry about all that."

I reached up a finger and placed it to his lips. "Shh… It's over. We're good. Just… let me help you from now on."

He nodded. "I will."

A knock sounded at the door, and we both jumped.

"Occupied!" I called out quickly.

"Hey, Rae. It's Teagan," she called through the door. "Let me know when you're done in there. I need to talk to you."

Venn and I quickly got to our feet. I started cleaning up while he pulled on his pants.

"I'll be right out!" I called.

"That goes for you, too, Venn," Teagan said.

My face went white, and I started laughing hard under my breath. Did she know what we were up to in here?

"Shh…" Venn chuckled, but he didn't seem to care.

I dressed quickly, then smoothed my hair down. When we stepped out of the bathroom, we heard voices in the kitchen. Ryland and Teagan sat at the table, waiting for us. Everyone else was still downstairs.

"What's up?" I asked innocently.

Teagan knotted her hands together and looked to Ryland. "We… we have something we have to tell you two."

My stomach sank as Ryland gestured to a dining room chair. This didn't sound good. I took a seat next to Venn, who looked as clueless as I felt. I grabbed Venn's hand beneath the table, and he squeezed it tightly.

"First off, I want to start by apologizing," Ryland said.

"Apologizing?" I furrowed my brow at him. "For what?"

"I haven't been very welcoming to you," he admitted.

"Don't say that…" I started, but it was kind of true.

Ryland held up a hand. "Let me finish. I never should've blamed you for what happened in your past lives. You had no control over that. Things have been hard on all of us lately. I'm sorry I made it harder for you."

A hint of a smile touched my lips. "Thank you, Ryland. Apology accepted."

I thought for a moment that was it, but I could tell by their faces that they wanted to tell us something else.

"What is it?" Venn asked, sounding worried.

Teagan gazed down at her hands. "We wanted you to know that I won't be able to come with you."

I gaped at her. "But you're our best fighter."

"I know," she said in a small voice.

I'd had my suspicions for a while, but I never knew how to bring it up. Now seemed like an appropriate time. "Did something happen on Gregor Island?"

Ryland and Teagan shared that look again.

Teagan shook her head. "No, it happened before. There was a reason I didn't go with you into the woods that night on the island, either—why Ryland and I went to the boathouse instead."

"Were you hurt?" I asked. "When they took you?"

She didn't look hurt, but something had definitely changed.

"No," Teagan said. "The exact opposite. I'm pregnant."

My jaw dropped, and Venn went speechless beside me. It took me a moment to process what she'd said, then I leapt to my feet and rounded the table.

I pulled her into a hug. "Oh my God!"

Venn finally found his voice and said, "Congratulations!"

He stood and gave Ryland one of those one-arm hugs guys shared. Ryland beamed, and Teagan hugged me back tightly.

"Thanks," Ryland said. "Now you get why Tea hasn't been able to help you. We just want the baby to stay safe."

"Why didn't you tell us?" I asked as I drew away from her.

Teagan smiled wide. "We were waiting, but we can't keep it in any longer."

"I hope we're not the first people you told," Venn said.

"No," Ryland assured me. "We just told Sondra and Fiona this morning, but we wanted to tell everyone individually rather than in a big group."

"It feels easier that way," Teagan said.

"Well, we're really happy for you," I told them.

Teagan ran a hand across her belly. "Thank you. We're just ready for all this to be over."

Venn chuckled. "Believe me, we all are."

"So, names?" I asked excitedly.

"We haven't decided yet," Teagan said. "We probably won't until we know whether it's a boy or a girl."

"How long do you have to wait?" I asked.

"Just a few more weeks." Teagan looked own at her belly. I hadn't noticed before, but now that I was looking for it, I saw she had a small bump.

"Anyway," she said. "You should probably head back downstairs. We have a lot more preparations to do before tonight, and we still have more people to tell."

When Ryland and Teagan told us about their baby, it felt like maybe things would turn out okay.

We only had a few more hours until we found out.

25

V enn stood at my side in the trees as I fiddled with Carla's bracelet. We'd arrived at Bryant Park over an hour ago, just before dusk, and there was still no sign of Matias.

"Do you think he figured out this is an ambush?" I whispered.

Venn placed his index finger to his lips to quiet me. I distinctly heard the brush of fabric as his arm moved. My senses were on high alert after the potion I drank. I could easily see through the darkness and feel the heaviness in the air, indicting further rain. I was also armed with one of Devin's cufflinks, a healing potion, a few weapons, and my trinket—a golden ring we'd gotten from Xander. I'd also drank one of those potions Clarita had said made one guy invisible, but I had yet to discover what superpower I'd drawn.

I heard the flapping of his suit coat in the wind before I saw him. Matias came down from the skies like an angel of death, levitating himself above the ground. He landed so softly in the grass that I didn't hear it. He straightened a lock of hair, then glanced around. Even without the silver eyes, he still looked sinister.

I closed my eyes and focused on my other senses, trying to get a feel for whether Matias was alone or not. He seemed to be, but I wasn't sure I trusted Devin's potions enough to say with certainty.

"Oh, Genevieve?" he sang, looking deep into the trees. We had at least fifty witches and shifters on our side. Genevieve had called in more favors than I thought. I was confident we were hidden well enough that he couldn't see anyone. "Come out, come out, wherever you are."

Sondra gestured to Venn and me, and the three of us stepped out of the trees as we'd planned if he was alone.

Matias turned in our direction with a smirk on his face. "Well, well, well, I didn't expect to see you here. Have you come to join the cause?"

"We've come to make a deal," I said boldly as we stopped several paces from him.

"And Genevieve?" he asked curiously.

"Dead," Sondra stated flatly.

Matias placed a hand on his chest, like he actually cared. "Oh, bless her. I really had hoped she'd join me."

Keep dreaming!

He dropped his hand, and his demeanor quickly shifted. It was like he could only bear to spare a few seconds for the news. "So, what kind of offer are you proposing?"

Matias began to circle us, like he was some sort of animal and we were his prey.

Sondra held her head up confidently. "A trade for the Owl."

Matias paused his pacing and threw his head back in maniacal laughter. "What could you possibly offer me that is of more worth than the Artifact?"

Venn shrugged. "Your life."

Matias's laughter quickly died, and he continued to circle us slowly. My gaze flickered downward, and I noticed he was tapping his leg rhythmically. He was trying to put some sort of binding spell on us without us noticing! I'd read about it in one of Genevieve's books.

I stepped out of the circle to break the spell before he could complete it. He looked over to me in dissatisfaction, but I kept innocence plastered to my face. He didn't seem to notice that I'd caught his intention.

"Are you threatening me?" Matias asked casually.

"Yes," Sondra said.

"We can do this the easy way or the hard way," I told him. "Either way, we'll be getting that Owl."

Matias stopped pacing and turned to look directly at us. "No. We do this my way. I'll be keeping the Owl, and you three will either join me or die. Besides, do you really think you can take me on by yourselves? In case you haven't noticed, I've taken your magic."

Matias held his palms up and began to levitate again. Lightning crackled out of his palms. "I am all powerful!"

And full of it.

"What will it be?" he challenged.

I looked to Sondra, then to Venn. They both gave me the same look, and I knew what I had to do.

I turned back to Matias. "It looks like we're playing this by your rules. Either way, one of us will die tonight. Time to find out who."

Anger built up inside of me, triggering the magic in the bracelet I wore. A blast shot out in front of me, sending Matias reeling through the air. He flipped a few times, then landed in the ground on his ass.

"Now!" Venn shouted.

Witches and shifters came flooding out of the trees. Carla and Adrien led the charge, letting out matching battle cries as they sprinted forward.

I quickly slipped the dagger out of my boot, while Sondra and Venn cocked the guns they'd gotten from Genevieve's. Gunshots rang out around me, but Matias stood with confidence, unharmed. He stuck his fingers in his mouth and let out a high-pitched whistle.

Predictable.

Men came out of nowhere, raining down from the sky like supervillains. They all looked like clones of Matias in their dark suits. His men went toward the witches and shifters racing out of the trees.

All around us, the park broke out into the sounds of battle. I heard gunshots and the sound of magical weapons *whizzing* through the air. People screamed in agony. But I shut it all out as I focused on Matias and sprinted toward him alongside Venn and Sondra.

I gripped a vial of explosive potion in my palm and threw it at him as soon as I was close enough. He flicked his wrist, and it went flying off its trajectory. The vial burst against the ground and sent one of Matias's men off into oblivion.

Shit. I only had one of those potions left.

I smelled the scent of brimstone before fire shot out of his palms. It was enough of a warning for the three of us to jump out of the way. Three fireballs shot over our heads in quick succession. He held his hands up again and muttered something under his breath. Nothing happened. He looked down at his hands like there was something wrong.

That'd be the trinkets, jackass.

The momentary pause was just enough time for me to jump to my feet and aim my dagger at his chest. At the flick of his wrist, it went flying out of my hand. I didn't think. I just reacted. I drew back my arm and slammed my fist into his face. Matias stumbled back a few steps and wiped the blood from his nose. He looked at me in complete and utter shock.

And that'd be the cufflink.

Another gunshot sounded, but Matias remained unharmed. He must've been doing something to the bullets to protect himself.

Matias threw out his hand, and I went flying backward several feet, knocking Sondra to the ground on my way down. I gasped for breath that had been stolen from me.

Venn quickly realized his gun was no use against Matias. He raced forward so fast that he was a blur in my peripheral vision. His fist slammed into Matias's face faster than my eyes could process.

The superpower potion, I realized. It'd given Venn superhuman speed.

I quickly got to my feet, as did Sondra. Her face twisted in rage as we raced toward him again. Matias slammed his fist against the side of Venn's head, casting him aside, then thrust his palm out at me. Lightning crackled from his palm and struck my shoulder. I was starting to realize it was one of his favorite spells. I went down where I stood, my muscles twitching.

As I tried to regain my strength, Matias shot a ball of red energy at Sondra's chest. She thrust her hands out on instinct and caught the magic in her hands, sustaining it as if she could still control magic.

She glanced down at the glowing ball with surprise, but it quickly melted away as she realized it wasn't hurting her. Matias's face paled as she shot the magic back in his direction. He ducked, and the magic struck one of his men beyond us. The magic continued straight through him, like the thing that had killed Devin. I shuddered to think that had almost just killed Sondra. Her super-human potion must've given her the ability to manipulate other people's magic.

"How did you—?" Matias started, but I'd already grabbed my knife from where it lay and gotten to my feet. I tackled him to the ground.

I didn't know how I got up so fast after the lightning strike. It should've stopped my heart, but my extra strength must've saved me. I didn't question it. I just fought.

My blade came down for his heart. He muttered a quick incantation, and my arm jerked to the side, like my blade had slammed into an invisible barrier above his chest. It sank into the grass at his side. A split-second later, it flew out of the ground and skidded across the grass, far out of reach, like Matias had used a telekinetic spell on it.

Fine. Whatever. I could fight without my blade.

Venn and Sondra were quickly at my side, coming to my aid. Their hands were inches from Matias when they both leapt back like they'd been shocked. I hadn't felt a thing.

Matias shoved me off of him, and my body rose into the air. My feet hung a meter off the ground, and a tight sensation squeezed my neck as if I were hanging from the gallows. I clawed at my throat but found nothing there. My heart hammered.

Matias chuckled as I hung there, gasping for breath. Venn and Sondra tried to reach him again, but they slammed into an invisible barrier. The sounds of fighting and death continued on around us. I couldn't look around to see who was still alive and who had fallen.

"Why aren't you... killing me?" I asked in the loudest voice I could manage. It sounded like only a whisper.

"Until your breath runs out, the offer's still on the table," Matias said, looking amused. "Join me."

He loosened his magical hold on me just enough to give me a chance to answer.

"I will—"

I was cut off as the sound of a throwing knife *whooshed* through the air. It sank into Matias's shoulder, and I fell to the ground. Matias's face contorted in anger as he ripped the knife from his flesh and turned on Fiona, who stood fifteen yards away from him, ready to throw another.

"Why don't you go to hell, asshole!?" she shouted.

In his anger, he flung a ball of black-colored magic at her. I gasped, but it never reached her. One second, she was standing in the line of fire. The next, she materialized three feet away.

Teleportation wasn't a usual witch gift. I'd only heard of two witches who were able to master it in all of history. Usually, witches avoided it because of how complicated it was. If you didn't do it right, you might leave a limb behind.

But Fiona was still in one piece. It must've been her superhuman potion. These potions were meant to be neat party tricks, not weapons, but they were serving us well tonight.

Matias stalked toward her. His eyebrows knitted in frustration while he shot magical energy at Fiona, only to miss every time. Venn and Sondra still hadn't broken through the magical wall he'd thrown up between them and were now trying to fight off some of his men.

I shot to my feet to help Fiona, but someone jumped in front of me. I caught a glimpse of his face in the moonlight, and I realized it was Ellwood—the witch from Seattle we'd seen on TV with Matias. On instinct, I slammed my heel into his chest. He stumbled back a few feet but remained on high alert as a fireball flew out of his palm. It hissed as it rushed by me, catching the end of my hair and singeing it.

"Is that all you've got?" I taunted.

Ellwood stood between me and Matias, as if protecting his master. He smirked and formed another fireball in his hand. If that was his only party trick, this was going to be easy. I threw myself forward and clipped his jaw with my fist. I didn't give him a chance to recover before I punched him a second and third time.

On the fourth swing, he threw his hands out and caught me by the wrist. Red-hot heat rose to his palm to burn the skin beneath the bracelet I wore.

I let out a scream and shouted, "Jackass!"

Using all my strength, I shoved my fingers into his eye socket and yanked down. Warm blood rushed over my fingers as he let out a pained screech. I kicked him in the abdomen, and he went down, clutching his bleeding eye socket.

"That's right," I snarled. "I play dirty."

I quickly rushed over to where my dagger lay in the grass and dove for it. When I rolled over, Ellwood was almost on top of me. I held my dagger upright, and he landed straight on it. Shock crossed his features, and a disgusting gurgle bubbled up out of his throat. Then his body went limp.

His blood rushed over me and soaked into my clothes, but I didn't give myself time to think about it. He would've killed me if I hadn't killed him first.

I shoved his body off of myself and stood. I turned my gaze back toward Matias, but before I could spot him through the chaos, a heavy weight fell down on me from out of nowhere. Someone had jumped on my back and was pinning me to the ground. My dagger had flown out of my hand. Whoever it was, they were strong. He must've been a shifter. His hands clamped down around my throat. I tried to throw him off of me, but he just held down tighter. I didn't recognize the man, but there was so much rage in his eyes, like he had a personal vendetta against me. The sky above me started to blur as he squeezed harder and harder.

"How does it feel?" he growled.

I gasped for breath, but couldn't answer.

"Huh?" he demanded, lifting me by the neck and slamming my head down into the grass again. "You're about to die, raven shifter. Say hi to Valkas for me in the afterlife."

A Soulless, I realized.

I tried to reach for my dagger, but it was inches out of reach.

Come on, I begged. I wasn't about to let this asshole kill me. Not after everything I'd faced. The dagger wiggled in the grass, like it heard my command. It was like Matias's focus was waning, like we were gaining back some of our powers.

Come on! I shouted in my mind, willing the dagger to come to me.

But it didn't move before the man above me grunted and I felt his hands leave my neck. Air entered my lungs again, and I sucked in greedy breaths.

When I looked up, Zoey was standing over him, and a knife stuck out of his back. She ripped it out of his flesh as he fell to the ground in a lifeless heap. She stuck a hand out to me and helped me to my feet.

"Thank you!" I cried. I'd definitely been wrong about Zoey.

"Thank me later," she said as she grabbed my shoulders and forced me to duck. An orange stream of magic flew over our heads and continued into the trees.

The sounds of fighting around me seemed to quiet as I focused on a figure in the trees. He ducked out of the way as the magic whizzed by him. The magic was bright enough to illuminate his features.

Cavanaugh? What was he doing here?

The answer was obvious. He was waiting to see if I'd fulfill my end of the bargain—a bargain I hadn't even taken yet.

Get your ass in here and fight if you want it so badly, I thought to myself.

"Down!" Zoey shouted.

Another stream of orange magic shot over us. This time, Cavanaugh didn't have time to jump out of the way. I threw my hands over my mouth as the magic slammed into his face. All I saw was burnt, bloody skin before his body crumpled to the ground. My guts ached as I witnessed him seizing in the trees.

It hit me that Cavanaugh was completely unprotected. I couldn't just let him perish this way. I abandoned Zoey and raced toward the trees.

"You idiot!" I shouted as I leaned down beside him.

He stared up at the canopy with glossed-over eyes as his body shook violently. His face was so distorted from whatever curse had hit him that it was barely recognizable. White foam had begun forming around his lips. I quickly reached into my pocket and pulled out the healing potion I had with me. I poured it into his open mouth. The potion was one of Devin's, so it would take a while to kick in. I hoped it was enough.

"You shouldn't have come! What were you thinking?" I demanded. I could hardly hear myself over the sounds of battle all around me.

Cavanaugh continued shaking, but he found control over his hand and reached out toward me. I took his hand in mine and squeezed tightly.

"I… had to… know…" He could barely get the words out.

Damn him and his curiosity.

I shook him as his eyes began to close. "No! You didn't come here just to die."

Idiot, idiot, idiot! I wanted to scream, but I didn't.

"Stay with me," I demanded.

Cavanaugh moaned something, but I couldn't make it out.

"What?" I asked desperately. "What is it?"

He reached into his pocket with trembling fingers, then pulled out his phone. I was completely baffled. Now was not the time to make a phone call.

"Maggie… Grover," he managed to choke out.

I had no idea what he meant. Did he want me to call her, whoever she was? He pressed a button on his phone, then his whole body went limp.

"Cavanaugh?" I shook him, but there was no response. "Cavanaugh!"

It was no use. He was already gone.

Pushing past the bile rising to my throat, I reached down for his phone to see what was so important that he wanted to tell me. But I didn't touch it before a rogue stunning spell slammed into me.

It felt like someone had smashed a brick into the side of my head. I fell to the ground on my side, unable to move. The world swam around me, and all I could do was take it in. All around the park were unmoving bodies. Some were covered in blood. Others had been ripped apart by magic. Some looked unharmed but were clearly dead. They mostly seemed to be from our side, too.

Screams continued from both sides. I tried to move my eyes to find Matias in the crowd, but I couldn't. Directly in front of me, I caught sight of Venn and Sondra taking on a moose shifter alongside Clarita and Amalia.

Carla and Adrien worked as one as they fought a witch with glowing blue magic. Carla ducked out of the way of the witch's attack, then maneuvered around him. She grabbed his hair and dragged his head backward so that Adrien could shove a potion vial down his throat. The two quickly ducked out of the way as the vial exploded in his mouth, sending bits of flesh in every direction.

My eyes caught Fiona, who had just wasted her last throwing knife on a guy who was advancing on her. He flicked his wrist, and it went flying in the other direction. Purple magic sizzled in his palms as he stalked toward her. I wanted to run in and protect her, but the stunning spell hadn't worn off yet. Feeling was returning to my fingers, but I could hardly twitch them.

The guy threw the magic at Fiona, and she blinked out of existence only to appear several feet away a second later. She reached to the ground to grab her knife she'd thrown at him, then appeared at his back. She aimed the knife at him, but he whirled around at the last second and grabbed hold of her wrist. She cried out in agony, so loud that it cut through the other screams.

No! I wanted to scream, but it only came out a whimper. *Fiona!*

The man squeezed harder, and Fiona shrieked louder. He must've been crushing her wrist! She flickered in and out of existence, but it was like he had some magical hold on her that didn't let her abilities work.

Fiona let go of her knife, and it fell to her feet. He yanked on her arm, and her whole body whipped around and landed hard in the grass. He shifted into a huge, terrifying wolf and bared his teeth at her.

"That's my sister, you asshole!" Ryland voice came, and he raced into my line of vision. He aimed his gun at the guy, but when he pulled the trigger, nothing happened. He tossed the empty gun aside and snatched up Fiona's knife from the ground.

Watch out! I wanted to say.

The wolf turned on Ryland and lunged. It knocked him to the ground, but not before Ryland sank the knife into its chest. The wolf let out a howl, then snapped its jaw at Ryland's face.

The spell was starting to wear off. I pushed myself upward, but my legs still weren't working.

"Ryland!" I shrieked.

But it was too late. Blood spurted out of Ryland's throat as flesh went flying everywhere. The wolf didn't hold back. He ripped Ryland apart before I could even blink.

"No!" I shouted.

The world seemed to slow as I realized what had just happened. It all happened too fast.

Fiona looked a little disoriented, but she quickly focused when she caught sight of her brother's body lying in pieces on the ground. I'd never seen her look so angry in her life. She got to her feet, then aimed herself at the wolf, letting out a battle cry as she launched herself on top of him.

The wolf rolled over and snapped its jaws at Fiona, but she only held on to him tighter. Her arm wrapped around his neck, and her legs secured around his middle. She squeezed his neck tighter and tighter, giving everything she had into the rage. The wolf bucked and bit at her, trying to get her off of him, but she wouldn't give up so easily. A huge gash ran along her arm where the wolf's teeth had caught her, but it was like she didn't even feel it—didn't see the blood dripping down her arm and into the grass.

The wolf went limp, and still she held on. She wasn't taking any chances.

The feeling returned to my legs, and I pushed myself to my feet. I stumbled a little as the spell wore off, then found my footing and raced across the grass toward them.

But before I could get to them, hands swooped down out of the air and lifted me. I screamed as I flew higher and higher above the park. Venn looked upward at the sound of my voice, and sheer fear washed over his face.

"Rae!" he screamed.

"Venn!" I shouted back. He got smaller and smaller the higher I rose, until he looked like a mere ant beneath me. I caught sight of a white stream of magic knocking him to his side, then the park disappeared from view.

"What are you doing to me?" I demanded. I didn't try to struggle, because I knew if he let go, I'd surely fall to my death. But I sure as hell deserved an answer.

"Relax," Matias's voice sounded in my ear. "This will all be over soon."

26

Matias flew us over the countryside and into Nocton. He dropped me ten feet above a tall apartment building. My ankles twisted under me when I landed on the rooftop, and I rolled across the concrete to slow my fall. He landed softly behind me.

I whirled toward him. "What is this!?"

"Isn't it obvious?" he asked, spreading his arms out wide. His brown hair was in disarray, and the buttons on his suit coat were ripped from the fight. He had a wild look in his eyes that made me uneasy. "I wanted to get you alone."

"Why don't you just kill me already?" I snapped. Seriously, what was the guy waiting for? Isn't that what he wanted?

Matias threw his head back and laughed. "Oh, Rachel. I don't want to kill you. You know what I want—what I've *always* wanted."

"You want me to join you. Why?"

He couldn't be that desperate. People had flooded in from all over the country to join him. What could I offer that the rest of them couldn't?

"Your power is unstoppable, Rachel, if only you knew how to use it."

"What makes you think I would *ever* take your side?" I demanded.

"Because it's your only option," he said like it was obvious.

"Why would you trust me?" I asked. "You could give me my magic back just to have me turn on you."

"I'd have no reason not to trust you once you saw the beauty of my plan," he said simply.

Pompous ass.

"I know what your plan is, and it goes against everything I believe in," I spat.

He raised an eyebrow. "Really, Rachel? You're against building a better world?"

"No," I stated firmly. "Just against your means. It won't work, Matias. Why can't you see that?"

"It will!" he roared, before quickly softening his voice. "It'd be a shame to kill you. It really would."

Why? I didn't get it. What was so much harder about killing me than all the other people he killed?

"You're one of the most powerful souls in all of history," Matias said. "You just need a little guidance. I could train you, Rachel. Together, we could unlock the magic that would allow us to live forever."

There it was. He'd trade a little training for immortality—because he knew he'd never figure that one out on his own. He wasn't powerful enough for it.

"And everyone else?" I asked. "Where do you stand on your followers?"

"Same place I always have," he said. "They will do as they are told or suffer the consequences."

"Then we have no deal," I snarled.

Matias and I struck at the same time. My bracelet blasted him backward as he shot blood-red magic at me. I dove behind an air-conditioning unit. The metal screeched and crumpled beneath the weight of his magic.

I quickly grabbed my last vial of magic. I tossed it over the air conditioning unit, then ducked down again. An explosion sounded, but it was at least twenty yards away from where I'd aimed. Matias must've deflected it.

My heart slammed against my rib cage. How was I possibly going to defeat him without magic to defend me? The only thing I *could* do was hope he wore out before I did. That, or surprise him.

I held my breath and listened to the sound of his light footsteps across the rooftop.

"Come on, Rachel," he taunted. "Let's not drag this out. We both know how this is going to end."

My whole body quivered. He was right. He was clearly holding the winning hand. But I'd beaten the odds before. I wasn't about to surrender.

He was only feet from me now. I leapt out from behind the safety of the air conditioner and grabbed him. I dragged him to the ground as my fingers tangled in the chain around his neck. It gave way, and the locket flew several yards away from us.

I shot another blast out of the bracelet. Matias reacted at the same time. He threw his palms out, and the blast reversed toward me. I went flying backward and flipped through the air. I almost landed on my feet, but my body kept moving over the lip around the edge of the roof. My feet slipped out from under me, and suddenly, I was falling.

Desperately, my hands reached out to grab anything. To my relief, I caught the edge of the roof with the tips of my fingers. I stole a glance beneath myself to see that my feet were dangling at least ten stories off the ground. My pulse quickened.

I quickly tried to pull myself up, which wasn't difficult with the extra strength the cufflink in my pocket gave me. But I barely made any headway before Matias's shiny shoe was pressing down on my fingers.

"Ah!" I screamed as the heavy pressure radiated across my right knuckles.

Matias pressed down on my fingers. He had that same wild look in his eyes I'd spotted earlier.

"I was going to kill you with magic," he taunted with a laugh, "but I think I like this idea better. Ironic that your wings won't save you now."

He leaned forward, and his suit coat opened. My eyes caught a bulge on the inside pocket.

"Please, Matias," I begged.

He smirked. "Ready to join me? Too late."

He pressed down harder on my hand and leaned even closer. "Rachel Collins hung from a wall. Rachel Collins had a great—"

As my last-ditch effort to survive, I reached up and tangled my fingers in Matias's inner pocket the moment he shoved me off the side of the building. The glorious sound of tearing fabric met my ears, and The Wise Owl tumbled out of his pocket and toward the ground with me.

It felt like I was falling in slow motion. My limbs reached out, as if I might catch something in the air that would stop my fall. I saw Matias's face go stark white as the Artifact fell out of his grasp. I knew the moment he lost his hold on it because I suddenly felt energized, like I could take on anything.

Shifter magic shot through me, and I spread my wings a moment before I was about to hit the ground. The jewelry I'd been carrying with me clinked to the pavement, but my enchanted clothing shifted with me.

A thrill swept through my body as I flapped my wings as fast as I could. I hadn't flown in what felt like ages, not since Valkas ripped my flight feathers out. I was glad to see they'd grown back, even when my magic was missing.

Behind me, magic slammed into a nearby building as it tried to knock me out of the air. It just barely missed my tail feathers as I dodged around it. I glanced down to the Owl in the alleyway below me to see it rising into the air.

I landed and shifted as fast as I could, then pointed my palms toward the Owl. It stopped around the third floor and wavered in the air as Matias and I fought against each other's magic.

I let out a cry of glee. I'd never done telekinesis before. I felt powerful. *Really* powerful.

I tugged harder with my magic, and the Owl went flying out of both of our magical holds. It smashed through a window in the building beside us and out of sight. Matias glanced over the edge of the building, his face paling.

I jumped and guided my body upward with my newfound power. Wind whipped my hair around, and lightning crackled out of my hands. I landed softly on the roof beside Matias.

He stepped back from the edge and smirked. "Two can play at that game, Rachel."

He held his palms upward. Lightning jumped out of them and connected with nearby buildings.

"*Quod dico facies*," I muttered under my breath.

Matias stilled at my puppeteer spell, but the lightning continued to crackle out of his palms. In my hands, I gathered water from the air and formed it into sharp knife-like icicles, then aimed them at Matias's chest.

"Any last words?" I asked.

He chuckled. "Yeah. You think that's going to work on me?"

Rage entered Matias's features, and his face began to turn red, as if he were trying to move a brick wall.

I didn't waste another second. I shot my ice knives at his chest.

They never made it. Somehow, he broke through my hold on him. His palms shot out in front of him, and the icicles melted in mid-air.

Anger swept through me. I'd show him no mercy. This ended *now*.

I thought back to all the incantations I'd read in Genevieve's books and shot anything and everything I could think of at him.

Stunning spell.

Transfiguration curse.

Freezing spell.

Pain curse.

He deflected every one of my cursed with magic of his own, then started throwing magic back at me. I dodged out of the way and put up a shield. I could feel it weakening with each curse he threw at me.

Using my telekinesis, I tried to lift him up into the air, but his magic pushed against mine. His feet remained on the ground.

"Give it up," I warned him. "You said yourself I'm powerful."

Matias chuckled. "So am I. Looks like we're going to have to do this the old-fashioned way."

Matias came at me so fast he was a blur. His hands tangled in my shirt as he tried to take me down. I grabbed hold of his wrists and shot straight upward, using my telekinesis to fly through the dark sky.

Matias's face was only inches from mine. When he laughed, I could smell his breath. It smelled like rot. That crazy look in his eyes was even more apparent now. Matias shifted our course as we went higher and higher. I fought against him, and we jerked in the other direction.

"Just die already," he snarled.

Matias yanked his right hand from my hold and slammed his fist into the side of my face. Pain shot across my cheek, but I responded with a punch of my own. My knuckles slammed into his nose, and his head snapped backward. I'd lost the cufflink when I shifted—since it wasn't enchanted like my clothes were—so it didn't do as much damage as I wanted.

"Never," I snapped.

A ball of red magic formed in his palm. I was acutely aware of his hand heading toward my chest. I let go of him and kicked off his abdomen to distance myself from him.

Magic rained down on me from all angles as a primal scream ripped out of Matias's lungs above me. I dodged around it, then reoriented myself so I could see him. Magic shot out of my hands.

Fireball.

Boils curse.

Shrinking spell.

Matias moved around each attack. I turned my gaze forward again and quickly corrected my flight as I almost slammed into the side of a tall building.

We were blocks away from where we'd started, right at the center of Nocton. Tall hotel buildings and conference centers rose around us. People on the street below looked like ants beneath the street lamps.

I heard the flap of his suit coat in the wind and dropped several feet to avoid him. But he quickly followed and grabbed hold of the back of my shirt.

I screamed as Matias dragged me higher and higher. We landed on the rooftop of the hospital next to a helipad.

Matias flung my body around with all his strength. My head cracked into the brick safety wall at the edge of the roof. My vision blurred, and when I reached up to cradle the area of impact, my hand came away covered in blood.

Matias stalked toward me, but my eyes couldn't focus on him. Double vision assaulted me.

Matias clicked his tongue. "You were a worthy opponent, Rachel. I really am sorry."

He reached out for me, and I quickly shifted to avoid his hold. But he found my feathers anyway and slammed my body back to the ground.

I gasped for breath as his hands clamped down over my small neck. It felt like he was crushing bone. I shifted back to human form to give myself a fighting chance, but he only squeezed my throat harder. His eyes went wide in crazed satisfaction.

I grabbed his wrists and tried to burn them, but he only smirked, like he enjoyed the pain. I tried to blast him back with my magic, but all it did was send a strong wind through his hair. I was too drained.

Tears rose to my eyes.

Please, I begged no one in particular. *I'm not ready to die.*

At the thought, figures began to form around me out of nowhere. At first, they looked like shadows. Then they faded to white. Five see-through beings stared down at me. Matias didn't seem to notice the spirits.

Mom? Dad?

They nodded like they could hear my thoughts speaking to them. Tears began to fall down my face as I looked between each of the faces.

Genevieve, Ryland, and Amalia were there, too. My gut sank at the sight of them. Amalia hadn't made it, either?

How are you here? I asked in my head.

"The potion you drank," Amalia said. "It made you a medium—just for tonight."

I began to cry harder. *Why are you here? I'll be with you soon.*

Mom shook her head. I couldn't believe I was seeing her face again. "Not yet, Rachel."

She leaned down and placed a transparent hand to my head. It felt like a cool breeze across my skin.

I hesitated. If I waited it out just a few more seconds, I could be with them again. We didn't have to move on to a new life. They'd waited in the afterlife this long for me. We could just stay there forever.

"Rachel," Dad whispered. "You can't give up. You have more work to do here."

"Please, Rae," Ryland begged. "Everyone else needs you."

"Fight him, Rachel," Genevieve encouraged. "You're stronger than him. You have more than he does."

More than he does? I thought to myself. Clearly, our powers were matched. I might've had more strength inside of me, but I hadn't exercised it. I'd need more time. Time I didn't have.

As my eyes flickered between each of my family's faces, I realized what Genevieve meant. I had a family. Matias didn't.

And that was what made me stronger than him.

Gathering all my strength inside of me, I found just enough for one last spell. I pointed my hand up toward the sky and closed my eyes.

This better work.

Red magic shot straight upward and into the clouds. It was so bright that it felt like the sun against my closed eyes.

Matias let out a frustrated scream and squeezed me harder. My airways were completely blocked off, and I could feel my consciousness slipping.

This is it.

I heard the sound of feet landing around me, then the low growl of a wolf—a familiar wolf.

Relief flooded through me. They'd seen my signal!

A primal growl ripped out across the night, then suddenly, Matias's hands vanished from my neck. I sucked in a deep breath, though my throat burned.

Yips, growls, and roars sounded across the rooftop. Shadows flashed by me. A fox, a raccoon, a lion...

The sound of an explosion burst across the roof the same time a bright green light lit up the night sky. The shadow of a wolf flew across my vision before I even had a chance to sit up.

My eyes followed Venn to see him roll across the rooftop and land beside the rest of the people who had come to my rescue. Jenna, Ronark, and Fiona had also been blasted back by Matias's magic. They got to their feet in their shifted form.

Everyone was here: Jenna, Venn, Fiona, Sondra, Clarita, Ronark, and Zoey. They all glared at Matias in rage.

I whipped my head around toward Matias and saw that he was on the ground. Three large gashes from Venn's claws marred his face, but he wore an expression of satisfaction.

I shot to my feet, cradling my neck with my hand. I faced Matias with my head held high.

Multiple pairs of footsteps approached, along with the sound of paws padding against the rooftop. I suddenly felt stronger—like just having my family here had restored my energy.

Sondra whispered just loud enough for me to hear. "Ready when you are."

"Perhaps I was wrong about you, Rachel," Matias chuckled, wiping the blood from his eyes. "I thought you were strong, but you're weak for relying on others."

"You're wrong," I said boldly. "I'm strong *because* of them."

He laughed. "You're nothing—"

"Now!" I shouted.

Matias lifted his palms, but we were faster. Sondra, Clarita, Zoey, and I used our magic to lift his body up in the air and bind his arms at his side. He struggled but couldn't get out of our hold.

"You're making… a big… mistake," Matias said through struggled breath.

"No," I said firmly. "I don't think I am."

Venn nudged my hand with his nose. I glanced down into his dark wolf eyes, and I was overcome with a sense of love—of belonging. Jenna came to my side in racoon form and sat at my feet. Warmth filled my chest.

My eyes swept over the others—the witches and shifters standing at my side and the spirits no one else could see. A magic I'd never felt before rose up within me. It felt strong, like electricity sizzling straight into my bones and across my skin. I knew what I had to do.

I walked forward until I was just feet from Matias's hovering form. "This is why your plan would never work. All you want is control."

He let out a chilling laugh. "How else do you get people to comply?"

"You treat them like *people*!" I shouted. "You listen. You compromise. You *love*!"

Matias's features hardened as he continued to struggle out of the witches' hold. "You can burn in hell, Rachel."

I smirked. "I'll meet you there."

I slammed my palm into his chest. Blinding white light shot out of my hand and into his body. He let out a scream so loud it echoed off the buildings around us. The white light built within him until his skin was lit up like the sun.

Boom!

Matias's body exploded in a dazzling array of tiny white stars. There was no blood. No flesh. Just a firework display of white light.

I dropped to my knees as all the energy drained out of me. The lights faded, and the city turned back to night.

I was vaguely aware of arms wrapping around me. It smelled like Jenna, then came Venn's scent as he knelt beside me. I looked up to Mom and Dad, who smiled back at me. A single tear streaked my face as the five spirits began to fade.

"I love you," I whispered out loud.

The five of them whispered back in unison. "We love you, too."

Then they were gone.

Jenna mistook my confession as directed at her. "I love you, too, Rugrat."

I dashed the tears from my cheeks. "How did you get here so fast?"

"We all felt our magic return, and it gave us the edge we needed," Jenna said. "We won the fight. But you were gone, so we came looking for you. We weren't far when we saw your signal."

Fiona knelt in front of me and drew me into a tight hug. "Did you get the Owl?"

My head snapped upward. "The Owl! We have to go back for—"

I was cut off by the sound of a helicopter coming in for a landing. I thought at first it belonged to the hospital, but then I noticed five other choppers hovering next to the building with guns trained on us.

Then came the sound of a voice over their speaker. "This is the DMR. Get down on the ground, and put your hands where we can see them."

<h1 style="text-align:center">27</h1>

We were all covered in blood and bruises. None of us had any fight left in us. And so, we did as we were told.

Fear whipped through me. If the DMR arrested us, I may never see my family again. I had one last chance to say what I wanted to.

"I'm sorry!" I called over the sound of the chopper.

"It's not your fault!" Venn shouted back.

"No, I mean, I'm sorry for how I treated you." I glanced between him, Jenna, and Ronark. "I overreacted. I should've listened to you."

"Relax," Jenna told me. "It's ancient history."

"Cavanaugh offered me a deal," I told them.

"A deal?" Sondra asked.

"A pardon," I clarified. "The Owl for full immunity on our crimes."

"No!" Fiona cried. "You can't take it. The Owl has to be destroyed."

"I know—" I started, but I cut off as the helicopter landed and a woman in a red pantsuit stepped out onto the helipad.

"Don't take it," Venn insisted. "We'll serve our time. It's not worth stealing magic from everyone else."

"If anyone makes it out of here," I said quickly, "the Owl smashed through an apartment window on Fifth Avenue. Get it, and destroy it."

The sound of the helicopter blades quieted as they slowed. The woman stopped directly in front of me, with three guys bigger than Ryland behind her. I looked up and realized I recognized her. She was the vice president of the Department of Magical Regulation, the woman I'd recognized in the photo in Cavanaugh's waiting room.

"Rachel Collins," she said in a tone I couldn't read.

"I'm not taking the deal, so you might as well arrest us," I snapped.

She blinked a few times, then said, "I think you misunderstand my purpose here. I haven't come to arrest you. I've come to help."

My jaw dropped. "What?"

Vice Pres Lady glanced around the roof. "It seems, however, you didn't need our help after all."

I gaped at her. "Who… who are you?"

She reached out her hand and helped me to my feet. Slowly, my friends also stood.

"Don't you know who I am?" she asked.

"You're the VP of the DMR," I answered.

She held her head high. "President now. Mr. Robertson couldn't take the pressure of recent events and resigned. But that's not what I meant. We met two years ago, and I've been searching for the Ravenite ever since."

She didn't sound angry. She sounded… relieved.

And then it hit me. I knew exactly where I recognized her from. Her hair was different, and her features softer, but it was definitely the same woman.

"I saved you from Ivan Valerik," I realized.

She nodded. "I'm Maggie Grover."

"Cavanaugh called you for backup?" I asked.

"Yes," she said. "I'm aware of the deal he offered you, Rachel, but he didn't tell me about it until *after* he spoke to you. He was under no authority to make the offer in the first place."

I crossed my arms. "Doesn't matter. I wasn't going to sign the contract anyway."

Maggie smiled. "I think you'll like my offer more."

"Oh?" I asked curiously.

"You are free to destroy The Wise Owl, and I will wipe out all evidence Cavanaugh gathered against you. You'll walk free."

Venn took a step forward, like he was protecting me. "In exchange for what?"

"Nothing," Maggie said. "You've already done your part. You saved us. How could I possibly ask for more?"

I was so overcome with emotions that I couldn't speak. Jenna squealed and wrapped her arms around me. Everyone else followed suit and rejoiced, but I could barely process their voices.

"One more thing, Rachel," Maggie said. Everyone around me quieted. "The Department of Magical Regulation will be changing now that I'm President. I've been working for years to create better, fairer laws. Now, I actually have a chance to see those laws put into place. I'd like to offer you a job as a consultant."

Jenna and Fiona squealed again.

"What?" I asked breathlessly. "Why me?"

"I read through the files Cavanaugh sent me. You have always used your magic to serve and protect. We need someone like that on our team, someone who is willing to do the right thing for everyone. Plus, you know the magical community better than anyone else in our department. You can give them a voice for once."

"I-I..." I couldn't think straight. This was all too much. It was like a miracle.

No, not a miracle, I thought. *Synchrony.*

I'd said it before. We were alive for a reason. Synchrony wanted us to restore the balance. And here was my opportunity to do that.

But then there was my family. I couldn't leave them and move to another city to take the job.

"I'll have to think about it," I finally said.

"Of course," Maggie replied. "Take all the time you need."

The thing was, I didn't need more time to think it over. I knew I'd take the job.

After tonight, nothing would ever be the same.

EPILOGUE

THREE WEEKS LATER

"*Every day is beautiful when you're sitting next to me.*"

Venn strummed the last chords on his guitar, and my heart melted. We sat on the back porch at the lake house, looking over the sloping lawn and out toward the water. The sun was warm on my skin, and a pleasant breeze rustled through the trees around us.

I took a deep breath of fresh air. "Venn... that was so beautiful. You really wrote that?"

He nodded sheepishly. "For you."

I couldn't help the wide smile that spread across my face. I reached over and cupped his face in my hands, then brought my lips to his. He fell into the kiss, his lips melting gently into mine. My heart lifted in my chest. I'd never felt so relaxed in my life.

I drew away from him but kept my hands on his face. He ran his fingers up and down my arm, soaking in the beauty of the moment.

"It was beautiful," I whispered. "I'm glad you're enjoying the new guitar."

We'd lost everything when the Soulless captured the family. I was glad to see him so happy when we'd gone into town earlier to pick up a new one.

Venn sat up straighter and adjusted the capo, then began strumming again. "I am enjoying it. So much."

I looked out over the lawn. Teagan leaned back in the grass and rubbed her belly. Fiona sat beside her, trying to perform a simple cleansing spell on a pair of flip flops.

Further down the lawn, Jenna and Ronark were doing yoga beside the water. Ronark instructed Jenna to stand tall, stretching her hands high above her head in Mountain pose. But Jenna's arms didn't stop above her head. They kept

578

moving until they were wrapped around Ronark's neck. Jenna dragged him closer to her, and their lips connected.

"Venn!" I pointed, and he looked up from his guitar to see Ronark hugging her back and deepening the kiss.

"Finally," he said with a chuckle.

I scoffed. "Come on. They shared a room at Genevieve's. Don't tell me they weren't fooling around then."

Venn shrugged. "Maybe they were. At least now they've made it public."

Jenna screamed as Ronark hoisted her up and threw her into the water. Her legs flailed, and she landed with a loud *splash*. I could hear Ronark chuckling from all the way up at the house. Jenna sucked in a deep breath of air when her head surfaced, then started for shore. Ronark reached out to help her out of the lake, but she pulled him in instead. The two laughed as they rolled around in the water and splashed each other.

I laughed while I watched them. "This is great."

"What is?" Venn asked curiously.

"*This.*" I gestured around me. "Being with all of you. It's just so… wonderful."

Venn smiled. He set his guitar aside, then took my hand in his. "*You're* wonderful."

He leaned over and pressed his lips to the side of my face. Warmth spread through my abdomen. I tilted my head his way and met his lips again. God, I'd never get sick of kissing this man.

"Where's Sondra?" I asked when he pulled away again. "It's too beautiful to be inside."

"She's probably working on house stuff," Venn said.

For all intents and purposes, the lake house was hers now, but she and Richard hadn't finished the official closing paperwork yet. Plus, she'd been having to deal with insurance claims on the old house, and I'd gotten the feeling that was a long and difficult process.

"I'm glad she's getting it all," I said.

"What do you mean?" He shot me a questioning look.

"Everything she dreamed of," I clarified. "Fiona told me all she ever wanted was to buy a house outside the city and lead a quiet life. This seems like the perfect place to do it."

After a beat, I spoke again. "What do you think she'll do now?"

Venn opened his mouth to answer, but before he could, Sondra stepped through the back door.

"I think I finally figured that out," she said.

I looked up at her curiously. "You sound excited."

"I am." She bounced on the balls of her feet and held her sketchbook in her hand. She took a seat beside us and gave us a wide smile. "Fiona and I talked about it last night. We're going to run retreats!"

"What kind of retreats?" Venn asked.

"Magical retreats!" Sondra exclaimed. "A place where witches can come to learn the basics of magic. We have to get approval from the Department of Magical Regulation, but I think with Maggie calling the shots, we have a good chance of this working."

"Yes!" I scooted to the edge of my chair, excited by her idea. "This is a great idea, Sondra. We could set this kind of thing up all over the place. No one would have to fear their magic if they're taught how to use it."

"We also thought of running classes for non-supernaturals," she said. "They could get a chance to interact with magic and learn more about it."

I sat back in my chair and chuckled. "Maybe *you* should be the one moving to D.C. to consult with the DMR."

She laughed and looked out over the water. "Nah, I'm good here."

She turned back to us. "What are you going to do in D.C., Venn?"

We exchanged a glance. We didn't tell anyone, as we only got the offer this morning.

He sat up straighter and rubbed his hands together. "Well... Rae talked to Maggie, and while she was discussing some of her reservations about working with the DMR, she mentioned the move out to D.C. and how it might be hard for me to find a job. So..."

Sondra's jaw dropped. "They offered you one?"

I nodded eagerly. "Yes! Along with a huge offer. They want Venn on their consultant committee as a shifter spokesperson. I'll be speaking for witches."

Sondra tossed her sketchbook aside and threw her arms around Venn. "Oh my God. That's great! You two are going to have so much fun."

"I think we will, too." Venn gazed at me with soft eyes.

"Hey," Sondra said quickly, changing the subject. "I have something I wanted to show you."

Sondra led us inside and told me to close my eyes. I covered my eyes with my hands, and Venn helped guide me over to the stairs. We stopped at the base of them.

"Okay. Open your eyes," Sondra instructed.

When I did, I saw my own face staring back at me. Sondra had completed the drawing she'd been working on and had framed it at the bottom of the stairs. My jaw dropped. I was speechless. It looked exactly like me, as if someone had snapped a black-and-white photograph of my face and printed it out. I couldn't believe her level of talent.

"Sondra..." I couldn't find the words.

"I'm starting up the wall again," she said proudly. "And I wanted your portrait to be the first."

Tears rose to my eyes, and I welcomed them. I turned to her and drew her into a hug. "Thank you. It's beautiful."

"Guys!" Fiona's excited voice came from the back door.

We turned to see her rushing into the house, waving her flip flops. She hurried over and shoved them into Sondra's hands.

"I did it!" she exclaimed. "I performed the cleansing spell."

Sondra looked over the flip flops. They looked brand new, not a spec of dirt on them. Her eyebrows shot up. "Wow. Fiona, this is great."

"I know! This means I'm officially a low witch, right?" She bounced on her toes.

"Yes," Sondra said, sounding impressed. "You performed magic, Fiona. You're officially a witch."

"Booya!" Fiona did a little dance in front of us, then turned to Teagan as she stepped inside.

Teagan smiled, looking amused at Fiona's dance.

"Told you!" Fiona hurried over to Teagan, then bent to her belly. "Hear that, little niece or nephew? I'm a witch!"

Teagan chuckled, then checked her watch. "Relax, Auntie Fiona. It looks like it's time to go."

"Oh, crap," Sondra said, checking the time. "You're right. Everyone in the van."

Sondra's brand-new minivan sat in the driveway, and we all piled in—after she performed a quick drying spell for Jenna and Ronark.

The drive only took about a half hour, but Clarita and Zoey were already there when we arrived at the Nocton Cemetery. We met them beside a fresh grave.

I bent down and placed my flowers below the headstone. We'd already said our goodbyes at the funeral, but it didn't feel any easier facing his grave again.

"We miss you already, Ryland," I said, already feeling myself choke up.

Venn placed a comforting hand on my shoulder. "We'll never stop missing you, bro. We'll always love you, in this life and the next."

Fiona knelt down next. She placed a kiss to the tips of her fingers, then pressed it against his name on the marble stone. "I'll never forget what you did for me, Ryland. But the crazy thing is, I know you'll be back. You told me when Mom and Dad died that I'd never have to live without you, and even though you're gone in this form, I know you won't be gone long. I love you, big brother."

Sondra knelt beside her and wrapped an arm around her shoulder. "Fiona's right, cousin. I can already feel you with us."

Teagan knelt beside the two of them. Silent tears streamed down her face. She placed a large wreath beside his grave. "You were always there when I needed you, and I know you won't let me down now. I finally decided on names for our baby."

Teagan glanced down and ran her hand over her belly. Everyone was completely silent as she spoke to Ryland like he was here with us. "Ryland, if it's a boy, and Genevieve, if it's a girl."

"Teagan," Fiona said, leaning into her. "Those names are beautiful."

Teagan dashed the tears away. We stayed at Ryland's grave for another few minutes in respectful silence.

Finally, Clarita spoke up. "Shall we?"

We followed her to another corner of the cemetery, where two other figures stood.

"Carla. Adrien," Sondra greeted, shaking their hands. "We're so glad you could join us."

"Anything to help," Adrien said.

We stopped beside Genevieve's grave. Clarita sat over Genevieve's body and gestured for the rest of the witches to join her. Carla, Adrien, Sondra, Zoey, Clarita, and I formed a circle in the grass, while the others stood off to the side.

Sondra waved to Fiona. "Come on. You're a low witch, aren't you?"

Fiona's eyes lit up, and she joined us around the circle. "I am now."

Clarita smiled, then turned to me. "The Owl?"

I pulled it out of my bag and placed it in the center between the seven of us. We'd retrieved it—along with my trinket, bracelet, cufflink, and the Leora Locket—the night of the fight, but with the funerals and everything that followed, we needed to take time to recover before we could perform the spell.

"Do you think we have enough witches to do it?" I asked.

Clarita cocked an eyebrow at me. "The question is not about our numbers. It is about our power. Do you believe we have the power to do this?"

It sounded like a trick question, but I answered honestly. "Yes."

She nodded. "Then there's your answer. Everyone, please join hands."

I took Clarita's hand on my left and Sondra's hand on my right. My eyes connected with Venn's momentarily, and I was filled with a sense of peace. This would work.

"Where did you find the spell to destroy something like this?" Fiona asked Clarita curiously.

Clarita gave a knowing smile. "I didn't."

Fiona shot her a questioning glance.

"Magic comes not from incantations, but from inside ourselves," Clarita explained.

"Which means we can write our own," Sondra said in realization.

Clarita nodded. "Precisely. I'd like everyone to repeat after me. *The Owl's power is too much to contain. Send it back to hence it came.*"

The spell began as a murmur at first, but as we all began to hear the words, we fell into a harmonious chant.

"*The Owl's power is too much to contain. Send it back to hence it came. The Owl's power is too much to contain. Send it back to hence it came.*"

I could feel the magic pulsing through my arms, in through my left and out through my right, around and around the circle.

"*The Owl's power is too much to contain. Send it back to hence it came.*"

The sky began to darken above us, and the air cooled around us.

"*The Owl's power is too much to contain. Send it back to hence it came.*"

Wind whipped by my hair as we continued the incantation. I pushed away the chill and focused solely on the magic inside of me, calling it to the surface and sending it out to share with the other witches around me. Their magic mixed with my own, until I couldn't distinguish mine from theirs. The pulsing of magic through my body transformed into a powerful, constant hum.

"The Owl's power is too much to contain. Send it back to hence it came."

The owl skull began to rise into the air. All eyes followed it as it rose higher and higher above our heads. Our incantation grew more intense the more we repeated it.

"The Owl's power is too much to contain. Send it back to hence it came. The Owl's power is too much to contain! Send it back to hence it came!"

The incantation grew so loud that it seemed to echo in my ears. I raised my voice, and the others around me followed suit.

"The Owl's power is too much to contain! Send it back to hence it came!"

The Owl continued to spin above our heads, but that was it. We needed more power!

As everyone else continued speaking the incantation, I sent another message out. *Genevieve, we're here because we need you. Your soul is still here with us. You still have power. Complete our circle, and help us finally defeat this magic.*

The earth rumbled beneath our feet, and thunder cracked above our heads. Suddenly, bone shattered, sending bits of dust all around us. All that remained was a broken portion of the eye socket. It fell to the ground as the sky lightened once again and the wind let up. The earth stilled.

Nobody moved. Nobody spoke.

The dirt rose to consume the last piece of bone, then swallowed the rest of the Owl whole.

Genevieve?

We'd destroyed the Owl! It was hard to believe that after all the effort we went through to retrieve it, it was finally gone. No one would ever be able to use it again.

A soft breeze brushed across my cheek, and in that moment, I knew. Genevieve had helped us from beyond the grave. And somehow—I could feel it deep down in my gut—that had brought her the peace she'd been looking for all these years.

"We did it!" Fiona exclaimed.

Teagan, Venn, Jenna, and Ronark all looked at us in awe.

Clarita took a deep breath, then broke the circle. "It is done."

"Wow!" I threw my arms around Sondra beside me, and she hugged me back. "I can't believe it!"

Sondra laughed and drew away. "I can. We all make an amazing team!"

Fiona leaned over to hug Sondra, too. "That, we do."

Venn came up behind me, and I rose to my feet to pull him into a hug. He squeezed me tightly. "Are you okay?"

"Yes!" I exclaimed as Jenna stepped up beside us. "Better than okay."

I kept one arm around him while I drew away, then placed the other around Jenna's neck. She beamed at me.

"Nothing has ever been better," I said, pulling them both close to me. "I have my family at my side, and that's what matters."

My gaze flickered over to Ryland's grave across the cemetery. "Though we didn't all make it."

Jenna's face fell, and she dropped her gaze. I could tell by the look in her eyes that she was thinking of Mom and Dad. I never stopped thinking of them either, but now, the memories that came to mind were warm and happy—as they should be.

"No, we didn't all make it," Venn said in agreement. His eye flickered with a hint of sorrow. He got that look on his face that he always got when he thought about Tyson.

"But you know what?" he said, perking up.

"What?" I asked curiously.

Venn rubbed his hand over my shoulder, then placed a kiss on the top of my head. "I think we're all finally at peace."

My heart warmed at the thought, and I smiled. Venn was right. My family may not all be with me in the physical sense of the word, but they were still here with me—in spirit and in memory. And that made all the difference.

As long as I had my family by my side, nothing could ever stop me.

THE END

ABOUT THE AUTHOR

Alicia Rades is a USA Today bestselling author of young adult and new adult paranormal fiction. When she's not dreaming up magical stories, she's either binge-watching paranormal shows, meditating, or spending time with her family. She has an unhealthy obsession with psychic characters and writes with a deck of tarot cards next to her computer.